James H. Graff, James Grant

The Scottish Cavalier

An Historical Romance

James H. Graff, James Grant

The Scottish Cavalier
An Historical Romance

ISBN/EAN: 9783337348809

Printed in Europe, USA, Canada, Australia, Japan

Cover: Foto ©Andreas Hilbeck / pixelio.de

More available books at **www.hansebooks.com**

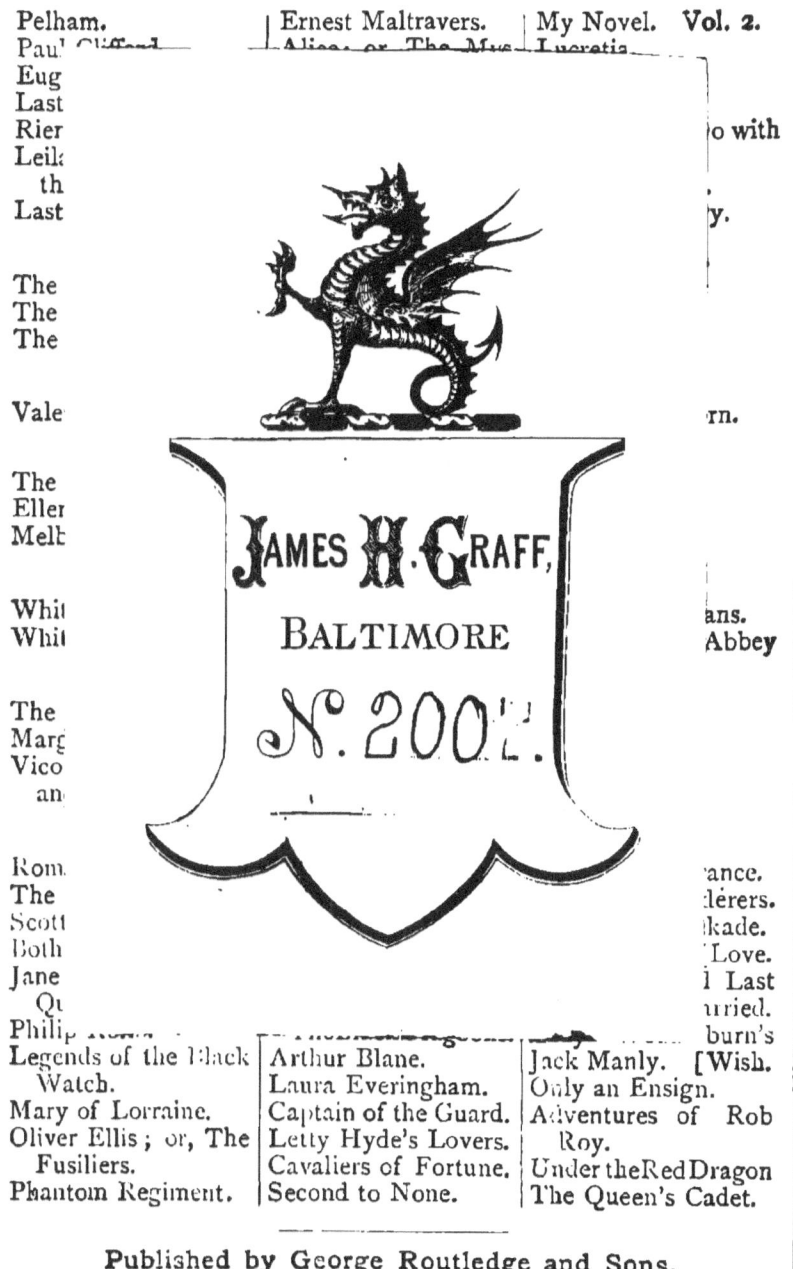

PREFACE.

FROM the historical and descriptive nature of the following tale, the Author intended that certain passages should be illustrated with notes, containing the local traditions and authorities from which it has been derived; but on second thoughts he has preferred confining these explanations to the preface.

History will have rendered familiar to the reader the names of many who bear a prominent part in the career of *Walter Fenton*; but there are other characters of minor importance, who, though less known to fame than Dundee and Dunbarton, were beings who really lived and breathed, and acted a part in the great drama of those days. Among these, we may particularise Douglas, of Finland, and Annie Laurie.

This lady was one of the four daughters of Sir Robert Laurie, the first baronet of Maxwelton, and it was to her that Finland inscribed those well-known verses, and that little air which now bear her name, and are so wonderfully plaintive and chaste for the time; but it is painful to record that notwithstanding all the ardour and devotion of her lover, the fair Annie was wedded as described in the romance. Her father, Sir Robert, was created a baronet in 1685.

The old halberdier and Hugh Blair (mentioned so fro-quently) are also real characters. The former distinguished himself at the battle of Sedgemoor, and by a *Royal Order*, dated 26th February, 1686, received "forty pounds for his good service in firing the great guns against the rebells " who were opposed to Sir James Halkett's Royal Scots. The tavern of Hugh Blair was long celebrated in Edinburgh. His name will be found in *Blackadder's Memoirs*, and frequently among the *Decisions* of Lord Fountainhall, in disputes concerning various runlets of Frontiniac, &c.

Lord Mersington was exactly the personage he is described in the following pages—an unprincipled sot. From *Cruickshank's History* it appears that his lady was banished the liberties of Edinburgh in 1674, for being engaged in the female assembly which insulted Archbishop Sharpe.

Of Thomas Butler, an unfortunate Irish gentleman connected with the ducal house of Ormond, who bears a prominent part in the second volume, an account will be found in the London papers of 1720, in which year he was executed at Tyburn as a highwayman.

The song mentioned so frequently, and the burden of which is *Lillebulero bullen a la!* was a favourite Whig ditty, and the chorus was formed by the pass-words used during the Irish massacre of 1641.

The principal locality of the story is the Wrightshouse or Castle of Bruntisfield, which stood near the Burghmuir of Edinburgh, and was unwisely removed in 1800, to make way for that hideous erection—the hospital of Gillespie. As described in the romance, it was a magnificent château in the old Scoto-French style of architecture, and was completely encrusted with legends, devices, armorial bearings, and quaint bassi relievi.

It was of great antiquity, and over the central door were the arms of Britain, with the initials J. VI. M. B. F. E. H. R.

Amid a singular profusion of sculptured figures represent-

ing Hope, Faith, Charity, &c., was a bas-relief of Adam and
Eve in Eden, bearing the following legend :—

𝕼𝖚𝖍𝖊𝖓 𝕬𝖉𝖆𝖒 𝖉𝖊𝖑𝖇𝖙 𝖆𝖓𝖙 𝕲𝖇𝖊 𝖘𝖕𝖆𝖓
𝕼𝖚𝖍𝖆𝖗 𝖜𝖆𝖗 𝖆' 𝖙𝖍𝖊 𝖌𝖊𝖓𝖙𝖎𝖑𝖊𝖘 𝖙𝖍𝖆𝖓 ?

Between them was a female representing Taste, and inscribed
Gustus. " On the eastern front of the castle was sculptured
a head of Julius Cæsar, and under it *Caius Jul. Cæsar, pri-
mus Rom. Imp.* On the eastern wing were figures of Tempe-
rantia, Prudentia, and Justitia, which it is remarkable were
among the first stones thrown down." (*Scots Mag.,* 1800.)
On the west wing was a Roman head of Octavius II., and
five representations of the Virtues, beautifully sculptured.
Sicut oliva fructifera, 1376, *In Domino Confido,* 1400, *Patriæ
et Posteris,* and many other valuable carvings, which are now
preserved at Woodhouselee, adorned the walls and windows.

The east wing was said to have been built by Robert III. ;
Arnot informs us, that the centre was erected by James IV
for one of his mistresses, and about the close of the last century, Hamilton of Barganie made many additions to it. How
the edifice obtained the name of *Wright's* or *Wryte'shouse* is
now unknown, as no proprietor of it who bore that name can
now be traced ; but the Napiers appear to have possessed the
barony from an early period, and their names frequently
occur in local records.

Alexander Napier de Wrichtysnouse appears as one of an
inquest in 1488. His coat armorial was a bend charged with
a crescent between two mullets. He married Margaret Napier of Merchiston, whose father was slain at the battle of
Flodden. In 1581, among the commissioners appointed by
James VI., " anent the cuinze," we find William Napier of
the Wrightshouse, (*Acta Parliamentorum*) and in 1590,
Barbara Napier, his sister. was convicted of sorcery, for
which on the 11th of May she was sentenced to be burnt at
a " stake sett on the Castellhill, with barrells, coales, heather,

and powder;" but when the torch was about to be applied, pregnancy was alleged, and the execution delayed. (*Calderwood's Historie.*)

In 1632, William of the Wrightshouse was a commissioner at Holyrood, *anent* the valuation of Tiends; and two years after we find him retoured heir to his father William in certain lands in Berwickshire; but in 1626, "*terrarum de Brounisfield, infra parochiam de Sanct. Cuthbert*" belonged to Sir William Fairlie of Braid. In 1649 he obtained a crown charter of his lands (*MS. Mag. Sigilli*), and in 1680, the last notice of this old family will be found in the *Inquisitionum Retornatarum*, where it ends in a female.

Thus about the close of the 17th century, the Napiers had passed away, and their barony was possessed by the laird of Pennicuick. All that now remains of them is their burial-place on the north side of St. Giles's cathedral, where may still be seen their mouldering coat-armorial, with this inscription :—

S. C. P.

Fam. de Naperorbm interibus,

Hic situm est.

EDINBURGH, *March,* 1850.

CONTENTS.

———◆———

CONTENTS.

CH. XXIX.—THE WHITE-HORSE CELLAR .... *Page* 229
XXX.—THE BETROTHAL 241
XXXI.—THE DEFIANCE 251
XXXII.—THE MARCH FOR ENGLAND................. 254
XXXIII.—THE HAWK AND THE DOVE 265
XXXIV.—A STATESMAN OF 1688 271
XXXV.—TRUST AND MISTRUST 275
XXXVI.—THE GUISARDS 279
XXXVII.—THE REVOLT AT IPSWICH 286
XXXVIII.—FREE QUARTERS 294
XXXIX.—THE REDEEMED PLEDGE 301
XL.—THE SWART RUYTERS 305
XLI.—LILIAN 311
XLII.—HOW CLERMISTONLEE PRESSED HIS SUIT 317
XLIII.—CLAVERHOUSE TO THE RESCUE 323
XLIV.—THE SECRET STAIR 328
XLV.—THE ATTEMPT 334
XLVI.—EDINBURGH—THE NIGHT OF THE REVOLUTION 339
XLVII.—SACK OF HOLYROOD...... 346
XLVIII.—THE VEILED PICTURE 356
XLIX.—LOVE AND PRINCIPLE 364
L.—THE PASS OF KILLYCRANKIE............... 372
LI.—THE LAST HOUR OF DUNDEE 378
LII.—ST. GERMAIN 384
LIII.—THE CAVALIERS OF DUNDEE 391
LIV.—THE 20TH OF SEPTEMBER, 1692............. 401
LV.—THE EFFECT OF THE POSTSCRIPTUM 410
LVI.—THE BATTLE OF STEINKIRKE 414
LVII.—A DISCLOSURE 423
LVIII.—WALTER FENTON AND THE KING 433
LIX.—THE RETURNED EXILE..................... 437
LX.—THE BUBBLE BURST 442
LXI.—LOVE AND MARRIAGE ARE TWO............. 448
LXII.—THE RING AND THE SECRET 453
LXIII.—THE IRON ROOM—THE DEATH SHOT 460

SCOTTISH CAVALIER.

CHAPTER I.

THE PLACE OF BRUNTISFIELD.

There is nae Covenant noo, lassie,
There is nae Covenant, noo ;
The solemn League and Covenant,
Are a' broken through.—OLD SONG.

ONE evening in the month of March, 1688, a party of thirty soldiers mustered rapidly and silently under the arches of the White Horse hostel, an old and well-known inn on the north side of the Canongate of Edinburgh. The night was dark and cold, and a high wind swept in gusts down the narrow way between the picturesque houses of that venerable street and the steep side of the bare and rocky Calton-hill.

Gathering in cautious silence, the soldiers scarcely permitted the butts of their heavy matchlocks to touch the pavement. In a loud whisper the officer gave the order to march, and they moved off with the same air of quietness and rapidity which characterized their muster, and showed that a very secret or important duty was about to be executed.

In those days the ranks were drawn up three deep, and such was the mode until a later period ; so, by simply facing a body of men to the right or left, they found themselves three abreast without confusion or delay.

"Fenton," said the officer to a young man who carried a pike beside him, "keep rearward. You are wont to have the eye of a hawk ; and if any impertinent citizen appears to watch us, lay thy truncheon across his pate."

This injunction was unnecessary : for those belated citizens who saw them, hurried past, glad to escape unquestioned.

1.   B

In those days, when every corporal of horse or foot was
vested with more judicial powers than the lord justice
general, the night march of a band of soldiers was studiously
to be avoided. Aware that some "deed of persecution" was
about to be acted, the occasional wayfarers hurried on, or
turned altogether aside, when forewarned that soldiers appeared, by the measured tread of feet, by the gleam of a gun-
barrel, or cone of a helmet glinting in the rays of light that
shot from half-closed windows into the palpable darkness.

These soldiers belonged to the regiment of George earl o
Dunbarton, the oldest in the Scottish army, and a body o·
such antiquity, that they were jocularly known in France a.
Pontius Pilate's Guards. With red coats, they wore moriors
of black unpolished iron; breast-plates of the same metal,
crossed by buff belts which sustained their swords, fixing·
daggers and collars of bandoleers, as the twelve little wooden
cases, each containing a charge of powder, were named.
Their breeches and stockings were of bright scarlet, and each
had a long musket sloped on his shoulder, with its lighted
match gleaming like a glowworm in the dark. The officer
was distinguished by a plume that waved from a tube on his
gilded helmet, which, like his gorget, was of polished steel;
while to denote his rank he carried a half-pike, in addition to
his rapier and dagger, and wore a black corslet richly en-
graved and studded with nails of gold, conform to the royal
order of 1686. He was a handsome fellow, tall, and well set
up, with a heavy, dark moustache, and a face like each of his
soldiers, well bronzed by the sun of France and Tangiers.

In that age, the closes and wynds of the Scottish capital
were, like those of ancient Paris or modern Lisbon, narrow,
smoky, and crowded, unpaved, unlighted, and encumbered
with heaps of rubbish and mud, which obstructed the gutters
and lay in fœtid piles, until heavy rains swept all the *débris*
of the city down from its lofty ridge into the loch on the
north, or the ancient *communis via* on the south. At night
the careful citizen carried a lantern—the bold one his sword;
for men generally walked abroad well armed, and none ever
rode without a pair of long iron pistols at his saddle-bow.

The late king had made every kind of dissipation fashionable; and after nightfall the gallants of the city swaggered
about the craimes or the Abbey-close, muffled in their cloaks
like conspirators; and despite the axes of the city guard, and
the halberds of the provost, excesses were committed hourly;
and seldom a night passed without the clash of rapiers and
the shouts of cavalier brawlers being heard ringing in the
dark thoroughfares of the city. Thieves were hanged, coiners

were quartered, covenanters beheaded, and witches burned, until executions failed to excite either interest or horror but with the plumed and buff-booted ruffler of the day, who brawled and fought from a sheer love of mischief and wine, what plebeian baillie or pumpkin-headed city-guard would have dared to find fault? Of this more anon.

Stumbling through the dark streets, the party of soldiers marched past the Pleasance Porte, above the arch of which grinned a white row of five bare skulls, which had been bleaching there since 1681. Every barrier of Edinburgh was garnished with these terrible trophies of maladministration.

Leaving behind them the ancient suburb, they diverged upon the road near the old ruined convent of St. Mary of Placentia, which, from the hill of St. Leonard, reared up its ivied walls in shattered outline. Beyond, and towering up abruptly from the lonely glen below, frowned the tremendous front of Salisbury craigs. The rising moon showed its broad and shining disc, red and fiery above their black rocks, and fitfully between the hurrying clouds, its rays streamed down the Hauze, a deep and ghastly defile, formed by some mighty convulsion of nature, when these vast craigs had been rent from that ridgy mountain, where King Arthur sat of old, and watched his distant galleys on the waters of the Roman Bodoria.

For a moment the moonlight streamed down the defile, on the hill of St. Leonard, with its thatched cottages and ruined convent, on the glancing armour of the soldiers, and the bare trees bordering the highway; again the passing clouds enveloped it in opaque masses, and all was darkness.

"Sergeant Wemyss," cried the cavalier officer, breaking the silence which had till then been observed.

"Here, an't please your honour," responded the halberdier.

"Where tarries that loitering abbey-lubber, who was to have joined us on the march?"

"The Macer?"

"Ay, he with the council's warrant for this dirty work."

"Yonder he stands, I believe, your honour, by the ruins of the mass-monging days," replied the sergeant, pointing to a figure which a passing gleam of the moon revealed emerging from the ruins.

"Mean you that tall spunger in the red Rocquelaure? To judge by his rapier and feather, he is a gentleman, but one that seems to watch us. So, ho, sir! a good even; you are late abroad to-night."

"At your service, sir," responded the other gruffly behind the cape of his cloak, which, in the fashion of an intriguing

2

gallant of the day, he wore so high up as completely to conceal his face.

"For King or for Covenant, sir?" asked the lieutenant,
who was Richard Douglas, of Finland.

"Tush!" laughed the stranger! "this is an old-fashioned
test: you should have asked," he added, in a lower voice,
"For James VII., or William of Orange! ha, hah!"

"Hush, my Lord Clermistonlee, by this light."

"Right, by Jove!" exclaimed the other, who was considerably intoxicated.

"Body o' me! it ill beseems one of his majesty's privy
councillors to be roving abroad thus like a night hawk."

"I am the best judge of my own actions, Mr. Douglas,"
replied the lord haughtily; but added in a whisper, "you are
bound for the Wrytes-house?"

"To the point, my lord," rejoined Douglas, drily.

"You will take particular care that the young lady—tush
I mean the old one—they must not escape, as you shall answer to the council. Dost comprehend me—the young lady
of Bruntisfield, eh?"

"Too well, my lord," replied the cavalier, drawing himself
up, and shaking his lofty plume with undisguised hauteur.
"Curse on the libertine fool," he exclaimed to the young
pikeman, as he hurried after his party; "would he make me
his pimp? By heaven! he well deserves a slash in the
doublet for casting his eyes upon noble ladies, as he would
on the *bona robas* of Merlin's Wynd."

The young man's hand gradually sought the hilt of his
poniard.

"What said he, Finland?" he asked, with a kindling eye
and a reddening cheek. "He spoke of the Napiers, did he
not?"

"Only to this purpose, that on peril of our beards the
ladies do not escape, especially the younger one. Hah! they
say this ruffling libertine hath long looked unutterable things
at Lilian Napier. He is a deep intriguer, and the devil only
knows what plots he may be hatching now against her."

"S'death! Finland, assure me of this, and, by heaven, I
will brain him with my partisan."

"Hush, lad, these words are dangerous. You are but a
young soldier yet, Walter," continued the officer, laughing;
"had you trailed a pike under Henry de la Tour of Auvergne, and the old Mareschal Crecqy, like me, you would
ere this have learned to value a girl's tears and a grandam's
groans at the same ransom, perhaps. But, egad, I had rather
than my burganet full of broad pieces, that this night's duty

had fallen on any other than myself; and I think, major, the Chevalier Drumquhazel (as we call him) might have selected some of those old fellows whose iron faces and iron hearts will bear them through anything."

"Why, Finland," rejoined the pikeman, "you are not wont to be backward."

"Never when bullets or blades are to be encountered; but to worry an old preacher, and harry the house and barony of an ancient and noble matron, by all the devils! 'tis not work for men of honour. The Napiers of Bruntisfield are soothfast friends of the Lauries of Maxwelton; and my dear little Annie—thou knowest, Walter, that her wicked waggery will never let me hear the end of it, if we march the Napiers to the Tolbooth to-night."

"You see the advantage of being alone in this bad and hollow-hearted world," said Fenton, in a tone of bitterness, "of being uncaring and utterly uncared for."

"Again in one of thy moody humours!"

"I have trailed this pike——"

"True; since Sedgemoor-field was fought and lost by Monmouth; but cheer up, my gallant. If this rascal, William of Orange, unfurls his banner among us, we will have battles and leaguers enough; ay, faith! to which the Race of Dunbar, and the Sack of Dundee, will be deemed but child's-play. And hark, for thy further contentment, I trailed a partisan for four long years under Turenne ere I obtained a pair of colours; and *then* I thought my fortune made; but thou see'st, Walter, I am only a poor lieutenant still—uncaring and uncared for. Bravo! 'tis the frame of mind to make an unscrupulous lad do his *devoir* as becomes a soldier. And yet I assure thee, friend Walter, if aught in Scotland will make a man swerve from his duty—ay, even old Thomas Dalzel, that heart of steel—'tis the blue eyes of Lilian Napier, of Bruntisfield. The beauty of her person is equalled only by the winning grace of her manner; and I swear to thee, that not even Mary of Charteris, or my own merry Annie, have brighter charms, a redder lip, or a whiter hand. Hast seen her, lad?"

"Oh, yes," replied the young man with vivacity, "a thousand times."

"And spoken to her?"

"Alas, no," was the response; "not for these past three years, at least."

There was a sadness in his voice, which, with the sigh accompanying his words, conveyed a great deal, but only to the wind; for the gayer cavalier marked it not.

" If we start the game—I mean these Dutch renegades on the Napier's barony, it will go hard with them in these times, when every day brings to light some new plot against the government. Napier of the Wrytes—'tis an old and honourable line, and loth will I be to see it humbled."

" What can prompt ladies of honour to meddle in matters of kirk or state?"

" The great father of confusion who usually presides at the head of our Scottish affairs. True, Walter, the rock, the cod, and the bobbins become them better; but I shall be sorry to exact marching-money and free quarters from old Lady Grizel. Clermistonlee is the source of this accusation, which alleges that her ladyship knows of an intended invasion from Holland, and that she hath reset two emissaries of the house of Orange. But a word in thine ear, Fenton; there are villains at our council-board who more richly merit the cord of the provost-marshal; and Randal Clermont, of Clermistonlee, is not the least undeserving of such exaltation."

" If the soldiers overhear, you are a lost man."

" God save King James and sanc King Charles, say I! but to old Mahoud with the council, which is driving the realm to ruin at full gallop. Hah! here comes, at last, this loitering villain, the macer," added Finland, as the moonlight revealed a man running after them. " Follow! why the deuce did you not meet us at the White-horse-cellar?"

" Troth, sir, just to tell ye the truth," replied the panting functionary, drawing his gilt baton from the pocket of his voluminous skirt, "it is a kittle job this, and likely to get a puir man like me unco ill will in such uncanny times—but I stayed a wee while owre late may be, birling the ale cogue, at Lucky Dreep's change-house in the Kirk-o'-field Wynd. However, sir, follow me, and we'll catch these traitors where the reiver fand the tangs—at madam's fireside."

" Follow thee!" reiterated the cavalier officer, contemptuously; "malediction on the hour when a Douglas of Finland and a band of the old Scottish musketeers are bent on the same errand with a knave like thee. Step out, my lads, and, Walter Fenton, do thou fall rearward again, and see that we are neither followed nor watched; for, egad! these are times to sharpen one's wits."

Thus ordered, our hero (for such is the handsome pikeman) fell gradually to the rear, and stopped at times to bend his ear to the ground and his eyes on the changing shadows of the moonlit scenery; but he heard nothing save the blustering wind of March, which swept through the hollow dells, and saw only the shadows of the flying clouds cast by the bright moon on the fields through which the soldiers marched.

They had now passed all the houses of the city, and were moving westward, by the banks of the Burghloch, a broad and beautiful sheet of water, upwards of a mile in length, shaded on one side by the broken woods of Warrender and the old orchards of the convent of Sienna; on the other, open fields extended from its margin to the embattled walls of the city. One moment it shone like a sheet of polished silver; the next it lay like a lake of ink, as the passing clouds revealed or obscured the full-orbed moon.

"What lights are those twinkling in the woods yonder?" asked Finland, pointing northward with his pike, on his party reaching the *rhinns*, or flat at the end of the lake.

"The house of Coates, sir—the old patrimony of the Byres o' that ilk."

"Harkee, macer, and the dark pile rising on the height, further to the westward?"

"The Place of Drumsheugh, sir, pertaining of auld to my Lord Clermistonlee. He was just the gudeman thereof before these kittle times. A dark and eerie place it is, where neither light has burned nor fire bleezed—a joke been cracked nor a runlet broached these mony lang years. He is a dour chield that Clermistonlee, and one that would—"

"Twist thy hause, fellow," said the pikeman, sternly, "for speaking of your betters otherwise than with the reverence that becomes your station."

"Ye craw brawly for the spawn o' an auld covenanter," muttered the macer between his teeth, as they entered the dark avenue that led to the place of their destination; "brawly indeed! but may-be I'll hae ye under my hands yet, for a' your iron bravery and gay gauds."

CHAPTER II.

THE PREACHER.

A stranger, and a slave, unknown like him,
Proposing much means little;—talks and vows,
Delighted with the prospect of a change,
He promised to redeem ten Christians more,
And free us all from slavery.—ZARA.

ON the succession of James VII. to the throne, the persecution of the covenanters by the civil authorities, and by the troops under Dalzel, Claverhouse, Lag, and officers of their selection, was waged without pity or remorse, and the mad rage which had disgraced the government of the preceding reign, was still poured forth on the poor peasantry, who were hunted from hill to wood, and from moss to cavern, by the cavalry employed in riding down the country, until by banishment, imprisonment, famine, torture, the sword, and the scaffold, presbyterianism was likely to be crushed altogether; but an odium was raised, and a hatred fostered, against the Scottish ministry of the house of Stuart, which is yet felt keenly in the pastoral districts, where the deeds of those days are still spoken of with bitterness and reprehension.

The parliament of Scotland was presided over by the duke of Queensbury, a base time-server: it appeared devoted to the new sovereign, and declared him vested with solid and absolute authority, in which none could participate, and had promised him the whole array of the realm, between the ages of sixteen and sixty, whenever he should require their services. Notwithstanding these and similar loyal and liberal offers, there existed a strong faction intensely averse to the rule of a Catholic king; and though only three years before Archibald, earl of Argyle, and the equally unfortunate duke of Monmouth, had both perished in a futile attempt to preserve the civil and religious liberties of the land, the unsubdued Presbyterians were still intriguing with Holland, and concerting measures with William, prince of Orange, for a descent on the British shores, the expulsion of James by force of arms, and thus breaking the legitimate succession of the crown. Suspicion of these plots, and the intended invasion, had called forth all the fury and tyranny of the Scottish ministry against those whom they supposed to be inimical to the then existing state of things.

A certain covenanting preacher of some celebrity, the Reverend Mr. Ichabod Bummel, and a man of a very different stamp, Captain Quentin Napier (an officer of the Scottish brigade in the service of the States-General), both supposed to be emissaries of the prince of Orange, were known to be concealed in the house of Bruntisfield, the residence of Lady Grizel Napier, widow of Sir Archibald, of the Wrytes, a brave commander of cavalier troops, who had fallen in the battle of Inverkeithing. Unluckily for herself the old lady was a kinswoman of the intercommuned traitor Patrick Hume, "umquhile designate of Polworth," to use the legal and malevolent phraseology of the day; and consequently, notwithstanding the loyalty of her husband, the eyes of that stern tribunal, which ruled the Scottish Lowlands with a rod of iron, had been long upon her. And now, attended by a macer of council, bearing a warrant of search and arrest, a party of soldiers were approaching her mansion.

An archway, the piers of which were surmounted by two great stone eagles in full flight, each bearing a lance aloft, gave admittance to the long avenue that curved round the eminence on which the mansion stood. As the soldiers entered, the measured tap of a distant drum was borne from the city on the passing night-wind, and announced the hour of ten.

Thick dark beeches and darker oaks waved over them; the gigantic reliques of the great forest of Drumsheugh, beneath whose shade in the days of other years, the savage wolf, the stately elk, the bristly boar, and the magnificent white bull of ancient Caledonia, had roamed in all the glory of un-bounded freedom, on the site now occupied by the Scottish capital.

The blustering wind of March swept through their leafless branches, and whirled the last year's leaves along the lonely and grass-grown avenue, a turn of which brought the detach-ment at once in front of the mansion.

The Wrytes-house, or castle of Bruntisfield, was a high and narrow edifice, built in that striking and peculiar style of architecture which has again become so common—the old Scottish. It was several stories in height, and had steep corbie-stoned gables with little round turrets at every angle, a lofty circular tower terminating in a slated spire, numerous dormer windows, the acute gablets of which were surmounted by thistles, rosettes, crescents, and stars. Every casement was strongly grated, and the tall fantastic outline of the mansion rose from the old woodlands against the murky sky in a dark opaque mass, as the soldiers passed the barbican gate, and found themselves close to the oak door, which closed the central tower.

The night was still and dark; at times a red star gleamed tremulously amid the flying vapour, or a ray of moonlight cast a long and silvery line of radiance across the beautiful sheet of water to the eastward. The turret-vanes, and old ancestral oaks creaked mournfully in the rising wind, and the venerable rooks that occupied their summits croaked and screamed in concert.

"A noble old mansion!" said Walter Fenton; "and if tradition says truly, was built by our gallant James IV for one of his frail fair ones."

"It dates as far back as the days of the first Stuart, and men say, Walter, that its founder was William de Napier, a stark warrior of King Robert II.; but fair though the man-

sion, and broad the lands around it, the greedy gleds of our
council-board will soon rend all pieccmeal. Soldiers, blow
your matches, and give all who attempt to escape a prick of
the hog's bristle."

The musketeers cautiously surrounded the lofty edifice,
resistance to the death being an every-day occurrence—but
the windows remained dark, and the vast old manor-house
exhibited no sign of life, save where between the half-parted
shutters of a thickly-grated window a ray of flaky light
streamed into the obscurity without. To this opening the
curious macer immediately applied his legal eye, and cried in
a loud whisper,

"Look ye here, sirs, and behauld the godly Maister
Ichabod himsel' sitting in the cosiest neuk o' the ingle between
the auld lady and her kinswoman. Hech! a gallows-looking
buckie he is as ever skirled a psalm in the muirlands, or
testified at the Bowfoot, wi' a St. Johnstoun cravat round his
whaislin craig."

"Silence!" said Fenton in an agitated voice, as, clutching
the haft of his poniard, he applied his face to the barred
window; "silence, wretch, or I will trounce thee!" and the
scowling macer could perceive that his colour came and went,
and that his eye sparkled with vivacity as he took a rapid
survey of the apartment. "Fool, fool!" he muttered, as a
cracked voice was heard singing—

> " I like ane owle in desert am,
>   That nichtlie there doth moan ;
> I like unto ane sparrow am,
>   On the house-top alone."

" The true sough o' the auld conventicle," said the bluff
old sergeant, merrily. " Hark, your honours, the game's
afoot."

According to the rank of the house and the fashion of the
present time, the room which Fenton surveyed would be
deemed small for a principal or state apartment ; but it was
richly decorated with a stuccoed ceiling, divided into deep
compartments, as the walls were by wainscoting, but in the
panels of the latter were numerous anomalous paintings of
scenery, scripture pieces, armorial bearings, and the quaint
devices of the Scoto-Italian school. An old ebony buffet,
laden with glittering crystal and shining plate massively embossed. The furniture was ancient, richly carved, and dark
with time ; stark, high-backed chairs with red leather cushions,
and tables supported by lions' legs and wyverns' heads. The
floor was richly carpeted around the arched fireplace, where
a bright fire of coals and roots burned cheerily, while the

grotesque iron firedogs around which the fuel was piled, were glowing almost red-hot, and the blue ware of Delft that lined the recess, reflected the kindly warmth on all sides. The ponderous fireirons were chained to the stone jambs—a necessary precaution in such an age; and on a stone shield appeared the blazon of the Napiers: *argent*, a saltire, engrailed, between four roses, *gules*, and an eagle in full flight, with the lance and motto, "*Aye ready.*" A tall portrait of Sir Archibald Napier, in the dark armour of Charles the First's age, appeared above it.

A young lady sat near the fireplace, and on her the attention of the handsome eavesdropper became immediately riveted. Her face was of a very delicate cast of beauty; her bright blue eyes were expressive of the utmost vivacity, as her short upper lip and dimpled chin were of archness and wit. The fairness, the purity of her complexion was dazzling, and her glittering hair, of the brightest auburn, fell in massive locks on her white neck and stiff collar of starched lace. A string of Scottish pearls alone confined them, and they rolled over her shoulders in soft profusion, adding to the grace of her round and beautiful figure, which the hideous length of her long stomacher, and the volume of her ample skirt, could not destroy. She was Lilian Napier.

Opposite sat her grand-aunt, Lady Grizel, a tall, stately, and at first sight, grim old dame, as stiff as a tremendous bodice, a skirt of the heaviest brocade, the hauteur of the age, and an inborn sense of much real and more imaginary dignity, could make her. Frizzled with the nicest care, her lint-white locks were all drawn upwards, thus adding to the dignity of her noble features, though withered by care and blanched by time; and the healthy bloom of the young girl near her made the contrast between them greater: it was the summer and the winter of life contrasted. Lady Grizel's forehead was high, her nose decidedly aquiline, her eyes grey and keen, her brows a perfect arch. Though less in stature, and softer in feature, her kinswoman strongly resembled her, and though one was barely eighteen, and the other bordering on eighty, their dresses were quite the same; their gorgeously flowered brocades, their vandyked cuffs, high collars, and red-heeled shoes, were all similar.

As was natural in so young a man, Walter Fenton remarked only the younger lady, whose quick, small hands toyed with a flageolet and a few leaves of music, while her more industrious grand-aunt was busily urging a handsome spinning-wheel, the silver and ivory mountings of which flashed in the light of the fire, as it sped round and round. Close at her

feet lay an aged staghound, that raised its head and erected
its bristles at times, as if aware that foes were nigh.

There was such an air of happiness and domestic comfort
in that noble old chamber-of-dais, that the young volunteer
felt extremely loth to be one of those who should disturb it;
but fairly opposite the glowing fire, in the most easy chair in
the room (a great cushioned one, valanced round with silken
bobs), sat he of whom they were in search, and whom the
macer had pronounced so worthy of martyrdom.

He was a spare but athletic man, above the middle height;
his blue bonnet hung on a knob of his chair, and his straight
dark hair hung in dishevelled masses around his lean, lank
visage and sallow neck. His face was gaunt, with red and
prominent cheek-bones; his eyes intensely keen, penetrating,
and generally unsettled in expression. He wore clerical bands
falling over that part of his heavily-skirted and wide-cuffed
coat where lapelles would have been, had such been the fashion
of the day; his breeches and spatterdashes were of rusty grey
cloth; his large eyes seemed fixed on vacancy, and his hands
were clasped on his left knee. When he spoke, his whole
face seemed to be convulsed by a spasm.

"Maiden," said he, reproachfully, "and ye will not
accompany me in the godly words of Andro Hart's Scottish
metre?"

"Think of the danger of being overheard, Mr. Bummel,"
urged the young lady, "I will sing you my new song, the
'Norlan' Harp.'"

"Name it not, maiden; for thy profane songs sound as
abomination in my ears!"

Lilian Napier laughed merrily, and all her white teeth glittered like pearls.

"Fair as thou art to look upon, maiden, and innocent
withal, the fear grieves me that ye are one of the backsliders
of this sinful generation. Thy 'Norlan' Harp' quotha?
Know that there is no harp save that of Zion, whilk is a lyre
of treble-refined gold. What saith the sacred writ,—'Is any
among ye afflicted, let him pray. Is any merrie, let him *sing
psalmes.*'"

"I wot it would be but sad merriment," laughed the young
lady.

"Peace, Lilian," said grand-aunt Grizel, while the solemn
divine fidgeted in his chair, and hemmed gruffly, preparatory
to returning to the charge.

"Maiden, when thou hast perused my forthcoming discourse, whilk is entitled, '*A Bombshell aimed at the Tail of
the Great Beast,*' and whilk, please God, shall be imprinted

when I can procure ink and irons from Holland (that happy Elysium of the faithful), thou shalt there see in words of fire the strait and narrow path, contrasted with the broad but dangerous way that leadeth to the sea of flame : and therein will I show thee, and all that are yet in darkness, that the four animals in the Vision of Daniel hieroglyphically represent four empires—Rome, Persia, Grecia, and Babylonia, and that the man of sin, the antichrist, and the scarlet harlot of Babylon——"

At that moment the staghound barked and howled furiously, upon which the preacher's voice died away in a quaver, and his upraised hand sank powerless by his side.

"The dog howls eerily," said the old lady. "Gude sain us ! that foretells death,—and far-seen folks say that dumb brutes can see him enter the house when a departure is about to happen."

"— And further," continued the preacher incoherently, when his confusion had somewhat subsided, "I will show thee that the blessing of Heaven will descend upon the men of the Covenant—"

"Yea," chimed in Lady Grizel, "and upon their children—"

"Even unto the third and fourth generation."

"My honoured husband was as true a cavalier as ever wore buff," said Lady Grizel, striking her cane emphatically on the floor ; "but some of my dearest kinsmen have shed bluid for the other side, and I can think kindly o' baith."

"But if the king," urged Lilian ; "if the king should permit—"

"Maiden !" cried Mr. Bummel, in a shrill and stern voice, "mean ye the bloody and papistical Duke James, who, contrary to religion and to law, hath usurped the throne of this unhappy land,—that throne from which (as I show in my 'Bombshell') justice hath debarred him,—that throne from the steps of which the blood of God's children, the blessed sancts of our oppressed and martyred Kirk, rolls down on every hand ! But the hour cometh, Lilian, when it is written, that he shall perish, and a new religious and political millenium will dawn on these persecuted kingdoms. On one hand we have the power of the horned beast that sitteth upon seven hills, and her best-beloved son James, with his thumbscrews, the iron boots, and gory maiden,—the savage Amorites of the Highland hills, who go bare-legged to battle—yea, maiden, naked as the heretical Adamites of Bohemia,—those birds or Belial, the soldiers of Dunbarton,—those kine of Bashan, the troopers of Claverse, of Lag, and Dalyel, the fierce Muscovite cannibal ; in England, the *lambs* of Kirke, and the gallows of the butcher Jeffreys—a sea of blood, of darkness, death, and horror! But lo! on the other hand, behold ye the dawn of a new morn of peace, of love, and mercy; when the exile shall be restored to his hearth, and the doomed shall be snatched from the scaffold,—for he cometh, at whose approach the doors of a thousand dungeons shall fly open, the torch of rapine be extinguished, the sword of the persecutor sheathed, and when the flowers shall bloom, and the grass grow green on the lonely graves of our ten thousand martyrs. Yea—he, the saviour—William of Orange!"

The eyes of Ichabod Bummel filled with fire and enthusiasm as he spoke; the crimson glowed in his sallow cheek—the intonations of his voice alternated between a whistle and and a growl, and with his hands clenched above his head, he concluded this outburst, which gave great uneasiness and even terror to the old lady, though Lilian smiled with ill-concealed merriment.

"You have all heard this tirade of treason and folly?" said Douglas to his soldiers.

"Hech me!" ejaculated the macer, drawing a long breath; "it is enough to hang, draw, and quarter a haill parochin, I think."

"The Dutch rebel!" exclaimed Douglas, whose loyalty was fired. "Soldiers, look well that none escape by the windows; close up, my 'birds of Belial;' and, harkee, Sergeant Wemyss, tirl at the pin there."

The risp rung, and the door resounded beneath the blows of the halberdier. Lilian shrieked, Lady Grizel grew pale, and all the blood left the cheeks of the poor preacher, save the two scarlet spots on his cheek-bones.

"Woe is me!" he shouted; "for, lo! the Philistines are upon me."

"The guards of Pontius Pilate, he means," said the soldiers, as they gave a reckless laugh.

A shutter flew open, and the fair face of Lilian Napier, with all her bright hair waving around it, appeared for a moment gazing into the obscurity without.

"Soldiers, soldiers!" she screamed, as the light fell on corslets and accoutrements. "O! aunt Grizel, we are ruined, disgraced, and undone for ever."

CHAPTER III.

THE OLD CLOCKCASE.

In the meanwhile
The king doth ill to throw his royal sceptre
In the accuser's scale, ere he can know
How justice shall incline it.

THE AYRSHIRE TRAGEDY.

THE entrance to the mansion was by the narrow tower already described, and which contained what is called in Scotland the turnpike, a spiral stair, turning sharply round on its axis. The small doorway was heavily moulded, and ornamented above by a mossy coat armorial, the saltire, and four roses. The door was of massive oak, covered with a profusion of iron studs, and furnished with two eyelet-holes, through which visitors could be reconnoitred, or, if necessary, favoured with a dose of musketry.

"What graceless runions are you, that knock in this way, and sae near the deid hour of the nicht, too?" asked the querulous voice of old John Leekie, the gardener, while two rays of streaming light through the eyelets imparted to the doorway the aspect of some gigantic visage, of which the immense risp was the nose.

"Gae wa' in peace," added the venerable butler, in a very blustering voice, "or bide to face the waur."

"Open, rascals!" cried the sergeant, "or we will set the four corners of the house on fire."

"Doubtless, my bauld buckie," chuckled the old serving-man; "but the wa's are thick, and the winnocks weel grated, and we gaed a stronger band o' the English Puritans their kail through the reek in the year saxteen hundred and fifty." The over-night potations of the aged vassals had endued them with a courage unusual at that time, when a whole village trembled at the sight of a soldier.

"Wha are ye, sirs, ?" queried the butler, Mr. Drouthy; "wha are ye?"

"Those who are empowered to storm the house if its barriers are not opened forthwith," replied the sonorous voice of Douglas; "so, up, varlets! and be doing, for the soldiers of the king cannot bide your time."

The only reply to this was a smothered exclamation of fear from various female voices within, and the clank of one or two additional heavy bolts being shot into their places; and then succeeded the clatter of various slippers and high-heeled shoes,

as the household retreated up the steep turnpike in great
dismay.

"Now, ye dyvour loons!" cried the old butler, from a shot-
hole, "we'll gie ye a taste o' the Cromwell days, if ye dinna
mak' toom the barbican in five minutes. Lads," he continued,
as if speaking to men behind, although, save the old and
equally intoxicated gardener, the whole household were
women; "lads, tak' the plugs frae the loop-holes. John
Leckie, burn a light in the north turret, and in a crack we'll
hae our chields frae the grange wi' pitchfork, pike, and caliver.
Awa' to the vaults and bartizan—blaw your coals, and fire
cannily when I tout my old hunting-horn."

These orders caused a muttering among the soldiers, who
were quite unprepared to find the house garrisoned and ready
for resistance. An additional puffing of gun-matches ensued,
and all eyes were bent to the turrets and those parts which
were battlemented; but no man appeared therein or thereon,
and the thundering was renewed at the door with great
energy. Suddenly the bolts were withdrawn, the door revolved slowly on its hinges, and the musketeers, who were
about to rush in, hung back with mingled indecision and
respect.

In the doorway stood Lady Grizel Napier, leaning on her
long walking-cane; her dark-grey eyes lit up with indignation, and her forehead, though marked by the furrows of
eighty years, still expressive of dignity and determination;
nearly six feet in height, erect and stately as lace and brocade
could make her, she was the belle ideal of an old Scottish
matron. She wore on the summit of her frizzled hair a little
coif of widowhood, which she had never laid aside since her
husband was slain at Inverkeithing; and the circumstance of
his having died by a Puritan's hand, alone made her somewhat cold in the cause of the Covenant. Her retinue of
female servitors crowded fearfully behind her, and by her side
appeared the silver-haired butler, armed with a huge partisan,
while a battered morion covered his head, as it often had done
in many a tough day's work; and behind him staggered the
old gardener, armed with a watering-pan, and a steel cap with
a peak behind.

"Gentlemen," said the old lady, in a tone of great asperity,
while striking her long cane thrice on the doorstep, and all
her frills seemed to ruffle with indignation like the feathers
of a swan; "Gentlemen, what want ye at this untimeous
hour? Know ye not that this is a house whilk we are
entitled by crown charter to fortify and defend, as well
against domestic enemies as foreign; and methinks it is a

daring act, and a graceless, to boot, to march with cocked matches, and bodin in array of war on the bounds of a lone auld woman like me. By my faith, in the days of my honoured Sir Archibald, ye had gone off our barony faster than ye came, king's soldiers though ye be."

"Excuse us, madam," replied Douglas, lowering his rapier, and bowing with a peculiar grace which then was only to be acquired by service in France: "we have a warrant from the lords of his majesty's privy council, to arrest the persons of certain Captain Napier, of a Scots Dutch regiment, and the reverend Mr. Ichabod Bummel, who are accused of being treasonable emissaries of the States-General—intercommuned traitors, and now concealed in your mansion. Your ladyship must be aware that implicit obedience is the soldier's first duty: surrender unto us these guilty men, otherwise your house must be ransacked by my soldiers—a severe humiliation, which I would willingly spare the baronial mansion of a dame of honour, more especially when I remember the rank and loyal service of her husband."

"Gude keep us, laird of Finland," replied the old lady, trembling violently and leaning on her cane. "O what doo. is this that hath come upon us at last? My dream—my dream—it forewarned me of this: as the rhyme saith—

> "A Friday nicht's grue
> On the Saturday tauld,
> Is sure to come true,
> Be it never sae auld."

On my honour—nae such persons—I protest to you——"

"Enough, Lady Grizel," replied Douglas, with a little hauteur; "positively we must spare you the trouble, if not the shame, of making those unavailing but humiliating assertions, which the laws of humanity and hospitality require. The sooner this affair is over the better; we crave your pardon, madam, but the king's service is paramount. Sergeant Wemyss, guard the door—follow me, Walter: forward, soldiers, and I will unearth this clerical fox!"

Rushing past Lady Grizel, while the startled household fled before them, the musketeers pressed forward into the chamber-of-dais; but the reverend Mr. Bummel had vanished, and no trace remained of him, save his ample blue bonnet, with its red cherry or tuft, and Walter Fenton was certainly not the last to perceive that the young lady had disappeared also.

"Search the whole house, from roof-tree to foundations," exclaimed Douglas; "cut down all who make the least resistance; but on your lives beware of plunder or destruction—away."

I.

A violent and unscrupulous search was made forthwith; every curtain, every bed and panel were pierced by swords and daggers; every press, bunker, and girnel—the turrets and all the innumerable nooks and corners of the old house were searched. Every lockfast place was blown open by musket-balls, and thirty stentorian voices summoned the miserable preacher "to come forth;" but he was nowhere to be found. Pale and trembling, between terror and indignation, propped on her long cane, the old lady stood under her baronial canopy on the dais of the dining-hall, listening to the uproar that rang through all the stone vaults, wainscoted chambers, and long corridors of her mansion, and regarding Richard Douglas, and his friend the young volunteer, with glances of pride and hostility.

Walter Fenton coloured deeply, and appeared both agitated and confused; but Douglas coolly and collectedly leaned against the buffet, toying with the knot of his rapier, and drinking a cup of wine to Lady Bruntisfield's health, helping himself from the buffet uninvited.

"Lady Grizel," said he, "by surrendering up these foolish and guilty men, whom. contrary to law, you have harboured and resetted within your barony, you may considerably avert the wrath of the already incensed council."

"Never, sir! never will I be guilty of such a breach of hospitality and honour. Bethink ye, sirs, the Captain Napier is my sister's son, and it would ill become a Scottish dame to prove false to her ain blude. The minister, though but a gomeral body, is his friend—one of those whom the people deem exiled and persecuted for Christ's sake—ye may hew me to pieces with your partisans, but never would I yield a fugitive to the tortures and executioners of that bluidy and infamous council." And to give additional force to her words, Lady Grizel as usual, struck the floor thrice with her cane.

"Lady Bruntisfield," said Walter Fenton, gently, "beware lest our soldiers, or that dog the macer, overhear you."

"Glorious canary this!" muttered the lieutenant, apostrophizing the silver mug—"hum—I believe your ladyship is a Presbyterian."

"Though unused to be catechized by soldiers," replied the dame, drawing herself up with great dignity, "I acknowledge what all my neighbours know. I am Presbyterian, thank God, and so are all my household, who never miss a sabbath at kirk or meeting; and our minister is one, who having complied with the government regulations, hath an indulgence to preach."

" This applies not to the spy of that rogue William of Orange—this pious Ichabod, whom we must hale forth by the lugs at every risk."

" Never before was I suspected of disloyalty to the Scottish crown," said Lady Grizel, sobbing, " and now in my auld and donnart days, with ane foot in the grave, it's hard to thole, sirs—it's hard to thole. How often hae these hands, wrinkled now, and withered though they be, laced steel cap, greave and corslet, on my burdly husband and his three fair sons. Ehwhow, sirs! how often hae my very heart pulses died away with the clang o' their horses' hoofs in yonder avenue. Ane fell at Dunbar—another in his stirrups at the sack of Dundee, and my fair-haired Archy, my youngest and my best beloved, the apple o' my e'e, was shot deid by the side of his dying father, on the field of Inverkeithing. Save my sister's grandchild, all I loved have gone before me to God— but though my heart be seared, and my bower desolate, O laird of Finland, this disgrace is harder to thole than a' I hae tholed in my time."

Touched with her sorrow, Walter Fenton and Finland approached her; but ere they could speak, a dismal voice, that seemed to ascend from the profundity of some vast tun, was heard to sing, " I like an owle in desert am," &c., and the verse was scarcely concluded when the officer burst into a violent fit of laughter.

" O, ye fule man!" exclaimed the old lady, shaking her cane wrathfully: " ye have ruined yoursel' and the house of Bruntisfield too!"

" Where the devil is he?" said Douglas. " Ah, there must be some panel here," he added, knocking on the wainscot with the pommel of his sword.

" He is not very far off, your honour," said the macer approaching, pushing his bonnet on one side, and scratching his head with an air of vulgar drollery and perplexity. " I'll wager ye a score o' broad pieces, Finland, that I howk out the tod in a moment."

" Then do so," said Douglas, haughtily, " but first, you irreverend knave, doff your bonnet in the Lady Bruntisfield's presence."

" There is something queer about this braw Flanders wag-at-the wa'," said the macer, approaching a clock, the case of which formed part of the wainscoting. It was violently shaken, and emitted a hollow groan. The macer opened the narrow panel, and revealed the poor preacher coiled up within, in great spiritual and bodily tribulation, and half stifled by want of air. His face was almost black, his eyes bloodshot, and his features sharpened by an expression of delirious terror bordering on the ludicrous.

" Dolt and fool !" exclaimed Walter, " what fiend tempted ye to rant thus within earshot of us ?"

" Gadso, I think the varlet's mad," said Douglas, laughing. " Dost think we will eat thee, fellow ?"

" Mad !—I hope so, for the sake of this noble lady."

" And the marrow in his bones, Fenton."

" Come awa, my man," said the macer, making him a mock bow ; " use your shanks while the ungodly Philistines will let you. Ye'll no walk just sae weel after you have tried on the braw buits my Lord Chancellor keeps for such pious gentle- men as you."

" From these sons of blood and Belial, good Lord deliver me !" ejaculated the poor man, turning up his hollow eyes, as he was dragged forth ; " ye devouring wolves, I demand your warrant for what ye do."

" Macer—your warrant ?" said Douglas.

Unfolding the slip of paper, the worthy official now reve- rentially took off his bonnet, and in a sing-song voice drawled forth—

" I, Michael Maclutchy, macer to the privy council of Scotland, by virtue *of*, and conform *to*, the principal letters raised at ye instance of Maister Roderick Mackenzie, ad- vocat-depute to Sir David Dalrymple, his majesty's advocat, summon, warn, and charge *you*, the said Reverend Mr. Hugh —otherwise Ichabod Bummel—is that richt, friend ?"

" Yea—I was so named by my parents Hugh, a heathenish name, whilk in a better hour I changit to Ichabod, signifying in the Hebrew tongue—' where is glory ?' "

" Weel—weel, mind na the Hebrew—charge you to sur- render peaceably—and sae forth ; it's a' there in black and white : subscribitur *Perth*."

" Fie upon ye !" exclaimed Ichabod, " ye abjurers of the Lord, and persecutors of his covenanted kirk."

" Away with him !" said Fenton to the soldiers.

" Truly ye are properly clad in scarlet, for it is the garb——"

" Silence, sir ; you make bad worse."

" Of your Babylonian mother."

" Peace !" cried Douglas.

" I liken ye even unto broken reeds——"

" On with the gyves, and away wi' him !" said the sergeant, and the poor crack-brained enthusiast was unceremoniously handcuffed and dragged away, pouring a torrent of hard scriptural epithets and invectives on his captors, and chanting suitable verses from Andro Hart's book of the *Psalmes*.

Lady Bruntisfield started as he was taken away, and was about to bestow on him some address of comfort and farewell, but the young volunteer interposed, saying with great gentleness,

"Pardon me, Lady Grizel—by addressing him you will only compromise your own safety and honour. O madam, I deeply regret your involvement in this matter! The privy council is not to be trifled with."

"Madam," observed Douglas, "I believe I have the honour of being not unknown to you?"

"You are the young laird of Finland, who wounded my nephew Quentin——"

"In a duel in Flanders—O yes—ha! ha! we quarrelled about little Babette of the Hans-in-Kelder, or some folly of that kind. I acquaint you, madam, with regret, that in consequence of this trumpeter of rebellion being found resetted here—your whole family——"

"Alake, laird, I have only my little grandniece."

"Your whole household must be considered prisoners until the pleasure of the council is known. In the interim," he added in a low voice, "I hope your kinsman will escape; though he has been no friend of mine since that time we fought with sword and dagger on the ramparts of Tournay, I would wish him another fate than a felon's, for a braver fellow never marched under baton. Meanwhile, Lady Bruntisfield, I am your servant—adieu;" and bowing until his plume touched the floor, he withdrew.

Leaving his veteran sergeant, and Walter the volunteer, with twenty men to keep ward, he returned to the city with his prisoner, who was immediately consigned to the iron room of the Tolbooth.

For a few minutes after his departure Lady Grizel seemed quite stunned by the dilemma in which she so suddenly found herself. She had now been joined by Lilian, who hung upon her shoulder weeping; for the privy council of Scotland was a court of religious and political inquisition, whose name and satellites bore terror throughout the land.

Sergeant Wemyss posted seven of his musketeers within the barbican, with orders "to keep all in who were within, and all out who were so;" after which he withdrew with the remainder to the spacious and vaulted kitchen, where, as occupying free quarters, they made themselves quite at home, d crowded round the great wood-fire that was roaring in the vast archway which spanned one side of the apartment, joked and toyed with the half-pleased and half-frightened maids, and compelled the indignant housekeeper (who, with Lady Grizel's cast coifs and fardingales assumed many of her airs) to provide them with a substantial supper, the least items of which were a huge side of beef, a string of good fat capons, and an unmeasured quantity of ale and usquebaugh for the soldiers; while his honour the halberdier insisted on wine dashed with brandy, swearing "by the devil's horns," and other cavalier oaths, "he would drink nothing but the best Rhenish." There was an immense consumption of viands, and as the revellers became merrier, they made the whole house ring to their famous camp-song,

"Dumbarton's drums beat bonnie, O,"

to the great envy of those luckless wights in the barbican, who heard only the bleak March wind sighing among the leafless woods, and witnessed through the windows all this hilarity and good cheer from which they were for a time debarred.

Mr. Drouthy the butler, and other old servitors, who had seen something of free quarters under the duke of Hamilton in England, entered heartily into the spirit of entertaining their noisy visitors, to whom they detailed the fields of Inverkeithing, Dunbar, and Kerbeister, with great vociferation, and ever and anon voted the Reverend Mr. Bummel a most unqualified bore, and declared that "the house of Bruntisfield was weel rid o' his grunting and skirling about owls and sparrows in the desert."

CHAPTER IV

A PAIR OF BLUE EYES.

Thou tortur'st me. I hate all obligations
Which I can ne'er return—and who art thou,
That I should stoop to take them from your hand?
FATAL CURIOSITY.

THE post of honour—that in the hall or lobby immediately outside the room occupied by the ladies—had been appropriated by the sergeant to Walter Fenton.

The young man placed his pike across the door of the chamber of dais (as the dining-hall was named in those Scottish houses, which, though to all intents baronial, were not castles), and then paced slowly to and fro.

A lamp, the chain of which was suspended from the mouth of a grotesque face carved on the wall, lighted the lobby or ambulatory, and dimly its flickering rays were reflected by a rusty trophy of ancient weapons opposite. An old head-piece and chain-jacket formed the centre, while crossbows, match-locks, partisans, and two-handed swords, radiated round them. A deer's skull and antlers, riding gambadoes, heavy whips and spurs, a row of old knobby chairs, and a clumsy oaken clock, which (like many persons in the world) had two faces, one looking to the lobby, the other to the dining-hall, ticked sullenly in a corner, and made up the furniture of the place.

Save the monotonous vibrations of the clock, and an occasional murmur of voices from the chamber of dais, no other sound disturbed the solitary watch of Fenton, unless when a distant shout of hilarity burst from the vaulted kitchen, and reverberated through the winding staircases and stone corridors of the ancient mansion.

Absorbed in meditation, the young man walked slowly to and fro, turning with something of military briskness at each end of the half-darkened passage, by the indifferent light of which we must present a view of him to the reader.

> "A young man, gentle-voiced and gentle-eyed,
> Who looked and spake like one the world had frowned on."

He seemed to be about twenty years of age; of a rather tall and very handsome figure, which his scarlet sleeves, and corslet tapering to the waist, and tightly compressed by a broad buff belt sustaining a plainly-mounted sword and dagger, tended greatly to improve. The check-plates of his burgonet, or steel cap, were unclasped, and his dark brown hair rolled over his polished gorget in the profuse fashion of the time; his pale forehead was thoughtful and intellectual in expression; but the gilt peak of his cap partly concealed it, and cast a shadow over a very prepossessing face of a dark complexion, and somewhat melancholy contour. His dark eye had a soft and pleasing expression, though at times it lowered and overcast. The curve of his lips, though gentle and haughty, and scornful, by turns, was ever indicative of firmness and decision. They were red and full as those of a girl, but short black moustaches, pointed smartly upward, imparted a military aspect to a face such as few could contemplate without interest — especially women. With the manner of one who has early learned to think, and hold communion with himself, his eye sparkled and his cheek flushed as certain ideas occurred to him: anon his animation died away; he sighed deeply, and thus immersed in his own thoughts, continued to pace to and fro, until at the half-opened door of the chamber of dais there appeared the fair face of Lilian Napier—a face so regular in its contour of eyebrow, lip, and nostril, that the brightness of her blue eyes, and the waving of her auburn ringlets, together with a decided piquancy of expression, alone prevented it from being insipid. She was looking cautiously out.

On recognizing her, Fenton bowed, and the girl blushed deeply, as she said hurriedly, and in a low voice,

"Oh joy! Walter Fenton, is it indeed you? how fortunate! but oh, what a night this has been for us all."

"Mistress Lilian," said he (the prefix *Miss* as a title of honour did not become common until the beginning of the next century), "need I say that it has been a night of sorrow and mortification to me. Yet, God wot, what could I do but obey the orders of my superiors?"

"Hush!" she whispered; for at that moment Lady Bruntisfield came forth, pale and agitated, with eyes red from recent weeping.

Tall in form and majestic in bearing, Lady Grizel Napier, as I have said before, was one of those stately matrons who appear to have departed with their hoops and fardingales. In youth, her face had possessed more than ordinary beauty, and now, in extreme old age, it still retained its feminine softness and pleasing expression. Undecided in politics, she was intensely loyal to James; while condemning his government, she railed at the non-conformists, and reprobated the severities of the council in the same breath. Like every dame of the olden time, she was a matchless mediciner, and maker of preserves, conserves, physics, and cordials, and, did a vassal's finger but ache, Lady Grizel was consulted forthwith. Like every woman of her time, she was intensely superstitious; she shook her purse when the pale crescent of the new moon rose above the Corstorphine woods; if the salt-foot was overturned, she remembered Judas, trembled, and threw a pinch over her left shoulder; she saw coffins in the fire, letters in the candles, and quaked at deidspales when they guttered in the wind. She listened in fear to the chakymill, or deathwatch, which often ticked obstinately for a whole night in the massive posts of her canopied bed. Witches, of course, were a constant source of hatred and annoyance; and, notwithstanding her great faith in the holy kirk (and a little in Peden's Prophecies), she had such a wholesome dread of the prince of darkness, that, according to the ancient usage, a piece of her lands adjoining the Harestane was dedicated to him, under the dubious name of *the gudeman's croft*, and, in defiance of all the acts against this old superstition (which still exists in remote parts of Scotland), it was allowed to remain a weedy waste, unsown and unemployed. With all this, her manners were high-bred and courtly, her information extensive, and there was in her air a certain indescribable loftiness, which *then* consciousness of noble birth and long descent inspired, and which failed not to enforce due respect from equals and inferiors.

On her approach, Walter Fenton bowed with an air in which politeness and commiseration were gracefully blended. Her bright-haired kinswoman leant upon her arm, and from time to time stole furtive and timid glances at the volunteer beneath her long eyelashes.

"Young man," said Lady Bruntisfield, "for a soldier you seem good and gentle. Have you a mother" (her voice faltered) "who is dear to you—a sister whom you love?"

"Nor mother, nor sister, nor kindred have I, madam. Alas, Lady Grizel, I am alone in the world; the first, and perhaps it may be the *last*, of my race," he added bitterly. "But what would your ladyship with Walter Fenton?"

"Ha! are you one of the Fentons of that ilk?"

"Nay, lady, I am only Walter Fenton of the Scottish Musketeers, and nothing more; but in what can I serve you?"

"How shall I speak it?—That you will sleep on your post, and permit this poor child—dost comprehend me?—oh, I will nobly reward you; and the deed will be registered elsewhere."

"Oh, no, no; beg no such boon for me," said the blushing and trembling girl; while the brow of the young man became clouded.

"You would counsel me to my ruin, Lady Bruntisfield; is it generous, is it noble, when I am but a poor soldier? Seek not to corrupt me by gold," he said hurriedly, on the old lady drawing a purse from her girdle; "for all I possess is my honour, the poor man's best inheritance; and yet, for the sake of Lilian Napier, I would dare much."

The deep blush which suffused the soft cheek and white brow of Lilian as the pikeman spoke, was not unobserved by the elder lady; and she said, with undisguised hauteur,—

"How is this, sir sentinel? ye know my kinswoman, and by that glance it would seem that ye have met before. Lilian, do thou speak."

Lilian trembled, but was silent and confused.

"I have often had the honour of seeing Mistress Lilian at my Lord Dunbarton's," said the young man, hastening to her relief.

"How, are you little Fenton?"

"The countess's page, madam."

"By my father's bones!" said Lady Grizel, striking the floor angrily with her cane; "I little thought a time would come when I would sue a boon in vain, either from a lord's loon or a lady's foot-page."

These words seemed to sting the young soldier deeply; fire sparkled in his eyes. But tears suffused those of Lilian.

"Madam," said he, firmly, "I am the first private gentleman of Dunbarton's Foot, and am so unused to such hauteur, that had the best man in broad Scotland uttered words like these, my sword had assuredly taken the measure of his body."

"I admire your spirit, sir," said Lady Grizel, gently; "but it might be shown in a more honourable cause than the persecution of helpless women-folk."

"Lady Grizel, a soldier from my childhood, I have been inured to hardship and trained to face every danger. My conscience is my own; my soul belongs to God; and my sword to the king and parliament of Scotland, whose orders I must obey."

"Then, gentle sir, be generous as your bearing is noble, and, in the name of God, permit my little kinswoman to escape. Alas, you know well what is in store for us, if we are dragged before that odious privy council—fine, imprisonment, torture——"

"Or banishment to Virginia," said Lilian, bursting into tears.

"God wot I pity you, Lady Bruntisfield, and would lay down my life to serve you. Retire—I will keep my post; your chamber has windows by which——"

"Alas! they are grated, and there are sentinels without."

Fenton stamped his foot impatiently.

"Birds' eggs aye bring ill luck; and oh! Lilian, ye thoughtless bairn, when ye strung up the pyets yesternight, I forewarned ye that something *would* happen. The thumbscrews and extortions of the council, yea! and banishment even in my auld age, I might bear, though the thocht of being laid far frae the graves of my ain kindred is hard to thole; but thee, my dear doo, Lilian—it is for thee my heart bleeds."

"Oh! madam, they cannot be such villains as to harm her—so young—so fair."

"You know not what I mean," replied Lady Grizel,

pressing her hands upon her breast, and speaking in an inco-
herent and bitter manner. " Lord Clermistonlee rules at the
council-board, and he hath seen Lilian. Wretch—wretch, too
well do I know 'tis for worse than the thumbscrews he would
reserve her ! "

She paused ; and Fenton starting, said, " Oh, whence were
all my unreasonable scruples ? Finland by his hints warned
me of Clermistonlee, that *roué* and ruffian, whose name brings
scandal on our peerage."

" Then let my dear aunt Grizel escape to some place of concealment, and, good Mr. Fenton, you shall have my prayers
and gratitude for life."

It was the young girl who spoke : her accents were low
and imploring ; and her whole appearance was very fascinating, for her timidity and mortification added the utmost
expression to her blue eyes, while her lips, half parted, showed
the whiteness of her teeth, and lent a sweetness and simpli-
city to her face. The tenor of her address made the heart of
Walter flutter, for love was fast subduing his scrupulous sense
of duty.

" Artless Lilian," said he with a faint smile, " Lord Clermistonlee aims neither at Lady Grizel's liberty or life. He
is a villain of the deepest dye ; and you have many things to
fear. It ill beseems a lady of birth to sue a boon from a
poor sworder such as I. Leave me to my fate, and the fury
of the council. I am, I hope, a gentleman, though an unfortunate one, and reduced to the necessity of trailing a pike
under the noble earl of Dunbarton ; but in spirit I can be
generous as a king, though my whole inheritance is to follow
the drum."

" I offered you money——"

" Lady Grizel," said Fenton, colouring again, " I hope that
the poorest musketeer who follows the banner of Dunbarton
would have rejected it with scorn. Though soldiers, we are
not like those rapacious wolves the troopers of Lag, of Dalzel,
or Kirke the Englishman. By my faith, madam, for six
shillings Scots per day I have often perilled life and limb in a
worse cause than yours ; and why should I scruple now ?
Escape while there is yet time. Lady Grizel, permit me to
lead you forth."

And, drawing off his leather glove, he offered his hand to
the old dame, who, struck by the gallantry of his manner,
said—

" You have quite the air of a cavalier, such as I mind o
in my young days, when the first Charles was crowned in
Holyrood."

"I pretend not to be a cavalier," said Walter, with a sad smile: "the camp is the school of gallantry."

"Fear for my Lilian makes me miserably selfish. I would rather die, good youth, than that a hair of your head should be injured; but that this delicate bairn should be dragged before that fierce council, like some rude cottar's wife—'tis enough to make the dead bones in the West-kirk aisle to clatter in their coffins! Ere we go, say what will be your inevitable punishment for this dereliction of duty?"

"A few days' close ward in the Abbey-guard, with pease bannocks and sour beer to regale on, and mounting guard at the Palace porch in backbreast and headpieces, partisan, sword and dagger, in full marching harness, for four-and-twenty consecutive hours,—that is all, madam," said he gaily, though the inward forebodings of his heart and his sad experience told him otherwise. "In serving *you*, fair Lilian," he added gently, and half attempting, but not daring, to touch her hand, "I shall be more than a thousand times recompensed for any penance I may perform. Believe me, it will weigh as a featherweight against what the council may inflict on Lady Bruntisfield. Now, then, away in God's name. Ye will surely find a secure shelter somewhere among your numerous friends and tenantry; but seek not the city, for Dunbraiken's guards are on the alert at every gate; and, above all, oh! beware of—of Lord Clermistonlee, who (if Finland suspects truly) has a deep project to accomplish."

"Heaven bless thee, good young man!" faltered the venerable Lady Grizel, laying her small but wrinkled hands upon his shoulders, and gazing on him with eyes that beamed with heartfelt gratitude. "Alack! alack! my mind gangs back to the time when three hearts, as brave and as gentle as yours, grew up from heartsome youth to stately manhood under this auld roof-tree; but, oh, waly! waly! the cauld blast o' war laid my three fair flowers in the dust."

A noise in the kitchen, and the loud voice of the halberdier calling fresh sentinels, now caused them to hurry away. To conceal about their persons such jewels and money as they could collect from the cabinets in the chamber of dais, to muffle up in their hoods and mantles, to give one glance of adieu to the portrait of the dark cavalier above the fireplace, and another of gratitude to Walter Fenton, were all the work of a minute,—and they were led forth to the avenue. Grey morning was breaking in the east, and the black ridge of Arthur's Seat stood in strong relief against the brightening sky; the wind had died away, and the waning moon shone cold and dim in the west, while, far to the northward, the dark opaque clouds were piled in shadowy masses above the bold and striking outline of the capital. There the great spire of the Gothic cathedral, the ramparts of its rock-built fortress, the crenelated towers of the Flodden-wall, and the streets within "piled deep and massy, close and high," were all glimmering in the first pale rays of the dawn, though the valleys below, and the woods around, were still sunk in the gloom and obscurity of night. A sentinel challenged from the dark shadow of the barbican wall, and his voice made the fugitives tremble with fear.

"Dunbarton," answered Walter; and on receiving the password, the soldier stepped back. "And now, ladies, whence go ye?"

"As God shall direct,—to some of our faithful tenant bodies, for safety and concealment," sobbed Lady Bruntis-field.

"Poor Mr. Fenton!" murmured Lilian; "I tremble more for you than for ourselves."

"A long farewell to our gude auld barony of Bruntisfield and the Wrytes—to main and holm, and wood and water," said Lady Grizel, mournfully; "we stand under the shadow of its green sauchs and oak-woods for the last time. Once before I fled frae them, but that was in the year fifty, when our natural enemies, the English, won that doolfu' day at Dunbar; and again our hail plenishing will be ruined and harried, as in the days o' the ruffianly and ungracious Puritans."

"Not by us, Lady Bruntisfield," replied the young man, slightly piqued; "we are the soldiers of the gallant Dunbarton, the old Royals of Turenne, les Gardes Ecossais of a thousand battles and a thousand glorious memories, and your mansion will be sacred as if in the hands of so many apostles. Farewell, and God speed ye! Would that I could accompany your desolate steps to some place of safety! but that would discover all." They parted.

"I have done," muttered Walter, striking his breast; "and from this hour I am a lost man!"

Hastily returning, he resumed his post, with his heart beating high with the conflicting emotions of pleasure and apprehension. Youth and beauty in suffering, danger, or humiliation, form naturally an object of interest and compassion; but Walter, though pleased by the conviction that he had done a good action, and one so fully involving the gratitude of Lilian Napier and her haughty relative, felt a dread of what was to ensue weighing heavily on his mind; for the Scottish privy council was then composed of men with

whom the proudest noble dared not to trifle, and before whom
the pride and power of the great Argyle, lord of a vast terri-
tory, and chief of the most powerful of the western clans,
bent like a reed beneath the storm.   Poor Walter reflected,
that he was but a friendless and nameless volunteer; and too
well he knew that the council would not be cheated of their
prey without a terrible vengeance.

Scarcely had he resumed his post in the corridor, when the
sergeant, whose brown visage was flushed with carousing, and
whose corslet braces were unclasped to give space for the
quantity of viands he had imbibed, reeled up with a relief of
sentinels, all more or less in the same condition.

"All right, an't please you, Master Walter?   I warrant
you will be tired of this post of honour, and longing for
a leg of a devilled capon, and a horn of the old butler's
Rhenish."

"I thought you had forgotten me, Wemyss.   You will
have a care, sir," said Walter, addressing the soldier who
relieved him, with a glance that was not to be misunderstood,
"that you do not disturb the ladies by entering the chamber
of dais: dost hear me, thou pumpkin-head?"

"Rot me, Master Fenton, I have clanked my bandoleers
before the tent of Monsieur of France, and I need nae be
learned now how to keep guard on king or knave, baron or
boor.   Dost think that I, who am the son of an auld vassal of
her ladyship's, would dragoon her out of marching-money?"

"'Tis well," replied the pikeman, briefly, as he retired, not
to the kitchen, but to a solitary apartment prepared for him
by the orders of his old patron, the halberdier.

CHAPTER V.

A PAIR OF RAPIERS.

If thou sleep alone in Urrard,
    Perchance in midnight gloom,
Thou't hear behind the wainscot
    Of that old and darken'd room
A fleshless hand that knocketh——
        HIGHLAND MINSTRELSY.

IN a dark old wainscoted apartment, in the small arched
chimney of which a coal fire was glowing cheerily, supper and
wine were sullenly laid for Walter by a sleepy and half-
frightened servant; but the first remained untouched and the
last untasted, at least for a time.   Removing his burgonet and
gloves, he sat with his elbow on the table and his forehead on

his hand, with his fingers writhed among his thick dark locks. He was again sunk in one of his gloomy reveries; but at times a smile of pleasure and animation unbent his haughty lip and lit up his handsome face like sunlight through a cloud; and it was evident he thought more of Lilian Napier's bright blue eyes, her innocence, and her fears, than the dangers and ignominy to which coming day would assuredly expose him.

The mildness, modesty, and beauty of the young girl, with the touching artlessness of her manner, had awakened a nearer and more vivid interest in his heart, one to which it had hitherto been utterly a stranger. It was the dawn of passion; never before, he thought, had one so winning or so attractive crossed his path; he had found at last the well-known face that his fancy had conjured up in a thousand happy reveries, and he was predisposed to love it. Her tears and affliction for the last relative (save one) whom fate and war had left, had increased her natural attractions, and a keen sense of her unmerited humiliation, and the risk he ran for her, by knitting their names together, all tended to raise a glow in young Walter's solitary heart; for having no living thing in this wide world to cling to, it was peculiarly susceptible and open to impressions of kindness and generosity; now it expanded with a flush of happiness and delight to which since thought-less childhood it had been a stranger; and in a burst of soldierlike enthusiasm, he uttered her name aloud, and drained the pewter flagon of Rhenish to the bottom.

As he set it down, a noise behind made him turn sharply round and listen; nothing was visible but the dark stains of the wainscoting, and its gilded panels glistening ruddily in the glow of the fire. From an antique brass sconce on the wall, the light of three great candles burned steadily on the old discoloured floor, the massively jointed arch of the fire-place, which bore a legend in Saxon characters, on three old pictures by Jamieson, of cavaliers in barrelled doublets, high ruffs, and peaked beards, and one of the famous Barbara Napier of Bruntisfield, who so narrowly escaped the stake for her sorceries, on a spectral suit of mail, and six old heavily carved chairs, ranged against the wall like grotesque gnomes with their arms akimbo; but although nothing was visible to create alarm, the aspect of the chamber was so gloomy, that certain tales of a spectre cavalier who haunted the old house, began to flit through Walter's mind, and he could not resist listening intensely; still not a sound was heard, but the wind rumbling in the hollow vent, and the creaking of the turret vanes overhead.

"Tush!" said he, and whether it was the faint echo of his

own voice or a sound again behind the wainscot, he knew not,
but he palpably heard something that made him bring the hilt
of his long rapier more readily to hand.   The portraits, like
all those of persons whom one knows to have been long dead.
when viewed by the dim candlelight had a staring, desolate,
and ghastly expression, and they really seemed to "frown"
over their high ruffs on the intruder, who would probably
have frowned in return, had he not, even in the harsh lines of
the old Scottish artist, traced a family likeness to the soft
features of Lilian Napier.   But there was a stern, keen, and
malignant expression in the features of the old sorceress, Lady
Barbara, that made Walter often avert his eyes, for her sharp
features seemed to start from the panel instinct with life and
mockery.

As sleep weighed down the eyelids of Walter, strange fancies
pressed thick and fast, though obscurely, on his mind; and
though once or twice the same faint hollow sound made him
start and take another survey of the apartment by the dim
light of the sconce and the dying embers of the fire, his head
bowed down on the table, and at last he slumbered soundly.

Scarcely had he sunk into this state, when there was a sharp
click heard; a jarring sound succeeded, and on the opposite
side of the room, about three feet from the ground, a panel
in the wainscoting was opened slowly and cautiously, and the
bright glare of a large oil cruise streamed into the darkened
apartment.   Beyond the aperture, receded a gloomy alcove or
secret passage, into the obscurity of which the steps of a
narrow stair ascended, and therein appeared the figure of a
man, who gazed cautiously upon the unconscious sleeper.
He was about thirty years of age, strongly formed, and possessing a handsome but very weatherbeaten countenance. He
wore a plain buff coat and steel gorget; his waist was encircled by a broad belt, which sustained a pair of long iron
pistols of the Scottish fashion, and a sharp narrow-bladed
rapier glittered in his hand.

Young Fenton still slept soundly.

The stranger regarded him with a stern and louring visage,
on which the lurid light of the upraised cruise fell strongly.
It betokened some fell and deadly intention, and the hostile
ferocity of its aspect increased as, slowly, softly, and ominously,
he descended into the apartment.

"Through which part of the iron shell shall I strike this
papistical interloper?" he muttered; "I will teach thee,
wretch, to think of Lilian Napier in thy cups."

His right hand was withdrawn preparatory to making one
furious and deadly thrust, which assuredly would have ended

this history (ere it is well begun) had not the subject thereof started up suddenly, exclaiming,—

"Back, rebel dog! on thy life, stand back!" and striking up the thrust rapier, drew his own, and throwing a chair between him and his adversary, he stood at once upon his guard.

"Malediction!" cried the stranger, furiously, "dolt that I was not to have pistolled thee from the panel."

"Wemyss, Wemyss!" exclaimed Walter, "The guard— what, ho, without there!"

"Spare your breath, for you may need it all," said the other, putting down his lamp, and barring the door. "This chamber is vaulted and boxed, and long enough mayest thou bawl ere thy fellow-beagles hear thee. Defend thyself, foul minion of the bloodiest tyrant that ever disgraced a throne. Strike! for by the heaven that is above, ere a sword is sheathed, this floor must smoke with the blood of one or both of us. Come on, Mr. Springald, and remember that you have the honour to cross blades with the best swordsman in the six battalions of the Scottish Brigade."

"You are——"

"Ha, scoundrel! Quentin Napier of Bruntisfield, by God's grace and King William's, a captain of the Scots-Dutch; so fall on, for I am determined to slay thee, were it but to keep my hand in practice for better work."

The blades crossed and struck fire as they clashed; each cavalier remained a moment with his head drawn back, the right leg thrown forward and his eyes glaring on his antagonist. Walter was ten years younger than his adversary, upon whom he rushed with more ardour than address, and consequently, in endeavouring to pass his point and close, received a slight wound on the hand, which kindled him into a terrible fury. Napier excelled him in temper, if not in skill; he parried all his thrusts with admirable coolness, until, perceiving that the youth's impetuosity began to flag, he pressed him in turn, the ferocity that sparkled in his eyes and blanched his nether lip revealing the bitterness of his intention; but in making one furious lunge, he overthrust himself, and was struck down with his sword-hand under him. Rage had deprived Walter of all government over himself; in an instant his knee was on Napier's breast, and his sword shortened in his hand with the intention of running him through the heart, for his blood was now up, and all "the devil" was stirred within him. He felt the deep broad chest of his powerful adversary heaving beneath him with suppressed passion and fury.

I.   D

"Captain Napier," said Walter, "for the sake of *her* whose name and blood you share—though you disgrace them—I will spare your life if you will beg it at my hands."

"Strike!" and he panted rather than breathed as he spoke; "Strike! life would be less than worthless if given as a boon by Dunbarton's beggarly brat O, a thousand devils! is it come to this with *me?*"

"Peace, fool!" exclaimed Walter, "peace, lest your words tempt me to destroy you. Accept life at my hands; they spared the blood of a better man upon the field of Sedgemoor."

"Be it so," replied the discomfited captain, sullenly receiving his rapier; "I accept it only that I may, at some future time, avenge in blood the stain thou hast this night cast upon the best cavalier of the Scottish Brigade." He ground his teeth. "D——nation, my throat is burning—any wine here?" He drank some Rhenish from a flask, and then continued: "Ho, ho, and now, since you know my hiding-place, doubtless for the sake of the thousand marks this poor brain-pan is worth, ye will deliver me unto our Scottish Philistines, those lords of council, who are steeped to the lips in infamy and blood."

"Perish the thought," replied Walter, sheathing his rapier with a jerk. "You are safe for me, and here is my thumb on't."

"Gadso, young fellow, I love thy spirit, and at another's expense could admire your skill in the noble science of defence. You fought at Sedgemoor—so did I."

"For the king?"

"Why—not exactly."

"For James of Monmouth?"

"Humph!"

"Then doubly are you a branded rebel."

"I had been a glorious patriot, had we won that bloody field. Young fellow, you must have early cocked your feather to the tuck of the drum! Art a Papist?"

"Nay, I am a good Protestant, I hope."

"And loyal to our Seventh James, the crowned Jesuit? Der tuyvel, as we say in Holland, 'tis a miracle!" and after drinking from the wine-flask, he resumed with greater urbanity: "When I remember how you permitted the Lady Bruntisfield and my kinswoman Lilian to escape, it shames me that I was not more generous; but the devil tempted me to blood in that infernal hole to which I must return."

"Now, sir, since the ladies are gone, you will undoubtedly starve."

"Nay, the whole household know of my concealment, and old Drouthy will not let me want for wine and vivres."

"They may inform."

"O never! I am their lady's only kinsman—the last of the good old line, and they are stanch servitors; a few among those, whom the courtly villany of these times hath left uncorrupted. 'Tis well I know all the outlets of the mansion, for it will become quite too hot for me after to-night. No doubt a band of your soldiers will be here at free quarters until the whole barony, outfield and infield, are as bare as my hand."

"In part you anticipate rightly."

"Henckers! then I must shift my camp among our Whig friends in the west until ——"

"Until what?" asked Walter, suspiciously.

"Thou shalt learn anon, and so shall all thy faction with a vengeance!" replied the captain, while a deep smile spread over his features. "Meantime, adieu, and may God keep us separate, friend! I trust to thine honour."

"Adieu!"

He sprang into the secret passage, closed the panel, and Walter heard his footsteps dying away as he ascended into the hollow recesses of the thick wall, and sought some of those secret hiding-places with which this ancient mansion abounded more than any other edifice in or around Edinburgh.

Morning came, and with it came an order from the king's advocate to bring the prisoners before the privy council, and to secure the persons of their entire household for future examination and thumb-screwing, if necessary.

The multiplied lamentations and exclamations of fear and sorrow, which rang through the house of Bruntisfield on the arrival of Macer Maclutchy, with this terrible fiat (which he announced with all the jack-in-office insolence peculiar to himself), and the clank of muskets and din of high words in the corridor or ambulatory, roused Walter from a second short but sound sleep, and starting, he raised his head from the table on which he had reclined.

Redly and merrily the rays of the morning sun rising above the oak woods streamed through the grated window of the chamber, and threw a warm glow on its dark-brown wainscoting. It was a sunny March morning, and the old oaks were tossing their leafless branches on the balmy wind; the black corbies cawed on their summits, and the lesser birds twittered and chirped from spray to spray; the clear sky was flecked with fleecy clouds, and its pure azure was reflected in the still bosom of the long and beautiful loch, that stretched away between its wooded banks towards the east, where the old house of Gifford and the craigs of Salisbury closed the background.

Walter felt his bruises still smarting from the **recent** **struggle**; he examined the place of his fierce visitor's exit, but failed to discover the least trace of it; every panel fitted close, and was immovable, for he knew not the secret. The whole combat appeared like a dream; but a scar on his hand, a notch or two on his sword, and several overturned chairs, still remained to attest the truth of it. Hastening to unfasten the door which Quentin Napier had secured with such deadly intentions, a little glove on the floor attracted his eye. He snatched it up. It was very small, and of richly-worked lace, tied by a blue riband.

"She has worn this. Oh, 'tis quite a prize," said the young man as he kissed it, and laughing at himself for doing so, placed it within the top of his corslet.

"My certie, here is a braw bit o' wark and a bonnie!" exclaimed Macer Maclutchy, bustling into the room. "Here is an order from the king's advocat to bring the leddies o' Bruntisfield to the Laigh Council House instanter, and the chamber o' dais is empty, toom as a whistle,—the birds clean awa, and the gomeral that stood by the door kens nae mair about them than an unchristened wean. My word on't, lads," he continued, flourishing his badge of office, "some here maun kiss the maiden or climb the gallows for last night's wark!"

After swearing an oath or two, which appeared to give him infinite relief in his perplexity, "Master Walter," said the old halberdier, "here is a devilish piece of business—an *overslagh*, as we used to say in Flanders. Rot me! I have searched every place that would hold a mouse, but the prisoners are not to be found! I have pricked with my dagger every bed, board, and bunker, and so sure as the devil—make answer, Halbert Elshender," he cried, shaking the sentinel roughly by his bandoliers, "answer me, or I will truncheon thee in such wise, thou shalt never shoulder musket more. Fause knave! where are the prisoners over whom I posted ye?"

"A lang day's march on the road to hell, I hope—the old one, at least," responded the musketeer, sullenly: "dost think I have them under my corslet?"

"Faith! General Dalyel will let ye ken, friend Hab, that a thrawn craig or six-ounce bullets are the price Scottish of winking on duty. Ye'll be shot like a cock-patrick. I pity thee, Hab—d—mme if I don't; you've blawn your matches by my side on many a hot day's work, and bleezed away your bandoliers in the face o' English, Dutch, and German; but my heart granes for the punishment ye'll dree."

"You are all either donnart or drunk!" exclaimed the

incensed soldier; "if the ladies were in the chamber when I first mounted guard, I swear by my father's soul, they are there yet for me. I neither slept nor stirred from the door; so they maun either have flown up the lum or whistled through the keyhole ——"

"Didst ever hear of a noble lady playing cantrips o' witch-craft like a wife o' the Kailmercat, or that auld whaislin besom, your mother, down by St. Roque?"

"What for no?—it rins in the family, this same science o' witchcraft, gif a' tales be true."

"See if such a braw story will pass muster with Sir Thomas Dalyel. Cocknails! I think I see every hair o' his lang beard glistening and bristling with rage!"

"And he will mind that my father was a stanch vassal o' the Napiers!" added the poor musketeer, in great conster-nation at the idea of confronting that ferocious commander. "What can I do or say?—O help me, Master Walter! Would to God I had been piked or shot at Sedgemoor!"

"Wemyss," said Walter, advancing at this juncture, just as the sergeant was unbuckling the soldier's collar of bando-liers. "The ladies are gone where I hope none, save friends, will find them. Elshender is innocent, for I freed them, and must bear the punishment for doing so; but next time, com-rade Hab, you take over such a post, see that your wards are in it."

"I had your word, Mr. Fenton," replied the musketeer in a voice between sorrow and joy; "your word at least in the sense, and we alway deemed you a gentleman of honour, though but a puir soldier-lad like mysel."

"True, true," replied Walter, colouring; 'will not the generosity of my purpose excuse the deceit?"

"Why, Mr. Fenton, I wish weel to the auld house, for I was born and bred under its shadow, and mony o' my kin hae laid down their lives in its service, and I can excuse it——"

"D'ye think my lord chancellor will, though?" asked the macer sharply, as he bustled forward, "or his majesty's advocat for his majesty's interest?"

"Or Sir Thomas Dalyel o' the Binns?" added the sergeant testily. "O! what is this o't noo—after I, from a skirling brat, had made a man and a soldier of thee? O! 'tis an unco scrape—a devilish coil of trouble, and I wish you weel out o't. Retain your sword, my puir child, but consider yourself under close ward until orders come anent ye. D—me! I once marched three hundred prisoners from Zut-phen to French Flanders, among them the noble count of Bronkhorst himself, and never lost but one man whom I pistolled for calling me a hireling Scot, that sold my king for a groat, whilk I considered as a taunt appertaining to the Covenanters alone. Gowk and gomeral, boy, what devil tempted thee to——but why ask? Yon pawkie gipsy's blue een——"

"Hush!"

"Hae thrown a glamour owre ye. Wherever women bide, there will mischief be. 'Tis a kittle job! What a pumpkin-head I was not to keep watch and ward mysel. Rot me! a young quean's skirling, or a carlin's greeting would hae little effect on me, for I have heard muckle o' baith in my time. Did no thought of our council prevent ye running your head in the cannon's mouth?"

"No; I saw women in distress, Wemyss, and acted as my heart dictated."

"Had they been two old carlins with hairy chins, gobber teeth, wrinkled faces, and hands like corbies' claws, I doubt not your tender heart would have dictated otherwise. But when next I set a handsome young lad to watch a young lass, may the great de'il spit me, and mak my ain halbert his toasting-fork!"

"Ay, ay," muttered Macer Maclutchy, whose jaws were busily devouring all the good things he could collect in buffet or almrie; "auld Hornie may do so in the end, whatever comes to pass."

"O Willie Wemyss, Willie Wemyss!" quoth the veteran halberdier, apostrophizing himself; "dark dool be on the hour that brings this disgrace upon thee, after five-and-thirty years o' hard and faithful service, under La. Tour d'Auvergne, Crequy, Condé, and Dunbarton! The deil 's in ye, Walter Fenton! You were aye a moody and melancholy chield, and I ever thought ye were born under some ill star, as the spae-wives say."

"Braw spark though he be," said the macer, "he's come o' the true auld covenanting spawn, Mr. Wemyss; and birds o' a feather—here's luck, sergeant, and better times to us a';" and so saying he buried his flushed visage in a vast flagon of foaming ale.

CHAPTER VI.

THE OLD TOLBOOTH.

Whether I was brought into this world by the usual human helps and means,
or was a special creation, might admit of some controversy, as I have never
known the name of parent or of kindred.—THE IMPROVISITORE.

MANY of the citizens of Edinburgh may remember the Old
Bank close, and the edifice about to be described. On the
west side of that narrow street, which descended abruptly on
the southern side of the city's central hill, stood in former
days a house of massive construction and sombre aspect. Its
walls were enormously thick and elaborately jointed; its passages narrow, dark, and devious; its stairs ascended and
descended in secret corners, and one led to the paved bartizan, which formed the roof. Many of its gloomy chambers
were vaulted. Over its small and heavy doorway appeared
the date 1569, encrusted by smoke and worn with time.
The whole aspect of the edifice was peculiarly dismal; the
walls were black as if coated over with soot, the windows
were thickly grated with rusted iron stanchells, and sunk in
massive frames, the little panes were obscured by the dust
and cobwebs of years.

It was the ancient prison of the city. In older days it had
been built by a rich citizen named Gourlay, and had held
within its walls the ambassadors of England and France.

From its strength it had been converted into a Tolbooth,
and was used as such until the time of the Solemn League
and Covenant, when the spacious and more famous prison
was adopted for that purpose; but the older, darker, more
obscure, and more horrid place of confinement was still used
at this time.

A party of the ancient City Guard, armed with swords and
Lochaber axes, buff coats, and steel bonnets, occupied one of
the lower apartments entering from the turnpike stair, at the
foot of which stood a sentinel with his axe, before the door,
which, though small, was a solid mass of iron-studded oak,
bolts and long bars.

In a small but desolate chamber of this striking old edifice
—the same in which the hapless earl of Argyle passed the
night of the 29th June, 1685, his last in the land of the
living—Walter Fenton was confined a prisoner; while the
Reverend Mr. Ichabod Bummel, Mr. Drouthy the butler, and
other servitors of Lady Bruntisfield, were in close durance in

the greater or upper Tolbooth. The roof, the walls, and the floor of this squalid apartment were all of squared stones, stained with damp and scrawled over with hideous visages, pious sentences, and reckless obscenity. Its only window was thickly grated within and without, and there in the sickly light the busy spiders spun their webs from bar to bar in undisturbed industry. It opened to a narrow, dark, and steep close of dreary aspect; the opposite houses were only one yard distant, and ten stories high; the alley was like a chasm or fissure; a single ray of sunlight streamed down it, and penetrating the cobwebs and dust of the prison window, radiated through its deep embrazure, and threw the iron gratings in strong shadow on the paved floor. Though the day was a chill one, in March, there was no fire under the small archway, where one should have been, and the only articles of furniture were a coarse and heavy table like a carpenter's bench, a miserable paillasse on a truckle bed-stead, and a water-flagon of Flemish pewter. One or two rusty chains hung from enormous blocks in the dirty walls, for the more secure confinement of prisoners who might be more than usually dangerous or refractory, and the whole *tout ensemble* of the chamber, when viewed by the dim and fast-fading light of the evening, was cheerless, desolate, and disgusting.

The day had passed away, and now, divested of his gay accoutrements, and clad in a plain unlaced frock of grey cloth, the young prisoner awaited impatiently, perhaps appre-hensively, the hour that would bring him before that terrible council whose lawless will was nevertheless the law of the land. Sunk in moody reverie, he remained with his arms folded, and his head sunk forward on his breast.

The shadow of the grating on the floor grew less and less distinct, for, as the light faded, his vaulted prison became darker, until all became blackness around him. Anon the pallid moon rose slowly into its place, and from the blue southern sky poured a cold but steady flood of silver light into the cheerless room, and again, for a time, the shadow of the massive grating was thrown on the discoloured floor. All around it was involved in obscurity, from amid which the damp spots on the walls seemed like great and hideous visages, mocking and staring at the captive.

Bitter were the thoughts, and sad the memories that thronged fast upon the mind of Walter Fenton; his dark eyes were lit, his lip compressed, but there were none to behold the changes; his handsome features were alternately clouded by chagrin, contracted by anger, and softened by love. Though ever proud in spirit, and fired by an inborn nobility of soul, never until now did he feel so keenly the dependence of his situation, or so fierce a longing for an opportunity when by one brilliant act of heroism and courage, he might place himself for ever above his fortune, or—die. And Lilian! Oh, it was the thought of her alone that raised these vivid aspirations to their utmost pitch; but his heart sank, and even hope—the lover's last rallying-point—faded away when he pictured the difference of their fortunes and positions in life. Scotland was then a country where pride of birth was carried to excess; and a remnant of that feeling still exists among us. He reflected that *he* was poor and nameless, compelled from infancy to eat the bread of dependence and mortification, and now in manhood, having no other estate than his sword and a ring, which, as he had often told Lilian with a smile (and he knew not how prophetically he spoke) "contained the secret of his life;" *she* the representative of a long line of illustrious barons, whose shields had shown their blazons on the fields of Bannockburn, Sark, and Arkinholme, the inheritrix of their honours, their pride, and their possessions. Poor Walter! but he was too thoroughly in love to lose courage altogether.

As a boy, he had sighed for Lilian, and he felt his enthusiasm kindled by her gentleness and infantile beauty, for then his heart knew not the great gulf which a few years would open up between them. The ardour of his temperament made him now feel alternately despair and hope, but the latter feeling predominated; for though the clergy railed at wealth and all the good things of this life, and took peculiar care to enjoy a good share thereof, the world was not so intensely selfish then as it is now; for a high spirit and a bold heart, when united to a gallant bearing, a velvet cloak, a tall feather, and a long sword, were valued more than an ample purse by the young ladies of that age, who were quite used to find in their ponderous folio romances, how beautiful and disinterested queens and princesses bestowed their hands, hearts, and kingdoms on those valiant knights-errant and penniless cavaliers, who alone, or by the aid of a single faithful squire, freed them from enchanted castles, and slew the wicked enchanters, giants, gnomes, and fire-vomiting dragons, who had persecuted them from childhood.

To resume: poor Walter was intensely sad, for deeply at that moment he experienced the desolate feeling, that he was utterly alone in this wide world, and that within all its ample space there existed not one being with whom he could claim kindred. He felt that it was all a blank. a void to him; but his thoughts went back to those days when the suppression of the rising at Bothwell, struck terror and despair into the hearts of the Presbyterians, and filled the dungeons of the Scottish castles, and the tolbooths of the cities, with the much-enduring adherents of the Covenant, beneath the banner of which his father was supposed to have died with his sword in his hand; so with her dying lips had his mother told him, and his heart swelled and his eye moistened, as he recalled the time, the place, and her tremulous accents, with a vivid distinctness that wrung his breast with the tenderest sorrow, even after the lapse of so many years.

During the summer of 1679, those citizens of Edinburgh whose mansions commanded a view of the Greyfriars kirkyard, beheld from their windows a daily scene of suffering such as had never before been seen in Scotland.

This ancient burial-place lies to the south of the long ridge occupied by the ancient city; it is spacious, irregular, and surrounded by magnificent tombs, many of them being of great antiquity, and marking the last resting-places of those who were eminent for their virtues and talents, or distinguished by their birth. It is a melancholy place withal. For three hundred years never a day has passed without many persons being interred there; and the hideous clay, the yellow and many-coloured loam, that had once lived and breathed, and loved and spoken, has now risen several feet above the adjacent street, against the walls of the great old church in the centre, and has buried the basements of the quaint and dark monuments that surround it. The inscriptions and grotesque carving of the latter, have long since been encrusted and blackened by the smoke of the city, or worn and obliterated by the corroding and fetid atmosphere of the great graveyard. There is not a spot in all the Lothians where the broad-leaved docken, the rank dog-grass, the long black nettle, and other weeds grow so luxuriantly; for terrible is the mass of human corruption, for ever festering and decaying beneath the verdant turf.

In the year before mentioned, this ancient city of the dead was crowded to excess with those unhappy nonconformists whom the prisons could not contain, for already were their gloomy dungeons and squalid chambers filled with the poor, the miserable, and devoted Covenanters. Strong guards and chains of sentinels watched by day and night the walls of the burial-ground; and then the buff-coated dragoon, with his broadsword and carbine, and the smart musketeer, with his dagger and matchlock, were ever on the alert to deal instant death as the penalty of any attempt to escape. The rising at

Bothwell had been quenched in blood; and these unhappy people had been collected—principally from Bathgate—by the cavalry employed in riding down the country, and being driven like a herd of cattle to the capital, were penned up in the old churchyard. And there, for months, they lay in hundreds, exposed to the scorching glare of the sun by day, and the chill dew by night—the rain and the wind and the storm! God's creatures, formed in his own image, reduced to the level of the hare and the fox, with no other canopy than the changing sky, and no other bed than the rank grass, reeds, and nettles, that sprung in such hideous luxuriance from the fetid graves beneath them.

It was a sorrowful sight; for there was the strong and athletic peasant, with his true Scottish heart of stubborn pride and rectitude, his weak and tender wife with her little infants, his aged and infirm parents. Their miseries increasing as day by day their numbers diminished, and other burial-mounds, fresh and earthy, rose amid the hollow-eyed survivors to mark the last homes of other martyrs in the cause of "the oppressed Kirk and broken Covenant." And all this terrible amount of mental misery and bodily suffering was accumulated within the walls of the capital, amid the noisy and busy streets of a densely-peopled city—and for what? Religion—religion, under whose wide mantle so many thousand atrocities have been committed by men of every creed and age; and because these poor peasants had resolved to worship God after the spirit of their own hearts, and the fashion of their fathers.

When the duke of Albany and York (afterwards James VII.) came to Edinburgh, the persecution was not continued with such rigour; but the progress of time never overcame the resolution of the Covenanters, though many noble families were reduced to poverty, exile, and ruin, while their brave and moral tenantry suffered famine, torture, imprisonment, and every severity that tyrannical misgovernment could inflict, until the Presbyterians were driven to the verge of despair; intrigues with the prince of Orange were set on foot, and for some years a storm had been gathering, which, in the shape of a Dutch invasion, was soon to burst over the whole of Britain.

Walter's memory went back to those days, when, amid the tombs and graves of that old kirk-yard, he had nestled, a little and wailing child, on the bosom of his mother, who, imprisoned there among the "common herd," had soon sunk under the combined effects of exposure, starvation, degradation, and sorrow; and he remembered when coiled up within her mantle and plaid, how he hid his little face in her fair neck, trembling with cold and fear in dreary nights, when the moon streamed its light between the flying clouds upon the vast and desolate church and its thick grave-mounds, with the long reedy grass waving on their solemn and melancholy ridges.

A mystery hung over the fortune of Walter Fenton. Of his family he knew nothing further than that his mother's name was Fenton, and his own was Walter, for so she had been wont to call him. Of his father he knew nothing, save that he had never been seen since the cavalry of Claverhouse swept over the bridge of Bothwell, scattering its defenders in death and defeat. He had heard that his father there held high command, but was supposed to have perished either in the furious *mêlée* on the bridge, or in the stream beneath it. Concealing her rank in the disguise of a peasant, his mother had been found in the vicinity of the battle-field, was arrested as a suspected person, sent to Edinburgh, and imprisoned with other unfortunates in the old church-yard.

Poor Walter used to remember with pleasure that they had always remained aloof from the other prisoners, and were treated by them with marked respect. Their usual shelter was under the great mausoleum of the Barons of Coates, the quaint devices and antique sculpture of which had often raised his childish fear and wonder; he recalled through the struggling and misty perceptions of infancy, how day by day her fair features became paler and more attenuated, her eye more sunken and ghastly, her voice more tremulous and weak, and her strength even less than his own; for (he had heard the soldiers say) she had been a tenderly-nurtured and fragile creature, unable to endure the hardships to which she was subjected; and so she perished among the first that died there.

One morning the little boy raised his head from the coarse plaid which on the previous night her feeble hands had wrapped around him, and called as usual for her daily kiss; he twisted his dimpled fingers in the masses of her silky hair, and laid his smiling face to hers—it was cold as the marble tomb beside them; he shrank back, and again called upon her, but her still lips gave no reply; he stirred her—she did not move. Then, struck by the peculiar, the terrible aspect of her pale and once beautiful face, the ghastly eyes and relaxed jaw, the child screamed aloud on the mother that heard him no more. He dreaded alike to remain or to fly; for, alas! there was no other in whose arms he could find a refuge.

A soldier approached. He was a white-haired veteran,

who had looked on many a battle-field, and speaking kindly to the desolate child, he gently stirred the dead woman with his halberd.

"Is this thy mother, my puir bairn?" said he.

The child answered only by his tears, and hid his face in the grass.

"Come away with me, my little mannikin," continued the soldier, "for thy mother hath gone to a better and bonnier place than this."

"Take me there too," sobbed the child, clinging to the soldier's hand; "oh, take me there too."

"By my faith, little one, 'tis a march I am not prepared for yet—but our parson will tell you all about it. Tush! I know the flams of the drum better than how to expound the text; so come away, my puir bairn; thy mother, God rest her, is in good hands, I warrant. Come away; and rot me, if thou shalt want while old Willie Wemyss of the Scots Musketeers, hath a bodle in his pouch, or a bannock in his havresack."

By the good-hearted soldier he was carried away in a paroxysm of childish grief and terror; and he saw his mother no more.

By the beauty of her person, the exceeding whiteness of her hands, and a very valuable ring found with her, she was supposed to be of higher rank than her peasant's attire indicated; and those apparent proofs of a superior birth, the soldiers never omitted an opportunity of impressing upon Walter as he grew older; and cited innumerable Low Country legends and old Scottish traditions, wherein certain heroes just so circumstanced, had become great personages in the end; and Walter was taught to consider that there was no reason why he should be an exception. But *who* his mother was, had unfortunately remained locked in her own breast; whether from excessive debility and broken spirit she lacked strength to communicate with the other captives, or whether she feared to do so, could not be known now; her secret was buried with her, and thus a mystery was thrown over the fortune of the little boy, which through life caused him to be somewhat of a moody and reflective nature.

William Wemyss, a veteran sergeant of Dunbarton's musketeers, became his patron and protector; and a love and friendship sprang up between them, for the orphan had none other to cling to. Wemyss often led him to the old church-yard, and showed him the grave where his mother lay—where the soldiers had interred her; and there little Walter, overcome by the mystery that involved his fate, and the loneliness of his heart, wept bitterly; for the soldier, though meaning well, was rather like one of Job's comforters, and painted his dependence in such strong colours, and reminded him how narrowly he had escaped being hanged or banished as "a Covenanter's spawn," that the heart of the poor boy swelled at times almost to breaking. Then the soldier would desire him to pray for his mother, and made him repeat a curious but earnest prayer, full of quaint military technicalities, in which the good old halberdier saw nothing either unusual or *outré*. Often little Fenton came alone to seek that well-known grave, to linger and to sit beside it, for it was the only part of all broad Scotland that his soul clung to. The weeds were now matted over it, and the waving nettles half hid the humble stone, which, with his own hands, the kind soldier had placed there. Walter always cleared away those luxuriant weeds, and though they stung his hands, he felt them not. It was a nameless grave too, for the real name of her who slept within it was unknown to him; and the desolate child often stretched himself down on the turf, burying his face in the long grass, and weeping, as he had done in infancy, on the poor bosom that mouldered beneath, retraced in memory, days of wandering and misfortune, of danger and sorrow, which he could not comprehend. Time, and that lightness of heart which is incident to youth, enabled him at last to view the grave with composure; but he sought it not the less, until after his return from Sedgemoor; he hastened to the well-known place, but, alas! the grave had been violated, and the charm of grief was broken for ever. *Another* had been buried there; the earth was freshly heaped up; and he rushed away, to return no more.

From childhood to youth the old sergeant was his only protector: though poor, he was a kind and sincere one; and the little boy became the pet of the musketeers.

A child, a dog, or a monkey, is always an object of regard to an old soldier or sailor; for the human heart must love something.

Little Walter carried the halberdier's can of egg-flip when he mounted guard, learned to make up bandoliers of powder, polish a corslet, to rattle dice on a drumhead, and to beat on the drum itself; to fight with rapier and dagger; to handle a case of falchions like any sword-player; and became an adept at every game of chance, from kingly chess, to homely touch-and-take. He learned to drink "Confusion to the Covenant," in potent usquebaugh without winking once, and swear a few cavalier-like oaths. Like all such pets, he was often boxed severely, and roundly cursed too, at the caprice of his nume-

rous masters, until the poor boy would have been altogether
lost, his ideas corrupted, and his manners tainted by the
roughness of camp and garrison, had not his humble patron
been ordered away on the Tangier expedition; and being
unable to take his little *protégé* with him, bethought him of
craving the bounty of his commander's wife, the countess of
Dunbarton, a beautiful young English woman, who was the
belle of the capital and the idol of the Scottish cavaliers.
Struck with the soldier's story, envying his generosity,
pitying the little boy, and pleased with his candour and
beauty, she immediately took him under protection, adopting
him as her page; and never was there seen a handsomer
youth than Walter Fenton, when his coarse attire (a cast
doublet of the sergeant's) was exchanged for a coat of white
velvet slashed with red and laced with gold, breeches and
stockings of silk, a sash, a velvet cloak, and silver-hilted
poniard; and his dark-brown hair curled and perfumed by
Master Peter Pouncet, the famous frizzeur in the Bow. He
parted in a flood of tears from his old patron, who slipped
into his pocket a purse the countess had bestowed on himself,
drew his leather glove across his eyes, and hurried away.

At Lady Dunbarton's he had often seen Lilian Napier; she
was then a little girl, and always accompanied her tall and
stately relative in the vast old rumbling coach, with its two
footmen behind and outriders in front, armed with sword and
carbine; for the noble dame set forth in great state on all
visits of ceremony. Lady Grizel's majestic aspect and frigid
stateliness scared and awed the little footpage; but the
prattle of the fair-haired Lilian soothed and charmed him,
and he soon learned to love the little girl, to call her his
sister, to be joyous when she came, and to be sad when she
departed.

Young Walter, from his well-knit figure, and a determined
aspect which he had acquired by his camp education, was as
great a favourite among the starched little demoiselles of the
countess's withdrawing-room, as his clenched fist and bent
brows made him a terror at times to the little cavaliers whose
jealousy he excited; and his military preceptors (the Old
Royals, then battling and broiling at Tangiers) had inculcated
a pugnacity of disposition that sometimes was very troublesome; and he once proceeded so far as to d—n the old
dowager of Drumsturdy pretty roundly, and draw his
poniard on the young lord her son, who, with his companions,
had mocked him as " a Covenanter's brat." The countess
made him crave pardon of the little noble, and they shook
hands like two cut-and-thrust gallants of six feet high.

But when their companions, with childish malevolence,
taunted poor Walter as "my lord's loon," "the soldier's
varlet," or "the powder puggy," epithets which always
kindled his rage and drew tears from his eyes, Lilian, ever
gentle and kind, wept with him, espoused his cause, and told
that "Walter's mother was a noble lady, for the countess
had her ring of gold;" and the influence of the little nymph,
with her cheeks like glowing peaches, and her bright hair
flowing in sunny ringlets around a face ever beaming with
happiness—was never lost, or failed to maintain peace among
them. And thus days passed swiftly into years, and the girl
was twelve and the boy sixteen when they were separated.
Walter followed his noble patron to the field, when the
landing of Argyle in the west, and Monmouth in the south,
threw Britain into a flame. Dunbarton, now a general officer,
marched with the Scottish forces against the former; but
Walter, as a volunteer, served under Colonel Halkett, with a
battalion of Scottish musketeers, at the battle of Sedgemoor,
where he felt what it was to have lead bullets rebounding
from his buff coat and headpiece. Since then he had been
serving as a private gentleman; but in a country like
Scotland, swarming with idle young men of good birth and
high spirit, who despised every occupation save that of arms,
preferment came not, and he had too often experienced the
mortification of seeing others obtain what he justly deemed
his due, the commission of King James VII.

His recent interview with Lilian had recalled in full force
all the friendship of their childhood and the dawning love of
older years; but the manner in which he was now involved
with the supreme authorities seemed to destroy all his hopes
for ever—in Scotland at least; and yet, though that reflection wrung his heart, so little did he regret the part he
had acted, that for Lilian's sake he would willingly run
again a hundredfold greater risk. The last three years of
his life had been spent amid the stirring turmoil of military
duty in a discontented country, where each succeeding day
the spirit of insurrection grew riper. In the rough society
with which he mingled, never had he been addressed by a
female so fair in face and so winning in manner as Lilian of
Bruntisfield; and thus the charm of her presence acted more
powerfully upon him. Her accents of entreaty and distress—
her affection for Lady Grizel struggling with anxiety for
himself, had in one brief interview recalled all the soft and
happy impressions of his earlier and more innocent days, and
love obtained a sway over his heart, that made him for a time
forget his own dangerous predicament, in pondering with

pleasure on the mortifications from which he had saved the ladies of Bruntisfield, the risks he had run for their sake, and consequently the debt of gratitude they owed him.

From his breast he drew forth her glove a hundred times, to admire its delicate texture and diminutive form; but he could not repress a bitter sigh when contemplating how slight were the chances of his ever again beholding the gentle owner, now when both unhappily were under the ban of the law,—she a homeless fugitive, and he a close prisoner, with death, imprisonment, or distant service in the Scots brigade his only prospects. Even were it otherwise,—and, oh! this idea was more tormenting than the first,—her heart might be dedicated to another; and she might, with the true pride of a noble Scottish maiden, deem it an unpardonable presumption in the poor and unhonoured pikeman to raise his eyes to the heiress of Sir Archibald Napier of Bruntisfield and the Wrytes. And thus, having introduced to the reader the grand feature upon which our story must "hinge," we shall get on with renewed ardour.

CHAPTER VII.

THE LAIGH COUNCIL HOUSE.

Ye holy martyrs, who with wondrous faith,
And constancy unshaken have sustained
The rage of cruel men and fiery persecutions;
Come to my aid, and teach me to defy
The malice of this fiend!—TAMERLANE.

THE moon had passed westward; the close was gloomy as a chasm; and Walter's prison became dark as a cave in the bowels of a mountain. The clank of chains and bars as the door was opened roused the prisoner from his waking dreams; a yellow light flashed along the heavily-jointed stone walls, and the harsh unpleasant voice of Macer Maclutchy cried authoritatively—

"Maister Walter Fenton!—now, then, come forth instanter. Ye are required by the lords of the privy council."

A thrill shot through Walter's heart: he endeavoured in vain to suppress it, and, taking up his plain beaver hat, which was looped with a riband and cockade à la Monmouth in the military fashion, he descended the narrow spiral stair, preceded by the macer carrying his symbol of office on his right shoulder, and attired in a long flowing black gown. Two of the town-guard, with their poleaxes, and Dunbraiken their captain,—a portly citizen, whose vast paunch, cased in corslet

A.   B

and backpiece, made him resemble a mighty tortoise erect,—
kept close behind; and thus escorted, Walter set out from
his prison, to appear before a select committee of the
dreaded privy council of Scotland.

Encumbered by his long official garb, Macer Maclutchy's
step was none of the most steady. He was evidently after
his evening potations at Lucky Dreeps; he wore his bonnet
cocked well forward; and such a provoking smirk of vulgar
importance pervaded his features, when, from time to time
he surveyed his prisoner, that the latter was only restrained
by the axes behind from knocking him down.

In those days the hour of dinner was about one or two
o'clock; but as the earl of Perth, the lords Clermistonlee,
Mersington, and others loved their wine too well to leave it
soon for dry matters of state, and the thumbscrewing of
witches and nonconformists, the evening was far advanced
before Walter Fenton was summoned for examination in the
Laigh chamber, where the council held their meetings under
the parliament hall, in a dark and gloomy region, where
lights are always burned even yet during the longest days
of summer.

Passing a narrow pend or archway (where, in the following
year, the Lord President Lockhart was shot by Chiesly of
Dalry), Walter and his conductors issued into the dark and
deserted Lawn-market, passed the Heart of Midlothian—from
the western platform of which the black beam of the gibbet
stretched its ghastly arm in the moonlight,—and reached the
antique Parliament-square, a quadrangle of quaint architecture, which had recently been graced by a beautiful statue of
Charles II. On one side rose the square tower and gigantic
façade of St. Giles, with its traceried windows, its rich battlements, and carved pinnacles all glittering in the moonlight,
which poured aslant over several immense piles of building
raised on Venetian arcades, and made all the windows of the
Goldsmiths' hall glitter with the same pale lustre that tipped
the round towers of the Tolbooth, the square turrets and circular spire of the Parliament-house, the whole front of which
was involved in opaque and gloomy shadow, from which the
grand equestrian statue of King Charles, edged by the glorious
moonlight, stood vividly forth like a gigantic horseman of
polished silver.

The square was silent and still, as it was black and gloomy.
A faint chorus stole on the passing wind, and then died away.
It came from the hostel, or coffee-house, of Hugh Blair, a
famous vintner, whose premises were under the low-browed
and massive piazza before mentioned. The deep ding-dong

of the cathedral bell, vibrating sonorously from the great stone chambers of the tower, made Walter start. It struck the hour of nine, and, save its echoes dying away in the hollow aisles and deep vaults of the ancient church, no other sound broke the silence of the place; and Walter felt a palpable chill sinking heavily on his spirit, when, guided by the macer, they penetrated the cold shade of the quadrangle, and by a richly-carved doorway were admitted into the lobby of the house, which was spacious and lofty enough to be the hall of a lordly castle. From thence another door gave admittance into that magnificent place of assembly where once the estates of Scotland met—

" Ere her faithless sons betrayed her."

Its rich and intricate roof towered far away into dusky obscurity; its vast space and lofty walls of polished stone echoed hollowly to their footsteps; and the bright moon, streaming through the mullioned and painted windows, threw a thousand prismatic hues on the oaken floor, on the grotesque corbels, and innumerable knosps and gilded pendants of its beautiful roof,—on the crimson benches of the peers,—on the throne, with its festooned canopy,—on the dark banners and darker paintings, bringing a hundred objects into strong relief, sinking others in sombre shadow, and tipping with silver the square-bladed axes and conical helmets of the town-guardsmen as they passed the great south oriel, with its triple mullions and heraldic blazonry.

From thence steep, narrow, and intricate stairs led them to the regions of the political Inquisition, and the wind that rushed upward felt cold and dewy as they descended. At the bottom there branched off a variety of stone passages, where flambeaux flared and cressets sputtered in the night-wind, and cast their lurid light on the dusky walls. And now a confused murmur of voices announced to the anxious Fenton that he was close to this terrible conclave, whose presence few left but on the hurdle of the executioner.

In an anteroom a crowd of macers, city guardsmen, messengers-at-arms, and officials in the blue livery of the city, laced with yellow, and wearing the triple castle on their cuffs and collars, a number of persons cited as witnesses, &c., lounged about, or lolled on the wooden benches. The ceiling of the apartment was low, and the deep recesses of the doors and windows showed the vast solidity of the massively-panelled walls. A huge fire blazed in a grate that resembled an iron basket on four sturdy legs, and its red light glinted on the varied costumes, the weather-beaten visages, polished headpieces, and partisans of those who crowded round it. The entrance of Walter Fenton and his escort excited neither attention nor curiosity ; and feeling acutely his degraded position, he sought a retired corner, and seated himself on a wooden bench. The groups around him conversed only in whispers. A murmur of voices came at intervals from the inner chamber; and Walter often gazed with deep interest at its antiquely-fashioned doorway, the features of which remained long and vividly impressed on his memory ; for he longed to behold, but dreaded to encounter, the stern conclave its carved panels concealed from his view.

Anon a cry—a shrill and fearful cry—announced that some dreadful work was being enacted within ; every man looked gravely in his neighbour's face (save Maclutchy, who smiled), and the blood rushed back on Walter's heart tumultuously. Deep, hollow, and heart-harrowing groans succeeded ; then were heard the sound of hammers and the creaking of a block as when a rope runs rapidly through the sheave ; then a low murmur of voices again, and all was still ; so still, that Walter heard the pulsations of his heart, and in spite of his natural courage, it quailed at the prospect of what *he* too might have to undergo.

Suddenly the door of the dreaded chamber flew open, and the common doomster and his two assistants, with their muscular arms bared, and their leather aprons girt up for exertion, issued forth, bearing the half-lifeless and wholly miserable Ichabod Bummel. His countenance was pale and ghastly; his teeth were clenched, and his eyes set ; his limbs hanging pendant and powerless, bore terrible evidence of the agonies caused by the iron boots, as his fingers, covered with blood, did of the thumbscrews. He groaned heavily.

" What has the gallows loon confessed, Pate ? " asked Maclutchy, eagerly.

" Sae muckle, that the pyets will be pyking his head on the Netherbow-porte when the sun rises the morn," replied Mr. Patrick Pincer, the heartless finisher of the law, whose brawny arms and blood-stained apron, together with all the disgusting associations of his frightful occupation, rendered him a revolting character. " He defied the haill council as a generation o' vipers ; boasted o' being a naturalized Hollander, and denied his ain mother-country."

" Wretch ! " muttered Bummel, " well might I deny the land that produces such as thee. But there is yet a time, and in Heaven is all my trust."

" Silence in court ! " said the macer, imperiously thrusting the brass crown of his baton in the sufferer's mouth. "Ay, ay, denying his ain country, eh?"

"Till my Lord Clermistonlee recommended a touch o' the caspie-claws, and wow, sirs, the loon stood them brawly, but when we gied him a twinge wi' the airn buits, my certie! they did mak' him skirl. Did ye no hear him confessing, lads?"

"What! what?"

"Ou, just onything they asked him. Treason, awfu' to hear; about a Dutch invasion, and a rebellion among the westland Whigs, to whom he showed letters from Hume o' Polwarth, Fagel the pensioner o' Holland, Dyckvelt the Flemish spy; and a' hidden whar d'ye think?"

"Deil kens; in his wame, may be."

"Hoots; sewit up in the lining o' his braid bonnet."

The poor fainting preacher had now the felicity of being stared at by a crowd who pitied him no more than the strong-armed torturers whose grasp sustained his supine and inert frame.

"Soldier," said he to one near him, "art thou a son of the Roman antichrist?"

"Na, I am Habbie, the son o' my faither, auld John Elshender, a cottar body, at the Burghmuir-end."

"Then, in the name of God," implored the poor man in a weak and wavering voice, "give me but a drop o' water to quench my thirst; for, oh youth, I suffer the torments of hell!"

The soldier, who seemed to be a good-natured young fellow, readily brought a pitcher of water, from which Bummel drank greedily and convulsively, muttering at intervals, "'Tis sweet —sweet as *aqua cœlestis*, whilk is thrice-rectified wine. Heaven bless thee, soldier, and reward thee, for I cannot." He burst into tears.

"Hath he taken the test?" asked Maclutchy, "and did he acknowledge the king's authority?"

"Ou, onything, and so would you, Maclutchy, gif I had ye under my hand, as I'll soon hae that young birkie in the corner."

"'Tis false!" cried Ichabod Bummel, through his clenched teeth; "and sooner than acknowledge that bloody and papist-ical duke, I would kiss, yea, and believe the book of the accursed Mohamet, whilk, as I show in my '*Bombshell aimit at the Taile of the Great Beast,*' was written on auld spule banes, and kept by the gude wife of the impostor in a meal girnel. But fie! and out upon ye, fiends, for lo! the hou

of our triumph and deliverance from tyrants and massemongers is at hand.   O, why tarry the chariot-wheels of
our Deliverer ? "

> " I like ane owl in desart am,
>   That nightly——"

" What ! " exclaimed Maclutchy, in legal horror, " would
ye dare to skirl a psalm within earshot o' the very lords o'
council, ye desperate cheat, the woodie !   Awa wi' him by
the lug and horn, or he'll bring the roof about us."   He was
hurried off.

Walter was deeply moved.   Pity and indignation stirred
his heart by turns ; but he had not much time for reflection ;
at that moment the drawling voice of the crier was heard,
calling with a cadence peculiar to the Scottish courts,—

" Maister-Walter-Fenton."

He became more alive to his own immediate danger, and
ere he well knew what passed, found himself in another
gloomy and panelled apartment, one-half of which was hung
with scarlet cloth.   On a dais stood the vacant throne, with
the royal arms of Scotland glittering under a canopy of velvet,
festooned and fringed with gold.

Scott has given us a graphic picture of this strange tribunal,
when it was presided over by the odious duke of Lauderdale.
Let us take a view of it as it appeared six years after, when
that scourge of the Presbyterians had departed to render at
a greater bar an account of his tyranny and enormities.

CHAPTER VIII.

THE PRIVY COUNCIL.

> 'Tis noble pride withholds thee—thou disdain'st
> Wrapt in thy sacred innocence—these mad
> Outrageous charges to refute.
>   SCHILLER'S MAID OF ORLEANS.

A LONG table, covered with scarlet cloth, extended from the
throne towards the end of the room where Walter stood.
Large, red-edged, and massively-gilded statute-books, docquets
of papers, inkstands, and the silver mace (now used by the
Lords of Session), lay glittering on the table, while a large
silver candelabrum, with twelve tall wax-lights, shed a lustre
on the striking figures of those personages who composed the
select committee of council.

On a low wooden side-bench lay certain fearful things,
which (in his present predicament) made the heart of Walter

quail; though on the field he would have faced, without flinching, the rush of a thousand charging horse; they were the instruments of torture then authorized by law; the *pilnie-winks*, the *caspie-claws*, and the *iron-boots*—all diabolical engines, such as the most refined cruelty alone could have invented. With these, both sexes, even little children, were sometimes tortured until the blood spouted from the bruised and crushed limbs.

The thumbikins were small steel screws like hand-vices, which, by compressing the thumb-joints, produced the most acute agony; and this amiable and favourite engine (which saved all trouble of cross-examining witnesses), was first intro-duced by one of the council, whose stern eyes were fixed on Walter Fenton, Lieutenant-General Sir Thomas Dalyel of Binns, a cavalier baronet of great celebrity, whose name is still justly abhorred in Scotland. He had long borne a com-mand under the Russian standard, where his humanity had not been improved by service among Tartars and Calmucks.

The boot was a strong box enclosed with iron hoops, between which and the victim's leg, the executioner, by gradual and successive blows, drove a wooden wedge with such violence, that blood, bone, and marrow were at last bruised into a hideous and pulpy mass.

Walter could scarcely repress a shudder when he surveyed those frightful engines, under the application of which so many unfortunates had writhed; but he confronted with an undaunted air the various members of that stern tribunal, which had so long ruled Scotland by the sword, and many of whose acts and edicts might well vie with those of the Inqui-sition, the Star-chamber, or any other instrument of tyranny and misgovernment.

Two earls, Perth, the lord chancellor, and Balcarris, the high treasurer, were present; they were both fine-looking men, in the prime of life, richly dressed, and wearing those preposterous black wigs (brought into fashion by Charles II.), the ends of which rolled in many curls over their broad collars of point lace. The bishop of Edinburgh, the lord advocate, and his predecessor, the terrible Sir George Mackenzie, of Rosehaugh, "that persecutor of the saints of God;"—(he whose tomb was, till of late years, a place so full of terror to the schoolboy), occupied one side of the council-board. Oppo-site sat John Grahame, of Claverhouse, colonel of the Scottish life-guards, the horror of the Covenanters (and to this hour the accursed of the Cameronians), but the handsomest man of his time. His face was singularly beautiful, and his black, magnificent eyes were one moment languid and tender as those of a love-sick girl, and the next sparkling with dusky fire and animation. When excited, they actually seemed to blaze, and were quite characteristic of his superhuman daring and unmatched ferocity.

Cruel as the character of the laird of Claverhouse has ever been held up to us, let us not forget the times in which he lived, and how much room there is for malevolent exaggeration. Even Wodrow allows that at times he showed compunction, mercy, and compassion. Mutual injuries, assassinations, and outrages heightened the hostility of spirit between the Scottish troops and the Scottish people to a frightful extent; but it is a curious fact, that the local militia and vassals of the landholders were, by far, the most severe tools of persecution. The *real* sentiments of the troops of the line were powerfully evinced by their joining *en masse* the banner of the Protestant invader. In making these remarks, let it not be thought we are attempting to gloss over the atrocities of the persecution, the records of which are enough to make one's blood boil even at this distant period of time. The darkest days of our history are those of which the industrious Wodrow wrote; but glorious indeed was the ardour and constancy with which so many of Scotland's best and bravest men gave up their souls to God in the cause of the " oppressed kirk and the broken covenant."

Claverhouse was splendidly attired; his coat was of white velvet, pinked with scarlet silk and laced with gold; over his breast spread a cravat of the richest lace, and on that fell the heavy dark ringlets of his military wig. Near him sat Sir Thomas Dalyel, colonel of the Scots Grey dragoons. This fierce soldier was in the eightieth year of his age; he was perfectly bald, and a lofty forehead towered above his keen grey eyes, that shone brighter than his polished gorget in the light of the candelabrum. To his stern features a noble and dignified aspect was imparted by a long white beard, that flowed over his plain buff coat, reaching to the buckle of his sword-belt. There was a very striking and antique expression in the fine face of the aged and detested " persecutor," that never failed to impress beholders with respect and awe.

There are but two others to describe, and these are of some importance to our history.

Swinton, of Mersington, a law lord, who was never known to have been perfectly sober since the Restoration, and whose meagre body, nut-cracker jaws, bleared eyes, and fantastic visage, contrasted so strongly with the upright and square form of the venerable cavalier on his right, and the dignified Randal, Lord Clermistonlee, who sat on his left.

A renegade Covenanter, a profligate, and debauched *roué*, steeped to the lips in cruelty, tyranny, and vice, the latter, after having squandered away a noble patrimony and the dowry of his unfortunate wife, still maintained his career of excess by gifts from the fines, extortions, and confiscations, made by the council on every pretence, or without pretence at all. He was forty years of age, possessing a noble form, and a face still eminently handsome, though marked by dissipation; it was slightly disfigured by a sword-cut, and, notwithstanding its beauty of contour, when clouded by chagrin and ferocity, and flushed by wine, it seemed that of a very ruffian, and now was no way improved by his ample wig and cravat being quite awry. His dark vindictive eyes were sternly fixed on Walter, who, from that moment, knew him to be his enemy. Clermistonlee, who was not a man to have his purposes crossed by any mortal consideration, had long marked out fair Lilian Napier as a new victim to be run down and captured. Her beauty had inflamed his senses, her ample possessions his cupidity—it was enough; his wrath, and perhaps his jealousy, were kindled against the young man by whose agency she had found concealment, after he thought all was *en train* by his accusing the baroness of Bruntisfield to the council, and procuring a warrant of search and arrest for intercommuned persons at her manor of the Wryteshouse. His brows were contracted until they formed one dark arch across his forehead; one hand was clenched upon the table, and the other on the embossed hilt of his long rapier, which rested against his left shoulder, and there was no mistaking the glance of hostility and scrutiny he bent upon the prisoner. The other members of the council were all highly excited by the revelations recently extracted from Mr. Ichabod Bummel (by dint of hammer and screw), concerning the intrigues of the Whigs with the prince of Orange. The letters of the exiled baron of Polwarth, and of Mynheer Fagel, the Great Pensionary of Holland, were lying before the lord chancellor, who played thoughtfully with the tassels of his rapier, while his secretaries wrote furiously in certain closely-written folios. Several clerks, macers, and other underlings who loitered in the background, were now ordered to withdraw.

"Approach, Walter Fenton," said the earl of Perth.

"Fenton," muttered General Dalyel, "'tis a name that smacks o' the auld covenant; I hanged a cottar loon that bore it, for skirling a psalm at the foot o' the Campsie Hills, no twa months ago."

"And of true valour, if we remember the old Fentons of that ilk, and the brave Sir John de Fenton of the Bruce's days."

continued the chancellor. "Young man, you of course know for what you this night compear before us?"

"My lord, for permitting the escape of prisoners placed under my charge."

"Prisoners charged with treason and leaguing with inter-communed enemies of the state!" added Clermistonlee, in a voice of thunder.

"And you plead guilty to this?"

"I cannot deny it, my lords."

"Good—you save the trouble of examining witnesses."

"A bonnie piece o' wark, young Springald!" said General Dalyel scornfully; "a braw beginning for a soldier—but ken ye the price o't?"

"My life, perhaps, Sir Thomas," replied Walter, gently; "yet may it please you and their lordships to pardon this, my first offence, in consideration of my three years' faithful and, as yet, unrequited service. Heaven be my witness, noble sirs, I could not help it!"

"By all the devils! Help what, thou fause loon?"

"Permitting the escape of Lady Bruntisfield and her kins-woman, the young lady."

"Aha! the young lady!" laughed Claverhouse and Balcarris.

"I was overcome by their terror and entreaties. Oh, my lords, I seek not to extenuate my offence."

"Plague choke thee!" said Dalyel, with a grim look; "a braw birkie ye are, and a bonnie to wear a steel doublet—a fine chield to march to battle and leaguer, if ye canna hear a haveral woman greet, but your heart maun melt like snaw in the sunshine. By the head of the king, ye shall smart for this! Sic kittle times thole nae trifling."

"I doubt not the young fellow was well paid for his un-timely gallantry," said Clermistonlee, with a provoking sneer.

"Any man who would insinuate so much, I deem a liar and coward!" said Walter, fearlessly: the eyes of the privy councillor shot fire; he started, but restrained himself, and the young man continued: "No, my Lord Clermis-tonlee! though poor, I have a soul above bribery, and would not for the most splendid coronet in Scotland change sides, as *some* among us have done, and may do again."

"Silence!" replied Clermistonlee, in a voice of rage, for he writhed under this pointed remark, having once been a stanch Covenanter; "silence, rascal, and remember that on yonder bench there lieth a bodkin of steel, for boring the tongue that wags too freely."

"Enough of this," said the chancellor, striking the table impatiently with his hand; "Mr. Secretary, attend, and note answers. Walter Fenton, you are doubtless well aware of where the ladies of Bruntisfield are concealed, and can enlighten us thereon."

"I swear to you, most noble earl, that I know not!"

"Ridiculous!" said his tormentor, Clermistonlee, who was under the influence of wine. "Say instantly, or by all the devils, if there is any marrow in your bones, we shall see it shortly:" with his gold-headed cane he significantly touched the iron boots that lay near.

"Hath he been searched according to the act of council, whilk ordains,—sae forth," said Mersington; "for some of Madam Napier's perfumed carolusses may be found in his pouch."

"Nothing was found on him, my lord," replied Maclutchy, "save a sang or twa, a wheen gun-matches, twa dice, a wine bill o' Hughie Blair's—the council's orders to the forces—and —and—"

"And what, sir?"

"A few white shillings, my lord."

"Whilk ye keepit, I suppose."

The macer scratched his head and bowed.

"Whence got ye that ring, sirrah?" asked the imperious Clermistonlee, suddenly feeling a new qualm of jealousy.

"Ring, my lord, ring!" stammered Walter, colouring deeply.

"Yea, knave, it flashed even now, and by this light seems a diamond of the purest water. A common pikeman seldom owns a trinket such as that."

"I cry ye mercy," said Dalyel; "had your lordship seen my brigade of Red Cossacks retreating after the sack of Trebizond and Natolia, ye would have seen the humblest spearman with his boots and holsters crammed to the flaps with the richest jewels of Asiatic Turkey. I myself borrowed a string of pearls from an auld Khanum, worth deil kens how mony thousand roubles. Gad! some pretty trinkets fall in a soldier's way at times."

"Sir Thomas," said Claverhouse, "I would we had a few troops of your Cossacks, to send among the westland Whigs for six months or so."

"S'death!" said the general, through his massy beard, "your guardsmen think themselves fine rufflers, and so they are, Claver'se, but I doubt muckle if in a charge they would have come within a spear's length of my Red Brigade. Puir chields! lang since hae they stuffed the craps of the wolves and vultures that hovered oure the bluidy plains of Smolensk."

"Well, my lords, about this ring," observed Clermistonlee, with ill-disguised impatience, while endeavouring to waken his majesty's advocate, who, oblivious of "his majesty's interest," had fallen fast asleep. "We all know that the Lady Bruntisfield has a god-daughter, grand-niece, or something of that kind—a fair damsel, however ; and 'tis very unlikely this young cock would run his neck under the gallows (whereon I doubt not his father dangled) for nothing. Fenton—harkee, sirrah, surrender the jewel forthwith, and say whence ye had it, or the thumbscrews may prove an awkward exchange for it."

"Do with me as you please, my lords ; but ah, spare me the ring. It is the secret of my life—it is all that I possess in the world—all that I can deem my own ;" pausing with sudden emotion, the young man covered his eyes. "It was found on the hand of my mother—my poor mother, when she lay dead among the graves of the Grey Friars."

"When, knave ? "

"In the year of Bothwell."

A cloud came over the face of Clermistonlee.

"In the year of Bothwell, my lords," continued Walter, in a thick voice ; "that year of misery to so many. I have been told my father died in defence of the bridge ; and my mother—she—spare to me, my lords, what even the poor soldiers who found me respected! It was preserved and restored to me by the good and noble countess of Dunbarton, when, three years ago, I marched against James of Monmouth."

"The true pup of the crop-eared breed!" said Clermistonlee, scornfully ; "false in blood as in name. Macer, hand up the ring. His mother (some trooper's trull) never owned a jewel like that."

The macer advanced, but hesitated.

"Approach, wretch, and, by the God that beholds us, I will destroy thee!" cried Fenton, inflamed with sudden passion ; and so resolute was his aspect, that Maclutchy retreated, and now Mersington and the king's advocate, who had been snoring melodiously, woke suddenly up.

"My lords, you trifle," said the earl of Perth.

"Halt, sirs!" added Claverhouse, who admired Walter's indomitable spirit ; "I cannot permit this ; let the lad retain his ring, but say, without parley, where those fugitives are concealed."

"On the honour of a soldier, I solemnly declare to you, Colonel Grahame, that I know not."

"It is enough," responded Claverhouse, whose deep dark eyes had gazed full upon Walter's with a searching expression which few men could endure. "Never saw I mortal man who could look me openly in the face, when affirming a falsehood."

"This is just havers," said Mersington; "jow the bell for Pate Pincer to gie him one touch of the boot."

"My lords, you may tear me piecemeal, but I cannot tell ye; and, were it otherwise, I would rather die than betray them."

"Hush!" whispered Claverhouse, who admired his spirited bearing; but Clermistonlee exclaimed in triumph,—

"Heard ye that, my lords, heard ye that? Gadso! a half acknowledgment that he can enlighten us anent the retreat of these traitresses, and I demand that he be put to the *question!*"

Now ensued a scene of confusion.

"Aye, the boot!" said Rosehaugh, Mersington, and one or two others. "Let him be remanded to the Water Hole—the caspie claws."

"My lords, I protest—" said Claverhouse, starting up abruptly.

"Hoity toity!" said Mersington; "here's the laird of Claver'se turned philanthropist! Since when did this miracle take place?"

"Since the cold-blooded atrocities this chamber has witnessed," began Claverhouse, turning his eyes of fire on the law lord; but the entrance of Pincer and his two subaltern torturers, whom that little viper, Mersington, had summoned, cut short the observation. Walter's blood grew cold; his first thought was resistance—his second, scorn and despair.

"Had the noble earl of Dunbarton, or all our blades, the old Royals, been in Edinburgh instead of being among the westland Whigs, ye had not dared to degrade me thus," he exclaimed, with fierce indignation. "I disclaim your authority, and appeal to a council of war--to a court of commissioned officers."

"Uds daggers!" said Dalyel, "I love thee, lad. Thou art a brave fellow, and the first man that ever bearded this council board."

"But we will teach thee, braggart," said Sir George of Rosehaugh sternly, "that from this chamber there is *no* appeal, either to courts of peace or councils of war. There can be no appeal——"

"Save to his majesty," added the chancellor, who, to please James VII., had recently embraced the Catholic faith.

"And of what value is the appeal, noble earl, after one's bones have been ground to powder by your accursed irons?'

"We do not sit here to bandy words in this wise," replied the chancellor; "macer, lead the prisoner to the anteroom, while his sentence is deliberated on."

After a delay of some minutes, which to Walter seemed like so many ages, so great was his anxiety, he was again summoned before the haughty conclave. The first whose malignant glance he again encountered was Clermistonlee, whose voice he had often heard in loud declamation against him, and he felt a storm of wrath and hatred gathering in his breast against that vindictive peer. The monotonous voice of the clerk reading his sentence with a careless off-hand air now fell on his ear.

"Walter Fenton, private gentleman in the regiment of Dunbarton, commonly called the Royal Scots Musketeers of Foot, for default and negligence of duty——"

"Anent whilk it is needless to expone," interposed Mersington.

"—— And for your contumacy in presence of the right honourable the lords of his majesty's privy council, you are to be confined in the lowest dungeon of the common prison-house of Edinburgh, for the space of six calendar months from the date hereof, to have your tongue bored by the doomster at the Tron-beam, to teach it the respect which is due to superiors, and thereafter to be sent as a felon, with ane collar of steel riveted round your neck, to the coal heughs of the right worshipful the laird o' Craigha', for such a period as the lords of the said privy council shall deem fitting—*subscribitur* Perth."

"Such mercy may ye all meet in the day of award!" muttered Walter.

"Withdraw," said Lord Clermistonlee, with a bitter smile of undisguised ferocity and malice. "Begone, and remember to thank Sir Thomas of Binns and the laird of Claverhouse, that your tongue is not bored this instant, and thereafter given to feed the crows."

Walter bowed, and was led out by the macer, while the council proceeded to "worry" and terrify the remaining prisoners, Lady Bruntisfield's household, and, after nearly scaring them out of their senses, dismissed them all (save two stout ploughmen, who were given to Sir Thomas Dalyel as troopers), with warning to take care of themselves in all time coming, and with a promise of a thousand marks if they gave intimation of their lady's retreat.

CHAPTER IX.

DEJECTION.

A mournful one am I, above whose head,
  A day of perfect bliss hath never passed;
Whatever joys my soul have ravished,
  Soon was the radiance of those joys o'ercast.
                    LAYS OF THE MINNESINGERS.

WALTER was conducted back to the prison-house in Gour-lay's Close, the Heart of Midlothian being already filled with nonconforming culprits.

Preceded by Macer Maclutchy and the gudeman or gover-nor of the establishment, who wore the city livery, blue, laced with yellow, and carried a bunch of ominous-like keys, Walter found himself before a little archway, closed by a strong iron door, which opened under the great turnpike stair of the edifice, and led to the lower regions—to a superstruc-ture of vaults, which, from their low and massive aspect, might have been deemed coeval with the days of the Alexan-ders. The light of the iron cruise borne by the gudeman failed to penetrate the deep abyss which yawned before them on the door being opened, and the cold wind of the subter-ranean chambers rushed upward in their faces. Slowly descending the hollowed and time-worn steps of an ancient stair, accompanied by his guard and conductors, poor Walter moved mechanically. The lamp, as it flared in the chill atmosphere, showed the dark arches and green slimy walls of massive stonework forming the basement story of the prison. He felt a horror creeping over his heart. A profound and dismal silence reigned there; for these earthy passages where the frog croaked, the shining beetle crawled, and the many-legged spider span in undisturbed security, gave back no echo to their footsteps. In the heart of a populous city, thought he, can such a place be? Is it not a dream?

"Adonai! Adonai!" cried a voice in the distance, so loud, so shrill, and unearthly, that the gudeman paused, and the macer started back. "How long, Oh Lord, wilt thou permit these dragons to devour thy people? Rejoice, ye bairns of the Covenant! Rejoice, O ye nations, for He will avenge the blood of his chosen, and render vengeance on his adversaries."

"Hoots! it's that fule-body Bummel blawing like a piper through the keyhole," said the macer, and knocking thrice on the cell door with his mace, added, "Gif your tongue had been bored with an elshin as it deserved, my braw buckie, ye

wadna hae crawn sae crouse. However, gudeman, his rebellious yammering will not disturb you muckle."

"The vaults are gey far doon—we would be deeved wi' him
else," replied the gudeman; "but he gangs to the Bass in
the morning, and there he can sing psalmody to the roaring
waves and the cauld east wind, wi' Traill, Bennet, Blackadder,
and other brethren in tribulation."

"By my word, keeping thae chields on the auld craig is
just feeding what ought to be hanged," responded the macer,
for these underlings affected to acquire the cavalier sentiments
of the day. A door was now opened, and Walter Fenton
heard the voice of the gudeman, saying,—

"Kennel up there, my man. You will find the lodgings
we gie to conventiclers and enemies of the king are no just as
braw as Gibbie Runlet's, doon at the White Horse. There
is a windlan o' gude straw in that corner to sleep on, gif the
rottons, and speeders, and asps, will let ye, and a mouthfu' o'
caller air can aye be got at the iron grate; and sae my service
t'ye."

"And keep up your spirits, Mr. Fenton," added the macer
with a mock bow, "for the toun smith, Deacon Macanvil, will
be doun in the morning to rivet round your craig the collar o'
thrall wi' Craighall's name on't, and sae my service t'ye, too."

The sneers of these wretches stung Walter to the soul, and
it was with difficulty he restrained an impulse to rush upon
them and dash their heads together. But the door was
instantly closed; he heard the jarring of the bolts as they
were shot into the stonework, the clank of a chain as it was
thrown across, and then the retreating footsteps of his jailers
growing fainter as they ascended the circular staircase. A
door closed in the distance, the echoes died away, and then
all became intensely still. He was now left utterly to his
own sad and mortifying reflections, amid silence, gloom, and
misery.

The darkness was oppressive; not the faintest ray of light
could be traced on any side, and he wondered how the chill
March wind swept through the vault, until, on groping about,
he discovered on a level with his face a small barred aperture, which opened to the adjoining close. In that high and
narrow alley, there was but little light even during the day;
consequently, by night, it was involved in the deepest obscurity.

The cold, damp wind blew freely upon Walter's flushed
face and waving hair, as he moved cautiously round his
prison, and feeling the dark slimy walls on every side, dis-

covered that it was a vault about twelve feet square, faced with stone, destitute, damp, frightful, and furnished only by a bundle of straw in a corner. On this he threw himself, and endeavoured to reflect calmly upon the perils by which he was surrounded.

He was naturally of an ardent and impetuous temper, and consequently his reflections failed either to soothe or to console him. His sentiments of hostility to Lord Clermistonlee were equalled only by those of gratitude to the laird of Claverhouse, by whose influence he had, for a time, been spared a cruel and degrading maltreatment ; but that, alas, was yet to be endured, and the contemplation of it was maddening. To be given as a bondsman or serf, girt with a collar of thrall or slavery, to work in the pits and mines of certain landholders, was a mode of punishment not uncommon in those vindictive days.

When the Scottish troops, under Lieutenant-colonel Strachan, defeated the brave cavaliers of Montrose in battle at Kerbister, in Ross, on the 27th of April, 1650, hundreds who were taken captive were disposed of in that manner. Some were given in thrall to Lieutenant-general Lesly, many to the marquis of Argyle, others to Sir James Hope, to work as slaves in his lead-mines, and the residue were all sent to France, to recruit the Scottish regiments of the Lord Angus and Sir Robert Murray.

Had his sentence been banishment to a foreign service, though it would have wrung his heart to leave his native country, and forego for ever the bright hopes and visions that had (though afar off) begun to lighten the horizon of his fortunes, he would have hailed the doom with joy ; but to be gifted as a slave to another, to drudge amid the filth, obscurity, and disgrace of a coal-mine,—oh, he looked forward to that with a horror inconceivable. ....

His mind became filled with dismal forebodings for the future. Though he still remembered with sincere pleasure the services he had rendered to the Napiers of Bruntisfield, his dreams of Lilian's mild blue eyes and glossy ringlets were sadly clouded by the perils to which they had hurried him.

All those proud and high aspirations, those intense longings for fame and distinction, for happiness and power, in which the mind of an ardent and enthusiastic youth is so prone to luxuriate, and which had been for years the day-dream of Walter Fenton, now suffered a chill and fatal blight. It is a hard and bitter conviction, that one's dearest prospects are

I.   F

blasted and withered for ever ; and to the heart of the young
and proud, there is no agony equal to that of unmerited disgrace and humiliation. Misery was Walter's companion, and
further miseries and degradations awaited him ; but happily,
the dark future was involved in obscurity.

CHAPTER X.

HOPE

Thou art most fair ; but could thy lovely face
Make slavery look more comely ? could the touch
Of thy soft hand convey delight to mine
With servile fetters on ?

BOADICEA, ACT IV.

THREE days passed away. Three, and still there was no
appearance of the dreaded Deacon Macanvil with his hammer
and rivets, and collar of thrall.

The monotony of the prison had been unbroken, save, each
morning, by the entrance of the gudeman of the Tolbooth
and a soldier of the Town-guard, bearing a wooden luggie of
fresh water and a slice of coarse bread, or coarser oaten cake
on a tin trencher, and to these poor viands, the gudewife of
the keeper, moved with pity for " such a winsome young
man," added a cutlet or two on the third day. For the first
four-and-twenty hours this mean fare remained untouched,
but anon, the cravings of a youthful appetite compelled him
to regale on it.

In a retired, or rather, a darker corner of this miserable
place, he reclined on his truss of damp straw, listening to the
lively hum of the city without, and the deep ding-dong of the
cathedral bells as they marked the passing hours.

Slowly the interminable day wore on.

Shadows passed and repassed the wretched aperture which
was level with the pavement, and served for a window. Feet
cased in white funnel boots garnished with scarlet turnovers,
gold spurs and red morocco spur-leathers, in clumsy Crom-
wellian calf-skins, or in brogues of more humble pretensions,
appeared and disappeared as the passengers strode up and
down the close; and many pretty feet and taper ancles in
tight stockings of green or scarlet silk set up on " cork-heeled
shoon," tripped past, the fair owners thereof displaying, by
their uplifted trains, rather more than they might have done,
if aware that a pair of curious eyes were looking upward from
the cimmerian depth of that ghastly vault.   Barefooted

children gambolled about in the spring sunshine; with ruddy and laughing faces they peeped fearfully into the dark hole, and on discerning a human face through the gloom, cried "A bogle, a ghaist!" and fled away with a shout.

Propped on his staff, the toiling water-carrier passed hourly, conveying limpid water from the public wells, even to the lofty "sixteenth story," for a bodle the measure. Lumbering sedans were borne past by liveried carriers at a Highland trot; and the voices that rang perpetually in the narrow alley, though enlivening the prison of Walter, only served to make his sense of degradation and captivity more acute.

Anon, all those sounds ceased one by one; the bells of evening tolled, the ten o'clock drum was beat around the ancient royalty, and died away in the depths of close and wynd, and night and silence stole together over the dense and lofty city. The last wayfarer had gone to his home, and a desolate sense of loneliness fell upon the heart of Walter Fenton.

"Alas, alas!" he exclaimed, "had my dear friend Lady Dunbarton been on this side of the border, I had not been thus persecuted and forgotten. And Finland, why tarries he? Friendship should bring him to me, for shame cannot withhold him; I have committed no crime."

So passed the fourth day.

Night came on again, and the poor lad felt an oppression of spirit, a longing for freedom, and abhorrence of his dungeon, so bitter and intense, that reflection became the most acute torment. He turned restlessly among the straw, its very rustle fretted him, and he started up to pace to and fro in the narrow compass of the vault. He muttered, moaned, and communing with himself, pressed his face against the rusty grating, while listening intently to catch a passing sound, and inhale the cool fresh breeze of the spring night.

Though so many thousand souls were densely packed within the fortifications of Edinburgh, and every house was like a beehive or a tower of Babel, at that hour the city was still as the grave. Walter heard only the throbbing of his heart. The last dweller in the close had long since traversed the lofty stair that ascended to his home; the heavy door at the foot of the prison turnpike stair had long since been closed, and its sentinel had withdrawn to smoke a pipe or sip a can of twopenny by the gudeman's well-sanded ingle. From the hollow recesses of its great rood-spire St. Giles's bell tolled eleven.

"Another night!—another—another!" exclaimed Walter; as he threw himself upon the straw, and wrung his hands in rage, in bitterness, and unavailing agony. "Another night! Oh, to be taught patience, or to be free!"

From a sleepy stupor that had sunk upon him, the very torpidity of desperation, he was roused by a noise at the grating: a face appeared dimly without, and a well-known voice said,

"Harkee, Fenton,—art asleep, my boy?"

"*Me voilà*—I am here!" he exclaimed, as he sprang to the grating and pressed the hand of his friend.

"You forget, Walter, that I am not calling the roll," laughed the officer; "but *me voilà* is very old-fashioned, my lad, and hath not been used by us these two hundred years, since the battle of Banje en Anjou. By all the devils, 'tis a deuced unpleasant *malheur* this!"

"I thought you had forgotten me, Finland."

"You did me great injustice; but, lackaday, with Wemyss and my party I have been for these three days worrying all the old wives and bonneted carles on the Bruntisfield barony, to take certain obnoxious tests under terror of thumbscrews and gunmatch. By my honour, I would rather that my lord, the earl of Perth, would march with his mace on shoulder, anent such dirty work, for I aver that it is altogether unbecoming the dignity and profession of a soldier. And mark me, Walter, all this tyranny will end in a storm such as the land hath not seen, since our fathers' days, when the banner of the Covenant was unfurled on the hill of Dunse."

"And are there no tidings of Dunbarton, our commander?"

"The deuce, no! there hath been no mail from London these fourteen days; the rascal who brought the bag had only one letter, and, getting drunk, lost it in the neutral grounds, somewhere on the borders. The earl was to have taken horse at Whitehall for the north, on the first of this month; 'tis now the penult day only, and he cannot be here for a week yet; so patience, Walter." Walter sighed.

"There are others here who have not forgotten thee, my dear Mr. Fenton," said a soft voice, as a pretty female face, lighted by two bright eyes, stooped down to that hideous grating. "But, forsooth, our good friend the laird of Finland, seems resolved to talk for us all, which is not to be borne. I think he has acquired all the loquacity of the French chevaliers, without an atom of their gallantry."

"A thousand moustaches!" stammered the officer; "my fair Annie, I had almost—"

"Forgotten me! you dare not say so; but O my poor boy Fenton. how sorry I am I see thee there."

"I thank you, Mistress Laurie, but the honour of this visit

would gild the darkest prison in Scotland—even the Whig
vault of Dunoter," said Walter, kissing the hand of the
speaker, whom he knew to be the betrothed of his friend, a
gay and lively girl of twenty, whose beauty was then the
theme of a hundred songs, of which, unhappily, but one has
survived to us—the effusion of Finland's love and poesy.
Long had they loved each other; but the father of Annie,
the old Whig baronet of Maxwelton, had engendered a furious
hostility to Douglas, in consequence of his soldiers having
lived at free quarters on his estates in Dumfriesshire, where
they made very free indeed, burned down a few farms, shot
and houghed the cattle, and extorted a month's marching-
money thrice over, with cocked matches and drawn rapiers.

"This visit is as unexpected as it is welcome," continued
Walter; "and, for the honour it does me, I would not
exchange—"

"Thy prison for a palace," interrupted Annie. "Now,
Mr. Walter, I know to an atom the value of this compliment.
which means exactly nothing. But we must not jest; I have
to introduce a dear friend—one who has come to thank you
personally for those favours of which you are now paying the
price. Come, Lilian, love," continued the lively young lady,
"approach and speak. My life on't! how the lassie trembles!
Come, Finland, we understand this, and will keep guard while
little Lilian speaks with her captive Paladin."

"You are a mad wag, Annie," said the cavalier, as he gave
her his ungloved hand; "but lower your voice, dear one, or,
soft and sweet as it is, it may bring down the gudeman and
all his rascals about us in a trice."

"How can I find words to thank you, Mr. Fenton?" said
the tremulous voice of Lilian Napier, whose small but beautiful face appeared without the massive grating, peeping
through a plaid of dark-green tartan, a mode of disguise then
very common in Scotland, and which continued to be so in
the earlier part of the last century. Like a hooded mantilla,
it floated over her graceful shoulders, and a silver brooch
confined it beneath her dimpled chin.

"Lilian Napier here!" exclaimed Fenton with rapture;
"ah, fool that I was to repine, while my miseries were remembered by thee!"

"Ah, sir! the Lady Bruntisfield has lamented them bitterly. Never can we repay you for the unmerited severity
and humiliations to which you have been subjected in our
cause. Oh, can I forget that but for you, Mr. Fenton, we
might have become the occupants of that frightful place, the
air of which chills me even here."

" Thee—O no, Lilian Napier, they could not have the heart to immure thee here ! "

" The lack of heart rather, Walter. "

" The idea is too horrible—but now," he continued, in a voice of delight, " you are speaking like my old companion and playfellow. 'Tis long—O, very, very long, Lilian, since last we conversed together alone. Do you remember when we gathered flowers, and rushes, and pebbles by the banks of the loch, and berries at the Heronshaw, and gambolled in the parks in the summer sunshine ? "

" How could I forget them ? "

" Never have I been so happy since. O, those were days of innocence and joy ! "

There was a pause, and both sighed deeply.

" Poor Walter, how sincerely I pity thee ! "

" Then I bless the chance that brought me here. "

" In that cold, dark pit—oh, 'tis a place of horror. Would to Heaven I could free you, Mr. Walter ! "

" Ah, Lilian, call me Walter, without the *Mr* Your voice sounds then as it did in other days, ere cold conventionalities raised such a gulf between us. "

" They can do so no longer," said the young lady, weeping : " we are landless and ruined now ; and O ! did not fear for my good aunt Grizel make me selfish, I would surrender myself to the council to-morrow. "

" S'death ! do not think of it. "

" We both accuse ourselves of selfishness—of the very excess of cowardice, and of blotting our honour for ever, by meanly flying, and transferring all our dangers to you. "

" Do not permit yourself to think so," said Walter, moved to great tenderness by her tears. " Dear Lilian (allow me so to call you, in memory of our happier days), leave me now— to tarry here is full of danger. If you are discovered by the rascals who guard this place, the thought of what would ensue may drive me mad : threats, imprisonment, discovery, and disgrace. Oh, leave me, for God's sake, Lilian ! "

" Besides, I may be compromising the safety of those good friends who so kindly have accompanied me hither to-night. Ah ! there is a terrible proclamation against us fixed to the city cross ; they style us those intercommuned traitors, the Napiers, umquhile of Bruntisfield. "

" Then leave me, Lilian—I can be happy now, knowing that you came—— "

" From Lady Grizel," said Lilian, hastily, " to express her sincere thanks for your kindness, and her deep sorrow for its sad requital, which (from what you told us) we could not have contemplated. Indeed, Mr. Walter, we have been very unhappy on your account, and so, impelled by a sense of gratitude, I came to—to—" and, pausing, she covered her face with her hands and wept, for the new and humiliating situation in which she found herself had deeply agitated her. She did not perceive a dark figure that approached her softly, unseen by her friends, who were gaily chatting under the gloomy shadow of a projecting house, and quite absorbed in themselves.

"Lilian, you were ever good and gentle," said Walter, altogether overcome by her tears, and pressing her hand between his own. "Deeply, deeply do I feel the mortification you must endure; but do not weep thus—it wrings my very heart."

She permitted him to retain her hand (there was no harm in that), but his thoughts became tumultuous; he kissed it; and as his lips touched her for the first time, his whole soul seemed to rush to them.

"Oh, Lilian, were I rich, I feel that I could love you."

"And if one is poor, can they not love too?" she asked artlessly.

"Oh, yes, Lilian—dear Lilian," said Walter, quite borne away by his passion, and greatly agitated; but his arm could not encircle her, for the envious grating intervened: "deeply do I feel at this moment how bitter, how hopeless, may be the love of the poor. But if I dared to tell you that the little page, Walter, who so often carried your mantle and led your horse's bridle—now, when a man, aspired so far——"

The girl trembled violently, and said, in a feeble voice of alarm, "Oh, hush—hush, some one approaches."

"Then away to Douglas, for he alone can protect you. One word ere you go: you have found a secure and secret shelter?"

"Humble and secret, at least."

"With the Lauries of Maxwelton?"

"Oh, no, their house is already suspected. In the poor cottage of my nurse, old Elsie Elshender, at St. Rocque—there we bide our fate in poverty and obscurity."

"And your cousin, Napier, the captain?"

"Hath fled to the west: but that person—he is certainly listening—adieu!"

"Remember me."

"How can I forget?" she replied, naïvely, as she arose to withdraw; but lo! the person started forward, and her hand, which was as yet glowing with Walter's kiss, was rudely seized in the rough grasp of the intruder. Fear utterly deprived the poor girl of power to cry out.

"Aunt Grizel—dear grand-aunt Grizel!" was all she could gasp, and she would have sunk on the pavement had not the eavesdropper supported her. He was a tall, stout gallant, and muffled, by having the skirt of his cloak drawn over his right shoulder, so as to conceal part of his face, then the fashionable mode of disguise for *roués* and *intriguantes*.

"Lilian Napier, by all the devils!" cried Lord Clermistonlee, in a tone of astonishment : he was considerably intoxicated, having just left the neighbouring house, where he had been drinking for the last six hours with the Lord President Lockhart. "Now I thought thee only some poor mud-lark, or errant *bona roba*. This is truly glorious. Thou shalt come with me, my beauty. What, you will scream? Nay, minx, then you have but a choice between the stone vaults of the Tolbooth and the tapistried chambers of my poor old houses of Drumsheugh and Clermistonlee—ha, ha!" and he began to sing the old ditty :—

> "There was a young lassie lo'ed by an auld man——"

"Help, Finland, help, for the love of God!" cried Lilian, dreadfully agitated ; but the lord continued :—

> "'With a heylillelu and a how-lo-lan!
> Her cheeks were rose-red, and her eyne were sky-blue
> With a how-lo-lan and a heylillelu!
> And this lassie was lo'ed by this canty old man,
> With a heylillelu and a how-lo-lan!'"

"By all the devils! I can sing as well as my lord the president, though he hath three crown bowls of punch under his doublet."

"Douglas, Douglas,—your sword, your sword!" cried Walter, grasping the massive grating, and swinging on the bars like a madman, essaying in vain to wrench them from their solid wrests ; but ere the words had left his lips, Lord Clermistonlee was staggered by a blow from the clenched hand of the cavalier, and Lilian was free.

"Fly, Annie," he exclaimed to his love ; "away with Lilian Napier to the coach at the close head. The devil! girl—art thou doited?—off, and leave me to deal with this tavern brawler. Fore George! I will truss his points in first-rate fashion." The girls retired in terror, and Douglas unsheathed his rapier.

"Beware thee, villain," exclaimed the other, drawing his long bilbo with prompt bravery, and wrapping his mantle round the left arm. " I am a lord of the privy council—to draw on me is treason."

" Were you King James himself, I would run you through the heart, for applying such an epithet to a gentleman of the house of Douglas."

" You will have it then—come on, plated varlet, and look well to guard and parry, for I am a first-rate swordsman."

Finland's cuirass rang with a rapier-thrust from his assailant, who fell furiously to work, lunging like a madman, and exclaiming, every time the fire sparked from their clanging blades, " Bravo, bilbo ! Excellent—come on again, Mr. Malapert, and I will teach thee to measure swords with Randal of Clermistonlee. Gads-o, fellow, thou art no novice in the science of fencing—crush me, what a thrust ! well parried—

" ' With a heylillelu, and a how——'

Damnation seize thee, man ! how came that about ? "

The sword of Finland, by one lucky parry, had broken the lord's rapier off by the hilt, and ripped up the skin of his sword-hand, with such force that he staggered against the wall.

" I hope your lordship is not hurt ! " exclaimed his antagonist, supporting him by the arm.

" Zounds, no ! a little only," replied Clermistonlee, whom the shock had perfectly sobered. Full of rage, he tossed his embossed sword-hilt over the house-tops, exclaiming, " Accursed blade, may the hands that forged thee grill on the fires of eternity ! "

It whistled through the air, and fell down the chimney of the dowager Lady Drumsturdy, where it stuck midway, and so terrified that ancient dame that, notwithstanding her hatred to " massemongers," she laid her poker and shovel .crosswise; but the mysterious noise in her capacious " lum " formed a serious case for the investigation of ghostseers and gossips next day.

" Harkee, laird of Finland," said Clermistonlee haughtily, " we must enact this affair over again in daylight ; meantime let us part, or the town-guard will be upon us with their partisans, and I have no wish that you should suffer for ripping up an inch or two of skin in fair fight; you will hear from me anon."

" Whenever your lordship pleases, I am your most obedient," replied Douglas, bowing coldly as he hurried to join the terrified ladies, with whom he had barely time to get into the hackney-coach and drive off, when the door of the prison opened, and a few of the town-guard, who had heard the clashing of the rapiers, rushed forth with lanterns and pole-axes; like modern police, exhibiting great alacrity when the danger was over, they seized Clermistonlee.

"Dare ye lay hands on a gentleman," he exclaimed, fiercely shaking them off. "Unhand me, villains, I am Randal Lord Clermistonlee! I was assaulted ——"

"By whom, my lord, by whom?" replied the guardians of the peace, cringing before this imperious noble.

"What is it to such rascals as thee?—oh, a knavish cloak-snatcher, or cut-purse, or something of that kind. Retire; I have always hands to defend myself."

The guard, with hurried and half-audible apologies, withdrew, and the brawling lord was left to his own confused reflections. He tied a handkerchief about his hand, and was about to withdraw, when a thought struck him: he approached the grating of the low dungeon, and placing close to it his face, which though unseen was pale with fury, while his dark eyes gleamed like two red sparks.

"Art there, thou spawn of the Covenant?" he asked in a husky voice: "Ah, dog of a Fenton, I will hang thee high as Haman for this night's misadventure."

The prisoner replied by a scornful laugh, and the exasperated *roué* strode away.

CHAPTER XI.

CLERMISTONLEE AT HOME.

Too long by love a wandering fire misled,
My latter days in vain delusion fled;
Day after day, year after year, withdrew,
And beauty blessed the minutes as they flew,
These hours consumed in joy, but lost to fame.——
HAMILTON OF BANGOUR.

THE town residence of Lord Clermistonlee was a lofty and narrow mansion of antique aspect; it stood immediately within the Craig-end gate, that low-browed archway in the eastern flank of the city wall, which, from the foot of Leith Wynd still faces the bluff rock of the Calton. With high pedimented windows and Flemish gables, Clermiston-lodging towered above the mossy, grass-tufted, and time-worn rampart of the city—the aforesaid portal of which gave entrance to it on one side, while the more immediate path from the great central street was a steep and narrow close, the mansions of which were as black as the smoke of four centuries could make them. Their huge *façades*, plastered over with rough lime and oyster-shells, completely intercepted the view to the south, while that to the north was shut in by the black cliffs of the bare Calton. and the Multrees-hill with the ancient suburb of St. Ninian, straggling through the narrow chasm that yawned between them, and afforded a glimpse of Leith and the far-off hills of Fife. At the base of the hill lay the last fragments of the monastery of Greenside, and opposite a thatched hamlet crept close to the margin of the loch, the broad sluice of which the irascible baillies of Edinburgh invariably shut, when they quarrelled with a colony of sturdy and "contumacious" weavers and tanners who had located there, and whose communication with Halkerstoune Wynd they could cut off at pleasure by damming up the waters of the loch. Immediately under the windows of the mansion lay the park, hospital, and venerable church of the Holy Trinity, founded by the queen of James II., about two hundred years before.

On the night described in the last chapter, a large fire burned cheerily in the chamber of dais; and the walls of wainscot, varnished and gilded, glittered in its glow. Supper was laid; carved crystal, plate, and snow-white napery gleamed in the light of the ruddy fire, and of four large wax candles that towered aloft in massive square holders of French workmanship. Over the mantel-piece, in an oak frame, amid the carving of which, grapes, nymphs, and bacchanals were all entwined together, hung a portrait painted by Jamieson, representing a pale young lady in a ruff and fardingale of James the Sixth's days, and having the pale blue eyes, exquisitely fair complexion, and lint-white locks, which were then so much admired. It was his lordship's mother, a lady of the house of Spynie.

Silver plate, a goodly row of labelled flasks (bottling wine was not then the custom), and various substantial viands, formed a *corps-de-réserve* on a grotesquely-carved buffet of black oak, for everything was fashioned after the grotesque in those days. The knobs of the red leather chairs, and the ponderous fire-irons, were strange and open-mouthed visages; the brackets supporting the cornices of the doors and the mantel-piece, were also strange bacchanalian faces grinning from wreaths of vine-leaves, clusters of grapes, and crowns of acanthus. Three long silver-hilted rapiers with immense pommels, shells, and guards, pistols, steel caps, masks, foils, and a buff coat richly laced with silver, lay all huddled in a corner, while the broad mantel-piece presented quite an epitome of the proprietor's character.

The massive stone lintel displayed in bold relief the legend carved thereon by his pious forefathers,

Blyssit be God for al his giftis, 1540.

but above it lay Andro Hart's " Compendious Book of Godly Songs," beside the " Gaye Lady's Manuall," and the " Banqvet of Jests or change or cheare imprinted at the shoppe in Ivie-lane, 1634," a book of ribald ditties, another of farriery, another of falconry, obscene plays ; Rosehaugh's " Dissertations" sent by the author, and used by Clermistonlee to light his Dutch pipe ; whistles, whips, hunting-horns, and drinking-flasks, cards, dice, hawks' hoods, an odd pistol, papers of council, warrants of search, arrest, and torture, mingled with challenges and frivolous *billets-doux*. A large wolfish dog, and a very frisky red-eyed Scottish terrier slept together on the warm hearth-rug.

Juden Stenton, the stout old butler, had stirred the fire and wiped the glasses for the tenth time, tasted the wine for the twentieth, and had made as many rounds of the table to snuff the candles, and re-examine everything ; he was very impatient and sleepy, and listened intently with his head bent low, a practice which he had acquired in the great civil wars. The clock in the spire of the Netherbow-porte struck midnight.

" Cocksnails !" muttered Juden, " twelve o'clock and nae sign o' him yet. What's the world coming to ? My certie, what would his faither the douce laird o' Drumsheugh hae thocht o' this kind of work ? He (honest man !) was aye in his nest at the first tuck o' the ten o'clock drum."

Juden was verging on sixty years of age ; his figure was short and paunchy, his face full and florid ; his twinkling grey eyes wore always a cunning expression, and had generally a sotted appearance about them, which made it extremely difficult to determine whether he was drunk or sober. His large round head was bald, and his chin close shaven, according to the fashion for the lower classes, few but nobles and cavaliers retaining the manly moustaches and imperial. A clean white cravat fell over his doublet of dark-green cloth, the red braiding of which was neatly curved to suit his ample paunch ; breeches of dark plush, black cotton stockings and heavy shoes, the instep of each being covered by a large brass buckle, completed his attire. A scar still remained on his shining scalp to attest the dangers he had dared in his younger days.

The last of a once numerous and splendid but now diminished household, old Juden Stenton was a faithful follower of Lord Clermistonlee, for whom he would have laid down his

life without a sigh of regret. He acted by turns butler and
baillie, cook and valet, groom, farrier, trooper, and factotum,
being the beau ideal of the stanch but unscrupulous serving-
man of the day, who changed sides in religion, politics, and
everything just as the laird did, and who knew no will or law
save those of his leader and master. When Clermistonlee
(then Sir Randal Clermont of Drumsheugh), ruined by the
mad excesses into which he had plunged at the dissipated
court of Charles II., in a fit of despair joined the insurgent
Covenanters at Bothwell Bridge, Juden put a blue cockade in
his bonnet, "girded up his loins," as he said, " and went forth
to battle for Scotland's oppressed kirk and broken covenant."
But when Sir Randal's name (in consequence of mistake, or
of some friendly influence in the Scottish cabinet) was omitted
in the list of the attainted, and he changed sides, obtaining—
none knew how or why—rank and riches under the persecutors, Juden changed too, and donning the buff coat and
scarlet, became a bitter foe to " all crop-eared and psalm-
singing rebels," and riding as a royalist trooper, suppressed
many a harmless conventicle, and hunted and hounded,
slashed and shot, or dragged to prison those who had been
his former comrades, for in political matters Juden's mind
was as facile and easy as that of a German.

He had too often less honourably acted the pander to his
lord, in many a vile intrigue and cruel seduction ; for of all the
wild rakes of the time (Rochester excepted) none had rushed
so furiously on the career of fashionable vice and dissipation
as Clermistonlee ; and even now, when forty years of age, he
continued the same kind of life from mere habit, perhaps,
rather than inclination.

But there was one chapter of his life which memory brought
like a cloud on his gayest hours, and which riot and revel
could never efface,—a sad episode of domestic mystery and
unhappiness. Clermistonlee, in the prime of his youth, had
been wedded to a lady of beauty and rank, of extreme gentleness of manner and softness of disposition. Like many
others, *the fancy* passed away ; repentance came, as his love
cooled or changed to other objects. He took the lady to
Paris, and there she died. . . . . . There were not wanting
evil tongues, who said he had destroyed her. A kind of
mystery enveloped her fate ; and even in his most joyous
moods, sad thoughts would suddenly cloud the lofty brow of
Clermistonlee, a sign which his kind friends never failed to
attribute to remorse. Many were the women who had trusted
to his honour, and found they had believed in a phantom ;
until, at the era of our story, his name had become (like that

of the marquis de Laval) a bye-word in the mouths of the people for all that was wicked, irregular, and bad.

"Twelve o'clock," muttered Juden: "braw times—braw times, sirs; I warrant he'll be roistering in the change-house o' that runagate vintner Hugh Blair, at the Pillars. A wanion on his sour gascon and fushionless hock! Waiting is sleepy work, and dry too. Gude claret this! My service to ye, Maister Juden Stenton," he continued, bowing to his reflection in an opposite mirror, "you're a gude and worthy servitor to ane that doesna ken your value. The members o' council maun a' be fu' as pipers by this time except Claverhouse, wha canna touch wine, and auld Binns, wham wine canna touch. Hech! here he comes; and now for a clamjamfray wi' the yettwards."

A violent knocking at the city gate close by announced the return of his master from a midnight ramble. The sentinel within opened the wicket of the barrier; and on demanding the usual toll required of belated citizens, a handful of pence, flung by the impatient lord, clattered about his steel cap. Clermistonlee entered, and, half dragging a little crooked man after him, rapidly ascended the flight of steps that led to the circular tower or staircase of his own house. In the low-pointed doorway, which was surmounted by an uncouth coronet, stood Juden with a candle flaring in each hand, bowing very low, though not in the best of humours.

"Od, that weary body Mersington is wi' him!" he muttered. "The auld spunge—he'll drink the daylicht in!"

"Light the way there, Juden," cried his master. "My good Lord Mersington is generally short-sighted about this hour."

"Double-sighted, ye mean," chuckled the decrepit senator. "Sorrow tak' ye, Randal, ye maun aye hae your joke—he! he! A cauld nicht this, Juden," he added, while hobbling up the narrow stair, with an enormous wig and broad-brimmed beaver overshadowing his meagre figure.

"A cauld morning rather, please your lordship," replied Juden somewhat testily, as he ushered them into the chamber of dais, and stirred the fire as well as the chain which secured the poker to the jamb permitted him.

"Be seated, Mersington. This way, my lord; take care of the table—devil! the man's blind," said Clermistonlee, as he somewhat unceremoniously pushed the half-intoxicated senator into one of the high-backed chairs of red maroquin.

Mersington was twenty years his senior, and never was there a pair of more ill-assorted gossips or friends. The one, a polished and fashionable cavalier *roué*; the other, a cranky

and meagre compound of vulgarity, shrewdness, and ignorance, who was never sober, but had obtained a seat on the
bench in consequence of his inflexible devotion to the government, to please whom he would have sent the twelve apostles
to "testify" at the Bow-foot, had it been required of him.
Clermistonlee unbuckled his belt, and flung his empty
scabbard to the one end of the room, his plumed beaver to
the other, and drew his chair hastily forward to the table.

"Where is your braw bilbo, my lord?" asked Juden.

"What the devil is it to thee?—'Tis broken. I will wear
the steel-hilted backsword to-morrow."

"The auld blade ye wore at *the* Brigg?"

": D—n Bothwell Brigg! How is Meg?"

"Muckle the same, puir beastie."

"I hope, knave, thou gavest her the warm mash, and
bathed her nostrils and fetlocks."

"Without fail. We maun tak' gude care o' her—the last
o' a braw stud of sixty, my faith! But when a mear hath
baith the wheezlock and the yeuk——"

"How! has she both?"

"Had ye, a month syne, tar-barrelled that auld carlin,
Elshender, owre the muir at St. Rocque, Meg would hae been
sound, wind and limb, frae that moment."

"'Sblood! Juden, dost think the cantrips of this old hag
have really bedevilled my favourite nag?"

"I'm no just free to say, my lord; but it *is* unco queer that
Meg (puir beastie!) should fa' ill o' sae mony things just
after Lucky Elshender flyted wi' ye for riding through her kail
for a near cut to the Grange, the day ye dined wi' auld
Fountainhall."

"By all the devils, Juden, if I thought this bearded hag
had any hand in the mare's illness, I would have her under
the hands of the pricker to-morrow," replied Clermistonlee,
who was deeply imbued with the Scottish prejudice against
old women. "We had before us to-day two hags, whom we
consigned to the flames; one for confessing witchcraft, and
the other for obstinately refusing to confess it."

Juden rubbed his hands.

"Ou aye—ou aye—he! he!" chuckled Mersington. "Hae
her up before the fifteen—a full blawn case o' sorcery—on
wi' the thumbikins; I have kent rack and screw bring
mony a queer story to light;—riding to Banff on a besom-
shank—sailing to the Inch in a milkbowie—bewitching wheels
that ane minute flew round as if the mill was mad, and the
next stood like the Bass Rock—raising a storm o' wind in the
lift by the damnable agency of a black beetle, 'ane golach,'

as Rosehaugh called it in the indictment. We had a grand case o' that lately in the northern courts."

"But the gude auld fashion o' tar-barrelling is clean gaing out in thae fushionless days," said Juden, whom Mersington treated with considerable familiarity. "We havena had a respectable bleeze on the Castle-hill these aucht years and mair."

"You may chance to have one very shortly," replied his lord impatiently, "if Meg gets not the better of her ailings soon. But enough of this.—Let us to supper."

"Blaid, as I live! Foul fa' the loon that shed it!" exclaimed Juden, in accents of intense concern, as his master drew off his perfumed gloves, and revealed the scar on his right hand. "Whatna collyshangie has this been, noo—and your braw mantle o' drab de Berrie—oh laddie, when will you learn to tak' care o' yoursel?" added honest Juden, who from force of habit still styled his lord as he had done thirty years ago.

"Pshaw! you have seen my blood ere now, I suppose."

"Owre often, owre often," groaned the old man. "You'll hae been keeping the croon o' the causeway, I warrant, majoring rapier in hand, as your faither was wont in his young days."

"No, no; I merely measured swords in Gourlay's close with one of the Scots musketeers."

"Aboot what? They're mad, unchancey chiclds, Dunbarton's men."

"A girl—the cursed baggage!"

"Burn my beard, if ever I saw dochter o' Eve that tempted me to encounter a slashed hide!" said Juden, with a tone of thankfulness, while his master tied a handkerchief round the wounded limb, and applied himself to the viands before him, attending to his friend with hospitality and politeness, and doing the honours of the table with peculiar grace.

A roasted capon, mutton and cutlets, oysters fried and raw, a gigantic silver mug of brandy and burnt sugar, a tankard of sack, and several tall silver-mouthed decanters of claret, with manchets of the whitest flour, oaten cakes, and fruit, composed the supper, on sitting down to which, Lord Mersington, with an affected air and half-closed eyes, by way of grace mumbled a distich then common among the cavaliers—

> " From Covenanters with uplifted hands,
> From Remonstrators with associate bands,
> From such Committees as governed these nations,
> From Kirk Commissions and their protestations,
> Good Lord, deliver us ! "

" Amen," said Clermistonlee, " d——n all kirk commissioners and sessions too !"

" The last keepit a firm hand owre such gallants as you,
before King Charles cam' hame," replied Mérsington, who,
like all meagre men, was a great gourmand, and was doing
ample justice to all the good things before him. Clermistonlee,
too, notwithstanding the lateness of the hour, did his part
fairly—but all times were alike to him, his irregular habits
and debauched life had by long custom made them so, and he
assailed the capon, the cutlets, the oysters, and sack tankard,
in rapid succession, while Juden stood behind his chair,
napkin in hand, with eyes half closed, and nodding head.

" Mersington, some more of the cutlets? My lord, you
must permit me—do justice to my poor house, a bachelor's
though it be. Juden, hand that dish of Crail capons from
the buffet."

The butler hastily placed before his master an ample dish,
containing a pile of small haddocks prepared in a mode now
disused and forgotten.

" Crail capons—allow me to help you ; and don't spare the
burnt sack, my lord."

" Thank ye :—weel, then, Clermistonlee, anent this business
of the Napiers," said Mersington, referring to a former conversation ; " what mean ye to do now, eh ?"

" Use every means to obtain their lands—and Lilian to
boot," replied his friend, after a brief pause, and while a
slight colour crossed his cheek. " I have taken a particular
fancy for that old house of Bruntisfield—ha, ha ! with the
parks adjoining. Faith, the lands run from the Hairstane to
my own gate at Drumsheugh, and from the Links, where
young Bruntisfield was slain long ago, to the house of the
Chieslies, beside the devil only knows how many tofts and
tenements within the walls of the city."

" A noble barony for a dowry ! "

" It will form a seasonable subsidy to my exchequer, which
is drained to its last plack at present. You know I have
long loved this girl."

" Or *said* so ; but the lands, he, he ! are forfeited to the
king, man ! "

" So were those of the Mures of Caldwell, yet Sir Thomas
of Binns now holds them as a free gift from the council, and
holds fast, too."

" Auld Dame Bruntisfield is but a life-rentrix; thou knowest,
man, that Captain Napier, of Buchan's regiment of Scots-
Dutch, is the next and last heir of entail."

L.

"Tush! I will have *him* under the nippers of the lord advocate ere long; when his head is on yonder battlements of the Nether Bow, the barony of Bruntisfield goes to Lilian Napier; and dost think, Mersington, that chitti-faced girl will stand in *my* way? I trow not. Maclutchy and some of our best-trained beagles are on the captain's track, and they will run him down somewhere in the west country, depend upon it. But 'tis neither hall nor holm, wood or water, that will satisfy me——"

"Odsfish, man! he, he! what mair would ye hae, Randal? There is the auld dame denounced a rebel, and in default of compearance, put to the horn: her moveable gudes and gear escheat to the king, conform to the acts thereanent, and sae are the heritable, but the council will soon snap them up. What mair would ye hae?"

"The person of little Lilian," said Clermistonlee, with a sinister smile, as he winked over the top of his great silver tankard.

"Hee, hee!" chuckled Mersington.

"I would give a thousand broad pieces——"

"If ye had them!"

"Crush me! yes—to discover where the young damsel is in hiding at this moment. Accustomed to subdue women from very habit, her piquant coldness and hauteur have inflamed, surprised, and offended me; and by all the devils, I will have her, though I should be tumbled down the precipice of hell for it," he continued, in the cavalier phraseology. "And this fellow, Fenton, this silken slave, who crossed me on the very night I had hoped to have her arrested (he ground his teeth), and that braggart, Douglas of Finland, who was so ready with his rapier to-night, let them look to it; my path shall not be crossed with impunity by man or devil."

"Nor is that of any lord of council, while a warrant of arrest and ward may be had from Mackenzie for the asking, like the *lettre-de-cachet* o' our French friends."

"True, my lord—our laws are severe; they are written in blood, like those of Draco, the Athenian. If this fellow, Finland, has the young lady concealed about Edinburgh, and if I thought he had a deeper aim in view than merely crossing me, I vow to heaven, I would make him a terrible example to all such rascally intermeddlers with the purposes of their betters."

His half-intoxicated companion looked slily at him over his inverted tankard, and replied,

"Get a warrant of search, and send every macer, messen-ger-at-arms, and toun guardsman after your dearie—he, he!

and proclaim at the cross by tuck of drum, that the right honourable the Lord Clermistonlee, baron of Drumsheugh, and knight of the Thistle, will pay one thousand marks of our gude Scottish money to the discoverer, or producer——"

"Hush, Mersington, you jest too much on this matter. Withered be my tongue for speaking of this project to thee; but the deed is done, and I might as well have proclaimed it by sound of trumpet at the Tron."

"You have been a wild buckie in your day, Randal," said Lord Mersington; "and when I think o' all the braw queans, gentle as weel as simple, that you have loved and abandoned, gude-lackaday! I marvel that the whinger of some fierce brother or father hath not cut short your career o' gallantry. How about your fair one in Merlin's Wynd?"

"Pshaw! I tired of her long ago."

"And Lady Mary Charteris?"

"By all the devils, 'tis very droll to hear you speak of a noble lady and a poor *bona roba* in the same breath. Mary is beautiful, magnificently so, but wary, proud, and poor; we would hate each other in a week. Now, I really think little Lilian Napier is capable of fixing all my wandering fancies into one focus for life."

"He, he!" chuckled Mersington, "I have heard you say the same o' twenty. But a peer of the realm, heir of—"

"The whole heraldic honours of the house of Clermont, which you see on yonder window-pane, *or*, three bars wavy embattled, surmounted by a lion *sable—argent*, a bend engrailed *gules*, and so forth. Ha, ha!"

"The coronet aboon them is a braw die, and ane that glitters weel in lassies' een."

"With Lilian Napier it has no more value than a peasant's bonnet. A thousand times I have endeavoured to gain her notice, by the most respectful attentions, which the little gipsy ever evaded, or affected to misunderstand, treating me with the most frigid coldness. The older lady, perhaps, is not indisposed towards me, but the memory of—Fury! always *that* thought! .... I never was crossed in my purpose, and now I mean to hang Quentin Napier, and marry his cousin forthwith. Ha, ha!"

"What, if he should discover and carry her off in the mean time?"

"Ah—the devil! don't think of that. I would give a hundred French crowns to have the right scent after her."

"I could do sae for half the money, my lord," said Juda, suddenly waking up from his standing doze.

" The deuce! fellow, art *thou* there? " exclaimed his master with stern surprise.

" Fallow, indeed! " reiterated the ancient servitor, indignantly. "Troth, I was the best o' gude fallows when I received on my ain croon here the cloure that Claverse meant for yours, in that braw tulzie on Bothwell Brigg."

" True, Juden; though I like not being overheard in some matters," replied the lord more kindly; "but as Colonel Grahame and I are now the best of friends, it would be better to recall the memory of bygone days as little as possible. Dost hear me? "

" And Alison Gifford—my lady that is dead and gone now, puir thing," continued Juden, spitefully and mournfully, knowing well that her name stung Clermistonlee to the soul. " Often and often, she used to say, ' you are a gude and leal servitor, Juden, and the laird (ye were but a laird then) can never think enough, or mak' enough o' ye, Juden; for ye are one that, come weal, come woe, peace or war, victory or defeat, will stick to the house o' Clermont, Juden, like a burr on a new bannet. But losh me! *he* docsna ken the worth o' ye, Juden!' " The pawkie butler raised his table napkin to hide " the tears he did *not* shed;" but the face of Lord Clermistonlee, which had gradually grown darker as he continued to speak, now wore a terrible expression. " Puir young Lady Alison! sae kind and sae gentle, sae sweet-tempered, blooming, and bonnie. You were aye owre rough and haughty wi' her, my lord——"

" Ten thousand curses! wretch and varlet! whence all this insolence, and why this maudlin grief? " cried Clermistonlee, in a voice of thunder. " Why speak of Alison? she sleeps in peace in the old aisles of St. Marcel, in Paris; and are her ashes to be ever thrown upon me thus? S'death! away, sirrah. Get thee gone, or the sack tankard may follow *that!* "

And plucking off his long black wig, he flung it full in Juden's face.

Without making any immediate reply, the latter picked up the ample wig, carefully brushed the flowing curls with his hand, and hung it upon the knob of a chair. He then turned to leave the room, but pausing, said slily—

" Then, my lord, ye dinna want to ken where this bonnie bird could be netted. I could cast your hawk to the perch in a minute."

" Art sure of that, sirrah? "

" My thumb on't, Clermistonlee, I will."

" You are a pawkie auld carle, Juden," said his master, in

an altered voice; "but tell with brevity what ye know of this matter."

"Lucky Elshender, a cottar body at St. Rocque, owre the Burghmuir yonder, was nurse to the Lady Lilian, yea, and to her mother before her. Though as wicked and cankered an auld carlin as ever tirled a spindle, or steered hell-kail, she was ane leal and faithfu' scrvitor to the house o' Bruntisfield, for her gudeman and his twa sons died in their stirrups by Sir Archibald's side, on that black day by the Keithing Burn. Sac, Clermistonlee, as she is a body mickle trusted by the family, if any woman or witch in a' braid Scotland can enlighten ye anent this matter, it is Lucky Elshender. And maybe my Lord Mersington (he's asleep, the gomeral body) will be sae gude as keep in memory, that there is not an auld wife in the three Lothians mair deserving o' a fat tar-barrel bleezing under her, in respect o' puir Meg's mischanter."

"Right, Juden," replied his master. "She may be brought to the stake yet, though the taste for such exhibitions is somewhat declining among our gentles. To-morrow I will have her dragged to the Laigh chamber; and if there is any truth in her tongue, or blood in her fingers, I warrant Pate Pincer's screws will produce both. Take these, Juden, as earnest of the largess I will give if the scent holds good."

But Juden drew back from the proffered gold pieces.

"If I am to serve ye, my lord, as a leal vassal and servitor ought, and as I served your honoured faither before ye, and my forbears did yours in better and braver times, ye will hold me excused from touching a bodle o' this reward, or ony other beyond my yearly fee and livery coat. Keep your gowd, Clermistonlee, for faith ye need it mair than auld Juden Stenton; and sae, as my een are gathering straws, I will bid your lordship a gude morning, and hie cannily away to my nest; for, by my sooth, there's the Norloch shining through the window-shutters like silver in the braid daylight." And so saying, Juden withdrew with a jaunty step, pleased with his own magnanimous refusal.

Though a good-hearted man in the main, and one, who (where his master's honour, interest, fancy, or aggrandisement were not concerned) would not have injured a fly, then how much less a human being, Juden Stenton had thus, without the slightest scruple, set fire to a train which might end in the ruin and misery of an already unfortunate family, and the dishonour and destruction of an amiable and gentle girl, in whose fortunes and misfortunes we hope to interest the reader still more anon.

CHAPTER XII.

THE COTTAGE OF ELSIE.

Ha! honest nurse, where were my eyes before?
I know thy faithfulness and need no more.
                    ALLAN RAMSAY.

SEVERAL days elapsed without our tyrannical voluptuary
being able to do anything personally in the discovery or
persecution of the Napiers.   His wounded hand from neglect
became extremely painful, and his late debauch with Mersington had thrown him into a state so feverish, that luckily he
was compelled to keep within his own apartments; but
obstacles only inflamed his passion and exasperated his
obstinacy.   It would be difficult to analyze the sentiments he
entertained towards Lilian Napier.   Love, in the purer,
nobler, and more exalted idea of the passion, he assuredly had
not.   His overweening pride had been bitterly piqued by her
hauteur.   The beauty of her person, and the inexpressible
charm of her manner had first attracted him, and, notwithstanding the studied coldness with which he was treated, the
passion of the *roué* got the better of judgment.   Lilian's great
expectations, too, had further inflamed his ardour; but all the
attentions which he proffered on every occasion with inimitable address, were utterly unavailing, and for the first time
the gay Lord Clermistonlee found himself completely baffled
by a girl.   Surprised at her opposition, his pride and constitutional obstinacy became powerfully enlisted in the affair,
and he determined by forcible abduction, or some such *coup-
de-main*, to subdue the haughty little beauty to his purpose.
Although he had been unable to prosecute his amour in person,
Juden and others had narrowly watched the cottage of old
Elshender, and brought from thence such reports as convinced
his lordship that she alone could enlighten him as to the
retreat of Lilian and Lady Grizel, if they were not actually
concealed within her dwelling.

Though a munificent reward had been offered for their
discovery, trusting to the well-known faith and long-tried
worth of their aged vassal, the ladies had found a shelter in
her humble residence, correctly deeming that a house so poor
and so near the city walls would escape unsearched, when
one at a distance might not.   There they dwelt in the strictest
seclusion and disguise on the very marge of their ample
estates, and almost within view of the turrets of their ancient
manor-house.

Since the torture to which the unhappy Ichabod Bummel had been subjected, and his subsequent imprisonment on the Bass Rock (where Peden of Glenluce, Scott of Pitlochie, Bennett of Chesters, Gordon of Earlston, Campbell of Cesnock, and others, endured a strict captivity as the price of sedition), Lady Grizel and Lilian hoped that their involvement with the Orange spies, and their flight, would soon be alike forgotten, especially now, when they were so utterly ruined and impoverished by proscription, that they were forced to share the bounty of their humblest vassal.

Near the old ruined chapel of St. Rocque, and close under the outspread branches of a clump of lofty beech-trees, by the side of the ancient loan that led to Saint Giles's Grange, nestled the little thatched cottage of Elsie Elshender. It was low-roofed, and its thick heavy thatch was covered with grass and moss of emerald green. The white-washed walls were massive, and perforated by four small windows, each about a foot square, but crossed by an iron bar; two faced the loan in front, and two overlooked the kailyard and byre to the back. The cottage had one great clay-built chimney, at the back of which was a little eyelet-hole, affording from the stone ingle-seats a view of the arid hills of Braid, and the solitary path that wound over their acclivities to the peel of Liberton, then the patrimony of the loyal Winrams. On one side of the door was a turf seat, on the other a daddingstone, where (in the ancient fashion) the barley was cleansed every morning, for the use of the family. This humble residence contained only a *but* and a *ben*, or inner and outer apartment, and both were furnished with box-beds opening in front with doors. The first chamber, though floored with hard beaten clay, was as clean as whitening and sprinkled sand could make it; a large fire of wood and peats blazed on the rude hearth; and in its ruddy light the various rows of Flemish ware, beechwood luggies, milkbowies, horn-spoons, and polished pewter arrayed above the wooden buffet or dresser, were all glittering in that shiny splendour which a smart housewife loves. Within the wide fireplace on a pivot hung a glowing Culross girdle, on which a vast cake was baking.

It was night, but neither lamp nor candle were required; the fire's warm blaze gave ample light, and a more comfortable little cottage than old Elsie's when viewed by that hospitable glow, was not to be found in the three Lothians. Three oak chairs of ancient construction, a table similar, a great meal girnel in one corner, flanked by a peat bunker in the other, and an odd variety of stoups, pitchers, and three-legged stools made up the background. On the table lay an

old quarto bible from which Lilian read aloud certain passages
every night, Andro Hart's "Psalmes in Scot's meter," and
the "Hynd let loose" of the "Godly Mr. Sheils," who was
then in the hands of the Philistines, and keeping the Reverend
Ichaboa Bummel company in the towers of the Bass.   Two
kirn-babics decorated with blue ribands, a quaint woodcut of
our first parents joining hands under what resembled a great
cabbage in the Garden of Eden appeared over the mantel-
piece, together with a long rusty partisan, with which the
umquhile John Elshender had laid about him like a Trojan
on the battle-field of Dunbar.

   Close by the ingle sat his widow Elsie enjoying its warmth,
and listening to the birr of her wheel.   She was a hale old
woman of seventy years, with a nose and chin somewhat
prominent ; her grey hair was neatly disposed under a snow-
white cap of that Flemish fashion which is still common in
Scotland, and over which a simple black riband marks widowhood.   Her upper attire consisted of a coarse skirt of dark
blue stuff, over which fell a short linen gown, reaching a little
below her girdle, which bristled with keys, knitting-wires,
pincushion, and scissors.   Similarly attired in a short Scottish
gown, which showed to the utmost advantage the full outline
of her buxom figure, her niece Meinie, a rosy, hazel-eyed, and
dark-haired girl of twenty, stood by the meal girnel baking
(*Anglicè kneading*), and as the sleeves of her dress came but a
little below the shoulder, her fair round arms and dimpled
elbows did not belie the pretty and merry face, which now
and then peeped round at the group near the fire.   Two of
these ought perhaps to have been described first.

   Disguised as a peasant, Lady Grizel no longer wore her
white hair puffed out by Monsieur Pouncet's skill, but
smoothed under a plain starched bigonet, coif, or mutch
(which you will), and very ill at ease the stately old dame appeared in her hostess's coarse attire.   By way of pre-eminence
she occupied the great leathern chair, in which no mortal had
been seated since the decease of John Elshender, who, for
forty consecutive years had hung his bonnet on a knob thereof,
while taking his evening doze therein, after a day's ploughing
or harrowing on the rigs of Drumdryan.

   Clad in one of the short gowns of Meinie, her foster-sister,
Lilian looked more graceful and decidedly more piquant, than
when at home rustling in lace, frizzled and perfumed ; her
fair hair was gathered up in a simple snood like that of a
peasant girl ; but never had peasant nor peeress more beautiful or more glossy tresses.   The poor girl was very pale ;
constant watching and anxiety, a feeling of utter abandon

ment and helplessness should their retreat be traced, had quite robbed her of that soft bloom, the glow of perfect health and happiness, her checks had formerly worn.

The cottage contained a secret hiding-place, constructed by that "pawkie auld carle," John Elshender, as an occasional retreat in time of peril, and therein the noble fugitives remained during the day, issuing forth only at night, when the windows closed by shutters within and without, and a well-barred door, precluded all chance of a sudden discovery. These precautions were imperatively necessary: had the fugitives been seen by any one, the exceeding whiteness of their hands, the softness of their voices, and, above all, the decided superiority of their air, would have rendered all disguise unavailing. In silence and sadness Lady Bruntisfield sat gazing on the changing features of the glowing embers; but her mind was absorbed within itself. Lilian was sewing, or endeavouring to do so; her downcast eyes were suffused with tears, and from time to time she stole a glance at Aunt Grizel. Every sound startled and caused her to prick her delicate fingers, or snap the thread, until compelled to throw aside the work; she then drew near her grand-aunt, bowed her head on her shoulder, and wept aloud.

"Lilian, love!" exclaimed Lady Grizel, endeavouring to command her own feelings, though the quivering of her proud nether lip showed the depth of her emotion; "for my sake, if not for your own, do not thus, every night, give way to unavailing sorrow and regret."

Lilian's thoughts were wandering to poor Walter Fenton in his prison, and she still wept.

"Marry come up! it would ill suit this little one to become the wife of a Scottish baron or gentleman of name," said the old lady, pettishly. "Lilian Napier! those tears become not your blood, whilk you inherit from a warrior, whom the bravest of our kings said had nae peer in arms. Bethink ye, Lilian! Ere I was your age, I had seen my two brothers, Cuthbert and Ninian, cloven down under their own roof-tree by the Northumbrian mosstroopers, and brave lads they were as ever levelled pike or petronel. O! yet in my ears I hear the clink of their harness as they fell dead on the flagstones of our hall; and never may ye hear such sounds, Lilian, for they are hard to thole. But I was a brave lassie then, and could bend a hackbut owre a rampart, or send a dag-shot through an English burgonet, without wincing or winking once: for my memory gangs back to the days of gentle King Jamie, ere the Scotsman had learned to give his ungauntled hand to the Southron."

" Fearfu' times, my leddy," said Elsie, " fearfu times! waly, waly, I mind o' them weel."

" They tell us we are one people now," continued the Scottish dame, with kindling eyes. " Malediction on those who think so! I am a Hume of the Cowdenknowes, and cannot forget that my brothers, my husband, and his three fair boys, poured their heart's blood forth upon English steel."

" Ill would it become your ladyship to do so," said Elsie, urging her wheel with increased velocity, and resolving not to be outdone in garrulity by Lady Grizel. " Weel mayest thou greet my bonnie bairn Lilian, for these are fearfu' times for helpless women bodies, when the strong hand and sharp sword can hardly make the brave man haud his ain ; but they are as nothing to what I have seen, when the doolfu' persecution was hot in the land. I mind the time when, trussed up wi' a tow like a spitted chucky, I was harled away behind that neer-do-well trooper, Holsterlie, and dookit thrice in Bonnington-linn, by Claver'es orders, and just as the water rose aboon my mutch, gif I hadna cried ' God save King Charles and curse the Covenant,' I hadna been spinning here to-night. Weary on't, I've aye had a doolfu' cramp since that hour."

" A piece of a coffin keepeth away the cramp, Elsie ; but 'tis an unco charm, and one that I like not."

" Gude keep us! how many puir folk I have seen in my time hanged, or shot, or writhing in great bodily anguish in the iron buits, wi' lighted gun-matches bleezing between their birselled fingers, and expiring in agonies awfu' to see and fearfu' to remember, and a' rather than abjure the Holy Covenant and bless the king."

" And rightly were they served, false rebels!" said Lady Bruntisfield, striking her cane on the floor.

" But let the persecutors tak' heed," continued Elsie, heedless of the dame's cavalier prejudices, " for their foot shall slide in due time (as the blessed word sayeth), the day of their calamity is at hand, and the sore things that are coming upon them make haste."

" O hush, dear Elsie," said Lilian, " you know not who may near you."

" True, Madame Lilian," continued the old woman, " and your words are a burning reproach against those who make it treason to whisper the word, unless to the sound o' drums, and shawlms, and organs. These are fearfu' times."

" Toots, nurse, I have seen waur, ' said Lady Bruntisfield impatiently.

" **Aye**, my leddy, in the year fifty, when the army o' that accursed Cromwell came up by Lochend brawly in array o' battle, wi' the sun o' a summer morning glinting on their pike-heads and steel caps ; marching they were, but neither to tuck of drum nor twang of horn, but to a fushionless English hymn, whilk they aye skirled on the eve o' battle. But our braw lads beat the auld Scots march, and my heart warmed at the brattle o' their drums and the fanfare o' the trumpets. O, their thousands were a gallant sight to see, a' lodged in deep trenches by Leith Loan, and the green Calton braes covered wi' men-at-arms, and bristling wi' spears and brazen cannon. On the topmost rock waved the banner o' the godly Argyle, and a' the craigs were swarming wi' his wild Hieland-men, in their chain jackets and waving tartans. An awfu' time it was for me and mony mair ! My puir gudeman (whom God sain) rode in the Lowden Horse, under Sir Archibald's banner (Heaven rest him too). That morning I grat like a bairn when hooking the buff coat on his buirdly breiest, and clasping the steel helmet on his manly broo (O, hinnie Lilian, ne'er may ye hae to do that for the man ye loe !) ere he gaed forth to battle for this puir cot, his little bairns, and me. But heigh ! it was a brave sight, and a bonnie, to see our Lowden lads sweeping the English birds o' Belial before them like chaff on the autumn wind, though my heart was faint, and fluttered like a laverock in the hawk's grasp, and I trembled and prayed for my puir man Jock. My een were ever on Sir Archibald's red plume——"

" Red and blue, gules and argent, were his colours, Elsie," said Lady Grizel, whose tears fell fast. " O, nursie, my ain hand twined them in his helmet."

" True, my leddy," continued the old woman, whose strong feelings imparted a force to her language, " my een were ever on that waving plume, for well I kent where the laird was, John Elshender was sure to be if in life. Aye, Lilian hinnie, Sir Archibald's voice was as a trumpet in the hour of strife. ' Bruntisfield ! Bruntisfield ! bridle to bridle, lads ! ' We heard him shout on every sough o' wind, ' God and the King ! ' and ever and anon his uplifted sword flashed among the English helmets like the levin brand on a winter night, and mony a gay feather and mony a gay fellow fell before it."

" Peace, Elsie, enough ! " said Lady Grizel, weeping freely at the mention of her husband, who had greatly distinguished himself in that cavalry encounter, where Cromwell's attack on Edinburgh was so signally repulsed. " If you love me, good nurse, I pr'ythee cease these reminiscences."

" Weel, my lady, but muckle mair could I tell doo Lilian

o' thesc fearfu' times," continued the garrulous old woman, who loved (as the Scots all do) to speak of the dead and other days ; " muckle indeed, for an auld carlin sees unco things in a lang lifetime. But, dearsake, your ladyship, dinna greet sae. for better times *will* come, and bethink ye they that thole overcome, for when things are at the warst, the're sure aye to mend; sac spake the godly Mr. Bummel to those who out-lived that fearfu' night in the Whigs' vault at Dunottar."

" Ah !" said Lilian shuddering, for she thought of Walter Fenton. " That was a dark dungeon, nurse, was it not ? "

" Deep, and dark, and vaulted, howkit in the whinrock, yet therein were ane hundred three score and seventeen o' God's persecuted creatures thrust, and there they expired in the agony and thirst, such as the rich man suffered in hell—where Lauderdale suffers noo. Ah, hinnie, it was a dowie place; the Water-hole of the town-guard is a king's chamber in com-parison ; it is black, damp, and slimy as a tod's den."

" Oh, madam, it is just in such a place they have confined poor Walter—I mean this young man whom we have involved in our misfortunes," said Lilian, in tears and confusion. " It is ever before me, since the night you sent me to him. Dear aunt Grizel, you cannot conceive all he endures at present, and is yet to endure."

" He is of low birth, Lilian, and therefore better able than we to endure indignity," said Lady Bruntisfield, somewhat coldly. " Yet I hope he shall not die—"

" Die !" reiterated Lilian, piqued at her kinswoman's cool-ness ; "ah, why such a thought ? "

" I sorrow for him as much as you, Lilian. The young man seemed good and gentle, with a bearing far above his humble fortune, and a comely youth withal."

Lilian made no reply, but a close observer would have per-ceived that her blue eyes sparkled and the colour of her cheek heightened with pleasure as Lady Grizel spoke.

" And said he of the council threatened him with torture ?" she continued.

" Clermistonlee—"

" Ah !" ejaculated Lady Grizel.

" Eh, sirs ? " added Elsie.

" Clermistonlee," continued Lilian, shuddering, " would have had him torn limb from limb, but for the intercession of Claverhouse."

" And for what does he hate the youth ? "

" Permitting *me* to escape, I presume," replied Lilian, raising her head with a little hauteur.

" Claver'se !" said Elsie, in a low voice ; " then this is the first gude I have heard o' him. Folk say he is in league wi' the de'il (Heaven keep us!) and that when the satanic spirit is in him, his black een flash like wildfire in a moss-hagg. Certes! I'll no forget that fearfu' day when he would hae dookit me to death for a word or twa."

"Colonel Grahame was guilty of most abominable ungallantry, Elsie; and yet I do not think he would have ducked me."

"Ungallantry, Lilian!" said Lady Grizel, grasping her cane, "ye should say a breach of law, ye sillie lassie. Our barony hath power of pit and gallows by charter from Robert the Auld Farrand, and it was a daring act and a graceless, to drag a vassal from our bounds, when I could have hanged her myself on the dule-tree, by a word of my mouth!" (Elsie winced.) "But he stood the youth's friend, you say?"

"Yes, and what dost think, nurse Elsie, so did old Beardie Dalyel!"

"Marvellous! but mind ye the proverb, *Hawks dinna pyke out hawks' een.* The lad wears buff and steel, and eats his beef and bannock by tuck of drum; and sae baith Claver'se and Dalyel showed him that mercy whilk a sanct o' God's oppressed kirk would hae sued in vain wi' clasped hands and bended knees."

"Ah, nurse, you don't know this young man. He is so mild-eyed and gentle, that Dalyel—"

"Meinie, ye hizzie, the cakes are scouthering. Dalyel! folk say his mother was in love wi' the deil; and my son Hab (a black day it was too when he first mounted his bandoliers), ance saw a kail-stock scorched to the very heart when the auld knicht spat on it—but fearfu' men are suited to fearfu' times."

"Hush, Elshender," said Lady Grizel; "they are indeed times when we must fear the corbies on the roof, and the swallow under the eaves. One might deem the council to have a familiar fiend at their command (like that fell warlock Weir, whose staff went errands), for nought passes in cot or castle on this side of the Highland frontier, but straightway they are informed of it. From whence could they have tidings that our gallant kinsman Quentin, and that fule body Bummel were at Bruntisfield? Landed at midnight from the Dutch frigate near the mouth of the lonely Figget Burn, they were secretly admitted to our house, in presence only of my baillie and most familiar servitors, who would not betray me. I rejoice the captain hath escaped their barbarities—but Ichabod, poor man,—I suppose his earthly troubles are well nigh over."

"A dreich time he'll have o't on the lonely Bass," said

Meinie, turning the savoury cakes, and blowing her pretty fingers. "There is naething there but gulls flapping and skirling, the soughing wind and roaring waves; but it will be a braw place to preach in, gif the red-coats let him. Oh, it would be the death o' me to be among these red-coats."

"Unless Hab Elshender were one," said Lilian; and Meinie blushed, for the linking of two names together has a strange charm to a young heart.

"Ou' aye," laughed the light-hearted girl; "but Maister Ichabod may cool his lugs blawing gospel owre the craigs, to the north wind, or gieing the waves a screed o' that blessed '*Bombshell,*' he aye havers o'. Better that than skirling a psalm at the Bowfoot, till the doomster's axe comes down wi' a bang, and sends his head chittering into a basket. Ugh!"

"Meinie, peace wi' this discourse, whilk beseems not!" said Elsie with great asperity. "I heard the lips o' the godly Renwick pray audibly, after his head lay in Pate Pincer's basket. Eh, sirs, what a head it is *now*. Yet the Netherbow guard watch it wi' cocked matches day and night, for there is mony a bold plot made by the Cameronians to carry it awa."

"But our unfortunate friend the preacher—how dearly, by his crushed limbs, has he paid for his zeal in the cause of the Dutch prince. Yet, as Heaven knoweth, I knew not that letters of treason to our Scottish nobles were in his possession, or never would he have darkened the door of Bruntisfield. He deceived me; let it pass. Sir Archibald, thou rememberest well my husband, Elsie?—'tis well that he sleeps in his grave. Oh, judge what *he* would have thought of our downfal and degradation."

"My mind misgives me, my lady, but Sir Archibald's kirk was the fushionless ane o' episcopacy, and, indeed, he just gaed wherever the troops marched, with trumpets blawing and kettle-drums beating waefu' to hear in the day o' the Lord."

This last speech somewhat displeased Lady Grizel, who struck her cane thrice on the clay floor, and there ensued a long pause, broken only by creaking of the beeches in the adjoining grove, and the birr of Elsie's wheel as it whirled by the ruddy fire.

"Come, your leddyship," said Elsie, "let bygones be bygones, and we'll be canty while we may. Meinie can sing like a laverock in the summer morning; sae, lassie, gie forth your best sang to please our lady, and then we'll hae our luggies o' milk, and bit o' your bannocks, a screed o' the blessed gospel, and syne awa to our rest, for it's waxing late."

Meinie of course was about to enter some bashful protest, when the soft voice of her foster-sister said,—

" Do, dearest Meinie, and I will join thee; 'twill raise the spirits of good aunt Grizel. Ah, if I had only my spinnet, the cittern, or even my flageolet here."

"What is your pleasure, then, Madam Lilian?" asked Meinie, curtseying, " *Lady Anne Bothwell's Lament*, or *The Broom of the Cowdenknowes ?*"

"Anything but the last," said Lady Bruntisfield. "The Knowes of Cowden hath passed away from the house of Hume, and bonnie though the golden broom may be, it blooms for us no more."

"Sing *Dunbarton's drums*, Meinie," said Lilian "you hum it from morning till evening."

"And so do *you*, madam," said Meinie, slily and bluntly; " but I loe the merry measure."

"Ewhow, that's because o' my wild son Hab," said Elsie, laughing. " Mak' speed, lassie, our lady waits."

Meinie made another low old-fashioned curtsey, and then, while continuing her task, sang the song and march composed for the Scots Royals, or Dunbarton's Musketeers, and which had then been popular in Scotland for some years. Lilian at times added her softer notes to Meinie's, and their clear voices made the rough rafters, hollow box-beds, and deep bunkers of the old cottage ring to that merry old air :—

> " Dunbarton's drums beating bonnie, O,
> Remind me o' my Johnnie, O,"

added Elsie, beating time with her feet to the mellow voices of the girls; but Lady Bruntisfield heard them not, for with her glistening eyes fixed on the glowing embers, she gradually sunk into a deep reverie. Animated each by her own secret thoughts, the girls sang with tenderness and enthusiasm, and all were so much engaged that none of the four perceived a *fifth* personage, who suddenly made his appearance among them.

In a corner of the cottage stood a great oak chest, apparently a meal girnel, but having a false floor, and being in reality the mouth of the subterranean place of concealment and escape, communicating with the grove behind the cottage. Such outlets were numerous in all large mansions; and the dangerous times of the Solemn League had caused the umquhile John Elshender to construct such a sallyport from his humble dwelling; and on several occasions of peril it had saved him from being hanged over his own door by Malignants, Covenanters, and English, or whoever had the upper hand ror the time. Slowly the girnel lid was raised, and the glowing firelight shone on the steel breast-plate and bandoliers of a musketeer. He was a ruddy-faced young man, with the prominent cheek-bones and shrewd expression of the Lowland peasantry: stout and athletic in figure, his keen grey eyes took a rapid survey of the cottage under the peak of his morion. His face expressed surprise and curiosity, but as the song proceeded, he stepped slowly and softly out, and when it was concluded stood close to the rosy and buxom Meinie.

"Hurrah!" he exclaimed, and gave her a resounding kiss on each cheek. The wheel fell from the relaxed hand of Elsie, and a shriek burst from Lilian, who believed they were betrayed, and threw herself before her aged kinswoman.

"Hab, Hab, ye graceless loon," screamed Elsie, as her son now kissed her, "how dare ye gliff folk this gate?"

"Hoots, Hab, ye've toozled a' my tap-knot," said Meinie, affecting to pout; "ye came on me noo like a ghaist or a spunkie."

"Heyday, Meinie, my doo! ye want to be kissed again; do ye think I have trailed a pike these eight years under my Lord Dunbarton, without learning to tak' baith castles and kimmers by storm?"

"Aye, aye, you are as bad as the warst o' them, I doubt not. Lassies, indeed—dinna come near me again."

"Hoity, toity, does she not want another kiss?"

"Haud, you wild loon," said his mother, in great glee; "do ye no see who are present?"

"An auld neighbour carlin, I think, and as bonnie a young lass as I ever saw on the longest day's march, d—n me."

Halbert suddenly paused, and became very much perplexed. The blood rushed into his swarthy face, as with an awkward but profound salute he said, in an altered voice,—

"I crave your pardon a thousand times, noble madam; and yours, sweet Mistress Lilian. My humble duty to ye both, though it is not long since I had the happiness to meet you. It goes to my heart to see you in attire so unbefitting your station. O, Lady Grizel, I ken oure well of all that has come to pass, for I was one of the thirty files of musketeers that were with Finland at the auld place on that sorrowful night last month. They are hard times these, my lady."

"Fearfu' times, my son," chorussed Elsie.

"True, Halbert," said the old lady. "Ruin and proscription now level the most noble with the mean, the most unoffending with the guilty, and blend all with the common herd. But, Halbert, I bid ye welcome, my man, and God bless ye!"

"And I too, Habbie," added Lilian; "for I cannot forget

when we bird-nested in the wood yonder, and gathered gowans and flowers on the sunny braes in summer. Oh! Hab, in all your soldiering, I will warrant ye have never been so happy as we were then."

The eyes of the soldier glistened.

"True it is, madam," said he, as slightly and bashfully he raised to his lip the beautiful hand she extended towards him; "true, indeed. I have spent many a happy hour under the canvass tent, and birled many a wine-horn merrily in the Flanders hostels and French cabarets; but never have I seen such happy hours as those we spent when we were bairns, amang the oak-woods of the auld place up by yonder. Often hath brave Mr. Fenton, when tramping by my side on the long dusty march, recalled their memory in such wise that my heart swelled under its iron case. And truly, honoured madam, though the same heart is wrung to see you dressed in cousin Meinie's humble duds, never saw I lassie that looked sae winsome. Od rot it, how came your ladyship to let that ill-omened corbie to darken your door? when sure ye might have been that dool and mischief would meet thereafter on your hearthstane. This goose Bummel——"

"Oh, Hab, ye gomeral, wheesht!" said Elsie, interrupting this somewhat laboured address. "Your notions o' ministers are gathered frae your tearing, swearing, through-ganging, horse-racing, and hard-drinking episcopal curates and chaplains, that swagger about wi' cockades in their bonnets and swords at their thighs, chucking every bonnie lass under chin, and gieing ilka sabbath a sleepy, fushionless, feckless, drouthie, cauldrifed discourse, whilk hath neither the due birr nor substantious, soul-feeding effect o' the true gospel, but savours rather o' the abomination——"

"Ahoi, mother, halt!—egad, or mind the iron gags, the fetterlocks, and thumbikins!" cried her son, with an alarm that was no way lessened by a violent knocking at the cottage door, where, at that moment, the iron ring of the risp was drawn sharply and repeatedly up and down.

The hearts of the poor fugitives forgot to beat! Insult, imprisonment, banishment, or worse, rushed upon the mind of Lady Bruntisfield; the dark, gloating eyes and terrible presence of Clermistonlee, upon that of Lilian: but Halbert Elshender snatched up his musket and blew the match till it glowed on his sun-burned face, an action which made the women grow paler still.

"Beard of the devil! Get into the girnel, Lady Grizel; and you, Madam Lilian—quick!" exclaimed the soldier in a vehement whisper.

"Hulbert," faltered Lady Bruntisfield, "your father was a leal and faithful vassal——"

"And I, his only son, will stand by you and yours to the death, even as he would have done. In—in—away to the Beech-grove, ere worse come of it. Mother, ye donnart jaud, doun wi' the lid, and pouch the key. And now, may I run the gauntlet from right to left, if you (whoever you are) that tirl the risp so hard get not a taste of King Jamie's new sweyne-feather!" He screwed his dagger or bayonet to the muzzle of his matchlock, and then demanded in a loud voice—

"Stand, stranger. Who goes there?"

"One who must speak with Lady Bruntisfield, whom I know to be concealed here. Open, and without a moment's delay."

"Lost—lost! Gude Lord, keep thy hand over *them* and us!" murmured Elsie, clinging to Meinie, as another loud and impatient blow shook the well-barred door, and found a terrible echo in the trembling hearts of the fugitives and their protectors.

CHAPTER XIII.

A REVERSE.

A fredome is a noble thing !
Fredome makes man to have liking
Fredome al solace to man gives,
He lives at ease that frely lives.
BARBOUR'S BRUCE.

WALTER was still where we left him in the eleventh chapter, an inmate of the city prison.

The gloom, monotony, and degradation affected his mind, not less than the confinement and noxious vapours of the place did his health, and he felt his strength and spirit failing fast. The longing for freedom became one moment almost too intense to be borne, and the next he sank into a listless apathy, careless alike of liberty and life. And as his health suffered, and his ardour died, his aspect became (though he knew it not) more haggard and ghastly on each succeeding day.

The recollection of Lilian's midnight visit, alone threw a ray of light through the gloom of his clouded fortune; over that event he mused, at times, with unalloyed pleasure. Anxiously he watched every night, animated by a faint hope that she might come again; but Lilian came no more.

"She came merely to thank me for my service, and I shall

soon be forgotten," he would say; and then came vividly on his mind, the blight and disgrace which had been heaped upon him, and the abyss into which he had been cast. Keenly and bitterly he now felt his loneliness in the world. All this he might have escaped, perhaps, but for the evil offices of the malevolent Clermistonlee; and when he contemplated how dim and distant was the prospect of ever again rising even to his former humble station, his heart was wrung; for, with the fetters of a coward and slave, he felt that he possessed the soul and the fire of a hero.

"Though poor and unpretending, I was a gentleman, so far as spirit, bearing, and manners could make me. I have done nothing that is vile or dishonourable; but *now*, after fetters have dishonoured these hands, and prison-walls enclosed me, can I ever again look my equals in the face? Yes! and may I perish, if Randal of Clermistonlee shall not learn that in time!"

He spoke fiercely; for he had now, from very solitude, acquired a habit of uttering his thoughts aloud. He could not suppress his dread that Lilian Napier, in the present proscribed and friendless state of her family, might too easily fall into the toils of that famous and powerful *roué*, whose crimes and excesses, in a country so rigidly moral, were regarded with a horror and detestation, that made women generally shun his touch as they passed him in the street, and his glance by the wayside. Remembering his parting words, the bitter threat, and the fierce aspect of his visage and polecat eyes when he last beheld him, Walter was justly under considerable apprehension, that he might again be summoned before the council, and either have his sentence altered to one of greater severity, or have its most degrading clauses carried into immediate execution. In fact, Lord Clermistonlee's temporary indisposition alone deferred such a catastrophe. Consequently day after day passed; the weeks ran on, but he never saw another face than that of a grim old city-guardsman, who each morning brought him a coarse cake, a bowl of porridge, and a pitcher of water; and, acting strictly to the tenor of his orders, withdrew without a word of greeting or condolence.

Thus day and night rolled on in weary and intense monotony, and poor Walter by turns grew more fierce and impatient, or more listless and apathetic. Sometimes he dosed and dreamed away the day, on his bed of damp and fetid straw, and by night paced slowly the floor of that little vault, every stone and joint and feature of which, became indelibly impressed on his memory.

But a crisis came sooner than he had anticipated.

One night he was roused from a deeper and heavier slum-
-er than usual by the unwonted light of a large lamp flashing
on his eyes; he started, awoke, and the glare blinded him for
a moment. Three persons were close beside him. One was
the odious, sinister, and hard-featured gudeman of the establishment; the second was the old soldier who acted as javel-
leur; and the third was a gentleman whose lofty bearing and
rich attire caused Walter to spring at once to his feet. He
was a dark-complexioned and very handsome man, bordering
on forty years of age; he wore a coat of rose-coloured velvet,
slashed at the breast and shoulders with white satin; his
breeches and stockings were of spotless white silk; his boots
of pale buff, and accoutred with massive gold spurs. His
voluminous black wig was shaded by his plumed Spanish hat,
the band of which sparkled with brilliants; while a long
rapier, gold-headed cane, and diamond ring showed he was
quite a man of fashion. It was George Douglas, the gallant
earl of Dunbarton.

"'Sdeath! Walter, my boy, I little thought to find you
here," said he. "Faugh! this place is like the old souter-
rains of Alsace or Brisgau; yet here it was that the great
Argyle once sojourned!"

"My lord—my lord!" exclaimed Walter, joyfully—"how
unexpected is this honour!"

"I returned only this forenoon from London."

"A long journey and a perilous, my lord. I congratulate
you on your safe return."

"Thanks, my boy. The countess suffered much, she is so
delicate, and my private coach, though carrying only six in-
side and six without (beside our baggage), rumbled so heavily
—but we were only five weeks on the way—a very tolerable
journey."

"Very; and still, my lord, I have heard of it being done in
three; but the roads——"

"O they are pretty good now, I assure you, till one reaches
the debateable land and the old boundary road at Berwick.
There are bridges over most of the rivers too; but the lonely
places swarm with footpads and highwaymen. Wilt believe
it? we had only one break-down by the way, and two encoun-
ters with gentlemen of the post. Ah! I winged one varlet
near the Rerecross of Stanmore one night, and to be a soldier's wife—egad how the countess wept! Immediately upon
my arrival at Bristo, I was waited on by the laird of Finland,
who told me your story, and, as Lady Dunbarton would not

rest until her young *protégé* was at liberty, I had to bestir myself, and so—am here."

"I am deeply indebted to your dear countess, my lord earl," replied Walter with glistening eyes; "I owe her a thousand favours, which I hope circumstances will never require me to repay."

"Thou art a fine fellow, Walter," replied the earl, striking him familiarly on the shoulder; "and thine inborn goodness of heart gains and deserves the love of all who know thee. The countess——"

"O would that I could thank her now for years of kindness and protection, when I was a poor and forlorn little boy!" exclaimed Walter with deep feeling.

"And why not, lad? a coach awaits us at the close-head, and you are a free man."

"Free! my lord, *free!*"

"Free as the wind, and without a stain on thy scutcheon."

"*My* scutcheon," repeated Walter coldly. "Ah, my lord, why jest with my nameless obscurity."

"Think not so ungenerously of me. The day shall come, Walter, when we may see the argent and bend azure of the old Fentounes of that ilk (I don't doubt the Lyon Herald will make thee a sprout of that ancient stock) quartered, collared, and mantled with your own personal achievements. Tush, lad, the wide world is all before you, and you have your sword. Think how many Scottish cavaliers of fortune have led the finest armies, and won the greatest battles, and the proudest titles in Europe! I have this moment come from the council chamber, where, with half a dozen words, I have reversed all thy doom, and had it expunged from their black books."

"I would, noble earl, that the same generosity had been extended to the Napiers of Bruntisfield."

"Nor was it withheld. What think you of that beautiful minx Annie Laurie of Maxwelton (I warrant thou knowest her—all our gay fellows do) waylaying me in her sedan. We met at the Cowgate stairs, which ascend to the Parliament House, and there desiring her linkboys and liverymen to halt right in that narrow path, she vowed by every bone in her fan, I should never get to council to-night—ha, ha! unless I pledged my word as a belted earl to have her friends the Napiers pardoned as well as thee. A brave damsel, faith! and would do well to follow the drum. 'Sdeath! I wish young Finland had her."

"And the Napiers——"

"Are pardoned; but they have fled, egad! nobody knows where. How exasperated Perth, Balcarris, and other high lying cavaliers were by the influence I seemed to possess over the votes at the Board, having won alike the noble Claverhouse, the ferocious Dalyel, and that addlepated senator, Swinton of Mersington."

"Lord Dunbarton, I have no words to express my feelings."

"Pshaw! in all this affair I see only the meanness of the despicable world. Deeming thee a poor and friendless lad, whose whole hope was the fortune of war, and whose only inheritance a poor half-pike, these blustering lords of council did not hesitate to misuse thee shamefully. Here thou art immured and forgotten, until one comes, on whom they reckoned not, but who, in addition to a coronet, writes himself knight of the Thistle, commander of the Scottish forces, and colonel of a devoted regiment of fifteen hundred brave hearts as ever marched to battle, and lo! his wish is law, his breath bears all before it. Walter Fenton, have a soul above the petty injuries of lordlings such as these, and cock thy feather not a whit the less for having endured their jack-in-office frowns."

Here the gudeman rattled his keys, and awe alone kept his constitutional impatience in check.

"And how did your lordship overcome the hatred of Clermistonlee, my most bitter persecutor?"

"O, he is quite a devil of a fellow that! Ha, ha! He got a rapier-thrust a few nights ago, which has luckily confined him to his apartments, and deprived the council of his pleasant company and amiable advice. Ah, he is a brave fellow, too, Clermistonlee; but though an expert swordsman and accomplished cavalier, he is, withal, too much of a *roué* and *fanfaron* for my taste. And harkee, Walter, I have one request to make ere we leave this abominable souterrain—that you will have no recourse to arms, for the severity with which as a privy councillor he may have treated you."

"Your lordship's wish was ever a law to me; but if I am set upon——"

"Zounds! then spare not to thrust and slash while hand and hilt will hold together," said the earl, as they ascended the spiral stair of the prison, preceded by the gudeman thereof, who never ceased bowing until they issued into the dark and narrow alley, then named Gourlay's or Mauchane's close. Walter's heart beat joyously, and his pulse quickened as the cool night wind blew upon his blanched but flushing cheek.

"He must have been a thoroughpaced tyrant, the constructor of this den of thine, gudeman," said the earl, surveying the prison as he handed some silver to the governor; "but I suppose we must pay largess, nevertheless;" and, taking the arm of his companion, they ascended the steep alley together. "You have followed my drums now, Walter, for, let me see——"

"Since Candlemas-tide '85, my lord."

"How, boy, for three years?"

"Ever since you defeated Argyle's troops at the Muir-dykes," said Walter with a sigh.

"Ha! is it so? I have been somewhat forgetful of thee in these bustling times, but shall make immediate amends. I have promoted many a slashed and feathered ruffler when thy quiet merit was passed unheeded. You fought under Halkett at Sedgemoor: it was a well-ordered field that, and had Lord Gray's horse properly flanked Monmouth's infantry, their lordships of Feversham and Churchhill might have had another tale to tell at St. James's. S'death, we are likely soon to have such scenes again, for there will be a convulsion in our politics that will make and unmake many a fair name and noble patrimony."

"This is a riddle to me, my lord."

"So much the better; my suspicions would be called treason to King James by the lords of the Laigh chamber. Our Scottish troops are concentrating fast round Edinburgh from the West and Borders; even our frontier garrison at Green-law is withdrawn here; so perhaps the Northumbrian thieves will get out their horns again, as they did in Cromwell's time after that day of shame at Dunbar. You will come with me to Bristo, of course?" continued the earl, as they issued into that main street which runs the whole length of the old city, and was long deemed for its bustle, breadth, height, and variety of architecture the most striking in Europe.

Then it was silent and empty, for the hour was late; the countless windows of the lofty mansions which shot up to a giant height on each side, in every variety of the Scottish and Flemish tastes, with fantastic fronts, of wood or stone, tur-reted, corbelled and corbie-stoned, gable-ended, balconied, and bartizanned, were dark and closed, or lighted only by the silver moon which bathed one side of the street in a flood of pale white lustre, while the other was immersed in obscure and murky shadow. The long vista of the Lawnmarket was closed by the gloomy and picturesque masses of the great Gothic cathedral, the façade of the Tolbooth, and the high narrow edifices of the Craimes, a street wedged curiously between St. Giles and the place now occupied by the Exchange.

A hackney-coach, like a clumsy hearse, one of the few introduced into Edinburgh only fifteen years before, and consequently deemed a splendid and luxurious mode of locomotion,
stood at the mouth of the pend or archway. The driver, a
tall, gaunt fellow, dressed in a plain gabardine of that coarse
stuff, with which a recent act of the Scottish parliament compelled the humbler classes to content themselves, stood bonnet
in hand by the heavy flight of steps which enabled first the
earl and then Walter to ascend into the recesses of the
vehicle. The door was closed with deliberation ; the driver
clambered into his place on the roof, and slowly and solemnly
his two horses dragged the lumbering machine up the Lawnmarket, over the rough and steep causeway of which it
rumbled like a vast caravan.

"We make great advances in the art of luxury, we
moderns," said the earl ; "Ah, twenty years ago there was
nothing of this sort. And there is that new invention, the
snaphaunce-lock, which is as likely to supersede the good old
match, as the screw-hilted dagger of Bayonne is to eclipse
the glories of the old sweynes-feather. Were you ever in
one of these Dutch conveyances before, Walter?"

"Once only, my lord, when I accompanied Lady Dunbarton to her grace of Lauderdale's levee at Holyrood."

"Though our preachers inveigh bitterly against them, as
dark places wherein to cloak wickedness and knavery, and in
opposition uphold the good old fashions of saddles, pillions,
and sedans, I think this is a pleasant and a useful contrivance
withal."

"But will you be pleased to remember that my present
attire is a very unfitting one for the presence of the countess?
soiled as it is by the contaminations of that noxious vault——"

"Right, Walter, and I had forgotten that my little Lætitia
is somewhat fatigued with her journey. You can pay your
devoirs in the morning, and tell Finland, Gavin of that ilk,
the Chevalier Drumquhasel, and such other of my cavaliers
as have arrived in the city, that we shall be glad to see them
at our morning *déjeûné* at Bristo. I have ordered a glorious
bombarde of choice canary to be set abroach ; so don't forget
to tell them that. But anent the Napiers," continued the
earl, " they are intimate friends of yours, I presume?"

" Friends ! " stammered Walter ; " alas, my lord, do you
think that the proud and stately old lady of Bruntisfield
would rank a poor and obscure lad like me among her friends?
Save your noble self and the countess, I have no friends on
earth—none."

" Ungrateful rogue ! thou forgettest thy fifteen hundred

comrades, each of whom is a friend. But, by all the devils, there is a mystery in this. 'Tis quite a romance. What tempted you to run tilt against the council in this matter? No answer. It will not pass muster with me, Mr. Fenton. A pretty demoiselle is enough, I know, to tempt any young gallant to swerve from his strict line of duty. I found it so in my bachelor days. There is old Mackay of Scoury, who now commands our Scots in the service of the States-General, openly deserted from us in Holland (when we followed the banner of Condé), and joined the enemy—for what? ha, ha! the love of a rosy little Dutch housewife, who had gained his weak side, the Lord knows how; for we Scots musketeers considered ourselves great connoisseurs in women, wine, and horse-flesh. Apropos, of Lilian Napier—I doubt not you know where this little one is concealed."

"I do, my lord," answered Walter, with vivacity.

"Heyday! I am right, then," laughed the gay nobleman, "you got a kiss, I warrant. *Point d'argent point de Suisses!* as we used to say of the Swiss gendarmerie, ha, ha!"

"Thanks, and the consciousness of doing a generous act, were my sole reward."

"Very likely; but I'll leave the countess to worm the secret out of thee. Ha, ha! 'tis very unlikely that a young spark would peril his life thus, and look only for a Carthusian's reward from a dazzling demoiselle of eighteen. Ho! I had served under Turenne, Luxembourg, and Condé, long ere I was thy age, and know well that a bright eye and ruddy lip—but here is the gate of the Upper Bow, and two fresh heads grinning on its battlement since I saw it last. Whose are they?"

"Holsterlee and some of his comrades dispersed a conventicle among the Braid hills lately."

"Poor rogues! If you do not mean to accompany me, we must part here; and in the course of to-morrow, if you know where the ladies of yonder old castle at Bruntisfield are in concealment, you will doubtless acquaint them with the decree I have obtained in their favour. But their kinsman, Quentin Napier, can neither be pardoned nor relaxed from the horn."

"'Tis well," thought Walter.

The Bow, a steep winding street that descended the southern side of the hill on which the old city stands, was then closed by a strong gate called the Upper Porte, under the shadow of which the coach stopped. On the right a heavy Flemish house projected over the street, on beams of carved wood; on the left, the house of Weir the wizard

frowned its terrors across the narrow way. A sentinel opened
the creaking barrier, received the nightly toll, and Walter,
after bidding adieu to the generous earl, was about to retire,
when the latter called him back.

"Harkee, Fenton ; you have far to go, and in these times,
when soldiers are openly murdered in the streets, my rapier
may be of some service should any quarrelsome ruffler cross
your path ; take it, for I have pistols."

"A thousand thanks, my lord," replied Walter, receiving
from the earl a long and richly-chased rapier sheathed in
crimson velvet.

He threw the embroidered belt over his should--, and
strode away with a feeling of pride and elation, to find himself once more a free and armed man ; while the great caravan occupied by the earl, rumbled down the windings of the
narrow street with increased speed, waking all the echoes of
its hollow stone staircases, and scaring those indwellers who
heard them through their dreams ; all sounds heard by night
in the Bow being fraught with imaginary terrors, and attributed to the wandering spirit of that diabolical wizard, who
a short time before had expiated his real and supposed enormities amid a blaze of tar-barrels on the castle-hill, and whose
uninhabited mansion was then viewed with horror, as it is
still with curiosity.

With a heart brimming with exultation, and glowing with
anticipations of happiness, which for the time made the
revolving world in all its features shine like a beautiful kalei-
doscope, Walter pirouetted and danced down the Lawnmarket
and through the narrow Craimes. Was it possible that but
an hour ago he was so very wretched and degraded? Was it
not all a dream, this new joy, a dream from which he feared
to awake? Ah, thought he, one requires to have tasted the
bitterness of captivity, to know the value and the glory of
freedom.

Again he wore a sword, and the consciousness of bearing
arms and having the spirit to use them, imparted to the cavaliers of other times a bearing, to which the gentlemen of the
present age are strangers.

As the clanking wicket of the Netherbow closed behind
him, the flap of a night-bird's wing caused an involuntary
thrill of disgust, he looked up to the central tower of the
Porte, and, faugh! a huge gled was winging away heavily
from the iron spike whereon a hideous head scowled at the
passers, and by the tangled locks that waved on the midnight
wind around its sweltering features, Walter thought he recognized the face of the preacher, Ichabod Bummel, of whose

fate he was still in ignorance. With pity and disgust he hurried on, and, without molestation or adventure, reached his quarters in the White-horse cellar—the place where this eventful narrative commenced a few weeks before—a spacious and ancient but long-forgotten inn, situated at the bottom of a small court opening from the Canongate. Rising from a great arcade, which formed of old the Royal Mews, this edifice is now remarkable only for its antiquity and picturesque aspect, its gables of carved wood, perforated with pigeon-holes, its enormous stacks of chimneys, and curious windows on the roof. At the time of our tale, there was always a body of troops billeted there, greatly to the annoyance of Master Gibbie Runlet, the host thereof, who found them neither the most peaceful nor profitable occupants of his premises.

CHAPTER XIV

WALTER AND LILIAN.

She's here! yet O! my tongue is at a loss;
Teach me, some power, that happy art of speech,
To dress my purpose up in gracious words,
Such as may softly steal upon her soul.

THE whole of the next day passed ere Walter Fenton found time to visit the fugitives; he was anxious to be the first bearer of the good tidings confided to him by the earl, and luckily intelligence did not travel very fast in those days. In Edinburgh there was but one occasional broad-sheet or news-paper, *The Kingdoms Intelligencer*, and a house situated a mile or two from the city wall, was deemed a day's journey, distant among wood, rocks, and water. Thus the rural residences of the Napiers, Lord Clermistonlce, Sir John Towcris of Inverleith, Sir Patrick Walker of Coates, and others, were situated in places over which the busy streets and crowded squares of the extended city have spread like the work of magic.

Walter had some difficulty in discovering the exact locality of Elsie's cottage, which was situated among a labyrinth of haw and privet hedges, and consequently the evening was far advanced before he presented himself at her humble abode, and caused the consternation described in a preceding chapter.

"I must speak instantly with those who are concealed here," said he; "I am a friend of the Lady Bruntisfield—the bearer of most happy tidings."

" I think I should know your voice," said Hab, still deliberating, and puffing at his match.

" And I thine, Halbert Elshender ; I am one of Lord Dunbarton's men."

"Welcome, Mr. Fenton!" exclaimed Hab, undoing the door briskly ; " I wish you much joy of being out of yonder devilish scrape."

" How are you back so soon, Hab ? By my faith, I thought you were browbeating the westland Whigs, and roistering at free quarters among the stiffnecked carles of Clydesdale."

"And so we were, sir, for three blessed weeks. Cocks' nails ! ilka man was lord and master, and mair of the billet he had, loundering the gudeman, kissing the gudewife, and eating the best in cellar and ambrie, and then settling the lawing with a flash of a bare blade or a roll on the drum, as Finland and yourself have dune too. But hech ! things are likely to be otherwise ; it's a bad sign when the nonconformist bodies begin to cock their bonnets in face of the king's so-diers, as they are doing now."

" Ay, 'tis thought there will be the devil to pay between King James and the English, who were ever jealous of the Stuart rule. The ladies of Bruntisfield are here, are they not ? "

" Maybe sae, and maybe nae," replied Hab cunningly, still keeping his match cocked.

" How ! " asked Walter, frowning, upon which Elsie cried in great alarm,

" Eh, sirs,—Hab, Hab, ye gomeral, speak the gentleman fair."

" To be plain, Mr. Fenton," asked Halbert bluntly, " came ye here as friend or foe ? "

" A late question, when I am within arm's length of you. Halbert Elshender, I pledge my honour I am here in honest friendship."

" And quite alone, sir ? "

" The deuce ! Sirrah, I am as you see," responded Walter impatiently. " Mistress Lilian is here, and her noble kins-woman too, I doubt not."

Hab winked knowingly, and knocked on the panels of the vast girnel, the front of which he opened, and the two fugitives forth stepped, pale and agitated. The first sight of Walter's military garb startled them ; but bowing profoundly, he said, in the formal fashion of the time,

" Lady Bruntisfield, your most obedient humble servant— Mistress Lilian, yours."

" Your servant, sir," muttered the ladies, and they all

bowed to each other three several times. Lilian blushed deeply.

"Ah," said Walter, " I have then the happiness to be remembered."

Lady Grizel, on adjusting her spectacles, immediately recognized him, and held out her hand with a smile, in which hauteur, kindness, and timidity were curiously blended.

"Welcome, young gentleman; though our fortunes are somewhat clouded now, I rejoice their shadow has not long blighted yours, and I congratulate you on your restoration to liberty."

"And I, in turn, wish you every joy at a sudden change of fortune. The decrees of council are reversed; your lands, your liberty, your coat armorial, are restored, and you are free to return to the ancestral dwelling of your family whenever it pleases you: to cast aside for ever that humble attire, though, believe me, fair Lilian, it never appeared to me so graceful or charming as at this moment."

Again Lilian blushed deeply; her bright eyes were full of inquiry and expression; her cherry mouth, half open, displayed the whiteness of her firm little teeth, and she never appeared so fascinating to Walter as, when laying her hand gently on his arm, she said,

"Ah, Mr. Fenton, is this indeed true?"

Of its truth the old lady appeared to have some doubts She remained for a few moments silent and motionless. Her first thought was one of rapture; her second of surprise and distrust, for might not this be a wile of Clermistonlee? might not the price of the young man's liberty be their betrayal to the council? But no! she suppressed the ungenerous thought, when, bending her keen eyes on Walter, she read the openness and candour expressed in his handsome face.

"This is indeed a reverse! O what joy," she exclaimed; "and yet 'tis strange," she added, striking her cane with great energy on the clay floor; "very strange withal, that no macer, usher, herald, or deputation of council hath come to me with intimation hereof. This is marvellous discourtesy in the earl of Perth, to a dame of honour, who hath had the privilege of the tabouret before the queens of France and Britain. Young man, were you specially commissioned to tell me this happy intelligence?"

"Not exactly," said Walter, colouring in turn; "but it is so pleasant to be the herald of joy, that I am glad another has not anticipated me. Indeed, as the reversal of your sentence was publicly proclaimed at the cross this forenoon, by the Albany Herald and Unicorn pursuivant, with tabard and trumpet, I am astonished you have not heard of it. But honest Hab's reluctance to admit me—"

"O teach me to be thankful," exclaimed Lady Grizel, raising her bright grey eyes and clasped hands to heaven; "to be grateful for this great and singular mercy. Then all our persecution is over?"

"My dear madam, it is so, and for ever."

Another burst of acclamation from Hab shook the cottage, and he kissed Meinie again in the excess of his exultation.

"O nurse Elsie, my dream is read," said Lady Grizel. "Last night I thought I saw Sir Archibald's favourite horse —ye mind his auld trooper, spotless Snawdrift. A white steed, ye know, Elsie, betokens intelligence; and his being spurgalled showed it would be speedy. His saddle was girth uppermost —"

"Whilk boded luck, and never mair may it leave the house o' Bruntisfield, thanks to the battling lord!" said Elsie, piously.

"I am unused to receive boons," said the stately dame; "but would be glad to know to what or to whom the house of Napier is indebted for this signal favour of fortune."

"To my generous lord and colonel, the princely Dunbarton, whom God long preserve! Here are the pardon and reversed decree of forfeiture; I received them from his countess, who desired me to bear them to you with her best regards."

"O, Mr. Fenton!" exclaimed Lady Grizel, whose artificial pride now quite gave way before the natural warmth and gratitude of her heart. And her broad silver barnacles became dim with tears as she received the documents which bore the well-flourished signature, "Perth, Cancellarius," and the seal of council. "God knows, good youth," she continued, pressing Walter's hand in hers, "that if I repined much at the sad occurrences of the last few weeks, it was for the sake of this fair child alone. Alake! at her age to be thrown into poverty and obscurity were to die a living death—but now—" Lilian, in a transport of tears and joy, threw her arms around her aged relative and kissed her.

"Poverty and obscurity!" thought poor Walter; "how can I dare to love a being so far above me, when these are all I have to share with her?"

With her snood unbound, and her bright hair flying in beautiful disorder, the lively girl rushed from Elsie to Meinie alternately kissing and embracing them, till honest Hab began to rub his mouth with his cuff in expectation of the favour going round; and in her girlish delight, she seemed a thousand times more charming than when clad in her long stomacher, and compelled to imitate Lady Grizel's starched decorum and old-fashioned stateliness of demeanour.

"Ah, good heavens," she suddenly exclaimed, "we are quite forgetting poor cousin Quentin."

"The deuce take cousin Quentin!" thought Walter, and he hastened to inform her that the council had resolved to cut the captain into joints the moment they could lay hands on him.

Meinie, whose cakes had long since been scorched to a cinder, now gave Hab a box on the car, and retreating from him with a pout of rustic coquetry, placed several three-legged stools near the fire, around which they seated themselves by desire of Lady Grizel, herself occupying the great elbow-chair, against which her tall walking-cane was placed by Elsie, with great formality. The venerable cottager was very lavish in her praises of Walter, for whom, as the bearer of such good tidings, she felt a cordial admiration; and, heedless of Lilian's confusion, continued to whisper it in her ear.

"A handsome cavalier, hinny. Saw ye ever sic een?—they glint like a goshawk's. His hair is like the corbie's wing wi' the dew on it; and his cheeks are like red rowan-berries. He is indeed a winsome young gallant, my doo Lilian!—no ane o' our law-breakers, who spend the blessed Sabbath in ruffling through the streets in masks and mantles, or dicing, drinking, or playing at shovel-board in a vile change-house, or playing at pell-mell like the godless Charles; but a gospel-fearing and discreet youth, as gude as he's bonnie, I doubtna."

"Oh, hush, Elsie!—he will hear you," said Lilian in a breathless voice.

"What did you say his name is, hinny?" asked Elsie, who was rather deaf.

"I never said," whispered Lilian; "but it is Walter Fenton—a pretty one, is it not, nurse?"

"Fenton?—he'll be ane o' the auld Fentons owre the water; as gallant and stalwart a race as ever Fifeshire saw."

"I hope so," sighed Lilian; "but, oh Elsie! there is some sad mystery about this poor young man. When a very little child, he was found nestled in his dead mother's bosom, in the kirkyard of the Greyfrairs, in that terrible time you will remember?"

"My bonnie bairn, it was indeed a fearfu' time; but, by his winsome face, I warrant him come o' gentle kin."

"Dost think so, dear nursie?"

"Not Claver'se himsel has an eye that glints wi' mair pride, or a lip that curls mair haughtily. True gentle blood can aye be kent by the curl o' the lip. I warrant his blude 's as gude as ony in braid Scotland."

"Oh, 'tis for that I pity and love him so much," said Lilian, artlessly. As she spoke, Walter, who was conversing with Lady Grizel, unexpectedly looked full towards her; he had removed his steel cap, and the long black locks beneath it flowed in cavalier profusion over his scarlet doublet. He never looked so prepossessing; and, fearing that he had overheard her, the cheek of the timid girl grew scarlet and then deadly pale; and to hide her confusion, she bent her face towards the old nurse, requesting her to bind up her hair.

"In ringlets and heart-breakers such as never Maister Pouncet fashioned, shall I twine thy bonnie gowden hair tomorrow, hinny," said the old woman, kissing with fond respect the white forehead of Lilian; for those were days when the highest and the lowest classes in Scotland were bound together by such endearing ties as never will exist again. "And nae mair shall your dainty arms and jimpy waist be bound wi' aught but Naples silk and three-pile taffeta."

"Ah! nurse Elsie, if my heart is always as happy and light as Meinie's, it will matter little what I wear."

"Sae said your lady mother, that's dead and gane; yea, and your great-aunt Grizel too (but silk and damask are grand braws, hinny); and, waes me! thae wrinkled auld hands hae braided the bonnie hair o' baith. And now the head o' ane is turned frae the hue o' the raven's wing to that o' the new-fa'n snaw; and the head o' the other, oh, waly! waly! lies low in the kirk vaults o' St. Rocque. I mind a time when the hair o' my lady there was as glossy as yours; yea, and her brow as smooth, and her cheek glowing like the red rowan-berry It is many a lang and weary year ago, and yet it seemeth but as yesterday, when your kinsman, umquhile Sir Archibald, first cam riding up the dykeside to Cowdenknowes, wi' my puir gudeman, John Elshender, astride his cloak-bags, on a high trotting mear; and weel I mind the time when first he drew his chair in by the ingle, and lookit awfu' things at Lady Grizel. Certes, but she was ill to please at her toilet after that. Frae morning till e'enin' there was nought but busking wi' braws, frizzling and puffing and perfuming; tying and untying, and flaunting wi' breast-knots and fardingales, and working wi' essence o' daffodils and gilliflower water. That was mony a year before that vile limmer Cromwell led his ill-faured host on this side o' the English bounds. He was a braw and a buirdly man Sir Archibald, though when last he rode frae the airwoods o' the auld place owre the muir, his pow was lyart enough. Methink I see him yet, as I saw him first, our brave auld laird! His green doublet o' taffeta, stiff wi' buckram, bombast, and gowden lace—his lang buff boots and clanking spurs—his broadsword and dudgeon-knife —and a bonnie ger-falcon on his nether wrist, wi' a plume on its head and siller varvels on its legs. Mony a sair gloom he gaed that braw chield, the laird o' Caickmuir; but Lady Grizel could never thole the Muirs, for they gained baith haugh and holm by pinglin' wi' base merchandise in Nungate o' Haddin- toun, when the Humes were winning the broomy knowes o' Cowden by the sharp spur and the long spear——"

"In fearfu' times, Elsie," said Lilian, laughing.

"Ay, indeed, hinny," continued the garrulous old woman. '' Fearfu' times they were, when the lord o' Crichton, wi' his fierce knights in their bright armour, on barbed horses, ravaged a' the west-kirk parochin to the castle-gate of Corstor- phin, ruining lord, laird, and tenant body alike,—giving the cottar's home, the baron's tower, and the priest's kirk to torch and sack. Fearfu' times they ever are, hinny, when Scottish braves and Scottish blades are bent on ilk ither in the fell stoure o' battle."

"Elshender," said Lady Grizel—(interrupting these remi- niscences, of which the reader is perhaps as tired as Lilian was)—"you have left the band on your wheel."

"Save us and sain us!" exclaimed the old woman, hobbling to her wheel. "The last time I did sae, the gude neighbours span on't the haill night, and ravelled a' my gude hawslock woo."

"Thou shouldst be more careful, Elshender," said Lady Grizel gravely, "It bodes ill luck; and a red thread should be tied to the rock.

> Red thread and Rowan tree,
> Mak' warlock, witch, and fairy flee.

I marvel, Lilian, that your friend and gossip, Annie Laurie, came not to visit us the moment she heard the proclamation of our innocence, and the council's injustice."

"Dear Annie was the first to fly hither when our fortune was at the lowest ebb," said Lilian timidly. "Ah, Heaven, if she should be ill! She knows how welcome are the bearers of happy tidings."

"And most welcome is Mr. Fenton!" said the old lady, pressing his hand so kindly, that Walter's heart leaped, and he scarcely dared to glance at Lilian. "Dear child, I tremble to think of all you have braved for our sake,—the torture, the bodkin, the dungeon! It was noble and generous. The hero of the old romance, Sir Roland of Roncesvalles, could not have done more."

"Spare me the shame of these thanks, madam. The honour of serving your ancient house is sufficient requital to one so—so nameless as I am. But, pray remember it is to my very good lord, the noble Dunbarton, you alone owe this happy change in fortune."

"And to-morrow, so early as decorum will permit, and when our servitors can attend in such state as befits our quality, shall he and his gentle countess (English though she be) receive our best thanks. The Lady Lætitia is the first of her nation," she added, and down went the cane on the floor; "yea, the first that Grizel Hume could ever thole. Lilian, we will immediately set forth on our return to the place of Bruntisfield."

"You will permit me to have the honour of escorting you, madam?"

"Thanks, Mr. Fenton,—There is a troop of horse at free quarters on the barony; and if——"

"They belonged to Dalyel's grey dragoons. They were withdrawn by the decree of council; and I heard their kettle-drums beating through the city this evening."

"'Tis well. Then we will return by coach, as it would be unseemly to do so on foot. We have long incommoded you, my poor Elshender."

"Gude, your ladyship, think not of it," replied Elsie; "all I hae is yours, and mair would be if I had it. I and mine ate of your bread and drank of your cup in prosperity, and may shame and dishonour fall on our grey hairs if in adversity we fail in our duty to the Napiers o' Bruntisfield!" Elsie wept: "and you especially, Hab, ye mickle gomeral, wi' the king's cockade in your bonnet!"

"Burganet, ye mean, Lucky; we soldiers of the king wear braw burganets of bright steel."

"But these are fearfu' times, my lady, when the superior is beholden to the vassal for a roof to cover them, and a mouthfu' o' meat; but think o't, madam; the auld house is dark and empty, and the auld survitors are scattered owre the barony among the tenantry, and the keys o' the barbican gate are owre the muir wi' the ground baillie, auld Sym o' the Greenhill."

"That loitering runnion should have been the first to present himself before us!" exclaimed Lady Grizel; "but I care not; let Hab and Meinie accompany us now, for our attire is too unseemly for appearance in daylight. I am impatient to return; for O, Elsie, thou knowest well this night on the old returning anniversary of my marriage and the laird's death, and dost think I will spend it under another roof than that of Bruntisfield, if I can avoid it?"

"Of course not, my lady—but ewhow! I'll be alone in this auld cot, to be scared by spunkies or gyre carlins, for there is no' a place in a' the Lowdens for deid-lichts, bodochs, and unco' things, like the auld massemongers' kirk doun the loan there."

"Peace, Elsie! and remember that there lie the bones of the Napiers for ten generations. Lay the bible on the table when we go," said Lady Grizel, with solemnity, "and place a four-leaved clover and rowan-tree sprig over the fireplace, and, dost hear me, Elshender, lay the poker and shovel crosswise above the gathering peat—"

"Crosswise?" muttered Elsie; "doth not that pertain to the auld papistical leaven o' idolatry?"

"It doth, I own, but the sign of the cross is a right good charm against the machinations of the evil one. You must have found that one made with red chalk on the bed-head, keepeth away both cramp and nightmare. My honoured mother used these marks, and by advice of Quentin, the abbot of Crossregal. O, Elshender, that is a long, long time ago, yet I mind it as yesterday."

"Cocksnails!" muttered Hab; "a jovial stoup of Barbadoes kill-devil were a far better charm, and I doubt not the abbot would have thought so too, eh, Master Fenton?"

"Dear nurse," said Lilian, "surely one so harmless and so pious as thee need fear nothing."

"Had ye heard the bummel o' the fairy boy's drum amang the lang grass in the loan and the stooks o' the hairst fields, brave though your bluid be, Lilian, it would turn, even as water. But if Lady Grizel requireth service of Hab and Meinie, it beseems no' the wife o' auld John Elshender to grudge it. Mony a year I have dwelt here, lang before the mirk Monanday, and ne'er saw aught that was unco, but I canna get owre my fears, though there is a horseshoe on the door where my puir gudeman nailed it forty years ago; there is a sprig o' rowan-tree owre the lintel, and the heart o' an elfshotten nowte, birselled wi' wax, and stuck fu' o' pins under the door step."

"A grand charm, Elsie," said Lady Grizel gravely; "no evil thing can enter or prevail against it."

"And so with these notable allies, gudewife, you think you will face out the terrors of one night alone?" said Walter impatiently, for soldiering had rubbed off much of that superstition which still exists in Scotland.

" I have courage to do whatever my lady requires o' me as
her bounden vassal," replied Elsie sharply ; " courage ! my
certie ! young sir, mony a lang year before you saw the light,
I learned to look without blenching on steel flashing in my
ain kailyard, and battle-smoke rowing owre holm and hollow.
A Scottish wife, maun, needs hae courage in thae fearfu'
times, when never a day passes without a son, a gudeman, or
a brother having to buckle on steel cap and corslet whenever
the laird cries, ' Mount and ride !' How mony a time and oft
has the bale fire at Libberton-peel, and the cry o' ' Horse and
spear !' made my douce gudeman crawl out frae his cosy nest
in that bein boxbed, wi' a heavy curse on the English, the
nonconformists, or malignants (or whaever kept the country-
side astir for the time), then donning morion, jack and spear,
he rode awa, de'il kens where, at Sir Archibald's bidding, for
they were aye together in drumming and dirdum, trooping
and travelling, hunting and hosting, sic as may we never see
again ! But alake ! there is a whisper gaing owre the land,
that waur is yet to come than the wildest persecutor could
think o'."

" Beard o' Mahoun !" said Hab impatiently, " you are at
your weary auld-world stories again. Let all bygones be
forgotten, mother, and as for the trooping and tramping of
those days, when my faither rode by laird's bridle, God send
we may soon have the same again ! But if our Lady means
to return to the old place to-night, the sooner she sets out the
better."

" True, Halbert," said Lady Grizel, " for the hour waxes
late ; but," she added, striking her cane on the floor, " we
will require a coach, for, late or early, we must return in such
state as befits us."

" Hab," said Walter, " hurry to the Portsburgh, and desire
the master of the inn there immediately to send his hackney
coach (I know he keeps one), with horses to drag it, and
link-boys conform."

" He is a dour auld carl, I ken," replied Hab, throwing off
his bandoleers, and preparing to start. " Our inquartering
there a month ago, has neither improved his temper or
gudewill. It will be the dead hour of night when I tirl his
pin, and he may refuse to obey me."

" How, if you say the coach is for a lady of quality."

" For me, Halbert ?" added Lady Grizel with dignity.

" Ay, madam, and ask my authority."

" Then show him the blade of your sword," said Walter :
" 'tis the best badge of authority to an insolent boor."

" But the auld buckie, though round as a puncheon of

Rhenish, can handle backsword and dagger, double and single falchions like any French sword-player; and look ye, Mr. Fenton, though a bare blade passed well enough in the Low Countries under Condé, or in the west under Claver'se, it will not do at all within sound of the Tron Kirk bell."

"Right, Halbert; we have neither law nor reason for browbeating the poor vintner; but faith, our living so long at free quarters has imparted to us a somewhat imperious mode of requiring service at all hands. Get the coach as you may, Hab, but be speedy."

"And Hab, my son," cried Elsie with anxiety, "keep the middle o' the gate till ye come to the place o' the Highrigs; and gif ye hear aught like the bummel o' a wee drum amang the lang grass or fauld-dykes by the wayside, neither quicken nor slacken your pace."

"For remember," added Lady Grizel, "it is equally unlucky either to meet or to avoid fairies or evil spirits."

"This cowes the gowan!" exclaimed Hab with a laugh, which awe for the old dame failed to restrain. "Lady Bruntisfield, a lad that hath heard Dunbarton's drums beating the point of war in the face of the Imperialists, need not care a brass bodle for all the fairies and witches in braid Scotland, and Gude kens, but there is plenty o' them—young anes, at least—eh, cousin Meinie?" and suddenly kissing her red cheek, he made a sweeping salute to the others, and sprang from the cottage.

Elsie now remembered that in her alternate joy and anxiety, the usual hospitality had been quite forgotten. Her nappy stone jars of usquebaugh and brown ale, with their attendant quaighs—crystal being then a luxury for the great and wealthy alone--cheese and bannocks of barley-meal were produced, and each person drank the health of all the rest with an air of solemn formality. The strong waters were tasted first for form-sake, and then their horns were replenished with the dun beverage of October, while their stools were all drawn close to the blazing fire, Lady Grizel, in the leathern chair, occupying the centre. Every face beamed with the purest happiness, and none more than that of Walter Fenton, and his handsome dark features, shaded by his clustering hair, glowing in the light of the fire and radiant with joy, formed an agreeable contrast to the paler and more interesting Lilian, whose eyes beamed with vivacity and drollery. Even old Elsie's face became dimpled with smiles, and she whispered in Meinie's ear, that "her auld een had never seen a mair winsome pair" than Walter and Lilian. Low as the whisper was, it reached the ear of the latter, or she divined its meaning, and it covered her with the most beautiful confusion, for to a young girl, there is nothing so indescribably charming, as when first her name is linked with that of a lover.

Though very happy, they were very silent. Lady Grizel was sunk in reverie; Lilian was a little abashed, and Walter, who was turning over his thoughts for a subject to converse on, was becoming more perplexed, until relieved by Elsie's loquacity, which found an ample theme in the terrors of the famous gnome or fairy boy, whose appearance about that time had caused no small consternation in Edinburgh. On the summit of the Calton—as all the gossips of the city were at any time ready to aver on oath—he was heard at midnight beating the role to the fairies, who came forth from under the long dewy blades of glittering dog-grass or heavy docken-leaves, from crannies in the rocks, and mole-tracks in the turf, to dance merrily on the Martyr's rock, in the blaze of the silvery moon. And, worse still, this same devilish gnome, by the clatter of his infernal drum, summoned weekly from the four quarters of heaven, the gyre-carlins and witches to Satan's periodical *levée*, and often the benighted citizen as he wended up the long and dreary loan from Leith (to which the ruins of a monastery, and a gibbet hung with skeletons, lent additional terrors), paused in dismay, when the din of the enchanted drum rang from the dark rocks on the gusts of the midnight wind, and the troop of gathering hags astride broomsticks and sprigs from a gallows-tree, swept like a storm through the air, bending strong trees to the earth, laying flat the ripening corn, and rumbling among chimney-heads, making the nervous indwellers cower under the bed-clothes, and tremble in the wooden recesses of their snug box-beds, while they murmured old charms against sorcery and the devil. Other witches of more aquatic propensities, were ferried across frith and bay in eggshells, sieves, and milk-bowies, to that damnable conclave, where plots were laid to blast their neighbours' kail or cattle, and work all manner of mischief, as the records of justiciary show. On all these appalling facts, Lady Grizel and Elsie descanted with such earnest seriousness, that Walter felt half inclined to shive with the rest, when the wind rumbled in the chimney as if flock of gyre-carlins were sweeping past it, to their *levée* o the Calton, about the bluff black rocks of which Lady Grizel averred emphatically, she had repeatedly seen them swarming in the bright moonlight, like gnats in the summer sunshine; and after evidence so conclusive, we hope nobody will doubt it.

CHAPTER XV

LOVE AND BURNT SACK.

HORATIO. 'Tis well, sir, you are pleasant.
LOTHARIO. By the joys
  Which my fond soul has uncontrolled pursued,
  I would not turn aside from my least pleasure,
  Though all thy force were armed to bar my way.
                                                N. ROWE.

THE evening of the night described in the preceding chapter had been a glorious one. The giant shadows of the rock-built city were falling from its central hill far to the eastward, and all its myriad casements were gleaming in the light of the western sky, where amid clouds of crimson, edged with gold, the sun's bright disc seemed to rest on the dark and wooded ridge of the Corstorphine hills, from whence it poured its dazzling flood of farewell radiance on all the undulations of the wide and varied scenery. On the vast and dusky mass of the hoary city which presented all the extremes of strong light, and deep retiring shadow, on the great stone crown of St. Giles, on the cordon of towers that girt the castled rock. and the stagnant lake that washed the city's base two hundred feet below, fell full the blood-red lustre of the setting sun.

The same warm tints glared along the western slopes of those bluff craigs and hills that rise to the westward, green, silent, stern, and pillared with basalt, rent by volcanic throes into chasms and gorges; where, though darkness was gathering, the slanting sunbeams shot through, and gilded objects far beyond. The loch, the city's northern barrier, usually so reedy and so stagnant, now swollen to its utmost marge by recent rains, was dotted by wild ducks and teals, that seemed floating in liquid gold, and like a polished mirror the water reflected its banks with singular distinctness. On one side appeared the inverted city, where gable, tower, and bartizan shot up so spectral, close, and dense, that it seemed like one vast fairy castle; on the other, a lonely and grassy bank, dotted with whins, alder-trees, weeping willows, and grazing sheep, while the old square tower of St. Cuthbert, rising above a clump of firs at one end of the loch, was balanced by the church of the Holy Trinity and its ancient orchard at the other.

On the northern bank of this artificial sheet of water flocks of crows were wheeling in circles among the furrows, and following the slow-drawn plough; and from the thatched cottages of St. Ninians, that nestled close to the ruins of an ancient convent, the smoke arose in long steady columns, and unbroken by the faintest puff of wind soared into the evening sky, and melted away into the blue atmosphere.

The sun had set.

The last rays died away on the cathedral spire, and Arthur's round volcanic cone ; the last wayfarer had been ferried across the loch, and had disappeared over the opposite hill ; successively the seven barriers of the city were closed for the night, and then the evening bell from the old wooden spire of the Tron rang on the rising wind. Though this evening had been a beautiful one, and all the gayer denizens of the city had flocked to the Lawnmarket and Castle Hill (then the only and usual promenades), the tall feather and laced mantle of Lord Clermistonlee had not been seen there.

From the windows of his chamber-of-dais he had long been surveying the view before described, but in one feature of it alone he seemed most interested. It was, where to the westward above the open fields named Halkerstoun's Crofts, he saw the smokeless chimneys of his empty, dismantled, and deserted mansion of Drumsheugh, which for many a year had been abandoned to a venerable colony of rooks and owls. The broad acres of fertile land that spread around it were now no longer his. Successively haugh, holm, farm, and onsteading, mill, and field had passed away to the possession of others, and of the noble estate acquired by his ancestors, and which he had gained as a dower with his fair cousin Alison, nothing remained but the silent and dreary mansion, which was fated soon (by his pressing necessities) to pass into other hands. To Clermistonlee this was the leading feature of the landscape, and long and fixedly he surveyed its square stacks of dark old chimneys that rose above the bare and leafless woods.

The expression of his face was fierce and unsettled ; his cheek was deeply flushed ; but that might be attributed to the briskness with which he and his gossip Mersington had pushed the tankard between them since dinner. They were both deep drinkers, and in the old Edinburgh fashion it was no uncommon thing for his lordship (when he gave a dinner-party) to lock the room door, and, in presence of his guests, send the key flying through the barred window into the Norloch, thereby intimating that there could be no egress until the last of a long array of flasks, which Juden mustered on the buffet, was drained to the bottom ; after which the door was unhinged, and all the guests were carried home by their servants in chairs or shoulder high.

One hand was thrust under the ample skirt of his shag dressing-gown ; the other drummed on the window-panes ;

but a stern expression gathered on his broad and lofty brow, and sparkled in his deep-set hazel eyes.

Mersington sat near the cheerful fire. His weazel-like visage was radiant at times with a malicious smile, which briefly gave way for one of sincere pleasure, each time he applied to his thin and ever-thirsty lips the tankard of burnt sack, which his affectionate hand never quitted for a moment. His mighty senatorial wig—the badge of his wisdom and power—hung on the chair-knob behind him, and his bald pate shone like a varnished ball in the evening twilight. His pale grey eyes wore their usual expression, by which it was impossible to detect whether he was drunk or sober ; but they often wandered to a panel opposite, where the following was chalked in a bold irregular hand :—

His honour the laird of Holsterlee bets the right hon. Lord Clermistonlee £10,000 of gude Scots monie payable at Whitsuntide—his mear Meg against Fleur de Lys, or Royal Charles. To be run at Easter on the sandis of Leith, God willing.

CLERMISTONLEE.
HOLSTERLEE, *Scots Guards.*

" Forsooth ! you are a proper man to start from the board, and turn your back on a guest thus," said Mersington. " Whistle a bar o' that oure again.

" ' There was a clocker, it dabbit at a man,
And he dee'd wi fear,
And he dee'd wi fear——'

" He—he, it seems to gie you as mickle comfort as the burnt sack."

" Perdition, man ! " exclaimed the other, wheeling so briskly round that he startled his guest in the act of taking another long, deep draught. " How can you jest with my distress ? I tell thee, friend Mersington, if the lands of Bruntisfield and the Wrytes, on which I have built my hopes, slip through my fingers thus, I may yet come to the husks and the swine-trough, like the prodigal of old. Behold my manor of Drumsheugh, on the brae yonder ; for these ten years a puff of smoke hath not curled from its chimneys ; the moss is on its hearths, and cobwebs obscure the gilding of its galleries and chambers ; the long grass waves in the avenue as it doth in the stable-court, where my good and careful father mustered eighty troopers in jack and plate the night before Dunbar was fought and won by Cromwell. My ancient tower of Clermiston is in the same condition ; and both are mortgaged to that prince of scribes and scoundrels, Grasper, the writer

in Mauchin's-close.   This match with Holsterlee, too!
S'blood! Juden says the mare is elfshotten, and our best
jockies opine that I can never win against Holster's racers,
which have won the city purse these five years consecutively."

"As for the race—he, he! to be off with the laird, swear
your mare hath been bewitched, and burn some auld carlin in
proof o't."

"D—nation! I am a ruined and impoverished man."

"He, he! the old gossips of Blackfriars-wynd tell another
story."

"What do they say?"

"That Clermistonlee can never come to want, as his friend
the de'il has given him a braw purse, with moudieworts' feet
on't, and sae lang as he preserves it, he shall never lack
siller."

"I wish to God he had! But where got ye this precious
information?"

"At the teaboard o' my Leddy Drumsturdy, nae further
gane than yesterday."

"Stuff and nonsense!"

"I hope sae; for just sic a purse brought the learned
Doctor Fian to stake in 1590. I've read the ditty against him
—he, he! but to come to the swine-trough, that would be an
unco pity, you have such a braw taste for getting up dinners
and suppers, that his grace the gourmand o' Lauderdale was
just naething to ye."

"Say rather Juden Stenton, my ground baillie, major domo,
squire of the body, and everything."

"Then your burnt sack is just perfection; but alake! you
now begin to see the end o' chambering, dicing, drinking,
racing, and wantonness. And puir Alison Gifford—faith, you
made her tocher flee fast enough."

"This admonitory tone becomes *thee* well," said Clermistonlee, with scornful emphasis; "and truly, thou art like one
of Job's comforters."

"He, he!" chuckled the senator, who had a strange fancy
for maliciously stinging his companion. "This is the end o'
spending puir Alison's money among horse-coupers, vintners,
panders, de'ils-buckies, and *bona robas*——"

"Hold, Mersington! I beg you will hear me with gravity.
My good cousin and gossip, at times I have found your advice
of the first value. You know how immensely fond I am of
Lilian Napier; and having been pretty fortunate with the
sex in my time (crush me! like what-is-his-name, I might
say, *Veni, vidi, vici*), I made the little minx an offer of mar-

riage, and, wouldst believe it? she really had the impudence to reject me."

"A braw buckie like you, Randal? For what?"

"Forsooth, only because I was a matter of some twenty years older than herself."

"Pest upon the gipsy! but then there is that plaguy entail——"

"Pshaw! I could soon have that broken. Lady Grizel hath the life-rent, and after her death (which cannot be far off), and failing the captain, the lands go entire to Lilian. Now her cousin, this gay spark in the service of their mightinesses the States-General, by his leaguing and intriguing with that Dutch intromitter, Orange William, and our rascally recusants, hath made the entail null—a dead letter—ha!"

"Faith, Randal, if you get your claws laid on the Bruntisfield barony, the rents thereof will puff your purse out brawly for a time. But, alake! it's like a sieve that aye rins out—ever filling, but never full. Bethink ye, man, there is the auld mansion, having the right of dungeon, pit, and dule-tree, wi' the grange, mains, yards, orchards, stables, doocot, bake and brewhouses pertaining thereunto (o'd, I've the haill inventory by heart). The four merk land o' auld extent named Nether Durdic, bounded by the Burghloch—the fishings o' that water, the rigs, rowme, and holm o' Drumdryan, wi' the farm-toun to the eastward thereof, holden o' the city for ane crown-bowl o' punch yearly, and ane armed man's service, and whilk payeth fifty-seven bolls o' wheat, twa firlots o' barley, forty-and-aught o' aitmeal, sixty-four gude fat capons, and sae forth—my certie! by twa women being relaxit frae the horn you have lost a' that, and deil kens how mickle mair."

"Fool—fool! this croaking maddens me!" exclaimed Clermistonlee, starting a second time from the table, and pacing about the room.

"Come, come, my lord," said Mersington, putting on h, wig; "he, he! ye may huff and hector at Juden as ye please, but these are hard words for a Swinton to swallow."

"I crave your pardon, gossip, but why torture me thus? I must have some signal and terrible revenge on Dunbarton, for his interfering with me in this matter. Could we not bring him under suspicion of the council?"

"A moral and physical impossibility."

"Juden would give him the contents of a carbine, if I gave him a hint anent it."

"It would be wiser to let him alone. You would have his chief, the marquis of Douglas, and every one of the name, on ye like a nest o' hornets, for they are a proud and thrawart race, that winna thole steering. Ye maun train your hawks at other lures. Od's fish, man! his mad musketeers would sack and slaughter the haill city."

"And Fenton!" continued the lord, grinding his teeth, "I would travel to Jericho to have him within reach of my rapier,—I would, d—n me—to pull his nose off. What a ravelled hesp is my fortune! My wounded hand, too——"

"He, he! how can you expect it to heal, when the haill blude in your body is turning into burnt sack and sugared brandy?"

"It has kept me from prosecuting this affair. But I am getting desperate, Mersington; between love of the girl, lack of her lands, and fear of poverty, nothing now can save me but a dash."

"Spoken like yoursel—like the wild Randal Clermont o' 1670. But what do ye propose?"

"To carry off Lilian. and make a Highland wedding of it —ha. ha!"

"Hee, hee! abduction, reif, and felony, anent whilk see the acts of the seventh parliament of James V. and James VI. Parliament twenty-first, chapter fourth—hee, hee! these would bear hard on your case, my birkie."

"Pshaw! am not I. too, a lord of the parliament? so, friend Mersington, reserve this musty jargon for the hall of the Tolbooth. How often hath a Scottish baron with his band ridden to its threshold with jack and spear, and while his trumpets blew defiance at the cross, laughed the fulminations of the three estates to scorn."

"Ye mean mad Bothwell, with his thousand spears; but Clermistonlee, wi' his man Juden, would cut a sorry figure riding up the gate on the same errand."

"But the mere abduction of a girl?"

"It canna be sae bad in law as abducting that dour auld carle Durie, the lord president, whom a mosstrooping loon, by orders o' Traquair, carried off bodily, across his saddlebow, frae the dreary Figget whins, and warded for sax calendar months in the vault o' a border peel. For my part, I have hated the name o' womankind since my Lady Mersington had me fined a thousank merks Scots, for that damned conventicle whilk, in my absence, she held on my lands. But Gude be thanked, I had my vengeance, by having her banished the liberties of the city, for hearing that recusant runnion, Ichabod Bummel, preach, whilk rid me and a' Bess-wynd o' her eternal clack. Faith, Clermistonlee, ye are welcome to abduct her, gif ye please—he, h "

"I thank you, gossip, but beg to decline," said Clermis tonlee, draining his tankard of sack; "but to show thee, most learned senator, the value and veneration I bear those acts you have just cited, I shall this very night carry off Lilian Napier, whom my spies inform me to be concealed somewhere to the south of the town. O, by all the devils, I'll easily find the place. My blood's up; I will make my fortune to-night, or mar it for ever."

His sallow cheek glowed, his dark eye flashed, and taking a very handsome pair of pistols from the mantelpiece, he began to load them with great deliberation, having previously summoned his faithful rascal Juden, by furiously ringing a handbell.

"What's in the wind, now, my lord?" he asked, rubbing his eyes, having been abruptly summoned from an afternoon nap.

"You will learn ere long," said his lord, with a sternness that made the bluff butler's eyes to dilate with surprise; "but see that you are as prompt to act as to ask questions. You must bear a message from me to the Place."

"Eh? to Drumsheugh—at this time?"

"To Beatrix Gilruth."

"My lord—I—I—" stammered Juden.

"Saddle a horse, ride round the loch, and tell her that tns young lass she wots of will be there to-night, and that she must have some of the old rooms in the north wing, those that overlook the rocks, prepared for her reception."

"Where the gipsy was put, that we harled awa frae the west country?"

"What, the wench whom Holsterlee took off my hands— the same. You stare oddly—dost hear me, fellow?—art thou sober?"

"As a judge, my lord."

"Then hear me and obey. Desire this hag, Beatrix, to have all prepared for my fair one's reception—fires lit and tapestry brushed; and, on peril of thine own life, be speedy and secret. Tarry neither there nor by the way, as I will want thee when the town-drum beats at ten o'clock."

"She's an uncanny body, Lucky Gilruth, though I mind the time when there was not a bonnier lass in a' the Lowdens." said Juden, scratching his rough chin with undisguised perplexity; "but now, the auld wrinkled hizzie, she deserves the tar-barrel as weel as Lucky Elshender."

"What the devil is all this to me?"

"It is a lonesome and eerie road across Halkerstoun's crofts by the lang gate, and on such an errand to such a woman, with the mirk night coming on——"

"Blockhead! thou hast been guzzling in the wine-cellar. Begone, or I will beat thee; but first have the mare saddled as well as the horse, and procure a good link, and fail not when the drum beats. I will ride the Duke, 'tis a strong old trooper, and used to carrying double—hah! Away, away, and on peril of thy life, speak of this to no man."

"You will find me as of auld, Clermistonlee, a hawk of the right nest."

"Look well to Meg's girths."

"Ay, my lord, a fidging mear should be weel girded—now then hoe! for the Place."

Juden drained a wine-cup that his master handed him, and in five minutes more the mare's hoofs rang on the causeway of the steep wynd, and died away as he descended into the deep gorge, under Neil's Craigs, wheeled through the Beggar's Row, and ascended the opposite bank.

CHAPTER XVI.

THE TEN O'CLOCK DRUM.

Du Chatel. The gates stand open; no man shall molest you.
  Count Dunois, follow me—you gain no honour in lingering here.
Raimond. Seize on this moment! the streets are empty,—
  Give me your hand.
                            SCHILLER'S MAID OF ORLEANS.

CLERMISTONLEE was well aware that the forcible abduction of a young lady of family (or quality, according to the phraseology of the time), would create no small degree of indignation against him; but confiding in his rank, and in the influence of the powerful faction to which he belonged; aware that never could he otherwise obtain possession of Lilian's person, and ultimately her property, goaded by dread of poverty rather than avarice, inflamed by his own wild fancies and irregular passions rather than by love, and spurred on by the taunts and advices of the half cunning and wholly malicious Mersington, he sat longing with the utmost eagerness for the time of action, the tuck of the ten o'clock drum, after the beating of which, all within the city walls usually became so silent and still. He knew also that the family of Napier had experienced a severe shock by their recent forfeiture, and a squadron of Dalyel's dragoons being quartered on their estate for three weeks past, and being yet under hiding (as the term was), the abduction of Lilian could be more easily executed; and if once within the barred doors and grated windows of his desolate mansion on the   of Drumsheugh, or the massive chambers of his still more lonely tower on Clermiston Lee, Lilian might bid farewell equally to mercy and to hope.

Aware of the lonely situation of Elsie's cottage on the verge of the great Burghmuir, fully two Scottish miles from the city cross, and knowing that the locality was always deserted after dusk, in consequence of the unsettled nature of the times, and a horde of footpads who infested the remnants of its forest and the deep quarries and moss-haggs through which the roadway wound, and which, independent of a gibbet, a ruined church and graveyard, deterred all and sundry, after the city gates were closed, from travelling that way after dusk—considering all those things, the noble *roué* had no doubt of being able to fire the little cottage, and, in the confusion, to bear away Lilian across his saddle-bow. And to cast suspicion in another quarter, he had desired Juden to have a bonnet or two, a grey maud and a Bible, to leave on the road close by, that the odium of the outrage might fall on the houseless Cameronians who lurked among the hills to the southward.

Tipsy as he was, when the time approached for Clermistonlee setting forth, Lord Mersington had still sense remaining to say, —" Tak' tent, Randal, my man—hee, hee!—bide ye a wee, ere worse come o't. You may bring king, council, and parliament about your lugs for this, and the Foulis o' Ravelstone, Congaltoun o' that ilk, and Merchiston himsel will swarm like a hornet's nest, and ' Horse and spear!' will be the cry through half the country's side—he, he!"

" Curses on thy everlasting chuckle!" muttered the other between his teeth, as with fierce impatience he thrust his brass-barrelled pistols into his embroidered girdle. " What the devil are Ravelstone or Congaltoun to me? If the worst comes, 'tis but flying to the west Highlands till the affair blows over. I can count kindred with some of the best who bear the name of Campbell."

" Kindred that will truss ye wi' a tow, and hand ye over for twenty merks to the first macer or corporal of horse that the chancellor sends after you. Remember how Assynt served Montrose thirty-eight years ago."

" Your suspicions wrong my Highland kinsmen, who are honourable men——"

" But true blue whigamores withal—hee, hee! and brawly you'll look coming up the Netherbow in a cart like Montrose, puir fellow! wi' the town halberds bristling round ye, and Pate Pincer wi' his axe maybe, and our noble friend Perth, sitting in the Lower Chamber wi' his finger on the acts of James the V. and VI., anent wilful fire-raising—hee, hee! and as for the lassie——"

"My lord, this is intolerable stuff!" said Clermistonlee, shrugging his shoulders; "you cannot be so young a politician as not to perceive that a storm is approaching, which will crush and confound together all the factions that now distract the land, and keep our swords for ever by our sides. All men see it, else whence this muster of troops and din of preparation on both sides of the border?"

"Storm—a storm said ye?"

"Yes, amid which, if we can hold our own bonnets on our heads, we will be clever fellows, Swinton."

"And whence blows the breeze, think ye?"

"'The Lowlands of Holland,' as the song says," replied the cavalier lord, drawing himself up with a scornful smile.

"Wheesht!—hee, hee, hee!" chuckled the other, waving one hand warningly, while burying his rat-like visage in the sack tankard to hide the cunning smile of intelligence that spread over it. Harkee, Randal, whare'er the de'il be laird, you'll be tenant—hee, hee!"

"I value a crash in politics at the worth of a brass tester, and bid hail to the day of hard blows and buff coats. Ha, ha! I may pick up a marquisate in the scramble," laughed Clermistonlee, flapping his hat over his eyes. "You will not accompany me to-night, being scarcely cavalier enough for this kind of work."

"Hoots, man, a double-gowned senator of the College of Justice, a lord of council and session, aiding and abetting in wilful fire-raising. Doth not the act say, 'Quha cummis and burnis folk in their housis will be guilty o' treason and lese-majestic?' and as for running off wi' the lassie Lilian, that is clearly a kidnapping o' the lieges, whilk, according to Skene and Sir Thomas o' Glendoick——"

"Gossip Mersington, there are overmuch wine and law in thee to-night to leave room for common sense. Ha! there goes the ten o'clock drum, and that loitering villain has not yet returned."

He threw open a window that faced the south, where the black mansions of the Netherbow towered up from the steep hill at the foot of which his house was situated. The sound of a distant drum, beat in slow, regular, and monotonous measure, was heard on the wind at intervals, as a drummer of the civic guard (an old corps of Scottish gendarmes, which existed from the fatal day at Flodden until 1818), ascended St. Mary's-wynd, his usual nightly round, after having descended the Bow, and beat along the once lordly and fashionable Cowgate, where kings have feasted royally, and where Scottish nobles and the ambassadors of foreign powers were

wont to dwell; but now the hideous abode of misery and
crime, and long since abandoned to the dregs of mankind.
On strode the drummer, and the gates of the Netherbow
revolved back at his approach: as he passed under its double
towers, its picturesque spire and high embattled arch, the
great street of the city, wide and lofty, but dark and deserted,
rang to the same monotonous chamade and all its echoing
closes, broad paved wynds and old arcades of wood or stone,
its circular stairs and oaken outshots gave back a thousand
reverberations as "the ten o'clock drummer" strode on, until
reaching the town guard-house, where he finished his peram-
bulation of the ancient royalty by a long and loud ruffle,
which scared the vultures from the skulls that mouldered on
the parapets of the prison, startled the rooks in the gothic
diadem of St. Giles, and made all its hollow vaults and high
arched aisles, where the dead of ages lie, give back the
warlike sound.

The drum rang loudly as it passed the archway that led to
the lodging of Clermistonlee, who threw down the window
with a crash, exclaiming,—

"Malediction on my messenger—I must mount and ride
without him. Ha! here comes the loitering rascal in time to
save his shoulders from a stout truncheoning."

A horse's hoofs rang in the court yard; Juden's heavy
boots clattered on the pavement as he dismounted and
ascended to the chamber of dais, puffing, panting, and looking very pale and disconcerted.

"So-so, fellow," said the irritated lord, "it has pleased you
to return at last."

"With God's providence, my lord."

"How, fool? What means this unwonted piety? Art
drunk, fellow?"

"Fie, Juden!" said Mersington, "a fou man and a fasting
horse should hae come faster home, hee, hee!"

"You saw this woman, Gilruth, and left my message, I
presume?"

"Yes, my lord, yes," gasped Juden.

"What the devil is all this? There is something wrong
with thee, Juden."

"Then to be plain wi' your lordship, I canna thole the auld
place after nightfa'. I aye think o'—think o'——"

"What?" asked Clermistonlee, furiously.

"O' puir Leddy Alison," whined Juden, half in sorrow, and
half in spite. "Eh, sirs! but the auld place o' Drumsheugh
is fu' o' her memory, and I seemed to hear her sweet low
voice 'n every sough o' the auld aik trees, and to see her

L   K

shadow in every glint their branches threw on the moor-
lighted avenue and auld grey house."

"Fool, fool," said Clermistonlee, in a subdued voice, "you
speak as if she had been murdered."

"Nor did she fare mickle better," muttered Juden, under
breath, however.

"Poor Alison!—so gentle and unreproaching," said the
lord, in a low musing voice. "Alison—once that name was
ever on my lips—her presence was ever with me, and her idea
raised a rapture in this hollow heart, to which it has since
been a stranger. Yes, my love was a very true one."

"While it lasted," said Mersington.

"Of course," rejoined the other, recovering himself. "I
loved her to distraction once; or thought so; and, by all the
devils, 'tis quite the same thing. She is dead now, and peace
be with her; but peril of thy life, Juden Stenton, trouble me no
more with such untimely elegies. And pray, Master Morality,
how have you dared to loiter away these two hours past?"

"Ask that elfshotten mear Meg," said the butler, testily.
"Either the cantrips o' Beatrix Gilruth, or Lucky Elshender
(baith o' whom are weel deserving o' the branks and tar
barrel, Mersington), hae clean bewitched that puir beast.
May I never lay head on a pillow to-night, if I wasna' spell-
bound on Halkerstoun's crofts, where I continued to ride and
spur, wi' the black Calton looming in front and St. Cuthbert's
kirk behind; but I never neared the one, or got further from
the other; and yet Meg was fleeing like the wind, or as fast
as ever she did for city purse or king's plate on the sands o'
Leith. The night was dark; a cauld wind swept owre the
crofts, and soughed among the kirkyard yews and lang nettles by the drystane dykes; red lights gleamed in the runnels
that bummel down the brae side, and redder stars were
shooting in the lift. A cauld perspiration burst owre me;
every hair bristled under my bannet——"

"Rascal, art mocking us?"

"Patience, my lord," groaned poor Juden. "I kent there
was a spell on me, and I tried to say some holy word or name;
but, as the deil would hae'd, the sounds aye stuck in my
throat; and there I sat, sweating and trembling, and spurring
a galloping nag that never progressed; and there indubitably
I must hae been until cockcrow, if I hadna——"

"What?" exclaimed his master, stamping with impatience.

"Made a grasp at a rowan-tree that grew near, and pu'ed
a bunch o' the last year's berries, when lo! the charm was
broken, and Meg shot awa like the wind; and I cleared the
lang gate as if the Paip and the Deil were behind me."

" And dost think, rascal, that I believe one word of this precious Tale of a Tub, foisted up to deceive me, for time spent in the village changehouse yonder ?   Ha, knave, remember the old saw—Good wine makes a bad head and a long story."

" My lord, as I left the place, auld Gilruth cried, ' A safe ride to ye, Juden,' and her eldritch laugh is yet dingling in my lugs."

" That makes it a clear case o' witchcraft," mumbled Mersington, who was now very tipsy.   " He-he !—we'll hae the carlin before us in the morning, Juden.   Ay, my lords, (macers, silence in court !), this is as clear a case o' witchcraft as ever came before us ; and the act under Queen Mary (puir woman) anent sorcery bears just upon it.   Your lordships will remember," continued the senator, who thought himself on the bench, " the cases o' Isabel Eliot and Marion Campbell, twa notorious witches, who, for renouncing their baptism, and dancing a jig wi' the deil, were burnt at the Cross wi' ten others in the September o' '78, for whilk see the record o' justiciary—hee-hee ! a braw bleeze ! "

" I will show a blaze on the Burghmuir to-night worth a dozen of it—ha, ha ! " laughed Clermistonlee, as he drew on his voluminous boot-tops of stamped maroquin with silver bosses.

" O'd, Clermistonlee, do ye really mean to burn Elshender's cottage ? " asked Juden, with delight.

" Yea, sink me ! from rigging-tree to ground-stone. " Juden rubbed his hands.

" If the auld witch is bedridden," said he, " it will save the provost a bundle o' tar-barrels, forbye a pock o' peats."

" And perhaps cure those spells which you think the hag hath cast upon my best nag.   And so, Mersington, you will not ride with us to-night?"

" No, by my faith ! "

" Then your learned lordship forgets one notable point of our old Scottish law, by which a *guest* becomes the bounden *ally* of his host."

" True ; but only if loons come against him wi' harness on, boden in effeir o' weir, as the Acts have it."

" As the chase after Lilian may be a hot one, omit not to spread most industriously that I am gone to the west, to England, to the devil, or anywhere, to put them off the right scent—ha, ha ! while I am luxuriating in the smiles of Venus in the recesses of my snug old house over the hill there.   Dost hear me ! By Jove, he's very drunk. Fetch me a tass of brandy and burnt sugar, Juden."

It was brought immediately, in one of those long glasses then made at the citadel of Leith. It set Clermistonlee's impatient blood on fire.

"Another for thyself, Juden, and then to horse, and away. Your servant, gossip Mersington ; if unfortunate, you will see me in the course of to-morrow ; if otherwise, the devil knows when. Marriage and hanging go by destiny—so do all other things—with a hey lilleu and a how lo lan."

"Aye, aye, awa ye neer-do-weel—ye deil's buckie ; I'll stay and keep the terrier company. The sack is glorious—the English port auld as the mirk Monanday a' sixteen hunder and fifty-twa ; a clear case o' sorcery, your lordship—o' dark dealing wi' the great enemy o' mankind—hee-hee!—and woman kind baith."

His head sank forward on his wine-bespattered cravat, and the senior senator of the College of Justice fell fast asleep.

CHAPTER XVII.

CLERMISTONLEE MAKES A SAD MISTAKE.

But if this young lady will marry you, and relieve us, O my conscience! I'll turn friend to the sex, and rail no more at matrimony.—THE LYING VALET.

ISSUING from a private gate in the northern flank of the city wall, at the foot of the court attached to his mansion, the lord and his staunch follower mounted in a narrow lane, over-hung on one side by gloomy trees, and on the other by the ancient hospital of the Holy Trinity. The great oriel, or triple window of its church was then faintly lighted by the beams of the rising moon, the silver disk of which seemed to rest on the sable ridge of Arthur's Seat. They passed through the Calton, then a straggling burgh, consisting of antique houses of Flemish aspect, but occupied by a very inferior class of citizens, and entered the long and solitary path called Leith Loan, which was formed by an ancient trench of the great civil wars ; hollowly rang their horses' hoofs between the black rocks of the Calton on one hand, and the steep bank of St. Ninian on the other, where the ivied and shattered walls of a convent presented in the bright moonlight a striking variety of light and shade.

To avoid every chance of recognition or surprise, Clermistonlee thus made a complete circuit of the city, leaving it on the side opposite to the scene of his operations. The night soon became as cloudy and dark as he could have wished it ;

for, as the fitful moon became involved in opaque masses of vapour, every object was rendered obscure and indistinct. On one side of the way lay the lake, like a sheet of ink, and beyond it rose up the stupendous cliffs and ramparts of the castle, and the gigantic outline of the city towering like a mighty bank of cloud, through which the lights of distant casements glimmered like far and fitful stars. On the other side spread open fields and solitary farms; the castles of the Touris of Inverleith, the Kincaids of Warriston, and two or three small and lonely hamlets.

"Clermistonlee," began Juden, closing up to his master as the Long Gate became darker and more lonely, for the cottages of St. Ninian were now far behind; "If the auld witch, Elshender, by keeking through a spule bane should divine our errand, our riding will be to little purpose, I reckon. She is an unco uncanny body, Lucky Elsie; and though her gudeman was a trooper, and did richt leal service in King Charles's wars, I would fain see her brought to the tar-barrel, for, wow, but I hate an auld blench-lippit, long-chaffit, sunk-eyed carlin, as I do sour ale or the deil."

The lord vouchsafed no reply to these sapient remarks, and Juden, feeling somewhat uneasy at his silence, the darkness, and their vicinity to the old Cross-kirk of St. Cuthbert, with its great square central tower and broad burial-grounds, studded with mossy tombstones and slabs half sunk in the long reedy grass, spurred nearer and spoke again.

"And then to think o' Meg, puir beastie! to fa' ill o' the wheezlock, the malanders, and deil kens a' what, the very night ye trampled down that auld cummer's kailcastocks, and wi' this match wi' Holsterlee to come off at Easter! Troth, my Lord Mersington has thumbscrewed and tar-barrelled scores o' auld besoms on the half o' sic evidence o' malice, and ungodly ill-will. And I would beg o' you to gie Mersington a hint, that she was the gossip of Helen of Peaston, who was burned ten years byegone. Od's fish! I saw the brodder o' the High Court run his steel pricker thrice into Beelzebub's mark on her bare back—a lang black teat whereat she suckled Hornie's imps, and she neither winced nor skirled. And for what I would like mickle to ken——"

"Silence."

"Doth not this auld deevil, Elshender, deserve the tar-barrel as weel as her neighbour cummer?"

"I tell thee, silence! Blow the match that must light the link."

"The link—now?"

"Thou hast it I hope, pumpkin-head?'

"Yes—yes, my lord—but, wow, I wish this desperate job weel ower."

"Art getting white-livered? Is this our first affair of the kind?"

"What, if the coach with the skeleton lady cam' rumbling up Leith Loan after us! It is about her hour noo. Burn my beard, if I wadna die o' sheer fright."

"Would to Heaven she came then, and rid me of a thorough household pest!"

"Ay, ay, but ye would sune find the want o' puir auld Juden. Wha would spice the Canary and Rochelle, mull the sack, and sugar the brandy like me? Wha then would doctor your nags, break your hounds, and train your hawks wi' leash and lure, and do everything ye can think o' frae birselling a crail capon to backing a troop-horse, and frae brushing your spurleathers, to being your stanch henchman on sic a hillicate errand as this? Hech, sir! I am picking up my thanks now for standing by ye wi' buff and bilbo on many a stormy day, fighting now for the kirk and then for the king— a bab o' blue ribands in my bonnet to-day, a cavalier's white feather the morn, just as it suited you to uphold one banner because the other was like to be beaten down."

"Rascal! let these be the last of those impertinent reflections which you permit yourself to make on my conduct. Recollect that as my bounden vassal, *my* will is thine, my word *thy* law—enough—and seek not as usual, old Mr. Pertinacity, to have the last word with me."

"I am mum, my lord." Juden checked his horse and fell to the rear in high dudgeon.

Making a complete circuit of the suburbs, they crossed the Burghmuir, where the turrets of Bruntisfield rose above the dark oaks of the olden time. Clermistonlee took a long survey of the stately old mansion and its domain, and greatly refreshed with the noble aspect thereof, pushed on with increased speed.

When they approached the little cottage it was dark and silent as the ruined chapel beside it, and the beechen grove which overshadowed them both. The smoke of the rested night-fire curled up pale and grey among the dark copsewood, from the massive clay-built chimney, but there was no other sign of life within. Concealing their horses behind a thick privet hedge, the conspirators approached the cottage, Clermistonlee unrolling an ample roequelaure of scarlet cloth to throw over Lilian as a muffler, the moment she rushed forth escape the conflagration.

"The hut is very still," said the lord. "Zounds! if she should be gone away."

"Impossible," responded Juden. "Jock, my sister's son, watched the place until mirk night came on. But hear me— one word, my lord, ere we come to the onset?"

"What the deuce is it now, thou most incorrigible prater?"

"Would it no be better to ding up the door and carry the lady off before I fire the bit placie, lest the flame bring those who might strike into the rescue?"

"True, Juden, you speak sensibly for once," replied his master, who staggered a little in consequence of his recent potations, and felt no ordinary excitement as the moment approached, when he hoped to clasp Lilian Napier in his arms, and bear her off in triumph. Clermistonlee had long been the wildest gallant of his time, and in such a desperate affair as this he felt quite in his element.

Poising a large stone aloft, he hurled it against the door with all the impetus he could lend it; but the barrier yielded not. An exclamation, half-smothered in the depths of a box-bed, showed that the inmates were sufficiently alarmed by the thundering shock, and poor Elsie lay quaking under the bed-clothes, in full conviction that the devil and his elvish drummer to boot, were about to force an entrance. Again and again Lord Clermistonlee hurled it against the cottage-door; but it remained fast as a rock, for several strong bars of wood inserted in the massive wall, gave it all that security which was then as necessary to the hut as to the palace. Juden raised aloft the flaring link, and its light streamed by fits on the thatched roof and whitewashed walls, on the divot seat in front, with woodbine and wild rose-tree clambering above it; on the high beech-trees that spread their arms to the night wind, scaring the rooks from their leafless nests, and the sparrows from the thick warm thatch which the blazing link menaced every instant.

"Reif and roist the obstinate yett!" exclaimed Juden, capering as the stone rolled back upon his shins, and Clermistonlee, exasperated by the unlooked-for delay, furiously thrust the link into the heavy thatch. The dense mass smouldered and smoked for an instant, while the dry straw below struggled with the thick stratum of green moss above, till the former prevailed, and a broad lurid flame shot upward, revealing the broad fields and pasture land, the rough dykes and budding hedge-rows, the dreary road that wound over the adjacent hills, the far recesses of the beechen grove, bringing forward the knotted branches and gnarled and ivied trunks in strong relief, from the darkness and obscurity of the wooded vista behind. Full on the roofless walls and pointed windows of St. Rocque fell the fitful light, and on the spacious burial-ground, where close and thick lay the headstones of those unfortunates who perished in the deadly pestilence of 1645. In a few minutes a mass of blazing thatch fell inwards through the bared and scorched rafters, and a terrific scream ascended from within. Fire now flashed through the little square windows of the cottage, and its whole interior became filled with yellow light; but the door still remained fast, while the shrieks that rang within made Clermistonlee tremble with apprehension.

"Fury and confusion!" he exclaimed, "she may be scorched to death by that flaming mass of thatch! Horror! aid me—fool and villain—to burst in the door! quick, or the accursed baillie of the Portsburgh with his trainband of souters and wabsters will be on us."

While he was speaking, the cottage door flew open, and, amid a shower of sparks, which she threw from her attire, a female rushed forth in a state of distraction.

"'Tis she, Juden!" cried Clermistonlee, "'tis she! I could know that purple hood among a thousand!" and rushing forward with a tipsy shout of triumph and rapture, he snatched up the slight figure, over which his stanch bravo threw the ample and stifling rocquelaure in a manner that showed he had practised it on former occasions, as it effectually pre-vented her cries from being heard. Tall, strong, and muscular, Clermistonlee, with perfect ease, placed his fair captive on the croupe of his horse, and, springing into the saddle, gave it the spur so suddenly, that it bounded into the air, and he lost a stirrup.

"Courage, Juden!" he exclaimed, while his heart panted with love and exultation; "to horse and spur for the place of Drumsheugh—but first assist me—confusion! I have lost a stirrup—quick, varlet, the curb-rein. So, now, look to thy petronel, for, by Jove! I hear a horn blowing somewhere."

Trembling with terror, and shaken furiously by the bound-ing of his restless horse, the muffled captive lay helpless in his bold embrace. One hand and arm were firmly clasped round her light and shrinking figure, the other held the reins of his powerful horse, which dashed along the road, clearing dyke and hedge at a bound, until gaining the summit of the Burghmuir, where the road was rendered dangerous by the ancient quarries, moss-haggs, and heron-shaws that bor-dered it.

"My dear Lilian, why will you struggle with me when I

tell that your efforts are vain; but fear not, gentle one, I wil. slacken my horse's speed, if you wish it." He spoke with the utmost deliberation and coolness; for he was too much used to such affairs to feel at all puzzled in making an apology; besides, he was very tipsy. "You have long rejected me, dear Lilian, and forced me to this act, for which I crave your pardon with the most abject humility—by all the devils I do! I am not one to stand on trifles, as thou knowest: no, sink me! and if it is in the power of man to bend a woman's will to his, thine shall bend to mine."

This address was in no way calculated to quiet the terrors of his prisoner: his lordship was becoming more and more confused and intoxicated, as every bound of his horse forced into his head the fumes of the wine of which he had partaken so freely; and so he continued in the same strain—

"What dost say, little one—my beloved Lilian, I mean— you will struggle, you will scream? Permit me to insinuate, my dear madam, that it will be worse than useless, for nothing can avail you now but pleasing me; a course I would advise you to pursue forthwith. I know some devilish fine women that would be proud to do it—crush me if I do not! My dearest Lilian, (what was I saying?) I will teach thee to love as I would wish to be loved. My heart and coronet are at your feet—will not sincere love beget love? By all the devils, I know it will! You will pardon all this to-morrow, for I know women forgive all that has love for an excuse; then how much more so you, that are ever so gentle and kind, when other dames are so haughty and cold; d——n them! amen. You think me a wicked ruffian, eh? Zounds! I am not at all so, but a very fine fellow in every respect, though an unfortunate victim of love to thee and fear of a few rascally creditors. My pretty Lilian, in fact I love thee so tremendously, that even the pen of Scuderi could never describe it; and I swear by this kiss, dear Lilian, and this—and this—a thousand furies! where am I?"

He became sobered in a moment, for, on removing the mantle to salute the soft cheek of the girl, instead of beholding, as he expected, the head of a seraph peeping forth from a mass of bright ringlets, lo, a ray of the sickly moon streamed on the hooked nose, peaked chin, grey-haired, and smoke-begrimed visage of Elsie Elshender.

"Horror!" exclaimed Clermistonlee, whose rhapsody this terrible vision had cut short.

"Avaunt, hag of hell!" and, trembling in every fibre with rage and disgust, he flung the poor woman from his arms, and goading his horse with the sharp rowels, dashed up the dark and rough Kirk Brae at a break-neck pace; while Juden totally unable to comprehend what had taken place in front, partly drew up as the female rolled by the way-side, near the gate of the place of Bruntisfield.

"Awa wi' ye! fie and out upon ye, ye sons o' the scarlet woman!" exclaimed Elsie, in great wrath and tribulation, for she soon recovered the use of her tongue. "May a' the plagues of Egypt fa' upon your ungodly heads! May the Lord send cursing, vexation, and rebuke! Out upon ye, fie, and a murrain upon ye!"

Juden was astonished; but no sooner did he hear her shrill voice, and behold by the moonlight her aged and withered visage, with long tangled hair falling grey around it, than he became seized with a superstitious terror, which the raising of her long skinny arm and crooked finger, as if to curse, completed; and he stayed not to hear the expected anathema.

"The first fuff o' a haggis is aye the hottest, but I'll not bide a second. Tak' that, ye accursed witch, until you are tar-barrelled!" he exclaimed, and fired his long horse pistol full in her face. Poor Elsie fell forward motionless, while Juden, without daring once to look behind him, dashed at full gallop after his lord, who had already crossed Halkerstoun's Crofts, and was nearing the village of St. Ninian.

CHAPTER XVIII.

THE GROWTH OF LOVE AND HOPE.

The lady of my love resides
Within a garden's bound;
There springs the rose, the lily there
And hollyhock are found.
An instant on her form I gazed,
So delicately white;
Mild as a tender lamb was she,
And as the red rose bright.
                LAYS OF THE MINNESINGERS.

IT is, perhaps, unnecessary to inform the reader that, thanks to the delay caused by Juden's cunning or superstition, Lord Clermistonlee's intended seizure of Lilian Napier had been attempted an hour too late. This was indeed fortunate. Had it been made earlier, blood and blows and loss of life must have undoubtedly ensued.

Exactly one hour before the unexpected visit which ended in the destruction of Elsie's cottage, and nearly terrifying the poor woman out of her senses, her late guests had all departed in one of those vast and solemn hackney equipages (before described) which crawled away over the Burghmuir like the mighty catafalco of a deceased hero, passed the end of the still and waveless Burghloch, and up the dark and gloomy avenue of Bruntisfield, after being nearly an hour in traversing a space which any modern cab will carry one over in three minutes. Like a true gallant of the day, Walter Fenton stood on the footboard behind, while Hab, with his matchlock slung, shared the driver's ample hammer-cloth, so that the ladies and their attendant Meinie (whose delight and wonder at being in such a vehicle must be duly commemorated) were pretty safe from those bold lads of the post who prowled about after nightfall with sword and pistol, making every unarmed citizen who chanced to pass that way, stand and deliver cloak and purse with so cavalier an air, that it was almost impossible to refuse.

With as much formality as if she was entering a conquered city, Lady Grizel received the keys of the barbican gate from her ground-baillie Syme, of the Greenhill, who, bareheaded, with three stout sons, bearing torches, and several of the old servants, who had found shelter in Syme's onsteading, and whose clamorous joy burst forth in loud pæans of triumph, as she was led by the baillie into the old baronial chamber of dais, the canopy of which, to the simple "tenant bodies" of those days, was fraught with more terrors than the chair of the Lord President Lockhart.

"A thousand welcomes to your ladyship," said Symon, bowing profoundly for the twentieth time.

"Thanks, Symon," replied Lady Bruntisfield, giving him her hand to kiss. "I hope your gudewife is well, and that your youngest bairn got over its hooping cough by the means I prescribed."

"My lady, wi' the advice o' a barber-chirurgeon——"

"A barber-guse! did I not tell ye to pass that afflicted bairn three times through a blackberry bush, whilk is an infallible remedy—but I'll see after it mysel to-morrow."

Lilian wept and laughed, and gave her hands to the servants to kiss, for her heart beat as joyously to find herself under the old ancestral roof, as if she had doubled Cape Horn since she last saw it. She kissed grand-aunt Grizel, and rushed from one dark and silent apartment to another, as if to gladden them by her happy presence, and looked forth with beaming eyes on the waving woods and the long expanse of the placid lake, whose dark bosom gave back the light of a thousand stars, and anon she paused to listen to that old familiar sound, the cawing of the rooks amid those great hereditary oaks, the remnants of the vast forest of Drumsheugh, which, in the days of St. David, surrounded the city and its castle on every side.

Meantime, standing under the old velvet canopy, and leaning on her walking-cane, Lady Grizel was listening with a kindling eye and glowing cheek to her ground-baillie, who poured forth a dismal and exaggerated report of the extortions and outrages committed on her tenantry by Capt. Crichton's troop of the Grey Dragoons, who had carried off all the baillie's own grain, "whilk he had laid up for seed; they had taken the best cow, and a notable nowte from the gudeman of Netherdurdie, and nae less than three bonnie servitor lassies frae the farmtoun of Drumdryan; they had toomed every corn-ark, meal-girnel, and beer-barrel in the barony, forby and attour, extorting riding-money three times owre wi' cockit carbines!" It was a lamentable story, and three energetic taps from the Lady Grizel's cane closed the tale.

She, however, found her own mansion scatheless, save where several drawers and lock-fast places had been forced and damaged during the search of Macer Maclutchy and other underlings in authority, for treasonable papers (and more especially loose cash), while in the cellars an empty runlet or two, and empty flasks in such number, that Drouthy, the butler, surveyed them in silence for ten minutes before he began to swear and count them—bore evidence of the strict search which Sergeant Wemyss and his musketeers had prosecuted in the lower regions of the house. The news of their lady's return spread to the Homegrange and neighbouring cottages like wildfire, and, half dressed, the good people came crowding to the mansion testifying by repeated acclamations their joy at her return and restoration to rank; for, save the honoured, envied (and, from that moment, hated) Elsie Elshender, none knew where she had been concealed for the past month. It was generally thought that she had fled to England, to the "Lowlands of Holland," or some other "far awa place." The affection which the Scottish tenantry ever manifested for the old families on whose lands they dwelt, whose banner their ancestors had followed, with whose name and fame, and hope, and happiness, or misfortune, their own were so interwoven, and under the wing of whose protection so many generations of their race had lived and died, was a noble sentiment of the purest love peculiar to the nation. It knit together in a manner which we cannot now conceive, the interests of the highest and the lowest—a remnant of the good old patriarchal times, which strongly marked the character of the people, and, like the endearing ties of clanship, was very different from the feudal tyranny that existed in other lands.

Late though the hour, the old house was crowded with glad faces; casks of ale were set abroach by Mr. Drouthy, and every ruddy cheek became flushed with joy and the brown October beverage; every eye was bright and moist; a buzz of happiness pervaded the spacious mansion, and rang in the dark woods around it. But midnight passed; the morning waxed apace, and now the baillie rang the household bell, as a warning for all to retire, and, making an obeisance, bonnet in hand, he set the example by trotting away on his plump Galloway cob.

Walter Fenton, as he had no excuse (though every wish), to stay, would have retired with the rest; but this Lady Grizel's hospitality would by no means permit; he remained without much pressing, and after the parting or sleeping cup had been passed round, they separated for the night, and Walter, in the same apartment which had witnessed his combat with Captain Napier, lay down on his couch, not to sleep, but to brood over bright and joyous visions of the future that were never to be realised. One moment his heart glowed with unalloyed rapture and unclouded hope; and the next he was half despairing when he compared his humble fortune with that of Lilian. His whole inheritance was military service: of his family he knew nothing but their name. He was a child of war and misfortune; and these, more than he could foresee, were to be his companions through life. He was poor and obscure; while Lilian, with her artless beauty and girlish sweetness of manner, inherited the name and blood of one of the oldest and proudest houses in the lowlands—barons to whom the Prestons of Gourton, the Kincaids of Warriston, and the Toweris of that ilk, were but mushroom citizens; and when he pictured the grey old mansion which sheltered him, so tall, so grim, and aristocratic in aspect and association, and the many acres of fertile field, of grassy pasture, and bosky wood that stretched around it, and weighed in the balance his half-pike......................

Lovers are the most able of all self-tormentors. His horizon became fearfully overcast, and his bright visions seemed to end in smoke, till hope came again to his aid. Poor Walter! he was now fairly in love, and for the first time; his heart was unhackneyed in the ways of the world, and he knew not that the time might come when, with an inward smile, he would wonder that he ever thought so. But between his own anxious fears, the cawing of the rooks and creaking of the turret vanes, grey morning began to brighten the far off east before he slept.

With the first blush of dawn, old Elsie Elshender arrived

with a confused but lamentable history of the disasters and
terrors of the night—of how she had been carried away by
the devil and Major Weir, on a high trotting horse—how
claps of thunder had rung around her cottage, and lightning
consumed it—and that it was not until she was able to repeat
the Lord's Prayer, that they assumed the forms of Lord Clermistonlee and his hellicate butler, Juden Stenton, and thereafter vanished in a flash of fire, leaving Elsie among the
nettles and whins at the avenue gate.

Lady Bruntisfield, who, seated in her arm-chair, cane in
hand, had listened to this wonderful narrative with great
gravity, was at no loss to attribute the enterprise to the proper personages, and though the indignation she felt was very
great, her alarm and uneasiness were greater. She now saw
to what lengths the passion and daring of this rash and profligate suitor might carry him. In consequence of his rank
and power (which the complaints of a hundred old women
could never shake), it was deemed expedient to commit the
affair to silence, but to be on their guard, and in future never
to go abroad without an armed escort—composed of old Syme
the baillie and his sons, or some such stout fellows, with
sword and pistol. Meantime, the burning of the cottage (a
loss which Elsie deeply mourned, for there she had dwelt a
wife and widow for more than forty years), was attributed by
some to the outcast Cameronians who lurked among the whins
of Braid, and by others to certain malicious spunkies, who
then inhabited the morasses to the westward.

At a late hour next morning Walter awoke. It was now
the month of April. The sun shone warmly from a bright
blue sky, streaked with fleecy clouds, that gleamed like
masses of gilded snow, as his radiance streamed aslant between
them. The grass and the budding trees were heavy with
dew, and the merry birds were chirruping and hopping from
branch to branch. as if their little hearts rejoiced at the approach of summer. The ravenous gled and the ominous rook
were soaring on their dark wings into the azure sky, and their
light shadows floated over the still bosom of the loch, scaring
the lonely heron that waded in its waters, till piercing up, and
further up they grew mere specks in the welkin, as they flew
towards the rising sun. The old mansion, with its tall smoky
chimneys and projecting turrets, gleamed cheerily in the red
sunlight that streamed down the long shady avenue, where
myriads of gad-flies wheeled and revolved in the golden beams
as they pierced and shot through the thickening foliage—
thickening and expanding under the warm showers and

warmer sun of April, the balmy month of fresh leaves and opening flowers, of fleecy clouds and bright blue skies.

The beauty of the spring morning, and the passages of the preceding night, made Walter feel joyous and gay. At his toilet he took more than usual care in folding his cravat of point lace, hooking his coat, of tight and spotless buff, with its bars of silver lace, and in twisting his smart moustachios. His thick dark locks escaped from under a bonnet of blue velvet, adorned with the cross of St. Andrew, and a single white feather. His breeches were of red regimental cloth, and his stockings of scarlet silk. A gorget of bright steel, and a long basket-hilted rapier, suspended by a buff shoulder-belt, were his only arms, and he was altogether a handsome and gallant-looking fellow. With a light step, and a lighter heart, he followed the servant, who ushered him into the chamber of dais, where Lilian arose from tinkling on the spinnet, and running towards him with that delightful frankness which made her so charming, bade him good morning.

For the first time since they were children, he found himself alone with her, and the young man felt seriously embarrassed. Lilian seemed so fresh, rosy, and beautiful, the touch of her hand was so gentle and graceful, and the purity of her complexion so dazzling, (exhibiting just enough of red to show perfect health), that she might have passed for the goddess of the season. The richness and neatness of her dress did full justice to her round and charming person; a well busked boddice and stomacher of black taffeta, edged round the fair and budding bosom with a deep tucker of rich lace, and short sleeves frilled with deep falls of the same, revealed her round and spotless arm, from the dimpled elbow to the slender wrist. Her bright glossy hair (Meinie had found her very difficult to please in its arrangement that morning) rolled over her shoulders in massive tresses, perfumed, and tied with a white riband, which drew them back from her delicate temples and beautiful ears. A carcanet of Scottish pearls—those found of old on the rocks of Orrock—encircled her neck, and a long sweeping skirt of black satin gave a stateliness to her air, which with the admirable contour of her nose and short upper lip, by their noble yet piquant expression, completed. Her blue eyes were beaming with delight, and a half blush played about her cheek as she glided towards Walter Fenton.

" My dear old friend," said she, after the usual compliments, " I hope you slept well in this poor house of ours, notwithstanding the ghosts that make it their special business to plague all visitors; but after the turmoil of last night, I can hardly doubt it."

" The redness of your cheek, gentle Lilian, shows me that you must have slumbered soundly, and have quite recovered the terrors of the last few weeks."

" O no, I scarcely slept at all, or did so only to dream I was still at poor Elsie's, hiding in the meal girnel. My head is buzzing still with the clamour of the tenantry (are they not all dear folks?) and old Syme of the hill, with his doleful catalogue of enormities, stoutrief and hamesucken committed by the troopers ; and then poor old Elsie with her mishaps! Ah, good heavens! if it was really the devil that ran off with her. But were not the poor vassals happy last night? O, I could have kissed every one of them; and I am so happy, Mr. Fenton, to find myself under this dear old roof again, that I could dance with glee if you would join me. But you, who were so kind when greater friends shunned and forgot us, you who have endured so much contumely for our sake, how can we ever recompense or thank you?"

" By ceasing to remember it as an obligation. O rather view it as a duty!" said Walter, in a low voice. " Madam Lilian, often ere this, I have by intentional remissness of duty, saved many an unfortunate from the dungeon and the cord. But they were poor recusant Cameronians whose escape was valued as little as their lives."

" As nurse Elsie says, these are indeed fearful times," replied Lilian, laughing ; " but truly, when I remember the kind and gentle little Walter I used to play with long ago, I think you must be much too tender hearted for soldiering."

" Under favour, Lilian," said Walter, feeling his heart flutter as she spoke, " a true soldier is ever compassionate; and the hand that strikes down a foe should be the first to succour and protect him when fallen. I am too well aware that in these days of religious persecution and political misrule, the Scottish soldier is often, too often indeed, the instrument——"

" Hush, friend Walter! art not afraid I will betray thee? Have you forgotten that horrid vault, the Tolbooth, and its grim gudeman?"

" Ah, the rascally clown, I have a crow to pluck with him yet; but I was only about to say, that in these days of ours——"

" Ah, you are about to speak treason again," said she, playfully. " I mean to be very loyal, and must not permit you, although there are none here who would betray you, unless it be the old corbies that croak on the chimney head. But come with me, and I will show you their nests in some strange places, I promise you: and I have flowers to visit, and my pigeons too, poor pets! I once thought never to behold them again. Come, Mr. Fenton, your hand; how beautiful the morning is!"

Charmed with her vivacity, Walter became every moment more delighted with Lilian Napier. With a very cavalier-like air which he had acquired among his Parisian comrades of the musketeers, who had returned from the French to the Scottish service only ten years before, he hastened to give her his ungloved hand, and they sallied forth into the garden, where the deep rows of Dutch boxwood that edged the walks, the leaden statues of satyrs, swains, and shepherdesses, the gravelled terraces and flights of steps, the old mossy sun and moon dial, and the fantastic arbours, were all in admirable keeping with the quaint old manor house that towered above them. Old John Leekie, the gardener, clad in his coarse sky-blue coat, and long ribbed galligaskins, reverently doffed his broad bonnet, and bowed his lyart head, as his young mistress passed, and patting his shoulder with her hand, bade him a "good morning." The old man's eye brightened as he surveyed the garb and bearing of Walter Fenton, and continued his occupation of hoeing up the early kail, with a sigh;

" For he thought of the days that were long since by,
    When his limbs were strong, and his courage was high : "—

and when he rode in the iron squadrons of the loyal Hamilton and stern Leslie.

"Gentle Lilian," said Walter, colouring deeply as he gazed on the fine old mansion, the walls of which were quite en-crusted with coats armorial and quaint legends, "it is when surveying so noble a dwelling as this that I feel most bitterly how hardly fortune has dealt with me."

"Tush, friend! hast never got the better of those old glooms and fancies yet? Read the motto over yonder window; ah! 'tis my dressing-room that," said the lively girl, pointing to a distich in Saxon characters, which was one of the many that adorned the edifice.

" Quhen Adam delved and Eve spanne,
    Quhair war a' the gentlis than ? "

"It is very true; but I, who am a soldier, cannot think of those things like a philosopher."

"Then do not think of them at all."

"How numerous are the coats and quarterings here; there is the eagle of the Ramsays, the unicorns of the Prestons, and the saltier of Napier."

"But, Mr. Walter, do you know that aunt Grizel asserts there is an ancient prophecy which says, that like the Scottish crown, the fortune of our house came with a lass, and will go with oue."

"Indeed!" rejoined Walter, considerably interested, "its fortune?"

"That is—you must understand—you know that," and here poor Lilian became seriously embarrassed, "that it came to the Napiers by marriage from the Wrytes, and by marriage it will go to others."

Walter's heart fluttered; he was about to say something, but the words died on his lips, and there ensued a silence of some minutes; Lilian, who sometimes became very reserved, being abashed by what she had said, and Walter stupidly pondering over it. Lilian was the first to speak.

"See you that old corbie on the branch of the dule tree, that horrid branch, all notched by the ropes of old executions?"

"He with the bald head now watching us?"

"The same: what think you aunt Grizel says? He saw my great grandsire and his train in all their harness, ride down the avenue when they marched with brave King James to Flodden."

"By that reckoning he must be—let me see—one hundred and seventy-five years old."

"O there are some older than that hereabouts; but come to the dovecot, and there we shall see birds of brighter plumes and better augury than these gloomy corbies."

As they approached the dovecot, a round edifice vaulted and domed with stone in the most ancient Scottish fashion, a tame pigeon winged its way from amid the scores that clustered on the roof, and after fluttering for a time over Lilian's head, alighted on her shoulder and nestled in her neck, rubbing its smooth and glossy head against her soft cheek, and even permitting Walter to stroke its shining pinions, which in the sunlight varied alternately from green to purple, and from purple to red and gold. On each leg it had a silver varvel with Lilian's cipher on it. As Walter caressed the beautiful bird, his hand often touched the soft cheek and softer tresses of the happy and thoughtless girl.

"How properly this gentle emblem of innocence and happiness greets you as its mistress."

"And am I not its proper mistress?" asked Lilian artlessly. "It is the bird of peace, too."

"And love—so that it well becomes the hand of beauty."

"Ah, you are beginning to be waggish now. It is just so that your friend Douglas of Finland—he with the flaunting feathers—addresses my gay gossip, Annie Laurie. You know Annie? She is considered the first beauty in the Lothians, and 'tis said (but that is a great secret, and you must not say I said so) that the young lairds of Craigdarroch and Finland are going to fight a solemn duel about her. She is much taller than me."

"Then she is too tall for my taste."

"Oh, but I am quite little ; you used to call me little Madam Lily once. But her hair is the most beautiful brown."

"I prefer," said Walter, taking up one of Lilian's heavy tresses, "I prefer the colour that approaches to gold."

"And her eyes are just like mine."

"They must be beautiful indeed."

"Ha, ha!" laughed the merry girl : "harkee, Mr. Fenton, did I not know positively to the contrary, I would think you had been in France."

"Wherefore, Madam?"

"Because," said she, roguishly, with half-closed eyes, "you twist all one's speeches into compliments so readily and bluntly, and so quite unlike our douce Scots' gallants (who always let slip the opportunity while they are making up their minds), that you quite remind me of Monsieur Minuette, who came here with the duke of York. Ah, you remember him, with his long sword—how like a grasshopper on a pin he looked ; and he tried stoutly with his frightful rigadoon and the Bretagne, to put our good old Scottish dances into the shade, and so out of fashion. And yet Aunt Grizel says that, to see the Lady Anne (she that is now princess of Denmark), so tall and stately, and Claverhouse, so graceful and courtly, dancing the Italian vault-step, enraptured everybody. O, it was quite a sight. But there jangles the housebell, and now let us hie to breakfast."

Once more she placed her hand in Walter's, and they returned to the chamber of dais, where Lady Bruntisfield, no longer disguised in the humble attire of a cottar, but in all her pristine splendour of perfumed brocade, and starched magnificence of point lace and puffed locks frizzled up like a tower on her stately head, welcomed Walter with a courtesy of King Charles the First's days, and kissed her grandniece.

After a long and solemn grace, the repast began. The most substantial breakfast of these degenerate days would dwindle into insignificance when compared with that which loaded the long oaken table of Bruntisfield House. In the centre smoked a vast urn of coffee, surrounded by diminutive cups of dark-blue china, flanked on the right by a side of mutton roasted, on the left by a gigantic capon ; a dish of wild ducks balanced another of trout, both being furnished by the adjacent loch ; broiled haddocks, pickled salmon, kippered

aerrings, pyramids of eggs, and piles of oat and barley-cakes;
wheaten loaves and crystal cups of honey were also there;
but chief above all towered a vast tankard of spiced ale;
beside it stood a long-necked bottle of strong waters to whet
the appetite, lest through the eyes it should fairly become
satisfied by the mere sight of so many edibles.

At the lower end of the board, the servants were accommodated with bickers and cogues of porridge and milk, which
they supped with cutty-spoons of black horn, while two
mighty trenchers of polished pewter held the magazines from
which they drew their supplies. The custom of domestics
sitting at the same table with their superiors was then almost
obsolete; but Lady Grizel, whose memories and prejudices
went back to the days of King James VI., still retained the
ancient fashion, and consequently all her household sat down
with her, save two old serving-men in green livery, with her
crest on their sleeves : these were in attendance each as an
écuyer tranchant, or cutting squire. On the party being
joined by the ground-baillie, Syme of the Greenhill, who, in
consequence of his being a bonnet-laird, was permitted to sit
above the salt, the important business of making breakfast
proceeded with all the gravity and attention such a noble
display deserved. Cheerful and good-humoured, though
punctilious to excess, like every noble matron of her time,
Lady Grizel Napier did the honours of the feast with that
peculiar grace which makes a guest feel so much at home.
She never once recurred to late events, but conversed affably
on the topics of the day, like Lilian, investing little trifles
with an air of interest that made them quite new and charming
to Walter; for though aged and failing fast, she still possessed that art so agreeable in a well-bred woman, that even
when she talked nonsense, one could scarcely have thought
it so; and certainly, when witches, spells, and ghosts were
the theme, the wise and gentle King James himself was
nothing to her in credulity.

"Symon, I hope ye obeyed my injunctions to the letter, in
the affair o' your bairn's hooping-cough," said the old lady,
who took an active hand in all the family matters of her
vassalage.

"Faith did I, my lady, but found the wee thing no' a
hair the better of it. It is an unco trouble, the cough, but
Lucky Elshender says, gif I put my forefinger down the
bairn's throat for fifteen minutes, it will never cough mair."

"I'll warrant it o' that," said the old lady, scornfully;
but how dare she prescribe for any bairn on the barony

without consulting me? I'll gang o'er in the gloaming and
see about it."

" Mony thanks to your ladyship."

An air or two on the virginals, and Lady Anne Bothwell's
touching *Lament*, performed at full length by Lilian in her
sweetest manner, concluded the visit, and Walter reluctantly
prepared to retire. Lady Bruntisfield and Lilian departed in
their sedans with two armed servants before and two behind
them, to pay a most ceremonious visit of thanks to Lord
Dunbarton and his beautiful countess, and Fenton, after accompanying them to the arch of the Bristo Port, left them to
the care of their retinue, and receiving a warm invitation to
visit them soon again, pursued his way in a maze of stirring
thoughts through the steep wynds, narrow closes, and
crowded streets of the city to his sombre quarters in the
Canongate.

CHAPTER XIX.

THE OLD SCOTTISH SERVICE.

The soul which ne'er hath felt a genial ray
Glow to the drum's long roll or trumpet's bray ;
Start to the bugle's distant blast, and hail
Its buxom greetings, on the morning gale—
Such the muse courts not.
LORD GRENVILLE

ON the return of Walter Fenton to the White-horse Cellar,
Douglas, who was lounging on the broad flight of steps in
front of the edifice, and chatting gaily with a buxom damsel
of the establishment, informed him that Holsterlee of the
Life Guards had just been there, saying that the earl of
Dunbarton and the lords of the privy council required his
attendance at the lower chamber—immediate attendance.

His mind became troubled at this information : though unconscious of having done anything new to incur displeasure, it
was with considerable anxiety he bent his steps to the precincts
of that dreaded tribunal.

The lairds of Craigdarroch and Holsterlee (or as the latter
was commonly called, Jack Holster), two of Claverhouse's
cavalier troopers lounged in the antechamber smoking their
Dutch pipes, while the yeomen of the Scottish guard in their
blue bonnets and scarlet doublets, armed with long daggers
and gilt partisans, thronged the parliament close and outer
lobby of the house.

Their presence in some degree lessened his anxiety, as the absence of the military police of the city, and the viler menials of the law, announced that matters of state, and not of inquisitorial persecution were before that powerful and extraordinary conclave.   He waited long in the well-known antechamber, whose features brought back a host of gloomy thoughts, amid which his mind wandered continually to the house of Bruntisfield ; but he endeavoured to mingle in the gay conversation of the two guardsmen, who talked nonsense as glibly and laughed as loudly as if they had been in Hugh Blair's tavern on the opposite side of the square, instead of being within earshot of those whose names were a terror to the land.   After all that was of importance to the state had been discussed and dismissed, Walter, on being summoned by the drawling and hated voice of Maclutchy found himself before the same bench of haughty councillors he had confronted a few weeks before ; but now its aspect was different; the rays of the meridian sun streamed cheerfully into their dusky place of meeting, and hangings which appeared sable before were now seen to be of crimson velvet, fringed and tasselled with gold, gilded chairs, and the throne surmounted by the royal arms with the gallant lion *in defence ;* the rich and varied dresses of the lords, massively laced and jewelled with precious stones, embroidered belts, and embossed sword-hilts, were all sparkling in the several flakes of light that gushed between the strong stanchells of the ancient windows into the gloomy and vaulted room.

The stern basilisk eye of Clermistonlee alone was fixed on Walter as before.

The lord high treasurer, the chancellor, and the sleepy Mersington, withdrew as our hero entered.   Near the head of the table stood the earl of Dunbarton in his rich military dress of scarlet, with the cuffs slashed and buttoned up to reveal the lawn sleeves below ; his gallant breast was sheathed in a corslet of polished steel, beautifully inlaid with gold, and over it fell his lace cravat and the sable curls of his heavy peruke.   His badge as commander-in-chief of the forces, an ivory baton with silver thistles twined round it, was in one hand ; the other rested on his plumed head piece.   The magnificence of his attire formed a strong contrast to that of the stern Dalyel, who wore a plain suit of black armour like that of a cuirassier of Charles I., but rusted by blood and perspiration, and defaced by sword cuts and musket balls, it was a panoply with which his long silvery beard and iron but dignified face corresponded well.   Making a half military obeisance to these lords of council, Walter, felt not a little reassured by the presence of his patron the earl and Sir Thomas Dalyel.

"Mr. Fenton," said the former, "we have much pleasure in presenting you with that to which your merits so much entitle you—a pair of colours in my ancient regiment of Royal Scots, vacant by the death of young Toweris of that ilk, who has been slain in a late camisadoe in the north, with some broken rascals of the Clan-Donald. You will therefore hear the king's commission read over, and thereafter sign your oath of fealty to us without delay, as the day is wearing apace." Taking up a small piece of parchment to which appeared the great seal of Scotland, the signatures of the king and secretary of state, and his (Dunbarton's) own seal with the four quarters of Douglas, the earl read the following, which we give verbatim :—

"I George, earl of Dunbarton, lord of Douglas, knight, baronet, and knight of the Thistle, lieutenant-general, and commander-in-chief of the Scottish forces, by virtue of the power and authority given to me by his most sacred majesty James VII., do hereby constitute you, Walter Fenton, gentleman, an ensign of the royall regiment of ffoote in that companie wheroff his honor the laird of Drumquhazel, chevalier of St. Michael, is captain. You are therefore to obey such orders as you may receive from his majesty and your superiors, as you expect to be obeyed by your soldiers according to the rules and discipline of war.

"Given under my hand and seal at the Bristo Port.

"DUNBARTON."

Though astonished at all this unusual formality, Walter bowed in pleased and grateful silence, and then he heard the stern voice of Major-General Dalyel.

"Maister Fenton, you will please to repeat after me, and sign your oath of fealty to this council and the three estates of the realm."

"Oath of fealty, Sir Thomas?" reiterated Walter, equally surprised and offended at this new proposal, which accompanied the long-wished-for gift. "My lords, though deeply grateful for this mark of your favour, I deplore that you should suspect me——"

"Sir," interrupted Lord Clermistonlee, hastily and haughtily, "at *present* we suspect you of nothing ; but the corruption of these times, when the very air seems infected with treason and disloyalty, have made an oath of fealty necessary from this time forth."

"To the king?"

"No; to the officers of state and the parliament of Scot

land; and woe unto those who shall break it. An act of council previous to one of the House, made it law an hour ago. Art satisfied, sirrah?"

"My lords, I like it not, for it implies a suspicion a man of spirit cannot thole," replied Walter, in an under tone, as he advanced to the table; and Clermistonlee, seized by a sudden fit of passion, was about to pour forth some of his furious and abusive ebullitions, when Dunbarton said mildly:

"Walter, an edict of council hath (as his lordship said) made this a law, which will be more fully confirmed by the three estates. Mr. Secretary, read aloud the oath of fealty, and the young gentleman will sign it."

"By my beard, he had better, or prepare for his auld quarters again," added Dalyel, sharply, striking his heavy toledo on the floor.

Thus urged, Walter heard the oath of allegiance, which the approaching crisis in the affairs of those factions that then rent both Scotland and England, rendered necessary for the security of the Government, promising "faithfully to demean himself to the estates of Scotland presently met;" and affixed his name thereto, little foreseeing how dear that oath was yet to cost him, and how unfortunate in its influence it was at a future time to prove to his fortunes. As if *he* foresaw it, a dark smile lit the sinister eyes of Clermistonlee; it was a peculiar scowl of deep and hidden meaning; and though Walter soon forgot it at the time, he remembered it in after years when the cold hand of misfortune was crushing him to the dust.

"I trust, young birkie," said the fierce Dalyel, with a keen glance, "that you will never again waver in the execution of your duty or military *devoir*; but be staunch as a red Cossack, and ever ready to do his majesty gude and leal service (*whatever be his creed*) against all false rebels and damned psalm-singers, whilk are the same."

"I will gage my honour for him," said Dunbarton.

"How readily my lord defends his loon," whispered Clermistonlee to Dalyel, but not so low as to be unheard; and the earl's cheek flushed—his brows knit; but he made no reply, save waving his hand to Walter, who withdrew.

The warm noonday sun streamed brightly down the High street; the musical bells of Saint Giles jangled merrily in the pure breeze that swept through the stone-arched spire; and Walter Fenton never felt so happy and light of heart as when he issued from the sombre Parliament-close into the bustle of that grand thoroughfare; and giving full reins to his fancy, allowed it to career into regions fraught with the most brilliant visions of the future—fame, fortune, happiness—all were there in glowing colours, but were—never to be realized.

Poor Walter! That hour laid the foundation of the airy palace of love, glory, and renown, which every ardent young man builds unto himself, and which indeed is the only fabric that costs nothing but the bitter achings of a seared and disappointed heart. To Walter it was the dawn of joy; his foot, he thought, was now firmly planted on the first step of the dangerous ladder of honour; and with his thoughts divided between war, ambition, and Lilian Napier, and with his heart glowing with exultation, he pulled forth the little scrap of parchment to re-examine it again and again, as he skipped down the crowded street, and a severe concussion against a tower of the Netherbow first roused him from his dreams. He was in excellent humour with himself, pleased with everybody, and enraptured with the lords of council, whose orders he was ready to obey in everything, whether they were to storm a tower or fire a clachan, march to England, or duck an "auld wife" in the North Loch.

"My stars are propitious to me to-day," said he aloud, as he half danced down the street towards the White Horse cellar. "O, may heaven give me but opportunities to win a name; and if the most unflinching perseverance, the most spotless loyalty, and a headlong valour, such as not even Claver'se can surpass, will bring me honour and renown, I feel that I *shall win them*. O, bravo for the roll of the drum! the rush of the charging horse! and the ranks of pikemen shoulder to shoulder! I am one of the Guards of St. Louis— King James's Scottish musketeers—the old *Diehards* of Dunbarton."

CHAPTER XX.

LES GARDES ECOSSAIS.

Thus shall your country's annals boast your corps,
  And, glorious thought! in times and ages hence,
Some valiant chief to stimulate the more,
  And urge his troops, the battle in suspense,
Shall hold your bright example to their view.
                                  RUDDIMAUN'S MAG.

LOUIS, surnamed the Saint, king of France, having taken the cross, sailed with a splendid retinue of knights, nobles, and soldiers bent on the delivery of Jerusalem from the profanation of the Moslem; and, landing in the East, laid siege to Damietta (in Lower Egypt), which he triumphantly wouby storm.   But, after enduring innumerable hardships and disasters by the sword, and by pestilence from the fetid waters of the marshy Nile and the lake of Menzaleh, he was overthrown in battle at Mansoura, and made captive by the soldan.

This was about the year 1254, when Alexander III. was king of Scotland.

In these eastern wars, St. Louis was twice saved from death by the valour of a small band of auxiliary Scots crusaders, commanded by the earls of March and Dunbar, Walter Stewart, lord of Dundonald, and Sir David Lindsay of Glenesk.   Those brave adventurers had the good fortune to rescue the French monarch, first from the scimitars of the followers of the king of the Arsacides, a Mahommedan despot ; and afterwards from the emissaries of the comtesse de la Marche. Our good King Alexander, sent ambassadors to congratulate St. Louis on his deliverance from these double perils ; and on his return from this first crusade, the two monarchs agreed that, in remembrance of these deeds of fidelity and valour, there should remain in France, in all time coming, " a standing company or guard of Scotsmen recommended by their own sovereign," and who should in future form the *garde-du-corps* of the most Christian king.

Such was the origin of the bravest body-guard that Europe ever saw, though our ancient historians are fond of dating its formation from the days of Charlemagne and Gregory the Great of Scotland.

The guard thus established by St. Louis marched with him to his second crusade, in the year 1270.   It was then led by the earls of Carrick and Athole, Sir John Stuart, Sir William Gordon, and other brave knights, most of whom perished with Louis of a deadly pestilence before the walls of Tunis, and under the towers of Abu Zaccheria.

This noble band of Scottish archers remained constantly in France, and were the only military corps in that country, until King Charles VII. added a few French companies to increase his guards, still giving the Scots their old pre-eminence and post of honour next the royal person.   Their leader was styled *premier capitaine* of the guards, and as such took precedence of all military officers in France.   When the French sovereign was anointed, he stood beside him ; and when the ceremony was over, obtained the royal robes, with all their embroidery and jewels, as his perquisite.   When a city was to be stormed, the Scottish archers led the way ; when it surrendered, the keys were received by their captain from the hands of the king.

Twenty-five of them, "in testimony of their unspotted fidelity," wore over their magnificent armour white hoquetons of a peculiar fashion, richly laced and embossed with silver. Six of them in rotation were ever beside the royal person—by night as well as by day—at the reception of foreign ambassadors—in the secret debates of the cabinet—in the rejoicings of the tournament—the revels of the banquet—the solemnities of the church, and the glories of the battle-field. These Scottish hearts formed a zone around the monarchs of France ; and.at the close of the scene, the chosen twenty-five had the privelege of bearing the royal remains to the regal sepulchre of St. Denis.

It would require volumes, instead of a chapter, to recount all the honours paid to the Scottish guard, and the glory acquired by them in the wars of five centuries.

Led by Alexander earl of Buchan, great constable of France, they performed good service in that great battle at Banje-en-Anjou, where the English were completely routed ; and at Verneuil, where Buchan died sword in hand, like a brave knight, and covered with renown,—at the same moment that Swinton, the gallant laird of Dalswinton, slew the boasting Clarence with one thrust of his border-spear.

In 1570 the guard consisted of a hundred cuirassiers, or *hommes-des-armes*, a hundred archers of the corps, and twenty-five "keepers of the king's body,"—all Scottish gentlemen of noble descent and coat-armour. They saved the life of the tyrant Louis XI. at Liege ; and at Pavia fought around the gallant Francis in a circle until *four* only were left alive,—and then, but not till *then*, the king fell into the hands of the foe. In gratitude for their long-tried faith and unmatched valour, they were vested with "all the honour and confidence the king of France could bestow on his nearest and dearest friends ; " and thus, in a little band of Scottish archers, originated the fashion of standing armies, and the nucleus of the great permanent forces of France.

" By this means," says an old Jacobite author, " our gentry were at once taught the rules of civility and art of war and we were possessed of an inexhaustible stock of brave officers, fit to discipline and to command our armies at home, and ever sure to keep up that respect which was deservedly paid to the Scots' name and nation abroad."

As Sir James Hepburn's regiment of pikemen they returned to Scotland in 1633, being sent over by Louis XIII. to attend the coronation of Charles I. at Edinburgh. On the commencement of the great and disastrous civil war eight years after, they loyally adhered to the king, and were then by the

cavalier army first styled the *Royal Scots.* On the reverse
of Charles's fortune and subversion of all order, they went
back to France ; and under Louis of Bourbon, duc d'Enghien,
shared in all the dangers and glories of that campaign on the
frontiers of Flanders, so famous for ending in the utter
destruction of the Spanish host, the death of the brave Condé
de Fuentes, the fall of Thionville, Philipsburg, Mentz,
Worms, and Oppenheim, till the waters of the Rhine reflected the flash of their armour ; and there fell the veteran
Hepburn, with his helmet on his brow, and the flag of
St. Andrew over him.

Returning in 1678, they re-entered the Scottish army as
the earl of Dunbarton's foot ; and eight years after served
against the ill-fated Monmouth, and suffered severely, being
attacked at Sedgemoor by his cavalry in the night, their position being discerned through the darkness by the glow of their
lighted matches.

At the Union in 1707, on the incorporation of the forces
as the British establishment—and when Scottish blood and
Scottish treasure were more than ever required to further the
grasping aims and useless wars of that age—the Royals, in
consequence of their high standing in arms and venerable
antiquity, were numbered as the *First,* or Royal Scots Regiment of Foot,—a title they have since maintained with
honour, and on a hundred fields have upborne victoriously
the same silver cross which the brave archers of Athole and
the spearmen of Buchan unfurled so gloriously on the plains
of Anjou, and at Verneuil, on the banks of the Aure.

Proud of themselves and of the honours their predecessors
had sustained untarnished in so many foreign battles, Dunbarton's musketeers felt an *esprit de corps,* to which at that
time few other military bands were entitled ; and it was with
a bosom glowing with the highest sentiments of this description, that Walter Fenton for the first time clasped on the
silver gorget and plumed headpiece of his junior rank, and
found himself really a standard-bearer of a regiment
deemed the first in Europe, and whose boasted antiquity had
become a jocular proverb, obtaining for it the name of Pontius Pilate's guard.

When next he paid his *devoirs* at the residence of the
Napiers, Lilian fairly blushed with pleasure to see him looking so gallant and handsome ; for, to a young girl's eye, a
nodding plume, a golden scarf, and jewelled rapier, were
considerable additions to an exterior otherwise extremely
prepossessing.

The paleness resulting from his confinement had quite

passed away; his olive cheek was suffused with the rich, warm glow of health; while buoyant spirits, new hopes, and high aspirations, lent a lustre to his eye and a grace to his actions, which was not visible before, when he felt himself to be the mere object of patronage and dependence—the poor private gentleman, with a brass-hilted whinger and corslet of black iron.

Again and again he visited the old turretted house on the Burghmuir, and drank deeper draughts of that intoxicating passion which, from its hopelessness, he dared hardly acknowledge to himself. Every day he became more and more in love, and felt that it would be impossible (with all his awe of Lady Grizel's fardingale and cane) to keep it long a secret from the being who inspired it.

CHAPTER XXI.

THE GLOVE.

Distrust me not, but unreserved disclose
The anxious thought that in thy bosom glows;
To impart our griefs is apt to mitigate,
And social sorrows blunt the darts of fate.
EVENING, a Poem.

A MONTH had passed away, and the summer came; it was a month of unalloyed happiness to Walter Fenton, who, at the somewhat solitary mansion of Bruntisfield, was a frequent and always a welcome guest; and there he spent every moment he could spare from his military duties, which chiefly consisted of being on guard at the Palace porch or privy council chamber, a review on Leith Links, before old Sir Thomas, of Binns, practising King James's new mode of exercise, by flam of drum, or "worrying" various unhappy old women to say "God save the king," pronounce the rising at Bothwell a rebellion, Archbishop Sharpe a martyr, and Peden an impostor.

Notwithstanding the early season of the year, the game in the woods had particularly taken his fancy; so had the herons, eels, teals, and trout of the loch; and rabbit-warrens, and foxes that lurked among the great quarries; and with Finland he generally contrived to finish the day's loitering at the hall fire, where Lady Grizel, with the birr of her silver-mounted wheel, performed a burden to the long and monotonous tales she inflicted, of the splendours of King Charles's court, the terrors of the wars of Montrose, and the spells and charms of sorcerers and witches — warnings, ghosts, and heaven knows what more; but all of which proved much more interesting to her hearers in that age, than it could to my readers in this.

Walter loved better to hear the wiry tinkling of Lilian's cittern or virginals, after the old lady had fallen fast asleep, and then Annie Laurie joined her clear merry voice to the deeper notes of Douglas; and they were ever a happy evening party when the pages of "Cassandra," or "The Banished Virgin," and other romantic folios of the day—luxury, music, and conversation, free and untrammelled as any lover could wish—made the hours fleet past on silken wings. Ever joyous and ever gay, it was a circle from which Walter departed with regret, and counted one by one the long and weary hours until he found himself there again.

Notwithstanding her violent prejudice against the obscurity of his birth, Lady Grizel warmly admired the young man for the frankness and courage he displayed, his general high bearing, and above all, for a certain strong resemblance which she averred he bore to her youngest son, Sir Archibald Napier, who was slain in the unfortunate battle of Inverkeithing, when Cromwell forced the passage of the Forth.

Lucky it was for Walter that this strong idea took possession of her mind. From that time forward she loved to see him constantly, to watch his actions and features, and to listen to the tones of his voice, until, to her moistened and aged eyes, the very image of her youngest and best-beloved son seemed to be conjured up before her; and so strong became her feelings when this fancy possessed her, that it would have been a relief to have fallen upon his neck and kissed him.

To her it was a living dream of other days—a dream that called back sorrow and joy, and a thousand tender memories from the mists that envelope the past; and Walter was often surprised to find her eyes full of tears when, after a long pause, she addressed him. Perhaps for nothing but this tender and mysterious source of interest, would she have permitted such an intimacy to spring up between the nameless soldier and Lilian, the last hope of her race, the heiress of the honours and possessions of the old barons of Bruntisfield and the Wrytes. But her mind was now becoming enfeebled by age, and prudence struggled in vain with her powerful fancies.

Lilian (but this is a secret known only to ourselves and her gossip Annie), admired young Fenton too, though with ideas widely differing from those of her grandaunt, because he was a very handsome lad, with a cavalier air, and locks curling

over a white and haughty brow; keen dark eyes, that were
ever full of fire, but became soft and chastened when he
looked on her. She soon deemed that the curl of his lip
showed a—

"Spirit proud and prompt to ire;"

but she never observed his moustachioed mouth without thinking what a very handsome one it was. His soft mellow voice
was deep in its tones, and she loved to listen to his words till
her young heart seemed to vibrate when he spoke. He was
generally subdued rather than melancholy in manner; but the
depth of his own thoughts imparted to all he said an interest,
that could not fail to attract a girl of Lilian's gentle disposition.

But his enthusiasm and his vehemence startled her at
times, when he spoke of the soldiers of Dunbarton, and of the
glory he hoped to win beneath those banners which Turenne
and the great Condé saw ever in the van of battle. Gratitude,
too, had no small share in her sentiments towards him, when,
reflecting on the risk he had so generously run to save her
dearest and (except one) her only relative from a humiliating
examination by the imperious privy council; and she shuddered to think how narrowly he had escaped the extremity of
their wrath; for every instrument of torture was then judi-
cially used at the pleasure and caprice of the judicial
authorities.

A month, we have said, had passed away: in that brief
time a great change had gradually stolen over the hearts of
Walter and Lilian Napier. No declaration of love had been
made on his part, and there had been no acceptance on hers;
but they were on the footing of lovers: secret and sincere,
each had only acknowledged the passion to themselves: to her
he had never whispered a word of the love that now animated
every thought and action; but she was not ignorant of his
affection, which a thousand little tendernesses revealed—and
love will beget love in others.

They both felt it, or at least thought so.

Though his dark eyes might become brighter or more languid, his voice more insinuating, and his manner more graceful and gentle, when he addressed her, never had he assumed
courage sufficient to reveal the secret thought that with each
succeeding interview was daily and hourly becoming more
and more a part of his existence. Often he longed to be an
earl, a lord, or even a laird like Finland, that then he might
throw himself and his fortune at her feet, and declare the
depth of his passion in those burning expressions, that

thousand times trembled on his lips, and were there chained
by diffidence and poverty.

He was very timid, too: what true lover is not?

A circumstance soon occurred, which, however trivial in
itself, was mighty in its effect on our two young friends; and,
by opening up the secret fountain of hope and pleasure,
altered equally the aspect of their friendship and the even
tenor of their way.

Lilian was fair and beautiful indeed; and (though not one
of those magnificent beings that exist only in the brains of
romancers), when gifted with all the mystic charms and
romantic beauty, with which the glowing fancy of the lover
ever invests his mistress, she became in Walter's imagination
something more angelic and enchanting than he had previously
conceived to exist; for a lover sees everything through the
medium of beauty and delight.

Notwithstanding the real charms of her mind and person,
she possessed a greater and more lasting source of attraction,
in a graceful sweetness of manner which cannot be described.
With a voice that was ever "low and sweet," and with all her
girlish frankness and openness of character, she could at times
assume a womanly firmness and high decision of manner,
which every Scottish maid and matron had need to possess in
those days of stout hearts and hard blows, when brawls and
conflicts were of hourly occurrence, as no man ever went
abroad unarmed; and the upper classes, by never permitting
an insult to pass unpunished, became as much accustomed to
the use of the sword and dagger as their plodding descendants
to handling the peaceful quill and useful umbrella.

On a bright evening in May, when the sun was sinking
behind the wooded ridge of the dark Corstorphine hills, and
when the shadows of the turrets of Bruntisfield and its thick
umbrageous oaks were thrown far across the azure loch, where
the long-legged herons were wading in search of the trout and
perch, where the coot fluttered, and the snow-white swan
spread its soft plumage to the balmy western wind, Walter
accompanied Lilian Napier and her fair friend, Annie Laurie,
in a ramble by the margin of the beautiful sheet of water, the
green and sloping banks of which were enamelled by summer
flowers.

The purple heath-bell, bowers of the blooming hawthorn,
the bright yellow broom, and a profusion of wild rose-trees,
loaded the air with perfume; for everything was arrayed in
the greenness, the sunlight, the purity, the glory of summer,
and the thick dark oaks of Drumsheugh towered up as darkly
and as richly, as when the sainted King David and his bold

thanes hunted the snow-white bull and bristly boar beneath their sombre shadows.

The charms of the beautiful Annie Laurie live yet in Scottish song, though the name and memory of the gallant lover whose muse embalmed them is all but forgotten.

Tall and fair, with a face of the most perfect loveliness, she had eyes of the darkest blue, shaded by long black lashes, cheeks tinged with red like a peach by the morning sun, and bright auburn hair rolling in heavy curls over a slender and delicate neck, imparting a graceful negligence to the dignity of her fine figure. Her whole features possessed a matchless expression of sweetness and vivacity; her nose was the slightest approach to aquiline ; her lips were short and full; her profile eminently noble. A broad beaver hat, tied with coquettish ease, and adorned by one long ostrich feather drooping over her right shoulder, formed her head-gear; while a dress of light-blue silk, with the sleeves puffed and slashed with white satin, and white gloves of Blois, fastened by gold bracelets, formed part of her attire. She carried a pretty heavy riding-switch, which completed the jaunty, piquant, and saucy character of her air and beauty.

The young ladies were walking together, and Lilian hung on the arm of her taller friend ; while her cavalier was alternately by the side of each.

Though loving Lilian, he conversed quite as much—perhaps more—with her gay companion, whose prattle and laughter were incessant ; for Annie invariably made it a rule to talk nonsense when nothing better occurred to her. Walter treated both with the utmost tenderness, but Lilian with the greatest respect ; he now felt truly what Finland had often averred, "that the girl one loves is greater than an empress."

"And so, Mr Fenton," said Annie, continuing her incessant raillery, "is it true that a party of Dunbarton's braves were out at the House of Linn yesterday, dragooning the poor cottars to pray for King James, to ban the Covenant, and all that?"

"It is but too true, I fear. Indeed I was on that duty, and at the Richardson's barony of Cramond, too."

"Oh, such valour!—to terrify women and children, and drive the poor millers and fishers away; to stop the mills, break the dams, spoil the nets, and sink the boats. Fie upon you! Don't come near me, sir. Alas for the warriors of the great Condé, how sadly they are degenerating! Oh, Mr. Fenton, we positively blush for you; do we not, gossip Lilian?"

"Fair Annie, you are very severe upon me. If I was on

M

such a duty, could I help it? A soldier must hear and obey."

"Even to ducking his mother, I suppose. Go to—I have no patience with such work! And was it by Finland's orders that all the old cummers of Cramond were sent swimming down the river tied to chairs and cutty-stools?"

"But they were very old, and ugly, too; besides the stream was very shallow. And as they were all caught in the act of singing a psalm in the wood of Dalmenie, what else could we do but duck them well for their contumacy? It was rare fun, I assure you, and Finland nearly burst his corslet with laughing; but I assure you, ladies, we only ducked the *old* women of the village."

"Aye, aye; the young would not get off scatheless, I fear," replied Annie, giving him a switch with her riding-rod; "I know soldiers of old. But, marry, come up! our Teviotdale lads would have given you a hot reception had you come among them with such hostile intentions."

"Then the worse would be their fare," said Walter, in a tone of pique. "When ordered by our superiors to *test* the people——"

"Heigh-day! Now, good Mr. Fenton, suppose you were commanded to *test* us in that rough fashion, because we would not pronounce Sharp a martyr and the Covenant a bond of rebellion, and said just whatever you wished of us; what then? For, in sooth, we would say none of those things; would we, gossip Lilian?"

"But then we should each be sent voyaging down the loch on a cutty-stool," said Lilian, joining her friend in a loud burst of merriment.

"On my honour, ladies," said Walter, very seriously, "these orders of council refer only to the rascal multitude. Who ever heard of a lady of rank being treated like a cottar-wife?"

"High and low share alike the vengeance of the council, and Argyle lost his head for some such bubble. I cannot forget how, in the January of '82, six years ago (faith, I am getting quite an old spinster!), Claver'se and his troop took a fancy to quarter themselves at our house of Maxwelton, because my youngest sister had been christened by that poor man Ichabod Bummel, who carries misfortune wherever he shows his long nose. The cavalier troopers ate and drank up all they could lay hands on, in cellar, buttery, and barn-yard; and I was terrified to death by the clank of their jack-boots and long rapiers, as they laughed and swore, and pursued the servants up one stair and down another. But Claver'se drew his chair in by the hall-fire, and taking me upon his knee, looked on me so kindly with his great black eyes, that I forgot the horror my mother's tales of him had inspired me with; and he kissed me twice, saying I would be the bonniest lass in all Nithsdale—and has it not come true? But Colonel Grahame is so ferocious——"

"Oh, hush, Annie," whispered Lilian, for the name of Claverhouse was seldom mentioned but with studied respect and secret hatred, from the fear of his supernatural powers.

"Tush, dear Lilian! I am resolved to assert our prerogative to say whatever we have a mind to. But to return to the raid of yesterday. Had you heard Finland describing how valiantly his soldiers marched into the little hamlet, with drums beating, pikes advanced, and matches lighted, driving wives and weans and cocks and hens before them, you would (like me) have felt severely that the brave cavaliers of Dunbarton, *Les Gardes Ecossais* of Arran and Aubigné, the stout hearts that stormed the towers of Oppenheim, had come to so low a pass now. If ever Finland goes on another such barnsbreaking errand, I vow he shall never come into my presence again."

"Under favour, fair Annie," said Walter, laughingly, "your heart would soon relent; for I know you to be a true cavalier-dame, notwithstanding all this severe raillery."

"I have heard her say quite as much to the earl of Perth; what dost think of that, Walter?" said Lilian.

"It is more than the boldest of our barons dared have done in these degenerate days; but he would find how impossible it is to be displeased with you, fair Annie. How is it, Madam Lilian, that you do not in some way assist me against the raillery of your gossip? Her waggery is very smarting, I assure you."

Ere Lilian could speak, the clear voice of Annie interrupted her by exclaiming—

"Aha, Mr. Fenton, you have dropped something from the breast of that superbly pinked vest of yours—is it a tag, a tassel, or what?"

"I know not," he muttered hurriedly, putting his hand in the breast of his coat.

"It fell among the grass," said Lilian.

"Oh, I have it, I have it!" added Annie, springing forward and picking something up. "'Tis here—on my honour, a glove!"

"A lady's—it fell from his breast," said Lilian, in a breathless voice.

"Of beautiful point lace—one of yours, gossip Lilian. O brave!—ha, ha!"

M 2

" Mine—mine, said you? " Lilian's voice faltered; she grew pale and red alternately, while adding, with an air of confusion, " You are jesting as usual, you daft lassie. Oh, surely 'tis a mistake ! "

" Judge for yourself, love. I saw you mark it ; here are your initials worked in beads of blue and silver."

" It is but too true—I lost it some weeks ago," faltered Lilian, whose timid blue eyes stole one furtive glance at the handsome culprit under their long brown lashes, and were instantly cast down in the utmost confusion. She was excited almost to tears.

" Forsooth, there is something immensely curious in all this, Mr. Fenton," continued the waggish Annie, twirling the little glove aloft on the point of her riding-switch. " We must have you arraigned before the high court of love, and compelled to confess, under terror of his bow string, to a jury of fair ladies, when and wherefore you obtained this glove."

" Now, Mr. Fenton, do," urged Lilian, entering somewhat into the gay spirit of her friend, though her happy little heart vibrated with confusion and joy as tumultuously as a moment ago it had beat with jealousy and fear. " Tell us when you got it, and all about it."

" The night Ichabod Bummel was arrested," replied Walter, who still coloured deeply at this unexpected discovery, for he was yet but young in the art of love.

" Aha, and Lilian gave it ! My pretty little prude, and is it thus with thee ? "

" Cease, I pray you, Annie Laurie," said Lilian, in a tone very much akin to asperity. " I hope Mr. Fenton will resolve this matter himself."

" Forgive me, Lilian—forgive me, madam. I found it on the floor after your escape, and I kept it as a token of remembrance. You will pardon my presumption in doing so, when I say, at that time, I thought never, never to meet you again, and assuredly could not have foreseen the happiness of an hour like this." He spoke in a brief and confused manner, for he was concerned at the annoyance Annie's raillery evidently caused Lilian. " Permit me to restore it," he added, with increased confusion, " or perhaps you—you will permit me—"

" What ? "

" To have the honour of retaining it."

" Oh no, no; how could you think of that? " said Lilian, hurriedly and timidly, as she took the glove from the upheld riding-rod, and concealing it in some part of her dress, continued, " now let us hear no more of this silly affair. Ah, Mr.

Walter, how sadly you have exposed yourself! To carry one's old glove about you, as Aunt Grizel does a charm against cramp, or thunder, or ill luck. 'Tis quite droll! Ah, good heavens!" she added, in a whisper, "do not *tell her* of this affair, Annie."

"Dost think I am so simple? Finland has taught me how one ought to keep one's own secrets from fathers and mothers, and aunts too."

"But to-morrow your sedan will be seen trotting over the whole town, up this close and down that, as you hurry from house to house, telling the wonderful adventure of the glove, and trussed up quite into a story in your own peculiar fashion, as long as the *Grand Scipio*, or any romance of Scuderi."

"For Lilian's sake, let me hope not, Mistress Laurie," said Walter, imploringly, to the gay beauty.

"Trust me for once, dear Lilian," said Annie, patting her cheek with her riding-switch, "I know when to prattle, and when to be silent. Dost really think, my sweet little gossip, that I would jest with thy name, as I do with those of my Lady Jean Gordon, Mary of Charteris, the countess of Dunbarton, or any of our wild belles who care not a rush how many fall in love with them, but bestow glances and kerchiefs, and rings and love-knots of ribbon, on all and sundry? I trow not. *Apropos* of that; I know three gentlemen of Claver'se Guards who wear Mary's favours in their hats, and if these ribbons are dyed in brave blood some grey morning, she alone will be to blame, for her coquetry is very dangerous. Young Holsterlee will be at the countess of Dunbarton's ball *à la Française* next week; observe him narrowly, and you will see a true love-knot of white ribbons at his breast; and if the young lords Maddertie and Fawsyde are there, you will see each with the same gift from the same fond and liberal hand. Ah, she is a wild romp! It was the Duchess Mary's late suppers, and Monsieur Minuette's Bretagne that quite spoiled her, for once upon a time she was as grave, discreet, and silent as—as myself."

"O you wag—such a recluse she must have been."

"Quite a little nun!" added Annie, and both the charming girls laughed with all the gaiety of their sex and the thoughtlessness of their rank.

Lilian was both vexed and pleased at the discovery that Fenton had for so many weeks borne her glove in his bosom; but from that time forward she became more reserved in his presence, and walked little with him in the garden, and still less in the lawn or by the banks of the loch.

She did not avoid his presence, but gave him fewer oppor. tunities of being alone with her. Did she think of him less?

Ah, surely not.

A lover is the pole-star of a young girl's thoughts by day and night, and never was Walter's image absent a moment from the mind of Lilian; for like himself she numbered and recounted the hours until they met again. Their meetings were marked by diffidence and embarrassment, and their parting with secret regret.

Walter, too, was somewhat changed, from the knowledge that Lilian had discovered his passion. His voice, which seemed the same to other ears, became softer and more insinuating when he addressed her. He was, if possible, more respectful, and more timid, and more tender. His imagination—what a plague it was, and how very fertile in raising ideal annoyances! One hour his heart was joyous with delight at the memory of some little incident—a word or a smile; and the next he nursed himself into a state of utter wretchedness, with the idea that Lilian had looked rather coldly upon him, or had spoken far too kindly of her cousin the captain of the Scots' Brigade.

Though the latter was a bugbear in his way, Walter did not seriously fear a rival; for he wore a sword, and, after the fashion of the time, feared no man. He dreaded most the loss of Lilian's esteem, for he dared not think that yet she linked love and his name together in her mind. Could he have read her heart and known her secret thoughts, he would have found a passion as deep as his own concealed under the bland purity and innocence of her smile, which revealed only well-bred pleasure at his approach.

Many days of anxious hoping and fearing, &c., passed, after the affair of *the glove*, but he saw Lilian thrice only. She kept close by the side of her grand-aunt Grizel, and the old lady seldom left her wheel and well-cushioned chair in the chamber-of-dais.

"Why did she not permit me to retain the glove?" he would at times say to himself. "Then I would have no cause for all my present doubts and fears. Had we been alone, perhaps she would have done so——"

Walter was right in that conjecture.

CHAPTER XXII.

A BALL IN THE OLDEN TIME.

Shades of my fathers, in your pasteboard skirts,
Your broidered waistcoats and your plaited shirts,
Your formal bag-wigs—wide-extended cuffs,
Your five-inch chitterlings and nine-inch ruffs;
I see you move the solemn minuet o'er,
The modest foot scarce rising from the floor.
SALMAGUNDI.

ON the south side of the city where the old Liberton road branching off enters it by two diverging routes, one by the narrow and ancient Potter-row, and the other by the street of the Bristo Port, a formidable gate in the re-entering angle of the city-wall, which bristled with cannon and overlooked the way that descended to the Grass-market, there stood, in 1688 (and yet stands), an antique mansion of very picturesque aspect. It is furnished with numerous outshots and projections, broad, dark, and bulky stacks of chimneys reared up in unusual places, and having over the upper windows circular pediments enriched with initials and devices, but now blackened by age and encrusted with the smoky vapour of centuries.

It is still known as the "General's House," from its having been anciently the residence appropriated to the Commander-in-chief of the Scottish forces. A narrow passage leads to it from that ancient suburban Burgh of Barony, the Potter's-row, where, doubtless, many a psalm-singing puritan of Monk's regiment, many a scarred trooper of Leven's iron brigade, and many a stern veteran of the Covenant have kept watch and ward, in the pathway which is still, as of old, styled, *par excellence*, THE General's Entry.

Its garden has now become a lumber-yard, and is otherwise encroached upon ; its stables have long since vanished, and mean dwellings surround and overtop it; the windows are stuffed with old hats and bundles of straw or rags ; brown paper flaps dismally in the broken glasses, and its once gay chambers, where the "cunning George Monk," the grave and stern Leven, Dalyel of the iron-heart, and the gallant Dunbarton feasted royally, and held wassail with their comrades, have, like all the surrounding mansions of the great and noble of the other days, been long since abandoned to citizens of the poorest and humblest class.

In 1688 its aspect was very different.

Standing then on the very verge of the city. it was deemed

in the country, though now the gas lamps extend two miles
beyond it, and dense and populous streets occupy the sites of
two straggling and unpretending suburbs of thatched cottages
and "sclaited lands." To the southward of the road, a
narrow rugged horseway, passed through fields and thickets
towards the great loch of the burgh, and ascending its
opposite bank, passed the straggling suburb named the
Causeway-side, where there were many noble old villas, the
residences of Sir Patrick Johnstone, of the laird of Wester-
hall and others, and sweeping past the ruined convent of St.
Catherine of Sienna, wound over the hill (near a gibbet that
was seldom unoccupied by sweltering corpses and screaming
ravens), towards the Barony of Liberton, a lonely hamlet with
a little stone spire, and the tall square tower of the Winrams,
in older days the patrimony of a lesser baron named Macbeth.

To the westward of the general's house were fertile fields
that extended close up to the defences of the city, then a long
line of lofty and embattled walls built of reddish-coloured
sandstone, strengthened at intervals by towers alternately of
a round or square form, which defended its various ports or
barrier-gates. Within this stony zone rose the dark and
massive city, which for ages had been increasing in denseness; for, in consequence of the nature of the times, and the
dubious relations of the country with its southern neighbour,
the citizens seldom dared to build beyond the narrow compass
of the walls.

From these causes, and in imitation of those bad allies the
French, Edinburgh, like ancient Paris, became deeper and
closer, taller and yet more tall; house arose upon house, street
was piled upon street, bartizan, gable, and tower, shot up to
an amazing height, and were wedged within the walls, till the
thoroughfares, like those of Venice, were only three feet broad,
and in some places exhibited fourteen tiers of windows.

An Act of the Scottish Legislature was found absolutely
necessary to curb the rage for stupendous houses, and in 1698
it was enacted, that none should be erected within the liberties
of the city exceeding five stories in height. Prior to the
middle of the seventeenth century Edinburgh could not boast
of one court or square save that of White Horse Hostel, if
indeed it could be termed either.

The access to these vast and imperishable piles was by
turnpike stairs, steep, narrow, dark, and mysterious. The
population of the city was then about 50,000; but as it
increased, so did the denseness of the houses; even the buttresses of the great cathedral were all occupied by little
dwellings, till the venerable church resembled a hen with a

brood under her wings. Year by year for seven centuries the alleys had become higher and narrower, till Edinburgh looked like a vast city crowded in close column on the steep faces of a hill, until the building of a bridge to the north, when it burst from the embattled girdle that for ages had pent it up, and more like another Babylon than a "modern Athens" spread picturesquely over every steep rock and deep defile in its vicinity. But to return:

On a dusky evening Walter Fenton and Douglas of Finland, muffled in their ample scarlet rocquelaures, which completely hid their rich dresses, came stumbling along the dark and narrow Potter's-row, towards the gate of the general's house, where a mounted guard of the Grey Dragoons sat motionless as twenty statues, the conical fur cap of each trooper forming the apex of a pyramid, which his wide cloak made, when spread over the crupper of his horse. Still and firm as if cast in bronze, were every horse and man. Each trooper rested his short musketoon on his thigh, with the long dagger screwed on its muzzle. This guard of honour was under arms to receive the general's military guests, and the fanfare of the trumpets and a ruffle on the kettle-drum announced that Sir Thomas Dalyel of Binns had just arrived.

In the entry stood a foot soldier, muffled in his sentinel's coat.

"One of ours, I think," said Douglas. "Art one of the old Die-hards, good fellow?"

"Hab Elshender, at your service, laird."

"Hah! hath the Lady Bruntisfield arrived?" asked Walter.

"Ay, sir," replied Hab, with a knowing Scots' grin; for he understood the drift of the question. "Ay, sir, and Madam Lilian too—looking for a' the world like the queen of the fairies."

Within the gate, the court was filled with light and bustle. Carriages of ancient fashion and clumsy construction, profusely decorated with painting and gilding, with coats armorial on the polished panels and waving hammer-cloths, rolled up successively to the doorway; sedans, gaudy with brass nails, red silk blinds, and scarlet poles; military chargers, and servants on foot and horseback in gorgeous liveries, all glittering in the light of the flaring links which usually preceded every person of note when threading the gloomy and narrow thoroughfares of Edinburgh after nightfall.

Impatient at every moment which detained him from the side of Lilian, now, when he could appear before her to the utmost advantage, Walter, heedless of preceding his friend sprang up the handsome staircase of carved oak, the walls of which were covered with painted panels and trophies of arms, conspicuous among which was the standard of the unfortunate Argyle, taken in the conflict of Muirdykes three years before. Here they threw their broad hats and red mantles to the servants, and were immediately ushered into a long suite of apartments, which were redolent of perfume and brilliant with light and gaiety.

Douglas, whose extremely handsome features were of a dark and olive hue, like all those of his surname generally, wore the heavy cavalier wig falling over his collar of point d'Espagne and gold-studded breastplate. Walter had his own natural hair hanging in dark curls on a cuirass of silver, polished so bright that the fair dancers who flitted past every moment saw their flushed faces reflected in its glassy surface.

Their coats and breeches were of scarlet, pinked with blue silk and laced with gold; their sashes were of yellow silk, but had massive tassels of gold; and their formidable bowl-hilted rapiers were slung in shoulder-belts of velvet embroidered with silver. Their long military gloves almost met the cuffs of their coats, which were looped up to display their shirt-sleeves—a new fashion of James VII.; and everything about them was perfumed to excess. Such was the attire of the military of that day, as regulated by the "royal orders" of the king.

Threading their way through a crowd of dancers, whose magnificent dresses of bright-hued satins and velvets, laced with silver or gold, and blazing with jewels, sparkled and shone as they glided from hand to hand to the music of an orchestra perched in a recessed gallery of echoing oak, they passed into an inner apartment to pay their *devoirs* to the countess, who for a time had relinquished the dance to overlook the teaboard—a solemn, arduous, and highly-important duty, which was executed by her lady-in-waiting, a starched demoiselle of very doubtful age.

Though rather diminutive in person, the countess of Dunbarton was a very beautiful woman, and possessed all that dazzling fairness of complexion which is so characteristic of her countrywomen. She was English, and a sister of the then duchess of Northumberland. Her eyes were of a bright and merry blue; her hair of the richest auburn; her small face was quite enchanting in expression, and very piquant in its beauty; while her fine figure was decidedly inclined to *embonpoint*.

She was one of the fashionable mirrors of the day, and the standard by whom the stately belles of Craig's-close and the

Blackfriars-wynd regulated the depth of their stomachers and the length of their trains—the star of Mary d'Este's balls at Holyrood, where, in the splendour of her jewels, she had nearly rivalled the famous duchess of Lauderdale ; and though an Englishwoman, notwithstanding the jealousy and dislike which from time immemorial had existed between the two kingdoms, she was, from the suavity of her manner, the brilliancy of her wit, and the amiability of her disposition, both admired and beloved in Edinburgh.

With a pretty and affected air, she held her silver pouncet-box in an ungloved and beautifully-formed hand, which was whiter than the bracelet of pearls which encircled it. Close by, upon a satin cushion, reposed a pursy, pug-nosed, and silky little lap-dog, of his late majesty's favourite and long-eared breed. It had been a present from himself, and bore the royal cipher on its silver collar. Near her, on a little tripod table of ebony, stood the tea-board, with its rich equipage, and a multitude of little china cups glittering with blue and gold.

The tea, dark, fragrant, and priceless beyond any now in use, was served by the prim gentlewoman before mentioned (the daughter of some decayed family), who acted as her useful friend and companion ; and slowly it was poured out like physic from a little silver pot of curious workmanship, a gift from Mary Stuart (then princess of Orange), and the same from which she was wont to regale the ladies of Holyrood.

Tea was unknown in London at the time of the Restoration ; and when introduced a few years afterwards by the Lords Arlington and Ossory, was valued at sixty shillings the pound ; but the beautiful Mary d'Este of Modena was the first who made it known in the Scottish capital in 1681. This new and costly beverage was still one of the wonders and innovations of the age, and was only within the reach of the great and wealthy until about 1750 ; but the royal tea-parties, masks, and entertainments of the Duchess Mary and her affable daughters, were long the theme of many a tall great-grandmother, and remembered with veneration and regret among other vanished glories, when, by the cold blight that fell upon her, poor Scotland felt too surely that "a stranger" filled the throne of the Stuarts.

Lady Grizel of Bruntisfield, and other venerable dowagers and ancient maiden gentlewomen (a species in which some old Scottish families are still very prolific), all as stiff as pride, brocade, starch, and buckram could make them, were sitting very primly and uprightly in their high-backed chairs, clustered round the countess's little tripod table, like pearls about a diamond, when the cavaliers advanced to pay their respects.

"Welcome, Finland," said the countess, addressing Douglas according to the etiquette of the country. "My old friend Walter, your most obedient servant. How fortunate!—we have just been disputing about romances, and drawing comparisons between that lumbering folio 'The Banished Virgin' and the 'Cassandra.' You will act our umpire. My dear boy, let me look at you : how well you look, and so handsome, in all this bravery ; doth he not, Mistress Lilian ? "

Lilian, who, in all the splendour of diamonds and full dress, was leaning on aunt Grizel's chair, blushed too perceptibly at this very pointed question, but was spared attempting a reply, for the gay countess continued :

"Remember, Walter, that the great Middleton, who became an earl, and lieutenant-general of the Scots' Horse, began his career like yourself, by trailing a partisan in the old Royals—then Hepburn's pikemen in the French service ; and who knoweth, my dear child, where your's may end ? Heigho! These perilous times are the making and unmaking of many a brave man. So, Mr. Douglas, we were disputing about—— (Madam Ruth, assist the gentlemen to dishes of tea)——about —what was it ?—O, a passage in the 'Cassandra.' "

" I shall be happy to be of any service to your ladyship," began Finland, with his blandest smile, while raising to his well-moustachioed lip a little thimbleful of the new-fashioned beverage, which he cordially detested, but took for form's sake.

" We are in great doubts whether Lysimachus was justified in running his falchion through poor Cleander, for merely desiring the charioteer of the beautiful princesses to drive faster. You will remember the passage. We all think it very cruel, and that no lover is entitled to be so outrageous."

Douglas knew the pages of his muster-roll better than those of the romance in question, but he answered promptly, " I think Master Cleander was an impudent rascal, and well deserving a few inches of cold iron, or a sound truncheoning at the hands of the provost-marshal. I remember doing something of that kind myself about the time that old mareschal de Crecqui was blocked up and taken in Treves."

" Ay, Douglas, that was when we were with the column of the Moselle," said the earl, who now approached and leaned on the back of the countess's chair. " It was shortly after the brave Turenne had been killed by that unlucky cannonball that deprived France of her best chevalier. We were in full retreat across the river. Some ladies of the army were with us in a handsome calèche, as gay a one as ever rolled along the Parisian boulevards. There was a devil of a press at the barrier-gate of Montroyale, and an officer of the regiment de Picardie was urging the horses of the vehicle to full speed, by goading them with his half-pike, regardless of the cries of the ladies, when Finland, by one blow of his baton, unhorsed him, and some say he never marched more."

"Oh! Mr. Douglas!" said the countess, holding up her hands.

"There was an old feud between us and the chevaliers de Picardie," continued the earl; "but the worst of this *malheur* was, that the poor officer was the husband of one of the demoiselles in question; and as she was extremely handsome, and Finland, by becoming her very devoted *serviteur*, endeavoured, during the remainder of the campaign, to make every amends for the loss he had occasioned her, the gallants of the army said——"

"Marry, come up! My lord, dost take my *boudoir* for a tavern or a sutler's tent. Fie! laird of Finland, you are worse than the Lysimachus of the romance. But what think *you*, Walter, of that hero becoming enamoured of the fair prisoner committed to his care, the Princess Parisatis? It would seem that in ancient times, as well as modern, that beauty must be a dangerous trust for a young soldier."

The earl laughed till he shook the perfume from his wig; Walter smiled, and stole one glance at Lilian. She, too, was smiling, and playing with her fan; but her long lashes were cast down, and her cheek was burning with blushes.

"So dangerous, indeed, is beauty," said the earl, "that had I any fair prisoners, I would entrust them only to old fellows with leather visages and tough hearts, ancient *routiers*, like Will Wemyss, or if they were remarkably handsome, why, I might keep them in my *own* immediate charge."

"Indeed, my lord—quotha?" said the countess, pouting.

"Believe me, dear Lætitia," said the handsome noble, patting her white shoulder, "they could not be in safer keeping than the wardship of your husband. He can never see beauty in others."

She smiled at the earl's compliment, and turning to the blushing Lilian, said:

"In sooth, madam, Walter Fenton was always somewhat addicted to gallantry, though Mistress Ruth and he were ever at drawn daggers while he was about me. While a boy, he was quite a little cavaliero; and when obeying my orders, always preferred a kiss to any other reward. But by my honour, little Walter was so pretty a boy, that I gave him enough to have made my lord the earl quite jealous. Even Anne of Monmouth and Buccleugh, never had a page so handsome and so gay; and I doubt not, boy, thou prove a true Scottish cavalier in those sad wars which all men say are fast approaching."

Walter's only reply was pressing to his lips the white hand of the beautiful Englishwoman; for his heart was too full to speak.

"And now, Walter," she continued, "as a mark of my favour, you shall dance with me, while Lord Dunbarton leads out the young lady of Bruntisfield. I have not been on the floor since the first cotillon with Claverhouse. Madam Ruth, you will please preside at the tea-board. Mr. Douglas—Finland, as you Scots name him, where is he?"

"Gone to look for the Lily of Maxwelton, I warrant," said the earl.

"Then he may even spare himself the trouble, poor man! she has been coquetting for this hour past with the laird of Craigdarroch, a gentleman of the Life Guards. On, on, or we shall be late for the cotillon. Ah, Walter, you are still looking after that fair girl Napier. She *is* very pretty; but are you really in love with her? You blush! Bless you, my poor boy, she is immensely rich, they say—and—but you shall dance with her next."

As they advanced among the dancers, a tall lady in scarlet brocade, with a stomacher blazing with diamonds, swept past. She was led by a gentleman gorgeously attired in a coat of pink velvet, lined and slashed with yellow satin, and looped and buttoned with gold. Like all the rest, his voluminous wig was of the most glossy black. His dark stern eyes glared for a moment upon Walter, as he bowed profoundly to the countess and passed on.

"'Tis Mary of Charteris, and that fearful man Lord Clermistonlee," said she. "We cannot omit him here, though we detest him. How handsome, how noble he looks; and yet, how repulsive!"

A crash of music burst from the arched gallery, and after a few preliminary flourishes, a cotillon commenced. This graceful dance was then the universal favourite, but has long been superseded or merged in the modern quadrille, where some of its figures are still retained. Though stately in measure and elaborate in step, the cotillon had none of that grave solemnity which characterises the latter. When our forefathers danced, they did so in good earnest, and the whole ballroom became instinct with life, action, and agile grace, as the dancers swept to the right and to the left, the tall ladies with their high plumage floating, trains sweeping, and red-heeled slippers pattering, while their pendants and lappets, flounces and frills, and pompoons and puffs were flashing, glinting, and waving among the curled wigs and laced coats, diamond-hilted swords and brocade-vests of the gentlemen. In what might (now) be deemed odd contrast with the richness of their attire, and the starched dignity of their demeanour, familiar and homely expressions were heard from time to time, such as,—

"My Leddy Becky, your hand—Drumdryan, your're a' gaun agee, man!—Pardon, my Lord Spynie, your rapier's tirled wi' mine—Haud ye a', my Leddy Pitnchar has drappit her pouncet-box! Hoots, Laird Holster, are you daft?—Pilrig, set to her Leddyship," and so forth.

Meanwhile Douglas wandered through the glittering throng in quest of his beautiful Anne, nodding briefly on all hands; for Dick, the laird of Finland, was one of those gay fellows whom everybody knew; but his fair one was nowhere visible. He began to wax fearfully wroth, and resolving to dance with no one else, continued his search until he found himself at the end of the suite of apartments, in a handsome little room wainscoted with gilt panels, and having a large sun gilded over the mantel-piece, from the centre of which, as from a reflector, a blaze of yellow light was thrown by an alabaster lamp.

Lord Mersington, accurately attired in black velvet, plainly laced with silver, Dalyel, with his long white beard and mail-rusted buff coat, looking as ferocious as ever, with his enormous toledo, and Swedish jingle-spurs, which in lieu of rowels had each four metal balls in a bell, and consequently made a great noise when he walked; the unfortunate president Lockhart, the "bluidy advocate," Mackenzie, the two ancient maiden dames of Pheesgil, Lady Grizel Napier, and Madam Drumsturdy, a tall and raw-boned dowager in black taffeta with pearls, plumes, and heart-breakers (or false ringlets) were all intently playing at the old-fashioned game of primero.

"Hee, hee, my Lady Drumsturdy," said Mersington, simpering like an ape at his partner in his attempts to be pleasing, "the general is a kittle opponent. A spade led."

"Your lordship will not turn my flank gif I can help it—'tis a knave;" replied the old cavalier, sorting his suit. "I ken primero weel. Mony a time and oft, d—n me! I have played a round game at it, and ombre, knave-out-o'-doors, post-and-pair on the head o' a kettle-drum, and mony a score of roubles I have swept off the same gude table: but troth,

Mersington, ye are waur to warsle wi' then a Don Cossack—
(play, Sir George)—o' whom God wot, I have had some experience in my time."

"Ay, ay—hee, hee—a diamond was played," said Mersington, as the card party exchanged glances of impatience,
confidently foreseeing the infliction of some of Sir Thomas's
Russian reminiscences.

"Speaking o' Don Cossacks," said he, starting off without
further preamble, and clanking his enormous spurs; "it was
just this time thirty years ago that we sacked Smolensko and
Kiow, after storming them from the Polanders. Dags and
pistols! but my squadron of Cossacks showed themselves born
deevils that day. Sabre and spear was the cry. Some braw
pickings we got, your ladyships, in that same province of
Lithuania, which to an industrious cavalier, who knoweth the
fashion of war, is as fine a place for free in-quartering as the
Garden of Eden would have been, d—n me!"

"Oh! Sir Thomas," said Lady Grizel, deprecatingly. "But
is it true that in Muscovy no man will either beck, bow, or
veil bonnet to a woman in the streets?"

"I hope no true-born Russ would undervalue himsel' so
far," replied Sir Thomas, stroking his silver beard. "He
would as soon put his head in the fire as bend it to any
woman, his ain mother even; and as for adoring beauty—
udsdaggers! a Muscovite would sooner think of adoring his
horse's tail. I assure you, ladies, that the great duke of
Muscovy himsel' would not permit his mother, wife, or
daughter to eat at the same buird wi' him, even if it were to
save their lives. 'Tis the law o' the land, and a very gude
ane too."

Here the old ladies held up their hands and eyes, but the
general continued,—

"They are fine cheilds, those same Russians though, and I
will at one sliver cut the throat of any loon that gainsayeth it.
Had your ladyships seen Salcroff's black cuirassiers sweeping
ten thousand wild Tartars before them, and driving them with
levelled lances into the foaming waters of the Vistula, it would
have been a sight to mind o'. Udsdaggers! that was different
work from riding owre a band o' puir psalm-singing deevils o'
Covenanters, just as ane would trot owre a corn-rig. Ay, *those*
were the days, and *that* was the service, for a pretty man.
My lord president, play, if it please you."

"You are an awfu' man, Binns," said Mersington; "a
perfect auld deil's buckie, and weel kent to be a most unre-
lenting tulzier that caresna whether a man crieth *quarter* in

our decent Scots' tongue, or in that o' an Englishman, Tartar, or other unco body, death being the doom o' all alike."

"And what for no, my lord?" rejoined this ferocious commander, knitting his formidable brows. "Are these times in whilk to show mercy to low-born rapscallions? A bonny spot o' work this is in the north: these deevils the Clandonald o' Keppoch and the fusileer guard hae been at it ding-dong wi' pike and broadsword every day for this week past. But I have heard that Captain Crichton is off on the spur wi' some horse and dragoons, to tak' a turn against the Hielandmen : and if he sends a pockfu' o' heads now and then to the council he will not be riding aboon the king's commission."

"Oh, Sir Thomas!" ejaculated Lady Grizel again, "the brav are ever merciful."

"So, please your ladyship, I have often ridden by the side of a certain cavalier, Sir Archibald Napier of Bruntisfield, whom Montrose esteemed as brave a man as put foot in stirrup; and, like mysel', *he* showed but small favour to the canting, crop-luggit, covenanting rapscallions o' his time. Puir Paton o' Meadowhead and Wallace o' Auchans, whom thrice at Pentland I had this very blade upraised to smite, were the only honest men that followed their banner. God sain them baith! for they were pretty men, and knew the wars like mysel'. Lady Drumsturdy, a spade, if you please."

"Sir Thomas," said the soft voice of Lady Grizel, "no marvel it is that the poor nonjurors shrink before you, even as from—from——"

"Our gude friend wi' the forkit tail," added Mersington, closing the sentence, while Dalyel's bushy beard shook with his laughter as he replied—

"Ou, ay; and like Claver'se, Glenæ, Lag, and a few mair o' our leal royal commanders, I am proof to lead and steel— ha, ha! Weel may these snivelling loons, who sold their king for a groat, and sacrificed their country for its d—n'd kirk, quail before the eye of a leal man and true. I am an auld gentleman trooper, and trailed a pike under the Muscovite eagle owre lang to hae mony remains o' tenderness, whilk is a failing I believe few folk will accuse me o'. Udsdaggers, Finland, I see you listening, my braw man. Your beard may grow white like mine (though, after the fashion o' these degenerate days, your chin is as smooth as a Christmas apple), but never will ye ride owre the spur-leathers in Tartar gore as I have done. Braw gallants as ye are, in your plate corslets and pinket doublets, laced and perfumed, tasselled and tagged, and jagged and bedeevilled like state trumpeters, ye would be

N

but puir hands at resisting a charge o' mailed horse or heavy dragoons."

"Under favour, General Dalyel," replied the handsome lieutenant, laughing, "I hope not; and Monmouth's cavaliers found lately, that a stand of Scottish pikes are still as firm as when levelled on the fields of Sark or Otterburn. By my faith, their spurred horses recoiled from our solid squares like water from a rock."

"Awa'," replied Sir Thomas, sternly; "it beseemeth not a laddie like you to venture an opinion on that fray at Sedgemoor. Had ye seen the field of Smolensko on the day that great battle was fought and won, then might ye speak o' sic matters. There, mair than a hundred thousand matchlocks and petronels rung like thunder in the frosty sky; bombs were bursting, cannon-shot and barbed arrow fleen' thick as hail; while helmet and corselet rang like siller bells to the clink o' scimitar and mace. Oh! for a deep wassail bowl to drink to the brave that fought there, for my auld heart warms to their memory. Like the wind o' their snowy deserts, the squadrons of horse swept with uplifted lances to the heidlong charge. Alexis on the right, Sinboirs on the left, and mysel', the leal laird o' Binns, in the centre wi' the eagle—whoop! then came a crash, and all gave way before us, like a Dutchman's dyke when the dam breaks. Loud aboon a' the din o' war thundered the great battle-drum of the Muscovite host, carried on four horses, and having aucht loons loundering on't wi' wooden mells. Sedgemoor!—It was bairns' play to such a field as Smolensko; and gif mortal man gainsayeth it, there is the hand that will right the matter. I mind the fray as if 'twere yesterday; and I assure you, Lady Grizel, that I had a braw supper that night on the field, cooked from a horse's flank by some of the Tartar women I kept about me."

Tired of this conversation, Douglas left the old beaux to do the agreeable to the brocaded dowagers of the Canongate, and lounged through the glittering rooms, continuing his search for Annie Laurie. Leaning on the arm of the handsome Claverhouse, who over a coat of white velvet, richly laced and slashed, wore a sash and gorget of burnished gold, with the collar of the Thistle, the countess of Dunbarton slowly promenaded past.

"Ah, laird of Finland," said she archly, "I know for whom you are still looking so anxiously."

"In sooth, madam, I scarcely know myself."

"All the better is such philosophy, for she has been coquetting all night with the young laird of Craigdarroch."

They parted. At that moment a flourish of music swept

along the painted ceilings, and the dancers began to arrange
themselves for a new cotillon. Douglas, now seriously angry,
cast a rapid and impatient glance round the bright throng,
and caught a glimpse of his fair one in all the glory of white
satin, white lace, and white pearls, her eyes sparkling with
pleasure, and the braids of her auburn hair with diamonds and
spangles. She was chatting gaily with Lady Mary Charteris,
one of those beautiful romps who flourished in ancient Edina,
notwithstanding the starched demureness of the time. Fearful of being anticipated, he advanced at once, and requested
her hand for the next dance.

"And now, Finland," said she, placing her soft hand in his,
"What have you to say for yourself?"

"How, fair Annie?"

"That until this moment you have never approached me;
and I have been forced to endure the vanity of Craigdarroch,
who, like all the Claver'se gentlemen-troopers, thinks he is
quite a paladin, because he guards the high commissioner,
rides with the parliament, and (like yourself) terrifies the old
cummers of the kailmarket, or some poor cock-lairdie, to
abjure the Covenant, or hang on the next tree. Is it not so?"

Douglas laughed as his merry mistress spoke; for Craigdarroch was the only man in Edinburgh of whom he felt a
little jealous, or whose influence he valued a rush. Tall and
handsome, an accomplished gentleman, an expert horseman
and fencer, and a brave and good-hearted fellow to boot,
young Fergusson was altogether a rival quite calculated to
create some uneasiness; and his whole regiment were a source
of dread to the beaux and dandies of the capital.

There was a certain dashing and indescribable bearing
attached to all the cavalier troopers of the Scottish life guard,
which, with the unusual splendour of their garb and armour,
their rank in society, courage in the field, and that high
esprit de corps which necessarily pervaded a band so very
exclusive and prætorian, made every one a formidable rival.
Thus, notwithstanding his own rank, figure, and bearing,
Douglas felt considerable anxiety whenever Craigdarroch
approached his mistress; nor could he at times repress a sigh
of anger and regret at her gaiety and volatility, which charmed
him one moment and provoked him the next.

The cotillon commenced. Happy Walter and his beautiful
Lilian were their *vis-à-vis*. They were chatting very gaily on
the trivial matters of the day—De Scuderi's last, but ponderous romance—the new comedy performed by his majesty's
servants, at the little theatre in the Tennis-court—new-
fashioned suits of Genoa velvet, laced with Bruxelles—gloves

of Blois—perfumes and balls of *pomme d'ambre*—a witch that was to be burned next day on the Castiehill, by the economical provost and baillies, in the same bonfire, lit in honour of the victory at Bothwell, on its eighth anniversary.

The whole city was agog "anent the worrying" (as the term was) of this famous sorceress, who had been unanimously condemned by a pious and intelligent jury (principally composed of Kirk elders), for sailing across to Fife, in a sieve instead of the Kinghorn cutter; for causing a neighbour's calf to have two heads; for raising a storm to sink the good ship *Charles the Second*, of Leith, by performing certain diabolical cantrips over a kail-blade full of water; and various other enormities, which made every hair in the wigs of the fifteen lords of session and justiciary stand on end with horror and amazement.

<hr />

CHAPTER XXIII.

TWO LOVES FOR ONE HEART.

Oriana sighed as if her heart were breaking, and said to herself, dear friend, in a woful hour the boon was granted.—AMADIS OF GAUL.

NOTWITHSTANDING the graces of her person, and richness of her attire, there were many bright and beautiful beings present who attracted more attention than the timid and retiring Lilian Napier; but in her whole air and manner it is not easy to imagine a girl more exquisitely ladylike. Her long eyelashes were drooped upon her soft and changing cheek, veiling her soft glances, and imparting to her eyes an expression of timidity and modesty, which lent additional charms to the fine features of her adorable little face. The ball delighted, the music exhilarated her; and she soon raised her head, like a flower when the dew is past. Her blue eyes were full of animation; her cheek was flushed; the most enchanting grace was in all her motions. She was glorious; and Walter felt that he adored her.

Her friend, gay Annie, outshone her in showy and dazzling beauty; but to those who knew and loved the winning manner of Lilian, and beheld how her cheek mantled with the emotions of her heart, while her eyes beamed with the purest good-nature and vivacity, she was indeed one without a *peer* (as the king said of her mailed ancestor), and one fair star that charms us thus, is worth a thousand of those brighter planets that shine alike on all.

But nothing could be more brilliant than the loveliness of

Annie. Tall, full, and graceful, in all the bloom of twenty, and radiant with health, white satin, and diamonds, she excited the admiration of her companions, while little Lilian touched their hearts. There were many fair girls present, who, like Mistress Laurie, had in their manners a considerable dash of Parisian coquetry, which is always excessively attractive to beaux, though a timid and retiring girl, like Lilian, is sure, in the end, to prove the most loveable and devoted.

At that time, the *tone* of society in Edinburgh was very different from what it had been during the rampant reign of Presbyterianism, and equally so from that which characterized it twenty years afterwards, when the gloom, depression, and humiliation of the country, and the empty desolation of the capital "communicated to the manners and fashions of society a stiff reserve, precise moral carriage, and a species of decorum amounting to moroseness." At the period of our narrative it was very different. The recent residence of foreign ambassadors and influence of a court, the existence of a parliament— (for *centralization*, that grand curse of Scotland, was then unknown)—the long intercourse with France, in the armies of which all younger sons and cavaliers of good family took a turn of service, had communicated a lightness to the manners of the aristocracy, very different indeed from the "moroseness" which succeeded the revolution, and still more so that great national paralysis, the union, which was so long a source of regret to our grandfathers.

Walter longed to change the commonplace tenor of the conversation, mentioned in the last chapter, and endeavoured gradually to broach the sentiments that lay nearest his heart ; but he either wanted tact, or the figures of the dance put him out, or a crowded room was not quite the place for it. The young lady too was somewhat reserved ; she remembered the affair of the glove, and thought it quite necessary to be so.

"So you will not go with me to-morrow to see this old witch burned ?" said he.

Lilian shuddered.

"Ah, how could you think of it ?"

"Lady Mary of Charteris is going—all the earl of Dumfries' windows are occupied, but I think I could procure you a seat somewhere, overlooking the Castle-hill."

"I would not go for the wealth of the Indies. Oh, is it not said that she confessed some horrible things ?"

"As you would have done, fair Lilian, if questioned in the same manner."

"And what did she reveal ?"

"That she was kissed and christened anew by the devil, whom she met at the Gallowlee one mirk midnight, when he imprinted his mark between her shoulders; and though the minister of St. Giles and my Lord Mersington ran a long needle thrice through the infernal signet, she neither winced nor betrayed the least uneasiness."

"Betouch us too! The wicked woman deserves to die—but her death—how horrible! And she really sold her soul? Oh, what appearance had the devil—and what said he?"

"If all be true that appears in the *Mercurius Caledonius*, which I saw to-day in Blair's coffee-house, Satan is a very well-bred and gentlemanlike man," replied Walter, laughing. "He wore a lowland bonnet, and had his nether foot in a buff boot to conceal its deformity. He was somewhat rough, and had a beard of iron wire. He kissed the witch whose spells had conjured him up, and said in husky French, 'Permettez-moi, madame,' adding thereafter in our kindly Scottish, 'What's your will, cummer?'"

"And so Monsieur Le Diable kissed her? He has long been proverbial for very bad taste. His witches are always so old, so ugly, so hideous!"

"After giving her all the power she required, Master Mahoud vanished in a whirlwind."

With all the credulity incident to the time, and though deeply imbued with a sense of the ridiculous, Lilian shuddered; but be it remembered, that the grave and learned senators of the College of Justice had that very morning trembled at the same appalling recital.

"And the power?" she faltered.

"Ample it was, indeed. She could brew hell-kail, and wherever it was sprinkled the soil was scorched, the herbs were blasted, and whoever trod thereon died. Water would not drown, nor hemp hang her. She could bewitch cattle that were without St. Mungo's knot on their tail."

"Mungo—poh! he was a papist."

"And blight children, and bring sickness on her enemies by roasting waxen images, and, in short, do more mischief than was contained in wise King James's Dæmonology, or the box of Pandora."

"Pandora—was she a papist too?—Away with this witch! she must indeed be an ill woman. But now, Mr. Fenton, do you really believe in all the charms of these old enchantresses?

"No, but I do devoutly in those of the young," he added gaily, as he led her down the dance, resigned her to Douglas, and turned to Annie Laurie, who whispered,

" Saw ye who overheard your *tête-à-tête* ! "

"No," he replied, laughing; "but perhaps it was the great subject thereof."

"One not much better, certes. He is behind you now."

Walter turned and beheld the large dark eyes of Lord Clermistonlee, fixedly regarding him with an expression too hostile to be misunderstood. He replied by a glance as haughty and as stern; but a cold and inexplicable smile curled the proud lip of the handsome *roué*, as he turned slowly away, and addressed himself to Lady Charteris, the beautiful blonde, who rustled in a ponderous suit of brocade, and stood five feet seven inches independent of "cork-heeled shoon," being in every sense of the word what the Scotch were wont to consider a "fine" woman, one of those stately and Patagonian beauties, of whom once in a time Edinburgh could always boast a large stock, but who appear to have vanished with the hoops and fardingales, the bobwigs and laced coats, the gentlemanly spirit and the sterling worth of the "last century."

In the middle of the cotillon, Fergusson of Craigdarroch, who had been looking unutterable things for some time, now approached, and twisting his moustachios, said with cold hauteur,

"Your humble servant, Mr. Douglas."

"Craigdarroch, yours," rejoined Finland, quite as coldly, and they surveyed each other from head to foot.

"I requested the honour of Mistress Laurie's hand for this cotillon."

"Indeed!" replied Finland, in the same cavalier tone, and raising his eyebrows with a well-bred stare of surprise. "You have forfeited it by being too late, however."

"You will not resign in my favour?"

"Zounds!" said Finland, frowning. Fergusson's cheek glowed with passion.

"You have your rapier with you?"

"Here, at your service," replied Douglas, in the same low tone, and bit his glove.

"Good. When the cotillon closes I will be in the garden, where the moonlight is bright enough to enable us to come to a proper understanding." Douglas nodded significantly, and his rival withdrew. Annie, who had been gaily chatting for a minute with some passer, had not heard what passed—Lilian Napier did, or at least, she saw enough to alarm her. Douglas went through the cotillon with his usual gaiety and grace; and after a short promenade, handed his unconscious partner to a seat; but instead of posting himself behind it as usual, to Annie's great surprise and indignation, he beckoned Walter Fenton, and they left the room together.

At that moment Lilian, with a pale lip and agitated eye, glided to the side of her friend, and whispered—

"Where has the laird of Finland gone?"

"I know not, and I care not," replied Annie, pettishly, flirting her large fan; "but the varlet left me abruptly enough, and 'tis not his wont. This comes of loving soldiers —fie!"

"O! Annie," said Lilian, in a breathless voice, "they have followed Craigdarroch to the garden. There has been a feud about your dancing with one when engaged to the other; and something terrible will assuredly come of it."

"Preserve me, Heaven! O, in my heedlessness I did so, and they will be fighting about it—blood ever comes of a Scotsman's quarrel. My God! Lilian—where is the earl— the countess—to whom shall I speak? Stay—let us not spoil the merriment around us. The garden, said you? I know the way, and if the cavaliers are there, I will soon make them sheath their rapiers, I warrant you."

Lilian took her arm; and though it was not easy for two such bright stars to leave their orbits unseen, they contrived, to elude observation, to glide down stairs, and reach the old-fashioned garden, on the rich flower-beds, leaden nymphs and Corydons, box-edged walks and thick green holly hedges or which, several flakes of strong light fell in long ruddy lines from the grated windows of the mansion.

The full round moon was sailing in summer radiance through clouds of fleecy whiteness, and threw her slanting beams in showers of silver on the shrubbery and terraces of the garden. All was still and silent; the agitated girls could not perceive any one; but, trembling, they listened fearfully for the clash of swords or the jingle of spurs.

"Oh! if they should have gone to the fields, where we cannot follow them!" murmured Annie, in great agitation. "God guide me!" she added, pressing her hands upon her temples, and displaying, as she did so, two beautiful and braceleted arms, that shone like alabaster in the moonlight. "O! if blood is shed for me, I will never smile more. Ah! surely they will not fight about such a trifle as my preference in a cotillon."

"Dear Annie, think you your love is a trifle to spirits as these? They *will* fight, and desperately too. Douglas bit his glove, and that, Aunt Grizel says, is an old border sign of deadly feud; Craigdarroch will never forgive it; and I saw his black eyes flash fire, as he bit his gauntlet in reply, and turned sharply away on his heel."

At that moment they heard the voice of Douglas. He was close by, but one of those dark holly hedges, so common in ancient gardens, interposed its thick impervious screen between them.

"'Tis well!" he exclaimed; "but ere we come to slash the doublets we were born in, Walter, unclasp this iron shell of mine: Craigdarroch is minus a corslet, and we must fight on equal terms. A merry moonlight, gentlemen, for a camisadoe. A clear field and no favour. Shall we fight with our buff gloves on?"

"That is as you please," replied another guardsman, the young laird of Holsterlee, who was Craigdarroch's second. "But speak softly, or Dunbarton's guard of dragoons may overhear us. Ah! gentlemen, this cometh of the sin of promiscuous dancing—men mingling with women, whilk is ane abomination in the sight of the Lord," he added in a singsong voice. "Ha, ha! so say the dogs of the Covenant. Are ye ready, sirs?"

"All ready," replied Craigdarroch, unsheathing his long troop-sword.

"Be brief, gallants," said Holsterlee, "and sink points on the first blood drawn. I hope the Earl's guests will not disturb us; but ere ye tilt at each other's throats, Finland, as a dear friend to both, I ask thee to apologize to Craigdarroch."

"Apologize to the devil!" rejoined Douglas, as he threw away his corslet and plumed hat, drew his rapier, and stood on the defensive, while his antagonist confronted him in the same manner. Handsome, richly garbed, graceful, and athletic, they would have formed a noble study for an artist, as they remained steadily watching each other, their eyes sparkling, and their long keen blades gleaming like blue fire in the moonlight. Such was the aspect they presented when the terrified girls hurried by a circuitous path towards them.

"Oh! Finland—Finland!" muttered Annie.

A well-bred man of the present day, on seeing a lady, whose hand he had engaged, dancing with another, would not take any unpleasant notice of it, however mortifying the preference might be; but not so the bold cavalier of the seventeenth century. To fight or be dishonoured were the only alternatives. Craigdarroch was infuriated, and Finland rapidly found his blood boiling up in turn; but ere a blow could be struck, his beautiful Annie, like a fairy or angel of peace, glided between them, and the menacing points of the rapiers were lowered at her approach.

"Sheath your swords this instant, sirs!" said she with a half-playful, half-earnest imperiousness, which the gentlemen showed no disposition to resist. "Up with them! and remember it was an ancient rule of chivalry that knights combatants became friends at a woman's approach. Come hither, Mr. Holster, and tell me what these gay rufflers have quarrelled about."

"Yourself, fair madam," replied Holsterlee, a tall athletic young man, whose fair complexion consorted ill with a sable wig, and in whose sporting air there was a certain jaunty swagger, bordering on the vulgar, but acquired chiefly by frequenting Blair's coffee-house at the Pillars, the race-course at Leith, and every tavern and stew wherever he happened to be quartered—Clermistonlee's furious dinner-parties, and the company of all the horsemongers, bucks, bullies, and courtezans in the city ;—" yourself, fair madam; and on my honour, I know no prize in all broad Scotland so well worth tempting buff under bilboa for."

"Prize, sir!" retorted Annie. "Do you talk of me as if I were your famous roan horse, or the city purse you expect it to win at Easter? Go to, sir! Certes, gentlemen, you honour me greatly by accounting me merely a sword-player's prize—the guerdon of a duello between two cut-throats! I am infinitely obliged to you," she added curtseying low. "But if you are determined to fight, O do so, good sirs," she continued, with a merry laugh; "but I am not for you, Finland, at all events."

"Indeed! madam," rejoined Finland, as he bit his nether lip, and grasped his sword. "Craigdarroch, then, I presume, is the favoured——"

"Nor he either, quotha!"

"Ha, ha!—ho, ho!" shouted Holsterlee. "May the great Diabolus roast me in my own ribs if this isn't good! Who then, fair Annie?"

"What is it to such as thee, sirrah?" she replied, stamping her pretty foot scornfully; but the beautiful rogue laughed as she added slowly, "I have not yet made up my mind whether to accept Sir Thomas Dalyel, of the Binns, or that very accomplished cavalier——"

"Who? who?" they all asked.

"Lord Mersington."

"Zounds!" laughed Holsterlee; "but that old cock hath a roost-hen already—a brave girl—a bouncer that can coquette and ruffle it, without snaffle or martingale; a thorough-pacer, by the Lord—ho, ho!"

"As this is her choice," said Douglas, who perfectly

understood the humour of his waggish mistress, "I think, Craigdarroch, we had better shake hands on't, as neither will be a winner in this affair."

"Yes, yes—shake hands like whipped school-boys, and quarrel no more. So, up with your rapiers!—or, as the comedy says, the dew will rust them. But as a penance on you, Mr. Douglas, for fighting without my express permission, I shall dance with the laird of Craigdarroch, and no one else, while you lead out old dame Drumsturdy, or some such witch, whose most devoted you must be for the remainder of the night."

"How droll! O! I shall die with laughing," cried Lilian, clasping her hands with delight at this happy conclusion.

"Nay—fair Annie," said Douglas, "under favour—I must implore——"

"Not a word, sir, of extenuation or excuse. You shall walk a minuet with old Lady Drumsturdy, who is as charming as patches, puffs, and rouge can make her."

Hosterlee laughed till the braces of his corslet started.

"Tush! Annie—O, by all the devils, I shall be the laughing-stock of the whole city."

"I care not."

"Gadzooks! I'll have a duel with old Dalyel next."

"I care not. And, ah! Mr. Fenton, I must find a way to punish you too. But come, Lilian, love—Craigdarroch, your hand."

Douglas joined in the laugh against himself, as Annie was led off by his rival, while Walter gave his hand to Lilian, and they hastened back to the ball-room in the happiest mood. Douglas, while loitering a little behind to clasp the braces of his cuirass, was attracted by the voice of Lord Clermistonlee, a man whom, of all others in Edinburgh, he disliked, in consequence of an old grudge between them, when they exchanged blows in a brawl at Blair's coffee-house. Though he scorned being a spy upon his lordship, the fact of his overhearing the name of Lilian Napier pronounced in a very audible whisper —his knowledge of the speaker's passion, and of what he was capable, formed a sufficient whet to his curiosity, and were, he deemed, quite a warrant for assuming the unpleasant part of eavesdropper.

Clermistonlee was standing near a gate, which afforded communication between the crowded courtyard and the quiet gardens, and through its iron bars the bright moonlight streamed upon the rich embroidery of his gay attire, on the brilliants of his hat-band, buckles, and silver-hilted rapier. Near him stood a stout and thickset old man in green livery

having a massive crest and coronet worked on each sleeve.
A broad belt encircled his waist, and sustained a heavy basket-
hilted sword.   He was a little intoxicated, and balancing himself on one leg, snapped his fingers while chaunting the merry
old catch—

> " Though I go bare, take ye no care
>   I nothing am a-colde ;
> I stuff my skinne so full within,
>   With jollie gude ale and old.
>
> Back and side go bare, go bare,
>   Both foot and hand go colde ;
> But bellie, God give thee gude ale enough,
>   Whether it be new or olde.
>
> I love no roste, but a nut-brown toste——"

" God's curse, rascal! " said his master, angrily, " in this
mood you will never arrange the matter satisfactorily."

" Trust me, my lord, trust me," stammered Juden, rubbing
his bald pate with a sudden air of perplexity, which showed
that the *matter* referred to had quite escaped him; " but
ane needs a lang spoon to sup kail wi' the deil, and you are
'cittler than the great serpent himsel."

" Gadzooks! old limb of Beelzebub, thou art drunk already;
but hear me, Juden, if you fail in this service to-night, old
though ye be, by the Heaven that hears us, I will handle my
whip in such wise that a coffin will be your next resting place."

The eyes of the fierce lord gleamed as he spoke, though his
face was pale with that white fury which is ever the index of
a bad and bitter heart, and is much more to be dreaded than
the red flush of passion that suffuses a generous brow.

" How many followers hath the dame of Bruntisfield in
her train to-night?"

" Four, my lord—her chairmen."

" Armed, of course?"

" Like myself, ilk ane wi' a gude basket-kilted whinger.
They are a' in Lucky Tippeny's Change-house outbye, birling
the ale cogue like sae many lords or troopers."

" All the better.   Here is money—join them, and spare
not to push the jorum till they become like blind puppies;
but, peril of thy life, Juden, keep sober, though ale, usquebaugh, and even wine flow like water, if the knaves will it.
When Lady Grizel summons them, if they are able to stand,
by the head of the king I will truncheon thee in famous
fashion.   Dost comprehend, jolthead?"

" The upshot, my lord, the upshot?"

" When Lady Bruntisfield's people are summoned—but
who is with you to-night?"

" The hail household—just Jock, my sister's son. Wha else would there be ?"

" The devil! that fellow is a born gomeral, like his uncle, and will spoil all."

" Jock's gey gleg at the uptak', and mair kenspeckle than ye think. My certie, my lord, there are mair fules in the world than Jock, puir man—fules that canna keep their fingers out of the fire."

" Silence, or I will certainly beat thee. When the Napiers' chairs are summoned, you will immediately bear off that containing the young lady Lilian, without the delay of a moment."

" No to Bruntisfield, I warrant?" rejoined Juden, with a bright leer of intelligence.

" 'Sdeath, no—to the place of Drumsheugh."

" Ha! ha! ha! My certie, gif this plot succeeds, there will be a braw clamjamfray in the toun the morn! But I hope the business will be owre in time to let me be at the tar-barrelling. 'Twill be a braw sight. O that it were Lucky Elshender's! then I might ride up Meg, puir beastie, to see hersel revenged for that weary fit o' the wheezlock ——"

" Silence, addlepate. I go to Beatrix Gilruth. Wo to thee, if one tittle of my injunctions be forgotten."

Juden bowed with a tipsy air of respect, and withdrew, while Lord Clermistonlee rolled his furred rocquelaure about him, and, stepping through the postern gate, issued into the Potter's-row, and hurried away at a quick pace.

" Good even, my lord," said Douglas, looking scornfully after him. " If I mar not your precious plot to-night, may I never march more!"

He sprung up the stair, and forgetful of the penance his playful mistress had assigned him, sought an opportunity of communicating to Lady Grizel or to Walter Fenton this new plot of Clermistonlee, but none occurred. The former was too deeply engaged with General Dalyel in the intricacies of ombre or primero, and the mode of impaling among the Tartars, and the latter in the more delightful occupation of squiring Lilian from room to room, or exchanging the hand-in-hand mazes of the merry couranto for a moonlight promenade on the flowery terraces of the garden.

Douglas became deeply anxious; the night wore apace, and the hour rapidly approached when the guests would be departing, for already had the roll of the ten o'clock drum rung through the thoroughfares of the city, and these late balls and suppers were but a new innovation of the time, an introduction by Mary of Modena.

CHAPTER XXIV.

BEATRIX GILRUTH.

Her heart was full
Of passions which had found no natural scope.
She hated men because they loved not her,
And hated women because they were beloved,
And thus in wrath, in hatred and despair,
She tempted hell.—
THE CURSE OF KEHAMA.

CLERMISTONLEE walked hurriedly forward, with his mantle rolled about him, his hat flapped over his eyes, and his sword-hilt ready at hand, for his amorous quarrels and politics had, through life, created him innumerable enemies. He muttered as he went, and his cheek flushed at times, though his nether lip was pale as marble, and under the broad shadow of his Spanish beaver his fierce dark eyes burned like two sparks of fire.

Inflamed by wine and the beauty of Lilian, who had never appeared so enchanting as in her ball-dress, he had deter-mined that very night to make another desperate attempt to obtain possession of her person, at whatever ultimate danger and odium. It was curious how strongly the sentiments of pride, avarice, and revenge, mingled with his love-musings ;— his matchless pride was fired by the idea of the woman he loved being given to another—he had revenge to be gratified because, with ill-disguised loathing, she had shrunk from his addresses, and avarice crowned all, as he doubted not if by fair means or foul he obtained her hand, the entail of Bruntis-field and the Wrytes would soon become a dead letter. In effect, it was so already. But once a prisoner in his power, even for a single night, he knew that shame and her injured reputation would *compel* her to become his wife.

Full of these thoughts, which crowded and chased each other in rapid succession through his unsettled brain, he strode forward at a quick pace, impatient for the triumphant consummation of his projects. The city was silent and dark, for the moon had now become obscured, and there were no lamps to light the narrow ways through which he hurried. In the High-street a few oil lanterns had been suspended about four years before by the provost, Sir George Drummond, of Milnab, and these at long intervals shed a pale and sickly light : but all the numerous alleys diverging from this great thoroughfare were still involved in Cimmerian darkness. Deserted as they were, the cogitations of Clermistonlee were often interrupted by scraps of conversations from belated passengers, or stair-head gossips, who were making all secure for the night, and maintained at the top of their voices a colloquy with their neighbours opposite.

"Ken ye, cummer, at what hour the morn that vile witch is to be worrit?" screamed one.

"When the Tron Kirk bell rings aucht. My Lord Provost, the baillies, and the captain of the guard are to eat the deid-chack at Hughie Blair's twa hours thereafter. Fie upon the greedy gleds that meet to revel and roister oure a puir sinner's departure, and to drink Gascony and Rhenish like spring water, though they be eightpence the quart, and at this time when a puir man's four hours' draught ——"

"But gif a' be true, nane hae sae well deservit bridle and faggot, since that monster o' iniquity, Weir, was burnt wi' his staff, whilk my ain faither, as honest a body as ever wore the blue ribbon at his lug, often met stoting down the Bow, for a plack's worth o snuff for its hellicate master. And mair, cummer ——"

But Clermistonlee hurried on, and passing the porte of the Potter's-row, hurried down the steep College-wynd, where picturesque edifices of vast strength and unknown antiquity towered up on each side of the way, and excluded the pale light of the stars. A single ray from a window revealed the rich dresses of two gentlemen who were slowly ascending.

"I insist upon giving you a Kelso convoy, my lord," said one.

"A devil of a dark night, Laird, especially for a summer one—but I vow to ye, Libberton, that my Lord Perth's claret has cast a glamour oure me."

"Hold up, Balcarris, or ye'll measure your length in the gutter: and that would be a braw place for the lord high treasurer to be found in the morning. Thank God, the gate is no a broad ane. I mind when Cromwell, that's now roasting in a pretty hot place—ahoa! who goes there? Draw, Balcarris—it's some spy o' the States-General—a keeper o' conventicles contrary to proclamation. Stand, ye deil's buckie—for king or covenant?"

"For the king!" cried Clermistonlee; and, irritated by their stopping the narrow way, he unceremoniously tumbled the inebriated laird of Libberton to the right, and the treasurer to the left, as he broke past and hurried into the Cowgate (the ancient *communis via*), then the residence of aristocratic exclusives. An old author,* who wrote in the sixteenth century, informs us, "that the nobility and chief senators o

* Munster Cosmograph. p. 42.

the city dwell in the Cowgate—*via vaccarum in quâ habitant patricii et senatores urbis:*" and that " the palaces of the chief men of the nation are also there : that none of the houses are mean or vulgar, but, on the contrary, all magnificent—*sed omnia magnifica.*"

The troubles of Clermistonlee were not yet over. On issuing into the High-street, a crowd of tipsy roisterers, young bucks, students, and Life Guards, burst out of Hugh Blair's tavern, with shouts of laughter and drawn swords, ripe for mischief. They beat back the axes of the watch, and joining hands in one long line, danced down the broad street, vociferously chaunting the merry old ditty—

" Now let us drinke,
Till we nod and winke,
Even as good fellows should do ;
We shall not misse
To have the blisse
Good wine doth bring men to ! "

" Hold fast, my brethren," cried one whom his lordship recognised to be the Reverend Mr. Joram, the famous cavalier chaplain of Dunbarton's Foot. " Hold fast—and every lass we meet must kiss us all from right to left ; aye, d—me! or drink a pint of hot sack at one gulp."

" Bravo !" shouted the rest. " Once, twice, thrice, and away ! "—and onward they came, hand in hand, dancing and singing with stentorian voices that made the whole street ring. Clermistonlee drew his rapier, and shrunk under the carved arches of those stone arcades which supported the houses on both sides of the way ; and, without perceiving him, this crowd of merry fellows passed on to beat the watch and terrify the sleepy denizens of other quarters. Glad of his escape— for he had confidently expected a dangerous brawl—Clermistonlee hurried down Mary King's close.

Debauched and *roué* as he was, he felt an involuntary shudder on descending into the gloomy precincts of that deserted street, a locality shunned by all since the plague had swept off its entire inhabitants. For a hundred years its houses remained closed, and gradually it became a place of mystery and horror, the abode of a thousand spectres and nameless terrors. Superstition peopled it with inhabitants, whom all feared, and none cared to succeed.

Those who had been foolhardy enough to peep through the windows after nightfall, saw within the spectres of the long-departed denizens engaged in their wonted occupations; headless forms danced through the moonlit apartments, and, on one occasion, a godly minister and two pious elders were scared out of their senses, by the terrible vision of a raw head and blood-dripping arm, which protruded from the wall in this terrible street, and flourished a sword above their heads, and many other terrors which are duly chronicled in that old calender of diablerie, "Satan's Invisible World."

Scarcely a foot's space from his elbows on either hand, the tall mansions rose up to a great height, empty, dark, and desolate, with their iron-barred and shadowy windows decaying and rattling in the gusts that swept through the mouldering chambers. Who Mary King was, is now unknown; but though the alley is roofless and ruined, with weeds, wallflowers, and grass, and even little trees, flourishing luxuriantly among the falling walls, her name may still be seen painted on the street corner. Clermistonlee was not without a strong share of the superstition incident to the time and country, and he certainly quickened his pace as he turned down the steep alley towards the dark loch, the waters of which rippled in little wavelets against the bank, then named Warriston Brae. The eastern sluice was shut, for there was a whisper abroad of coming strife, in which the city might require all the strength of its fortifications; and thus in a few weeks the loch had risen many feet above its usual margin. The ferryboat was chained to a stake, against which it jarred heavily, as the west wind swept over the darkened water.

It was down this steep bank that the earl of Arran and his son rushed, after being defeated in their famous feudal battle in the High-street; and finding a collier's horse at the edge of the loch, leaped upon its back, and though both were sheathed in complete armour, forced it to swim them over to the opposite bank. And down the same place, the wild young master of Gray dragged the fair mistress Carnegie, whom, sword in hand, he had torn from her father's house, and boated over the loch, attended by twelve men-at-arms.

Lustily the impatient lord thundered at the door of the ferryman's cottage; but it was long ere the unwilling Charon of the passage attended his summons.

"Hallo, boatman! Harkee, fellow, truss your points and come forth," he cried in his usual overbearing manner. All cavaliers of the time spoke thus towards inferiors; but Clermistonlee carried it to an outrageous extent. "Come forth, rascal, or I will chastise thee so tremendously, that thou wilt never pull paddle again, in this world at least."

"Awa, ye impudent limmer, awa!" replied a voice from the profundity of a box-bed. "Is that the way to ding at a douce man's yett? Awa, ye misleared loon, or I tak' my dag frae the brace, and send a bullet through your cracked harnpan."

I.   o

A terrible oath burst from Clermistonlee, for he was frenzied by wine, passion, and delay. "Insolent runnion! attend me, or by —— I will beat down the door, and twist thy whaisling hause! Beware thee, fool," he added in a low tone; "I am the Lord Clermistonlee!"

On hearing that terrible name, the affrighted boatman sprang from bed; an exclamation of fear and much anxious whispering followed. The door was immediately opened by a lean and withered old man, whose face was a mass of wrinkles. Scarcely daring to raise his grey twinkling eyes, he stood lamp in hand, cringing and bowing his bald head with the most abject humility before Clermistonlee, who cut short his muttered apologies by saying—

"Unmoor, dyvour loon, and pull me across the loch, if you would be spared the beating I owe you."

The old ferryman hurriedly dragged his leather galligaskins over his hodden grey breeches, donned his skyblue coat and broad bonnet, and bowing at every step of the way, though inwardly cursing the summons from his cosy nest and gude-wife's side, led the proud baron towards the little boat, for the use of which he paid a yearly rental to the city. They stepped on board; he unlocked the mooring-chain and shoved off.

Fed by the springs of the castle-rock and the rivulets that gurgled down its northern bank, the loch had of late become considerably swollen, and now rose high upon the bastions of the Well-house tower. It was without current, and, save the ripple raised by the soft west wind, was still and motion-less as a lake of ink.

Clermistonlee, with his rocquelaure rolled around him, and his broad beaver with its heavy plumage shading his face, lounged silently in the stern, watching the gigantic features of the city as they rose in sable outline behind him, towering up from the lake like a vast array of castles, or a barrier of splintered rock, a forest of gables and chimneys, whose sum-mits shot upwards in a thousand fantastic shapes.

To the westward, from a cliff of perpendicular rock, three hundred feet in height, rose the towers of the castle. Beneath the gloomy shadow of this basaltic mass the loch vanished away into obscurity; but from under its impending brow there gleamed a light that tremulously shed one long red ray across the dark bosom of the water. It shone from the guard-fire in the Well-house tower. Save the measured dash of the oars, and the creaking of the boat, all was so still that Clermistonlee heard the pulsations of his own evil heart.

Suddenly the moon gushed forth a glorious blaze of light

between the flying clouds. Magnificent was the effect of that silver splendour, and wondrous was the beauty it lent to that romantic scene. High over the jagged outline of the tall city it streamed aslant, and its thousand points and pinnacles became tipped with instant light. The great stone turrets, the massive towers and angular bastions of the castle, and its perpendicular cliffs, were thrown forward, some in silver light, while others remained in sombre shadow. To its base the still loch rolled like a silver mirror, while the dewy alders. the waving osiers, and bending willows that fringed its northern bank, shone like fairy trees of gleaming crystal.

Even the old boatman paused for a moment and looked around him. City, rock, wood, and water, all shone in the magnificent moonlight; but once more the gathering vapours obscured the shining source, and the whole faded like a vision. The varied masses of the city and its stupendous fortress sank again into darkness, and once more the sheet of water rolled to their base a black and fetid lake. At that moment the boat grounded, the passenger sprang ashore, and addressed the boatman in his usual style :—

"Peril of thy life, knave, tarry till my return, or thy fee will contain more cudgel-blows than bonnet-pieces."

"Yes, my lord, yes," stammered the poor man, whose teeth chattered with cold and fear ; meanwhile his imperious employer sprang up the bank, and hurried on till, reaching the Lang Dykes, a road which led westward, and which he traversed until he gained the Kirk-brae-head, where on one hand the road branched off towards the castle rock, and on the other plunged down between thick copsewood towards the secluded village of the Dean, which lay at the bottom of a deep dell overhung by the richest foliage.

By the margin of the loch, and surrounded by an ample churchyard, where the long grass waved and the yew-trees cast their solemn shadows on many an ancient grave, where the moss-grown headstones, half-sunk in earth, and obliterated time, marked the resting-place of the dead of other days, the old cross kirk of St. Cuthbert reared up its dark façade, with a gloomy square tower and pointed spire surmounting the nave and transept. There slept all the ancestors of Clerestonlee ; he cast but a glance at its vast outline and hurried on. The occasional stars alone gleamed through its mullioned windows, for the tapers of the midnight votary had long since been quenched on the altars of Cuthbert and St. Anne, the mother of the Virgin.

Under a mouldering gateway, where two stone wyverns, with forked tails and outspread wings, reared up on their mossy columns, Clermistonlee paused for a moment—for a host of strange fancies and burning thoughts, the memories of other days, crowded fast upon his mind as he surveyed the long gloomy vista beyond.

It led to his mansion of Drumsheugh.

The avenue was long and dark; thick oaks and beeches, clothed with the most luxuriant foliage of summer, formed a leafy arcade, which seemed dark and impervious as if hewn through the bowels of a mountain.

"Long, long it is," thought he, "since the hoof of the trooper's horse, or the blast of the hunter's horn, the voice of mirth, or the merry voice of a woman awoke these lonely echoes. Alison—Alison—pshaw! I am another man now," he added aloud, and endeavoured to whistle a fashionable couranto, as he walked up the grass-grown avenue, at a pace which soon brought him to the door of the house, where again he made a brief pause.

The mansion was a high and narrow edifice, built on the very verge of a cliff, overhanging the Water of Leith, that struggled through a deep and wooded gorge a hundred feet below, and the rock was so abrupt, that a plumb-line could have reached without impediment, from one of the turrets to the rocky bed of the river.

The house had the usual Scottish gablets, turrets at the angles and machecoulis between. Its windows were all thickly barred, dark, silent, and in many places broken. The vanes creaked mournfully in concert with the rooks and the wind, that sighed through the ancient oaks. All else was silent as the grave. There came no sound from the mansion; none from the empty stalls of the stable court, and none from the tenantless perches of the falconry.

On the door-lintel, notwithstanding the darkness, Clermistonlee could decipher, *I fear God onlye*, 1506, a legend placed there by his pious forefathers, to exclude witches and evil spirits, on whom it was supposed that the name of the Deity would act as a spell of potence. The present lord was as evil a spirit as the city contained; but the legend neither affected him or his purpose, and he furiously tirled at the risp, and kicked at the door till the whole house rang to the noise. A ray of light streamed through the keyhole, and vizzying all of the door, on the green leaves and dewy grass, and the approach of a slip-shod female was heard.

"Who knocks so late?" asked a shrill voice. "A proper hour and a pleasant to disturb folk. Marry, deil stick the visitor," she added, **withdrawing the ponderous bolts,** and opening the door.

"As of old, good Beatrix, you are still without fear," said
Clermistonlee.

"Why? because I am without hope," she rejoined, in a
fierce tone. "Fear! what should I fear? Did I not know
it was thee? But what fool's errand or knavish purpose
brings thee here now?"

"Silence, Mistress Malapert!"

There was a momentary pause, and a terrible glance—one
at least of intense expression passed between those two. A
sentence will explain it.

When Clermistonlee was but a youth, Beatrix, though
ten years his senior, was among the first of his loves, and by
her own futile endeavours to ensnare the heir of a powerful
baron, became one of the first victims of his gallantry; she
was then a beautiful and artful woman; but gradually her
beauty faded, her arts failed, and her spirits sank : abandoned
by her friends, and despised by her betrayer, she had long,
long since lost sight of every hope of marriage, or of regain-
ing an honourable position in life, and now she had sunk so
low as to be a mere abject dependant, a vile panderer to the
amours of her early lover—an entrapper of others ; and when
the old mansion was abandoned to the crows and spiders, she
had remained there, a half-forgotten pensioner on his bounty
—a creature only to be remembered when her vile services
were required. Now she was old, wrinkled, and hideous; but
Clermistonlee, in his fortieth year, seemed as gay and as
young as in the days when first he pressed her to his bosom.
Beatrix was now fifty!

These ten years made a world of difference between them.

He felt all her eagle glance conveyed, but uttering a very
cavalier-like malediction, strode along the passage or ambulatory, with his bright spurs clanking, and his white plumes
waving as gallantly as they had done twenty years before.
How different was the aspect of Beatrix! Crime, mental
misery, and a life of disease and dissipation made her seem
many years older than she was. She stooped much at times,
and was poorly clad in garments that, like herself, had seen
better days. Her head was covered by a dirty long-eared
linen cap, beneath which a few grizzled hairs escaped to wander over a face that, like her hands and neck, had by the use
of lotions and essences become a mass of saffron wrinkles.
Her eyes were grey, hollow, keen, and unpleasant in expression ; her lips thin and colourless, and grey hairs were appearing on her chin.

"Zounds!" thought Clermistonlee, as he loathingly gazed
upon her ; "can this old kite be the creature I once loved?"

By the course of time and desertion, the house seemed as much dilapidated as its occupant; but an air of desolate grandeur pervaded its lofty chambers and echoing corridors. Masses of the frescoed ceiling had in many places fallen down, in others the wainscoting had given way, revealing the rough masonry behind. The once gaudy tapestry hung mouldering on its tenter-hooks, and a dreary air of dusky dampness was everywhere apparent. A thousand spiders spun their nets undisturbed across the unopened windows and unentered doorways; and through the rattling casements the hurrying clouds were seen afar off chasing each other in masses across the pale-faced moon and paler stars, that twinkled through the tossing trees.

Traversing an ambulatory, on the discoloured walls of which old pictures and older trophies hung decaying, Clermistonlee was about to enter the hall; but its vast space rang so hollowly to his tread, and its gloom so much resembled that of a church at midnight, that he drew back overpowered by some superstitious feeling, and entered a small apartment which adjoined it, and had in earlier days been named the Lady's Bower.

A fire burned cheerily on the hearth; the furniture and the tapestry were fresh; the gilding and scarlet marquise of the high-backed chairs unfaded; a large mirror gleamed over the carved buffet, which two grotesque imps sustained on their heads; and several old portraits, in the warm glow, looked complacently out of their round oak frames.

"And 'tis *here* you have made your lair!" said Clermistonlee, throwing himself into a chair.

"Yea: it was *her* boudoir—her bower. Hast thou forgotten that too?" responded the woman, setting down her lamp, and surveying him with a malicious eye.

"Well! old dame, and what recks it thee?" asked the lord, impatiently. "Art alone—of course—eh?"

"Alone!" reiterated the woman, bitterly—"when am I ever otherwise? Alone—and why! Because I am old and hideous now. Yet there was a time when it was otherwise. Yea—I am ever alone, save when the knave and the fool (on whose scanty bounty I am too often dependent), prompted by the devil, come hither to visit me."

"Dependant? have I not given thee a fee of four hundred pounds Scots per year, and what the devil more?"

"Between your own necessities and your butler's villany, not a plack of it have I seen since Lammas-tide."

"This shall be seen to. Come, come, Beatrix, my merry old lass, thou art as petulant as when I led you into the chamber twenty years ago. You want gold, I know; but, faith! I have devilish little of that." He spread a few French crowns on the table.

" 'Tis but white money," said the hag, her eyes sparkling as, with clutching hands, she swept the coins into her lap.

"Greedy gled! if thou art faithful, the gold will come in bushels anon."

"On what ill errand come ye now? Is there any one to be poisoned—hah! any poor flower to be torn from its stem, and trod under foot when its perfume is gone?"

"Harkee! Lucky Gilruth," said the lord, striking his clenched hand on the table; "thou knowest me well, I think."

" O would to heaven I had never, never known thee!" said Beatrix, with a tearless sob. "I know little of thee that is good."

"What know ye that is bad?"

She gave him a glance of scorn and fear.

" Say forth, old Barebones—I care not. I am one——"

" Who never spared a man in his hatred, or a woman in his lust! A renegade covenanter!—a relentless persecutor of the pious and the holy!—a perjured lover!—a faithless husband! —a false friend!—one to whom Lord Solis of old, and the Marquis de Laval, were as saints in comparison. Randal Clermont, thou art a fiend in the form of a man!"

"With a bcylillelu and a how-lo-lan! ha! ha!" laughed Clermistonlee, shaking back his feathers and long cavalier locks, while regarding Beatrix with a sardonic glance, for her words stung him deeply. "And I know *thee* for one whom the tar-barrels and thumb-screws await, if ye prove false to me. Ay, woman, I doubt not my learned gossip, Mersington, would soon find the devil's mark on that poor hide of thine. But I came to arrange, not to quarrel with thee—ha! ha! I want my fortune read."

Beatrix gave him a long steady glance; her bleared eyes were glaring with insanity, and a certain degree of intoxication; but she quailed before the dark basilisk eye of her former lover, for the ferocity of her expression relaxed, and she burst into a horrid laugh.

" Thy fortune? ho, ho! I tell thee, Randal, that the blade is forged and tempered that will drink thy heart's blood!"

" Gadzooks! likely enough; for I do not expect to die in bed," replied Clermistonlee, calmly, yet nevertheless exasperated by her reply, as he knew from old experience the value of her prophecies. " But I trifle. I know, good Beatrix, you can be faithful, and will serve me as of old. Here is my hand—shall I be fortunate in love?"

"How often these twenty years hath that question been asked of me; and where now are those anent whom ye asked it? Fortunate? I doubt not ye will be more so than she whose portrait is there;" and suddenly withdrawing a veil from a panel, she displayed the portrait of a pale young lady, in a rich dress and high ruff. Her features were soft and beautiful; her hair fair and in great profusion; and her parted lips appeared to smile with inexpressible sweetness. Clermistonlee turned pale, and averted his face, for the portrait seemed full of life and expression.

"Cover it!" said he, in a husky voice; "Cover it!—dost hear me? or must I blow the panel to pieces with my pistols, that these upbraiding eyes may look on me no more?"

"Wretch, ye dare not!" said Beatrix, scornfully, while gazing with something like pity on the fair face the pencil of Vandyke had traced in other times. "Yes, Lady Alison, I hated thee in life, but in death I can respect thee. Oh! Randal, she shared thy wedded love; but was it more fortunate than mine? It was, it was; for she is at rest in her grave, while I still linger here."

"Pity you are not there too! Enough! I am tired of these eternal complaints; and were ye fair as Venus——but look to my hand—what say its lines to-night?"

In her long, lean, and wrinkled fingers she took his ungloved hand, and he half withdrew it, with ill-concealed disgust.

"Ha!" screamed Beatrix, in a terrible voice; "you shrink from my touch now. Oh! Randal, Randal!" she added, in a tone of intense bitterness, "to kiss these faded hands was once a boon of love to thee. Oh! Randal Clermont, have you so quite forgotten these days as to feel no pity for the being you once loved so well?"

"Hum!" muttered the lord impatiently.

"How different was I then from what I am now!" she exclaimed, pressing her hands upon her breast, as if it would burst.

"The deuce!" Clermistonlee whistled.

"Yes, base and ungrateful! the hand that now ye loathe was then white as the new-fallen snow, and these grey locks were like the dewy wing of the raven. My eyes could then look love to thine, that flashed with the youth, the joy, and the brightness of twenty summers. Who that saw us then, would dream that we are the same? I am no longer young, no longer lovely, and thou—art still a man."

"Crush me if this is not ridiculous! art nearly done, old lady?"

" No; there is a rival in thy way!"

" S'death, I know that too well. 'Tis that spawn of the Covenant, young Fenton of Dunbarton's Foot. But I am still trifling. Listen, beldame, and lay my words to heart. A brisk young damsel will be here in an hour hence. See that the turret that overhangs the rocks is prepared for her reception, for I swear by all that is holy, she shall never leave this roof until she is mine; yea, as much as——"

" As I once was, and many more have been, hah!"

Clermistonlee laughed loudly. " I have arled thee, Beatrix, and woe if thou failest or playest me false, for the hemp is twisted that shall strangle, and the faggots oiled that shall consume thee. Yet more. The eyes of the council have long been on thee for suspected sorcery, and dealing in love-potions and medicinal charms—the red hand of Rosehaugh is over thee, wretched Beatrix, and ere long thou mayest know the full value of the protection I afford thee. Enough! we know each other, I think."

" Not quite," replied Beatrix, with an air that startled her proud tormenter : " Vain fool! ye know not that by a word I could crush thee to nothing—yea, to the dust beneath my feet. Randal Clermont, I could reveal that, would smite thee like the scorching lightning. But no! my lips shall remain sealed until ——"

" When ?"

" When the measure of my wrongs and my vengeance *is full!*"

" Pshaw! thou art but a woman—a fool," replied Clermistonlee, jerking on his buff gloves carelessly, but feeling somewhat surprised by her manner.

" When will this new victim be here ?" asked Beatrix, with a ghastly grin.

" I have said in an hour, if all goes well. Prepare the old turret for her—that cage hath held a wilder bird ere now; nay, nay, none of that kind of work," said he, changing colour as Beatrix took a poniard from the mantelpiece ; " nothing of that sort will be required—once in a lifetime—tush! I will be back anon—till then, adieu." He hurried away with evident confusion, and rushing down the avenue without looking once behind him, leaped into the boat and was pulled over to the city.

" Will your lordship be crossing the water again this nicht?" asked the boatman, with the utmost humility.

" That is as may be ; what recks it to such as thee, fellow ?" rejoined the passenger haughtily, as he tossed a few coins into the extended bonnet of the ferryman, sprang up Mary King's-close, and hurried towards Bristo.

CHAPTER XXV

THE SEDAN.

ADURNI.—I will stand
The roughness of the encounter, like a gentleman,
And wait ye to your homes, whate'er befal me.
THE LADY'S TRIAL.

LORD CLERMISTONLEE, as he anticipated, reached the earl of Dunbarton's house just when the company were separating. The guard of horse was drawn up in the court-yard in courtesy to the guests. Lumbering old-fashioned carriages were rolling solemnly away; sedans, borne by liveried chairmen, and having lighted links flaring in the night-wind before and behind them, were carried off at a trot through the dark and devious windings of the city. The court on the north side of the mansion was becoming comparatively still and empty, and Clermistonlee, with no small anxiety for the success of his plot, looked on all sides for his faithful Juden; but that pink of butlers and factotum of his household was nowhere visible, and he searched in vain for the green livery of Clermont faced with scarlet.

At this crisis a sedan approached, bearing the blazon of Napier in a widow's lozenge. It was borne by two men, in whom, though attired as public chairmen, Clermistonlee recognized Juden and his nephew Jock, a strong, lank-bodied fellow, who acted as valet, groom, errand-boy, turnspit, &c., at his lordship's lodging. He had coarse pimply features, high cheek-bones, and a shock head of red hair waving under a broad bonnet, piggish eyes, and a mouth of vast circumference. His whole vocabulary consisted of a deep guttural *cry*, with which he replied to everything and everybody. Half knave, half idiot, he was just the kind of ally required by Clermistonlee, to whom he was intensely devoted, and to whom he looked up as something more than a demigod.

" I am glad you have doffed the green and scarlet," said the lord. " You have been a thought beyond me to-night, Juden. Have her ladyship's sedans been summoned?"

" Half an hour syne, my lord."

" Indeed !" rejoined the other, in a breathless voice, and letting fall the rocquelaure which muffled his face. " Mistress Lilian is not departed! Rascal, if she has ——"

" Hooly and fairly: we have just come for her, by her ladyship's orders," grinned Juden. " A weary tramp we had to Bruntisfield wi' the auld dame (devil tak' her.); but we coupit her at Dalryburn—ha, ha!"

"How, sirrah? where were her chairmen?"

"Where they are even now, in the water-hole of the town-guard, a dungeon vaulted wi' stane, dark as pitch, and half fu' o' water. Gif your lordship does na ken sic a place, owre weel do I, for there I passed fifteen weary days and eerie nights after Bothwellbrig, shivering like a rat in an ice-house."

"Gomeral! is this a place for thy pestilent reminiscences of Bothwell? Ye obeyed my orders?"

"To the letter o' the law, as my Lord Mersington says. I have made Lady Grizel's servitors as fu' as strong October, reeking usquebaugh, ay, and a three-gallon runlet of gude red Rhenish, at sixpence the quart, could make them. But then, by way o' repaying my hospitality, they began misnaming your lordship."

"What said the knaves?"

"That ye were but a cock-laird o' Cramond, for a' your baron's coronet, and a fause Whig and misleared Covenanter at heart."

"Foh! it matters not," replied Clermistonlee. "I will have all those varlets under my thumb ere long, and then I will teach them the respect that is due to my coronet. A cock-laird! By all the devils, they shall have their tongues bodkinned, and their ears nailed to the Tron, as a terror to all such plebeian rascals. But what didst thou, and this great baboon thy nephew, when these rascals made so free with our family?"

"We sweeped the house wi' the hair o' their heads—eh, Jock?"

"Ay," gaped the personage appealed to.

"My birse rose at the first word, and drawing my whinger, I fell on like a Stenton. Jock threw owre the buird and settles, and laid about him wi' a three-leggit stule. The gudewife o' the change-house scraighed like a howlet, and a' gaed to wreck. Shelves o' dishes and tin flagons, caups and luggies, Leith crystal and Delft ware, iron pots and pewter trenchers, a' flew like a hail-storm, and we laid about us like naething that I mind o', but the tulzie at Bothwell, when Dalyel's troopers broke the brig-ward, and fell on us sword in hand."

"Bothwell again! Rascal, how often must I tell thee to recur to those days no more?"

"In burst the toun-guard, wi' axe and pike, and carried them a' to the water-hole, as disturbers o' the peace."

"And how did you escape?"

"At the very sight o' the red wyvern on my sleeve, the loons let me go, as if my gude braid-claith had been iron in a white heat; and sae I am here."

"Excellent! for this night her people are safe. Thou art a priceless fellow, Juden."

"When Lady Grizel's men were summoned, we changed our coats, and in their places came as ye see. We bore her awa to the place o' Bruntisfield, and are now, by her orders, returned for Madam Lilian."

"Heaven is propitious to me to-night. But I fear me, thy dullard of a nephew may spoil all."

At that moment the voice of the earl's chamberlain was heard summoning "Mistress Napier's chair," and with much pretended bustle, Juden and his cunning nephew, in their assumed character of hack-chairmen, carried it up the broad flight of steps into the brilliantly lighted lobby, while, with a beating heart, Clermistonlee withdrew a little, to observe the issue of his plans.

He waited what appeared to be an age; for Juden and his nephew had been desired to remain in the court without for a time; and when again they were summoned, Lilian Napier was in the chair, and when it was brought forth, the little blinds of scarlet silk were so closely drawn that Clermistonlee could not discern the least part of that fairy form, over the beauties of which he revelled in fancy; and his swart cheek glowed, his pulses quickened, as his unscrupulous serving-men approached at a slow trot, carrying with ease the sedan, though it was ponderous with black leather, gilded nails, and armorial bosses.

Equally pleased and surprised that Walter Fenton was not escorting it, Clermistonlee (who had pre-arranged to leave him dead among the fields) silently opened the gate of the court which led to the westward, and shrinking behind the shadow of a wall, almost held his breath as the vehicle passed which contained that fair being for whose possession he was risking so muc_ dium and danger; but neither were new to him. Regardless of the feelings of others, and dead to every sense of honour, save that bull-headed valour which made the cavaliers of his day fight to the death for matters of less value than a soap-bubble, he had long been accustomed to gratify without a scruple his strong and unruly passions.

He breathed more freely as his followers traversed the deserted road that led to the barrier of Bristo, and thence striking westward, proceeded by a narrow horseway leading to the thatched hamlet and manor-house of Lauriston,—

suburb a few hundred yards from the city wall, which, with its row of embattled bastelhouses, rose on the right hand.

It was a long and monotonous line of crenelated wall, the outline of which was broken only by the spire of the old Greyfriars' kirk (which was accidentally blown up in 1718, by powder stored therein by the thrifty baillies of Edinburgh), the turrets of Heriot's Hospital, and at intervals a fantastic stack of great black chimneys studded with oyster-shells. On the left were fields of waving grain, and rows of foliaged trees, that spread over the gradual slope to the sandy margin of the beautiful lake. The little village was buried in silence and sleep; all was hushed under the green thatch of its humble cots. Scarcely a star was visible; it was nearly midnight, and utter solitude surrounded them.

Poor Lilian! Her daring abductor had not as yet formed any defined plan of ultimate procedure. His first object was to have Lilian completely at his mercy, and nowhere could she be more so than in the strong and solitary house of Drumsheugh, watched by the infamous being introduced to the reader in the preceding chapter.

Within the grated chambers of that house, which he had made the scene of a thousand enormities, Clermistonlee hoped soon by terror, persuasion, or force, to overcome the repugnance Lilian had so long expressed for his addresses. The cold, but decided refusal of old Lady Grizel, the startled dismay and ill-concealed *hauteur* of Lilian, when but a few months before he had made a somewhat abrupt and unexpected proposal for her hand, now rose vividly to his mind, and spurred him on to triumph and revenge.

He contemplated with a malicious satisfaction, that even if to-morrow, or a week hence, he should free Lilian from durance, she would go forth with a stain upon her reputation, and imputations upon her honour, worse than death to a girl of her delicacy and spirit,—imputations which ultimately might force the proud little beauty into his arms, when the web of his machinations was stronger, and when even her lover would shrink from her as from one contaminated.

Then would be his hour of triumph! and——but here his cogitations were interrupted by the yelling of a great wolf-dog, which thrust its black nose through the barbican-gate of the Highriggs, and barked furiously.

Clermistonlee had hoped that, fatigued with dancing and the lateness of the hour, sleep had overpowered Lilian, and now he trembled lest she should awake, and by her cries summon aid to her rescue from this old baronial mansion, which terminated the Portsburgh. In wrath, he thrust with his long rapier at the dog; but its baying redoubled, and, in great consternation, Juden and Jock hurried northward down the slope at their utmost speed. To the joy of Clermistonlee, his fair captive expressed no alarm, and the curtains of the sedan remained undrawn. Her voice was unheard; and no sound broke the stillness of the place, save the wind sweeping over the fields, and the tramp of the chairmen's feet, as they ascended by a narrow bridle-path to the ancient gate or Drumsheugh.

"She is mine at last!" exclaimed the triumphant *roué*, through his clenched teeth, as they entered the damp, gloomy avenue. "Ha! Master Fenton, I have the odds of thee! Ha, ha! Not all hell itself could save her from me now."

At the base of a tower, where a small doorway gave entrance to the house, Juden, who was in front, to his great tribulation, saw Beatrix Gilruth, with a long pikestaff in one hand, and an iron cresset in the other. She held it aloft at the full stretch of her meagre arm, and fitfully the flame streamed in the night-wind, casting a bright but uncertain glare on her pinched, unearthly features, her sunken eyes, matted hair, and tattered attire, on the moss-green walls, the grated windows, and striking façade of the ancient mansion, and the thick trees that grew around it, revealing the dewy leaves and threads of silver gossamer that spread from branch to branch—but Beatrix was the most striking object, for the wildness of her air imparted to her the aspect of an antique Pythoness, a sorceress, or a maniac. Juden fearfully eyed her askance.

"Gude e'en to ye, cummer," said he breathlessly.

"Evening? ye feared gowk!" retorted Beatrix. "'Tis the dead hour of midnight, as ye may know by putting your net oure the kirkyard dyke, where mair may be seen than ye reckon on. Behold the light that dances in yonder hollow."

Juden looked down the long avenue, which the dense foliage caused to resemble a leafy tunnel, and saw afar off a lambent and uncertain light playing in the distance.

"'Tis a corpse-candle!" screamed Beatrix. "It glints above the grave of an unchristened wean. Hah, fool! frightened as ye are for it, the day is not far off when the same deidlicht will be dancing amoug the grass that covers your own."

Perspiration burst over Juden's brow, while the woman, enjoying the terror she created, uttered a wild laugh.

"My lord—Jock—I tak ye to witness she foretells my weird; a clear case o' malice and sorcery as ever came before the Fifteen. But I defy ye, Lucky Gilruth, for the barrels are tarred that shall send thee to the fires o' eternity, ye shameless limmer." Juden trembled between pious confidence and deadly fear—like one who in a dream defies a fiend.

"Hark to St. Cuthbert's bell!" continued Beatrix, who appeared to find a satisfaction in the fear and aversion she created. "Now shall ye behold the spirits of the dead, that many a time and oft on this returning night, I have seen rush forth from yonder woods,—Sir Patrick of Blackadder, and his slayers, Douglas, Hume, and Clermistonlee. Like the driven cloud, they fly without a sound along the gloomy avenue—pursuers and pursued, their swords flashing and their hell-forged harness glinting, as they sweep like shadows oure the dewy grass, with the stars shining through the ribs of their skeleton horses, till the spirit of Blackadder plunges into the loch, as it did on his dying day—then red flash their petronels, and the pure water sparkles around them like diamonds in the moonlight—an eldritch yell arises from its shining bosom, and all is over!"

"What mummery is this, thou eternal babbler?" said Clermistonlee, in a voice of suppressed passion. "Woman, Beatrix, silence, lest I strangle thee!"

The sedan was now within the vaulted ambulatory of the mansion, and the door was securely bolted by Juden, while his master, who had begun to feel no little surprise and anxiety at the silence maintained by Lilian, advanced hurriedly to the chair; but first whispered to his old paramour :—

"A word, Beatrix,—is the wainscoted room in the turret prepared for the reception of this little one?" Beatrix nodded. "Peril of thy head, woman, if it were not," he added scornfully, and raised the top of the sedan, while his assistants respectfully withdrew. "Fair Lilian," said he, commencing one of his made-up fine speeches, but not without apparent confusion, "fair Lilian, and not less beloved than fair, pardon this duplicity, for which the excess of my love can be my only, my best excuse. My love—alas! my dear girl, you have known it long, and too long have you slighted it. But on bended knee, behold!—I beseech you to pardon me—Lilian—dearest Lilian——"

"Ha, ha! ho, ho!" laughed a deep and sonorous voice within the sedan. "Horns of Mahoud! if this is not exquisite!" and, instead of beholding Lilian's fair face, shaded by silken ringlets—lo! the exasperated lover was confronted by the bushy periwig, swart visage, and black moustachios of Dick Douglas, of Finland. "Ho, ho! your lordship has been prodigiously outwitted;" and the cavalier laughed as if he would die.

"A thousand furies! draw! Finland, draw!—your life shall pay for this!" exclaimed Clermistonlee, recoiling and laying hand on his sword.

"As you please, right honourable; but I hope, most noble lord, your rascals mean to carry me back to the city—ha, ha!"

"Not unless it be cold and stark upon a bier. Zounds! sir, I believe you know I am one who will not brook being trifled with."

"Your lordship must know me for the same," replied Finland, gravely. "I care not a straw what view you may take of this night's adventure, and will now, or at any time, render due satisfaction for it, with my sword, body to body. I am generally to be found either at my quarters in the White Horse-cellar, or in Hugh Blair's coffee-house."

"Or the laird of Maxwelton's—ha!"

"Where your lordship had better not present yourself; and so, gadzooks! your most obedient. Harkee! Mother Gilruth, undo the barrier; you know me, I think, old one, eh?" and he threw a few coins in her apron, saying, "I can be as free of my flesh and gold as either lord or loon."

Beatrix, whose grey eyes gleamed with malice and avarice, clutched the money with one hand, and shook a poniard at the donor with the other; while Clermistonlee, who was boiling with passion and mortification, again approached him. Douglas started, and half unsheathed his glittering rapier; while Juden, who considered his lord's affront as one offered to himself, snatched an old partisan from the wall, and prepared to fall on.

"Hold! Juden—back!—not now—not now!" said his master, waving his hand.

"'Tis well, my lord," said Douglas, "delay so long as you please. We expect to march southward shortly, and I would regret to be left behind with a slashed skin, when Dunbarton's drums were beating the point of war in the face of an enemy. Yes—by all the devils, I would wish rather to fall à la coup de mousquet, than by the rapier of Randal Clermont."

"Your wish may be frustrated if you speak thus insolently," replied Clermistonlee, who admired the cavalier's bearing, though exasperated by the trick he had played him. "But be it so, Finland. Were not this hand fettered by a longing for revenge—a longing which beyond the morrow I cannot control, and which compels me to retain my sword for the heart of another enemy, God wot, I would slay you where you stand. As a swordsman, you are aware I am unmatched in the three Lothians."

"Pshaw!—on the ramparts of Lisle, after three passes, I

disarmed Monsieur de Martinet, of the Regiment du Roi; and *he* was the first swordsman in France and Flanders. I believe we are pretty equal. But, my lord, he for whom you reserve your skill and fury is my friend—my friend is my second self; and I tell thee, Randal Clermont, lord and baron though ye be, that when I think of what might have been the fate of Lilian Napier under this accursed roof, and in the hands of thee and thy hell-doomed harridan, I am sorely tempted to have at thy throat."

"'Sdeath! these are words rarely addressed to Clermistonlee. Begone! sirrah, ere from high words we come to hard blows. Away! and remember that the time is not far distant when this night's prank shall be dearly atoned for."

"When that hour comes, Finland will never fail," replied the cavalier, throwing his broad beaver jauntily on one side, as with one hand on his rapier, and the other twirling his moustache, he strode away, singing—

> "She is all the world to me,
> And for my blue-eyed Annie Laurie,
> I would lay me down and die."

CHAPTER XXVI.

ADVENTURES OF THE NIGHT CONCLUDED.

COUNT. What an unaccountable being! But it won't do. Steinfort, we will take the ladies home, and then you will try once again to see him. You can talk to these oddities better than I can.—THE STRANGER.

RAGE, mortification, and love (if so his passion can be named), possessed by turns the proud heart of Clermistonlee; but every idea soon became absorbed in one deep and concentrated longing for revenge—revenge upon Douglas of Finland and Walter Fenton, especially the latter, as being the most dangerous and hated—his rival.

He considered and re-considered every charge upon which he could possibly subject their conduct to the scrutiny of the council, and their persons to its torture and dungeons. It was in vain. The high character of Finland on one hand, and the influence of Dunbarton on the other, rendered all such attempts utterly futile; and with a savage exultation, the baffled lord resolved to trust to his own unerring hand for disabling, maiming, and, perhaps, slaying the young ensign; and he resolved, on the first opportunity, to put in practice a species of outrage, which was far from being uncommon in

L.   P

those unsettled times, when our bold forefathers fought to
the last gasp, rather than yield one inch of the causeway to a
man of a family or a faction whom they held at feud.

While the *dénoûment* (recorded in the preceding chapter)
was taking place at the desolate old mansion of Drumsheugh,
gay Annie Laurie, with her usual vivacity and wit, was
relating to the earl and his beautiful countess, and to Lilian,
who, with Walter Fenton, had tarried in the bower or
boudoir after all the other guests had departed, the plot of
the famous *roué;* and how, by her contrivance, Douglas had
been carried off in the sedan to mortify and disappoint him.

Poor Lilian trembled and changed colour as she felt alternately fear and indignation at the lure that had been laid for
her; but Walter kindled up into a red-hot passion; the
countess became agitated; and the earl hurriedly buckled on
his walking-sword, saying,—

" This must be looked to. My fair but thoughtless Laurie,
mischief will come of this. Douglas is a brave spark, and
somewhat too prompt in the use of his hands; while Clermistonlee is wary as a wolf, and blood will be drawn. Fenton, order the household guard to horse: we will ride round
and arrest them, ere worse come of it."

" Yes, yes," exclaimed the little countess, clasping her
white hands; " away, away—but oh, will it not make both
your deadly enemies? Heavens! what a land is this for
blows and outrage!"

" Fear not, dear Lady Dunbarton," said Annie. " When
Douglas left me, he pledged his sacred word of honour not to
fight Clermistonlee until I gave permission. That promise
ties his sword to its sheath, unless his honour requires it
should be drawn, and then ill would it become a Laurie of
Maxwelton to fetter the hand of any brave cavalier."

" You are a perfect enchantress, fair Annie," said the earl,
pressing one of her silken ringlets to his lips; " one that can
rule our wildest gallants, and bend them to your will like the
Urganda of Amadis."

" Nay, my lord, if you talk much thus, I shall be deemed a
witch in earnest. You lords of council deem suspicion equal
to guilt. Is not the poor creature who is to be burned to-
morrow merely *suspected* of sorcery?"

" On application of the boot, she confessed all the lord
advocate asked her; but let us not canvass the decrees of the
High Court or Privy Council. In these our days, the decisions
of such tribunals will not brook much scrutiny. But Clermistonlee shall answer to me for this attempt. 'Sdeath! to abduct my

guest, and the fairest that ever graced our roof-tree: but say, Madam Lilian, what punishment doth he deserve?"

"Good, my lord, leave him to the reproaches of his own evil conscience."

"The answer beseems your artless gentleness, fair Napier; but you know not the infamy he intended for you. 'Tis horrid! 'tis damnable!"

"And, belted baron though he be," began Walter, handling his rapier, for his wrath increased while the earl spoke, "a day shall come——"

"Tush! my boy. Art beginning to ruffle it already? His lordship is the best hand either with rapier or dagger, single or double falchion, in all broad Scotland, while you are but a new-fledged soldier, whose burganet is bright as a new carolus. When you have followed the drum as long as I, you will learn to view everything with more coolness; though I ever loved a young gallant that was ready-witted and quick handed in defence of his mistress and honour. Clermistonlee is a thorough-paced rascal, and, though invited here for state purposes, God wot he is the only unwelcome guest under the roof-tree of Dunbarton. When I bethink me how he treated his wife and kinswoman Alison Gifford, my blood bubbles up to boiling heat. Poor Alison! I used to love thee in my boyish days; but—hah! 'tis past like a tale that is told."

Twelve o'clock had rung from all the city bells, and the time was waxing outrageously late according to the punctilious ideas of the age. Lilian, in great anxiety to be gone, accepted the countess's chair, while Walter, muffled in his rocquelaure, and having his sword girt close, followed as her escort, and bade adieu to their noble friends whose suite of apartments now seemed deserted, sad, and desolate, after the departure of all the gay and beautiful forms that had thronged them but an hour before; and the only traces of whom were here and there a faded or forgotten bouquet, a stray glove, a scarf, a riband, or a fontange. The lights waxed dim and few, for, like the joyous spirit of the *fête*, their lustre had passed away. Walter had too much of the continental gallantry that then distinguished the Scottish gentles, to act the mere part of escort. He threw the chairman's slings over his own shoulders, and fairly carried his lady-love home.

Dismissing the sedan at the barbican gate, he led Lilian up the steps to the door of the house, lingering at each; for there was something on his lips which he longed, but dared not to utter. Ere he pulled the ring of the risp, he softly pressed her hand, and said, in a very gentle voice,—

" Lilian, dear Lilian. restore the glove of which you deprived me."

" Glove—glove!" reiterated Lilian, in a great flutter.

" Forgive me. dear madam—oh, you cannot have forgotten,
when last we walked by the loch yonder."

" Foh! what a droll request, Mr. Fenton."

" All night you have called me Walter. Alas, I shall be
very wretched if you refuse this little boon."

" I am sorry for that; but you must learn that Aunt
Grizel's marmoset carried it off from my toilet-table, and
quite tore it to pieces."

" Ah, the provoking ape! But, dear Lilian, do not be so
cruel as to cloud this dream of joy by dismissing me without
a token of—of your favour to-night. I will not see you often
now—we leave Scotland very soon, 'tis said."

Walter's voice trembled, for a first love (while it lasts) is
always a timid and a true one. His passion was rapidly
mastering him. Lilian soon began to tremble too, but had
sufficient tact to answer with a tone of raillery,—

" I owe you something for your chairman's fee—ah, rogue
Walter, you are pulling my glove off! Come, sir, tirl the
risp, or must I stand here all night?"

The risp rang; but first she permitted him to untie and
remove a glove from her hand, which he immediately pressed
to his lips. His heart glowed within him—his feelings became tumultuous and impetuous; at all risks he would have
pressed her to his heart, and transferred to her soft cheek that
burning kiss; but unluckily the door was opened at that
instant by a sleepy old servant (who still carried the pewter
flagon which he had drained in the spence an hour before),
and Meinie Elshender, who appeared very coyly in a very
becoming dishabille, with all her fine hair gathered up, *en
papillotes.*

Pleased with all the passages of the night, Walter retired,
and preserved in his gauntlet the little blonde glove which his
braced corslet of steel prevented him from consigning to his
bosom—the romancer's grand emporium for all tokens of love
and friendship, save—cash.

Happy Walter walked briskly forward between fields and
hedges, shaded by trees that were now clothed in the heaviest
foliage of summer, and skirted the western *rhinns* of the lake,
where the scared coots squatted among the sedges at his
approach. The vast expanse of water lay still as death; its
dark unruffled bosom reflecting only the occasional stars
and the masses of flying cloud which by turns revealed and
obscured them.

The deep bark of a watchdog in some lonely cot made him start at times, as it echoed among the copsewood; so did every distant sound, and every peculiar shadow attracted his scrutiny. He kept his sword-hilt ever at hand. Perilous to all, the times were especially so to the soldiery, whose duties, dictated by the tyranny of the council, and the mistaken bigotry of James VII., made them obloxious to all, but more so to the oppressed Covenanters, whose vengeance and hatred had been terribly evinced on several occasions.

It was the patrician regiment of Claverhouse they more particularly reviled and abhorred; and several of his reckless cavaliers had perished by the most villanous assassination. One was actually shot dead in open day in the streets of Edinburgh; and soldiers were often barbarously murdered in their solitary billets in the country. The indiscriminate ferocity with which the guilty districts were invariably scourged for those outrages, served but to make matters worse. It has been remarked by some one, that though there were laws for everything in Scotland, even to the shape of a woman's hood, still it remained the most lawless kingdom in Europe.

Walter knew that his only personal enemy was Lord Clermistonlee, yet every sound kept him on the *qui vive*, and interrupted the gayer visions of his fancy, and his happy anticipations of the morrow, when he had made an appointment to escort Lilian to the Castlehill and Luckenbooths, then the favourite promenades of the loungers of the time.

CHAPTER XXVII.

THE FENCING LESSON.

Host. What say you to young Master Fenton? he capers, he dances, he hath the eye of youth, he writes verses, he smells April and May; he will carry't, he will carry't; 'tis in his buttons; he will carry't.
Page. Not by *my* consent, I promise you!
MERRY WIVES OF WINDSOR.

WITH the fumes of a late debauch still obscuring his faculties, Clermistonlee sat next morning with his head reclined on his hand, and breakfast before him, but untasted. His lordship was in a decidedly bad humour. It was the 22nd of June, and he had been early aroused by the cannon of the castle and the citadel of Leith saluting in honour of the anniversary of the victory at Bothwell; and the deep boom of the artillery, as they pealed over the city, drew many a groan from the burning hearts of the subdued faction.

The morning was beautiful; a thin gauzy mist was curling up from the loch, and rolling round the green foliage of the Trinity Park, and the sable rocks of the Calton.

In vain the fragrant coffee, new manchets hot from the oven, the fragment of a collared pig, a great silver flagon of spiced ale, a trencher of kippered salmon, and other viands sent up their odours, or were displayed before him in tempting array. Juden, napkin in hand, bustled nervously about the room; one moment dusting the buffet, which already shone like a mirror, or repolishing the row of plate tankards that glittered upon it; and the next, turning to his pettish master, whose attention he endeavoured yet half dreaded to attract.

The fierce dark eyes of Clermistonlee were red and blood-shot; his face was pale, and a stern smile of sinister import curled his proud yet handsome lip; his rich bobin vest was awry and unbuttoned, the lace cuffs and broad collar of his shirt crumpled and soiled; his overlay of *point d'Espagne* tied carelessly. One hand was thrust into the wide pocket of his rich dressing-gown, the other supported his unshaven chin; one foot exhibited a maroquin slipper, the other was cased in a handsome funnel boot of white buff, garnished with a gold spur and scarlet spur-leather. His lordship was regularly blue-devilled; and, though he sat motionless, a storm of fiery passions were smouldering in his haughty bosom.

In the grate, among torn billets, faded bouquets, love-knots, stray gloves, and innumerable corks, lay his glossy black wig, just where he had flung it the preceding night; his broad hat, with its cavalier plume, lay crushed under the buffet, where a favourite Skye terrier had for an hour past been engaged in a vain attempt to masticate the quills of the ostrich feathers. The arrangement of the chairs on one side of the room showed that the *roué* had reposed there during the night, or morning rather, after the failure of his attempt upon Lilian. A book lay near him : it was Sir William Hope of Hopetoun's " Complete Fencing Master ; " and he glanced at it from time to time."

" What hour is it ? " he asked suddenly.

" It will be ten gin the time," replied Juden, dusting the buffet again; " but I think, my lord, a drap coffee, or spiced October, a crail capon, or a slice o' the kipper, would do ye mair gude than graning and glooming for a' the world like your grandfather in the painted chalmer. Here are eggs fresh frae Moutriehill owerbye. Had ye been up in the braw cauler air like me this morning, ye would hae the appetite o' a hawk or a lang famished bratch."

" Like thee, fool!—And where the devil didst bestow thy self this morning ? "

" Just awa' up at the tounheid, to see that auld witch tar-oarrelled. It was a braw sight! Every place was crowded wi' folk—every window crammed wi' faces, and every lum-heid and bartisan loaded wi' skirling weans and shouting laddies. And there was auld Magnus the provost, the baillies and the councillors, a' majoring up the causeway in their scarlet gowns, wigs, and cocked beavers, with the city sword. mace, and banner borne before them, wi' drums beating and halberts glinting. Dunmore's dragoons lined the street.

" Certes, it was grand, my lord, and a bleeze weel worth riding to Birgham to see. She maun hae been a horrid witch, that auld carlin, for gude kens was a dooms ugly ane. She was trussed wi' a tow, like a chicken for the spit; and a devilish black beetle, her familiar spirit, tied round her neck in a crystal vial. 'Twas na brunt wi' her, but, God sain us! when the flames touched it, gaed up into the sky, wi' a flaff o' sparks and a clap like a thunder. She sceaighed for a tass o' water before the fire was lighted. 'Gie her nane,' quoth my Lord Mersington, ' Gie her nane, ye loons ; gin the auld jaud's dry, she'll burn better.' Then a' body lough and threw up their bannets, as if they had been making a Robin Hude.

" Auld Sir Thomas o' Binns was there, and he leugh too, till the tears came rowing owre his beard ; for there is nae-thing that born deil likes better than a tar-barrelling, unless it be a back-handed slash at the hill-folk. And ken ye, Cler mistonlee, that a' body said she would hae slippit the claws o' the council and the fifteen to boot, but for the notable speech o' my worthy Lord Mersington, who laid down the law and quoted the acts o' Estate in a way whilk was most most edify-ing to hear."

" What is all this cursed cataract of words about?—Or what are you prating?"

" Prating ? " reiterated Juden, a little put out. " Ou, just that if your lordship would condescend to break your fast— "

" To eat!—no, the first morsel would choke me like a burning coal. No, Juden ; away with the table, and bring me the quilted gloves and a bundle of foils."

Clermistonlee impatiently pushed aside the table, and in doing so, overturned the great ale-tankard.

" What are ye aboot, laddie?—are ye daft?" exclaimed Juden, wiping up the streaming liquor in a state of high excitement. " The best damask buirdelaith—he's gane clean wud! The last o' four dizzen o' my lady's Flanders plenish-ing—he's daft—keepit for high days. O Randal! hae some respect for yoursel,' if you have nane for *her* whose bonnie hands worked your cipher in the corner o' this very buird-claith."

"Silence, pest!" cried his master in a voice of thunder; but the destruction of the table-cloth was a matter of no small importance to the thrifty old butler, who continued to wipe and mutter,

"The damask buirdclaith—the best in the aik napery-kist—sae braw wi' its champit figures, the very ane that his high-ness the duke (James the Seventh that is now) dined off wi' Lag, Lauderdale, and the auld laird. Fie upon ye, Clermis-tonlee! sic wickedness and waste would hae driven your faither daft—wae's me!"

"Art done with this cursed gabble?"

"Indeed I'm no, my lord."

"When you are, fool, go and bring the foils."

"Is that a' the breakfast you are for?"

"Rascal, begone! or by ——" Juden trotted off, napkin in hand, ere his passionate lord could finish. He returned in a few minutes with foils, masks, and gloves. Clermistonlee then threw off his dressing-gown; and as he grasped one of the long heavy foils, his cheek reddened and his eye sparkled in anticipation of successful revenge and signal triumph.

"Now, Juden, my trusty knave," he began, in a milder tone; "you know that in my affair with this young minx, Lilian Napier—though I have been foiled in divers ways—that it would ill become *me* to draw bridle when such game is in view."

"Ay, my lord; many a shy bird we have flown our hawks at, but never saw I ane that cost the trouble this pretty paro-quet hath done."

"She loves a young spark of Dunbarton's musketeers—a nameless and beggarly varlet, who in infancy was found among the covenanting rabble in the Greyfriars kirkyard—"

"Aboot the time o' Bothwell—o'd I mind it weel."

"And, forsooth," continued the lord, stamping with impa-tience, "Dunbarton's baby-faced countess, in imitation of proud old Anne of Monmouth, would needs have a pretty page to hold up her train when she walked, sit by her knee in coach and boudoir, carry her lap-dog to church when the bishop preached; to kiss her dainty hand at all times, and God knows what more.

"This fair lady's toy hath now become a man with a beard on his chin, and a sword at his side; and after trailing a pike for these three years past beneath our Scottish pennon, hath obtained a pair of colours u his patron's band. and presumes to ruffle it in scarlet and lace among the best gentlemen in Scotland; and cocks his beaver *à la cavalier* in the faces of the boldest and the best. But these are trifles. This mis-begotten minion hath become my rival—*mine*. Ha, ha! Juden—and to be crossed in purpose by a cur like this! Zounds! I shall burst......... This very noon he will be flaunting his feathers with other triflers; and if it is in the power of mortal man to dash his rapier in a thousand pieces—to nail him to the pavement through steel and bone, and to drench his sark in his heart's best blood before her very face, by Jove! this right hand will do it. But ere venturing on so public a trial of my skill, I would fain have a bout with thee; so come on, my old boar at bay—have at thee."

Entering at once into the spirit of the anticipated conflict, he attacked Juden with as much ferocity as if he had actually been his foe and rival. He thrust and lunged forward with such fury and rapidity, that Juden, being stout, pursy, less agile, and older by twenty years, was sorely pressed; but being perfect master of the broadsword, backsword, and dagger, he stood his ground like a thoroughbred sword-player; and for a time nothing was heard but their suppressed breathing, and the clash of the foils.

The cheek of Clermistonlee was crimsoned with passion, and his dark eyes flashed with the energy of every cut and thrust; for, in the excitement of the lesson, he seemed to forget that he was not engaged with Walter, waxing wroth when his most able thrusts were parried with such force that his sword-arm tingled up to the very shoulder. Under old General Lesly and the duke of Hamilton, Juden had often hewn a passage, sword in hand, through the solid ranks of the English pikemen; and though somewhat blown, he re-mained perfectly cool, and when he had breath to spare, assumed the part of an instructor.

"My lord, my lord—hoots, laddie! this will never do. You forget yoursel, and show owre mickle front."

"'Sdeath! how so?"

"Mind ye—hand and arm, body and sword, should be dressed in one line; and inclining forward, ye should lunge *so*."

"Pest! fellow—dost take my bobin vest for buff coat or pyne doublet?"

Juden laughed as his master spoke.

"Rough lessons are suited to rough work. It was just sae at Dunbar; my whinger whistled through a fat Southron's brisket. Touts! my lord—what na way was that to fient forward? I ken a wile worth twa o' it. Lurch forward sae

—making an opening and pawkily inviting lunge; when giving a *riporte* at him, ye may *lock in*, as the masters of fence say; that is, seize his sword-arm by twining your left round it—close your parade shell to shell, in order to disarm him, whilk ye sall do just *so*;" and suiting the action to the word, Juden suddenly closed up and wrenched away his lordship's foil.

"God confound thee, fellow!" exclaimed the fiery lord, exasperated to find himself so adroitly disarmed; while his bluff old butler, delighted with his own skill and vigour, laughed till his eyes swam.

"My lord," said he, presenting the hilt of the foil, "ye will find yoursel mickle the better o' this rough lesson when crossing blades with our young spark; for my mind sairly misgies me, that Dunbarton's cavaliers are kittle callants to warsle wi' But ye ken, Clermistonlee, there is no a man in the three Lowdens that could hae dune what I did now. Hech! I am ane o' auld Balgonie's troopers, and mony an ell o' gude English bone and braidcloth I've cloven in my time."

"Well—enough of this, Juden. Bring me a tass of hocheim dashed with brandy—the last runlet—and then I will go abroad. Get me my walking boots and short wig, a buff under-coat, and my scarlet suit bobbed with the white ribands; my hat—ah, thou damnable cur!—the terrier has torn to shreds a feather, which, with its gold drop, cost me six silver pounds at Lucky Diaper's booth. But it matters not—I may never don another. I will wear my white beaver with the yellow feathers; and get thee thy bonnet and whinger, and follow me. Be brisk, for the morning wears apace."

In five minutes the embossed cup of hock had been brought and drained, and his lordship attired. With his noble features shaded by his broad hat and its waving feathers, his black wig curling over the shoulders of his scarlet satin coat, which was stiff with silver lace and white ribands, Clermistonlee had quite the air of a finished gallant. A perfumed handkerchief fluttered from one pocket, a gold snuff-box, with a lady's picture on the lid, glittered in the depth of the other. His long bowl-hilted rapier, with a grasp of embossed silver and a sheath of crimson velvet, hung behind from an embroidered shoulder-belt: one hand dangled a gold-headed and tasselled cane—the other carried the long buff glove, and was bare, according to the vanity of the time, for displaying the sparkle of a splendid diamond ring.

Juden buttoned his green coat close up, buckled on a heavy basket-hilted spada, and drawing his broad blue bonnet

over his red burly visage with the air of a man intent on
something desperate, followed his master, respectfully keeping a few paces behind on their gaining the crowded street,
which was to be the grand arena of their operations.

CHAPTER XXVIII.

THE LUCKENBOOTHS.

He comes not on a wassail rout,
  Of revel, sport, and play ;
Our sword's gart fame proclaim us men
  Long ere this ruefu' day.
                              OLD BALLAD.

THE bell tolling eleven in the clock-tower of the Netherbow
Porte, made Clermistonlee quicken his pace in issuing from
the gloomy alley of his house into the broad and magnificent
High-street, along the far-extending vista of which, and on
its thronging crowds and infinity of shining windows, the
summer sun poured down its morning glory. Round the
Fountainwell there was the same bustle that may be seen at
the present day : thrifty and noisy housewives quarrelling
with the watercarriers, whose shining barrels upborne on
leather slings, were then the only means by which water was
conveyed to the houses ; and a few old men, the last remnant
of another age and more primitive state of society, yet linger
around the old fountain, and climb to the loftiest mansions of
the ancient wynds, supplying the water which the reservoir
cannot force to so great a height.

Carved and gilded coaches rumbled slowly over the rough
causeway, and sedans borne by liveried chairmen were
bearing the owners to morning visits. The street was
crowded with passengers and loungers dressed in all the
colours of the rainbow. The heads of the ladies were covered
by hoods of silk and velvet, while the wives of citizens were
forced to content themselves with a plaid muffler pinned
under the chin.

Gentlemen still wore the plain Scottish bonnet, or the vast
cavalier hat, looped up and plumed ; snug burgesses and
staring countrymen thronged past, attired (conform to Act of
the Estates) in linsey-woolsey, hodden-grey, tartan, coarse
blue bonnets, and ribbed galligaskins, a style of dress which
formed a strong contrast to the splendid vestments of their
superiors, whose silks and velvets, slashed and laced, were
glittering everywhere in the sun.

A few officers of the Fusilier Guards in their gilt breast-

plates, scarlet coats, and white scarfs, cavaliers of Claver'se
regiment, and other "bucks of the first fashion," in all the
magnificence of laced taffeta, long rapiers, perfumed scarfs,
and tall feathers, were lounging about the pillars of the
Venetian arcade, in front of Blair's Coffee-house, or jested
and flirted with those passing fair ones who flaunted their long
trains under the cool shade of the Mahogany-lands, as certain
old balconied edifices that have long since disappeared were
named.

Jangling in mid air under the gothic crown of the old
cathedral, the musical bells rang merrily, mingling with the
busy hum that floated upward from the dense population
below. The gift of Thomas Moodie, a citizen, these bells
had been hung there in 1681. In one of the recesses formed
by the buttresses of the church, a man was reading to a
crowd, that listened intently, around the barrel on which he
had perched himself. It was the *Caledonius Mercurius,* from
the columns of which he was detailing some of Louis the
Fourteenth's religious persecutions under the intolerant
Mazarine which now and then brought a muttered execration
from the listeners.

Paunchy and gorbellied citizens, whose shops were in the
gloomy recesses of the Luckenbooths, the cruicks of the Bow,
or cellars of the Lawnmarket, were grouped about the city
cross, which, with its tall octagon spire and unicorn, was for
ages one of the chief beauties of the city. On one side of it
stood the Dyvours-stane, whereon sat a row of those unfortunates who, for misfortune or roguery, were, by act of the
council, compelled to appear there each market-day at noon,
in the bankrupt's garb—a yellow bonnet, and coat, one half
yellow, the other brown, under pain of three months' imprisonment.

On the other side groaned a wretched woman, who, for the
heinous enormity of drinking the devil's health had just
undergone the triple punishment of having her tongue bored,
her cheek branded, and her back scourged.

The cross was the 'Change of the city, and on the spot
where it stood, every Wednesday our traders yet meet to buy
and sell, and to consult with sharp clerks to the signet, and
more sharping solicitors, where bargains are daily made as of
old, but requiring ratifications more binding than merely
standing on "our lady's steps" at the east end of St. Giles,
or the pressure of wetted thumbs on a certain mysterious
stone which was there kept for that purpose.

With a velvet mantle floating from his left shoulder, a long
yellow feather waving over the right, and having in his

carriage all that indefinable air which the consciousness of rank and spirit seldom fail to impart, Clermistonlee walked hastily up the street, poking his nose into the hood of every woman that passed. He kissed his hand to fair Annie Laurie, as she sailed out of Peebles-wynd with her fan spread before, and her vast fardingale behind her : he made a long step to cross the grave of Merlin (whose stone coffin for ages marked the street he had been the first to pave), he roundly cursed the sooty Tronmen who did not make sufficient way for him, kicked a water-barrel ten yards off, and laid his cane across the shoulders of the aquarius, its owner, bowed to the gay fellows under Blair's pillars, and with the air of a man who knew he was pretty well observed, made a pirouette near the cathedral, surveying all around him, but without seeing the person of whom he was in quest.

"Juden," said he to that respectable personage, who stuck close to his skirts, "I see not this knave, with whom I would fain come to blows while my spirit is in its bitterest mood."

"Right, my lord ; but I warrant they will be cooing and billing on the Castle-hill yet."

"They—whom ? Dost mean to tell me that Lilian Napier hath appeared there with her spark ?"

"Hath she no ? By my faith, 'tis the toun gossip," said Juden, who, notwithstanding his devotion to his master, thought there could be no harm in rousing his fierce spirit to the utmost. "Mony a summer even in the balmy gloaming have they been seen in the King's-park, where none but lovers gang, as your lordship kens, for there yoursel and bonny Lady Alison——"

"Silence !" said Clermistonlee, through his clenched teeth ; "always these memories—ever reminding me of *her* whom I would wish to forget for ever, as the dead should be forgotten. But the park and the hill !—Gadzooks, varlet ! I believe thou liest, for Fenton hath not known her many months, I believe. I hope, too, the girl is over modest thus to exhibit herself. Come on ! by all the devils, come on !" and, giddy from passion and the fumes of his last night's wine, he turned abruptly, and made a circuit of the Parliament-square. Though it was false that Lilian had ever appeared on those solitary promenades, which then were the usual resort of avowed lovers (for such was the custom of the time), and though Clermistonlee could scarcely believe the tidings of Juden, they served the end that worthy aimed at, and became an additional gall to his spirit, and whet to his ferocity.

The idea of a young lady of family and fashion appearing

with her lover in such a place as the King's-park, may excite
a smile; now it is the resort of the artisan, the student, and
the sewing-girl; but in those days it was the common place
for afternoon promenades and assignations, ere the phases of
society among the middle and upper classes of the Scottish
capital underwent so complete a change.

"My lord," whispered Juden, approaching his master
sidelong, "what think ye o' keeping the croon o' the causeway
this morning?"

"Much as you love me, sirrah, you are ever prompting
me to blows and danger, and then seem wretched until I
am safe again. Gadso! dost think, thou gomeral, that I am
in humour to indulge the quarrelsome mood of every fool who
deems the length of his rapier and pedigree, entitle him to
maintain it for himself? Besides, the fashion went out with our
fathers, and he who would now march down the street in
defiance of all mankind, would be deemed a blustering
swash-buckler, and pitiful *fanfaron*, worthy only of a sound
cudgelling. No, no; for one alone must I keep my rapier
bright, and by Jove! yonder he comes—she is with *him*,
too—she leans on his arm—he talks, and she smiles—
D——nation! How happy they seem!—and this is the
minx who rejected my love, and despised my coronet.
Follow me, Juden, for now I will show thee a brawl such as
this street hath not witnessed, since old Crauford and the
covenanting major fought with sword and dagger from the
Bowhead to the Tronbeam!"

Swelling with fury, he advanced to the entrance of the
Luckenbooths, and Juden, like a true Scottish retainer, felt
his wrath rising in proportion with that of his leader. The
narrow pile of buildings they traversed extended the whole
length of the cathedral and the Tolbooth which adjoined it;
dividing that part of the High-street into two narrow alleys.
Expedience, the increasing population, and the political relations of the country with England, which required every
citizen to be within the walls, can alone account for this singular erection of one street in the centre of another.

Some of its tall ghostly edifices were very old and picturesque, having modern outshoots supported by grotesque
oak pillars forming arcades below; under these were the
Laigh cellars (*i. e.* low shops), where the merchants exhibited
their goods, and called public attention to them as noisily
and importunately as the shopmen of the Bridges did until
1818, and those of St. Mary's Wynd do at the present day.
Between the deep gothic buttresses of the cathedral were
clustered a multitude of little shops called the Craimes,

similar to those which still disfigure the magnificent façades of Antwerp and other great continental churches. This was the centre of the city, the place of bustle, crowd, and business, dust in summer, mud in winter, and noise at all times.

Quite unconscious of the fiery spirit that followed him, Walter Fenton led Lilian slowly through this narrow and crowded street, where they stopped often to survey the various things displayed under the piazza, and laughed and chatted gaily, for the young lady was very well pleased with her cavalier officer, who she thought never looked so handsome in his rich military dress and tall ostrich feather.

There was something very pretty, racy, and piquant in the beauty and attire of Lilian, whose hood of purple velvet, tied with a string of little Scots pearls, permitted her fair hair to fall in front, dressed à la négligence. Her ruff was starched as stiff as Bristol board, and her long rustling skirt of crimson silk, stuck out like a pyramid all round, from the velvet bodice, which was laced round a little bust, to Walter's eyes, the most charming in the world. Her gloves were highly perfumed, and so was all her dress; altogether the young lady of Bruntisfield was very charming; everybody knew her, smiled on her, and made way with that native politeness which, alas! is no longer characteristic of the lowland Scots. A lame old liveryman who had ridden in Sir Archibald's troop, limped behind, as their esquire and attendant.

"What are ye boune for buying the day, my winsome lady?" said a buirdly vendor of groceries; "what are ye buying? Plumedames sixpence the pound—the new herb wise folk ca' tea, and fules ca' poison, only fifty English shillings the pound—oranges, nutmegs, and lemons frae the land o' the idolatrous Portugales—Gascony, Muscadel, and Margaux, the wines o' the neer-do-weel French—aughteen pence the Scots quart—what are ye for buying, madam?"

"Or if you lacked a sharp rapier, sir," cried a bare-armed swordslipper, leaning over his half-door, and taking up the chant; "a corslet o' Milan that would turn a cannon-ball. I have spurs o' Rippon steel, dirks of Parma, pikes of Culross, blades of Toledo, pistols of Glasgow, and gude Kilmaurs whittles, the best of a'."

"O what a Babel it is!" said Lilian.

"Or a warm rocquelaure to wear in the camp, my handsome gentleman?" cried Lucky Diaper, a brisk and comely haberdasher, in a quilted gown, high-heeled shoes, and lace-edged coif. "What are ye buying, my Lady Lilian? You will be setting up house, I warrant, and are come to seek for the plenishing. Walk in, sir—walk in, madam. I have cushions o' velvet for hall-settles, and window-seats stuffed with Orkney down—buird-claiths of worsted and silk, servants (or napkins, as the Southrons ca' them), o' Dornick and Flanders damask, some sewit, and others plain—crammasie codwairs, and sheets just without number. What want ye, my bonny leddy, and *when* does the bridal come off ?"

"Malediction on her chatter!" muttered Clermistonlee, who lounged at the door. Walter smiled, Lilian blushed and trembled between diffidence and anger; but her reply was interrupted by the entrance of a customer, who, lifting his bonnet respectfully to her, tendered his order to Lucky Diaper, who immediately reddened up with indignation, and eyeing him askance, said sharply,

"Set ye up, indeed, wi' a *couleur-du-roi* coat of three pile taffeta; it's like the impudence that makes ye speir before your betters are served. My certie! what is this world coming to when a loon o' a baxter comes speiring for the like o' that? Awa wi' ye, man, awa! Galloway-white, drab-de-frieze, or buckram conform to the Act o' Apparel are gude enough for one of your degree!"

The unfortunate baker was forced to retreat, for the draper of 1688 thought very differently from one of the present day.

"Ay, Madam Lilian, there was that ill-faured wife o' Baillie Jaffray, who bydes up the Stinking Style (just aboon the Knight o' Coates' lodging), gaed down the gate not an hour ago, wi' a hood o' silken crammasie wi' champit figures as red as her ain neb, and a mantle wi' passments sewit round the craig o't. What think ye o' that for a wabster's wife in the Lawnmarket? I mind the time when sic presumption would have found her a cauld lodging in the Water-hole. That was in 1672, when the Apparel Act was strictly enforced, and nane but gentlefolk daured to ruffle it on the plainstanes in silk, taffeta, lace, or furring, broidery or miniver; but the times are changing fast. I am getting auld now; and neighbours say, am far behind the world.

"Bonny Florentine blue that is, my lady; and weel would it become your sweet face, if pinkit out wi' red satin *à-la-mode*. Lack ye a sword-knot, young gentleman, blue and white, our auld Scottish cockade? In what can I serve ye? A' the cavaliers of my Lord Dunbarton ken me; for I had a fair laddie once, that fell in their ranks at Tangier (rest him, God!), far, far awa' among the blackavised unco's."

When a pause in the bustling dealer's garrulity permitted her to speak, Lilian requested so much of the finest blue velvet as would make a scarf for the shoulder, with fringe and embroidery thread, and spangles of gold and silver.

"I see, madam—I ken," resumed Lucky Diaper, with a smirk of intelligence; "'tis a scarf for this winsome gentleman. Oh, hinny, ye needna blush; I mind the time when your lady mother came here to order a braw plenishing for her bridal and bedecking for her chamber-of-dais; and a blithe woman I was to serve her! Blue taffeta?—you'll be taking the very best Genoa, I warrant. It is a pleasure to serve gentlefolk; but it gars my heart grieve when loons like that baxter body think o' decking their ill-faured heads and hoghs in my fine Florence silk and Sheffield claith. Come, bustle, lassies, and show my Lady Lilian our velvets."

Two spruce and buxom shop-girls, in short overgowns, with snooded hair and bare arms, laid several rolls of velvet before Lilian, who immediately made her selection, and, anxious to escape the infliction of any more observations from Lucky, desired her to give it to the lame serving-man, and note it in the books of the steward, Syme of the Hill. All the shop-women curtsied profoundly, as Lilian took the arm of Walter, and swept again into the morning bustle of the Luckenbooths.

Chafing at their delay, Clermistonlee had been looking with imaginary interest into the window of a bookseller's booth (the sign of which was "Jonah"); but he heard not the chatter of the proprietor, whose tongue supplied the place of newspaper puff, review, and publishing list. His lordship's thoughts were elsewhere than among the red-lettered and quaintly illustrated tomes before him.

"What are you for buying, this braw day, my noble lord? There is the knight of Rowallan's 'Trve Crvcifix,' the 'Banished Virgin,'—a folio that will please you better;—the three volumes of 'Astræa;' the 'Illustrious Bassa,' imprinted by Mosely, the Englishman, in St. Paul's Churchyard, fresh frae London, by the last waggon, only three weeks ago; the last poem o' bluidy ——, my noble Lord Advocate, Sir George o' Rosehaugh, 'Clelias Country House and Closet,' whilk, as the Lady Drumsturdy said in this very buith yesterday, is the most delichfu' book since the days o' Gawain Douglas or Dunbar——"

"Sirrah, I want neither your books nor your babble; when I lack either, I will know where to come," said the haughty lounger, suddenly remembering where he was, and whence came the cataract of words that poured on his ear. Turning, he saw those for whom he was in wait, entering the Lawnmarket, the loftiest and most spacious part of the street, and where at that early part of the forenoon the thronged pavement was almost impassable. The moment for action had come! The heart of Clermistonlee beat like lightnin. He beckoned Juden (who had condescendingly been tasting the vaunted usquebaugh of various dealers), and hurried after them into the denser crowd and full glare of the noonday sun.

Quite unconscious of what was about to ensue, Walter and his fair companion, with the lame servant limping behind them, wended slowly up the busy street, chatting and laughing with low and subdued voices, till the blow of a heavy rapier ringing on Walter's backplate of steel, and the words—

"Turn, villain, and draw or die!" thundered in his ear, making him start round with his hand on his sword, and Lilian uttered a low breathless exclamation of dismay on beholding Clermistonlee,—the dreaded and terrible Lord Clermistonlee, tall, strong, and fierce-eyed, standing on his defence; while a dense crowd, whose attention the wanton insult immediately attracted, closed round on every hand.

All was clamour and uproar in a moment, and cries of "A fray, a fray!—the guard, the guard!—redd them!" burst from a hundred tongues. Walter's wrath was boundless on finding himself anticipated, insulted, and defied by the very man he had resolved to call to account on the first opportunity.

"Strike, rascal!" cried Clermistonlee.

"Thou double villain! why molest me thus in the public street?"

"That the public may the more readily behold thy cowardice. Wilt strike, man, or shall I spit upon thee as a cream-faced coistral?"

"For these words all the blood in your body could never atone. You will have it then? Come on, proud lord!" replied Walter, while with his sword he waved back the people, whose applause seemed in favour of Clermistonlee, as a townsman and peer, and late events had made the army in bad odour with the populace.

"O good people, part them—stay them for the love of God!" urged the plaintive voice of Lilian, and it thrilled through Walter's heart.

"Place, gentlemen! fall back, fellows—clear the causeway!" cried Douglas of Finland, pushing through the crowd.

"Give the gentlemen room," added Jack Holster, coming up at the same moment. "Now, gallants, to it blade and shell. Gentlemen of the Royal Guards, draw, that we may see fair play to the king's commission;" and he unsheathed his sword.

"Mistress Lilian, permit me—you must—entreaties are unavailing," said Finland, leading away the pale and sinking girl, in whose ears the clash of the rapiers rang terribly, and she saw them flashing in the sunlight above the heads of the dense and shouting mob, till reaching the booth of Lucky Diaper, where she burst into a passion of tears, and here we will leave her for the present.

Drawing his rapier, Douglas rushed back to separate the combatants, or take part in the brawl if necessary. Clermistonlee pressed forward with the greatest fury, determined to slay his antagonist, who, knowing how much *he* had to dread, if a man so high in rank, a lord of the Parliament, privy councillor, and head of a feudal family, perished by his hand, fought only to defend himself, or, if possible, to disarm or disable his furious enemy. At times their long keen rapiers were visible for a moment—but a moment only. Like blue fire, the bright blades flashed around them; but the skill of both was so admirable, that as yet not a wound had been given.

The people laughed when the tall plumes of Clermistonlee were shred from his hat by a back stroke, and floated away over their heads; and in turn they applauded, as Walter (still fighting strictly on the defensive) was driven by the impetuosity of his enemy backward to the wall of the Tolbooth, and cries of—

"Weel dune the gudeman o' Drumsheugh—up wi' the Red Wyvern—the auld leaven o' the Covenant for ever!" rang on every hand, and Juden exerted his lungs like a Stentor.

With a glowing heart and cheek, Walter found the conflict going against him, and that his adversary was becoming exhausted, on which he pressed vigorously in turn, and gaining more than the ground he had lost, drove Lord Clermistonlee towards the arch of Byre's Close, and then the rabble waved their bonnets and shouted—

"Hurrah for the cavalier! Weel done, my brave buckie! doon wi' the persecuting lord!" and so forth; but Walter despised their praise, and continued pressing forward till the fury of his antagonist on finding himself driven back, step by step, amounted almost to madness. Just at this successful crisis, Walter found his arms violently seized by some one behind, and pinioned in such a manner that he was placed completely at the mercy of his antagonist.

Jealous for the honour of his lord, Juden, who had worked himself into a very becoming fit of passion, had watched with kindling eyes and half-drawn sword, the various turns of the combat; and now, on beholding the master whom he loved as though he had been his own and only son, driven backward, breathlesss and exhausted, and in danger of being compelled to yield or die, he could no longer restrain himself, but rushed upon Walter, and pinioned his arms, exclaiming—

"Now, my lord, now ; put your bilbo through his brisket. Devil's murrain on you, Randal, strike for Clermont, or never strike again !"

Surprise, for an instant, kept mute the shout of shame which rose to every lip ; and Walter struggled furiously with the stout old butler. The eyes of Clermistonlee glared malignantly, and twice he raised his long sharp rapier for a deadly thrust, and twice he lowered its point. Walter's life seemed to hang by a hair, and how the fray might have ended it is impossible to say ; but just when Jack Holster, by a blow of his hunting whip, levelled Juden on the pavement, Lord Mersington came running with a remarkably unsteady gait, out of Blair's coffee-house, with his senatorial robes gathered about his waist, his wig awry, in one hand a roll of interlocutors, in the other a wine-flagon, which, in the hurry, he had forgotten to leave behind him.

"Haud, ye loons ! haud, in the sacred name of the king !" he exclaimed, throwing himself boldly between them. "This is breaking the peace o' the burgh—clean contrary to the act saxteenth James Sext, whilk ordains that nae man shall fight, or provoke another to the combat, under pain of death, and escheat o' moveable gudes and gear. What, is it *you*, Clermistonlee—hee, hee, hee ! ye born gomeral, to be brawling like a wild Redshank on the plainstanes in open day ? Come, come, gossip, this will never do. Stand back, I charge ye baith in the sacred name of his majesty the king !"

"My lord of Mersington, I am the best judge of my own conduct," replied his friend, fiercely.

"But one far owre lenient—hee, hee ! I am legally constituted judge and justiciar baith o' the haill country ; or up wi' your rapiers, gallants, or I shall commit you, Randal, to the iron room of the Tolbooth, and this braw spark o' Dunbarton's to the water-hole, whilk being fifteen feet below the causeway, is a fine place for cooling hot spirits."

Mersington's efforts were unavailing, for he was a man whom few respected. Jack Holster and Craigdarroch pulled him back very unceremoniously by his scarlet robes; for which he thrust his roll of papers into the face of one, and hurled the wine-pot at the head of the other.

Again the rapiers clashed together ; but at that juncture Baillie Jaffroy, a portly magistrate, the curve of whose round paunch was finely delineated by his braided coat of purple broadcloth, and its front row of vast horn buttons, displaying his gold chain (the badge of civic power) rushed with a party of the lord high constable's guard from the lobby of the Parliament House, and bearing back the crowd with levelled partisans, separated the combatants.

Neither of them were arrested.

Clermistonlee, followed by Juden (who had acquired a black eye and broken head), retired suddenly into the lower council-chamber, where the baillie, in dread of such a formidable personage, could not follow, and therefore turned the whole torrent of his magisterial wrath and indignation upon Walter Fenton, as being, he well knew, less able to withstand them. But Dougles of Finland, Gavin of Gavin, Holsterlee, and other military gallants, with drawn swords, carried him off triumphantly to Hugh Blair's famous establishment at the pillars, from whence, on the dispersion of the crowd, he rejoined Lilian : and so ended the last single combat witnessed in the High-street of Edinburgh.

CHAPTER XXIX.

THE WHITE-HORSE CELLAR.

To eat cran, pertick, swan, and pliver,
And everie fisch that swyms in river;
To drink with us the newe fresch wyne,
That grew vpon the River Ryne;
Fresch fragrant Clarets of France,
Of Angiers, and of Orliance,
With comforts of grit daintie.

DUMBAR TO JAMES V.

IT was now the autumn of 1688.

The evil genius of James VII., and the influence of his advisers, were fast hastening him and his house to destruction. His measures for the re-establishment of the Catholic faith, in all its pristine power and ancient grandeur, exasperated the whole nation, and the Episcopalians in the south, and the sourer Presbyterians in the north, joined in one united voice against him.

Many powerful nobles of both kingdoms were in exile. With these, and with the intermeddling prince of Orange, a close correspondence was maintained by the friends of the intended revolution. Even the Scottish and English forces, on whose valour and fidelity the unhappy king too much relied, were foes to his religion ; and certain obnoxious measures. in his military administration, tended to alienate from his cause all but the most romantic and devoted of his sub-jects.

It was evident that a great crisis was at hand. The king, in the month of September, sent an express to the privy council, requiring them to place the country on the war establishment. The standing army was increased, the militia embodied, the garrisons put in a state of defence, the High-land clans, ever loyal and ever true, were ordered to assemble in arms, and beacons were erected on Arthur's Seat and other mountains, to alarm the country. Similar preparations to repel William of Orange were made by the English govern-ment, whose forces, thirty thousand strong, under the earl of Feversham, were concentrated about London. But James's measures in the south ruined his influence everywhere, and the cheers of the English troops, on the acquittal of the bishops being known in the camp at Hounslow, proved that he had lost their sympathy for ever, and could rely on their support no more.

The regular forces of Scotland were cantoned in and around the capital, ready at an hour's notice to march for England, a measure which was vigorously and wisely opposed in council by Colin, earl of Balcarris, the lord high treasurer. Mal-contents were secretly flocking to Edinburgh from all quarters; and Master Magnus Prince, the sycophantic provost, with his bench of baillies, sent a dutiful letter to James VII., assuring him " of their most hearty devotion to his service, and being ready with their lives and fortunes to stand by his sacred person upon all occasions, and praying for the continuation of his princely goodness and love towards his ancient city."

The Presbyterians conducted themselves with more than their ordinary boldness, and in the streets openly chanted psalms and *Lillibulero bullen a la;* the government and its friends were full of anxiety, and remained on the alert. The Whigs spoke boldly, and the cavaliers with somewhat less confidence, of the great preparations of the Dutch for the invasion of Great Britain,—of the frigates, fireships, trans-ports, horse, foot, and artillery, assembled at Nimguen, and of the Scottish and English noblesse who in exile crowded beneath the unfurled banner of the Stadtholder. Thus,

" While great events were on the gale,
And each hour brought a varying tale ; "

none were more loyal in drinking his majesty's health in Hugh Blair's best Burgundy, and the Hocheim of the White-horse, than Walter Fenton and his cavalier comrades of the Scots musketeers ; none squeezed the orange more emphatically, and none handled so roughly those luckless wights whom they found chanting *Lillibulero*, and none drained their vast bumpers more earnestly to the undamning and double damning of the pumpkin-headed and twenty-breeched Dutch.

It was the afternoon of a September day; the last detachment of Dunbarton's Foot had marched into Edinburgh, from the famous expedition against the Macdonalds of Keppoch, in attacking whom they had been co-operating with a battalion of the Guards, and the horsemen of the celebrated Captain Crichton, whose memoirs were edited by Dean Swift; and now to enjoy a complete military *réunion*, all the cavalier officers of the ancient corps sat down to a banquet in the great dining-hall of the White-horse cellar.

The long apartment was lighted by several windows that faced the Calton-hill, which towered away to the north and westward, covered with whin and broom, where the fox, the hare, and the weazel yet made their lairs unheeded and unhunted. The hall was spacious, elegant, and hung with arras, and a great painting by Jameson, our Scottish Vandyke, the pupil of Rubens, hung over the yawning fireplace. It was a fanciful representation of the fair Mary, on that favourite white palfrey, which a hundred and fifty years before had given a name to the hostel, when the range of stabling below it had been occupied as a mews of the Scottish kings. Beneath this hung the battered headpiece and Jedwood axe which Gibbie Runlet had wielded—and wielded well, as the king's rebels knew to their cost—in the wars of the glorious Montrose.

The sturdy legs of the old oak buffet appeared to bend under the load of glittering crystal, shining plate, and various good things piled upon its shelves, while underneath in columns dark and close, were ranged in deep array the flasks of good old wine, from the cool vaults of the White-horse cellar, and covered with the undisturbed dust and cobwebs of years of long repose.

Clad in their rich military dresses, bright steel, and spotless scarlet, glittering with jewels and gold lace, the row of cavalier guests on each side of that long and festive board, presented a very gay and striking appearance, as the setting sun shone full upon them, and caused the whole vista of the dinner-table to glitter with sparkling objects, and the curling steam of the smoking banquet. In a great chair, with high back and stuffed arms, rough with carving and rich with nails and scarlet leather, sat the portly master, Gilbert Runlet (that host of immortal memory), with a vast red face, that seemed like the harvest-moon rising at one end of the table; while the great rotund form spreading out below it, a yard in diameter, loomed like a mountain, closing the long perspective of the board.

Gibbie had been for twenty years the most substantial burgess of the Canongate; and as a stanch and irascible royalist, had long "ruled the roast" at the council-board of that ancient burgh. The beau ideal of a jovial host, he laughed and talked, and helped on all sides incessantly, yet never appeared to be behind any one in emptying his own plate or tankard, which were replenished and emptied with wonderful celerity.

But the dinner! A flourish of trumpets announced it; and well it deserved the compliment of such a preliminary. A huge sirloin, which balanced a baron of beef, was undergoing a rapid process of diminution under Gibbie's long carving whinger; six collared pigs, bristling with cloves, and having flowers stuck in their nostrils, stood erect on great platters. Around them were hares, turkeys, geese, ducks, and chickens, roasted, stewed, fricasseed, and boiled. There was a vast silver salt-foot at each end, two grand epergnes of flowers and pea-cocks' feathers, two great salads, two hundred little manchets, venison, hams, salmon, flounders, crabs, and Crail capons,— all placed pell-mell without order of courses, among tarts, trifles, confections, pyramids of jelly and plumdames, and puddings and fruit of every description, disposed in orna-mental figures of trees, birds, &c.

But, far above all this wilderness of viands towered a great edifice, representing a fortress; the towers were of pie-crust, with ramparts of wax; the cannon and sentinels were sugar-paste; the bullets were little *bon-bons;* the moat was filled with wine, and from the keep hung a flag with St. Andrew's silver saltire. This erection elicited great admiration from the guests, by whom it was unanimously named the castle of Tangier, beneath the towers of which so many of their brave comrades had found a soldier's grave.

The feast proceeded in gallant style, amid unrestrained hilarity and bursts of military merriment. All did justice to the good things before them; while the servants, or *écuyers tranchans,* were kept on the alert pouring forth Rhenish, Gascony, Muscadel, port and sherry, and the rich and luscious wine of Frontiniac, as if there had been a conflagration in the stomach of every guest.

On the right of the host sat the regimental minister, the

Reverend Doctor Jonadab Joram (who, by the courtesy of the Scottish service, had the rank of major), a bluff and jovial personage, whose merry eyes twinkled on each side of a bottle-nose, and who could stride and swagger, drink and play with any man—one who winked knowingly at landladies, kissed their daughters, and, if he chose, could have out-bullied a Mohock. He was brimful of jocularity, which had cost him a duel or two in Flanders, and was known to be "up to" a great many things not very consonant to the dignity of his cloth.

On the left of the host sat the chevalier laird of Drum-quhasel, a tall, stark, and sunburned soldier, on whose breast sparkled several French orders; and near him was the chirurgeon, who was the very counterpart of the divine, a laughing, bullet-headed, merry-faced little man, about sixty years of age. Like his clerical brother, he was in the habit of averring that he had been broiled at Tangier, half-drowned at Bergen-op-zoom, and wholly frozen in the Zuider Zee; blown up in Flanders, and trod down in Alsace, for he always charged in the line-of-battle, and consequently neglected his professional duties; or like many sons of the healing god, was wont to introduce its topics at unseasonable times; and he was then, in the style of a lecturer of the old College of Physic, at the Cowgate Port, employed in tracing the spinal marrow of a hare, for his own amusement and the edification of Jerry Smith, a gay fellow with a curly periwig and thick moustache, the same who afterwards entered the English service and became so famous for his gallantries at Halifax, in Yorkshire.

There were present many handsome young sparks, whose first fields had been Sedgmoor in the south, or Muirdykes in the north; and their smooth chins and fair faces contrasted well with those war-worn cavaliers, whose service included the Scottish battles of Dunbar and Inverkeithing, the sack of Dundee, and the fight at Kerbister, and whose sparkling stars and crosses attested the good deeds they had performed under Henri d'Avergne, Le Mareschal Turenne, and the great Condé of glorious memory, especially old Drumquhasel.

When the Duc d'Enghien charged the Mareschal de l'Hôpital so successfully that the Spanish infantry, till then deemed the finest in the world, were swept before the victo-rious French, there was not a chevalier of St. Louis who distinguished himself more than old John of Drumquhasel, who, with his own hand, cut down the famous Count de Fuentes, for which he was thanked by Monsieur of France

at Versailles, and had a chaplet placed upon his head by
Mademoiselle La Fleur, the reigning favourite of the time.

Douglas was joyous and gay; but Walter was somewhat
reserved and abstracted; he foresaw that this great military
réunion would interfere with his evening visit to the Napiers,
and he was bored by the gaiety of the young, as much as by
the prosing of the older soldiers around him.

"Hector Gavin, harkee," said the divine to a tall officer
whose looped doublet and black corslet announced him lieutenant of the grenadiers, a species of force introduced about
ten years before,—"Master Gibbie, our right honourable host,
informs me that there are some excellent pigeons in the case-
mates of that same castle of Tangier before you; and if you
will so far favour me——"

"With pleasure, Joram. By my faith, I should know
something of the mode of attacking the place! It wants the
lower cavalier, with its thirty brass culverins, that swept the
gorge of that avant-fosse. Ha! I have breached the upper
parapet," said Gavin laughing, as he cut down the pastry.

"Ay, Hector, odsbodikins!" replied the divine. "I saw
thee push on at the head of our pikemen, like a true Scottish
cavalier, when the old Tangier regiment of England were
thrown into confusion by the shower of petards. Demme!
Hector, the recollection of that hot work makes me thirsty
as dry sand."

"Is the sack tankard empty, doctor?" asked Douglas.

"Drained to the lowest peg, laird."

"Tush, Joram; mayest thou be turned into a gaping oyster,
as the play-book saith, and drink nothing but salt water all
the days of thy life! You were talking of a shower of
petards, doctor: I remember when we marched with Condé
into Franche Compté with displayed banners, we beleaguered
the castle of a certain seigneur, which resembled one of our
Scottish peel-houses; and therein a brave cavalier of Spain
commanded a corps of tall Irish pikemen. For three days
they abode the salvoes of the demi-cannon, which battered
their outer ravelins, and breached the great barbican. I led a
hundred of our Scottish lads and sixteen German reformadoes
to the assault, with pike and pistol bent. By my faith, doctor,
the loons fought like so many peers of Charlemagne. Each
man flung a petard as we advanced. Crush me! a shower of
petards. Pho! my fellows were blown to ribands—their
very entrails were twisted round the trees and ramparts; but
Condé took the place at push of pike—put all the Irishry to
the sword, and placed in the châtelet a garrison of the Compté

de Bullioncs Scottish pikemen, and the good old Regiment de Picardie."

"Doctor Joram," said Walter, "I have heard much of your famous duel with a chevalier of that regiment, but never the particulars. About some fair demoiselle was it not?"

"You were never more mistaken in your life, Master Fenton. We measured swords in the purest spirit of *esprit du corps*. I will tell you how it was. We were with the army that invested Doesburg, where the famous adjutant Martinet was killed by a cannon-ball within a pike's length of me. We had long been at feud with that Regiment de Picardie, anent certain points of precedence and posts of honour, which was a state of matters not to be borne by us who represent Les Gardes Ecossais of the sainted Louis, while the Battalion de Picardie was but one of the mere *vieux corps* of Charles the Ninth's time. The Sieur de Guichet, their captain-lieutenant, and I came to high words about it, in a certain house——of——of——.''

"Ay, ay, doctor, we all know the place," said two or three cavaliers, amid loud laughter. "Madame Papillotes' little château on the banks of the Issel: she always accompanied the army. A nice billet for your reverence, truly."

"De Guichet quarrelled with me about precedence and right of *entrée*, though as chaplain of the Scots Royals, in the line of battle I rode next to Dunbarton himself. 'Tush! monsieur,' said I, laying hand on my sword, 'remember I am a Scottish cavalier, and chaplain to the guards of Pontius Pilate.' '*Nombril de Beelzebub!*' said the irreverent rascal, 'I believe you rightly name yourselves the guards of Monseigneur Pilate, for had the old *routiers* of the Regiment de Picardie kept guard on the Holy Sepulchre, they would not have slept on their posts as the Scots Musketeers must have done.' 'This to a clergyman?' I exclaimed. 'Have at thee, d——d runnion!' and attacking him, sword in hand, I disarmed him at the third pass; and ever afterwards Messieurs the Regiment de Picardie cocked their beavers the other way when passing us in the breach or on the Boulevards.''

"'Tis a brave old band," said Gavin of that ilk. "I saw them on the plains of Nordlingien. You remember how gallantly they repulsed a charge of the Count de Merci's steel-clad lancers. We had just formed square, with Sweyns' feathers in front, to repel their onfall, when Monsieur de Martinet (whom all the world knows of), adjutant of the Regiment du Roi, galloped up, rapier in hand, with an order from Monseigneur le Duc d'Enghien to form line in battalion

with the horse and dragoons on the wings: but my lord of
Dunbarton was too old a soldier to hear him amid the roar of
such a battle; and luckily a cannon-ball took Martinet's
charger in the crupper, on which he scrambled away. But
only conceive, sirs, to form line in face of a horse-brigade!
By my sooth, wild Hielandmen would have known better,
and I marvel that Monseigneur d'Enghien and Monsieur de
Martinet so greatly forgot their boasted *tactiques de guerre;*
but, as I said to my Lord Dunbarton," *et cetera* and so forth.

Such was the tiresome small talk with which those "hunger
and cold-beaten soldiers" (to use a camp phrase of the day)
maintained a cross-fire at table, and it differed very little from
what one may hear in a similarly constituted party of the
present day. The younger members of the company, whose
whole experience of war had been confined to repelling a foray
on the Highland frontier, a brawl in a Whig district, or a
review on the Links of Leith before Sir Thomas Dalyel, his
grace the lord high commissioner, and the ladies of his mimic
court, were somewhat more peaceable in the tenor of their
conversation, which went not beyond a duel at St. Anne's-
yard or in Hugh Blair's, the Leith races (where yesterday the
long pending match between Jack Holster's horse and Clermistonlee's mare had ended in the defeat of the latter), of Reid
the mountebank, and the feats of his famous "tumbling
lassie" at the Tennis Court theatre, where they had all been
the preceding night to behold "The Soldier's Fortune" by the
celebrated Otway, for whom they had a fellow-feeling, as he
had lately been a cornet of dragoons in Flanders. The merits
of the new-fashioned iron hat-piece covered with velvet, which
the English were now substituting for the old helmet, were
warmly discussed. Mistress Annie Laurie, Jean Gordon,
Lady Dunbarton, and other fair belles, new tawny beavers,
silver-hilted swords, horses, and wines, and various frivolities
were all descanted upon, while the bright wine flowed and the
laughter increased apace.

Dinner was over, and the vast wilderness of viands had
undergone a great and melancholy change; the collared pigs
were minus heads and legs; the great platters of turkeys,
geese, and ducks, stewed hares and fricasseed rabbits, the
lordly baron and the knightly sirloin, and everything else
were in the same plight; while the noble castle of Tangier
had been completely sacked, demolished, and its garrison of
baked and spiced cardinals, capuchins, and fantails given up
to the conquerors. The servants cleared the polished tables,
and one placed before Gibbie, the host, a great chased silver

tankard, the pride of his heart, for it was the production of George Heriot. It was mantling with purple port, and Gibbie (whose orb-like visage, by eating and drinking, was flushed like the setting October sun), laid his hand upon the cup, and looked round the board with his great saucer eyes to see that every guest's horn was filled; for the toast he was about to propose was,—

"The health of his sacred majesty James VII., with peace at home, and war and confusion to his enemies abroad."

Gibbie, we say, with a rubicund visage beaming with loyalty and hospitality, had just upheaved his ponderous bulk for this purpose, when the rapid and ominous clatter of hoofs in the inn-yard attracted the attention of all; and the Reverend Doctor Joram exclaimed,

"Egad, here comes my Lord Dunbarton and the young laird of Holsterlee! Gentlemen, the old game must be afoot; but what can be in the wind now?"

"A rising among those crop-eared curs in the west, I warrant," replied the laird of Drumquhasel. "Men say that false villain Clelland, the covenanting colonel, and Dyckvelt the Hollander, have been in the land of the whigamores, blowing the trumpet of sedition, and preparing the way for southern invasion and northern rebellion."

The earl hurriedly dismounted, and abstractedly threw the reins of his horse to Holsterlee his gentleman-in-waiting, who exclaimed,

"'Sdeath, Dunbarton, you forget that a cavalier of the guard is not like one of Douglas's Red troopers or Dunmore's Grey dragoons."

The earl asked pardon, and laughed as he ascended the flight of steps that led to the inn door; while Jack vociferously summoned the *peddies* or horse-boys, and tossing to them the reins of the chargers, jerked his long bilbo under his arm, and sprung up the steps, three at a time, after the general.

"Place for the most noble lord the earl of Dunbarton—place for the general commanding!" exclaimed a servant, ushering in the noble visitor, and all present arose at his entrance. His dark and handsome features were slightly flushed, and not without a marked expression of anxiety, while the saucy face of Jack Holster was extremely animated, and he. displayed rather more than usual of his jovial and reckless swagger.

"Gentlemen," said the earl; "the old banner that waved so often and ever victoriously in the vanguard of Condé and Turenne, is again to be unfurled before a foe."

" South or west ?" asked a dozen of eager voices.

" In the land of our ancient enemies."

" By my soul I rejoice at that," said Douglas. " I have no fancy for bending our fire on ranks that speak our mother tongue, and wear the broad blue bonnet."

" Well said, my true Douglas !" exclaimed Drumquhascl. " I knew this muster of force aimed at the recapture of Berwick. Dags and pistols ! *there* is the hand (and he struck it clenched on the table) that will pull their d—d red cross from the ramparts when the time comes."

" Ye mistake, gentlemen, and you in particular, chevalier major ; but know that the time hath come which shall prove who among us are true cavaliers, and who false-hearted Whigs. Wilt credit me, that the insolent Dutch prince William of Orange has at last put his great armament in motion, and that a hundred sail of the line, frigates, fireships, and four hundred transports have unrolled their canvass to the wind ? Herbert leads the van, Evertzen the rear, and William the centre. He has with him fifteen thousand good soldiers," continued the earl, consulting a royal despatch from Whitehall : " some of these are the hireling dogs of the Scottish brigade, who are led by Hugh Mackay, laird of Scoury, and carry a red banner."

" Scoury ?" exclaimed Douglas ; " how—the old rascal who deserted from us in Holland ?"

" The same. Why, my dear fellow, this man is a mere Swiss, and pricks his ears whenever drums beat, without caring a rush which side wins if the rix-dollars are sure. The prince's guards and Brandenburgers under Count Solmes, knight of the Teutonic order, and grand commander of the bailiewick of Utrecht, march with a white standard."

" Bravo ! we will know all the rogues by head-mark."

" The Dutch and French Protestant refugees, under Velt Mareschal Frederick duc de Schomberg, carry a little blue banner," continued the earl, still consulting his despatch. " Mynheer Goderdt van baron de Ginckle, on whom the would-be usurper hath bestowed the earldom of Athlone, commands the cavalry ; Mynheer Bein Tenk, who expects the dukedom of Portland : and Arnold Joost van Keppel, the earldom of Albemarle ; Massue de Rouvigny, who is to be earl of Galway ; General le Baron de Sainte Hippolite ; D'Auverquerque, Zuylestein, and Caillemote, with all our banished lords, Argyle, Shrewsbury, Macclesfield, Dunblanc, and the devil knows how many more runaways and wild soldiers of fortune, the riddlings of rapine and scum of European wars, all crowd beneath his banner as to a bridal !"

"They are welcome!" exclaimed Finland, with enthusiasm.
"Up, gallants, all for God and King James!" and drawing
his sword, he flourished it aloft, and drained his wine-horn
to the bottom. Every man followed his example, save Gibbie
Runlet, who, having no rapier to draw, contented himself by
draining his wine-tankard, which he did without once removing his large saucer eyes from the face of the earl, to whose
muster-roll of hard-named invaders he listened with the aspect
of one astounded.

"Our dogs of citizens have already caught the rumour, that
their Dutch saviour is coming with his fireships and swart
Ruyters," said "Holsterlee; and in anticipation of their great
political millennium are chanting the *Lillibulero* with might
and main; yea, under our very beards, as we rode down the
Canongate. By the horns of Mahoud! we have tough work
before us, gentlemen. Fifteen thousand Hollanders under
baton, said you, my lord?"

"Pooh!" said Doctor Joram; "King James's English
troops alone are enough to eat them up."

"Will they be inclined to do so, reverend sir?" replied the
earl. "I fear me greatly."

"Then God help church and king!" ejaculated the minister,
gulping down a sigh and his sack together.

"Gentlemen," said Dunbarton, looking around him with
sparkling eyes, "the great, the terrible crisis to which our
leaders and our statesmen have so long looked forward, has
come at last; and to the hearts and swords of his faithful
soldiers, King James can alone trust the fortunes of his house.
I have received most urgent despatches, written by himself,
from Whitehall, and all our available force must, to-morrow,
march for England; Hounslow is the rendezvous; church
and king our *cri de guerre!* The privy council meets secretly
in the gallery at Holyrood; they will sit in ten minutes.
Farewell, my good friends and gallant comrades," continued
the earl, bowing with a heaviness of heart that was apparent
to all; "I will see you at daybreak, when the *générale* beats.
For the palace, ho! come Holsterlee."

"Away, gallants, to your fair ladies and gay lemans," exclaimed the latter, with a tragi-comic air; "away, to dance a
merry couranto, and have one last daffin with the belles of the
Cap-and-Feather close; a last horn at Hugh Blair's; a last
dish of oysters and a game at shovelboard in Bess-wynd; a
last camisadoe with the students and city watch, for we
march to-morrow, and when the guards and the royals go,
well may our ladies rend their silken tresses, and exclaim

'Ichabod, Ichabod, auld Reekie, for thy glory hath de
parted!'"

In a few minutes the jovial party was completely broker
up; many of them had taken leave, hurriedly, on those very
missions Mr. Holster had enumerated; some to bid farewel
to mothers, wives, and sweethearts; some to have a last Horr
of wine with old familiar friends; others to prepare for thei
sudden departure; while those happy spirits, who had neithe:
preparations to make, nor friends to leave behind them, clus
tered round the appalled landlord, and pushed the wine-cuj
more briskly than ever.

But Gibbie's spirit and vivacity had evaporated; he looke
forward to blood and blows, trooping and free-billeting, witl
no small horror, and on the departure of his military patrons
beheld a gloomy perspective of fines, persecutions, and annoy
ance from the Whig enemies of the government, who woul
undoubtedly usurp place and power in absence of that arme
force, on the presence of which the authority of James VII.
in Scotland, alone depended.

The moment the earl retired, Walter had thrown himsel
on horseback, and galloped away by the base of St. John'
Hill, and skirting the village of the Pleasance, dashed alon
the banks of the Burghloch, a place "then shaded by man
venerable oaks," and reached the house of Bruntisfield jus
as the sun began to dip behind the wooded summit c
Corstorphine.

END OF THE FIRST SERIES

THE
SCOTTISH CAVALIER.

———◆———

CHAPTER XXX.

THE BETROTHAL.

O love, when womanhood is in the flush,
  And man's a young and an unspotted thing!
His first-breathed word and her half-conscious blush
  Are fair as light in heaven,—as flowers in spring—
The first hour of true love is worth our worshipping.
                              THE MAID OF ELVAR.

THE red evening sun was setting, and his rays, piercing the
half-stripped trees of Bruntisfield, fell on the old mossy dialstone, which they never reached through the thick foliage of
summer. It was about the hour of five, and the western sky
shed a crimson glow over the whole landscape; the loch lay
calm and unruffled as a vast sheet of polished crystal, reflecting in its bright surface the ruddy clouds, the blue sky, and
the bordering trees, whose foliage was now assuming the warm
tints of autumn, presenting alternately the darkest green, the
brightest yellow, and most russet brown. The fallen leaves
rustled among the withered sedges of the lake, and the wild
swan, the black duck, and the water-hen floated double "bird
and shadow" on its surface, while the tall heron waded among
the eel-arks that lay half-hidden by the reeds and waterlilies
at the margin.

The rustle of the dark-brown woods, and the deepening
gloom of the hills, marked the decline of the day and year,
and Walter's heart became chilled and sad as he galloped up
the long dark avenue, which was strewed with the spoil of
the past summer—that happy summer which had passed away
for ever.

Lilian sat within the deep bay of a window in the chamber-
of-dais, busily embroidering Walter's long-promised scarf:
it was of blue velvet, having thistles of silver worked with

II.   R

St. Andrew's crosses alternately. For many weeks her nimble little fingers had plied the needle on it, and now it was nearly finished. The tramp of hoofs made her look down the far-stretching avenue, which, with its arching elms and sturdy oaks, formed a long vista to the eastward, where it was terminated by an ancient and grass-tufted archway; beyond it, the bluff craigs of Salisbury and Arthur's ridgy cone, mellowed in the distance, shone redly in the light of the setting sun, above the green and waving woods.

The blood rushed to Lilian's snowy temples: she sprang from her seat, her eyes beaming with delight, which rapidly gave place to surprise on observing the hurried and disordered air of Walter, who was minus cloak and plume. Never before had he come on horseback, and her mind misgave her there was something wrong.

She cast a timid glance at aunt Grizel. Lulled by an old and favourite ditty, which for the thousandth time the affectionate Lilian had sung to her, the old lady had fallen fast asleep in her great leathern-chair, with her relaxed hand on the spinning-wheel, the gay silver and ivory virrels of which glittered in the light of the cheerful fire. She slept profoundly.

Lilian threw on her hood and hurried to the door, where Walter had dismounted, and was in the act of slipping his snaffle-rein through one of the numerous rings in the wall—necessary appendages to the door of a manor-house, and quite as requisite as the "louping-on stane" in those days, when every visitor of consideration came on horseback.

With a charming mixture of frankness and timidity, the blushing girl held out both her hands in welcome to her lover; but there was a sadness in his smile that made the colour leave her cheek and the lustre fade in her eye.

"Lilian—dear madam—Lilian, I see you for the last time!" he exclaimed, as he took her hands in his, and raised them to his lips.

"The last time?" reiterated Lilian, faintly.

"Oh, are not these sad and bitter words? But so it is, Lilian; the fatal hour has come—our dream is over. We march for England to-morrow. The Dutch invaders are on the ocean, and in the hearts and swords of his faithful soldiers, poor King James can alone rely in the struggle that is to come."

"O Walter, what horror is this?"

"All the land is on the alert. A red beacon will blaze to-night from Arthur's rocky peak, and from Stirling in the west, to the Ochils in the north, will be sent tidings that will rouse the distant clans, and all Scotland will arise in arms. But oh! how adverse will be the motives of many who draw the sword! I have come to bid you adieu, Lilian—a long adieu; for many a battle must be fought and won ere again I stand on the threshold of your home—this happy home—the memory of which will cheer me through many a melancholy hour."

"Ah, Walter, the horrors of aunt Grizel's girlhood are again come upon us. What a sudden blow it is! We have been so happy—and you go—" Tears choked her utterance.

"This instant, Lilian," said Walter, overpowered at the sight of her tears; "this instant. God! I have only a few minutes to spare, even to bid you adieu."

"And Lady Grizel, too," said Lilian, in a breathless voice, for she was too artless to conceal her deep emotion; "she to whom you have always been so kind, so attentive—you surely will bid her adieu?"

"I could not be so ungrateful as to omit such a duty; but, dear Lilian, let us walk once more in the garden—you know our favourite place, by the old mossy fountain. Ah, Lilian, refuse me not," urged Walter, who saw that she trembled and hesitated. "I have much to say that I must not leave unsaid; for never again (how bitter are these words!) *never again* may an opportunity come to me; never again may I bend my eyes on yours, or hear the sound of your voice—oh, Lilian—"

Never had Walter trusted himself so far: he was earnest, impetuous, and confused. Lilian glanced timidly at his sparkling eyes, and then at the darkening woods, and trembling between love and timidity, permitted him to draw her arm through his, and lead her into the ancient garden, the thick holly hedges of which entirely screened them from observation.

The heart of Lilian foreboded that a scene was to ensue; but a spell was upon her—a power which she could not resist threw a chain of delight and fear around her, and bound her to the side of Walter. She seemed to be in a dream: the very air grew palpable, and she felt only the beating of her little heart. Equally wishing and dreading the coming *dénoûment*, she was almost unconscious of whither Walter led her.

He, poor fellow! was something in the same frame of mind. Though he had full time to rally his thoughts, reflection served but to make him more confused, and instead of the passionate avowal which, a moment ago, had trembled on his lips, his intense respect for Lilian brought him down to the merest commonplace, and again the favourite words of Finland came truthfully home to his mind, "the girl one loves is greater than an empress."

"It is very sad to think that—that peradventure we are walking here for the last time," said he.

This was not quite what Lilian expected, and somewhat reassured, she murmured a polite reply.

"You will not forget me when I am far, far away from you, Lilian?"

"Oh, no—how could I forget?" said she, bending her timid eyes kindly and sadly upon him. There was a charm in her answer that bewildered her lover, and, unable to resist longer the ardour and impulses of his heart, he threw an arm around her, and, pressing her right hand to his breast, exclaimed, in a voice that trembled with emotion, "I love you, Lilian—I have dared to love you long—oh, may I hope you will forgive me?"

He paused; but Lilian could make no reply. An instant she was pale, then a deep blush crimsoned her cheek, her long lashes veiled her humid eyes—and for the first time Walter pressed his lips to hers as she sank upon his breast.

"Oh, Lilian," he resumed, after a long pause, " now on the eve of parting, and perhaps for ever, I could not leave you with this great secret preying upon my heart—without saying that *I loved you*. The hope, that when I am gone, you will think of me with sentiments more tender and more endearing than those of mere friendship, will be my best incentive to become worthy of them. Dear Lilian, I am poor and nameless; save my heart and my sword, and the sod which shall cover me, I own nothing in all this wide world; but than mine, never was there a love more generous or more true. Long, long, adorable Lilian, have I loved you in secret, and loved you dearly."

There was no art in his declaration; it came straight from the soul, and his words, rich, deep, and full of feeling, thrilled through the agitated heart of the young girl. He sought no reply, no other avowal of her reciprocal love, than her beautiful confusion and eloquent silence. Immovable and breathless, she lay within his embrace, with the deepest blushes overspreading her whole face and neck. Her mild eyes were shaded by their lashes, and the charming expression of modesty imparted by their downcast lids increased the emotion of Walter, and closer to his breast he pressed her passive form, till her heart throbbed against his own.

O love, when womanhood is in the flush!'"

Walter was intoxicated. The purple hood of Lilian had fallen back, and the braids of her fair hair drooped upon his breast; his dark hair mingled with them, and their locks sparkled like gold in the glow of the set sun, as its last rays streamed down the long shady walk.

Short as the interview was, an age seemed to be comprised within its compass; the lovers were in a little world of their own—or with them the external world seemed to stand still. They were all heart and pulse, and overwhelmed with an emotion which the orthography of every human language has failed to portray.

But anon, the first glow of ardour and excitement passed away, and the memory of their parting fell like a mountain on their hearts. Lilian hung half embraced by Walter's arm; and a shower of tears relieved her.

Ah, could the evil-minded Clermistonlee have witnessed this scene!

The sun set behind the dark woods of Corstorphine; its last rays faded away from the turret vanes and seared foliage of Bruntisfield; the oaks and loch of the Burghmuir grew dark, as the shadows of the autumnal gloaming increased around them, and warned the lovers of the necessity of retiring and—separating.

Never was the glowing memory of that interview forgotten by Walter Fenton; and it cheered him through many an hour of sorrow, humiliation, and misery; through the toils of many a weary night, and the carnage of many a dangerous day. How happy and how well it is for us that the future is covered by an impenetrable veil that no mortal eye can pierce, and no hand draw aside!

The swans had quitted the lake, and the last glow of the day that had passed, was dying away upon its glassy surface, when hand in hand, the girl and her lover, contented, if not supremely happy, left the garden. There, by the old fountain of mossy and fantastic stone-work, on the pedestal of which a grotesque visage vomited the water from its capacious throat into a stone basin, they had plighted unto each other their solemn troth, according to the simple custom of the time and country.

There was no witness but the evening star that glimmered in the saffron west. There was no record but their own beating hearts.

Standing one on each side of the gushing fountain, and laving their hands in the limpid water, they called upon God to hear and register their vows of truth and love—vows which were, perhaps less eloquent than deep, but uttered with all the quiet fervour of two young hearts as yet unseared and unsoured by the trouble, the duplicity, the selfishness, and the bitterness of the world.

Poor lovers! It was their first hour of delight; and even then, though by them unseen, a human visage of livid and terrible aspect was steadily regarding them from the thick foliage of a dark holly hedge, with eyes like those of a serpent —eyes that glared like two burning coals, and seemed full of that dire expression with which the superstitions of Italy gift the possessors of the *mal-occhio*. The lips were colourless and white, the teeth were clenched; it was all that a painter could portray of agony and mortification. As they arose from the fountain, it vanished; footsteps crashed among the fallen leaves and withered branches, but the lovers heard them not.

Lilian, though she still wept from over-excitement, and the approaching separation which had so suddenly called all these secret feelings to empire and control in her bosom, with sensations of mingled happiness and grief too intense to find vent in words, hung on Walter's arm, and thus clasped hand in hand with more apparent composure, they slowly returned to the house and entered the chamber-of-dais.

Its panels of polished oak, the silver plate on the buffet, the china jars, and japan canisters, on the grotesque ebony cabinets, glittered ruddily in the light of the blazing fire. A noble stag-hound, with red eyes and wiry hair, Lilian's lap-dog, and a favourite cat, were gambolling together on the hearth, and tearing the snow-white wool from the prostrate spinning-wheel. Lady Grizel still slept soundly; but Lilian stole to her side, kissed, and awoke her by murmuring in a broken voice, and with a sickly attempt at playfulness,

" Awake, aunt Grizel, Mr. Fenton has come to bid us farewell. He marches by crow of the cock, and we may not see him again for—for many a weary day."

" My dream is read!" exclaimed the old lady, starting. " O, Lilian, lass! what is this you tell me? Walter, my poor bairn, come to me; for whence are ye boune?"

" For England, madam."

" England! alake, alake! and I was dreaming of Sir Archibald," replied the venerable dame, whose eyes were glittering with tears. " I saw him standing there, before the oaken cabinet, in his buff coat, steel cap, and plume, just as I saw him last when under harness; and oh! but he seemed young and winsome, with glowing cheeks and bright locks of curling brown. ' Archibald,' I cried, and stretching my arms towards him, I strove to say mair; but O! Lilian, the **words** died away in whispers on my lips. He walked over to the buffet, and took up his silver tankard, which other lips have never touched since his own. It was empty. Sairly he gloomed as he wont when aught crossed him, and flang down the cup. I heard the clank of his jangling spurs as he turned lightly about, saying, 'Fare-ye-weel, my jo Grizel, horse and spear's the cry again,' and strode away. But O, his face, and the flash of his dark-browed eye; they come back to me, a vision from the grave. I awoke, and there stood Walter Fenton— his living image. O, Lilian! my doo, something sad is at hand. Blows and blood ever followed such visions as mine hath been this night. It forebodes deep dool, and dark misfortune."

"Dear aunt Grizel, why such dreary thoughts?" said Lilian, no longer able to restrain her tears; "though we are losing our dear friend Mr. Fenton—one, I hope, after Sir Archibald's own heart."

"True, he hath the bearing of a Napier, and the very eye of my young son, and, sooth, he was a stalwart cavalier as ever danced a gay galliard, or spurred a horse to the battle-field. And you are boune for the south, Walter? War and blood, more of it yet—more of it yet—when will the wicked cease from troubling? Well it is for ye, boy, that ye have no mother to weep this night the bitter tears that I have often shed for mine. Three fair sons, Walter, hae gone forth from this auld roof-tree, three stalwart men they were, and winsome to look upon, blooming and strong as ever braced steel ower gallant hearts; but hardalake! ere the sun sank owre the westland hills, the last o' them lay by his father's side, cauld and stark on the banks of the Keithingburn.

"But I trow," she added, striking her cane on the floor, "many a braw English cap and feather lay on the turf ere that came to pass." The keen grey eyes of the spirited dame flashed bright through their tears, for strongly at that moment the Spartan spirit of the old Scottish matron glowed within her breast. "England? Alace! and what is stirring now that our blue bonnets maun cross the border again? Smooth water runs deep. I aye thought we were owre sib wi' the south to byde sae long."

"Madam, we march as friends and allies to assist in repelling invasion from its shores. William of Orange, with a great armament, now bends his cannon on the English coast, and by daybreak to-morrow we march for King James's camp. I must leave you instantly, for I have not a moment to spare. My Lord Dunbarton requires my presence at Holyrood, where General Douglas of Queensbury is to address

officers of the army.   Farewell, dear madam ; think kindly of
me when I am far, far away from you, for never may we meet
again," and half kneeling, he kissed her hand.

"Then ere thou goest, my poor boy, drink to the roof-tree
of one who loves thee well, and who may never behold thee
more.   Ye hae the very voice of my youngest son ; and O,
Walter, my auld heart yearns unto ye even as a mother's
would yearn unto her dearest child."

Walter's heart swelled within him as the kind old lady laid
her arm round his neck.

"Lady Bruntisfield," said he, in a low voice, "often have I
known how sad a thing it was to feel oneself alone in the
world, and never will the memory of these kind words be
effaced from my heart."

Lilian, blushing and pale by turns, with eyes full of tears,
brought from the almry a silver cup of wine, and after she
and Lady Grizel had tasted, Walter drained it to the bottom,
as he did so uttering a mental blessing on the house of
Bruntisfield.   The rich Gascon wine fired his heart, and gave
him courage to sustain the separation.

"'Tis a sad and sudden parting, Walter," said Lady Grizel,
weeping unrestrainedly with that old-fashioned kindness of
heart which has long since fled from the land.   "How long
will you be away from us ? "

"That depends on the fortune of war, madam."

"Puir bairn ! ye mean the misfortune.   Alace ! we live in
waefu' times.   Year after year an auld Scots wife seeth the
fair flowers that spring up around her trod down and destroyed.
How many fair sons are reared with mickle pain and toil to
be cut down by the sword of the foemen !   Thrice in my time
have I seen the balefire blaze on Soutra-edge and Ochil Peak,
and thrice have I seen the haill flower o' the country-side
wede away.   And well it is, Walter, that thou hast no other
mother than myself to mourn for thee this night ; for, as I
said before," she continued, in the garrulous musing of age,
"my mind gangs back to the happy days and the fond faces
of other times, when I have laced the steel cap owre comely
cheeks whose smiles were a' the world to me.   Then the balefire was lowing on ilka hill, and *mount and ride* was the cry.
O, when will men grow wise (as that fule body Ichabod said
with truth), and let the wicked kings of the earth gird up
their loins and go forth to battle alone ?

"Thine, Walter Fenton, is owre fair a brow for the midnight dew to lie upon, and the black corbie to flap its wings
aboon in the stricken battle-field," continued the old lady,
weeping, as "tremulously gentle her small hand" put back

the thick dark locks from Walter's clouded brow, and kissed it, while Lilian sobbed audibly on hearing her speak so forebodingly. The heart of the young man was too full to permit him to reply, but at that moment he felt he had done this kind and noble matron a grievous injury in gaining the love of Lilian without her consent. So reproachfully did the idea come home to his heart, that he was about to throw himself upon his knees, and in the ardour of his temper, pour forth an address in confession and exculpation—but his courage failed, and never again had he an opportunity.

Compelled at last to assume his bonnet and rapier, he felt his heart wrung when reflecting that he was, for the last time, with the only two beings on earth actually dear to him, that in another moment he would be gone, with the wide world before him, and that world all a void—a wilderness.

Lilian threw over his shoulders the scarf her fingers had embroidered, and as the reverend lady blessed him, the tears started into his eyes; he kissed their hands, and hurried away. Both arose to accompany him to the door; but while Lady Grizel searched for her long cane, he had yet a moment to give to Lilian. The light in the entrance hall fell full upon her face; it was pale as death, and never until that moment had Walter felt how intensely he loved her.

"Once again, farewell, dear Lilian," said he, putting a ring upon her finger; "wear this for my sake, and forget not this night—the twentieth of September. O, Lilian, this ring is the dearest, the only relic I possess, and it contains the secret of my life. On my mother's hand it was found, when cold, and pale, and dead, she lay among the tombs of the Greyfriars, in the year of Bothwell: you know the rest, and will treasure it for my sake. If your lover falls, Lilian, for you it will be some satisfaction that he died beneath the Scottish standard, fighting for his king by the side of the brave Dunbarton! Who would desire a better epitaph?"

"Walter," implored Lilian, in a piercing voice, "for the love of God, if not for the love of me, speak not thus!"

"Thou shalt hear of me, Lilian, if God spares me, as I hope he will, for thy sake," replied Walter, whose military pride neither love nor sorrow could subdue. "My name shall never be mentioned but with honour, for I have sworn to become worthy of thee, or to—die! And if our soldiers prove as they have ever done, leal men and true, many a helmet will be cloven, many a corselet flattened, many a pike blunted, and bullet shot, ere the banner of King James shall sink before these plebeian Dutch! Farewell: forget not the twentieth of September!"

Another mute caress, and Lilian was alone : a horse's hoofs rang among the strewn autumnal leaves ; but the sound died away, and Lilian heard her heart beating tumultuously.

As his horse plunged forward down the steep avenue, the starting of the saddle-girths compelled Walter to rein up near the gateway, and while adjusting the buckles, he became the unconscious listener to another leave-taking, which was accompanied by loud and obstreperous lamentations. It was Meinie Elshender bidding adieu to her kinsman and sweetheart, Hab, who was reeling about in his bandoleers, under the influence of various stoups of brandy.

"Now, Hab, you fause loon, dinna say no! You *will* forget me in the south, as you did in the west. Soldiers are a' alike."

"Roaring buckies are we, lassie!"

"Twa-faced varlets, that kittle up their lugs when the drums beat, and make love wherever they gang," replied Meinie, sobbing heavily. "You will be taking up with some English kimmer, I ken, and forgetting puir Meinie Elshender, that lo'es ye better than her ain life ; and ——"

"If I do, may ——"

"Ewhow! and the rambles we've had together in many a red gloaming by the heronshaws and quarrel-holes. O, Hab, you're a fause ane, and will forget me—for the truth is no in ye !"

"Dear Meinie, if I do may ——"

"Dinna swear, ye fule ; for I may weary waiting on ye."

"May the de'il jump down my throat with a harrow at his tail ! There now, will you believe me ? Hoots, lass, we'll be back by the Hallowen time to douk for apples in the muckle barn, sow hemp-seed in the Deil's-croft, roast nuts in the ingle, pu' kail castocks, and gang guisarding by Drumdryan and the Highriggs. Hech, how !

'Dunbarton's drums beat bonnie, O !'

Kiss me again, lass, and keep up your heart for a month or two more, when again I will have my arm around ye, and your red cheek pressed to mine ;" continued poor Halbert, to whom that hour was never doomed to come, "and many a brave story I will tell ye of how our buirdly Scots chields clapper-clawed the ill-faured Holanders."

"Hab, ye ill-mannered loon !" cried Elsie. "Hab, ye ungratefu' vassal, daur ye gang awa' without paying your *devoirs* to my lady ?"

"Bid her good-bye for me, mother," replied Halbert in a faltering tone, as the old woman hobbled up and threw her arms passionately around his neck. "My father was her bounden vassal; but his son is the king's free soldier. Say gude'en for me, for I have not another moment to spare, even for Meinie. Fareweel, dear mother; I never expected to leave you again, but for those who follow the de'il or the drum—Hoots, mother, havers!" exclaimed the soldier, as the poor woman sobbed convulsively on his breast. "I thought we had a' this dirdum oure before."

"Fareweel, my bairn, my winsome Habbie! On this side o' the grave we sall never meet mair. England is a far awa' and an unco' place, and long ere ye return I will be laid in the lang hame of my forbears. But fearfu' times will come and pass ere the grass is green and waving oure me. Mind your Bible, Hab, for your faither (peace be wi' him, for he had none wi' me) ever gaed forth to battle with a whinger in one hand, and the *blessed book* in the other. Beware o' the errors of episcopacy and idolatry, for yo're gaun to the hot-bed o' them baith."

"O yes; ou' aye," muttered Hab impatiently.

"Now gang, my bairn, and God will keep his hand owre ye in the hour of strife, for he ne'er forgets those by whom his power and his glory are remembered."

And while Hab dashed off towards the city, the old woman with upraised hands implored, with Scottish piety and maternal fervour, a blessing on the footsteps of the son that had departed from her—for ever.

CHAPTER XXXI.

THE DEFIANCE.

'Tis well for thee, Sir, that I wear no sword,
Else it had soon decided which should claim,
And which for death's colde arms exchange the dame.
OLD PLAY.

WALTER had listened longer than he intended, and for a moment he felt keenly how sad a thing it was that there were neither parent nor kindred to bless his departing steps. The sincere grief of the humble cottar had deeply moved him; but two kind kisses were yet glowing on his cheek, and the remembrance that there were two gentle beings who sorrowed for his departure, and sighed for his return, filled his heart with joy.

The ardour of youth, and his old enthusiastic spirit, blazed up within him as he galloped back to the town. There, bustle and confusion reigned supreme. The streets were thronged with citizens and soldiers ; and, though the hour was late, the hum of many voices showed that all were upon the *qui vive*.

As he passed the old house of the High-riggs, in the gloom of the autumnal night, he nearly rode over a man whose grey plaid and broad bonnet indicated him to be a peasant.

" Hollo, friend !—I crave your pardon."

" Goode'en to you, Mr. Fenton ; you ride with a slack rein for a cavalier," replied the other in a thick voice, after a brief pause.

" Ha ! you know me, and it seems as if your voice was not unfamiliar ; but the night is so dark. You are——"

" Captain Napier, of the Scots-Dutch," replied the other in a low voice.

" Astonishment ! Unwary man, know you not that the council have placed a price on you, dead or alive ? Is it madness that prompts you to venture, in this Cameronian disguise, within a city swarming with royal troops ?"

" No, sir," replied the other haughtily ; " but the service of William, prince of Orange."

" For God's sake, sir, hush ! These words are enough to raise the very stones in the streets against you."

" Enough, young spark. I have been too long under the ban of Scotland's accursed misrulers not to have learned caution. But I know that he who addresses me is a man of honour."

" I thank you, sir, for the compliment."

" I believe you to be honourable as I have found you brave, and will trust you when I cannot do better. I am bound for England, on the shores of which William of Orange will soon pour his legions like another Conqueror. Hark you, Mr. Fenton, we are rivals in love as we are foes in faction ; and, though the goal we aim at is the same, our paths are widely different. The scene I saw and overheard this evening by the fountain, makes me long with the hatred of a tiger rather then the spirit of a Christian man to slay you ; for, by the might of God ! no mortal shall ever cross the path or purpose of Quentin Napier, while his hand can hold a rapier or level a pistol !

" Walter Fenton, from my boyhood, I have loved that amiable girl, and there was a time when I fondly thought she loved me too. Necessity forced me into the ranks of the Stadtholder. In the campaigns in Zealand and Flanders, amid the turmoil of war, her image almost faded from my mind ; but when again we met, my memory went back to the pleasant days of our younger years—all the first hopes and fond feelings of my heart returned to their starting-place. 'Twas thou that didst destroy this spell! And well it is for thee, youth, that I am unarmed; for strong in my heart at this moment, is the power of the spirit of darkness."

"Sir," replied Walter, scornfully, "this is the mere Cameronian cant of the Scots brigade; and had I pistols——"

"The dust beneath our feet should drink the heart's blood of one or both of us! By the heaven that hears me, it should be so!"

At that moment the balefire on the cone of Arthur's Seat suddenly burst forth into a lurid flame, and, flaring on the night wind in one broad forky sheet, seemed to turn the dark mountain into a volcano, and, tipping its ridgy outline with light, brought it forward in relief from the inky sky beyond. The turreted battlements of Heriot's Hospital, and the casements of the towering city, were reddened by the gleam, and a faint light glowed on the pale contracted features of Quentin Napier. He smiled grimly.

"How long have I looked forward to the time when yonder blaze would redden on our Scottish hills! The time hath come! Farewell," he said, grasping Walter's hand with fierce energy, while his voice became deep and hoarse; "blows will soon be struck, and we may—*we must*—meet in the field. When *that* hour comes, spare me not; for by the Power who this night heard your plighted troth, and from His throne in heaven hears us now, I will not spare thee."

"Till then, adieu," replied Walter, with something of pity mingling in his pride and scorn.

"But that you may fall by other hands than these, is the best I can wish you. You were generous once, and I respect while I abhor you."

They separated.

A ferocious rival and uncompromising traitor were within his grasp, and effectually he might have crushed both in one: but he could not forget that this stern and cold-blooded partisan was the kinsman of Lilian Napier, and one who trusted in his honour.

As he urged his horse towards the Bristo Port, the great forges of the foundry, where formerly the Covenanters had cast their cannon, were in full operation, and the rays of those lurid pyramids of fire, that shot upwards from their towering cones, produced a wild and beautiful effect as they fell on the fantastic projections and deep recesses of the old suburbs, and the long line of crenelated wall which girdled the city, on the dark and ancient college of King James, and on the groups of anxious citizens gathered at their windows and outside-stairs, conversing in subdued tones on those "coming events" which were already casting their shadows before. As Walter passed, their voices died away, and many a lowering eye was bent upon him, while not a few shouted injurious epithets, and chanted " *Lillibulero bullen a la,*" the Marseillaise hymn of the Scottish revolutionists.

The arcades or piazzas in the High-street were crowded by a noisy mob. The whole city seemed on tip-toe from the High-riggs to the Palace Gate, and many an eye was turned to where, like stars upon the west and northern hills, the answering balefires threw abroad the light of alarm. No man had yet dared to assume the blue cockade of the Covenant; but the faces of the "sour-featured Whigs" were become radiant with hope in anticipation of their coming triumph and revenge. Guarded by Buchan's musketeers, the Scottish train of artillery was drawn up near the Tron, wheel to wheel, limbered and ready for service ; while cavalier officers, with their waving plumes and scarfs, guardsmen, and dragoons in their flashing armour, galloped hurriedly from street to street.

Women were wailing, and soldiers crowding and revelling in and around the hostels and taverns, and the whole city was one scene of universal confusion, noise, and dismay. Followed by six of his splendidly accoutred cavaliers, Claverhouse (now Major-General Viscount Dundee) dashed up from the palace at full gallop. All shrunk back as he swept forward on some mission of importance to the duke of Gordon, "the cock of the north," who commanded in the castle of Edinburgh, and, fired by the gallant air of Claverhouse, Walter felt his heart glow with ardour for the military splendour of the coming day.

CHAPTER XXXII.

THE MARCH FOR ENGLAND.

The neighynge of the war-horse prowde,
  The rowleinge of the drum;
The clangour of the trumpet lowde,
  Be soundes from heaven that come.
Then mount, then mount, brave gallants all,
  And don your helmes amaine ;
Death's couriers—fame and honour—call
  Us to the field againe.

SCOTS SONG.

LED by General James Douglas, a brother of the duke of Queenberry, the Scottish army was to march to London in three columns or divisions. He commanded the foot in person; Major-General Viscount Dundee led the cavalry; the laird of Lundin the train of artillery.

By grey dawn on the 21st of September, the boom of a cannon pealed from the ramparts of the castle over the city, and echoed among the craigs of Salisbury and the woods of Warrender and Drumsheugh. It was the warning gun; and immediately the varying cadence of the cavalry trumpets sounding *to horse*, and the infantry drums beating the *générale*, an old summons that has often gained the malison of the wearied soldier, rang within the narrow thoroughfares of Edinburgh.

> "I thought I heard the General say,—
> 'Tis time to rouse, and march away!"

Poor Lilian had passed a restless night; she slept only to dream, and awoke only to weep, and to feel that no tears are more bitter than those shed unseen by lonely sorrow in the solitude of night. Many a young heart was crushed with grief, and many a bright eye sleepless and tearful in anticipation of the morrow's separation, perhaps for ever. Many a fierce and enthusiastic religioso looked forward to the march of his countrymen as a relief from thraldom, and the dawn of a day of vengeance on the upholders of "the Great Beast."

Now that morrow was come, and the ruddy sun arose above the Lammermuirs to shed his morning glory on the woods of russet brown, from the bosky depths of which the lark, the gled, and the eagle were winging their way aloft.

Lilian looked forth from her turret-window, and the very brightness of that beautiful morning, in contrast to the gloom of her thoughts, made her heart feel more sad and lonely. The stern façade of the ancient château gleamed in the light of the rising sun, and the few flowers of autumn lifted up their heavy petals as the warm rays absorbed the diamond dew. Hastily and less carefully than usual, the duties of the toilet were dismissed, and deeply the young girl sighed as she braided her auburn hair, for now there was no one whom she cared to please. Bright and cloudless though the morning, to her a gloom seemed to veil everything; but she mastered her grief until Meinie Elshender, her tirewoman, burst into an uncontrollable fit of lamentation over the departure of her lighthearted Hab; upon which Lilian, infected by her sorrow, could no longer restrain herself, and the two girls wept together.

"Oh, Lady Lilian, another hour will see our braw lads owre the hills and awa! Hech-how!" sobbed the disconsolate bower-maiden, "I am glad that muckle tyke, Tam o' the Riggs, is no gaun too. I'll be sure o' *him* gif puir Hab's shot by the Hollanders. Eh, sirs, that ever I should see this day!" and she sobbed comfortably between sorrow and satisfaction.

"Oh that Annie of Maxwelton would come!" said Lilian; "she is ever so lighthearted, so joyous and gay—her presence were a godsend. Poor Annie! another week would have seen her wedding-day, and now her Douglas must follow Dunbarton to battle—perhaps to death."

"Yonder are her chairmen," replied Meinie as a sedan appeared in the avenue; "and my Lady Dunbarton's English coach, and madam this and my lady that—ewhow, sirs; we'll hae a fu' hall to-day."

Numerous vehicles were seen approaching. The troops were to march southward by the Burghmuir, and many ladies of rank and fashion were arriving, to behold their departure from a platform erected within the orchard-wall of Bruntisfield, and overlooking the rough old quarries and deep marshy ground that bordered the Burghloch. Lilian flew down to the barbican, and embraced her friend. Though as gaily attired as usual, Annie was very pale, and the breeze of the morning when it lifted her heavy locks, showed the pallor of the beautiful cheek below. Her innocent gaiety and coquetry had fled together; her spirit had evaporated, and tearful and sad, she sorrowfully kissed her paler friend.

The orchard was higher than the roadway, which its wall overlooked like a rampart, and there numerous high-backed chairs were placed for the convenience of the ladies, who were every moment arriving, each in a greater state of flutter and excitement than the last, to view the troops on their line of march. Various pieces of tapestry were spread over the parapet, and an ancient standard or two, and several branches of laurel tastefully arranged by the gardener, made the orchard-wall like a balcony at a listed tournament.

Lady Grizel was merry and grave by turns, but always stately and hospitable. With her the day had long since passed, when the march of a mailed host could raise other sensations in her bosom than those of pity for the young and brave who might return no more. The beautiful countess of Dunbarton veiled her anxiety under an admirable placidity of face and suavity of manner; while Lilian, Annie Laurie, and many other fair girls who had lovers and relations "under harness," were clustered together, a pale and tearful group that conversed in low whispers.

The moss-grown trees of the ancient orchard spread their faded foliage over them; behind rose the striking outline of the old manor-house, with its round projecting turrets and high-peaked gables glowing in the early rays of the sun, which streamed redly and aslant from the southern ridge of Arthur's Seat, lighting with a golden gleam the mirrored lake that rolled almost to the orchard wall. A light shower had fallen just before dawn, and everything was brightened and refreshed. The dew yet glittered on the waving branches and the bending grass, and white as snow the morning mists rolled heavily around the base of the verdant hills, or curled, in a thousand vapoury and beautiful forms, in the saffron glory of the rising sun. The dewy autumnal breeze was laden with balm and fragrance. The first-fallen leaves rustled in the long grass; the corbies and wood-pigeons were wheeling aloft, and the swan and the heron floated on the still bosom of the loch.

Bright though the morning, and beautiful the scenery, the group assembled near Bruntisfield were thoughtful and reserved; any little chit-chat in which they had indulged while Lady Grizel was detailing the duke of Hamilton's march for England in her younger days, died away, when the far-off notes of military music and the increasing hum in the city, announced that "they were coming."

"Hark!" said Lady Dunbarton, "now they are approaching. 'Tis by Lord Dundee's advice they march through the entire length of the city, from the Girth Cross to the Portsburgh, that their array may intimidate the false Whigs, who are hourly crowding in from all quarters."

Beneath where the ladies were seated, the roadway was thronged with cottars from the adjacent hamlets; and many an eye was turned wistfully to the road that wound by the western rhinns of the loch towards the old baronial manor of the Lawsons, that on the Highriggs, as before mentioned, terminated the ancient suburb of Portsburgh. From thence a dense mass was seen debouching: the sound of the drum, and the sharper note of the trumpet, were heard at intervals, while pikes glittered, banners waved, and hoofs rang, and every heart beat quicker as the troops approached; for, even in our own matter-of-fact age, there are few sights more stirring than the departure of a regiment for foreign service; but then it was the entire regular force of the kingdom en masse on the march for another land. Dense crowds occupied the whole roadway; for though the Scottish government had few friends, all the idlers of the city were pouring forth from its southern gates.

England was still a foreign and rather hostile country, and London was "an unco and far-awa place" (much more so than Calcutta is now); and persons on their departure, therefore, received the condolences of their friends; on their return, were welcomed by joy and congratulation, and were regarded with wonder and interest like the ancient mariners who had doubled Cape Non. And thus the Edinburghers, according to their various hopes, fears, hates and wishes, regarded with unusual anxiety the departure of their countrymen.

Save our brave Highlanders, fifty-seven years afterwards, this was the last Scottish host that ever marched into England.

First came an advanced guard of horse grenadiers, who wore scarlet coats over their steel corslets, and had high fur caps; they were armed with long muskets, bayonets, and hammer-hatchets, and wore grenado-pouches on their left side, to balance the cartridge-boxes on the right.

Led by the laird of Lundin, master of the ordnance, next came the train of artillery, with trumpets sounding and kettle-drums beating; the matrosses marching with shouldered pikes on each side of the polished brass cannon; the fire-masters on horseback, distinguished by waving plumes and golden scarfs. Nearly sheathed in complete armour of Charles the First's time, four gentlemen-of-the-cannon rode on each side of the great flag-gun, which was drawn by eight horses. The Scottish standards—one with St. Andrew's cross, the other with the lion, gules—were displayed from its carriage, on which sat two little kettle-drummers beating a march. It was followed by the gins, capstans, forge-waggons, and a troop of horse with their swords drawn.

Then the column of cavalry filed past; all fierce and select cavalier troopers, many of them inured to service by the civil wars of eight-and-twenty years. Claverhouse's life guardsmen, in their polished plate-armour, wearing white horsehair streaming from their helmets;—all were splendidly mounted, and rode with the butts of their carbines resting on their thighs. They were greeted by a burst of acclamation from the ladies, for these dashing horsemen were the Guardi Nobili, the Prætorian band of Scotland. Douglas's regiment of red-coat horse, and the earl of Dunmore's dragoons, the Scots Greys in their janissary caps, buff coats, and iron panoply, brought up the rear.

Next came the infantry; the two battalions of the Fusilier Guards, clad in coats, breeches, and stockings, all of bright scarlet, with white scarfs and long feathers; the officers marching with half-pikes, and the soldiers with lighted matches; the battalions of the Scots Musketeers in their round morions and corslets of black iron; the earl of Mar's fusiliers, Wauchop's regiment, &c. &c., poured past in rapid and monotonous succession, till the rear-guard of horse and a few pieces of artillery, with a long line of sumpter-horses, bidets, and peddies, or grooms, closed the rear.

From a cloudless sky, full upon their long line of march, the bright sun poured down his morning splendour; the blare of the brazen trumpet and the ringing bugle-horn, the clashing cymbal and the measured beat of the drum, rang in the echoing sky and adjacent woodlands; while, like the ceaseless rush of a river, the tread of many marching feet, the tramp of the horses, the clank of chain-bridles, steel scabbards, and bandoliers, the lumbering roll of the brass cannon and shot-tumbrils of the train, filled up the intervals of the air which all their bands were playing,—the famous old Scots march, composed for the guard of King James V.

Never before had Walter Fenton felt such exultation, or so proud of the banner that waved over his shoulder; and his heart seemed to bound to every crash of the martial music that loaded the morning wind. It is impossible to portray the glow of chivalry that stirs a heart like his at such a time.

Amid the dust of the long array in front, the innumerable bright points of armour, and accoutrements, and weapons, were sparkling and flashing, and, when viewed from the distant city, the host of horse and foot, with standards waving, resembled a vast gilded snake sweeping over the Burghmuir, and gliding between its old oak trees and broomy knolls towards the hills of Braid. It was a scene which no man could behold without ardour and admiration, or without that gush of enthusiasm which stirs even the most sluggish spirit—

> "When hearts are all high beating,
> And the trumpet's voice repeating
> That song whose breath
> May lead to death,
> But *never* to retreating."

"Ah! Douglas," said Walter to his friend, "I feel that all the romance of my boyish dreams is about to be realized. My breast seems too narrow for the emotions that glow within it. Love——"

"Yes, Fenton, *it* is the most powerful of all human passions; but a desire for military glory is scarcely less strong. Yet, bethink thee, Fenton, how sadly an old veteran's memory retraces the ardour of such an hour as this."

"To me it almost counterbalances the pain of parting from yonder dear girl;" and, while speaking, he bowed repeatedly to Lilian and kissed his hand, for they were now beneath the orchard wall. Long and sad was the glance he gave that fair face, every feature of which was indelibly impressed on his heart. Her vivacity was gone, and her cheek pale; her heart was wrung with anguish, though it fluttered with the excitement around her. Even the gay Annie was unusually grave, and her dark blue eyes were humid with the heavy tears that trembled on their long black lashes.

"Farewell, Annie," said Douglas, looking up to her with intense feeling. "Farewell, my love. 'Horse and spear' is the slogan now."

The aspect of Dunbarton's Royals elicited a burst of applause, and the ladies threw flowers among their passing ranks. That surpassing state of discipline and steadiness which they had acquired under the great De Martinet (that phœnix of adjutants and paragon of drills), whose fame is known throughout all the armies of Europe, had not passed away.

From the richness of their accoutrements, they seemed one mass of vivid scarlet and polished steel. The musketeers and pikemen (every corps had still a proportion armed with that ancient weapon) wore a close round morion of iron with cheek-plates clasped under the chin : those of the officers were of burnished steel, surmounted by dancing plumes of white ostrich-feathers. The cuirasses and gorgets of the captains were of the colour of gold ; the lieutenants' were of black, studded with gold ; and those of the ensigns were of silver,—and all had embroidered sword-belts and crimson scarfs with golden tassels. The corslets of the soldiers were of black iron, crossed by their collars of bandoliers, little wooden cases, each containing a charge of powder ; the balls were carried loose in a pouch on the left side, balanced by a priming-horn on the right. Their scarlet coats were heavily cuffed and richly braided, and each was armed with a sword in addition to his bright-barrelled matchlock. With tall fur caps, and coats slashed and looped, led by Gavin of that ilk, their grenadiers marched in front, with hammer-hatchets, slung carbines, swords, daggers, and pouches of grenades. Such was the aspect of the regular Scottish infantry of that period ; and certainly it was not a little imposing.*

At the head of his regiment rode the brave earl of Dunbarton, with the curious mask or visor (then appended to the helmet) turned upward, revealing his dark and noble features ; his coat of scarlet, richly laced, was worn open to display his corslet of bright steel, which was inlaid with gold. The military wig escaped from beneath the plumed headpiece, and flowed in long curls over his shoulders ; and he rode with his baton rested on the top of his long jack-boot. Still more gaily armed and accoutred, the handsome viscount of Dundee rode on his left ; and on the right, the dark-visaged

* Royal Orders of the day.

and sinister-eyed James Douglas of Queensberry, the general commanding, managed a spirited black charger ; and on passing the ladies, the three cavalier leaders bowed until their plumes mingled with their horses' manes.

The venerable Sir Thomas Dalyel, attired in his antique buff coat, steel cap, and long boots, and with his preposterous white beard streaming in the wind, galloped up, baton in hand, to pay his *devoirs* to Lady Grizel and her visitors— making, as he reined up, such a reverence as might have been fashionable at the court of his ferocity the czar of Muscovy. A crowd of tenants and cottars who loitered near, shrank back with ill-disguised fear and aversion as the " auld persecutor " approached.

" A fearfu' man, whose face is an index o' his heart," muttered Elsie Elshender, shaking her clenched hand at him behind Meinie's back. " 'Tis just such a beard the warlocks and the deil have on, when they meet the witches at their sabbath on the Calton." As she spoke, the keen stern eye of the veteran cavalier chanced to fall full upon her, and the old woman trembled lest he might divine her thoughts, if he had not overheard her words—so great was the terror entertained of his real and imaginary powers.

" Ye say true, Cummer Elsie," whispered Symon, the ground baillie, a grim old fellow, clad in hodden grey, wearing his Sunday bonnet and plaid, a staff in his hand, and a broadsword at his side. " He hath the mark of the beast on his frontlet. Hah! I have seen as muckle bravery displayed in the moss o' Drumclog, but the cheer of the oppressor was changed ere the gloaming fell. But better times are coming, Elsie ; better days are coming, and then sall ' the children of Zion be joyful in their king.' "

Sir Thomas Dalyel, who

> " Like Claver'se fell chiel,
> Was in league wi' the deil,"

and had of course been rendered bullet-proof in consequence of this infernal compact, from his style of conversation was ill calculated to soothe the anxious fears of those he addressed.

" How, Sir Thomas ?" said Lady Grizel Napier, " I know not that you were boune for England."

" Nor am I, please you, madam," replied the old cavalier, standing in his stirrups, erect as a pike. " I am getting owre auld in the horn now. Eighty years, saxty of whilk were spent under harness, are beginning to tell sairly on me at last ; and that frosty auld carle, Time, hath whispered long that my marching days are weel nigh over. But, please God,

I may die in my buff coat yet, gif the tide of war rolls northward I would fain see a few more blows exchanged on Scottish turf before I am laid below it."

" I marvel not, Sir Thomas," said the gentle young countess of Dunbarton, "that the sight of these passing bands rouses your nobler spirit, when I, who am so timid, feel myself inspired with a false ardour and courage."

" Most noble ladies, the heart would indeed be a cauld one, that felt nae fire in sic an hour as this. By my faith, even my auld troop-horse, grey Marston, kittles up his lugs at the fanfare o' the trumpet, like a Don Cossack at the cry of plunder. Puir Marston," he added, patting the neck of his charger, "I fear our fighting days are now gone by, unless the Dutch rapscallions come north, whilk may God direct, that auld Tammas o' the Binns may strike three strokes on steel for Scotland and his king, ere this baton is laid on his coffin-lid. 'Tis a brave sight, ladies, and Douglas hath under his banner some brave lads as ever marched to battle or breach. But I like not this new invention, whilk is callit the bayonet, preferring the good old Sweyn's feather, which repels the heaviest brigade of horse like a stane dyke.

" Lady Grizel, I heard you speak just now of the Marechal-General Lesly. He was a d——d auld round-headed cur, and his brigades of sour blue-bonnets were no more to be compared to our lads that marched to Worcester, than egg-shells are to cannon-balls. But had you seen the Muscovite host on the march for Samoieda, in that year when we beleaguered and sacked and overran the whole shores of the Frozen Ocean, ye would have seen marching to their last campaigns some of the prettiest cavaliers that ever ate horseflesh or slashed the head off a Tartar. Now, God's murrain on the southern clodpoles!" began Sir Thomas, commencing some fierce tirade against the English, for he was a Scot of the oldest school.

" Fie, knight of Binns!" said Annie Laurie; " you forget that my Lady Dunbarton is southland bred."

" Sweet mistress, I crave pardon of her gentleness. But I am owre auld to pick my words now. I say as my fathers have said; I think as my fathers have thocht."

" Your servant, Sir Thomas.—Ladies your humble servant!" said that unconscionable bore, Lord Mersington, who at that moment rode up with Clermistonlee. " Hee, hee, general— seeing your auld friends awa again—' bodin in effeir of weir,' as the acts say?"

" Yes, my lord. You, too, hae seen some work like this in your time."

"Ay. At Dunbar I rode in the troop of the College of Justice, and exchanged the judge's wig for the trooper's morion; ye ken, when drums beat, laws are dumb."

"Then Heaven send they may beat for ever and aye. A bonnie like troop o' auld carlins your lordship's justiciars were, and merrily we stark cavaliers of the French and Swedish wars laughed when Monk's regiment of foot, whilk are now denominate the Coldstreamers, routed ye like sae mony schule bairns."

"Under favour, Sir Thomas, I hold that to be leasing-making, hee, hee! and though we laugh owre it now as auld gossips, I mind the day when blades had been drawn on it."

Clermistonlee, while endeavouring with equal skill and grace to curb his restive horse, fixed his dark gloating eyes on Lilian Napier, and gave her a profound bow; but, well aware of what his intentions had long been towards her, instead of acknowledging it, she coldly turned away, and took the arm of Annie Laurie. She was too gentle to glance disdainfully, but an indignant blush crimsoned her cheek, and she withdrew to another part of the parapet. Clermistonlee bit his proud lip with vexation; but the fierce gleam of his dark eye passed unobserved by all save Juden, who, like his shadow, was never far off.

"My lord Clermistonlee, we will hae but a toom toun now, when our brave bucks and braw fellows have a' marched southward," said Dalyel.

"Many a fair damsel sees her stout leman for the last time," replied his lordship, with a soft smile at Lilian; "but keep bold hearts, fair ladies—there are as handsome fellows left behind as any that march under the baton of James Douglas."

"As gude fish in the sea as e'er cam' out o't, hee, hee!"

"True," retorted Annie Laurie; "but such gay fellows as your lordships are too economical of their persons to suit the taste of a bold border lass."

"Indeed, Mistress Laurie! But according to love à la mode, one leman is quite the same as another."

"Whilk," said Sir Thomas Dalyel, with a deep laugh, interrupting a sharp retort of Annie's, "whilk were the very words a certain Muscovite damsel sain to me, after her husband's head had been chopped off by the ungracious Tartars. I construed it into a hint that I was to occupy his place, and I was but owre happy, for 'tis a cold country, the land of the Russ and——but, dags and pistols! here cometh the rear-guard already! and as there are some lads marching owre yonder brae, with whom I would fain confer for the last

time, I must crave your ladyship's pardon, with leave to follow
the line of route."

Erect in his stirrups, with toes pointed upwards and baton
depressed, the old cavalier made a profound obeisance, and
notwithstanding his great age dashed at full gallop through
the crowd amidst an ill-repressed shout of hatred and
execration from amongst it.

" An auld ill-faured persecuting devil!" said Elsie
Elshender, shaking her withered hand after him; " a tormentor o' God's worthiest servants, a Cain among the sons o'
men—a fearfu' tyrant, and suited to fearfu' times. Gude
keep us ; look at the doken blade he spat on ; there is a hole
brunt clean through it."

" His horse's hoofs mak' runnin' water boil," added Syme
the baillie's wife in a low voice.

" Silence, cummers !" said Juden Stenton, " or you'll hae
the steel jougs locked round your jaws the morn, and may-be
get a het tar-barrelling after, for speaking sae freely o' your
betters."

Sir Thomas reined up alongside of the three generals, whom
for several miles he bored with musty maxims, obsolete
tactics, and strange advice, *anent* the superiority of Sweyn's
feathers over the screwed dagger (or bayonet), and furiously
condemned the slinging of carbines in budgets in lieu of
shoulderbelts. as in the days of Montrose—expatiated on the
method of forming square with the grenadiers covering the
angles, and making the bringers-up (or third rank) entirely of
musketeers. He particularly impressed upon General Douglas
the method of posting musketeers among the horse and dragoons in alternate regiments—a tactic of that Star of the
North, the great Gustavus of Sweden, and used by Prince
Rupert at Long Marston-moor,—and after a fierce tirade
against Sir James Wemys's leather-cannon for field service,
and a few words about the Muscovites, this veteran soldier of
fortune bade them adieu near the Balm-well of St. Catherine,
which lay yet a ruin, just as Cromwell's puritans had left it
thirty-eight years before, when sixteen thousand of them en-
camped on the Gallachlaw-hill. There Dalyel parted with
" bluidy Dunbarton, Douglas, and Dundee," never to meet
again ; for though he saw it not, the hand of death was
already stretched over the venerable " persecutor," and exile,
war, wounds, and death were the portion of the others.

Long, long remained the fair young countess watching the
glittering columns as they wound over the Burghmuir, and
ascended the hills of Braid, and until the faintest tap of the
drums died away on the wind, and the helmets of the rear-

guard flashed a farewell ray in the evening sun, as they disappeared over the distant hills.

Then the grief of Lilian could no longer be restrained, for
a heavy sense of utter desolation fell upon her heart.

"Oh, Annie, Annie!" she exclaimed, and throwing herself
upon the bosom of her friend, burst into a passion of tears.

The bustle, the glitter, and the music, all combined, had
caused an unnatural degree of excitement, and had sustained
their spirits while the troops were pouring past, enabling
them to behold with calmness a thousand tender partings.
All now were away—silence and stillness succeeded—the excitement had evaporated, and they experienced an unnerving
reaction which rendered them miserable, and they wept without restraint for the lovers that had left them—perhaps for
ever.

CHAPTER XXXIII.

THE HAWK AND THE DOVE.

O wae be to the orders, that marched my love awa,
And wae be to the cruel cause that gars my tears' dounfa`,
The drums beat in the morning, before the screich o' day,
The wee fifes played loud and shrill, and yet the morn was grey;
The bonnie flags were a' unfurled, a gallant sight to see,
But waes me for my soldier-lad, that marched to Germanie.
MOTHERWELL.

THE intense sadness of Lilian for some days after the march
of the troops, soon led Lady Grizel to suspect that her heart
and hopes were away with the Scottish host; and the blush
that ever suffused her cheek on Walter's name being mentioned, convinced the old lady that her conclusions were just.
Lilian knew well what was passing in the mind of her grand-
aunt, and as she had never hitherto concealed a thought from
her, she threw herself upon her neck, and with tears, blushes,
and agitation, which made her innocence appear more than
ever charming, confessed how she and Walter Fenton had
plighted their solemn troth, and showing his ring, implored
her pardon and her blessing upon them both.

"God bless thee, mine own dear child!" said the kind old
lady; "though poor Walter Fenton hath nothing on earth
but his heart and his sword, and though I might wish a
longer pedigree than he, good lad, can boast of, still I esteem
him for his manly bearing—I love him for his generosity:
and I have ever loved thee, Lilian, much too well to withhold aught on which thy happiness depends. May the kind

God bless thee, my fair-haired bairn! and may thy love be fortunate and happy as it is innocent and pure!"

Lilian's heart was full, and she wept on the breast of her kind old kinswoman.

After a time the idea did occur to Lady Bruntisfield, that the first-love of her grand-niece, who since the captain's out-lawry had become the only hope and last representative of an old baronial race, should be a nameless and penniless soldier, about to become a partisan in a dangerous civil war, was a matter for serious deliberation; but her blessing had been given, her honour had been pledged, and neither could be now withdrawn. She remembered, too, that if William con-quered in the coming struggle, that Lilian would be dowerless; for on her own demise, the lands of Bruntisfield and the Wrytes (of which, as before stated, she had but a life-rent) passed to her nephew, the captain of the Scots Dutch, as next heir of entail; and she knew that the crafty Lord Clermis-tonlee, who had long been Lilian's avowed suitor, based his mercenary and ambitious hopes mainly on breaking this law, by bringing the unfortunate captain under the ban of the council, now no difficult matter, as he had openly joined the standard of the prince of Orange.

Though his lordship's rank made him, in one respect, an eligible suitor, his general character for cruelty, debauchery, and every fashionable vice, caused him to be viewed with detestation by all, save a few wild and kindred spirits; and there were current certain dark, and, perhaps, exaggerated stories concerning the death of his lady several years before; and these, more than anything else, led every woman, in that moral age, to regard him with secret horror.

Yet all admitted that he was pre-eminently a handsome man, and that none dressed so magnificently, danced more gracefully, had better-trained hawks and hounds, or fleeter racers, than Randal, Lord Clermistonlee. Notwithstanding all this, Lady Grizel would rather have seen her dear-loved Lilian in the coils of a boa-constrictor than in his arms; and as the image of the daring roué came vividly before her, she blessed poor Walter more affectionately, and kissing her fair grand-niece again, made her feel more happy than she ever thought to have been in the absence of her lover. Rendered buoyant in spirit by the hopes which the affection and appro-bation of her venerable kinswoman had kindled anew within her breast (for love and hope go hand in hand), she retired to the garden, to view, for the hundredth time, the spot where she had plighted her faith and love to Walter Fenton—a species of *hand-fasting* in those days so solemn and binding, that it was almost esteemed a half-espousal.

Day was closing, and the old knotty oaks creaked mournfully in the evening wind: now their October foliage was crisped and brown; the branches of many were bare and leafless, and the voice of the coming winter was heard on the hollow gale; while the fallen leaves and faded flowers, the apparent exhaustion and decay of nature, increased the idea of desolation in her mind, and poor Lilian's heart swelled with the sad thoughts that oppressed it. Seated by the mossy dialstone, resigned to solitude and to sorrow, she yielded to the grief that gradually stole over her, and wept bitterly.

How vividly she recollected all the circumstances of that dear interview, and Walter's last injunction—"Remember the hour beside the fountain, and forget not the 20th of September!" The hour was the same, and the fountain was plashing with the same monotonous sound into the same carved basin, and the voice of Walter seemed to mingle with the echo of the falling water.

"Walter! Walter!" she exclaimed, and dipping her hands again in the water, pressed to her lips the pledge he had given her at parting—his mother's ring, the only trinket he had ever possessed in the world; and though small its apparent value, it contained a secret that was yet to have a potent influence on the fortunes of both.

On the preservation of that ring depended the life of Walter and the mystery of his birth.

Absence had now rendered more dear to her that love which preference, chance, and congenial taste had previously made the all-absorbing feeling of her heart.

"And he was here with me three weeks ago! Only three weeks! Alas! dear Walter, if years seem to have elapsed since then, what will the time appear before we meet again? Oh, that I had the power of a fairy, to behold him now!" She turned her eyes to the south—to where, above its thick dark woods, the embattled keep of the Napiers of Merchiston closed the view. There she had last seen the Scottish host winding over the muir, and remembered the last flash of arms in the sunlight, as a straggling trooper disappeared over the ridge. Her heart yearned within her, and her agitation increased so much that she reclined against the cold dialstone, and covered her face with her hands.

At length she became more composed, and her grief gave way to softer melancholy, as the sombre tints of the balmy

autumnal evening crept over the beautiful landscape. The
sun was setting, and, amid the saffron clouds, seemed to rest
afar off, like a vast crimson globe above the dark pine-woods
that cover the ridges of Corstorphine. The bright flush of
the dying day stole along the level plain from the westward,
lighting up the grated casements, the fantastic chimneys, and
massive turrets of the old manor-house, and the gnarled
trunks of its ivied beeches and old " ancestral oaks."

Pouring aslant from beneath a screen of dun vapour like a
thunder-cloud edged with gold, the sun's bright rays gave a
warm but partial colouring to the scenery, glittering on the
dark-green leaves of the holly hedges, then gaudy with clusters of scarlet berries, and rendering more red the crisped
and faded foliage that bordered the shining lake. White
smoke curled up from many a cottage-roof embosomed among
the coppice ; and as the sunbeams died away upon the stir-
less woods and waveless water, Lilian recalled many an
evening when, at the same hour, and in the same place, she
had leant upon Walter's arm, and surveyed the same fair
landscape ; and the memory of his remarks, and the tones
of his voice, came back to her with a fond but painful distinctness.

Her favourite pigeon, with the snow-white pinions and
silver varvels, alighted on her shoulder, and nestled in her
neck ; but the caresses of her little pet were unheeded.
Lilian neither felt nor heard them ; her heart was with her
thoughts, and these were far away, where the Scottish drums
were ringing among the border hills and pathless mosses.
The face, the air, the very presence of her lover, came vividly
before the ardent girl ; like a vision of the second sight, she
conjured them up, and his voice yet sounded in her ears as
she had last heard it—softened, tremulous, and agitated ; but,
alas ! now mountains rose and rivers rolled between them,
and kingdoms were to be lost and won ere again she felt his
kiss upon her cheek. The dove seemed sensible of the sorrow that preyed upon its mistress, and, nestled in her soft
bosom, lay still and motionless, with bowed head and trailing
pinions.

" By Jove ! she *is* a magnificent being," said a voice.
" Now, fair Lilian—now, by all that is opportune, you must
hear me."

She started, but was unable to rise, from confusion and
fear. Lord Clermistonlee stood beside her. His dark velvet
mantle half concealed his rich dress, as the plumes of his
slouched hat did the sinister expression of his proud and impressive features. He was armed with his long sword and

and had a brace of pistols in his girdle. A large hawk sat on his wrist, and the expression with which his large dark eyes were fixed on the shrinking girl, found au exact counterpart in those of the hawk when regarding the trembling dove, which cowered in the bosom of its mistress. From the ardour of his glance, and a certain jauntiness in his air, it was evident that he was a little intoxicated, as usual.

Lilian, in great terror, looked hurriedly around her. She was at the extremity of a spacious garden, and now the evening was far advanced. Save old John Leekie, the gardener, none could be within hearing; and the cry she would have uttered died away upon her lips. Even had that venerable servitor approached, he would soon have been knocked on the head by Juden Stenton, who lay close by, concealed like a snake in the holly hedge.

"My lord, to what do I owe this sudden visit?"

"To the attractive power of your charms, my beauty."

"Permit me to pass you," said Lilian, sharply.

"Nay, my dearest Lilian," replied the lord, taking her hand, and retaining it in spite of all her efforts to the contrary. "The very modesty that makes you shrink from my polite admiration invests you with a thousand new attractions."

"Doubtless," said Lilian, with as much scorn as her gentleness permitted, "politeness is the peculiar characteristic of your lordship; and yours is not less flattering than your admiration."

"My adorable girl! you transport me—you open up a new vista of hope to me in these words," said Clermistonlee, with something of real passion in his voice. "You must be aware there are few dames in Scotland that would not be flattered by my addresses; and that few men in Scotland, too, would dare to cross me. For thee alone my heart has been reserved. On this fair hand let me seal——"

"Nay, nay, my lord," urged Lilian, struggling to be free, and becoming excessively frightened.

"By every sparkle of those beautiful eyes, and the amiable vivacity that illumines them," continued his lordship, making a theatrical attempt to embrace her,—"suffer me to implore——"

"Help! help, for God's sake!" exclaimed Lilian. "My lord, this insolence shall not pass unpunished."

"Death and the devil! Dost mock me, little one? Is it insolence thus to fall at your feet?—thus to pour forth my soul in rapture, where a king might be proud to kneel?"

"My lord, you are the strangest mixture of pride, presumption, and absurdity, in all broad Scotland," said Lilian, spiritedly. "I command you to unhand me, and to remember that there is a pit under the house where much hotter spirits than yours have learned to become cool and respectful."

He released her.

"The pretty moppet is quite in a passion. My dear Lilian, why so cruel? Am I indeed so hateful that you despise me?"

"O, no," said she, gently, touched with his tone, for his voice was very persuasive, and his presence was surpassingly noble. "I cannot hate one who has never wronged me; and I dare not despise aught that God has made."

"Then you only respect me the same as the cows in yonder park?"

"Heaven forbid, my lord, I should rate you so low!"

"Joy! beautiful Lilian. I now perceive that you *do* love me; and that coy diffidence alone prevents you revealing the sentiments of your heart." And throwing his arms around her, he embraced her, despite all her struggles, and though the girl was strong and active. Thrice she shrieked aloud; and having one hand at liberty, seized Clermistonlee by his perfumed and cherished moustaches, giving him a twist so severe, that he immediately released her, but still interposed between her and the house. His eyes sparkled with ill-concealed rage.

"Hoity toity!" he muttered, stroking his moustaches, and surveying her with a gloomy expression. "May the great devil take me if I understand you!"

Lilian now began to weep, and murmured—

"I request your lordship to learn——"

"That thou lovest another? Damnation, little fool! art still favouring that beardless beggar, whom some Dutchman's bullet will hurl to his father in the bottomless pit?"

"Wretch!" exclaimed Lilian, with undisguised contempt. "In heart and soul, Walter Fenton is as much above thee as the heavens are above the earth!"

Stung by her words, the eyes of Clermistonlee glared, and his lips grew white: he looked round for some object on which to pour forth the storm of rage and jealousy that blazed within him. He saw the poor dove which nestled in Lilian's breast, and, prompted by wickedness and revenge, suddenly snatched it away, and tossed it into the air; then, quick as thought, he slipped the jess of scarlet leather that bound the fierce hawk to his nether wrist, and like lightning, it shot after the terrified pigeon, and soared far in air above it.

With fixed eyes and clasped hands, Lilian watched it; and so intense was her fear for her favourite, that, in the imminence of its danger she quite forgot her own. The stern eyes of Clermistonlee were alternately fixed on the soaring birds and on Lilian's pallid face; and he grasped her tender arm with the force of a vice with one hand, while pointing upward to the dove with the other.

"Behold! thou foolish vixen," said he—"*thou* art the dove, and *I* am the hawk; and thus shall I conquer in the end!" Even as he spoke, the hawk soused down upon its quarry, and both sank to the earth.

The pigeon was dead!

Lilian never spoke; but bent upon her tormentor a glance of horror, scorn, and contempt, so intense that he even quailed before it, while darting past him, she rushed towards the house.

The intruder then leaped the garden wall; and, followed by his stout henchman, hurried towards Edinburgh.

CHAPTER XXXIV

A STATESMAN OF 1688.

Call you these news? You might as well have told me,
That old King Coil is dead, and graved at Kylesfield.
I'll help thee out——.

AYRSHIRE TRAGEDY, ACT II.

SOME weeks after this, at a late hour one night, Lord Clermistonlee was seated by the capacious fireplace in his chamber-of-dais. He was alone. A supper of Crail capons and roasted crabs, a white loaf, and wine posset, had just been discussed; and he was resorting to his favourite tankard of burnt sack, when a loud knocking was heard at the outer gate.

His lordship was decidedly in a bad humour: satiated with a long career of gaiety, he had resolved to give this night to retirement, to reverie, and to maturing his plans against Lilian, whose beauty and manner in the last interview had inspired him with something like a real passion for her. He remembered with pain the hatred and the horror expressed in her parting glance. The memory of it had sunk deeply in his heart, and he bitterly repented the destruction of her favourite pigeon; for he felt that this cruel act had increased the gulf between them.

The knocking at the gate recalled his thoughts.

"'Sdeath!" said he, "who dares to knock so loud and late? Ha! it may be a macer of council; we have had no news from London for these fourteen days past. Now, by all the devils, who can this be?"

A person was heard ascending the stair, and singing in a very cracked voice the Old Hundredth Psalm. Clermistonlee started, and looked around for a cane, marvelling who dared to insult him in his own house. A psalm! he could hardly believe his ears.

"Pshaw!" said he, recognizing the voice, as Juden ushered in Lord Mersington, who entered unsteadily, balancing himself on each leg alternately : his broad hat was awry, and his wig gone ; but a silk handkerchief tied round his head supplied its place. The learned senator was in one of his usual altitudes.

"How now, gossip?" said Clermistonlee, impatiently; "whence this unwonted piety?"

"Out upon thee, son of Belial! Dost not see that the spirit is strong within me?"

"Rather too plainly ; but sit down, man—thy tankard of burnt sack hath grown cold. Juden prepares it nightly quite as a matter of course. Any news from our army yet?"

"None, none," replied the other, shaking his head with tipsy solemnity ; "but if matters go on as they seem likely to do, I maun een change, Randal, or the grassy holms and bonnie mains o' Mersington will gang to the deil before me ; and I'll hae my canting hizzie o' a wife back frae the west country to deave me wi' ranting psalms, and declaring against the crying sin o' the mass, papacy, prelacy, Arianism, and a' the rest o't." A glance of deep meaning accompanied this.

"And I, to mend my fortune, must fly my hawks more surely. *Bon gré, mal gré,* Lilian Napier must become Lady Clermistonlee, or my lord of that ilk must boune him for another land."

"Hee, hee!—and you are fairly tired o' following mad Mally Charteris, Maud o' Madertie, and my Lady Jean Gordon —hee, hee!"

"Stuff!—name them not. I am sick to death of all damsels who owe their beauty to sweet pomade, cream of Venice, Naples dew, and the devil's philters. Ah! the blooming glow of health and loveliness that renders so radiant the gentle Lilian arises from none of these."

"Ou' aye, ou' aye!" muttered Mersington, as he buried his weason face in the tankard. "You have been an awfu' chiel in your time, Randal, and would restore the auld acts o' King Eugene III. gif the council would let ye—he, he!"

"By all the devils, I would!" laughed the *roué*, curling his moustaches, as he lounged in his well-cushioned chair; "thou knowest, good gossip, that the great horned head of the law always gave me a strong *goût* for vice."

"But Eugene's law would matter little to you, Randal— hee, hee! Ye have but few women married within your fief or barony now."

Clermistonlee bit his lip as he replied:

"You taunt me with my poverty, gossip; but remember, that though I have lost my manor of Drumsheugh, I consider that of Bruntisfield as being nearly mine. Sir Archibald was an old cavalier, and stanch high churchman; and if the current of affairs (here his voice sank to a whisper) goes against the king, we may easily prevail upon the council to forfeit these lands to the state for ancient misdemeanors."

"And for the leal service done to the cause of grace in 1670, I would move that the council bestow upon my noble friend, the Lord Clermistonlee—hee, hee!—the haill in free heritage and free barony for ever, with all the meithes and marches thereof (as the form in law sayeth), auld and divided as the same lie in length and breadth, in houses, biggings, mills, multures, &c., hawking, hunting, fishing, eel-arks, &c., with court, plaint, and herezeld, and with furk, fok, sack, sock, thole, thame, vert, wraik, waith, ware, venison, out-fangthief, infangthief, pit and gallows, and sae forth, with the tower, fortalice, or manor place thereof, and the couthie wee dame hersel into the bargain."

"By Jove, thou art mad!" exclaimed Clermistonlee, who had listened with no little impatience and surprise to this rhapsody which the law lord brought out all at a breath.

"Hee, hee! the haill barony o' Bruntisfield is a braw tocher!—think o' its pertinents, forbye the lands o' Puddock-dub, whilk yield o' clear rental ten thousand merks after paying kirk and king!"

"King and kirk, you mean."

"I say kirk and king—hee, hee! The times are changing, and we maun change wi' them."

"Zounds! I believe the old fool is too drunk to hear me. Harkee! gossip Mersington, you know I lost a thousand pounds to that addlepate, Holsterlee, on our race at Leith, where my boasted mare failed so devilishly."

"Had ye tar-barrelled the carlin Elshender, it would hae been another story," grumbled Juden, as he replenished the tankards.

"A drowning man will cling to straws. By all the devils, on that race hung the partial retrieval or utter ruin of my

II.   T

fortune! 'Tis a debt of honour—the money is unpaid, and must be discharged with others, even should I turn footpad to raise the testers."

"'Tis an auld song, Randal—the fag-end of a career o' wickedness and depravity—birling the wine-cup, and flaunting wi' *bona robas*," replied Mersington, practising his now snuffling tone, and shaking his head with solemn but tipsy gravity, in the new character his cunning led him to assume. "A just retribution on the crying sins, blasphemies, and enormities, anent whilk see the act (damn the act!) committed in the days o' your dolefu' backsliding. I doubt you'll hae to take a turn wi' the Scots Dutch, like Jock, the laird's brother."

"My drivelling gossip," said Clermistonlee, with consider-able hauteur, "you forget that it beseems not a baron to be so roughly schooled by the mere goodman of Mersington!"

"Byde ye there, billy," exclaimed the other. "Gudeman, quotha! we hold our fief by knight's service, of the Scottish crown; and ken ye, Randal, that such as hold their lands of the king direct are styled lairds; but such as held their tacks of a subject were styled gudemen; a custom hath lately gone into disuse, as Rosehaugh saith in his folio on Precedence."

"Laird or lord, I care not a brass bodle. No man shall assume the part of monitor to me! Again and again I have told thee, Mersington, that my whole soul, for this year past, has been bent upon the possession of Lilian Napier, and her acres of wood and wold; and dost think, gossip, that I, who have subdued so many fine women (yea, and some deuced haughty ones, too), shall be baffled by a little moppet like this? Come, good gossip, assist me with thy advice. I have ever found your invention fertile, your advice able, your cunning matchless. Canst think of no new plan, by which to——Hah! who the devil can that be, now?" he exclaimed, as another furious knocking at the outer gate cut short his adjuration; and he listened anxiously, muttering, "'Tis long past midnight; some drunken mudlark, I warrant."

"A macer o' council, my lord," exclaimed Juden, entering hurriedly, and laying a square note before his master, who let fall his wine-cup, as he examined the seal, which bore the coronet and collared sleuth-hound of Perth. A red glow suffused the dark cheek, and sparkled in the eyes of Clermis-tonlee, as he deliberately opened a billet which he previously knew to be of the most vital importance to himself and to the nation. It was addressed "ffor y[e] Right Hon[ble] my very good friend the Lord Clermistounlee," and ran thus:—

" DEAR GOSSIP,—There is the devil to pay in the south—
all is lost! Craigdarroch, a trooper of the guards, hath
brought intelligence that our army, like the English (God's
murrain on the false knaves!), hath *en masse* joined the invader—that James has fled and William reached London.
Meet us at the Laigh council chamber without delay.

" Yr assured friend,
" PERTH, *Cancellarius.*"

Overwhelmed with consternation, Clermistonlee stood for
a moment like a statue; then, crushing his hat upon his head,
he stuck a pair of pistols in his belt, snatched his cloak and
sword, and tossing the note to Mersington, to read and
follow as he chose, rushed away in silence, with his usual
impetuosity.

Mersington, who had regarded his actions with a stare of
tipsy wonder, took up the note, and contrived to decipher its
contents. As he did so, his features underwent a rapid
change; fear, wrath, and cunning by turns contracted his
hard visage, and completely sobered him. At last, a sinister
leer of deep meaning twinkled in his bleared eyes; he quietly
burned the note, brushed his large hat with his sleeve,
adjusted it on his head, and assuming his gold-headed cane,
departed for the board of the privy council.

From that hour his lordship was a true-blue Presbyterian.

CHAPTER XXXV

TRUST AND MISTRUST.

March! march! why the deil do ye no march?
    Stand to your arms, my lads, fight in good order;
Front about, ye musketeers all
    When ye come to the English border.

LESLY'S MARCH.

As before related, the Scottish army advanced into England
in three columns.

It was by the express desire of James VII., and contrary
to the wish of the council, that these forces left Scotland,
where William had many adherents, especially in the western
shires. There the old spirit of disaffection was subdued, but
far from being extinguished. The privy councillors had proposed to retain their troops, and in lieu thereof to send to
their frontiers a corps of militia and Highlanders, thirteen
thousand strong; but James was urgent for the regulars

T 2

immediately joining him at Hounslow, and they marched accordingly.

On the first day of October the Scottish army crossed the Tweed, and drew up on English ground, when General Douglas (to quote Captain Crichton, the cavalier trooper who served in the Grey Dragoons) "gave a strict charge to the officers that they should keep their men from offering the least injury on their march; adding, that if he heard any of the English complain, the officers should answer for the faults of their men."

That night the Scottish drums were ringing in the streets of "merry Carlisle." There Douglas halted for the night, and Dunbarton's regiment bivouacked in a field on the banks of the Eden. Provisions were brought from the city in abundance, fires were lighted, and the cooking proceeded with the utmost despatch.

English troops kept guard at the gates of the city, which was inclosed by a strong wall, and Saint George's red cross waved on the castle of William Rufus—the same grim fortress where, a hundred and twenty-one years before, Mary of Scotland experienced the first traits of Elizabeth's inhospitality.

General Douglas, who commanded the Scottish troops, was a traitor at heart, and deeply in the interest of William. On the morning after the halt at Carlisle, he ordered the Viscount Dundee, with his division of cavalry, to march for London by the way of York; while he in person led the infantry and artillery by the road to Chester. Anxious that William should land before the army of James could be strong enough to oppose him, Douglas, by a hundred frivolous pretences, and by every scheme he could devise, delayed the march of his infantry, which did not form a junction with the English under the Earl of Faversham, at London, until the twenty-fifth of October.

James VII. had now under his command a well-disciplined and well-appointed army, led by officers of distinguished birth and courage, and he awaited with confidence the landing of his usurping son-in-law. The whole of his troops were quartered in the vicinity of London.

For many reasons, the people of England, like those of Scotland, were prepossessed against all the measures of King James, and to his brave army alone did this unhappy monarch look for support in the coming struggle; but notwithstanding that for years he had been a father rather than a captain to his soldiers, and had watched over their interests with the most kingly and paternal solicitude, quarrels and disgusts broke out between them, and he was yet to find that he leant on a broken reed. The strict amity subsisting between him and Louis of France, excited the jealousy of the nation, who dreaded an invasion of French and Irish Catholics, to enforce the entire submission of the Protestants.

Never were fears more groundless ; but the Irish appear to have been particularly obnoxious to the English soldiers, who flatly refused to admit them into their ranks. The officers of the duke of Berwick's regiment, on declining to accept of certain Irish recruits, were all cashiered, and the evident weakness of his position alone prevented James from bringing them to trial as mutineers.

Finding that the civil and ecclesiastical orders opposed him in every measure, James unguardedly made a direct appeal to his English army, by whose swords he hoped to enforce universal obedience. Anxious that each regiment in succession should " give their consent to the repeal of the test and penal statutes," he appealed first to the battalion of the earl of Lichfield, which the senior major drew up in line before him, and requested that " those soldiers who did not enter into the king's views should lay down their arms."

Save two catholics, the entire regiment instantly laid their matchlocks on the ground !

Astonishment and grief rendered James speechless for a time ; but his native pride recalled his energies.

" It is enough, my soldiers," he exclaimed haughtily. " Resume your arms ! Henceforth I will not do you the honour of seeking your approbation."

Hurried on by the secret advices of the Jesuits, by his religious enthusiasm (bigotry, if you will), and by the evil genius that has seemed to haunt his race since the days of the first Stuart, James rendered yet wider the breach between him and his army. He distributed catholic officers and soldiers throughout the different English regiments, " and many brave protestant officers, after long and faithful service, were dismissed, without any provision, to favour this fatal scheme." The quota of Irish troops joined him at London, and, on chapels being established for the celebration of mass, the murmurs of the protestants became loud and unrestrained, and a storm of indignation was raised, which in these days of toleration, we can only view with a smile.

The ill-advised appointment of the pope as sponsor for the young prince of Wales, the vile and unfounded rumours concerning whose birth the hapless king felt keenly, and the universal approbation with which the secretly dispersed manifestoes of the coming invader were received throughout the land, showed James that his throne was crumbling beneath him. The brave old earl of Dartmouth, who lay at the gun-fleet, with thirty-seven vessels of war, and seventeen fire-ships, in consequence of a storm, was unable to attack the armament of William, who arrived at Torbay on the 5th of November, and immediately landed his Dutch, Scots, English, and French troops, under their several standards.

James, who had no small share of courage and military skill, now threw himself entirely on that army, which he had spent so many anxious years in fostering, training, and disciplining. He despatched his son, the famous duke of Berwick, to take possession of Portsmouth, and prevent the inhabitants declaring for the invader, who was then on the march for Exeter; meanwhile he hurried to Salisbury plain, and placed himself at the head of twenty battalions of infantry and thirty squadrons of cavalry, with a resolution to defend his crown to the death : but, alas! the spirit of disaffection, disloyalty, and ingratitude had already manifested itself in the camp. The desertions were numerous and alarming, while sullen discontent and open mutiny so greatly marked the conduct of those who remained, that, save a few of the Scottish regiments, James found none on whom he could rely.

Lord Colchester, son of the earl of Rivers, with many of his regiment, were among the first who deserted to the standard of the invader; Lord Cornbury, son of the earl of Clarendon, followed, with three regiments of horse.

Lord Churchill, who, from a page, had been raised by James to the peerage and a high military command, also betrayed the blackest ingratitude, by forming a plot to seize his royal benefactor, and deliver him as a bondsman to the prince of Orange. Failing in this, he deserted with several troops of cavalry, and took with him the duke of Grafton, a son of the late king. Many officers of distinction informed the earl of Faversham, their general, "that they could not in conscience fight against the prince of Orange," and thus, hourly, the whole English army fell to pieces.

The spirit of disaffection soon spread into the Scottish ranks. Douglas, the perfidious general, with his own regiment of Red dragoons, openly marched off to William with the Scottish standard displayed, and their kettle-drums beating, a circumstance which deeply affected James, for this was a corps on which he had particularly relied; but the treason of Douglas was ultimately avenged by a cannon-shot on the banks of the Boyne. James was a Stuart, and naturally founded his hopes on the soldiers of the nation from whence he drew his blood.

A battalion of Scots' foot guards next revolted under a corporal named Kempt, and then every regiment went over in succession under their several standards, save a troop of Dundee's guards, a corps of dragoons, and the Scots' Royals, fifteen hundred strong, which yet remained loyal and true.

These repaired to Reading, where the gallant nobles, Dunbarton and Dundee, by exerting all their energies, re-mustered ten thousand men in ten days.

The former, with his single regiment alone, offered to attack the Dutch, and by a more than Spartan example of heroism and rashness, to shame their faithless comrades.

Meanwhile the Dutch drums beat merrily up for recruits, which poured to the banner of the invader on all hands, and horses were brought to mount the cavalry and drag the artillery.

All was lost!

The unhappy king, deserted nearly by all, found none near him to whom he could apply for consolation or advice, or in whom he could confide. By the instigation of Lady Churchill, even his daughter, the Princess Anne, left him, and retired to Nottingham. On finding himself now, when in the utmost extremity of distress, abandoned by a favourite daughter, whom he had ever treated with the utmost affection and tenderness, James raised his eyes and hands to heaven, and bursting into a passion of tears,—

"God help me!" he exclaimed, in the greatest agony of spirit; "God help me now, for even my own children, in my distress, have forsaken me!"

*　　*　　*　　*　　*　　*　　*

CHAPTER XXXVI.

THE GUISARDS.

O mother, thus to fret is vain--
My loss must needs be borne ;
Death, death is now mine only gain—
Would I had ne'er been born.
God's mercies cease to flow—
Woe to me, poor one, woe;
BURGER'S LEONORA.

WALTER had now been absent many weeks, and the constant fears expressed by Lady Grizel, with all the querulous and tedious prolixity of age, in no way tended to soothe the anxiety of Lilian. She was excessively superstitious, though guileless, kind, and simple, and daily saw terrible omens of

impending ill.   Black corbies flapped their wings incessantly
on the steep gables, and the dead-bell was never done ringing
in the crannies of the old house.   Strange sounds rumbled
behind the wainscoting, shrouds guttered in the candles,
coffins fell out of the embers, and the indefatigable deathwatch rang the live-long night in the recesses of her old tester
bed.   Her kindly-meant, but ominous insinuations, and her
dreams of stricken fields and riderless horses, nearly drove
Lilian to distraction, while old Elsie Elshender, who had been
admitted to her confidence, failed not to make matters worse
by shaking her palsied head mysteriously, and saying,—

   "It boded ill-luck to be betrothit wi' a dead woman's ring."

   So passed the first weeks of their separation in tears and
dark foreboding, save when Lilian was with Annie Laurie,
whose joyous buoyancy of spirit banished care and fear together.   Of Lord Clermistonlee she had seen nothing of late,
save on one occasion, when he had followed her from the
Abbey porch to the Bowhead; but as she was attended by
Drouthy, the butler, and another liveryman, well armed with
swords and pistols in their girdles, she was under no apprehension.

   The state of Edinburgh was daily becoming more and more
alarming.

   As yet there had been no tidings of William's landing; but
his friends were on the alert.   Under Sir George Munro, a
strong division of militia occupied the city; but on the march
of the regular troops, these failed to prevent the disaffected
from making the capital the focus of their operations.   No
sooner had the Scottish army crossed the borders, than the
Presbyterians, and all revolutionary spirits, crowded to Edinburgh well armed, and there held secret and seditious meetings, which were attended by the earls of Dundonald, Crauford,
Glencairn, and others.

   The subtle Mersington, the proud earl of Perth, the reckless Lord Clermistonlee, and others of the haughty council,
were made aware of all this by their numerous spies; but the
formidable tribunal which had so long ruled the land by the
sword and gibbet, was now completely paralysed by the appearance of many "sulky blue bonnets" crowding the streets;
they failed to arrest a single individual, though treason, like a
hundred-headed hydra, stalked in daylight through their
thoroughfares, and declaimed in their public places.   The
lords had no tidings of events in the south; all their despatches
from the king being effectually intercepted by Sir James
Montgomery, a revolutionist.

   And now came hoary Christmas; but it seemed not as of

old. It was a dreary one to poor Lilian; and the forebodings that hung over bolder hearts, chilled hers with apprehension. Old Arthur's bare ridge and rocky cove, the great chain of the Pentlands, and all the lesser hills that lie around them, were mantled with shining snow; the deep glens were impassable, and many flocks had perished in them. The cold norlan blast howled over the bleak Burghmuir, then a wide and frozen heath, save where, in some places, a venerable oak spread its glistening branches in the sparkling air. Above the lofty city to the north, that towered afar off on its ridgy hill, the dun smoke of a myriad winter-fires ascended into the clear mid air, and overhung its spires and fortress like a thunder-cloud, portentous of the storm that was brewing among its denizens. The great loch of the burgh lay frozen like a sheet of shining crystal; and there a few jovial curlers, forgetful of the desperate game of politics, shot the ponderous stones along their slippery rinks.

The great Yule-logs crackled and blazed merrily, as in other days, in the wide stone fireplace of the dining-hall, and old familiar objects and beloved faces glowed in its light; but Lilian's heart and thoughts were far away, and she seemed wholly intent on watching the sparks as they flew up the broad tunnelled chimney.

The eve of Christmas was dark and gloomy. The moon was enveloped in clouds, and not a star was visible; but the frozen snow that covered the whole ground gave, by its whiteness, a reflected light. The hollow wind blustered in the bare copsewood and rumbled in the chimneys, and a very social but hum-drum party of old friends formed a circle round the fireplace in the chamber of dais.

Old Lady Grizel occupied her great cushioned chair, with her spinning-wheel on one hand, and her cup of milk posset on a tripod table at the other. The neighbouring laird of Drumdryan, a plain, hard-featured man, in an unlaced coat and hideous wig; Sir Thomas Dalyel, in a gala suit of laced buff, rather cross and irritable with a lumbago contracted in Muscovy; and the dowager Lady Drumsturdy, all stomacher, starch, and black satin, with Mistress Priscilla, her daughter and exact counterpart, occupied the foreground; while honest Syme of the Greenhill, in his plain hodden-gray coat, a flaming red vest, with ribbed galligaskins rolled over his knees, and his fat, comely dame, with her serge gown, laced coif, and bunch of household keys, sat respectfully a little behind.

While the two lairds were accommodated with silver tankards, which Mr. Drouthy replenished again and again with the burnt sack, then so much in vogue, the bluff **ground** baillie, in virtue of his humbler station, drank nut brown ale from plain pewter. Everything in the apartment was trimmed with green holly branches, and a misletoe bough hung from the great dormont-tree of the ceiling, under which the long-bearded old cavalier saluted Lady Grizel's faded cheek with much good humour and courtesy

"Yes, Simeon, it was the case," continued the latter, who was engaged in some prosy reminiscence of King Charles the First's days. "A fiery dragon *was* seen in the west, and it flew owre the Muirfute hills, towards the castle of Dunbar; and, that day month, a mournful field was fought and lost there."

"I weel mind the time, your ladyship," replied Simeon, scratching his galligaskins where he had received a thrust from a Puritan's pike; "but the fleeing dragon, wi' its fiery tail, was thought to portend——"

"Just such things, Simeon, as the bright lights in the north hae portended this month past. And ye ken, Sir Thomas, that the miraculous shower of Highland bannets whilk preceded the irruption of the ill-faured Redshanks into the west, in the December of '84, was another wonderful and terrible omen."

"True, Lady Grizel," replied Dalyel, taking a sip from his tankard; "but ane partaking owre mickle o' the leaven o' the auld Covenant (d—n it!) for an auld cavalier like myself to believe; unless auld Mahoud was the merchant that made sae free wi' his gear. He has owre lang been poking his neb in our Scottish affairs."

"O' which my late lord (rest him!) had most ocular proof," said Lady Drumsturdy, in a low impressive voice; "when he saw him, wi' horns and tail, dancing on the walls o' Blackness, in the hour o' its upblawin', in the year 1652."*

"Cocks' nails!" muttered Drumdryan, "here's the snow coming down the lum;" and he shook the flakes from his wig.

"You are sitting owre far ben the ingle, laird."

"We'll hae a storm this night, sirs," said Simeon. "I ken by the sough o' the norlan wind—it's gey driech and eerie."

"'Sdeath! I hope not," said Drumdryan. "I've a score o' braw bell-wethers owre the muir at the Buckstane; and I lost enough at Martinmas-tide, when twa hundred black faces were smoored in the Glen o' Braid."

"And there has been no word from England since the snow fell—six weeks?" said Lilian, sighing.

"Some say the roads are deep, sweet mistress," said General Dalyel; "and others say the Orangemen are deeper;

* See Nichol's *Diary*.

but the deil a scrap hath reached the council since that rin-
awa' loon Craigdarroch arrived; and gude kens wha's hand
may be strongest by this time. But God bless the king and
the gude auld cause!" continued the old cavalier, draining his
tankard.

Drumdryan did the same, adding cautiously—"The king,
whae'er he be!"

"Out upon ye, laird!" exclaimed Lady Grizel, with great
asperity. "Wha could he be but his sacred majesty king
James VII., whom I pray the blessed God to counsel wisely
and protect."

"'Live and let live' has ever been my maxim, Lady Grizel;
but such words may cost ye dear, if the next news frae Berwick be such as I expect," replied the sly laird, drinking with
quiet composure.

Rage bristled in every hair of Dalyel's beard, and his eyes
glistened like those of a rattlesnake. He could not speak:
but the old lady, whose loyalty, fostered by that of the umquhile baronet, was tickled by these observations, brought her
chair sharply round, and, striking her long cane emphatically
on the floor, said to the shrinking delinquent—

"Shame on ye, Drumdryan!—is your blood turning to
water, or what? Gif ye expect bad tidings, it is time that ye
donned your buff coat and bandoliers, and had your steed in
stall wi' garnessing and holsters. And mair let me tell thee,
sir laird—but what is that I hear;—singing and mumming,
eh? What is it, Simeon?"

"Guisards!" exclaimed Lilian, looking from the window
down the snow-covered avenue—"guisards with links glinting
and ribbons flaunting. A braw band, in sooth!"

At that moment a faint but merry chorus was heard upon
the night wind that rumbled in the wide stone chimney, and
a loud knocking wrung on the barbican gate.

"Drouthy," said Lady Grizel, "away with ye to the buttery, and get some cogues of ale ready for the loons; and bid
Elsie prepare some farls of bannock and cheese, while John
the gardener lets them into the barbican, where we will hear
them sing. Let twa men keep the door with partisans, that
none may cross our threshold. In my time I heard of some
foul treachery done by masked faces. Wow, but the knaves
are impatient," she added, as the knocking was energetically
renewed at the outer gate. "And, Drouthy, d'ye hear, take
a gude survey of them through the vizzy-hole."

The butler trotted off.

"Lady Grizel," said the general, rubbing his hands, "ye
speak like a prudent dame; and a usefu' helpmate meet Sir

Archibald maun hae found ye, for he saw hot work in his time."

"Kittle times mak' cautious folk," said the malcontent Drumdryan slowly ; but wi' a' that, general, had I feared snow, my braw bell-wethers——"

"D—n you, and your bell-wethers to boot!" growled the fierce old royalist. "Here come the guisards," and, save him, all rushed to the windows ; the veteran cavalier, whose lumbago chained him to his bolstered chair, fidgetted and stroked his beard with a most vinegar expression of face.

Lilian clapped her hands with delight at the merry scene below.

From time immemorial, it has been the custom in Scotland for young people of the lower class, in the evenings of the last days of the old year, to go about from house to house in their neighbourhood, disguised in fantastic dresses, whence their name, *guisards*. The usual practice was to present them with refreshment; but that custom has departed with the other hospitalities of the olden time. They dance and sing a dog-grel rhyme, adapted to the occasion or the person they visit ; but while the catholic faith was the established one of Scotland, in their songs, the guisards were wont to proclaim the birth of Christ, and the approach of the three kings who were to worship him ; and some trace of this ancient religious ditty was discernible in the song sung by the visitors at Bruntisfield.

There were ten or more men, all stout, athletic fellows, each bearing a blazing torch, the united lustre of which lit up the deepest recesses of the old façade, under which they performed a fantastic morrice-dance to their own music. They were all furnished with enormous masks, of the most grotesque fashion ; from these rose head-dresses like sugar-loaves, covered with bells, beads, and pieces of mirror. Their attire was equally *outré*.

One was clad in the skin of a cow, having its horns fixed to the crown of his head, and the long tail trailing behind him in the snow. Another was furnished with an enormous nose, from which ever and anon a red carbuncle exploded with a loud report ; and a third had nearly his whole body encased in an enormous head, which had a face expressive of the most exquisite drollery. Under this prodigious caput the diminished legs appeared to totter, while the jaunty waggery of its aspect was increased by a little hat and feather which surmounted it.

But the principal figure was a tall, fierce, and brawny, but very graceful man, clad in a fantastic robe of scarlet, with his legs curiously cased in shining metal scales : he had a black face of dreadful aspect, from three hideous red gashes, in which the blood was constantly dropping. He wore a crown of green ivy-leaves and scarlet holly-berries, wreathed among the sable masses of a voluminous beard and shock head of parse hair. Through the openings of his scarlet robe, close observers might have observed a corslet glint at times. All were accoutred with swords and daggers.

Dancing in front, the red masker brandished his sputtering torch, and chanted in a deep bass voice the following rhyme :

" Trip and goe, heave and hoe,
Up and down, and to and fro ;
By firth and fell, by tower and grove,
Merrily, merrily let us rove ! "

Then the whole choristers struck in while whirling round, they brandished their torches and jangled their bells.

" Hogmenay ! Hogmenay !
Trois Rois la ! Homme est né !

Never before had so droll and jovial a band of guisards been seen ; and Lady Grizel, preceding all her guests, came cane in hand to the doorway, to see their grotesque morrice-dance, and listen to their rhymes ; and while the servitors were busy regaling them with ale, cheese, and bannocks, Lilian brought a cup of wine, which, in courtesy, she tendered to their leader. As he approached, she could not repress a shudder, so formidable was his aspect—so tall his stature—so large and dark the eyes with which he regarded her through that terrible mask, down the gaping lips of which he poured the ruddy Burgundy, and again tendered the cup to the fair Hebe who brought it.

As Lilian received it, his strong arm was thrown around her.

" *Homme est né !*" he shouted, in a voice like a trumpet. There was a confused discharge of pistols—swords were seen to flash, and in an instant all the torches were extinguished. There was a stifled shriek ; and the whole party were seen rushing down the avenue, leaving the barbican gate locked behind them.

" Clermistonlee !" exclaimed Lady Grizel, and swooned away in the arms of her people.

" Boot and saddle !—horse and spear !—ride and rescue !" exclaimed old Dalyel, forgetful of his lumbago and everything but the danger of Lilian. Rushing to the hall, no readier weapon than the poker was at hand ; but, alas ! it was chained to the stone pillar of the chimney-piece. Shrieks and outcries filled the mansion. Old Simeon, the baillie, John Leekie, the gardener, and others, snatched such weapons as came to hand; and, headed by Dalyel, who was now armed with his great Muscovite sabre, sallied forth to find themselves *within* the barbican, the strong iron gate of which defied all their attempts. The fierce old soldier rent his beard, and swore some terrible oaths in the Tartar, Russ, and Scottish tongues, till ladders were procured and the walls scaled.

They rushed down the avenue to find only the traces of many feet in the snow, the extinguished torches strewn about, the marks of horse-hoofs and coach-wheels, which, instead of going towards the city, wound over the Burghmuir towards the Castle of Merchiston; and, after many turnings and windings—made evidently to mislead pursuers, were lost altogether among the soft furzy heath at the Harestone, the standard-stone of the old Scottish muster-place.

CHAPTER XXXVII.

THE REVOLT AT IPSWICH.

I scorn them both! I am too stout a Scotsman,
To bear a Southron's rule an instant longer
Than discipline obliges.

SCOTT.

UNCONSCIOUS of this bold abduction, a whisper of which would have driven him mad, on the very night it took place, Walter Fenton was seated with Douglas of Finland in the public room of a large hostel or tavern in the central street of Ipswich.

It was the sign of the "Bulloign Gate:" the house was curious and old-fashioned; and on entering, one descended several steps, in consequence of the soil having risen upon the walls. Its fantastic front presented a series of heavy projections, rising from grotesquely-carved oak beams, diagonally crossed with spars of the same wood; little latticed windows, and two deep gloomy galleries, and projecting oriels, over which the then leafless woodbine and honeysuckle clambered, and from thence to the curious stacks of brick chimneys, and broad Swiss-like roofs, with their carved and painted eaves.

The host, a bluff and burly Englishman, with the whole of his vast obesity encased in a spotless-white apron, and exhibiting a great, unmeaning, and bald-pated visage, every line of which receded from the point of his pug nose, sat within the outer bar, where countless jugs of pewter, mugs of Delft, and crystal goblets shone in the light of a sea-coal fire, that roared and blazed in the wide fire-place of the public room.

At a table in one corner of the latter, a ponderously fat Southern was engaged in discussing several pounds of broiled bacon and a small basket of eggs. Over the great pewter trencher his round flushed face beamed like a full moon, while he had the wide cuffs of his coat turned up, and a great napkin, like a bib, tucked under his chin, to enable him to sup without spotting his glossy suit of drap-de-Berri.

Near him were several groups of saucy-like citizens, in short brown wigs and plain broad-cloth suits, playing at tric-trac, knave-out-o'-doors, and drinking mulled beer or egg-flip; while from time to time they eyed the Scottish officers askance, and whispered such jokes as the prejudices of the lower English still inspire them to make upon aliens. These they did, however, very covertly and quietly, not caring to enter into a brawl with two such richly-clad and stout cavaliers, armed with sword and dagger, and whose comrades, fifteen hundred in number, were all in the adjoining street.

Our friends sat silent and thoughtful, drinking each a posset of wine. Walter's eyes were fixed on the glowing embers of the fire and the changing figures they exhibited; while Finland seemed wholly intent on reading two papers pasted over the mantel-piece. One was the sailing notice of "the good ship *Restoration, which* was to sail from the Hermitage-bridge, London, for Leith, on the penult of next month, ye master to be spoke with on ye Scots-walk, where he would promise civility and good entertainment to passengers." The other was a proclamation, signed W. R., regarding the quarters of the Scottish forces in divisions. The cavalier's brow grew black as his eye fell on it; and he sighed, saying:—

"Matters are now at a low ebb with the king. Religion and misfortune have fairly check-mated him, as we say at chess."

"Measter, say rather his curst Scottish pride and obstinacy," said a great burly fellow, whose striped apron and greasy doublet announced him to be a butcher. Finland gave him a scornful glance; but being unwilling to engage in a brawl, was about to address Walter again, when the corpulent citizen, having gorged himself to the throat, now felt inclined to be jocular; and looking at the long bowl-hilted rapiers and poignards of the Scots, said:—

"Sword and dagger! by my fecth, thee art zo well vortified, that if well victualled, as thy coontryman, lousy King Jemmy, zaid to the swash-bookler, thee wouldst be impregnable. He was at Feversham by the last account," resumed the butcher, "with that long-nosed Jesuit, his confessor, about to embark vor France or Ireland—devil care which. Here is a long horn, lads, that king and confessor may gang to the bottom together."

"Silence, rascal!" said Walter. "Remember that we wear the king's uniform."

"Dom! and wot care I?" said the bumpkin, pushing forward with every disposition to annoy and insult, while a dozen of his townsmen crowded at his elbow. "Have ye not changed sides, like the rest of your canny coontrymen, and joined King William?"

"We have not!" replied Douglas, fiercely, making a tremendous effort to keep down the storm of passion and national hostility that blazed up within him. "Our solitary regiment alone remains yet true to James VII., over whom (with all his faults) I pray heaven to keep its guard. I abhor his religion, and despise the bigots by whom he is surrounded, as much as you may do, good fellow; but I cannot forget that he is our rightful king; and for him, as such, I am ready to die on the field or the scaffold, should such be my fate."

The fire of his expression, the dignity of his aspect, and the splendour of his attire, completely awed the English boors, and for a moment they drew back.

"You mistake, good people, if you think that, like too many of our comrades, we have changed banners. No! we are still the faithful subjects of that king who heirs his crown by that hereditary right which comes direct from God. This Dutch usurper (whom the devil confound!) hath made us splendid offers if we will take service with him, and march to fight for his rascally Hollanders under Mareschal Schomberg, instead of our good and gallant Dunbarton; and, to intimidate us, is even now enclosing us in your town of Ipswich by blocking up the roads with troops. But let him beware! we have stout hearts and strong hands, and Dunbarton may show him a trick of the Black Douglas days, that will cool the Dutchman's courage, despite his black beer and Skiedam. Yes, Fenton; the arrival of Schomberg to command us *bon gré mal gré* will bring us to the tilt."

While Douglas spoke with animation and energy, the Ipswichers had gazed upon him with open mouths and eyes, not in the least comprehending him; but their champion, suddenly taking it into his head that he was defied, threw his hat on the ground, and tucked up his sleeves, saying:

"Dom, but I'll vicht thee for a vardin, and ye have zo much

about thee. Dom thee and all thy lousy coontrymen; they should be droomed out o' the town, before they get fattened up among us. Come on, my canny Scot, and if I doant lace thy buff coat for all its tags and tassels, I aint Timothy Tesh of the Back Alley."

"Hoozah!" shouted the rabble in the room and at the doorway, where they had collected in great numbers on hearing high words in the tavern.

"Sawney, hast anything else than oats in thee pooch?" cried one.

"He hath some brimstone, I'll warrant," added another.

"Oot upon thee for a vile Scot that zold his king for a groat, to zave his precious kirk."

"Come on, Measter Scot, and I drub thee in vurst-rate style as old Noll did thy psalm-sing countrymen at Dunbarfield. Rat thee! my vather was killed there."

"Heyday, my canny Scot, wilt try a fall with me for a copper bawbee? Dom thee and thy mass-moonging race of Stuarts to boot. May ye all go to hell in the lump!"

"Ware your money, my masters, there are Scots thieves among us," said the host, entering into the spirit of his townsmen.

Walter and Douglas exchanged mutual glances expressive of the scorn they felt.

"Silence, knaves!" cried Finland, kicking over the table, dashing all the jugs to pieces, and drawing his sword. "This is but a poor specimen of that southern spirit of generosity and hospitality of which (among yourselves) we hear so much said. Bullying and grossly insulting two unoffending strangers, who are guiltless of the slightest provocation; and I tell thee, butcher, that were it not beneath a gentleman of name and coat-armour to lay hands on your plebeian hide, I would break every bone it contains."

Flushed with ale and impudence, and encouraged by the presence of his friends, the fellow came resolutely forward; he was immensely strong and muscular, but rage had endued Douglas with double strength, and seizing him by the brawny throat, he dashed him twice against the wall with such force, that the blood gushed from his nostrils in a torrent, and he lay stunned without sense or motion.

His comrades were somewhat appalled for a moment; but gathering courage from their numbers, and enraged at the rough treatment experienced by Mr. Tesh, they snatched up the fire-irons, stools, and chairs, and commenced a simultaneous assault upon the two cavaliers, who, rapier in hand, endeavoured to break through them and gain the doorway, where now a dense and hostile crowd had collected, who poured upon them a thousand injurious taunts and invectives.

The affair was beginning to look serious. Fired by their insolence and the old inherent spirit of national animosity, Walter Fenton lunged furiously before him, and shredding the ear off one fellow, slashed the cheek of a second, ran a third through the shoulder-blade, but was borne to the ground by a blow from behind. Walter's sword-hand was completely mastered, and he struggled with his heavy assailants, unable to free his dagger or obtain the least assistance from Finland, who, with his back to the wall, was fighting with rapier and poignard against the dense rabble that pressed around him.

Walter struggled furiously. The moment was critical, but he was saved by the timely arrival of an officer with a few of the Royal Scots, who burst among them sword in hand.

" Place, villains—make way," he exclaimed, with the voice and bearing of one in high authority. " I am George, earl of Dunbarton ! "

They fell back awed not less by his demeanour than by the weapons of his followers.

" Chastise these scoundrels, Wemyss," said he to a serjeant who followed him. " Lay on well with your hilts and bandoliers ; strike, Halbert Elshender, for it is beneath a gentleman to lay hands on clodpoles such as these."

Thus urged, the soldiers, who required little or no incentive to make use of their hands against their southern neighbours, laid on with might and main, and, clearing the house in a twinkling, drove the clamorous host out with his guests ; after which they overhauled the premises, and set a few of his best runlets abroach.

" A thousand thanks, my lord earl, for this timely rescue," exclaimed Finland. " But for your intervention I must indubitably have hurried some of those rogues into a better world."

" And I had been worried like an otter by a pack of terriers," said Walter ; " however, I have had blood for blood."

" The old moss trooper's justice, Master Fenton," said serjeant Wemyss, drinking a flagon of wine. " God bless the good cause, and all true Scottish hearts."

" Here is to thee, Wemyss, my noble halberdier," said the frank carl, drinking from the same cup ; " and I would to the powers above, that this night King James had under his standard ten thousand hearts like thine. But time presses—

away, lads, to the muster-place, for hark, our drums are beating."

"The *générale !*" exclaimed Fenton and Finland, as the passing drums rang loudly in the adjacent streets.

"Yes, gentlemen, the crisis has come," said the Earl; "an hour ago, De Schomberg arrived to deprive me of my command."

"By whose orders ?"

"The Stadtholder's."

"We know him not, save as an usurper," said Walter Fenton; "and rather than obey his Mareschal, we will die with our swords in our hands."

Wemyss flourished his halbert, the soldiers uttered a shout, and poured forth to the muster-place.

It was a clear frosty night; the whole sky was of the most beautiful and unclouded blue. Seven tolled from the bells of St. Peter's church. The winter moon, broad, vast, and saffron-coloured, rising above a steep eminence called the Bishops'-hill, poured its flaky lustre through the narrow and irregular streets of Ipswich, which, in 1688, differed very much from those of the present day. There terror and confusion reigned on every hand, for, on the drums beating to arms, the mayor and inhabitants feared that the Scots would burn and sack the town, which assuredly they would have done, had Dunbarton expressed a wish to that effect.

Save where the bright moonlight shot through the crooked thoroughfares, the whole town was involved in gloom and obscurity; but every window was crowded with anxious faces, watching the Scots hurrying to their alarm-post, while the flashing of their helmets and the clank of their accoutrements impressed with no ordinary terror the timid and the disloyal.

By this time King James had fled from Whitehall, and under an escort of Dutch troops, was—nobody knew where. William was in possession of his palace, from whence he issued orders to the troops, and proclamations to the people, with all the air of a conqueror and authority of a king. The entire forces of Britain had joined him, save sixty gentlemen of the Scottish Life Guards, and a few of the Scots' Greys (who were on their way home, under Viscount Dundee), and the Royals, whom, from their number, discipline, and known faith to James, the Stadtholder was very desirous of sending abroad forthwith, under command of the marshal-duke of Schomberg, a venerable soldier of fortune, whose arrival at Ipswich on the night in question had brought matters to a sudden issue.

Clad in a plain buff coat, with a black iron helmet and breastplate, Dunbarton galloped into the market-place of Ipswich, where the two battalions of his musketeers were arrayed, three deep, in one firm and motionless line, with the moon shining brightly on their steel caps, their glittering bandoliers, and the gleaming barrels of their shouldered arms. As he dashed up, the four standards—two of white silk, with the azure cross, and two with the old red lion and *fleur-de-lis*—were unfurled, and a crash of prolonged music rang through the echoing street, and many a bright point flashed in the moonlight as the arms were presented, and the hoarse drums rolled the point of war, while the handsome earl bowed to his holsters, as he reined up his fiery horse before his gallant comrades. The music died away, again the harness rang, and then all became still, save the hum of the fearful crowd, and the rustle of the embroidered banners.

" Fellow-soldiers of the Old Royals ! " exclaimed the earl, " at last the hour has come which must prove to the uttermost if that faith and honour which have ever been our guiding-stars, our watchword and parole, still exist among us—when we must strike, or be for ever lost ! Through many a day of blood and danger we have upborne our banners in the wars of Luxembourg, of the great Condé, and the gallant Turenne ; and shall we desert them now ? I trow not ! Oh ! remember the glories of France and Flanders, of Brabant and Alsace. Remember the brave comrades who there fell by your side, and are now perhaps looking down on us from amid these sparkling stars. O, my friends, remember the brave and faithful dead !

" Shall it be said that the ancient Royals, Les Gardes Ecossais of the princely Louis, so faithful and true to the race of Bourbon, deserted their native monarch in this sad hour of his fallen fortune, and at most extremity ? No ! I know you will serve him as he must be served, till treason and rebellion are crushed beneath our feet like vipers—I know you will fight to the last gasp, and fall like true Scottish men—I know ye are prepared to dare and to do, and to die when the hour comes ! "

A deep murmur of applause rang along the triple ranks.

" *That hour is come !* Even now, Frederick de Schomberg, the tool and minion of the Dutch usurper and his parricidal wife, is within the walls of Ipswich, empowered to deprive me of my baton, which I hold from the parliament of Scotland, and to lead you—where ? To the foggy flats and pestilential fens of Holland, the land of agues and hypocrisy, to fight for his beggarly boors and pampered burgomasters,

and to encounter our ancient comrades of France—the bold
and beautiful France, whose glories we and our predecessors
have shared on a thousand immortal fields. Between us and
our home lie many hundred miles. De Ginckel, with three
thousand Swart Ruyters, hovers on the Lincoln road to inter-
cpt us; Sir John Lanier, with two squadrons of English
ivalry, awaits us on another; while that false villain Maitland, with a foot brigade of our Scottish guards, is pushing
on from London to assail our rear. But fear not, my good
and gallant comrades, for by the blessing of God, by the holy
consecration of these standards, by the strength of our hands,
by the valour of our hearts, and the justice of our cause, we
will cut our way through ten thousand obstacles, and reach
the far-off hills of the Scottish highlands, where the loyal
clans are all in arms, and wait but the appearance of Dundee
and myself to sweep like a whirlwind down on the Low-
lander!"

A loud shout from fifteen hundred men rang through the
market-place, and the brave heart of Dunbarton swelled with
exultation at the devotion of his loyal soldiers, and anger at
the desertion of their false comrades. He was not, however,
without considerable anxiety as to the issue of this decided
revolt, or rather appeal to arms, at such a distance from their
native land, and in a place were they were so utterly without
sympathy, succour, or friends—where to be a Scotsman was
to be an enemy. But the very desperation of the attempt
endued him with fresh energy. Ere he marched his devoted
band, he addressed Gavin of that ilk, a tall gigantic officer,
with a rapier nearly five feet long—

"Go to the house of the town treasurer, and tell him
instantly to hand you over £10,000 for the service of King
James, under pain of immediate military execution. If the
villain demur——"

"I'll twist his neck like a cock-patrick," said Gavin.

"You will rejoin us at the bridge of the Orwell."

"And how if these rascally burghers make me prisoner?"

"Then, by the blood of the Black Douglas!" said the earl,
passionately, "I will not leave one stone of Ipswich standing
upon another."

Gavin strode away, and his tall feathers were seen floating
above the heads of the shrinking crowd that occupied the
lower end of the market-place.

"And harkee, Finland!" continued the earl, "take young
Walter Fenton and fifty tall musketeers, break open the
English government arsenal, and bring off four pieces of
cannon which I understand are there; press horses wherever

you can get them ; blow up the magazine ; and join us at the
bridge—forgetting not, if you are invaded, to handle the
citizens at discretion, in our old Flemish fashion. By
Heaven, they may be thankful that I have not treated their
town of Ipswich as old John of Tsercla, the Count Tilly, did
Magdeburg. Away, then !"

CHAPTER XXXVIII.

FREE QUARTERS.

FALSTAFF. 'Sblood ! 'twas time to counterfeit, or that hot termagant Scot
had paid me scot and lot too.—HENRY IV.

THE redness of the moon passed away as it ascended into
the blue wide vault, and its cold white lustre was poured
upon the level English landscape that spread at the feet of
the Scottish soldiers, as they began to ascend the heights, or
gentle eminence to the northward of Ipswich. Above the
winter smoke of the dense little town, the spires of its churches
stood out in bold relief, like lances glittering through a sea of
gauze ; and the *wich* or bend of the beautiful Orwell swept
in a silvery semicircle, like a gleaming snake, among the
fallow fields and leafless copsewood ; and far around the
scenery spread like a moonlit map or fairy amphitheatre. All
was still in the town below ; at times a light twinkled, or a
voice rang out upon the quietness that reigned there, but the
Scots Royals, who were halted on the brow of an eminence,
over which wound the northern road (the way to their distant
home) heard nothing to indicate the success of their comrades.

Anon a vast blaze gleamed broadly and redly on the night,
revealing a thousand striking objects unseen before,—the
church of St. Peter, with its gleaming windows, and the
Gothic façade of Wolsey's ruined college. A loud explosion
followed, a shout rose up from the town below ; then all
became still, and it seemed, as before, to float in the calm
misty light of the silver moon.

"Finland has blown up the English magazine," said the
earl ; "and here he comes."

The clatter of hoofs and wheels ringing in the narrow
streets, and rumbling above the hollow bridge of the Orwell,
approached ; steel caps flashed in the moonlight above the
parapet, the gleam of arms was reflected in the surface of
the river, and in a few minutes Douglas, Walter Fenton,
Gavin of that ilk, and their party seated on the tumbrils,

dashed up with four pieces of beautiful brass cannon, marked with the broad arrow and red rose of England, and drawn by twelve horses, captured for the occasion.

"Bravo, Finland!" exclaimed the earl; "here are four braw marrows for old Mons Meg."

"Would to heaven, my lord, they were in the Maiden Castle alongside of her, with the standard of the Cock o' the North waving over them!"

"How so?—art faint-hearted, man?"

"Tush, I am a Douglas.—Ask Gavin."

"What news, my tall grenadier? You have the rix-dollars, I hope."

"My lord earl, the devil a tester. This English burgomaster was not a whit dismayed by my threats, but assailed me with a band of tip-staves; so, with drawn rapier, I was glad to beat a retreat, and gain Finland's band with my skin whole."

"And what think you inspired him to beard us thus?" asked Walter.

"By the head of the king, I care not!" said Dunbarton, setting his teeth, and rising in his stirrups. "I will hang him from yonder steeple, and inquire after."

"Jeddart justice all the world over," muttered old Wemyss.

"He had received news that Sir John Lanier, with his regiment of dragoon guards and Langstone's horse, have already reached Saffron Walden, in which case it were madness in us to tarry."

"Gavin, must we then retreat?" said the earl, colouring with passion. "Who brought these evil tidings?"

"An English gentleman."

"Pshaw—I don't think he can be relied on."

"I know him to be a man of good repute," replied Gavin; "Sir Tufton Shirley, of Mildenham. He fought for the king at Sedgemoor. I warrant him brave and honourable as any cavalier in his country."

"Be advised, noble earl," urged the grim old laird of Drumquhasel; "every moment is worth the life of a brave comrade."

"Indubitably so," added the Reverend Dr. Joram, as he spurred a prancing mare which he had borrowed unconditionally, with holsters and saddle-bags, from the host of the Bulloign-gate. "As Sir John Mennys saith in his Musarum Deliciæ—

> "Hee that fights and runnis away,
> May live to fight——"

Ye know the rest, sirs."

"We are not wont to make such reservations, reverend ʌr; but you are in the right," replied the earl. "March in silence, comrades, and with circumspection. Keep your ranks close, and your matches lighted—forward!"

About midnight they passed Needham, a town on the Orwell. All was dark and silent; scarcely a dog barked as they marched through its deserted streets, and continued their way, by the light of the stars, across the fertile country beyond. The fugitive Scots marched with great care and rapidity; four hundred miles lay between them and their native land, a long and perilous route, on which they knew innumerable dangers and difficulties would attend them.

De Ginckel, the Dutch earl of Athlone, Sir John Lanier, and Colonel Langstone, with six regiments of horse and dragoons, and Major Maitland with a brigade of the renegade Scottish guards, were pressing forward by various routes to intercept and cut them off. No man dared, on peril of his life, to straggle from the ranks; for, as Scotsmen and loyalists, they were doubly enemies to the English peasantry, who would infallibly have murdered any that fell into their hands, as they had done all the Scottish wounded and stragglers after the battle of Worcester. And thus, animated by anxiety, hope, and the exhortations of the gallant Dunbarton and his cavaliers, they marched, all heavily accoutred as they were, with such amazing rapidity, that, long ere daybreak, they had left Bury St. Edmunds, with its ancient spire and once magnificent abbey, twenty miles behind them.

Making detours through the fields, cutting a passage through walls, hedges, and fences, they avoided every town and village, and more than once were brought to a halt by Gavin, who led the avant guard, declaring that he saw helmets glittering in the light of the waning moon. They forded the waters of the Lark, and the cold grey light of the winter morning began to brighten the level horizon, throwing forward in dark relief the distant trees and village spires, as they came in sight of Ely, without having encountered their Dutch or English foemen.

The cold was intense; and the same white frost that powdered the grassy lawns and leafless trees, encrusted the iron helmets and corslets of the soldiers, whose breath curled from their close ranks like smoke from a fire. To Scotsmen even the most hilly parts of the landscape appeared almost a dead level, where Ely, with its fine cathedral and street, that straggled on each side of the roadway, seemed floating in a sea of white mist, through which the Ouse wound like a golden thread. Shorn of its beams by the thick winter haze, the morning sun, like a luminous ball of glowing crimson, as-

slowly into its place, and the great tower and pinnacles of Ely cathedral gleamed in its light as if their rich gothic carving had been covered with the richest gilding, and the tall traceried windows shone like plates of burnished gold.

The reverend Dr. Joram, who had dashed forward with cocked pistols to reconnoitre, returned to report, with military precision, that "it was a fair city, open, without cannon or fortifications of any kind; and that, if it contained soldiers, they kept no watch or ward. And I pray Heaven," he added, " we may get wherewith to break our fast."

"We will march in with drums beating," said the earl. "*Allons, mon tambour major!* Give us the old Scottish march, with which stout James of Hepburn so often scared the Imperialists in their trenches on the Oder and the Maine."

With drums beating, standards displayed, and matches lighted, the solid column marched into the little city of Ely just as the tenth hour rang from the cathedral bells, and halting, the earl sent to the affrighted mayor to demand peaceably three hours' quarters and subsistence for 1,500 Scots in the service of king James. The mayor, who on the previous night had despatched a most loyal address to the new King William, was considerably dismayed to find the city so suddenly filled by the soldiers of a nation he equally feared and detested: but to hear was to obey. The determined aspect of young Walter Fenton, with his features flushed and red by the long and frosty night march, his drawn rapier, and Scottish accent and fashion of armour, made the mayor use every exertion to get his unwelcome visitors peaceably billeted on the terrified citizens, who expected nothing less than immediate sack and slaughter.

To the earl he sent a flowery invitation to breakfast, thus anticipating Dunbarton, who had proposed to invite himself. The other cavaliers quartered themselves on any houses that suited their fancy; and Walter Fenton, Finland, and their jovial chaplain took possession of a handsome old mansion at the extremity of the city, having with them Wemyss and a few soldiers, to prevent treachery, surprise, or inattention on the part of the occupants, whom they desired to prepare a substantial breakfast, on peril of their lives, ere the drums beat to arms.

It was an ancient, oriel-windowed house, with clusters of carved chimneys rising from steep wooden gables, around which the withered vine and dark-green ivy clambered; its gloomy dining-hall, lighted by three painted and mullioned windows, was floored with oak, and curiously wainscotted. A great pile of roots and coal was blazing in the projecting fire-place, and a shout of approbation burst from the frozen guests as they clattered in, and drawing chairs around the joyous hearth, threw aside their steel caps, and demanded breakfast as vociferously as if each was lord of the mansion, and the venerable butler looked from one to another in confusion and dismay.

"Fellow, where is thy master?" asked Finland; "why comes he not to greet the king's soldiers, if he is a true cavalier?"

"To be plain, sir, his honour took horse, and rode off whenever your drums were heard beating down-hill."

"Some rascally old roundhead! and why did he ride—was he afraid we would eat him?"

"I know not, sir; but a bold horseman *is* my master; and he dashed into the Ouse as if he saw the game before him."

"Or the devil behind!" added the clergyman. "Mahoud! a thought strikes me—he crossed the Ouse—what if he be gone to warn De Ginckel of our route? The Swart Ruyters were last seen at Haverhill."

"Convince us of that, doctor," said Walter, "and we should burn this fair house to the ground-stone."

"Gadso, lad; let us have breakfast first. Harkee, butler——"

"Thou se'st, reverend sir," began the old servant, trembling.

"Avaunt, caitiff! dost thou *thou* me? 'I am come of good kin,' as the old morality saith," cried Joram; "fetch me a pint of sack posset, dashed with ginger, and a white loaf, while breakfast is preparing; and if you would save your back from my riding-rod, and your master's mansion from the flames, see that our repast be such as not even Heliogabalus could find a fault with."

"And bring me a wassail bowl of spiced ale," said Finland.

"And me a stoup of brandy, master butler," added Serjeant Wemyss.

"And me the same," chorussed Hab Elshender and the soldiers at the lower end of the hall; while his reverence the chaplain, stretching himself before the ruddy flames, began the old ditty of the Cavaliers of Fortune.

> "Now all you brave lads, that would hazard for honour
>   Hark! how Bellona her trumpet doth blow.
> Mars, with many a warlike banner,
>   Bravely displayed, invites you to goe'
> Germani, Denmark, and Sweden, are smoking,
>   With a band of brave sworders each other provoking,
>   Marching in their armour bright,
>   Summonis you to glory's fignt,
>   Sing tan ta, ra, ra, ra, ra, ra'"

As his reverence concluded, he drained the sack posset, which the white-haired butler placed obsequiously before him.

"Many a time and oft have I heard my father chant that old Swedish war-song," said Finland. "He commanded a regiment of Ruyters under Gustavus."

> "O Vivat! Gustavus Adolphus, we cry,
>   With thee all must either win honour or die!
>   Tan ta, ra, ra, ra, ra, ra!"

sang the chaplain; "O 'tis a jolly anthem. Here's to his memory—Gustavus Adolphus, the friend of the soldier of fortune—the Cæsar of Sweden—the star of the north! I perceive, gentlemen," continued the divine, "that there are virginals and music in yonder oriel window. What say ye—shall we summon the rosy English dame, whose dainty fingers I doubt not, press those ivory keys, that she may sing us some of the merry southern madrigals King Charles loved so well?"

"Nay, doctor, by Heaven!" said Walter, as the thought of his absent Lilian (for whose sake all the sex were dear to him) flashed upon his mind. "If there are ladies here, no man shall molest them while I can hold a rapier."

"Hear this young cock o' the game," said Joram, angrily; "he cocks his beaver like a mohock already."

"Well spoken, young comrade," said Finland; "our clerical friend hath mistaken his avocation. Instead of entering holy orders, he should have been purveyor to old Dalyel's Red Cossacks."

"'Sdeath! gentlemen," said the divine, colouring; "I only jested, and you turn on me like so many harpies. But as for you, Mr. Fenton, my pretty cavaliero, *who* proposed burning the mansion to the ground-stone?"

"I knew not that it contained ladies."

"My lady comes of an old cavalier family, noble sirs," said the old butler, with great perturbation; "and would herself appear to greet you, but illness——"

"It is enough, good fellow," replied Finland; "how is she named?"

"She is a daughter of old Sir Tufton Shirley."

"Then God bless her!" said Joram; "her father's hall of Mildenham can show the marks of Cromwell's bullets. And your master, gaffer Englishman—*his* name?"

"Marmaduke Langstone," answered the servant hesitatingly.

"Who commands a corps of Red dragoons on the borders of Bedfordshire?"

"The same."

"Then hell's malison on him for a false, canting, prick-eared, round-headed, double-dyed traitor!" exclaimed the chaplain, furiously, as he attacked a cold sirloin, with the same energy as if it had been the proprietor. "He is now tracking us from place to place; but if he comes within reach of our cannon—Gadso! let him look to it."

A sumptuous breakfast of cold roasted beef, venison pies, broiled salmon, white manchets, cheese, butter, eggs, milk, possets of sack, tankards of spiced ale, coffee, &c., had been spread on the table of the dining-hall, by the timid English servants, whose dread and aversion of their unwelcome guests often made the latter laugh outright.

"I am glad," said Walter, as he breakfasted, "we have taken quarters in the house of so false a traitor. I should like much to have a horse; and, for the service of King James, I will mulct him of the best in his stable."

Wemyss and other soldiers, who occupied the lower end of the long oak table, were feasting, with all the voracity of famished kites, on the rich viands; but while hewing down the great sirloin in vast slices, Hab Elshender declared that he "would rather have a cogue of brose at his mother's ingle-neuk, than the best that bluff England could produce."

"And well I agree with thee, friend Hab," said the veteran Wemyss. "My heart misgives me, we will be sorely forfoughten, ere we see the blue reek curling from our ain lumheeds. But here is to Dunbarton—God bless his noble heart, and the good old cause."

"Good Wemyss, and you, my brave lads," said Dr. Joram, from the head of the table, "I crave to drink with you."

"Thanks to your reverence—thanks to your honour," muttered the soldiers, bowing and drinking.

The meal was a very protracted one; but the moment it was over, Dr. Joram muttered a hasty blessing, called loudly for more wine, lighted his great pipe, unbuttoned his vest and with Finland sat down to a game of tric-trac; the soldiers began to examine their bandoleers and muskets, and Walter repaired to the ample but nearly empty stables, where, from among the indifferent farm horses the necessities of war had left behind, he selected a fine-looking charger, high-headed, close-eared, square-nosed, and broad-chested, and having saddled, bridled, and caparisoned him to his entire satisfaction, led him forth just as the *générale* was beaten. Mounting, he galloped to the muster-place, well pleased with the acquisition the law of reprisal and the fortune of war entitled him to make.

CHAPTER XXXIX.

THE REDEEMED PLEDGE.

Ha! dost thou know me? that I am *Lothario?*
As great a name as this proud city boasts of.
Who is this mighty man, then, this *Horatio,*
That I should basely hide me from his anger?
FAIR PENITENT.

REFRESHED by their halt at Ely, the soldiers of Dunbarton pushed on towards "Merry Lincoln," the merriment of whose citizens would probably be no way increased by their arrival. Marching by the most unfrequented route to avoid the highway, they pursued a devious path through fallow fields and frozen lawns, and sought the shelter of every copsewood.

The level plains of fertile England could oppose but few and feeble obstacles to the hill-climbing Scots, accustomed from infancy to the rocky glens and pathless forests of their rugged mountain home; however they found it necessary to abandon the four pieces of English cannon, which were spiked and concealed in a thicket, and thus unencumbered, they hurried on with increased speed.

Walter's heart grew buoyant and gay as the day wore apace, and the picturesque villages with their yellow thatched cottages and ivy-covered churches, the old Elizabethan halls and brick-built manors of Cambridge and Lincolnshire, were passed in rapid succession. He knew that every pace lessened the distance between Lilian and himself, and before the sober winter sun descended in the saffron west, he hailed with pleasure the old town of Crowland, with its great but ruined abbey, the walls of which were buried under masses of luxuriant ivy.

Far over the gently undulated landscape shone the purple and yellow rays of the setting sun; Crowland Abbey, its old fantastic houses and village spire, on the summit of which the vine and ivy flourished, and all the winter scenery were bathed in [warm light. The Scots were descending a slope towards the town, when a shot fired by the avant guard, gave them an *alert;* then the voice of Dunbarton was heard commanding his brave musketeers to halt, while Gavin of that ilk came galloping back from the front.

" My lord earl," said he, "we have seen the glitter of steel above the uplands yonder."

" Then we have been brought to bay at last. With six

thousand horse on our flanks, it was not likely we would pass the ridings of Yorkshire without a camisado. Strike up the Scottish point of war, and let these knaves show themselves.

The shrill fifes and brattling drums rang clear and sharp in the pure frosty air, and ere the last note had died away, a body of horse appeared on an opposite eminence. Their broad beaver hats and waving feathers, polished corslets and scarlet coats, declared them English.

" 'Sdeath," said the earl, " they are Langstone's Red Dragoons, so De Ginckel's Black Riders are not far off."

" 'Tis but a troop of sixty, my lord," said Walter.

" Dost think they are within range?" asked Gavin, as his grenadiers began to open their pouches and blow their fuses.

" Scarcely, and we have no ammunition to spare; so if they molest us not, I freely bid them good speed in God's name."

A single cavalier was now seen to spur his horse to the front, and after riding along the roadway a few yards, to rein up and fire a pistol in the air. By the military etiquette of the time, this was understood to be a challenge to single encounter, or to exchange shots with any cavalier so inclined.

Full of ardour, and youthful rashness, and burning to distinguish himself, Walter Fenton exclaimed,

" I accept the challenge of this bravadoer; you will permit me, my Lord Dunbarton?"

" Doubtless, my brave lad, but beware; yonder fellow appears an old rider; his harness is complete *à la cuirassier*, as we used to say in France."

" Scaled all over like an armadillo, as we used to say at Tangier," added Dr. Joram. " Speed thee, Fenton, and show the rebel villain small mercy."

Walter galloped within a few paces of his adversary, who had now reloaded his pistol. His powerful frame which exhibited great muscular strength, was cased in a corslet of bright steel, buff coat and gloves, and enormous jack boots, fenced by plates of iron; his head was defended by an iron cap covered with black velvet, (a fashion of James VII.), and was adorned by a single feather; he carried a long carbine and still longer broadsword. His hair was cut short, and his chin shaved close in the Dutch fashion. He levelled a pistol between his horse's ears with a long and deliberate aim at Walter, whose eye was fixed in painful acuteness upon the little black muzzle and stern grey eye that glared along the barrel.

He fired!

The ball grazed the cheek-plate of Walter's morion, He never winced, but felt his heart tingle with rage and ex- ultation, as in turn he levelled his long horse-pistol at the Williamite trooper, who was reloading with the utmost cool- ness. Walter fired, and with a loud snort, a strange cry, and terrific bound, the strong Flemish horse of his adversary sank to the earth, and tore up the turf with its hoofs. Its brain had been pierced. The rider lost his pistol by the plunge, but adroitly disengaging himself from the twisted stirrups, high saddle, and convulsed legs of the fallen steed, he un- sheathed his long sword, and brandished it, crying—

" *Vive le Roi Guillaume!* come on, young coistrel !"

While the cheers of his comrades and a brisk ruffle on their drums made his heart leap within him, Walter sprang from his horse, and throwing the reins to Hab Elshender, drew his slender, cavalier rapier, and rushed to encounter his strong antagonist, but a glance sufficed to stay his forward step and upraised hand, and to lull the excitement of his spirit.

" Captain Napier !" he exclaimed, on recognizing beneath the dark head-piece, the stern, unmoved, but not unhandsome features of Lilian's kinsman, and his rival.

" I told thee, Fenton, we would meet again," said Napier, coldly, and sternly, " and I swore when that hour came to spare thee not. It hath come, so do unto me, as thou wilt be done by."

" For the sake of her whose name and blood you inherit in common, I would rather shun than encounter you. Your life —I spared it once."

" Why remind me of that ?" said Napier, furiously, while his cheek reddened. " 'Tis better to die than remember that the boldest heart of the Scots Brigade owes its existence to the favour of a beardless moppet like thee! bethink thee, man," continued Napier, sneeringly, "the entail—your sword can break it in a moment ; Quentin Napier is the last of his race, and then Lilian becomes an heiress."

" Away, sir," replied Walter, sadly and calmly, as he dropped the point of his sword, "you have mentioned the only thing that in an hour like this, unnerves my hand to en- counter you."

At that moment a drum of Dunbarton's beat a charge.

" Hark ! your comrades are impatient," said Napier, scorn- fully ; " fall on, you nameless loon, for here shall I redeem the pledge I gave or die," and swaying his sword with both hands, he attacked Walter with great fury and undisguised ferocity.

His courage was well met by Walter's address, but his

bodily strength and weight of weapon were far superior, and he pressed on pell mell, until a deep gash in the right cheek reminded him of the necessity of coolness.   The wound which would undoubtedly have roused another man to additional fury, had the effect of giving Napier a caution, that enabled him to parry Walter's successive cuts and thrusts with great success.   Without the least advantage being gained on either side, the combat continued for three or four minutes, during which the greatest skill in swordsmanship was exhibited by both cavaliers, in their attempts to pass each other's points, until a stone in the frozen turf caught Walter's heel, and he was thrown to the earth with great force.   Ere he could draw breath, the captain sprang upon him like a tiger, and with his sword shortened in his hand, and a knee pressed upon his breast, he exclaimed in a fierce whisper through his clenched teeth,

"Now I have thee! now your life is in my hand, but even now will I spare it, if here before the God that is above us, ye swear for the future to renounce all hope and thought of Lilian Napier—now, yea, and for ever!"

"Never!" gasped Walter, panting with rage and shame, for an exulting shout from the Red dragoons stung him to the soul; "never; by what title dare you impose such terms on me?"

"By the right of a kinsman and betrothed lover who would save her from contamination, by becoming the wife of an unknown foundling, a beggarly varlet, a soldier's wallet boy— ha!" and he ground his teeth.

Walter felt stifled as his corslet was compressed beneath the heavy knee of his conqueror, and he made many ineffectual struggles to grasp his poniard, but it lay below him.

"Renounce — renounce! swear — swear!" hissed Napier through his teeth.

"Never, never," groaned Walter.

"Then die!" shouted Napier; and raised his shortened sword which he grasped by the blade; but endued with new energy at the prospect of instant death, Walter, by a vigorous effort of strength, with one hand flung his adversary from him, and pinning him to the earth in turn, unsheathed his long dagger, and while labouring under a storm of wrath and fury, drove it twice through the joints of his shining gorget, but unable to withdraw it after the second blow, sank upon his enemy, and they lay weltering together in blood.

"My bitter and my heavy curse be on thee, Walter Fenton!" hissed the dying Napier through his chattering teeth,

" and if thou gettest *her*, may the curse of heaven, and the
curse that fell on Jeroboam be thine! mayest thou die child
less, and be the *last* as thou art the *first* of thy race!" He
fell back and expired.

CHAPTER XL.

THE SWART RÜYTERS.

With burnished brand and musketoon.
So gallantly you come ;
I read you for a bold dragoon,
That lists the tuck of drum.

ROKEBY.

WHEN Walter Fenton recovered, he found himself on
horseback, and his comrades on the march, beyond Crowland,
and the setting sun was about to dip below the far-off horizon.
A throng of thoughts chased each other through his mind,
but sorrow was the prevailing one. The rage he had felt
against Napier for his taunts, the hatred for his rivalry, and
animosity for his politics, had all passed away ; he felt now the
keenest sorrow for his fate, and remorse that he had fallen by
his hand.

The thought did flash upon him, that by the fatal issue of
the encounter, Lilian was indisputably heiress of Bruntisfield
and the Wrytes, but shrinking from contemplation of it, he
dismissed it from his mind, as unworthy to be dwelt upon.
By him the warm congratulations of his friends were unheeded
and unheard; his whole mind was absorbed in the idea that
he had slain the only kinsman of his beloved Lilian, and
destroyed the last of a long and gallant race, and already in
anticipation he beheld her tears, and heard the sorrowful reproaches of the proud Lady Grizel.

The appearance of the advanced party of Langstone's
troopers, whom the earl knew belonged to Sir John Lanier's
brigade of English horse, had considerably increased the
dread of the retreating regiment. There was now every prospect of being enclosed and cut off, for independent of infantry
pouring from twenty different roads upon their route, there
were 6,000 horse following them on the spur from the eastern
and western counties. Actuated by loyalty, by dread of cap-
ture and consequent disarmment, decimation, captivity, or dispersion, they marched with great rapidity, and to cheer them
on, the earl and his officers constantly encouraged them by

II.   x

enthusiastic addresses and encomiums, to which the brave Royals responded by shouts and cheers.

Shrill blew the fifes, and the braced drums rang briskly, as they entered upon a dreary wold to the northward of Crowland, a grassy and heathy waste, or down, over which the fading light of the setting sun shone in all its saffron splendour. On debouching from the road over which the tall poles, with the slender stems of the hops twining and clambering, though leafless and faded, formed an archway through the thick and dense hop gardens that bordered each side of the way, the advanced guard uttered a shout of surprise and defiance, and halted till the main body came up.

Goring his horse, Dunbarton dashed to the front, and beheld a dense column of darkly-armed cavalry formed in line across the moor, about a gunshot distant. They were motionless as statues, and the setting sun shone full upon their serried files and glittering weapons; they were solderlike in aspect; their helmets and corslets were of unpolished iron, as black as their long jack-boots; their yellow coats, heavily cuffed, and with looped skirts, proclaimed them Dutch. Their horses were large, heavily jointed, and as phlegmatic in aspect as their riders, for the whole brigade stood motionless and still as a line of bronze statues. Even their blue standards, with the white *fess*, hung pendant and unmoven.

A little in advance of the line was an officer on horseback, motionless, inert, and seemingly fast asleep; he was a man of vast rotundity, and cased in a capacious cuirass of polished steel, which gave him the aspect of a mighty tortoise, or some great bulb of which the gilt helmet formed the apex. An enormous basket-hilted sword swung on one side of him, and a brass blunderbuss on the other; while a great tin speaking-trumpet, like that of a Dutch skipper (then common in all armies, and last used by the brave Lord Heathfield), was grasped in his right hand. So utterly lifeless seemed the whole array, that if any other proof was wanting, it alone would have proclaimed them Hollanders.

"Dutch, by all the devils!" cried Dunbarton, galloping back to the Royals. "'Tis the Baron de Ginckel and his Swart Ruyters. Pikes against cavalry! Gavin, throw your grenadiers into the centre. Finland, Drumquhasel, brave gentlemen, march me your companies to the front. Musketeers, blow your matches, open your pans, and prepare to give fire!"

"Shoulder to shoulder, my boys!" cried Dr. Joram; "though the number of Gog be countless as the sand on the sea-shore, fear not!"

"God save King James! Hurrah!" cried the Royals, as the pikemen rushed forward to form the outer faces of the square, in which Dunbarton resolved to cut a passage through the Dutch, as there was no time for a protracted fight by taking advantage of the localities ; for other troops were pressing forward on every hand. Like a vast hedgehog with all its bristles erected, the band of Scots, in one dense mass, debouched upon the wold, with their fifteen hundred helmets and myriads of bright points gleaming in the last flush of the set sun. The stout pikemen, with their long weapons charged (or levelled) from the right haunch before them, formed the outer faces of the square ; and the musketeers, with their smoking matches and polished barrels, the rear-rank ; in the centre were the grenadiers, with their open pouches and lighted grenades, clustered round the Scottish standards, beneath which the old national march was beaten by twenty drums, as the whole column moved, with admirable order and invincible aspect, towards the centre of that long line of horse, whose flanks, when thrown forward, would quite have encircled them.

With his half-pike in his hand, Walter marched in front of the first face, and he felt a glow of ardour burn within him as they neared the Swart Ruyters—for so these horsemen were named, from their black armour.

The moment the Royals advanced, De Ginckel placed his great trumpet to his mouth, and puffing out his cheeks, in a voice of thunder, bellowed an order to break and form squadrons, for the purpose of attacking the Scots on every side. Hoarsely and deeply, in guttural Dutch, rang the words of command, as each successive captain gave the order to his troop ; and the whole line became instinct with life and action. Swords and helmets flashed, and standards waved, as the heavy iron squadrons, galloping obliquely to the right and left, formed in two dense columns, preparatory to charging.

"We will be assailed on every hand," exclaimed the earl ; "but be firm, my brave hearts, and quail not, for our lives and liberties depend upon the issue of this conflict. Halt! pikemen ; keep shoulder to shoulder like a wall."

"*Vivat!*" cried the Dutch dragoons ; "gluck! gluck! *vivat* Wilhelm!"

On they came in heavy masses, but ere their goring spurs had urged their ponderous chargers to the gallop, the voice of Dunbarton was again heard—

"Musketeers, open your pans—give fire!"

"Hurrah! down with the Stadtholder, and death to his birelings!" cried the Scots ; and the roar of six hundred muskets seemed to rend the very air, and reverberated like thunder over the echoing heath. From each face of the square, above the stands of pikes, six ranks poured at once their volleys, three kneeling and three firing over their heads, according to the old Swedish custom of the Scots when formed in squares. Two hundred grenades soared hissing into the air, sank and burst, and the effect was tremendous on the advancing Dutch.

More than a hundred and fifty troopers and horses fell prone on the frozen heath, dead or rolling in the agonies of death, and were fearfully trampled and kicked as the rearward squadrons, instead of dashing onward, reined up simultaneously, and appalled by the slaughter, and aware of the inutility of attacking a square of resolute infantry, began to recoil.

A shout of fierce derision burst from the retreating Scots, as De Ginckel, like a vast Triton blowing on a conch, galloped from troop to troop, bellowing in furious Dutch the order to advance, accompanied by a storm of hoarse abuse; but his Ruyters were immovable, and he beat both officers and men with the bell of his trumpet in vain. While reloading and blowing their matches, the musketeers continued retiring with all expedition towards a thick coppice that grew on the margin of the moor about a mile distant. The Dutch cavalry reformed, for pursuit. The roadway on the snow-covered moorland was scarcely visible in the grey twilight; on the right, it branched off towards Boston, and on the left towards Folkingham.

Dunbarton knew not the exact route, but his whole aim for the present moment was to reach the copsewood, where he would be less assailable by horse.

When but a quarter of a mile from this friendly bourne, a drum was heard to beat within its recesses, a long line of bright arms flashed under its dark shadows, and as if by magic the fugitive band beheld Maitland's brigade of the Scots Guards two thousand strong, drawn up in firm array, with the red matches of their shouldered muskets gleaming like a wavy line of wildfire in the twilight of the evening.

The shout of wrath and dismay that burst from the soldiers of Dunbarton, was immediately succeeded by another; for lo! a dense body of cavalry debouched from the Boston road, forming line at full gallop as they spread over the wold, while another, in dark and close array, came leisurely up at a trot from the ancient town of Folkingham, and all their trumpets sounded at once in martial and varying cadence, as they came in sight of the fugitives, and reined up for further orders.

" Lanier's troopers on the right ! " said Finland.

"Marmaduke Langstone on the left!" added Dr. Joram ; " hemmed in—lost—there is nothing for it now but surrender to the Philistines."

" Or die in our ranks ! " said Walter Fenton.

"Right, my young gallant," replied the earl. " All is indeed lost now ; but discretion is oft the better part of valour, and by yielding for the present we may the better serve King James at a future period, than by being shot on the instant, and thus ending our lives and our loyalty together.

What say ye, cavaliers and comrades?" Though the earl spoke thus lightly, his heart was throbbing with smothered passion, and the murmur that broke from his soldiers was expressive rather of wrath and fury than acquiescence to his advice.

Then a dead silence followed, and not a sound was heard throughout the different bands arrayed on the level waste, but the clank of accoutrements, as two Dutch officers, de-spatched by the baron de Ginckel rode up to Langstone and to Lanier, to communicate the orders of their leader, who was rapidly advancing with his strong column of Ruyters, so dis-posed as completely to cut off all hope of flight in any direc-tion.

In spite of his natural courage, Walter felt his heart now become a prey to intense sadness, if not apprehension. Jaded and wearied by excessive fatigue, his comrades were dispirited and little inclined for new strife, to engage in which, so far from their native land, and when hemmed in by forces so much more numerous, would have been madness. He con-templated with horror being a prisoner to the Dutch or English, to be banished perhaps to the West Indies or some far foreign station, or to endure a protracted captivity, and a shameful death ; in either case, perhaps never again to behold his Lilian and his loved native land,—for to a Scotsman the love of home is a second being—a part of his existence. So much was he occupied with these sad thoughts, that he was not aware a flag of truce was approaching, until he saw an English cavalier rein up his horse within a few yards of him. The stranger bowed gracefully, saying—

" Sir Marmaduke Langstone would speak with the earl of Dunbarton; he is bearer of a message from Goderdt de Ginckel, earl of Athlone."

" Say forth, Sir Marmaduke," replied the noble Douglas ; " if it be such as a Scottish earl may hear without dishonour What says mynheer of Athlone? "

The Englishman laughed and replied,—

"He desires me to acquaint your lordship and those gallant Scots who have so rashly revolted from King William——"

"You mistake, sir; we never joined the banner of the Stadtholder, and cannot be termed revolters."

"Then ye are rebels by the laws of the land."

"Not of England, as we owe it neither suit nor service."

"Then ye have broken the laws of your own country."

"Under favour, Sir Marmaduke! we hold our commissions from the Scottish parliament, from whom we have received no orders, since we marched south among you here; and you sadly mistake in naming those rebels, who still wear the king's uniform."

"My lord," rejoined the English knight, haughtily, "I have no time to argue these niceties with you. De Ginckel desires me to inform you, that he will grant such terms as might be expected by any other foreign foe who hath marched on English ground, with drums beating and standards displayed; and these are, life and kindness, on an unconditional surrender of arms and all martial insignia, yielding yourselves prisoners at discretion."

The swarthy cheek of the earl grew gradually crimson with passion as Langstone spoke; but an expression of shame and mortification succeeded.

"Alas, alas!" said he, looking sadly on the silk standards that rustled in the evening wind. "Are those old banners that were wrought for us by the noble demoiselles of Versailles to be thus dishonoured at last? Often have they been pierced by the bullets, but never sullied by the touch of a foe!"

"We will yield to our ain kindly folk," cried Sergeant Wemyss and several soldiers; "we will yield us to Major Maitland and the Scots Guards."

"You must surrender to the Swart Ruyters alone, my brave hearts!" cried Langstone.

"And what if we do not?" asked Dunbarton.

"Good, my lord, the consequences will be frightful—unconditional surrender, or utter extermination—Dutch terms. On every hand you are hemmed in, and every road to your native land is blocked up by enemies. My noble lord," and here with generous confidence the brave Englishman rode close to the levelled pikes, "be advised by one who wishes well to Scot as to Southern. If one cannot fight prudently to-day, better be fighting a year hence, than have the sod growing green over us. Shall I ride back to the baron, and promise your surrender?"

"Be it so; but deeply do I grieve that Sir Marmaduke

Langstone, whose family has ever been distinguished for valour and loyalty, is the propounder of such bitter terms to George of Dunbarton."

"The times are changed, my lord; live and let live is my motto; had such been the maxim of James II., this sword, which *my* father drew for *his* at Marston, had not this day been drawn against him. Liberty of conscience is dear to us all, and I respect the high principles of those soldiers who rushed to the standard of our deliverer."

" Then learn still more to respect the chivalry and generosity of the few whose principles of loyalty bound them to their unhappy king in the darkest hour of his distress and misfortune."

"Decide, my lord, decide—for the Swart Ruyters are closing up troop upon troop."

"We will yield our national standards to the Scottish Guards—our arms and persons to De Ginckel."

"It is enough," replied Sir Marmaduke, as he wheeled round his horse, and rode towards the immense Dutch commander, whose Ruyters with the brigades of Scotch and English, had now hemmed in the fugitives, as it were in a large hollow square.

Far off, at the horizon of the frozen heath, the winter moon, shining red and luminous, rose slowly into the blue sky, eclipsing the light of the diamond-like stars as it ascended; and its pale splendour fell brightly and steadily on the fitful weapons and the dark masses of half-mailed men, among whom they gleamed—on the white and powder-like frost that glittered silvery and clearly on every blade of grass, and on the dark spots that dotted the plain to the southward.

There many a rider and horse were lying stiff and cold.

CHAPTER XLI.

LILIAN.

I love thee, gentle Knight! but 'tis,
  Such love as sisters bear;
O, ask my heart no more than this,
  For more it may not spare.
                KNIGHT TOGGENBURG.

THE image of Clermistonlee and his threats came painfully upon Lilian's memory. She shrieked for aid, but her cries were lost in the vacuity of the old-fashioned coach in which she was being carried off. She strove to open the windows,

but they were immovable as those of a castle, and she resigned herself to tears and despair. The vehicle was rumbling
and jolting over a waste of frozen snow; here and there, a
farm-house or a congealed rivulet were passed, but everything appeared so strange and new, when viewed in their
snowy guise by the twilight of the mirky winter night, that
Lilian had not the most remote idea in what direction she
was taken; and shuddering with cold and apprehension, the
poor girl crouched down in a corner of the coach, and abandoned herself to grief and wretchedness.

The excessive chill of the night, and prostration of spirit
under which she laboured, produced a sort of stupor, and
when the coach stopped, she was unable to move; but a tall,
dark man, muffled and masked like an intriguing gallant of
the day, lifted her out. As one in a dream, who would in
vain elude some hideous vision, she attempted to shriek; but
the unuttered cry died away on her lips, and she closed her
eyes. A strong embrace encircled her; a hot breath—(was
it not a kiss?)—came upon her cold cheek, and she felt herself borne along; doors closed behind her, and by the warmth
of the altered temperature, she was aware of being within a
house.

She was seated gently in a chair; and now she looked
around her. A large fire of roots was blazing on the rough
stone-hearth; its ruddy glow rendered yet more red the bare
walls and strongly-arched roof of a hall (built of red sandstone), such as may be seen in the old fortlets of the lesser
barons of Scotland. The windows on each side were deeply
embayed by the thickness of the wall, and a deep-browed arch
spanned each; they had stone seats covered with crimson
cushions, and foot-mats of plaited rushes.

The hurrying clouds and occasional stars were seen through
the strong basket-gratings that externally defended these
prison-like apertures. The hall was paved, and its rude
massive furniture consisted only of a great oblong table of
oak, several forms or settles, a few high-backed chairs, and
one upon a raised part of the floor, at the upper end, had a
canopy of crimson cloth over it, announcing that it was the
state-chair of the lord of the manor. Swords, pikes, arque-
buses, hunting and hawking appurtenances, with a few veiled
pictures, were among its ornaments.

A great almery, or cupboard (so called from the old hospitable custom of setting aside food as *alms* for the poor),
occupied one end of the apartment, and an ancient casque
surmounted it. Various bunkers of carved oak, bound with
iron, occupied the other. On the right hand of the doorway,

a stone lavatory, covered with magnificent sculpture, projected from the wall. This old-fashioned basin was furnished with a hole to carry off water, and was an indispensable convenience to every ancient dining-hall.

With one rapid glance of terror Lilian surveyed the whole place, and started from her chair to be confronted by one whose aspect made her instinctively shrink back. The keen and hawk-like eyes of Beatrix Gilruth were fixed upon her with an expression at once menacing, searching, and scornful. There was something in the wild visage of this inexplicable woman that excited curiosity, while her air terrified, and her withered person repelled approach.

"Who are you, woman?" asked Lilian firmly, as, stepping back a pace, she surveyed her from head to foot; "and what are you?"

"*What* am I?" reiterated the other, with a voice that thrilled, while her grey eyes gleamed with a blue light, and she ground her teeth. "I am what thou shalt be, my pretty minx, ere ye leave these walls, perhaps."

Lilian, terrified by her aspect and her answer, sank into a chair, saying, as she clasped her hands and looked up imploringly from her bright dishevelled hair, "Woman, for the love of God, say where am I?"

"In the tower of Clermistonlee."

"So my soul foreboded; but can *he* have dared thus far?"

"What will he not dare that man can do?"

"Oh Heaven, protect me!"

"Neither the heaven that is above us, nor the hell that is beneath, will protect you, pretty one; but you will be made what many as fair have been—the toy, the plaything of an hour, to be cast aside when some new fancy has seized the wayward mind of your lord and betrayer. Look at that veiled portrait——"

At that moment three distinct knocks were heard against the almery. Lilian started and turned pale.

"Yes, yes," said Beatrix scornfully, addressing the knocker, "you are impatient. There was a time—but it matters not —I bide mine; and my long-delayed vengeance will wither thee up, false lord, even as if the lightning of God had scorched thy perjured soul."

Low as this was uttered, it reached the ears of Lilian; she became doubly terrified, and a momentary feeling of utter abandonment made her cover her face with her hands and weep bitterly. But suddenly starting up, she said with energy—

"I will go hence, madam; and whatever be the danger, I

will risk it.   But the snow, the darkness, and the distance—oh, horror!—aunt Grizel—gossip Annie—what will they think of this?—what will become of me?"

"Stand," said Beatrix, interposing.   "Are you mad, to think of leaving this roof in the middle of a winter night? Remember the dreary lea of Clermiston, the rocks and the frozen marshes of Corstorphine,—you are fey, maiden, to think it."

"Begone, thou ill woman," replied Lilian, contemptuously; I will go, and I dare thee to stay me."

"Then," rejoined Beatrix spitefully, "remember the barred windows, the bolted gates, and the good stone-walls.   Pooh! maiden, take tent and bide where ye are; for I swear ye can never go from hence, but at the pleasure of my lord."

"Insolent!   Know ye who I am?" asked Lilian.

"The young lady of Bruntisfield," answered Beatrix coldly; a wayward lass with a braw tocher, it seemeth,—one who prefers a younger cap and feather than my lord.   Ha! hath he not sworn—(and mark me, maiden, he never swears in vain!)—that he will compel thee yet to beg his love at his hand as a boon, even as humbly as he now sues thine."

"In sooth!" retorted Lilian, with angry surprise.   "He will surely have the aid of some such witch as thee, to work so modern a miracle."

"Witch, quotha!" replied Beatrix, whose withered cheek began to redden with passion.   "Lilian Napier, there was a time when these grey, grizzled locks were once as bright and as glossy as thine; when this brow was as smooth, this faded form as round, yea, and as beautiful; this step as light, and this poor face as fair, as thine now are.   So beware thee of taunts, maiden; for the time is coming (if thou art spared) when thou mayest be loathsome as I now am, and loathing as I now do.   That hour is coming; for Clermistonlee hath an evil eye, beneath whose baleful influence all that is good and beautiful in woman will wither and die.   Oh! Lilian Napier, what a tale of love and weakness, shame and misery, sin and horror, would the history of my life reveal!   But my hour of revenge is coming.   Yes——"

Again three knocks louder than before rang on the almery; and Beatrix, trembling, ceased to talk, and busied herself in laying a supper on the hall-table.

"Oh, Walter! Walter!" murmured Lilian, "if you knew of this—if you were here to protect me!"   Her tears flowed freely.

"Walter!" reiterated Beatrix, musing; "can it really be the same?   No, it is impossible; and yet, why not?   He is your lover, then, this Walter?" she asked in a low voice, while laying some cold grilled meat, confections, and wine from a buffet. "I know he is—that blush tells me (when did my cheek blush last?). He is young and handsome, I warrant?"

Lilian nodded an affirmative.

"And men say he is brave?"

"Oh, yes! brave as a hero of romance," said Lilian in the same low tone; for there is nothing so pleasing to love as to hear the object of it praised. "And so noble, so generous! If true worth gave a title, my dear Walter would be a belted earl."

"Instead of being a poor standard-bearer in the ranks of Dunbarton."

"You have seen him then?" said Lilian, her blue eyes beaming, as she almost forgot her present predicament in the thought of her lover. "Is he not handsome, good woman?"

"It *is* the same!" exclaimed Beatrix, in her shrillest tone. "Walter, the powder-boy—the soldier's brat—hah!"—she ground her teeth, and clenched her shrivelled hands like knots of serpents—"I bide my time. Oh, I will be fearfully avenged!"

A third time there was a knocking on the almcry, and Beatrix muttered—

"I am dumb—I will speak no more."

She pointed to the supper-table, and, throwing herself into a chair, fixed her sunken eyes upon the red, glowing fire, and lost in her own wild thoughts, continued to jabber with the rapidity and restlessness of insanity. It was evident that she was partly deranged,—a discovery which, while it raised the pity of the gentle Lilian, increased the dread and the horror of her situation.

Clermistonlee, with his faithful rascal Juden, were both within earshot. The former had sufficient tact and experience to know that it would be better to defer any interview with Lilian until next morning, by which time he hoped she would be a little more familiarized with her situation; and leaving Juden, who was ensconced in the recesses of the almery, to be a check upon the troublesome garrulity of his only female domestic, he retired to a snug apartment, where, enveloped in his shag dressing-gown, and comforted by a great tankard of his favourite mulled sack, and several books of "ungodly jests," he practised all his philosophy to enable him to endure this temporary separation from Lilian, consoled by the idea that she was completely in his clutches, within his strong tower, which he was entitled to defend against all men living;

and well aware that, in the political storm which in another week would convulse all Scotland from the Cheviots to Cape Wrath, the abduction of a girl—more especially the daughter of a " persecuting cavalier"—would be less regarded than the wind blowing over the muir.

As the still, quiet night wore on, and the fumes of the wine mounted into his head, very strange ideas floated through the brain of the *roué*. Again and again the thought of Lilian being so utterly in his power intruded itself upon his heated imagination ; he felt his blood begin to glow : his mind became confused ; he endeavoured to combat his constitutional wickedness, and, by aid of his repeated potations, and a highly-seasoned grillade, dozed away the night very comfort-ably in a well-cushioned chair ; while his leal henchman was in the same happy state of oblivion, through the medium of various stoups of ale, which he imbibed in the spence or buttery.

Not so did poor Lilian pass the slow and heavy hours.

The repast prepared for her was left untouched, she re-sisted every invitation to repose, and resolved on passing the night by the hall-fire ; until, reflecting that she would be quite as safe in one part of the tower as in another, and wishing to be alone, that she might weep unseen, she was ushered by Beatrix up a narrow stair into a little sleeping apartment, the greater part of which was occupied by a great hearse-looking tester, or canopy bed. The only light in the chamber came from the fire-place, where a heap of logs and coals were blazing, and diffusing a warm glow on the dark wainscotted walls, the oaken floor, and rude ceiling, which was crossed by a massive dormant-tree of oak, covered with grotesque and hideous carving.

There was something very gloomy and catafalque-like in the aspect of the gigantic bed in which Lilian was to repose ; its massive posts of dark oak and darker ebony were covered embossage, and the deep crimson curtains, with heavy fringes, fell in shadowy festoons, while four great plumes of feathers surmounted the corners in sepulchral grandeur. It stood upon a raised dais of three steps, and on the back, amid a wilderness of bassi-relievi, flowers, angels, satyrs, and ivy, appeared the coronet and gorgeous blazon of Clermistonlee.

" I cannot sleep here, good woman," said Lilian, shudder-ing ; but the noise of the closing door, and the bolt jarring outside, was her only reply. She found herself alone. Her first impulse was to fasten her door within securely ; her second to examine the chamber, by the light of the fire. In the deep little window stood a beautiful cabinet, on the upper

part of which were a mirror and all the usual appurtenances
for a lady's toilet, but of the most costly and elegant description, with all the perfumes, oils, essences, and lotions then
most in vogue.   She turned from them with disgust to survey
the walls, for the fear of secret entrances was impressed
powerfully upon her mind by her knowledge of the number
that existed in her own home; but, upon examination, she
found nothing to increase her dread, save the cabinet, the
doors of which were locked, and returned an unusually
hollow sound when she touched them.

Alternately a prey to fear and indignation, she walked
about the little apartment, or sat by the fire weeping and
praying, until sleep began to oppress her; and, unable longer
to resist its effects, with an audible supplication to Heaven
that the morrow might bring about her release, she threw
herself (without undressing) on the bed, and almost immediately fell fast asleep.

CHAPTER XLII.

HOW CLERMISTONLEE PRESSED HIS SUIT.

A strong dose of love is worse than one of ratafia; when once it gets into
our heads it trips up our heels, and then good night to discretion.
                                            THE LYING VALET.

FROM an uneasy slumber that had been disturbed by many
a painful dream, Lilian started, awoke, and leaped from the
bed.   The embers of the night fire still smouldered on the
hearth-stone, and the rays of the red sun rising above a
gorge in the Corstorphine hills, radiated through her grated
window as through a focus.   Pressing her hands upon her
temples, she endeavoured to collect the scattered images that
had haunted her sleep.   She had dreamt of Walter.   He
seemed to be present in that very chamber, to stand by her
gloomy bed, and smiled kindly and fondly as of old.   He
bent over to kiss her, but, lo! his features turned to those of
Lord Clermistonlee; the great tester-bed, with its plumage
and canopy, became a hearse; she screamed, and awoke to
find it was day.

Now all her former fear and indignation revived in full
force, and she wept passionately.   Reflecting how completely
she was at the mercy of Clermistonlee, whose character for
reckless ferocity, and steady obstinacy of purpose, she knew
too well; she resolved to endure with patience, and await

with caution an opportunity for release or escape. How little she knew of what was acting in Edinburgh! And her beloved kinswoman, so revered, so tender, and affectionate, but so aged and infirm.

"O horror!" exclaimed Lilian, wringing her hands, "this must have destroyed her."

"Open, Madam Lilian," said the voice of Beatrix Gilruth, as she knocked at the door; "open, my lord awaits you at breakfast in the hall."

Lilian hesitated; but aware that resistance would not better her fortune, with her usual frankness ran to the door, opened it, and despite the repulsive sternness of Gilruth's aspect, impelled by a sense of loneliness, and a wish to gain her friendship, she bade her good morning, and lightly touched her hand. Her air of innocence and candour impressed the misanthropic heart of Beatrix, and she smiled kindly. While leading her before the mirror to assist in arraying her for breakfast, the bosom of the unfortunate castaway could not repress a sigh, and a scanty tear trembled in either eye, as she writhed her withered fingers in the soft masses of Lilian's hair.

"I will show thee, my bairn, what a braw busker I am," said Beatrix, "though 'tis long since these poor fingers have had aught to do with top-knots and fantanges."

Resigned and careless of what was done with her, Lilian remained with a pale face of placid composure and grief, gazing unconsciously upon her own beautiful image as reflected in the polished mirror; and though she marked it not, there was a vivid and terrible contrast between her statue-like features, and those of her tirewoman—keen, attenuated, and graven with the lines of sorrow, rage, bitterness, and misanthropy; the true index of that storm of evil passions and resentful thoughts that smouldered in her heart.

At length the captive was arrayed so far as the skill of Beatrix would go; her dress (that in which she had left home) was long, flowing, and heavily flounced in the French fashion, derived from Albert Durer, who represented an angel in flounced petticoats expelling Adam and Eve from Paradise —hence flounces were all the rage. She wore long and heavy ruffles of the richest lace, a string of pearls and amber was twisted among the bright braids of her beautiful hair; a diamond drop depended from each of her delicate ears, and a rich necklace, like a collar, with a pendant, encircled her neck, the whiteness and purity of which never appeared in greater splendour, than when contrasted with the faded skin of poor Beatrix. Passive under her hands, Lilian allowed her great natural beauty to be thus dangerously enhanced, and when she stood up, her rather diminutive stature being increased by her high-heeled maroquin shoes, and the grace with which she wore her commode and floating flounces, caused the poor woman, whom so many fair ones had successively supplanted, to utter an exclamation of delight.

"Come," said she, "my lord awaits you; how pleased he will be."

"Oh, my God!" exclaimed Lilian, in deep anguish; "and was it to please him you have thus arrayed and attired me. Fie upon thee, ill woman!"

"Here at least his bidding must be obeyed implicitly, as when a hundred of his men stabled their horses in the barbican stalls. He is a dangerous man, hinny, and never tholed thwarting, though the hour is coming when he shall thole bitter vengeance, and dree the deepest remorse. But I bide my time—I bide my time."

As she led Lilian into the hall, Clermistonlee advanced to receive her, with an imperturbable air of assurance, gallantry, and devotion. Through one of the deeply-recessed windows, the light of the morning sun fell full upon his noble face and figure, which the richness of his dress displayed to the utmost advantage. He wore an embroidered suit of light blue satin slashed with white: he had round his neck the gold collar of the thistle, and had over his left breast the green riband and oval badge of the order; a diamond-hilted rapier sparkled in a baldrick that was stiff with gold embroidery; his flowing peruke was redolent of perfume; his ruffles were miracles of needlework, and his brilliant sleeve buttons flashed whenever his hands moved.

Hateful as he was at all times to Lilian, now he was more so than ever; surprise, indignation, fear, and contempt, agitated her by turns, and she gazed on him in painful suspense, awaiting his address. He had evidently made his toilette with more than usual care, and resolving to give Lilian no time for reproaches, he led her at once to a seat, saying,

"My dear girl will no doubt be in a prodigious passion with me, but ladies are kindly disposed to forgive every little mistake that has love for its excuse. 'Tis but a dismal old peelhouse this, dear Lilian, but I hope you slept well. The wind sings in the corridors, the corbies scream on the roof, and all that, but with a clear conscience you know, oh, yes, one may dose like a top, or a lord of sessin.

"A clear sharp morning this; I rode as far as Craigroyston before sunrise There is nothing so improves one's complexion as a gallop in the morning air. Apropos! what do you think of this embroidered suit? 'Tis the last fashion from Paris; that old villain Saunders Snip, in the Craimes, brought it direct from thence last month. On a good figure it is quite calculated to make an impression. Look'ee, fair Lilian; these ruffles cost me twenty guineas a pair, not a tester less, I assure you; and the sleeve buttons are the first of their kind, and were made by Monsieur Bütong, the eminent Parisian jeweller, for that glorious fop, the Comté d'Artois, who presented them to a friend of mine in the Scots Archers.

"But this tie of my overlay, ha! that is a contrivance of my own; graceful, is it not? exactly—I knew you would think so. Droll, is it not, that our tastes should be the same? You see, my dear girl, at what trouble I have been to please you. Smile again, dear Lilian," continued his lordship, whose overnight potations the morning ride had failed quite to dispel; "by Heaven, you look divine: where shall I find words to compliment the beauty of your appearance this morning!"

"You really seem to require all your verbosity for praising yourself, my lord," said Lilian, coldly.

"Now—now, do not be so angry," said Clermistonlee, taking her hand in spite of all her efforts to prevent him.

"I am justly so, my lord," replied Lilian, making a strong effort to restrain her tears under an aspect of firmness and determination. "By what right have you dared to bring me here and detain me prisoner?"

"Hoity, toity—right, dear Lilian? the right of a most devoted lover."

"My lord, you will be severely punished for this. The law——"

"Ha, ha! Lilian, there is no law now, no order, morality, nor anything else. The world is turned upside down, (at least Britain is)—revolutionized, bewildered, and the old days of battle and broil, reiving and rugging, have come back in all their glory. In this desperate game, my girl," he added, through his clenched teeth, "Clermistonlee must repair his fortune or be lost for ever; but enough of this; let us to breakfast, and then we will talk over matters that lie nearer our hearts. Nay, nay, no refusal—breakfast you *must* have."

He led her towards the long hall-table, where, thanks to Juden's catering and ingenuity, a noble repast was laid, in the profuse style of ancient gourmandizing; and the unscrupulous factotum who stood near with a napkin under his arm, and a long corkscrew in his hand, surveyed Lilian with something between a smirk and a leer, which was sufficient to increase the fear that oppressed, and the anger that swelled within her breast. She withdrew, saying, with a voice that trembled between indignation and apprehension,

"Spare me this continued humiliation. Oh, my Lord Clermistonlee, if there remain within your breast, one spark of that bright spirit which ought ever to be the guiding-star of the noble and the gentleman, you will restore me to my home, to the only relative (save one) whom death has left me in this wide world. Be generous, my lord," continued Lilian, touching his hand with charming frankness; "oh, be generous as I know you are brave and reckless. Restore me to my home, and I pledge my word you will never be questioned concerning my abduction. I will pass it over as a foolish but daring frolic. Hear me, my lord, in pity hear me."

Clermistonlee trembled beneath her gentle touch; but answered with his usual air of raillery,—

"Hoity, toity, little one! art going to read me curtain lectures already? My dear Lilian, it is too bad really! The abduction? Oh, the ardour of my love will be a sufficient excuse for that; and as to being questioned—I don't think any person will permit himself to question me, if he remembers that I am the best hand at pistol, rapier, and dagger, in broad Scotland.

"Beside, dear Lilian, (why dost always shrink? dost think, child, I am going to eat thee like a rascally ogre) if thou wouldst save thine honour," here his voice sank involuntarily into an impressive whisper, "become mine. Thou shouldst be well aware that after living in the power of one who is so tremendous a *roué* by habit and repute, no woman could go forth into the world without lying under suspicions of a very unpleasant nature. The roisters at Blair's coffee-house have got hold of the story, for it hath made a devil of a noise in the city, and in the mouths of the Bowhead gossips, and Besswynd scandal-mongers, our little affair will be quite a romance."

This cruel speech, which was uttered with the utmost coolness and deliberation by Clermistonlee, who played the while with his gold sword-knot, came like ice upon the heart of the unhappy Lilian, who could not but secretly acknowledge that it was too true. She grew pale as death, and, unable to reply, gazed upon her tormentor with a look of such intense aversion, that he could not repress a haughty smile of astonishment.

"Ha, ha! for what do you take me.°"

II.   F

"For a monster!" murmured Lilian, in a voice almost inarticulate.

"Oh—oh! you regard me as a poor sparrow doth a gerfalcon."

"Alas!" said Lilian, weeping as she sank into a seat, "the simile is but too true."

"You are very unpolite, Madam Lilian; a gerfalcon is between the vulture and the hawk."

Lilian answered only by her tears, and his lordship began to get a little provoked.

"A devil of a breakfast this, my pretty moppet," he continued, with an air of composure; "when these vapours have passed away, peradventure you will condescend to hear my addresses—meantime consider yourself quite at home, and for Heaven's sake (or rather your own), do take a share of such humble cheer as this my poor house of Clermiston affords." And without troubling her farther, he threw back the curls of his peruke, and attacked the devilled duck, the cold sirloin, and wassail-bowl of spiced ale, the smoking coffee and hot bannocks, forthwith.

Within the recess of a window, reclined upon the cushion of one of those stone side-seats so common in old Scottish towers, Lilian sat with her face covered with her hands, and shaded by the masses of her fine hair which fell forward over her drooping head. The glory of the red morning sun streamed full upon her tresses and turned them to wreaths of gold. She seemed something etherially beautiful, and the sensual lord felt his heart beat with increased ardour as he gazed on her from time to time; but aware, from old experience, that it was useless to press her to partake of his luxurious breakfast, he resolved to trouble her no more until the first paroxysm of her indignation had evaporated.

Juden and Beatrix having finished their luggies of porridge and ale at the lower and uncovered part of the table, were now engaged, the former in making lures of feathers and raw meat to train two young hawks that sat near him on a perch, with their long lunes or leashes coiled round it; and the latter, while affecting to occupy herself with some household matter, from the bay of an opposite window, watched with a keen, restless, and often malicious expression, the *nonchalant* lord and the unhappy Lilian, for whom, at times, she felt something akin to pity, and fain would have set her at liberty; but the keys of the tower-gates were buckled to Juden's girdle, and every window was closed by a grating like a strong iron harrow.

In the faint hope of some rescue approaching, Lilian gazed

earnestly from the window she occupied. It faced the south, and overlooked the then dreary waste of Clermiston Lee, which, with all the undulating country extending to the base of the Pentlands, and that gigantic range, towering peak abovo peak, as they diminished in the western shire of Linlithgow, were covered with one universal mantle of dazzling snow. Afar off above the hills of Braid the level sun poured its red rays through a hazy sky across the desolate landscape; the thickets, bare and leafless, stood like cypress groves in the waste; the dim winter smoke from many farm-house and cottage *lum* of clay, ascended in murky columns into the frosty air, but around the lonely tower on the Lec, there was an aspect of stillness and desolation that struck a chill upon Lilian's heart.

Far off, on the Glasgow road, that passed the picturesque old church, the thatched hamlet and Foresters' Castle of Corstorphine, a strong square fortress flanked by round towers, a solitary traveller, muffled in his furred rocquelaure and leathern gambadoes, or grey maud and worsted galligaskins (according to his rank), spurred his horse towards the city; but such occasional passers were all beyond the reach of Lilian. The bridle-road to the town was hidden, and not a foot-print stained the spotless mantle of the level Lee. At times a hare or fox shot across it, from the woods or rocks of Corstorphine, but no other living thing approached, and the heart of poor Lilian grew more and more sad as the dreary day wore on, and night once more approached.

CHAPTER XLIII.

CLAVERHOUSE TO THE RESCUE.

The winter cold is past and gone,
  And now comes on the spring;
And I am one of the Scots Life Guards,
  And I must fight for the King.
                My dear!
And I must fight for him!

OLD SONG.

BY orders from William of Orange, who had taken posses sion of James's palace, and issued from thence his sounding declarations and imperial mandates, Goderdt de Ginckel, with the utmost expedition, marched the captured Scots towards London, where the Stadtholder (though he had not yet been crowned) was intent on revenging, by the lash and bullet, this signal instance of resistance to his authority. In consequence of this event, he had the first "Mutiny Act" framed, but being an edict of the English parliament, it could in no way apply to Scottish troops.

Aware of the *esprit de corps* and indomitable valour of the old musketeers, and fearful of revolt or rescue, De Ginckel sent Lieutenant Gavin, twenty other officers, and five hundred privates, in charge of Sir Marmaduke Langstone, direct to London, towards which place he marched the remainder by another route; keeping near his person and under sure escort, Lord Dunbarton, Walter Fenton, Finland, and other officers, whose hostility of spirit was more undisguised than their comrades, De Ginckel advanced some miles in rear of the main body of his Black Horsemen. The earl was destined for the Tower of London; Walter and his brothers in misfortune for the cells of Newgate.

In every town and village through which they were marched, dense mobs of "the rascal multitude" attended and loaded them with every insult and opprobrium, such as the vulgar, the cruel, and the wicked are ever ready to hurl upon the fallen or the unfortunate. Marrowbones and cleavers were clattered around them; effigies of King James, and a figure meant to represent a Scotchman, were carried or kicked along the streets before them, and, amid yells and hootings, *warming-pans* were everywhere displayed from the windows at their approach; at that time a famous mode of insulting the Jacobites, being a palpable hit against the legitimacy of the young prince of Wales.

"Fie upon the Scots! Out upon thee, mon! No warming-pan king! William for ever, and down to hell with all Scots, papists, and massmongers! Hurrah!" yelled the rabble on every hand, while vollies of mud, stones, dead cats, &c., were showered on them from every hand. Meanwhile their Dutch escort rode on each side with the most phlegmatic indifference, every man seeming as if fast asleep in his voluminous breeches and wide jack-boots.

"Down with the race of Gog—the soldiers of the priests of Baal!" cried an old puritan; "down with Scots Jemmy and his cursed Jesuits!"

Weak and exhausted by constant marching, lack of food and sleep, dispirited by misfortune, and disfigured by mud and their torn and soiled attire, in the captives no one could have recognized the dashing cavaliers who passed northward a day or two before. They had all been deprived of their horses and arms, and been robbed of everything of value— their cuirasses, purses, rings, &c.,—by their guard. De Ginckel was as brutal and merciless as a Carrib Indian, and repeatedly struck the unfortunate cavaliers with his speaking-trumpet.

"Ach Gott!" he often cried to his Ruyters; "if von ob de brisoners escape, ye shall answer for him, body for body, by cast ob dice on de kettle-trum-head!"

"My good comrades, and gallant gentlemen," said the earl of Dunbarton to the little group that marched around him, "were it not that I feel in my heart assured that an hour of vengeance and retribution will come, I would die of sheer spleen and mortification, for the insults we are compelled to put up with."

"I pity these bluff-headed Saxon boors, because they know no better," replied Walter, staggering, as a stone struck him on the temple; "but De Ginckel——"

"My dear fellow," said Finland, bitterly, "'tis a sample of the good old southern hospitality and kindness of which we hear so much in romance, and so little in history."

"But," continued Walter, "I despise these poppy-headed Dutch poltroons in their black iron doublets, and would risk my share of heaven to have De Ginckel under my hands on Scottish ground, with none to interfere, and no weapons but our rapiers and a case of good pistols."

"You speak my thoughts," said the earl, through his clenched teeth. "My malediction on Langstone and his Red Dragoons. Had they and such as they been good men and true, we had not been reduced to this misfortune; and our misguided king, instead of being a houseless fugitive, had dwelt in Windsor still, where now the usurping Stadtholder keeps court and council. Sirs, of a verity we live in strange times!"

As they had now crossed the Nen, had left behind old Peterborough (with the hoary fane where St. Oswald's bony arm worked miracles of old), and were marching through the open country, being free from the yells and missiles of the mob, they could converse with tolerable freedom, though at times De Ginckel thundered silence through his trumpet, or a Swart Ruyter, more waggish or wickedly inclined than his soporific comrades, pushed his horse sidelong to tumble one of the captives among the half-frozen mud that encumbered the roadways. Their mortification and dejection increased at every step of their retrograde march, and even the lively sallies of Dr. Joram failed to enliven them.

The sombre evening was closing, when De Ginckel, with his Ruyters and their captives, after traversing the fenny district between Cambridge and Lincoln, came in sight of Huntingdon, where, as Dr. Joram remarked, "the devil's god-son, that prime rascal, old Noll, first drew breath." The dying light of the winter sun tipped the spires of the ancient town-hall and the church of All Saints, and glimmered on the sluggish windings of the Ouse. The prisoners were pursuing a lonely road : on one side lay a thick copsewood, and on the other one of those wide and desolate fens then subject to the inundations of the Ouse, whose waters in many places formed deep and solitary meres or tarns. Within the recesses of the wood, the quick eye of Walter had soon detected the glitter of arms, to which he drew the attention of the earl.

" It matters not," replied the dejected noble, " no arms now glitter under James's standard; we are lost men, my dear lad. It will be black tidings for my little Lætitia, when the accursed Tower of London holds the last lord of Dunbarton."

" And what thinkest thou, Walter, our dear lassies will say when they hear we are in Newgate ? " asked Finland.

" 'Twill be rare news for the Lord Clermistonlee," replied Walter, in a fierce whisper. " But look, gentlemen !—behold ! In heaven's name, are these friends or foes ? "

As he spoke, a troop of horse, clad in brilliant armour, with their white plumes waving in the evening wind, and their long uplifted rapiers flashing in the setting sun, and all gallantly mounted on matchless black horses, filed forth from the copsee, and drew up like magic on the roadway, about a hundred yards in advance of the Swart Ruyters, who instantly reined up. One cavalier, splendidly accoutred, rode to the front, wheeled round his snorting horse that pawed the air, and issued his orders with stern rapidity—

" Gentlemen of the Scottish Guard, prepare to charge ! Uncase the standards ! Sound trumpets ! "

The banneroles were unfurled, the trumpets sounded, the kettle-drums ruffled, and each brave cavalier pressed forward in the saddle, as if impatient for the order to rush to the charge.

" Ach tuyfel ! " shouted De Ginckel through his trumpet ; " Scots Horse—der tuyfel ! Sabre de brisoners—cut dem into de towsand becies ! Fall on, you Schelms ! " But there was no time.

" 'Tis Claverhouse, and the remains of his regiment. I would know his black steed among a thousand horse ! " exclaimed the earl. " Now God be with thee, thou gallant Grahame, for at last our hour of vengeance is come ! Oh for a sword ! How gallantly they formed line ! Now, now ! forward, my Scottish hearts ! "

The dark eyes of the proud Douglas gleamed with fire, as

the deep and distinct order, "Cavaliers of the Life Guard—forward! *charge!*" burst from the lips of Dundee; and with the force of a whirlwind, the sixty Scottish Guardsmen, bridle to bridle and boot to boot, rushed with their uplifted swords to the onset.

"Unsling carbines—blow matches—fire!—tousand tuyfels!—no!—traw sworts!" bellowed De Ginckel through his trumpet, as the front rank of his Ruyters recoiled in confusion on the rear.

"Gentlemen, prepare to save yourselves!" exclaimed the earl of Dunbarton, as the Dutch troopers cast off the cords that bound the prisoners to their waist-belts.

"Heaven save us!" ejaculated Dr. Joram; "'tis a perilous case this, truly!"

"To the rescue, Claverhouse! A Grahame! A Grahame! God for Scotland and James VII.! To the devil with the Stadtholder! hurrah!" cried the Life Guards.

It was a critical moment for the dismounted prisoners, who were hemmed in among the hostile horsemen, and each felt his heart beat like lightning, and his breath come thick and fast, for death or deliverance were at hand.

Between the close files of the Swart Ruyters, Walter Fenton saw the full rush of the advancing troop, in their shining harness, and chief of all, the lordly viscount of Dundee, a lance-length in front, with his sword brandished aloft, and his white ostrich-feathers streaming behind him, his cheek glowing, and his wild dark eyes flashing with that supernatural brightness which was the true index of his fierce and heroic spirit. Though the Dutch were as four to one, the Scottish cavaliers were fearless.

There was a tremendous shock—a flashing of swords, as their keen edges rang on the tempered helmets and corslets of proof—a furious spurring of horses—and Walter felt himself beaten to the earth, as if by the force of a thunderbolt; the light left his eyes, and he heard the voice of Claverhouse exclaiming enthusiastically—

"Well done, my Scots' Life Guard! Well done, my berry-brown blades!"

"Come on, De Ginckel!" cried Holsterlee. "Hand to hand, old gorbelly. Come on! for here are the hand and sword that shall punch a hole in thine earl's patent!"

A heavy hoof struck the head of Walter, as a horse plunged over him, and the Dutch recoiled in utter confusion.

He remembered no more.

Hewn down by the long swords of the Ruyters, poor old Wemyss and Halbert Elshender lay dead beside him.

CHAPTER XLIV

THE SECRET STAIR.

Chloris ! since first our calm of peace
Was frighted hence, this good we find,
Your favours with your fears increase,
And growing mischiefs make you kind.
EDMUND WALLER.

HEAVILY and slowly passed the cloudy winter day at Clermiston, and evening found Lilian seated, full of tears and misery, by the great fire that rumbled in the arched chimney, and threw a ruddy glow on the rough architecture of the ancient hall. According to old etiquette, there were but two chairs, one for the lord of the manor and the other for his lady ; the additional seats were mere stools. Lilian occupied one of these chairs, and her suitor the other. On one of the stone benches within the ingle sat Juden Stenton, still trimming hawks' lures ; opposite was Beatrix, spinning with all the assiduity of Arachne. These from time to time regarded her with furtive glances, which roused her anger not less than the presence and odious attentions of their lord did her apprehension. She felt a load accumulating on her breast, as the night wore on ; anxiety was impairing her strength and weakening her fortitude, and whenever Clermistonlee addressed her, she answered only by tears. Touched at last by her sorrow, a sentiment of generosity at times would prompt him to return her to her home ; but other thoughts came with greater power, and the momentary weakness was immediately dismissed.

"Psha !" thought he ; "'tis only a woman."

Sitting close by her, he spoke from time to time in a low voice ; and the scorn, malice, and jealousy which lighted up the keen grey eyes and pinched features of the fallen and forgotten Beatrix on these occasions, filled the gentle Lilian with a horror and pity which she could not conceal. The presence of this unfortunate woman, who, with the indefatigable Juden, formed now his entire household, was a curb for the present on the vivacity of his lordship's passion, and seemed to restrain it within the decorous bounds of gentle whispering. He soon tired of that, and ordering supper to be laid, took advantage of the domestics' absence to draw his chair still nearer Lilian, and take her hands within his own. She was so humbled, so gentle and broken in spirit, that she permitted them to remain, and the passiveness of the action made the heart of Clermistonlee glow with additional ardour.

"She loves me in secret," thought he; "but how charming is her coyness — how enchanting her modesty! My dear Lilian——"

"My lord, oh cease to persecute me thus. What wrong have I done you? In what have I offended, that you should make me so utterly miserable?"

"What a soft, low, charming voice! Does it offend you, to hear the sighs of the most honourable love that ever warmed a human heart?"

"This is the mere cant of love-making—flirtation—the phrases you have addressed to hundreds. My lord, I know their full value, and despise them. 'Tis enough! I can have no love for you."

"Indeed!"

"None—so for heaven's sake spare me more of this humiliation, and let me begone to the house of Bruntisfield."

"Now what strange infatuation is this? No love for me?" mused the egotist. "Why, damsel, when I was in London with Charles, all the women were mad about me—I was quite the rage. Rochester and I led the way in everything. But that was before Bothwell Brig." He glanced at a veiled picture that often attracted his eye, and disturbed the current of his thoughts. "No love for me!" he resumed, after a pause. "My pretty one, does my zeal offend you?"

"Like your flattery, it does; and my captivity here—a captivity which, I fear, will ever be a stain upon my honour, makes me abhor you."

"Abhor? Oh! 'tis a word never said to me before. Provoking Lilian! But," he added, maliciously, "you are right —your honour is lost, and there is only one way to redeem it."

She gave him a momentary glance of inquiry and disdain. Clermistonlee drew a ring from his finger. Lilian started back.

"Never—never! death were better."

"Hah—then you are still thinking of him—this beggarly boy—this nameless soldier—this so-named Fenton. 'Tis a cursed infatuation, madam; for doubtless, soldierlike he will forget you, while the flower of your youth is wasted in fruitless reliance on his constancy and advancement to honour and fortune."

"Forget me?" reiterated Lilian, raising her bright blue eyes to the speaker. "Oh no, he never will forget me! Dear, dear Walter," she added, weeping bitterly; "I know thy worth and truth too well to lose my own."

"He *will* forget thee," said Clermistonlee, angrily.

"Never!" replied Lilian, energetically clasping her hands. "In the busy city, and on the lonely hills, in the hour of battle and storm by sea and land, he will ever think of me—ever, ever!"

"But he may be slain?" said the lord, maliciously.

"Cruel—cruel!"

"What then—hah?"

"No second choice would ever make me violate the solemn vow I pledged to him—that plight which I called on heaven to witness and angels to register."

Clermistonlee made no reply, but her fervour and her words stung him to the soul; her eyes sparkled and her usually pale cheek glowed; but he knew that it was for the love and by the recollection of another; his first thoughts were those of wrath; his second spleen and sorrow. He arose and stepped aside a little.

"Unfortunate that I am!" said he, with something of sadness and real love in his tone and manner. "By what witchcraft am I so hateful to her; but I must quit her presence for a time at least, or lose all hope of her favour for ever."

He walked to and fro, while Lilian, resigned again to tears, covered her face with her handkerchief.

"Beatrix," said Clermistonlee, in a fierce whisper to the shrinking woman, as she laid supper on the long dark oaken board, over which six tall waxen candles flared from a great iron candelabrum. "Beatrix Gilruth—hear me, old shrivel-skin! Hast never a love-philtre about thee? Ere now I have known thee to my own cost use such things."

She gave a keen and fierce glance with her sunken eyes, and drawing him into one of the deeply-bayed windows, pointed to where the square keep and round towers of the castle of Corstorphine threw a long dark shadow across the frozen lake that, like a mirror before its gates, lay shining in the cold light of the winter moon.

"You see yonder castle?" she said.

"Yes."

"And the aged sycamore beside the dovecot-tower?"

"Yes—yes."

"Then remember how, nine years ago, the lord of that fair mansion perished under its shadow; and how his own good rapier, urged by the hand of the woman he had wronged, was driven—yea, to the very hilt—in his false and fickle heart. Often at mirk midnight have I seen the dead-light glimmering on his tomb in St. John's kirk, and illuminating the west window of the Foresters' aisle."

She gave him a glance so expressive of hatred, fear, contempt, and reproach, that he almost quailed beneath it ; and as she pointed to the veiled portrait, he turned abruptly away. Her words and allusion had evidently a deep effect on Clermistonlee. He was about to retire, but paused irresolutely, turned, and paused again. Then kissing Lilian's hand, he said in a gentle tone—

"Forgive me if I have offended, but love for you makes me perhaps act unwisely. Adieu, dear Lilian : if my presence is obnoxious, I hasten to relieve you of it. Till to-morrow, adieu ; and pleasant dreams to you."

He bowed profoundly, and retired to his own apartment followed by Juden, who kept close to his heels, as a spaniel would have done.

"Will you not sup, Madam Lilian ? " asked Beatrix in a kinder tone than usual.

"Sup—oh, no ! "

"Bethink you, lady ; the whole day hath passed, and you have tasted nothing but a posset of milk with a little sack. Still weeping ! 'Twas so with me once ; but I shall never weep again, until I have wrung tears of blood from my betrayer."

"Now you are going to frighten me again. A light, if it please you, good woman ; I will retire. Another night under his roof ! My poor aunt Grizel   how bad, how wicked is this ! "

"My lord desired me to ask if you wished to read a little : it may compose your mind."

"Oh, yes !—a thousand thanks, kind Beatrix. Bring me a Bible, if you have one."

Beatrix laughed.

"A Bible ! when was one last seen in the tower of Clermiston ? Not since the days of auld Mess John, I warrant ; and his was torn up by the troopers for cartridges. There is nothing here but a rowth of evil play and jest books, and some anent hawking, hunting, and farriery ; and others, my bairn, that suit only—women like me."

"Poor Beatrix ! " said Lilian kindly, touching her hand, for the exceeding humility of her manner raised all her pity. Beatrix surveyed her for a moment, with a troubled and dubious expression. Seldom was it that a word of compassion or commiseration fell upon her ear. Her heart was touched ; a moisture suffused her eyes ; but fearing to betray her feelings through the outward aspect of moroseness and misanthropy she had assumed, she set a light upon the cabinet of the bedchamber, and hurried away.

Again, as on the preceding night, Lilian fastened the door; and though the number and complication of its ancient iron locks somewhat reassured her, her heart sank when she surveyed the great gloomy tester-bed, with its dais, its solemn plumage and festooned canopy—the sombre wainscoting, and well-barred window, past which the changing clouds were hurrying in scudding masses, alternately obscuring and revealing stars. Kneeling at a chair near the fire, she prayed long and fervently, and, with innocent confidence, arose more assured and courageous, though aware that, by anxiety, want of food and rest, her natural strength and spirit were greatly impaired. A folio volume lay upon the cabinet; it was covered with purple velvet, on which a coat-of-arms and these words were exquisitely embroidered:—"Alison, Lady Clermistonlee, on her marriage-day, ye penult Maij, 1668."

The hand of her tormentor's unhappy wife had probably worked these words: all the dark and mysterious stories concerning her misfortunes and her fate came crowding upon the mind of Lilian, and filled her with melancholy forebodings. Perhaps, thought she, this was her chamber, and that her bed, where often she had wept away the dreary night in unseen and unregarded sorrow. Full of mournful interest, she unclasped and opened the volume. It was the *Bentivolio and Urania* of Nathaniel Ingelo, one of the prosy and metaphorical romances of the seventeenth century. The first words arrested her, and she read on:—

"He was no sooner entered within the borders of the forlorn kingdom of Ate, than the unhealthfulness of the air had almost choked his vital spirits; and being removed from the gladsome sun by a chain of hills, that lifted up their heads so high that they intercepted the least glance of his comfortable beams: it was dark and rueful. He chanced to light upon a path that led to Ate's house, which was encompassed with the pitchy shade of cypresse and ebon-trees, so that it looked like the region of death. As he walked, he perceived the hollow pavement made with the skulls of murdered wretches. At the further end of this dismal walk he espied a court, whose gates stand open day and night; in the midst whereof was placed the image of cruelty, with a cup of poyson in one hand, and a dagger wet with reeking bloode in the other. Her hairs crawled up and down her neck, and sometimes wreathed about her head in knots of snakes; fire all the while sparkling from her mouth and eyes   ."

This dismal passage in no way tended to alleviate the perturbation of her spirits; and hastily closing the volume, she prepared to retire. Aware that proper repose was absolutely

necessary to enable her to sustain all she might have to encounter or endure from Clermistonlee, remembering the
apparent security of her apartment, and somewhat reassured
by the cheerful blaze thrown by the fire upon the dark brown
panelling and high old-fashioned bed, she slowly and reluctantly began to undress, often pausing to re-examine her
room; but perceiving nothing more to alarm her: gathering
up the bright tresses of her hair into a caul, she unrobed and
sprang into bed. The sleep and the heaviness that preyed
upon her now completely evaporated: and more awake than
ever, she felt only the keenest sensations of fear, and her
prevailing horror was Clermistonlee. By the light of the
wood fire, that poured its broad blaze up the massive stone
chimney, she surveyed the room with watchful eyes, that
ached from the very intensity of their gaze, and the shadows
of the carved posts seemed like those of giants thrown against
the panelled wall.

Weariness overcame her, and she was about to drop asleep,
when a sound was heard, and one of the doors of the cabinet
rattled and opened; a cold wind blew upon her face; and by
her recumbent position, she beheld a steep staircase winding
away down into darkness she knew not where, between the
masonry of the massive wall. She would have screamed,
but terror chained her tongue; and almost fainting, and
afraid to move or breathe, she continued to regard it with the
most painful anguish and intense alarm. But up that dark
and mysterious outlet, so suddenly disclosed, no sound came
but the night wind, which moved the oak-door of the cabinet
mournfully to and fro.

Lilian's strength seemed utterly to have left her; and,
though painfully anxious to learn the secrets of this staircase,
which communicated so immediately with her bedchamber,
she lacked equally strength to rise, and presence of mind to
examine it.

But the current of air that swayed the door to and fro,
closed it; the sound rumbled away in the far echoes of the
tower, and all became still. Now more alarmed by the reflection that she was sleeping in this remote room alone, with
a secret entrance, she bitterly regretted her imprudence in
undressing, but had not the courage to rise and repair what
a certain prophetic apprehension made her fear had been very
unwise.

Excessive lassitude at last completely overcame her, and
she slumbered.

CHAPTER XLV

THE ATTEMPT.

Once in a lone and secret hour of night,
When every eye was closed, and the pale moon
And stars alone shone conscious of the theft,
Hot with the Tuscan grape, and high in blood,
Haply I stole unheeded to her chamber.
                              FAIR PENITENT.

WHEN Clermistonlee retired from the hall to the study or parlour, which was the only comfortably-furnished apartment in the dreary old tower, he resigned himself to reflection, and sipping his mulled sack, a great tankard of which Juden placed unbidden, and quite as a matter of course, at his elbow. His thoughts at first ran in the usual channel,—a determination to possess Lilian, from the double incentives of passion and pecuniary necessity. He was on the brink of ruin ; and her property, or expectations of it, were ample and noble. She was very unprotected ; the land was convulsed and trembling on the verge of a great civil war, though as yet no tidings had reached Edinburgh of what was passing in England ; and so, as the sack diminished in the tankard, his lordship's thoughts became in proportion more strange, more amorous, and confused. His brain wandered. He was restless and uneasy ; his flowing dressing-gown seemed to fit him like a horse-hair shirt ; and his disturbed manner was not unobserved by his faithful and subservient factotum.

The latter attempted some consolation, after his fashion ; but it was not palatable.

" Begone to the bartizan ! " exclaimed his master, angrily, " and bring me instant tidings if anything seems astir in the country about us. I expect news from the city hourly. Leave me."

Juden vanished.

" The deevil tak' lovers and lords ! " he muttered, as he drew his broad worsted bonnet over his cross visage, and ascended to the bartizan of the tower, and setting his teeth hard, as he faced the keen north wind, took a survey of the dreary and snow-covered landscape. On the passing wind ten o'clock came sullenly from the spire of St. John of Corstorphine ; then all was deathly still, save the sough of the winter breeze as it swept over the dreary lee, and whistled through the open corbels of the projecting tower.

Juden had no particular fancy for enacting the part of warder in so cold a night, and after taking a rapid survey of the extensive waste, he was about to descend again, when an unusual redness in the sky to the eastward arrested him. It rose in the direction of the city, and resembled the lurid and wavering glow of a great conflagration. The red blaze was rapidly spreading and crimsoning the edges of the dusky clouds above, and throwing forward in strong relief the southern edge of the Corstorphine Hills, and the dark pines that shaded them. Astonished, perplexed, and alarmed, Juden continued to gaze in the direction of the light, until a loud holla startled him, and he perceived a man on horseback close to the foot of the tower.

" Ho !" cried Juden through his hand, for the wind blew keen and high. "What want ye, friend ?"

" No a night's lodging, or I wadna come here," answered the other testily. " Closed gates and dark windows betoken cauld cheer and a caulder ingle."

" Beware o' your tongue, friend," replied the butler from aloft. " Langer lugs than yours hae been nailed to the tower yett. You have come frae Edinburgh, I warrant ?"

" Troth have I, on the spur, man, so open the yett, Juden Stenton."

" What's a' the steer there this night ?"

" Gif you had been there ye wad ken," responded the other with sulky importance. " I bear a letter for my Lord Clermistonlee on the king's service, *which* king Gude kens and the deil cares."

" Thir are kittle times, friend," replied the butler, warily ; " so if King James himsel' came to the peel o' Clermiston this mirk night, not a bolt would be drawn, or a lock undone. Tie the letter to this twine, gossip, and sae gang your way in peace."

Rendered cautious by the nature of the times, and by being constantly on the alert against force and treachery, the wary old servitor lowered over the wall a string, to which after sundry curses the horseman tied a letter, and Juden towed it up, "hand over hand."

" Ill folk are aye feared," said the stranger ; " and I doubt there are but few clear consciences in Clermistonlee. My horse is sair forfoughton wi' my ride frae the West-port ; he fell at the Foulbrigs, and was nigh swept awa, when fording the Leith doon by there ; but I maun een ride on to his honour the laird o' Niddry without a stirrup cup or a ' God save ye. Out upon Clermiston and its ill-mannered loons !" and dashing spurs into his horse, the servant galloped at a hunting pace away to the westward, and disappeared among the hollows at the verge of the Lee.

Anxious to learn the contents of a letter in which he doubted not he had as much interest as his lord, Juden hurried down the corkscrew stair from the bartizan, and repairing to the little study where his half-muddled master was gazing dreamily into the fire, and imbibing his sixth cup of sack, he placed the little square billet before him. Clermistonlee tore it open, and read hurriedly,

"Dear Gossip,

"A glorious revolution hath been accomplished, (and I am just drinking to its success in sugared brandy), but Satan seems to have broken loose in the city, whilk the rascal sort hath fired in six different places. The acts of estate and council are mere nullities. Your presence is required by the council anent ane address to the new king. We are to have a grand onslaught to-morrow against Baal's prophets, the host of Pharaoh, and a' that, ye ken.

"Yrs. at service,

"MERSINGTON."

"*Postscriptum.*—Keep the bonnie bird in the cage close; her kinsman Napier hath been slain by young Fenton, and ye know how the entail stands. Vale! King William the Second of Scotland for ever!"

Clermistonlee's first impulse was to start up and buckle on his sword, exclaiming,

"My gambadoes, Juden; the red leather ones—saddle Meg, and, peril of thy life, look well to—but no—no! I will not. Thou mayest go to the devil, Mersington, with thy drunken scrawl, the address, and the council to boot. I leave not Clermiston to-night. Napier slain—and by Fenton! By George, how the plot is thickening! 'Tis glorious. Juden, don your shabble, and ride to the city; tell my gossip Mersington in the *matter* pending, mark me, knave! in the matter pending to use my name as he shall deem fitting."

Juden replied by a leer of deep cunning (for he too was something of a politician), and, animated by an intense curiosity to know what was acting in the city, hurried away, and in ten minutes had left far behind him the dreary tower and frozen muir, above which its dark outline reared like that of a spectre.

As the fumes of the wine mounted upward, the heated imagination and inflamed passions of Clermistonlee got completely the better of his senses. Thoughts of Lilian's beauty and helplessness came vividly before him ; but such reflections instead of kindling his pity, roused all his passion for her to an ungovernable height. Draining a cup of brandy to make him yet more reckless of consequences, and snatching a candle, he staggered from the room, and descended the narrow stone stair that led from his apartment.

He knew that he was alone, for Beatrix was under lock and key ; yet he stepped with singular caution. Every stone in the rough walls seemed a grotesque face, regarding him with mockery and wrath ; he saw a figure in every shadow, heard a step in every whistle of the midnight wind. He dared not look at portraits as he passed, lest their eyes might seem to move ; and thus, though the entire consciousness of his dark intent came broadly and appallingly home to his heart, such was the influence of his ungoverned passions that a spirit of the merest obstinacy urged him to finish what he in part commenced, and the high pulsations of his heart increased at every step which brought him nearer to the chamber of his victim.

He entered the hall. The feeble rays of his upheld candle seemed only to reveal the size and darkness of the place, and the grey winter twilight that struggled through its thickly grated and deeply-arched windows. The embers of the fire still smouldered on the hearth, and, reddening when the hollow wind rumbled down the wide chimney, threw the shadows of the great oaken table, the dark grotesque cabinets and highbacked chairs in long and frightful figures on the paved floor.

Entering the almonry, he opened a door, within it, which revealed a narrow passage in the wall that communicated with the secret outlets of the place, and led directly to the *cabinet* in Lilian's room.

He stood within it, and the warmth of its atmosphere increased the ferment of his blood. Unconscious of the proximity of so dangerous a visitor, the innocent girl slept soundly, but lightly.

Shading the light with his hand, he gazed impatiently upon the slumbering beauty.

Her hair, which overnight she had put up with the carelessness so natural to grief, had now escaped from the caul, and rolled over the pillow in masses that glittered like gold in the rays of the uncertain light. She was very pale, but a slight glow began to redden her cheek, and it was graced with a smile of inexpressible sweetness.

Twice he approached, and twice drew back irresolute

·An unseen hand seemed to restrain him; the air of perfect innocence pervading the presence of the sleeping girl protected her for a time; and scarcely daring to breathe, the intruder continued to gaze upon her. She slept softly. At last, tears fell over her cheeks, and she tenderly murmured—

"Dear Walter, have I not said that I love you?"

Clermistonlee, on whose bent-down cheek her soft breath came, started at these words as if a serpent had stung him. One of those fierce, malicious, and scornful smiles, which so often imparted to his handsome features a fiendish expression, contracted them but for a moment; another of intense sadness and languor replaced it. At that instant, unable longer to restrain himself, he clasped her in his arms.

"Lilian!" he exclaimed, "dear Lilian, be not alarmed—it is I."

A piercing shriek, that startled the furthest recesses of the old and desolate tower, burst from the lips of Lilian; it was one of those deep and wailing cries of pain and horror which, when once heard, are never forgot.

"Villain, unhand me! Oh! spare me, my lord—spare me for the love of God!"

"Be calm, Lilian—why should you fear me? Do I not adore you? Yes; I prize your love beyond the possession of life. Dear girl, look not on me thus. I am the most devoted of lovers, and by this kiss, dearest——d—nation!"

He attempted to kiss her; but, endued with new strength by rage and fear, her little hands clutched fiercely his thick moustaches, and twisted his head aside, as she had done once before so effectually.

"Hear me!" he continued, "hear me, sweet Lilian; I came but to say that I loved thee——."

"Love me! oh! horror!—leave me, or I shall expire—leave me!"

At that moment a loud explosion, followed by the fanfare of trumpets and the ruffling of kettle-drums beneath the walls of the tower, arrested all the faculties of Clermistonlee, and by throwing his thoughts into another channel, covered him with shame; and he started back, the image of astonishment and irresolution.

Not so Lilian; her presence of mind was instantly restored. Springing to a window, and fearlessly dashing her hands through the panes of glass, she cried in agonized accents—

"Help! help! for the love of the blessed God! Help me, or I perish!"

"Lilian! Lilian!" cried a voice that filled her with transport. It was that of Walter Fenton.

A glance sufficed to show her a gallant troop of horse halted beneath the tower in the grey morning twilight. Again she would have spoken, but the strong hand of Clermistonlee dragged her furiously back into the apartment.

CHAPTER XLVI.

EDINBURGH—THE NIGHT OF THE REVOLUTION.

Meanwhile, regardless of the royal cause,
His sword for James no brother sov'reign draws.
The Pope himself, surrounded with alarms,
To France his bulls, to Corfu sends his arms;
And though he hears his darling son's complaint,
Can hardly spare one tutelary saint.

TICKELL, *Edit* 1749.

FROM the hour in which Lilian had been torn from her, the aged Lady Grizel had never raised her head. Affection and horror, wrath and insulted pride, had all aggravated to the utmost the weakness and debility consequent to exceeding old age; and by her weeping domestics the venerable dame was borne to her great chair in the chamber-of-dais, where she remained long insensible to all that passed around her.

The storm and hurry of political events employed otherwise Sir Thomas Dalyel and those friends who might have served her in this dilemma; and now she found herself quite deserted.

Syme, the baillie, and the whole male population of the barony, had fruitlessly searched the Burghmuir for the remainder of the night and morning; but, for reasons which will shortly be apparent, any application to the privy council or magistrates of Edinburgh would have been utterly futile, as their attention was amply occupied by more important matters than the abduction of a girl.

Long fits of stupor, succeeded by querulous bursts of passion, left the poor old lady so weak, that, as Elsie related to Sir Thomas of Binns, "between the night and morning, she cried on Sir Archibald *to save* her doo Lilian; and then she just soughed awa like a blink o' the sunshine, and lay back under her canopy in the chaumer-o'-deese, a comely corpse to see as ever was streekit."

The old lady did not die, however, but recovered her sense by having a pistol fired at her ear by the rough old Muscovite trooper, "a cure for the vapours, whilk," he said, "he had often seen practised on Samoieda."

As before related, in consequence of the vigilance of Sir

James Montgomerie, the privy council and people of Scotland had been kept for several weeks in a state of painful uncertainty as to the fate of James's affairs in England; but a letter from Lord Dundee reached the Scottish ministry, expressive of apprehensions for the issue of a conflict between the troops of the king and those of his invader.

To ascertain the true aspect of affairs, they despatched into England a man named Brand, a baillie of Edinburgh, who basely betrayed his trust by carrying his despatches straight to the prince of Orange, to whom he was introduced by Dr. Burnet.

On Craigdarroch's arrival at the Scottish capital, and others with similar tidings of the desertion and dissolution of the army, the flight of James, and success of William, the long threatening storm burst forth in all its fury. Scotland at that time swarmed with brave and hardy soldiers, skilful officers, ruined barons, and desperate vassals—the veterans of the covenant, and the endless wars of Sweden, France, and Flanders; thus, ingloriously as the campaign had passed over in the south, a cloud was gathering on the Highland hills, that threatened to descend, as of yore, in wrath and blood on the fertile Lowlands.

Infuriated by the severities of what was called the "twenty-eight years' persecution," the Lowland population were ripe for armed revolt, and the capital, to which they flocked in overwhelming masses, became the grand centre of their operations, and the scene of newer atrocities. The greatest outrages were committed upon the persons and property of those unhappy catholics, episcopalians, and cavaliers, who fell into the hands of this wild mob.

Perth, the lord chancellor, fled; the privy council, which had been severe to the nation, in proportion as it was servile to James, despatched an immediate address to William, and none were more cordial in their offers of dutiful service than Provost Prince, and the worthy council of Edinburgh; those very men who had so lately declared to the unfortunate Stuart, that they "would stand by his sacred person on all occasions." Now they were equally prompt in offers to his dethroner, to whom they complained bitterly " of the hellish attempts of Romish incendiaries, and of the just grievances of all men, relating to conscience, liberty, and property."

For three days the capital was in the power of a mad and lawless rabble, who, rendered furious by bigotry and intoxication, committed the most dreadful atrocities.

The houses of all who were obnoxious to them were plundered and given to the flames, and all effects of value were scattered in the streets. There were episodes of horror ensued such as Edinburgh had never witnessed before. The streets were filled with the smoke of burning houses; the air was sheeted with flame; the shrieks of the perishing inmates, the howls of their destroyers, and the crash of falling masonry, rang night and day. The college of the Jesuits was levelled to the dust; crosses and relics, statues, pictures, and vestments were borne aloft through the streets, and consigned to the flames amid yells of derision.

The ale and wine found in the cellars of the cavaliers inflamed the inborn savagism of the multitude, who were urged by their ministers to commit a thousand nameless atrocities. For three days they continued in a state of perfect intoxication (says Lord Balcarris in his " Memoirs"), and in open daylight, in the crowded streets of the city, committed upon the persons of many catholic ladies such outrages as cannot be written, and "without any attempt being made by the authorities to restrain such brutality." (Pp. 22, 27.)

Of all the members of the old government, none was more obnoxious to the people than Sir George Mackenzie, of Rosehaugh, the celebrated lawyer and essayist, who had rendered himself an object of intense hatred by the severity with which he had stretched the criminal laws to answer the views of the government; and who, in his office of public prosecutor, had obtained the unenviable soubriquet of " the persecutor of God's saints," " the blood-thirsty advocate," " bluidy Mackenzie;" and to this hour his vaulted mausoleum at Edinburgh is regarded with hatred and loathing by the old Cameronians and "true-blue" presbyterians.

His mansion in Rosehaugh-close was soon made the object of attack. The night of the third day had closed over the city, and still the scene of tumult and frenzy, the din and the flames of destruction loaded the air with sounds of horror and outrage.

In great anxiety for his personal safety, the unhappy statesman heard with no ordinary perturbation the increasing roar of sounds, like the chafing of a distant sea; the mingling of a myriad human voices, and the rush of feet, which betokened the approach of a vast mob.

With drums beating before them, and armed with various weapons, the thousand bright points of which gleamed in the lurid blaze of the uplifted torches, a dense mass of ragged, squalid, and insane-looking men, poured like a human flood into the deep and narrow alley, at the foot of which still stands the house of Rosehaugh. Begrimed with smoke and filth, maddened by intoxication and excess, their yells, as they resounded between the solid walls of the narrow street, rang like those of fiends from some deep abyss, and the heart of Mackenzie died away within him. To appeal to their pity would be like craving mercy from the waves of an angry ocean; there was no escape, no remedy, no bribe, no hope; for among that terrible mob were the fathers, the sons, the brothers—yea, and the mothers—of those who at his instance had perished in thousands, by the sword, by the torture, and the gibbet, or were lingering out a miserable existence as slaves and bondsmen in the distant Indies.

"My God! my God! for what am I reserved?" he exclaimed, as from a lofty upper window he surveyed the dense mass of madmen, who, wedged in the alley below, impeded each other's motions. Conspicuous above all, raised on the shoulders of two strong men, whose arms and faces were smeared with blood and blackness, there was upborne a man, whose sad-coloured garments and white bands announced him a preacher; his gaunt visage and long hair of raven hue waving around a face ghastly, though flushed with passion, his large hazel eyes glowing like those of a tiger, his upraised hands clenching one a Bible, and the other a broadsword, declared him a wild enthusiast (another "Habakuk Mucklewrath").

It was Ichabod Bummel, who had escaped from the damp vaults of the wave-beaten Bass, and had now come to take vengeance on Mackenzie for his exile, his captivity, his crushed bones, and long persecution.

"Come forth, Achan, thou troubler of Israel!" he shrieked; "come forth, thou destroyer of the good and just, thou persecutor of the saints of God! come forth, thou thing that art accursed, or we will burn thee in the ruins of thy dwelling, and salt them with salt. Courage, my brethren! Oh, is not this a brave hour and a glorious one? For lo, the time is come when the host of Pharaoh shall be discomfited and striken as of old. Achan, thou persecutor of the covenanted kirk, behold me towering amid Baal's prophets, four hundred and fifty men, as the book saith!"

This rhapsody was responded to with yells of ardour, and the din of hammers rang like thunder against the strong oaken door of the mansion, while many bullets were discharged at the windows, which were securely grated. A door of massive oak closed the entrance of the turnpike stair, and though the whole house resounded under the energy of the blows, the barrier refused to yield, though gradually it was falling in splinters, a process too slow to suit the fierce impatience of the increasing mob.

" Let fire be brought," cried Ichabod, "let the mansion be consumed, that its flames may be as a light to the house of Judah. Know, O thou persecutor of God's covenanted saints, that a sword is this night upon the inhabitants of Babylon, and upon her princes, and her mighty men; for it is the load of graven images, and they are mad upon their idols."

Urged by this blasphemous application of Scripture, burning brands were heaped by the people against the door, and soon the increased yells of satisfaction announced to the miserable advocate that the barrier was rapidly giving way, and that in another moment the reeking hands of the destroyers would be upon him. He threw round a glance of agony, the barred windows denied all hope of escape, and now his stern soul sank at the prospect of a cruel and immediate death, when lo! one tremendous yell of another import brought him once more to the shattered windows. "It is a dream!" he exclaimed.

A troop of the Royal Life Guards, with their bright arms flashing in the light of the waving torches, were hewing and treading down the mob like a field of rye; and chief above all shone one cavalier—it was Dundee—the gallant, the terrible Claver'se, that man-fiend, whom all deemed six hundred miles away. There was no mistaking the splendour of his armour, the nobility of his air, the ferocity of his purpose.

"Close up—fall on, gentlemen; no quarter to the knaves!" he exclaimed, while, standing erect in his stirrups, he showered his blows on every side, his white plumes rising and falling in unison with his trenchant rapier.

"Hey for King James! Ho for the cavaliers! Down with the rebels—down with the whigamores!" cried Holsterlee and others, as they pressed forward, and the rabble grovelled in the dust beneath the tremendous rush of the heavy horses, and their riders in steel and buff. In a minute the narrow alley was cleared of the living, and piled knee-deep with dead and dying. The shrill voice of Ichabod, as he was borne off by his disciples, was heard dying away in the distance, like that of an evil spirit carried away by a stormy wind.

By something like a miracle, Lord Dundee had traversed the whole of hostile England, and though menaced on every hand by great bodies of troops, had reached his native capital in safety; bringing with him not only the sixty cavalier troopers (who of all his cavalry alone remained stanch to him), but with them Walter Fenton, Lord Dunbarton, Finland, and other officers retaken from De Ginckel. They now rode under his orders as gentlemen-troopers, mounted on heavy black chargers that had whilome belonged to the Swart

Ruyters; and the whole, with standards displayed, had entered the city about an hour before the assault on Rosehaugh's house.

The reverend Dr. Joram, late chaplain to the Royal Scots, also bestrode a horse which he had taken as his spoil in battle; and had donned a trooper's corslet, with which his clerical bob-periwig consorted as oddly as with the fierce and tipsy expression of his flushed and florid face, and with the stern cock of the Monmouth beaver that surmounted it. The gallant divine had recently imbibed so much wine that he could scarcely keep his saddle.

Of the fate of their captured comrades they as yet knew nothing; but Gavin of that ilk, with twenty other officers and five hundred men, were then at London, close prisoners; the rest had returned to their colours; and after a time, the whole seeing the futility of resistance, ultimately embarked peaceably under the orders of their new commander, the veteran duke de Schomberg. None were punished, "as the new government had not yet been fully recognized in Scotland."

Rosehaugh had been saved from a terrible immolation; but the services of the night were not yet over. Claverhouse, with his cavaliers, retired to a quiet part of the city, under protection of the castle batteries, where a brave garrison of catholic soldiers, led by the duke of Gordon, remained yet stanch to James.

"My lord earl," said Dundee to Dunbarton, "we must be somewhat economical of our persons and horses, when encountering these mad burghers and drunken saints, and not forget that we are the last hope of the king in this hotbed of presbytery and rebellion."

"True," replied the earl, "and I rejoice that we have but few to regret, and few to mourn for us if we perish in the struggle on which we are about to plunge."

The eyes of the viscount filled with dusky fire.

"Dunbarton," said he, "I am alone in the world. Our grateful king has given me honours to which none can succeed, for I have cast the die by which they are lost for ever; and nowhere can my coronet be more gloriously surrendered than on the battle-field."

"I thank Heaven that the countess, my dear little Lætitia, is in England," said the earl, pointing to the lurid flames that from the blazing houses of the Abbey-hill flashed along the shadowy vista of the Canongate, glowing redly under the arch of the Netherbow, and throwing forward in bold relief a thousand fantastic projections of the old Flemish mansions that reared up their giant fronts on either hand. "I thank

Heaven that she is in a safer place than this poor city of wild fanatics."

"Would that I could say the same of Lilian!" thought Walter, with a deep sigh. "Can she be safe amid all this dreadful uproar?"

At that moment a dense rabble approached, with drums beating, torches blazing, and weapons glinting.

"To the palace! to the abbey!" cried a thousand hoarse voices. "Let us pull doon the temple of the idolater, and gie his fause gods to the flames!" and they swept forward, greeting the troop of guards with yells of hatred and menace.

They were led—by whom? Lord Mersington, with his wig awry, his clothes soiled with dust, and his face flushed with exertion! The earl of Balcarris relates "that this fanatical judge, with a halbert in his hand, and drunk as ale and brandy could make him," led on the rabble to the assault of time-hallowed Holyrood; but before reaching the eastern extremity of the city, his followers were joined by the trained bands in their buff coats and bandoliers, the magistrates, and other authorities, who vested this lawless mob with an air of order and official importance.

"Will those villains really dare to molest the palace of our kings?" said Dundee, his eyes kindling, as he looked after the revolters, and reined up his impatient horse.

"What will they not dare?" rejoined Dunbarton; "but I doubt not they will experience a warm reception. Wallace, who commands the guard, is a brave cavalier as ever drew sword, and the traitors will make nothing of it."

"Under favour, my lords," said Fenton, "they are in great numbers, and I have misgivings as to the issue."

"Wallace—he is an old friend of mine," said Finland. "'Sdeath! we've seen some sharp work together on the frontiers of Flanders; and with your permission, my lords, I will take a turn of service with him to-night."

"As you please," replied the viscount; "Dunbarton commands here, though he rides in my troop. Go—ha, ha! two heads are better than one."

"I go, then; and yonder fanatical senator may beware how he comes within reach of my hand."

"Thy riding-whip, say rather."

"I volunteer also," said Walter, who was under great anxiety to have an opportunity of visiting Lilian.

"And I too," added the reverend Jonadab Joram. "I long to encounter with Bible and bilbo, yonder preacher of sedition, that urges on this unhanged rout of traitors. For know ye, gentlemen, (hiccup) that one preacher is better in Scotland than twenty drummers to find recruits for the devil's service; so, in his own phraseology, I will gird up my loins, and g' forth to battle against them. Come on, gallants! Ho, for King James, and down with the whigamores! Rub-a-dub rub-a-dub——"

"Beware, sirs, for the good cause has not many such spirits to spare," said Claver'se, as they dashed spurs into their horses, and making a detour down one narrow wynd and up another, reached, without interruption, the deep-groined arch-way of the palace porch, an ancient gothic edifice, heavily turreted and battlemented.

CHAPTER XLVII.

SACK OF HOLYROOD.

'Twas a dream of the ages of darkness and blood,
When the ministers' home was the mountain and wood;
The musquets were flashing, the blue swords were gleaming,
The helmets were cleft, and the red blood was streaming;
The heavens grew dark, and the thunder was rolling,
When on Welwood's dark muirland the mighty were falling.
ANONYMOUS.

"WELCOME, gentlemen," exclaimed Wallace; "I never stood in such need of advice and comradeship."

He was a handsome man, above six feet in height; his gold-coloured cuirass and buff coat, laced with silver, announced him a captain; the slouch of his broad Spanish hat, with its drooping plumes, and the tie of his voluminous white silk scarf, gave him inimitable grace.

"Welcome, Finland, to share the poor cheer and hard-fighting of Holyrood. By Mahoud! but times are changed with the king's soldiers. I have endured a three days' siege here, and matters are not likely to mend."

"No; a rabble, many thousands strong, by all the devils! the very riddlings of St. Ninian's and the Beggar's-row, are at this moment approaching, and if one of your guard be left alive by daylight it will be a miracle."

"Dost think so?" rejoined Wallace, as he led them to a table in the outer court of the palace, where a lantern placed on a table revealed a few drinking-horns, a keg of eau de vie, and some objects of a more unpleasant nature, the dead bodies of several soldiers, shot by the rioters during the day. "You hold out a dark future to us, Finland, and, nevertheless, like the true soldier I have ever known thee, come to take a turn of service with us,"

"As you see," replied Finland, laughing, as he filled a horn from the keg unbidden.

"Drink with me, gentlemen," said Wallace.

"With all my soul!" hiccupped Dr. Joram.

"This keg of brandy was lately in the cellars of the Jesuits, and some friendly rogue trundled it our way. God bless the good old cause! my service to ye, sirs. Hark, comrades—drums!" he added, as he drained and threw down the cup.

"'Tis the march of the trained bands," said Walter.

"Indeed!" rejoined Wallace, sternly. "Let all the whig-amore scum of Scotland come, they are welcome. I am one of the good old race of Elderslie, and I thank Heaven that in an hour like this, it hath been the hap of one of my name to have entrusted to his care the defence of the palace of our princes, and yonder holy fane, the sepulchre of their bones— one of the fairest piles that ancient piety ever founded, or modern fanaticism destroyed." His swart countenance lighted up, and signing the cross (for this noble cavalier was a true catholic), he drew his sword.

"Hark, a chamade!" said Walter Fenton; "now let us hear what these rascals have the impudence to say;" and the three cavaliers repaired to the porch, leaving the divine to continue his *devoirs* to the brandy-keg. They beheld a very extraordinary scene.

Wallace's company was an Independent one. It was something less than a hundred strong, and had the great porch of the palace and the two lesser gates of the boundary wall to defend. In the former there were sixty musketeers drawn up, as it was the point of the greatest danger; the remainder were posted at the small gates, which were well secured by internal barricades. The great façade of the magnificent palace, with its deep quadrangle and six round towers, loomed through the starless gloom of the winter night; lights flickered in the gallery of the kings of Scotland, and through the lofty casements of its long corridors and echoing chambers, for there many proscribed catholic and cavalier families, terrified women, and helpless children, had fled for refuge. And from the great western windows of the chapel royal shone "the dim religious light" of the distant altar, where many a devout worshipper, in the ancient faith of our fathers, sent up, with catholic fervour, the most solemn prayers to God for conquest and for succour.

How different was the scene without those sacred walls, with their shadowy aisles, their glimmering shrines and marble tombs—their dark, deep, solemn arches, and mysterious echoes.

Through the strong gate of vertical iron bars that closed the dark round archway of the porch, the cavaliers beheld the long vista of the Canongate, extending to the westward. Its long perspective of ancient and picturesque edifices, turrets, outshots, and gables, was vividly lit up by the crimson glare of the blazing houses on the Abbey-hill, to the northward of the palace.

A dense mob that had gathered in the Cowgate, provided with weapons and torches, mingled with trained bandsmen, and having drums beating, and the earl of Perth's effigy, borne aloft before them, after traversing the West Bow and High-street, maltreating all they met, were now descending the Canongate; and the light of their brandished flambeaux streamed through the groined portal of the palace, glittering on the helmets and arms of the soldiers drawn up within it in close array, and beyond on the tall outline of the tower of James V

As the drums of the trained bands continued to beat the point of war, the rabble poured forth from all the diverging wynds and alleys, until like a river swollen by a hundred tributary streams, the dense mass that debouched upon the open space around the ancient Girth-cross of the once holy sanctuary, covered the whole arena. The united roar of ten thousand angry voices swelled along the lofty street, and the red torchlight revealed many an uncouth visage, distorted by drunkenness, fanaticism, and ferocity. Several muskets and pistols were incessantly discharged, while stones, sticks, fragments of furniture, dead cats, and every available and imaginable missile were hurled in showers over the battlements of the porch, and strewed the pavement of the court within.

In front were Grahame and Macgill, two captains in the trained band, armed with their buff coats, steel caps, and half-pikes; several baillies, in their scarlet gowns and gold chains; Lord Mersington, reeling about and brandishing a partizan, his senatorial wig and robes in a woeful plight; the Rev. Ichabod Bummel, bare-headed, and spurring like a madman a short, plump, and active Galloway cob of which he had possessed himself, and over the flanks of which, his long spindle shanks and scabbard trailed upon the ground. On each side were the Marchmont and Islay heralds, the Unicorn and Ormond pursuivants, in their tabards blazing with embroidery, and their tall plumed bonnets; behind was a confused forest of uplifted hands, and weapons, swords, pikes, staves, and halberts, which flashed incessantly in the wavering glare of the brandished torches, and chief above all were the effigy of the chancellor, and a great orange and blue standard; the first the colour of the Revolutionists, the second of the Covenanters.

The houses of the earl of Perth, the lairds of Niddry, Blairdrummond, and others, were blazing close by, and the sky was sheeted with fire. The contents of their cellars were rolled into the streets and staved, and the rich and luscious wines of France, the nut-brown ale, and crystal usquebaugh streamed along the swollen gutters, where hundreds of rioters were wallowing like pigs in the kennel, and were trod to death beneath the feet of the mighty host that swept over them. After a flourish of trumpets, the senior herald cried with a loud voice,—

"In the name of the lords of his majesty's privy council, I, the Islay herald-at-arms, summon, warn, and charge *you*, Captain William Wallace, under pain and penalty of loss of life and escheat of goods——"

"Yea, and the loss of salvation," screamed Ichabod, with a voice of a Stentor, as he brandished his Bible and bloody sword. "Woe unto ye who march against God with banners displayed! Woe unto ye who would build up the walls of Jericho, which the Lord hath casten down! Take heed, ye vipers and soldiers of Jeroboam, lest the curse that fell on Hiel, the Bethelite, fall upon ye also! Woe unto ye, worshippers of the Babylonian harlot, the mother of sin, for the hour is come when it is written that ye shall perish!"

"——And escheat of goods and gear," continued the herald, "forfeiture of name and fame."

"Surrender, ye d—d loons!" cried Mersington, "or hee hee, we'll gie ye cauld kail through the reek, conform to the Acts of Estate."

"Sound trumpets for silence!" exclaimed the herald indignantly; but now the voice of Mr. Bummel was again heard.

"Oh, for one moment of the hand that smote the foes of Zion!" he exclaimed, raising to heaven his sunken eyes that in the torchlight seemed to fill with a yellow glare. "Oh, for God's malediction on the brats of Babel! Lo! I see a sign in the lift—they are delivered unto us, that we may dash them against the stones. On, on, and spare not! smite and slay! death to the false prophets! death to the soldiers of the idolatrous James!"

"I, the Islay herald-at-arms——"

"Haud your d—d yammering!" cried Captain Graham, of

the trained bands, interrupting in turn; "close up, my trained men! come on, my buirdly Baxters, and couthie craftsmen—advance pikes—musketeers, blow matches—give fire!"

"Give fire!" re-echoed the deep voice of Wallace within the groined portal. A loud discharge of musketry took place, and the bullets of the mob rattled like a hailstorm against the walls, or whistled through the archway of the porch.

Three soldiers fell dead, but nearly forty of the rabble were shot, for every bullet fired by the "Brats of Babel" killed at second hand. Still they pressed forward with undiminished courage, and assailed the three gates of the palace at once, and pressing close to the bars of the portal, fired their muskets and pistols through with deadly precision on the little band within. Here Wallace commanded in person, with a bravery worthy of his immortal name, and encouraged by his animated exhortations, his gallant few, though falling fast on every hand, stood firm, with a resolution to die, but never surrender.

Walter Fenton and Finland commanded each about twenty musketeers at the lesser gates, which the insurrectionists assailed pell-mell with hammers and pickaxes, and as nothing but a cruel death could be expected if this mob of infuriated madmen obtained entrance, the poor soldiers fought as much for their lives as for honour and protection of the palace and chapel royal. From a platform of planks and furniture, overlooking the south back of the Canongate, Walter's party poured a fire upon the mob with deadly effect; the palace wall was high, the gate strong and well secured, so they hurled ponderous stones and swung hammers against its solid front in vain.

So it fared with Finland, who defended the northern doorway of the royal gardens near a little turretted edifice called Queen Mary's Bath. This experienced soldier had speedily made four loop-holes through the strong wall, and the rioters, as they approached the gate, were shot down in such rapid succession that an appalling pile of dead and dying lay before it, forming a barrier so hideous, that their companions began to recoil in dismay, and poured a storm of bullets and abuse from a distance.

The blaze from the Abbey-hill illuminated the whole garden, and the dark buttresses, the square tower, the deep-ribbed doorway, and tall lancet windows of the beautiful church of the Sancta Crucis were all bathed in a blood-red hue by the flaring sheets of flame that ascended from the burning houses.

"St. Bride speed you, my gallant Douglas!" cried Wallace,

who, anxious for the maintenance of his post, made a hurried round of the walls. "Art keeping the knaves in check?"

"Let the deed show," replied Finland. "By my faith! their dead are lying chin deep without the barrier. 'Twas a brave stroke in tactics this enfilade of the approach; and the flames of yonder great mansion enable my bold hearts to aim with notable precision."

"'Tis the noble lodging of the great chancellor," rejoined Wallace, turning his flushed face towards the ruddy glow; "and I grieve deeply that many noble dames of the first quality are likely perishing amid yonder flames; however, death is preferable to dishonour at the hands of fanatical clowns. This day they dragged my sister through the streets ....and in open day—my God!" He ground his teeth and smote his breast.

"Malediction!" exclaimed Finland; "can we not succour them?"

"Impossible," replied the other, resuming his military nonchalance. "I cannot spare a man. Bonnie black-eyed Maud, of Madertie, and merry Annie, of Maxwelton, are both yonder; this morning they fled to the house of Perth. God sain them both—now I must see how fares young Fenton." He hurried away, leaving Finland transfixed by what he had revealed.

"Follow me, some of ye," he exclaimed; "let six maintain the post. Come on, gallants, we will save these noble dames, or die."

His party had now been reduced to twelve; but forgetful of everything save the probable danger of Annie, he rushed through the garden followed by six soldiers armed with pikes, and leaving the precincts of the palace by a secret doorway near the old royal vault, hurried through the narrow suburb of Croft-an-Righ, and felt his heart leap as the hot glow of the burning houses was blown upon his cheek, and the sparks fell like red hail around him. The roar of voices and of musketry still continued around the palace with unabated vigour; but here the mob lay generally wallowing in the liquor that flowed along the street, or were busy in revelling around piles of wine flasks, runlets of wine, and barrels of ale, or hurrying away with whatever plunder they had saved from the fast-spreading conflagration.

The house of the chancellor, a lofty edifice, with turrets at the angles, steep roofs, and great stacks of chimneys, stood a little way back from the street, with a row of tall Dutch poplars before it; but these were now blackened and scorched by the forky flames that rolled in volumes from the windows, and clambered over the sinking roofs. The smoke ascended into the clear air in one vast shadowy pillar, and showers of sparks were thrown as from the crater of a volcano. Not one of the inmates was visible, for every window was full of flame, and Finland felt distraction in his mind as he gazed upon the blazing house ; but suddenly several females appeared upon the stone gutters and upper bartizan, waving their handker-chiefs, and crying in piteous accents for mercy and for succour ; but they were unheeded by the mob, or, if heard, only treated with derision.

"A ladder, a ladder!" exclaimed Finland, whose arms and attire were so much disfigured by smoke and dust, that he seemed in no way different from the other armed citizens that thronged the streets. "Death and confusion! a hundred bonnet pieces for a ladder ; my brave friends, my good com-rades, your pikes—truss them into a ladder. Ere now I have led an escalade of such a turnpike. Bravo, my bold hearts!" and with the silent precision of practised campaigners, the soldiers with their scarfs trussed or tied their six pikes into the form of a scaling-ladder. In a moment it was placed against the wall. "Guard the passage," cried Finland, as he disappeared through one of the upper windows.

The heat and smoke were so great that he could scarcely breathe ; for the old mansion being all wainscotted, burned like a ship, and ancient paintings, costly hangings, carpets, furniture, books, and all the magnificent household of the great chancellor, was crumbling to ashes beneath the relentless flame.

The hot conflagration often drove Finland back, and made his very brains whirl ; but he found other passages, across the yielding floors, and ascending from story to story, at last felt gratefully the cooler air upon his flushed and scorched face as he stepped upon the flame-lighted bartizan, and Annie, with a wild hysterical laugh, threw herself into his arms, and immediately swooned.

"Your hand, Lady Madertie—away, away!" cried he; "we have not a moment to lose ;" and bearing his burden like a child, he attempted to descend the staircase ; but lo! the forked flames shot up the spiral descent, and drove him back upon the platform, which was thirty feet in height.

All retreat was cut off.

Annie was insensible ; and Finland, as he leant against the parapet and pressed her to his breast, and felt the masses of her soft hair blown against his face, became giddy with despair. At a little distance Matilda of Madertie, a beautiful blonde, was kneeling before her crucifix, and praying with all the happy fervour of a true Catholic ; her long dark hair was streaming over her shoulders. Near her were several female servants, crouching against the parapet, and who, exhausted by the energy of their shrieks, and the near approach of death, lay in a kind of stupor, without motion, and seeming scarcely to breathe. Finland thought only of Annie; but a glance sufficed to show that their fate was sealed.

The whole of the lofty house beneath the turret where they stood was an abyss of flames, and the glare, as they flashed upward and around him, compelled him to close his eyes ; and thus a prey to grief and horror, he moved to and fro upon the toppling wall until the slate roofs sank crashing into the flaming pit with a roar, and now one vast sheet of broad red fire ascended into the air, making the calcined walls that confined it rend and tremble ; a shout came up from the street below ; the whole city, the hills, and the sky seemed to be on fire. The flames came closer to Finland—he felt their scorching heat; the next seemed to sweep his cheek, and Annie's waving locks and his own, that mingled with them, were burned away together.

"Laird of Finland," cried a soldier from below, " the tree —the tree ! "

" 'Tis death at all events," replied the cavalier; and quick as light, with his long scarf, he bound the slender waist of Annie to his own, and stretching from the wall, got into the lofty and strong poplar tree, and began to descend slowly and laboriously. A shout burst from the soldiers in the garden below.

"God receive us ! " cried Maud of Madertie, holding up her crucifix to heaven. At that moment the wall gave way beneath her, and she disappeared for ever.

Finland's desertion of his post proved ultimately fatal to the defence of Holyrood, which, by the efforts of Wallace, Walter Fenton, and the church-militant, Dr. Joram, was protracted until eleven at night. Then the soldiers of Finland, having been all shot down, a party of the trained bands, led by Captain Grahame, broke down the gate with sledge-hammers, and then the armed mob, roused to an indescribable pitch of frenzy and ferocity by the liquors they had imbibed, the resistance and slaughter, and the exhortations of the religious maniacs who led them, crowded like a hell disgorged into the outer court and inner quadrangle of the palace.

Taken thus in flank, the soldiers of Wallace were almost immediately destroyed. That brave cavalier was hewn down,

II.   2 A

his body was hacked to pieces, his entrails torn out and cast into the air. Many of his soldiers who surrendered were shot in cold blood, and all the wounded perished. Walter Fenton, gathering a few of the survivors upon his platform, still continued to fire upon the sea of madmen that swarmed around them.

Conspicuous among his followers, upon his prancing Galloway cob, towered the tall and ghastly figure of Mr. Ichabod Bummel; and, urging the work of death, he sent his powerful voice before him wherever he went.

"No quarter to the birds of Belial!—smite them both hip and thigh. On, ye chosen of Israel, who now, in the good fight of faith, shall extirpate the heathen, sent forth even as the Jews were of old."

"Pick me down yonder villain," cried Fenton to his soldiers; and bullet after bullet whistled past the head of the preacher, but he seemed to bear a charmed life, and escaped them all.

"On, on to the good work, and prosper!" he cried. "Smite and slay! smite and slay! lest the curses that befel Saul for sparing the Amalekites fall upon ye."

Thus urged, the people hewed the soldiers limb from limb, and the bodies of the dead shared the same fate. Seeing all lost, Walter and Dr. Joram had torn the cavalier plumes from their hats, and leaped upon their horses, hoping to cut their way through the press, or escape unknown. But, alas! Joram was recognised by the terrible Ichabod, who, urging his Galloway towards him, brandished his sword, and ex-claimed with stentorian lungs—

" 'Tis a priest of Baal, and this night will I send him howling to his false gods! Come on, Jonadab Joram, thou wolf in sheep's clothing."

" Approach, thou d—ned, round-headed, prick-eared, covenanting, and rebellious rapscallion!" cried the doctor in great wrath, urging his horse towards his clerical antagonist; but the crowd was great between them, and they were enabled to glare at and menace and bespatter each other with scriptural abuse and very hard names, for some time before they came within sword's point; for they were both intoxicated, the one with brandy, and the other with an enthusiasm that bordered on insanity. "Come on, thou villanous whigamore," cried Joram, flourishing his long rapier; "thy glory and thee shall depart to the devil together!"

" Out upon thee, and the bloody papistical duke whom thou servest, and hast blasphemously prayed for; but the curse that fell upon Jeroboam hath already fallen upon him—he shall die without a son, and be the last of his persecuting race, despite the brat in the warming-pan."

"On thy carcase, foul kite, will I avenge this treason against the Lord's anointed?" replied Joram, spurring his horse.

"Thou fool!" shrieked Ichabod, with a hollow laugh; "was that accursed tyrant who fiddled while Rome blazed beneath him the anointed of the Lord?"

"Have at thee, trumpeter of treason!"

"Caitiff and firebrand of hell, at last I have thee!" and their swords flashed as they fell upon each other like two mad bulls. The superior strength and skill of the cavalier chaplain quite failed him before the ferocious enthusiasm of the presbyterian, whose long broadsword, swayed by both hands, was twice driven through his body at the first onset.

"King and high kirk for ever!" cried poor Joram, as he fell forward with the blood gushing from his mouth; but, still unsatisfied, Ichabod seized him as he sank down, writhing one hand in his hair, and throwing the body across his saddle-bow, he slashed off the head, and held it aloft, a grinning and dripping trophy.

"Behold," he exclaimed, in an unearthly voice, "behold the head of Holofernes!"

All was over now. Walter gave a hurried glance around him. The palace was being sacked by the rabble, who carried off all they could lay their hands upon; but it was upon the beautiful chapel, that venerable monument of ancient art and David's pious zeal, that the whole tide of popular fury was poured. In five minutes it was completely devastated. The tall windows, with their rich tracery and stained glass, were destroyed; the magnificent tombs of marble and brass, the grand organ, the altar, with its burning candles and great silver crucifix, the rich oak stalls of the thistle, with the swords, helmets, and banners of the twelve knights,—were all torn down, and the beautifully variegated pavement was stripped from the floor.

All the wood and ornamental work, the pictures, reliques, furniture, vestments, &c., were piled in front of the palace, and committed to the flames amid the yells of the populace, whose cries seemed to rend the very welkin. Dashing spurs into his horse, Walter gave him the reins, and sweeping his sword around him, right, left, front, and rear, he broke through the crowd, and, followed by a score of bullets, galloped up the Canongate and escaped,—the sole survivor of that night's slaughter at Holyrood.

2 A 2

CHAPTER XLVIII

THE VEILED PICTURE.

To the Lords of Convention 'twas Claver's that spoke,
Ere the King's crown shall fall there are crowns to be broke ,
So let each Cavalier who loves honour and me,
Come follow the bonnet of bonnie Dundee.

SCOTT.

SKIRTING the city, Walter soon left the roar of the angry multitude far behind him ; he was galloping among fallow fields, hedge-rows, and solitary lanes, and the silence of the country was a relief to his excited spirit after the fierce tumult of the last six hours. The snow had melted ; Dairy-burn, and other little rills that traversed the dark fields, gleamed like silver threads in the starlight.

Walter passed the loch, and reached the old place of Drum-dryan ; the house was ruined and desolate, roofless and win-dowless, and the roadway was strewn with fragments of furni-ture. His anxiety increased, and, goring his horse onward, he dashed up the dark dewy avenue of Bruntisfield, and reined up at the barbican-gate. The perfect silence, unbroken even by the barking of a dog, and the strong odour of burned wood, had in some sort prepared him for the sight he wit-nessed. There, too, had been the hand of the destroyer, and a great part of the once noble mansion was a bare, blackened, and open ruin. Its corbie-stoned gables and round turrets stood bleakly in bold relief against the starry sky ; and from the depths of its vaulted chambers, the remains of the smoul-dering conflagration sent forth at times a column of smoke into the calm winter atmosphere. The court and garden were strewn with broken furniture, torn hangings, books, and household utensils.

The sudden snorting of his horse drew Walter's attention to two corpses that lay near the outer door. They were those of John Leekie, the gardener, and Drouthy, the aged butler, who, like true vassals, had both "with harness on their backs," perished at their lady's threshold. Both had on cors-lets and steel caps, and one yet grasped a broken partisan.

Full of dire thoughts of vengeance, Walter galloped back to the city, every corner of which was now overflown with the tide of confusion and uproar that had been so long concen-trated around Holyrood. He naturally sought the Castle-hill, where Dundee and Dunbarton, with their sixty followers, who of all the Lowlands seemed now alone to remain true to their fugitive king, were drawn up under the cannon of the Half-moon.

"So the villains have sacked Holyrood," said Dundee, smiling grimly.

"To their contentment," replied Walter. "Poor Finland, our jolly chaplain, Wallace, and a hundred brave soldiers, have gone to render a last account of their faithful service; and I alone, survive, my lords."

"To avenge them, add, sir. 'Tis the hope of repaying with most usurious interest this heavy account of blood that alone makes me bear up," replied Dundee with enthusiasm; "and God give me inspiration, for I feel I am the last hope of the old house of Stuart."

At that time certain persons who styled themselves a Convention of the Estates were assembled in conclave, and thither went the brave Dundee, though conscious that, personally or politically, he was the bitterest foe of every man present.

"My lords and gentlemen," said he, observing the chill that fell on the assemblage when he appeared—"I have come here as a peer of the realm, to serve his majesty James VII. and the parliament of Scotland! and I demand that, if the latter has no occasion for my service, it will at least protect my friends and self from the insults of the base-born rabble."

With one voice this hastily collected and illegally constituted assembly exclaimed—"We cannot and will not!"

"Then farewell, sirs," replied the viscount, with a smile of pride and scorn. "When again I appear before you, it will not be to entreat, but to command—it will not be to plead, but to punish; and now, let my trumpets sound *To horse!* In the country of the clans, the hills are as steep, the woods are as pathless, the glens as deep, and the rivers as rapid, as in the days of the Romans; and again from the wild north shall the whole tide of Celtic war roll on the traitor Lowlands, as in the days of the great Montrose. When again you hear the voice of Dundee, my lords of Convention,—*tremble!*"

He clasped on his headpiece and retired. As the jangle of his sword and spurs descending the stone turnpike died away, a deep silence pervaded the dusky hall; for the threats of this chivalric soldier, when united to their foreknowledge of his dauntless courage, his unflinching loyalty, his loftiness of mind, and intense ferocity, threw a chill upon the more cold-blooded and calculating revolutionists. But soon the gallant blare of the trumpet, the stirring brattle of the brass kettle-drums, the clang of iron hoofs, and jingle of steel scabbards

and chain bridles, awaking all the echoes of the great cathedral, and the hollow arcades of the dark Parliament-square,
announced the march of the Life Guards—those sixty brave
gentlemen who, of all his once numerous and fondly cherished
army, now alone remained stanch to the hapless James.

Dark looks were exchanged, and as the music grew faint,
all seemed to breathe more freely. Then the querulous voice
of Lord Mersington was heard, and in the half-lighted hall,
his dwarfish figure, clad in his senatorial robes, was dimly
seen on the rostrum, and, as he addressed the Convention,
from the effect of his recent potations and over exertion, he
swayed on his heels like a statue on a pivot. His speech was
somewhat to the following purpose.

"That for sae mickle as the vile and bloody papistical
James, duke of Albany and York, having assumed the regal
sceptre without the oath required for due maintenance of religion, and having altered the ancient constitution of the kingdom by ane exertion of tyrannous and arbitrary power, had
forfeited all richt to the crown of Scotland, now and for ever;
that it be forthwith settled on the Stadtholder William, and
Mary his spouse; that there be made a list of grievances to
be redressed, and a new act framit, anent witchcraft, papacy,
prelacy, and ither abominations."

The last echoes of the trumpets of Dundee had died away
under the arch of the Netherbow Port, and the motions of
Mersington were carried with universal approbation. "Thus,"
says the author of "Caledonia," "the revolution in England
was conducted constitutionally by the Parliament; but in
Scotland, unconstitutionally by the Convention. The English
found a vacancy of the throne, the Scots *made* one; the one
grave and regarding law, the other vehement and disregard-
ing it."

With a heaviness of heart, a deep and morbid sadness
against which he struggled in vain, Walter rode down the
steep Leith Wynd. He was now a private trooper under
Dundee, and leaving Lilian far behind him; for he was going,
he foresaw, to perish under the fallen banner of a desperate
cause and ruined king; but soon the clash of the cymbals,
the fanfare of the trumpets, the tramp of the stately horses,
the high bearing of their gallant riders, and that innate loftiness of soul, which made Dunbarton and Dundee rise superior to their fortune, and seem to set fate at defiance, communicated a new ardour to his heart, and it soon beat respon-
sive to the martial music, as the troop of cavaliers traversed
the city's northern ridge, and riding by the Long Gate saw

the morning sun rising afar off above the snow-clad Lammermuir, gilding Preston Bay, the far hills of Fife, and the shining waters of the dark blue Forth.

Dundee rode near Fenton, who finding, more than once, the dark and pensive eyes of this singularly handsome soldier fixed upon him with something of that foredoomed expression, indicative of his future fate and fame, he ventured to ask, " Whither go you, my lord ?"

" Wherever the shade of Montrose shall direct me," was the thoughtful and poetical reply. " Believe me, Mr. Fenton," he continued, after a pause, "under whatever circumstances, or however oppressed by fate, I will acquit myself before God, the world, and my own conscience. Yes !" he exclaimed, with flashing eyes, and striking his gloved hand upon his corsleted breast, "I will hazard life and limb, estate and title, name and fame, yes, I would peril even my salvation, were it possible, in the cause of my honour and allegiance; and if I cannot save the throne of King James, at least I will not survive its fall—so the will of God be done !"

There was something sublime in his aspect as he spoke; his dark and lustrous eyes were full of fire; his face, the manly beauty of which few have equalled, and none surpassed, was suffused with a warm glow, and the proud curl of his moustached lip, showed the high spirit of achievement that burned within him. The soul of the great Montrose seemed indeed to inspire him, and in such a moment all the darker and weaker points were forgotten. His ardour was communicated to Walter, whose heart beat fast as he exclaimed,—

" Noble Dundee, to victory or the grave, to the field or the scaffold, I will follow thee, and in that hour when I fail in my duty or allegiance, may woe betide me, and dishonour blot my name !"

Dundee pressed his hand and replied,—

" In the wilds of the pathless north, ten thousand claymores will flash from their scabbards at the call of Dundee. The loyal and gallant clans have not forgotten the glories of Alford, Inverlochy, and Auldern, when the standard of James Grahame, of Montrose, was never unfurled but to victory. Again, like him, will I lead them against this Dutch usurper, whom, in an evil hour, I saved from death upon the battlefield of Seneff. Yes, after he had fallen beneath the hoofs of Vaudemont's Reitres, I saved his life at the risk of my own, and horsed him on my own good charger, when, could his future ingratitude to me, and the usurpation of this hour have been foreseen, my petronel had blown his brains to the wind."

"Ha! what wants his grace of Gordon?" said Dunbarton, as the flash of a cannon broke from the dark castle wall, and a puff of white smoke curled away on the clear morning air, while the echoes of the report reverberated like thunder among the black basaltic cliffs of the great fortress, past which they were riding. A little arched postern to the westward opened, and a soldier appeared, waving a white flag from the brow of the steep rock, which the turretted bastion overhung. The troop halted, and their kettle-drums gave three ruffles in honour of the duke.

"Tarry for me, gentlemen comrades," said Claverhouse, "while I confer with ' the cock of the north,' " and galloping to the base of the castle rock, he dismounted, and notwithstanding his steel harness, buff coat, and jack boots, clambered with great agility to the postern, where he held a conference with the duke of Gordon.

What passed was never known; but each is said to have needlessly exhorted the other to loyalty and truth.

The multitude, who from a distance had watched the departure of the hated Dundee, fled back to the city, and reported to the lords of the convention, that "there was a coalition and general insurrection of the adherents of the bluidy Claver'se," and thereupon a dreadful panic ensued. The city drums beat the point of war; the duke of Hamilton and other revolutionists, who had for weeks past been secretly bringing great bands of their vassals into Edinburgh, where they were concealed in cellars and garrets, now rushed to arms, and the members of Convention, confined in their hall, were terrified and put to their wit's end by the uproar. Lord Mersington, it is related, exchanging his senatorial robe and wig, "for ane auld wife's mutch and plaid," fled to his lodging, and appeared no more that day; but their fears were causeless, for Dundee, and the devoted cavaliers who accompanied him in his chivalric but hopeless enterprise, were then passing the woods and morasses of Corstorphine, on their route to the land of the Gaël.

At a hand gallop they soon flanked the grey rocks and pine-covered summits of those beautiful hills, and the sequestered village lay before them, with the morning smoke curling from its moss-roofed cottages, its broad lake swollen by the melting snows, but calm as a mirror, save where the swan and dusky waterouzel squattered its shining surface; the ancient kirk peeped above a grove of venerable sycamores, and to the south stood the castle of the old hereditary Foresters of Corstorphine.

"What castles are these on the right and left?" asked Dundee. "I warrant Mr. Holster can tell; he knows everything and everybody."

"Yonder hold with the loch flowing almost to its gates, is the house of the Lord Forester," replied the cavalier trooper, "a leal man and true."

"And that tall peel on the muirland to the north?"

"The tower of Clermiston, my lord."

"What! the house of Randal Clermont—um—a converted covenanter, and worshipper of the rising sun, eh?"

"'Tis said his name is at the address sent by the turncoat council to the Stadtholder," said Dunbarton.

"Assure me of that," exclaimed Dundee, sharply reining up his horse, "and by all the devils, I will hang him from his own bartizan, lord and baron though he be! Halt, gentlemen, we will pay these lords a visit; they, or their stewards, must pay us riding money, for the king's service. My lord earl, and thirty of you gentlemen, will detour across to Clermiston, while I will ride down to make my *devoir* to the Forester of these hills—forward, trot."

The troop separated, and Walter somewhat unwillingly accompanied Lord Dunbarton, whose party galloped in single files along the muddy and rough bridle-road that led over the lea to the gate of the solitary tower. They encircled the barbican wall, which was built partly on fragments of low rock, without being able to find entrance, the great gate being securely fastened, and the stillness of the place seemed to imply that it was uninhabited. A shriek, echoing through the vaulted recesses of the tower, rang out upon the clear morning air; a window was dashed open, and a female hand, white and bleeding, appeared, while a voice calling for aid made the blood of Walter Fenton rush back upon his heart.

"On, on, good sirs!" he exclaimed, leaping from his horse; "some work of hell is being enacted here!" and he rushed against the tower gate, making fruitless efforts to burst it open; but they were as those of a child against the solid planks of the barrier.

"By Mahoud's horns, Clermistonlee is at his old tricks again!" cried Jack Holster, leaping from his saddle, and unslinging his carbine. "He hath a lass in his meshes; alight gallants all, or the fair fortress will be won by storm, while we dally in the trenches."

"Would to God I had a petard!" exclaimed Walter; "this gate is like a wall."

"Unsling your carbines, gentlemen," said the earl of Dunbarton. "A volley at the lock—give fire!"

Thirty carbines poured their concentrated volley upon the gate; it was torn to fragments, and an aperture formed which admitted the troopers; to creep through, and rush on with his drawn rapier, were to Walter a moment's work. By pulling the leathern latch of a long oak pin which secured the door of the tower, they procured ingress, and rushed up the turnpike stair to the hall, at the very moment that Lilian was just sinking backwards, with her hands clasped in despair, while Lord Clermistonlee, enraged by her outcries, and the new and pressing danger, was endeavouring with ferocious violence to drag her into some place of concealment.

"False villain!" exclaimed Walter, springing upon him with his rapier. "I have a thousand insults to avenge; but this, and this, and this, repay them all!" and he made three furious lunges at his rival, who escaped two by the intervention of Dunbarton, who vigorously interposed; but he received one severe wound in the left shoulder. Infuriated by the sight of his own blood, and being a man of great strength and agility, he grappled fiercely with Walter, breathlessly exclaiming, in accents of rage—

"Woe betide thee, thou unhanged rascal! A sword! a sword! lend me a sword, some one! Juden! Traitors, I am a lord of parliament, and dare ye slaughter me under the rooftree of my own fortified house? This is hership and hamesucken with a vengeance! Death and confusion, villains; recollect I am unarmed!"

"Lend him a sword, some of you," said Walter.

"Oh, no, no; spare him," moaned Lilian, who was supported by the earl of Dunbarton.

"Base-born runnion, and son of a dunghill!" exclaimed Clermistonlee, with that intense ferocity and scorn which he could so easily assume at all times; "an hour will come when this insult shall be fearfully repaid——" here the clenched hand of Walter struck him down. Staggering backward, making a futile attempt to recover himself, his clutching hands tore away the veil that concealed the portrait already mentioned. The face it revealed instantly arrested the forward stride and menacing sword. of Walter Fenton, who stood irresolute, trembled, and the sinking sword half fell from his relaxed hand, as he muttered—

"What is this coming over my spirit now? That face seems like a vision from the grave to me!"

" 'Tis the Lady Alison, my lord's late wife," said the shrill but sullen voice of Beatrix.

"Pshaw!" rejoined Walter; "then my weakness is over. Give him a sword, gentlemen. In fair stand-up fight I will meet him here, with case of pistols, sword, and dagger, or anything he pleases."

"O part them, for the sake of mercy!" implored Lilian.

Juden came in at that moment, clad in his steel bonnet and buff jack, and swaying an enormous partisan, was rushing upon Walter Fenton like a wild boar, when Holsterlee laid him flat with his clubbed carbine. The swooning of Lord Clermistonlee closed the brawl for the time; loss of blood, over-drinking, and over-excitement, had quite prostrated all his energies. Walter immediately sheathed his sword, and, kneeling down, was the first to tender assistance; for " compassion ever marks the brave."

Clermistonlee was borne away to his own apartment by the growling Juden, whose thick pate was little the worse of Holsterlee's stroke; and Lilian was now Walter's next and immediate care.

The disorder and scantiness of her attire, the pallor and horror of her aspect, and her presence in such a place, had previously informed him of all, and no sooner were they in a more retired apartment, than, throwing herself into his arms, she wept bitterly. Meanwhile, the unscrupulous cavaliers were ranging over the entire household, breaking open every press, cabinet, and girnel, with the butts and balls of their carbines, in search of wine, vivres, or anything else that suited their fancies. Juden kept always a full larder, and its contents furnished a sumptuous breakfast. Several whole cheeses, a cask of ale, and a thirty-gallon runlet or two of canary, were trundled into the hall; and a hearty repast, with the usual military accompaniments of mirth and laughter, was enjoyed by the hungry troopers, whose appetites a night spent in their saddles, and a ride in the keen air of a winter morning, had sufficiently whetted.

In a few minutes Lilian, with faltering accents, had informed Walter of her abduction, of the hours of suffering she had endured, and her anxiety to return to Lady Grizel; but, alas! poor Lilian knew not that perhaps her only relative had perished in the conflagration of her old ancestral home.

Aware that Dundee meant to halt for an hour or so, to await despatches from the earl of Balcarris and the ex-lord-advocate, Walter resolved without delay to accompany Lilian to Edinburgh, and there convey her to some place of safety, ere he cast himself upon the world for ever; for from that hour he was like a reed tossed upon the waves of misfortune. By the assistance of Jack Holster, he had Clermistonlee's favourite mare prepared for Lilian; and, after refreshing her with a milk-posset made by the cynical Beatrix, they departed for the city at a quick trot: the plain buff-coat, steel cap, and accoutrements of Walter, enabling him to pass for a Royalist or Revolutionist, as occasion required.

As soon as they began to converse, the pace of their horses was checked, and they proceeded slowly: forgetful of Claver-house and of his pledged word, Walter remembered only the presence of Lilian; and their minds were so much absorbed in their mutual explanations and plans for the future, that they marked not the tardiness of their progression towards Edinburgh.

CHAPTER XLIX.

LOVE AND PRINCIPLE.

My promised husband and my dearest friend;
Since heaven appoints this favoured race to reign,
And blood has drenched the Scottish fields in vain,
May I be wretched and thy flight partake?
Or wilt not thou for thy loved Chloe's sake,
Tired out at length submit to fate's decree.

TICKELL.

"AND this is the fate to which you have dedicated yourself?" said Lilian, weeping; "to become a follower of that fierce Dundee in the desperate course on which he is about to fling himself. Oh, Walter Fenton, this is the very folly of enthusiasm. Too surely can we see that the hand of fate is against the house of Stuart."

"Lilian," replied her lover, with mournful surprise, "the daughter of an old cavalier house should have other thoughts than these. Remember, dear Lilian, there is not in Europe a royal race for which so many of the good and the gallant, the brave and the loyal have from the foughten field and the recking scaffold given up their souls to God. Let no man judge harshly of those whose splendour is dimmed for a time; for the hour *shall* come when in the full zenith of their pride and power, the old line of our Scottish kings——"

" 'Tis all a dream, Walter. The entire nations are against them. I feel a presentiment that they and their followers are doomed to wither and perish like brands in the burning."

"My faith! art turning preacher, lassie?"

"Oh, what a prospect for thee, Walter!"

"The world is all before me; and I can always preserve my honour, my heart, and my sword. But thou, Lilian——"

"Am beside thee, dear Walter," said she, with touching artlessness; "and is not happiness better than honour?"

"True, true," replied the young man, while he kissed her hand, and his eyes filled with tenderness. "Ah, Lilian, it is the thought that I am leaving you, perhaps for ever, that alone unnerves me for the deadly venture in which we are about to engage. Hopeless though the cause of James may be, we have sworn not to survive it; and, come weal or woe, we will unfurl his standard on the northern hills, and if it waves not over us in victory, it shall never do so in defeat or dishonour; for to the last man we will perish on the sod beneath it. Your memory alone will make me sad—but am I singular? How many of these my brave companions have gentle ones to leave, mothers who bless, and sisters who love them, while I am alone. Save thee, there is nothing that binds me to this world. What of it is mine? The six feet that shall make my grave!"

"O! most ungrateful Walter," said Lilian, in a low voice of confusion and tenderness; "is not all that I have yours, manor and lands? are not these possessions ample? Greedy gled," she added, smiling; "what better tocher would you have?"

"Lilian," sighed Walter, in a thick voice, as he pressed her hand to his heart, "it may not be, dearest—yet awhile, at least."

The blushing girl gave him a timid and startled glance of inquiry.

"I am solemnly pledged to Dundee."

"Cruel Claverhouse! has he more charms for you than I have?"

"You know that my heart is full of you, Lilian; but there is also room for ambition in it. I cannot live ignobly and obscure; as such I would be unworthy to possess you. I would feel myself a nameless intruder under the rooftree of your crested ancestors, whose armorial blazons on every panel and window-pane, would shame my meaner birth, and put me to the blush."

"Ungrateful! after all I have urged and said. 'Tis a dream, Walter, a mere dream, but one that will make the world dark—oh! very dark to me."

"'Tis very true; I am choosing the path of proscription,

danger, and death; but the fortune of war may better the prospects of my faction."

"After years of separation, perhaps."

"With happiness in prospect, they would soon pass, dear Lilian."

"Oh, this wicked Claverhouse! he hath quite cast a glamour over you. How can you talk so calmly of years of separation? What may not be lost in that time?"

"My life on the field, or scaffold, perhaps."

"Your life is mine, Walter; it was pledged to me. Have you forgot the 20th of September, and the hour by the fountain?"

"Dearest girl, how could I ever forget it? 'Tis true, Lilian, that we are in the very flower of our days; the bloom of our youth and existence is at its full; love, tenderness, beauty, and susceptibility, all glow within our hearts."

"And will not the roll of years make them dull, diminish their force, and cool their fervour? Oh, heavens! I am quite making love to you," said Lilian, blushing crimson; "but danger and the risk of losing you have endued me with great boldness."

"But time will never diminish the love I bear thee, Lilian; and the memory of this hour's bitter struggle—this conflict between a love that is irresistible and the strong ties of honour, that bind me to the banner of Dundee, will haunt me to my grave!" Tears started into his eyes.

A silence ensued. Poor Lilian had nothing more to urge; and despite of all her gentleness, felt both intensely grieved and mortified, if not quite piqued, at Walter, whose heart was wrung by an agony too acute for words. As they rode past the thick woodlands that shelter the venerable church of St. Cuthbert, they heard a shrill but cracked voice chanting slowly,—

"I like ane owl in désart am, &c."

"By Jove! 'tis the villain who slew poor Joram," exclaimed Walter, drawing a pistol from his holsters; but the voices of two other persons finishing the verse, arrested him. "Astonishment! 'tis the voice of Finland!" said Walter, as he spurred his horse close to a fauld dyke, on the other side of which he saw—what? Annie Laurie, and his old friend and brother cavalier, Finland, on their knees, beside Mr. Ichabod Bummel, chanting a psalm in most dolorous accents.

"By all the devils!" said Walter, almost bursting with laughter; "'tis the age of miracles this! What, ho! Dick

Douglas and Mistress Anne Laurie, singing hymns among the heather, like two true laverocks of the persecuted kirk."

"Woe unto thee, thou troubler of the just in spirit!" cried Mr. Ichabod, unsheathing his broadsword. "I have plucked the youth and the maiden like brands from the fire which is fated to consume all such unrepentant persecutors of Israel as thee."

"I have seen a new light," said Finland, giving Walter a sly wink of deep meaning.

"And so have *I*," added Mistress Laurie, demurely: "and command thee, Walter Fenton, thou man of sin, to treat this holy expounder of the Gospel with becoming reverence."

"Annie—oh, Annie!" cried Lilian, as she boldly leaped the mare over the fauld dyke, and threw herself into the arms of her friend.

"My service to you, Mr. Ichabod," said Walter, bowing to the rawboned preacher; but quite unable to unriddle the mystery of this rencounter, he whispered to Finland (while the slayer of Joram was engaged with Lilian), "What the devil does all this mean, Dick!"

"Learn in a few words," replied Finland, who was in as miserable a plight as dust, smoke, and a hundred bruises could make him. "Annie and I had a most miraculous escape amid the horrors of last night. I will tell you of it anon,— 'twas quite a devil of a business. As for me, I am well used to such camisadoes, having been blown up at Namur, and twice nearly drowned in the Zuiderzluys; but how my adorable Annie escaped, Heaven, who saved her, can only know. We were in the hands of the most villancus mob the world ever saw; they were about to hang me from the arm of the Girth-cross; and Annie—oh! my blood bubbles like boiling-water when I think of what they intended for her; when this leathern-jawed apostle, who, with all his psalm-singing and whiggery, hath some good points of honesty about him, brought us off, sword in hand; we bundled out of the city, without blast of trumpet; and here we are. As a gentleman of cavalier principles," said Finland, colouring, "you may marvel that I would condescend to chant a psalm like a mere clown or canting herdsman; but as we are utterly at the mercy of this Ichabod Mummel or Bummel, I had no choice. He needs must——tush! you know the musty old saw."

"It is enough, maiden," said the preacher, replying to something Lilian had said, and taking, with an air of real kindness, the little hand of the shrinking girl within his own great bony paw, "I know thee to be the kinswoman of that

godly matron, Grizel Napier, who, though wedded to as cruel
a persecutor as ever bestrode a war-horse—yea, and though
leavened in their wickedness withal, sheltered me in the days
of my exceeding tribulation, when there was a flaming sword
over Israel, and when, as a humble instrument in the cause
of that great saviour of the kirk (whose coming I foretold in
my *Bombshell*, whilk hath not yet the luck to be printed), I
came from Holland to this land of anarchy, and had nowhere
to lay my head. She clothed and sheltered me, for the sake
of that loved kinsman who is now no more, slain by some
accursed persecutor, whom I would smite—yea, maiden, both
hip and thigh, if I had him within reach of this good old
whinger, that so oft hath avenged the fall of our martyrs ! "

Walter instinctively grasped his sword, startled by the stern
energy of the preacher, who continued—

" It is enough, maiden—with me ye are safe, and to a place
of peace I will conduct you and your friend ; but for these
two sons of the scarlet woman—these slaves of Jezebel, who
have been nursled in the blood of our saints and martyrs, and
in whom it grieves me to think ye have garnered up your
hearts, I may not, and *cannot*, with a safe conscience, protect
them. Let them depart from me in peace ; let them follow
him who, ere long, will be called to a severe account for all
his dark misdeeds—John Grahame of Claverhouse."

" 'Tis sound advice, Mr. Bummel," said Walter, tightening
his reins, and drawing off his glove. " By Heaven ! I had
quite forgotten ; he will have crossed the Forth by this time,
and it will require some exertion of horseflesh to rescue my
honour.   Finland, we must go.   Mount Lilian's horse.
Lilian," he added, in a low and tremulous voice, " farewell
now ; commend me to Lady Grizel, and bid her bless me ;
farewell, Lilian—we must part at last ; " and stooping from
his horse, he gently pressed her to his steel-cased breast, and
kissed her.

" Oh ! Walter, remain—remain," murmured Lilian.

" It cannot be—it is impossible now ; I am pledged to
Grahame of Claverhouse." And afraid to trust himself longer
within hearing of her soft entreaties, lest love might overcome the stern principles of loyalty in which he had schooled
himself, he leaped his horse over the fauld dyke ; and while
he felt as if his very heart was torn by the agony of that
separation, he dashed along the road to the west, leaving
Finland to follow as he chose.

With a mind overcharged by sad and bitter thoughts,
Walter galloped madly on, retracing the way he had come

with Lilian; his mind seemed a very whirlpool, and the events of the last twenty-four hours a dream. A steep old bridge, which the roadway crossed near the ancient manor of Sauchtoun, was ringing beneath his horse's heels, when a distant shout made him rein up.

"Hollo!" cried Finland, as he came after him breathlessly on the panting mare; "what the devil—art gone mad, Walter? Oh this tormenting love—ha! ha!"

"I envy this happy flow of spirits, Finland!"

"Then you envy me the possession of all that fate hath left me in this bad world. This devilish commotion hath confiscated my free barony of Finland, and torn my arms at the cross; still I am more gay than thee, who hath nothing to lose."

"And after parting with one you love," continued Walter, almost piqued by his friend's lightness of heart: "parting, perhaps for ever——"

"Tush, man—I am used to such partings. I have had many a love that was true while it lasted; but none like the passion I bear my dear Annie. My first flame was a blue-eyed demoiselle of the Low Countries (her mother was a *fleuriste* in Ghent). I thought I loved her very much; but somehow at Bruges, Mons, and Bergen-op-Zoom, 'twas ever the same; I always left some one with a heavy heart; and cursed the *générale*, when in the cold foggy mornings it rang through the dark muddy streets, waking the storks on the high roofs above, and the drowsy boors in their beds below. I know that the wheels of fate and fortune are ever turning; some points may, and others must, come round to their first starting-place, so I always live in hope. I was very sad in Ghent when our drums beat along the street of St. Michael, and I bade adieu to my fair one, coming away, I remember, by the window instead of the door."

"How—why?"

"I don't know, man," laughed Douglas: "but so we often left our billets in French Flanders. But I assure thee, laa, that under all this gaiety my heart is as heavy as thine; for I vow to thee, that the recollection of Annie, with her beseeching blue eyes, her dark clustering hair and pallid cheek, the touching cadence of her voice, and the words she said to me, are imprinted on my heart as if the hand of Heaven had written them there. By the bye, I have composed a famous song about her."

"A song!"

"Music and all. I wrote it on the night we were about to

back the old house of Bruntisfield, in search of yonder spindle-shanked apostle. Ah! if in my absence Craigdarroch should dare—but ho! yonder are some of our friends halted under a tree upon that grassy knowe."

"There is something odd being acted there. Does not yonder white feather wave in the steel bonnet of Dundee?"

"He is permitting some false Whig to sing his last psalm under *the* convenient branch where he is doomed to feed the corbies. Dundee is very kind in that way sometimes."

Recrossing the stream called the Leith, they rode towards a knoll that rose amid the marshy ground near the castle-loch of Corstorphine. There a dozen of the cavalier troopers were dismounted, and leaning on their swords or carbines, were holding their bridles in a cluster round Dundee, who was still on horseback, and in the act of addressing a dis-armed prisoner, in whom with surprise and sorrow they recognized the young laird of Holsterlee.

Cool and collected, with folded arms, he firmly encoun-tered the large dark eyes of Dundee, which were fixed with stern scrutiny upon him. The group of his comrades sur-veyed him with glances of mingled scorn and pity.

"Holsterlee!" said the viscount, who held in one hand a long Scots pistol, in the other a letter; "how little could I once have suspected that you, the best cavalier of the king's life-guard, and one in whose loyalty and high spirit I trusted so much, would stoop to this dishonour! The attempt simply of deserting to take service with this vile usurper, though bad enough in itself, is as nothing compared to the treachery which this stray letter has revealed. Fool and villain! thou knowest that I am the last hope of the king's cause in Scot-land, and that if I fall it will be buried in my grave; and yet thou art in league with this accursed Convention to destroy me! A thousand English guineas for my head, thou villanous scape-the-gallows and companion of grooms and horseboys, who hast squandered away a fair repute and noble patrimony among rakehelly gamesters and women of pleasure, dost thou value the head of a Scottish peer at a sum so trifling? hah!" He uttered a bitter laugh. "What," he resumed, "hast thou to urge, that I should not hang thee from the branch of this beech-tree?"

"That I am a gentleman," replied Holsterlee boldly; "a lesser baron of blood and coat-armour by twelve descents, and should not die the death of a peasant churl or faulty hound."

"Right!" exclaimed Dundee, whose dark and terrible eyes

began to fill with their dusky fire. "A gentleman should die by the hand of another, for every punishment is disgraceful. DEATH is the only relief from the consciousness of crime. Thou shalt have the honour of perishing by the hand of the first cavalier in Scotland. *Thus* shalt thou die—now God receive thy soul!" and pointing upward with his bridle-hand, he levelled the pistol and fired. The ball passed through the brain of Holsterlee, and flattened against the plastered wall of a neighbouring cottage. The body sank prostrate on the turf, quivered for a moment, and then lay still and stiffening, with upturned eyes and relaxed jaws.

This act, which was the most terrible episode in the life of the stern Dundee, threw a chill on the hearts of his comrades; but he did not permit them to remain gazing on the lifeless remains of one who had ridden so long in their ranks, and who was the gayest fellow that ever cracked a jest, shuffled a card, or handed a coquette through the stately cotillon or joyous couranto.

"Our nags are somewhat breathed after the hot chase he gave us, gentlemen," said Dundee, deliberately reloading his pistol, and endeavouring under an aspect of external composure to conceal the immediate sorrow, remorse, and anger that too surely preyed upon his heart. "To horse! sling carbines—forward—trot!" and away they rode in silence, leaving the cold remains of the dead man lying on the grassy sward, with his blood-dabbled locks waving in the morning wind, while the gleds and ravens wheeled and croaked around him with impatience.

But he felt not the one, and heard not the other.

He was stripped by the cottagers, and as his dress was remarkably rich, to prevent further inquiry they interred him where he lay between the bare beech-tree and the old cottage wall.*

* On removing the walls of an old cottage near Tynecastle, a mile west ward of Edinburgh, in 1843, the remains of a skeleton were found buried close by; the skull had been pierced by a bullet. In the plastered wall of the edifice a ball was found flattened against the stone.—*Edin. Advert.*, April 8, 1843

CHAPTER L.

THE PASS OF KILLYCRANKIE.

Heard ye not! heard ye not! how that whirlwind the Gaël,
Through Lochaber swept down from Lochness to Lochiel—
And the Campbells to meet them in battle array,
Came on like the billow, and broke like its spray!
Long, long shall our war-song exult in that day!

IAN LOM, OF KEPPOCH.

THE *revolution* might be said to be now fully achieved; save Dundee, Balcarris, and a few of their followers, all had submitted to the new sovereign whom these two nobles would rather have slain than acknowledged. Dundee had been required by a trumpet to return to the Convention; he treated the summons with scorn, and after cutting his way through a party sent to intercept him, reached the Highlands a proscribed fugitive, branded as an outlaw and traitor, and stigmatized with every epithet that Presbyterian rancour, heightened by the remembrance of his former military excesses, could heap upon him.

Colin, earl of Balcarris, the high treasurer, was captured and thrown into a dungeon. The weak and servile Melville, the crafty and fanatical Stair (the Scottish Talleyrand), and the not less crafty duke of Hamilton, were now at the head of the government, and these, though all staunch Presbyterians were by the king united in council with a few of the high-church nobles, an intermixture which inflamed the animosities of both parties, and sowed the seeds of hatred, discord, and confusion.

With his troop of faithful cavaliers, Dundee continued to wander from place to place in the Highlands until the beginning of May, 1689, when he appeared at the head of about two thousand clansmen led by Sir Donald Macdonald, the chiefs of Glengarry, Maclean, Locheil, and Clanronald—all names which shall ever be associated with the purest ideas of chivalry, generosity, and valour. He had only about one hundred and twenty horse, but they were composed entirely of gentlemen, and were commanded by a Sir William Wallace, a brave cavalier; Walter Fenton was his cornet, and carried the standard.

Lieutenant-General Hugh Mackay, of Scoury, now commander-in-chief of the Scottish forces, colonel-commandant of the Scottish brigade, and privy councillor of Scotland, marched against him at the head of nearly five thousand foot, and with two regiments of cavalry. Neither the fall of Edinburgh Castle (which Sir John Lanier demolished), nor the disappointment of assistance from Ireland which James had promised him, could damp the ardour of the brave Dundee. Deficiency of provisions had compelled him to shift his quarters frequently, and his devoted followers had endured the most severe privations; but under these they disdained to complain, when they knew that Dundee shared them all. Like Montrose, he was eminently calculated for a Highland leader. In his buff coat and headpiece he marched on foot, now by the side of one clan, and anon by the ranks of another, addressing the soldiers in their native Gaelic, flattering their long genealogies, and animating the fierce rivalry of clanship by reciting the deeds of their forefathers, and the sonorous verses of their ancient bards.

"It has ever been my maxim, Mr. Fenton," said he to our friend on one occasion, "that no general should command an irregular army in the field without becoming acquainted with every man under his baton."

On the 17th June, 1689, he marched to the Pass of Killycrankie, where one of the most decisive battles in Scottish history was bravely fought and fruitlessly won. Dawn was brightening on the hills of Athole; and Walter, who, quite exhausted by a long series of hardships, cold, starvation, and a pistol-shot wound, was sleeping under his horse's legs, was aroused by the sonorous and guttural cry of a sentinel, who screamed out in Gaelic—

"Hoigh, Mhic Alastair Mhor! Hark to the war-drum of the Saxon!"

It was the morning of a battle! Walter's first thought was of Lilian; his second of the prospects of victory. The dear image of Lilian made him rise superior to his fortune. Since they had so abruptly separated, he had never heard from her; and it was now many months. How long the time seemed! Amid his dreamy musings, the gentle expression of her face often came powerfully to his recollection, with all the vigour of a deeply impressed vision; and recollection summoned the tones of her sweet voice to his heart like the memory of some old familiar air, and all the gushing tenderness of his soul was awakened. But with these remembrances too often came bitterness and despair, and he kissed with all a lover's fervour the scarf her hands had wrought him. Gleams of memory, and vivid visions of happiness, which he foresaw too surely could never be realized, made his heart swell alternately with tender recollections and joyous anticipations, that died away to leave him hopeless and despairing. Now they were on the brink of a battle which Walter welcomed with anxious joy, for it would be not less decisive as to the issue of his love, than for the fortune of James and the fate of the British people.

It was a glorious morning in June; the purple summer heather, the long yellow broom, the wild briar and honeysuckle, that clambered among the basaltic cliffs, loaded the air with a rich perfume; while, through the savage and stupendous gorge of Killycrankie, the rising sun poured a flood of golden lustre, bringing forward in strong light the wooded acclivities of those sublime hills, that heave up to heaven their scaured and wooded sides, involving in dark shadow the deep rocky chasms, through which the foaming Garry rushes to mingle its waters with the rapid Tummel—chasms so profound, and hidden by the overhanging foliage, that the roar only of the unseen water was heard, awakening the echoes of the dewy woods and shining rocks.

Nothing in nature can surpass the wild grandeur and imposing sublimity of this mountain gorge, the frowning terrors of which, in after years, so impressed a brigade of Hessians in the last of our Scottish wars, that they refused to penetrate what appeared to them to be the end of the habitable world. Save the mountain torrent foaming down from the lofty hills, appearing one moment to hurl its spray against the shining rocks, and urge masses of earth and stones along with it, and disappearing the next, as it plunged into the bosky woodlands,—all was still as death in that Highland solitude, when, in steadiness and order, Dundee drew up his little host at its northern verge, admirably posted on well-chosen ground, two miles from the mouth of the pass; the only road to his position being the ancient pathway that wound along the face of the precipitous cliffs, where the least false step threatened instant destruction even to the most wary passenger.

Dundee's band—for it was indeed no more, though named an army—was only two thousand strong, and composed of various little parties, which were the nucleus of the corps he expected yet to form. On the right was the *soi-disant* regiment of Sir John Macdonald; a small body of the clans, under the illustrious chiefs of Locheil, Glengarry, and Clanronald. the Atholemen under Ballechin, Wallace's troop of horse, and a corps of three hundred half-clad and miserably accoutred Irishmen, composed the main body. Dundee's old troop, in which rode the Earl of Dunbarton, his officers, and several Highland gentlemen, formed the reserve of cavalry. The Highlanders, arrayed each in the picturesque tartan of their native tribes were formed in close ranks, with their filleadhbegs belted about them; their brass-studded targets, long claymores, ponderous poleaxes, and long-barrelled Spanish rifles, shining in the rays of the meridian sun.

The brandishing of weapons and clan-standards, and the fierce notes of war and defiance, as the various pibrochs rang among the echoing hills, announced that the troops of Mackay were in sight. And now the brave and anxious Dundee, clad in his rich scarlet uniform, with the tall plumes waving on his polished headpiece, his fine features full of animation, and his black eyes alternately clouded by anxiety, or flashing with valour and energy,—galloped from clan to clan, inspiring them by every exertion of graceful gesture and military eloquence to add that day to the fame of their forefathers.

The murmuring hum which, from afar off, announced the drums of Mackay, grew more and more palpable, and increased until the hoarse and sharp reverberations of the martial music rang between the steep impending rocks of the long mountain pass through which the foe was penetrating. Anon the Scottish standards, the red lion with the silver cross, and one with that of St. George (borne by Hastings' regiment), and the yellow banners of the Scots brigade, appeared at intervals of time, and weapons were seen flashing through the openings of the chasmed rocks and sable woods of drooping pine.

The day had passed slowly in anxious expectation: it was evening now, and the sun had verged to the northwest, but from between gathered masses of saffron clouds streams of dazzling light were radiating; and the setting rays, as they poured aslant on the mountain sides, made the deep pass seem darker as it receded beyond them. The rattle of the drums, and the blare of trumpet and bugle, the clank of bandoliers and tread of feet, rang with a thousand reverberations between the brows of that tremendous gorge, as the army of Mackay debouched from its windings, and formed successive battalions on the little level plain or hollow, above which the fierce and impatient Highlanders, "like greyhounds in the slips straining upon the start," were formed in array of battle. Undauntedly they surveyed the measured steadiness and precision of the Lowland soldiers, whose silken standards fluttered gaily above their moving masses of polished steel caps, their screwed bayonets, and long pikes, that were ever flashing in the setting sun

Sir James Hastings' English regiment, and those of Leven
and Mackay belonging to Scotland, were arrayed in that
bright scarlet which was to become so famous in future wars :
but the battalions of Balfour, Ramsay, and Kenmore, wore
the black iron caps, the scarlet hose, and yellow coats of the
Scotch-Dutch brigade.   The cavalry corps of the Marquis of
Annandale and the Lord Belhaven wore coats of spotless buff
and caps of polished steel.   Their numbers, discipline, and
order would have stricken with dismay any other volunteers
than the Highlanders, whose hearts had never known fear,
and who had long been accustomed to rout both horse and
foot with equal speed and success.   As the practised eye of
Mackay reconnoitered the position of Dundee, he pointed to
the clan, and said to young Cameron of Locheil, who rode
near him—

" Behold your father and his wild savages ; how would you
like to be with him ?"

"It matters little," replied the young man haughtily;
" but I recommend you to be prepared, or my father and his
' wild savages ' before night may be nearer you than you
would wish."

The reports of a slight skirmish between the right wing of
the Highlanders and Mackay's left, made the hearts of all
beat quicker ; and in the interval, Dundee exchanged his
scarlet coat for one of buff, richly laced with silver ; and over
it he tied a scarf of *green*, which the Highlanders considered
ominous of evil. Leaping on horseback, he galloped to the
front, and a shout of impatience burst from the Highland
ranks.

It was now eight o'clock, and the sun was dipping behind
the hills, when a simultaneous volley ran from flank to flank
along Mackay's line ; and while the roar of the musketry
rang from peak to peak, and rebellowed along the sky and
among the hills like thunder, with a thousand echoes, Dundee
gave the order to charge ; and in deep silence, and like a
cloud of battle, the race of old Selma came down !

Reserving their fire until within a pike's length of King
William's troops, the Highlanders poured upon them a deadly
volley ; and throwing down their muskets, drew their claymores, and, under cover of the smoke, charged with the fury
of an avalanche, striking up the levelled bayonets with their
studded targets, and hewing down with sword and axe, routed
the Lowland soldiery in a moment.

The brave Maclean cut the left wing to pieces ; while Hastings' Englishmen, on the right, had equal fortune from the

Camerons and Macdonalds. Dunbarton, at the head of sixteen mounted cavaliers, actually routed the whole artillery,
and seized the cannon; while, led by Finland, the remainder
of the troop broke among the dense and recoiling mass of
Mackay's regiment, riding through it as easily as through a
field of rye. King William's Dutch standard was captured
by Walter Fenton, who, after a short conflict, drove his
sword through the corslet of the bearer, and, spurning him
with his foot and stirrup, bore off the trophy.

Meanwhile Finland encountered a mounted cavalier, and
had exchanged blows before he recognised Craigdarroch, his
rival, in the leader of Annandale's Horse, whom his brave
little band had now assailed, and with whom they were main-
taining a desperate and unequal combat of one to five.

"Surrender, Finland!" said Fergusson, haughtily.

"Have at thee, rebel!" cried his adversary, and by one
blow struck his rapier to pieces. His sword was raised to
cut down the now defenceless trooper, and end their rivalry
for ever, but, animated by chivalric generosity, he spared him.
and pressed further on the broken ranks of the enemy.

Carrying aloft the Dutch banner, Walter Fenton rode
towards Dundee, who was applauding Sir Evan Cameron of
Locheil, and urging his clan yet further to advance. Dundee
(whose panting horse was in the act of stooping to drink of a
mountain runnel), with his eyes of fire turned to the disordered
masses of Mackay, was brandishing his sword towards them,
when a random bullet pierced his buff coat above the corslet,
and buried itself in his shoulder under the left arm.

The sword dropped from his hand; a deadly pallor overspread his beautiful features; he reeled in his saddle, and
would have fallen, but Walter supported him, and held before
his eyes the yellow standard of the Stadtholder.

"Now, God be thanked, they fly!" said he, in a voice
which showed how intense were the torments he endured;
"you are a brave lad, Fenton—the dying hour of Claver'se is
at hand, but he will not forget you. Meet me at the house
of Urrard in an hour, if all goes well and I survive till then.
Make my dutiful service to the noble Lord Dunbarton, and
desire him to assume the command. Adieu;" and placing
his hand on the orifice to staunch the blood, he rode over the
field at a rapid trot.

In a mass of disorder, horse and foot, musketeers, pikemen,
and cavalry, the soldiers of Mackay were driven like a flock
of frightened sheep down the narrow pass, while the fierce
clansmen, swaying, with both hands axe and claymore, "cut

down," says an old author, many of Mackay's officers and soldiers, "through skull and neck to the very breast; others had their skulls cut off above their ears like nightcaps; some had their bodies and crossbelts cut through at one blow; pikes and swords were cut like willows, and whoever doubts this may consult the witnesses of the tragedy." Thanks to the skill of Dundee and the valour of the Highlanders, never was a more decisive victory won. Mackay lost his tents, baggage, artillery, provisions, and his standards; he had two thousand men slain and five hundred taken prisoners. Such was the battle of Killycrankie, or *Rinn Ruaradh*, as it is still named by the peasantry, who attribute the ultimately fata, effects of the victory to the circumstance of Dundee wearing *green*, a colour still esteemed ominous to his sirname. A rude obelisk of rough stone still marks the place where the death-shot struck him, and is pointed out by the mountaineers with respect and regret as the *Tombh Claverse.*

The grief and consternation that spread through the Highland ranks on the fall of their beloved leader becoming known, prevented the pursuit being followed with sufficient vigour, otherwise few would ever have reached the southern mouth of that terrible pass.

"Dundee hath assuredly been slain," said General Mackay, as he breathed his sinking charger at the other extremity of Killycrankie, two miles from the field. "I am convinced of it: otherwise we would not have been permitted to retreat thus far unmolested."

CHAPTER LI.

THE LAST HOUR OF DUNDEE.

Oh last and best of Scots! who did'st maintain
Thy country's freedom from a foreign reign;
Now people fill the land, now thou art gone,
New gods the temples, and new kings the throne!
ARCHIBALD PITCAIRN.

Now the battle was over, and the fury of the conflict with the fierce energies it excited had passed away together. In that narrow gauge lay more than two thousand slain; and the broad round moon, as its shining circle rose above the dark ridge of the far-off mountains, poured its cold lustre on the distorted visages of the writhing wounded, and more ghastly lineaments of the pallid dead. While the Highlanders were plundering the baggage, and carousing on the provisions of Mackay (who was then retreating to Stirling), Walter Fenton rode to the house of Urrard, and repaired to the presence of his leader.

Within a little wainscotted apartment, lighted by four long candles, that flared in a brazen branch, stretched upon a low canopied bed lay the great and terrible Dundee. On his proud heart of fierce impulses and high aspirations, the hand of the grim monarch was now laid surely and heavily. His fine features were sharpened, pale and ghastly, by agony and approaching death. He breathed slowly. His Monmouth wig was laid aside, and his own raven hair, which formed a strong contrast with the whiteness of his skin, flowed over the pillow like the tresses of a woman.

"Can this be Claverhouse?" thought Walter.

His blood-stained buff coat, his sword and helmet, lay near him on a chair, and around the couch were Dunbarton, Finland, the great Sir Evan of Locheil, Glengarry, Clanronald, Grant of Glenmorriston, and other leaders, who leaned on their swords, conversed in low whispers, and watched with unfeigned sorrow the ebbing life of the only man who could lead them like Montrose.

The whole of his dying energies were now directed to one object, a despatch to his exiled king, containing an account of the glories he had gained in his cause, and the long career of service he had sealed with his own gallant blood. Though every muscle of his face was contracted at times with the agony he endured, when stretching from bed to write at the low table beside it, supported by his brother David Grahame, who was sheathed in steel *à la cuirassier*, he finished this memorable and disputed letter with singular coolness, appended his name, and instantly falling back, closed his eyes and lay motionless, as if in death.

"He is gone," whispered the agitated earl of Dunbarton to the stern Locheil. "There lies the strongest pillar of the good old cause."

"*Hereditary right will face the rocks!*" replied the chieftain in Gaelic, as he grasped his dirk; "cursed be the green scarf that wrought this evil work to Scotland and to us!"

Their voices seemed to call back the fleeting spirit; and, controlling the painful trembling of the limbs, Dundee opened his bloodshot eyes, and looked slowly round him.

"Do not persist," said he to the surgeon, who approached. "I know that all is over—let me die in peace. Approach, Mr. Fenton—unfurl that standard;" and his wild dark eyes

flashed with their old energy at the sight of the Stadtholder's
banner. "You will, at all risks, bear this despatch and that
trophy to the hands of King James, and say they are the
last—the best—the dying bequest of Dundee."

Walter's heart was full; he could only lay his hand upon
his breast, and bow a grateful assent.

"To Colonel Cannon I bequeath my baton and authority;
let him use them well in the king's service, if he would wish
to die in peace when he comes to lie *here*."

"Colonel Cannon!" muttered the Highland chiefs, as they
drew themselves up, exchanged glances of *hauteur*, and
twisted their moustaches.

"Be merciful to our prisoners," continued the sufferer in a
voice more weak and quavering, and stopping often to take
breath; "be merciful to them, for they are our countrymen.
Release and bid them return to their homes in peace; say
that such was the last wish of Dundee. Many have styled
me merciless in my time, sirs, and bitterly will they speak of
my spirit when it is far beyond the reach of mortal malevolence. I have done fierce and stern things, but I have been
hurried to do them by an irrevocable destiny, and a tide of
circumstances incident to these our troubled times. Every
iota of what I have done was foreordained—ha! do not your
Presbyterians tell us so? But grateful—deeply grateful is the
conviction to my passing spirit, that my friends will ever
remember my name with honour, and my foes with fear. I
feel more bitterness in dying after a victory than I could have
endured by a defeat; for *it* would have made life worthless,
and death welcome. Oh, may this day's great achievement
be an omen of future success, and a second Restoration! Go,
my comrades; continue in that path of earthly glory which I
must quit for ever; and let ye who survive to behold our
beloved king fail not to tell him—that—that John Grahame,
of Claverhouse—with his last breath blessed him—and—
died."

Falling back, he immediately expired, just as daylight
(which at that season scarcely passed away) brightened in
the east.

All started and bent over him; but the fierce spirit of that
remorseless cavalier had fled for ever, and his magnificent
features, as the rigidity and pallor of death overspread them,
assumed the aspect of a beautiful marble statue. A groan
that burst from the lips of his brother, as he knelt down and
closed his eyes; the heavy sobs of a few aged Highlanders;
and the low wail of a lament, as the pipers of Glengarry

poured it to the mountain-wind and echoing woods of Urrard, were the only sounds heard within that gloomy chamber, where the terror of the Presbyterians—the idol of the cavaliers, and the last hope of James, lay prostrate, to rise no more. Though by one faction styled the *last and best of Scots*—by the other, a murderer and outlaw; yet, by the cause for which he died, and the manner of his death, he closed in glory a life of singular ferocity and turbulence.

His remains were hurriedly interred in the rural kirk of Blair Athol; and the cause of King James was buried with him. His brother assumed his title; but died in great obscurity in France in 1700. The buff coat of Dundee, bearing the mark of the fatal ball, and stained with his blood, together with his helmet and other relics, are still preserved in the ducal castle of Blair.

Remembering the dying desire of their leader on the day after the battle, the Highland chiefs liberated all the prisoners on parole of honour not to serve against the king, Colonel Fergusson, of Craigdarroch (notwithstanding all the exertions of his generous rival Finland) "being excepted," says Captain Crichton, in his Memoirs, "on account of his more than ordinary zeal for the new establishment."

In those days the uncertain means of communication between towns, and the great deficiency of certain information of public events, caused many strange and varying rumours of the Highland war to be circulated in the Lowlands, where the only newspaper was the *Caledonius Mercurius*, which had been published occasionally since the Restoration. But the astounding intelligence of the victory at Killycrankie, and the fall of Dundee, spread like wildfire through the low country, to which he had so long been a terror and scourge. The defeat of Cannon at the Haughs of Cromdale, and the utter prostration of James's banner in the north, was soon followed by his disaster at the Boyne, in Ireland, where the loss of a decisive battle compelled him again to seek refuge in France.

Poor Lilian, at home in the then secluded capital of Scotland, heard of those stirring events at long intervals; and to her they were a source of deep interest, and of many a sigh and hour of tears; but of Walter she heard no tidings. Whether he lay mouldering in the Pass of Killycrankie, among the haughs of Cromdale, or was wandering among the wildest fastnesses of the north, with the doom of proscription and treason hanging over him, she knew not; and time in no way soothed or alleviated the agonies of her suspense. On the return of Colonel Fergusson, whose apostacy had opened an easy path to preferment under the new order of affairs, she learned some faint rumours of his departure to France with the other officers of Dundee—for that horizon where the sun of the exiled Jacobites was setting—the lonely palace of St. Germain. Though the tidings fell like ice on the heart of the poor girl, any certainty was preferable to suspense; and with her good aunt Grizel, she could only weep for the poor youth they loved so well, and pray and hope for happier times. To lighten the solitude his absence caused, she could not even hope for a letter; all intercourse with the court of the exiled king being proscribed under pain of banishment and death; and thus slowly the melancholy summer of 1690 passed on.

With the accession of William, and total subversion of the old high-church party, all the sourness and severity of Presbyterian discipline (which at times compelled the proudest peers to endure a rebuke on the ignominious repentance-stool, or at least before a congregation) was resumed by the overbearing clergy in full sway. From the innate cavalier sentiments of her family, and the wavering politics of Aunt Grizel, Lilian had never been a very rigid Presbyterian; and now looking upon the triumph of "the kirk" as having driven her lover into exile, she felt her heart further than ever removed from Presbytery. She had still to endure the persecution of Clermistonlee, who, having in a few months spent all the Revolution had enabled him to extort by fines from his old cavalier friends, was now more reduced and desperate than ever; and, as a last shift, was compelled to dispose of his tower of Clermiston for a trifling sum to his more cautious gossip Mersington; and though the gaming-table replenished his exchequer at times, gaunt starvation stared him hourly in the face.

Though the native kindness and exceeding gentleness of Lilian's manner had always given this indefatigable suitor some hope of ultimate success, he soon found that, besieging her whenever she went abroad, and keeping spies upon her when at home—pestering her with presents, and letters the most flattering and submissive his ingenuity and skill could indite, did not bring him nearer the summit of his wishes. As his funds waxed lower, his perseverance increased; and he brought a new ally into the field, in the person of our old friend Mr. Ichabod Bummel, whose zeal for the Revolution had procured him an incumbency in the city, where, every Sunday, he had the felicity of preaching in a pulpit of his own, quoting that immortal work the *Bombshell*, railing at the exiled king, and all other "bloody-minded massmongers," are "dinging" many successive bibles to "blads" in the true Knox-like energy of his discourse. This meddling preacher, after the abduction of Lilian, and the scandalous reports the kirk party had so industriously circulated concerning it, had long deemed it, in his own phraseology, "a shameful and malapert fact, unseemly to men, and abominable in the sight of Heaven, that these twain should remain unwedded;" and by his influence, Clermistonlee was duly cited before the kirk session. Resistance was in vain, for now the clergy had suc ceeded to the council's iron rod; and temporal proscription and spiritual excommunication invariably followed delay.

Clad in a sack of coarse white canvass, and on his knees before a staring congregation of stern Presbyterians, he "confessit his manifold sins and enormities," as the records of the kirk show, "and was rebukit by the godlie Mr. Bummel for the space of ane hour, being comparit to ane owle in ye desart;" and it appears that the minister, in his ire, made such direct reference to the abduction of Lilian, in language so pointed, so coarse, and unseemly, that, overwhelmed with shame and horror, the poor girl, unable to bear the scornful scrutiny and malevolent glances of her own sex, sank down in the gloomiest recesses of the old family pew, and swooned.

This event, together with the cruel inuendos industriously circulated by the gallants and gossips of the city, was her crowning misfortune; from that hour her peace was blighted, and her fair fame blotted for ever. Her friends pitied and acquaintance shunned her. She endured the most intense grief and bitterness of soul that a sensitive and delicate woman could feel; for even the very children of the Whig faction pelted her sedan when it entered the city, and called her "My lord's leman," "Clermistonlee's minion," and the "Deil's dearie."

The united effects of grief, shame, mortification, and in-sulted pride, were soon visible on her health; her cheek grew blanched and thin, her eyes dim; and though she did not weep, her sorrows lay deeper, and the canker-worm preyed upon her suffering heart. And not the least offensive to her feelings were those offerings of friendship which were mingled with condolence, when Lady Drumsturdy and others advised her to think seriously of the long and assiduous attentions of Clermistonlee; in short, "*after all that had taken place*," to receive him as her husband; that being, in their opinion, the only way to restore her forfeited honour.

The inuendo concealed under this odious advice provoked the anger of Lilian, whose concern was increased by perceiving that Lady Grizel, and her own bosom friend and gossip, Annie, were beginning to be of the same opinion. Thei countenance, and the hope of Walter's return, had alone sustained her so long ; but now a sense of utter desolation sank upon her soul, and her brain reeled with the terrible thoughs that oppressed it.

CHAPTER LII.

ST. GERMAIN.

And it was a' for our richtfu' kmg,
We ere left Scotia's strand, my dear ;
And it was a' for our richtfu' king,
We saw another land, my dear.

OLD SONG.

AGITATED by feelings such as few have experienced, on an evening in the summer of 1690, Walter Fenton found himself pursuing the dusty highway from Paris to St. Germain, the place where the hopes and the fears, the loyalty and the sorrows of the Jacobites were centred.   He wore a plain suit of unlaced grey cloth, very much worn, a hat without a feather, and a plain walking-sword.   He carried under his arm a small bundle, with particular care, for it contained a few necessaries and all he possessed in the world—his commission, the long-treasured letter of Dundee, and the Dutch standard he had taken at Killycrankie.   These were now his whole fortune.

That day he had walked from Senlis without tasting food, and was quite exhausted.   After spending his last sou on a glass of sour vin ordinaire at a small cottage, near the Wood of Treason (where Ganelon in 780 formed his plot which betrayed the house of Ardennes, the peers of Charlemagne, and occasioned the defeat of Roncesvalles), he grasped his bundle, and pushed on with renewed energy. His handsome features were impressed by an air of sadness and deep abstraction, for the acute achings of present sorrow struggled with the gentler whisperings of hope, and though his feet traversed the hard flinty roadway from Paris, his thoughts were far away in the land of his childhood, and his wandering fancy luxuriated on the memory of many a much-loved scene he might be fated to behold no more, and many an episode of tenderness and love that would never be reacted again.

How vividly he recalled every glance and graceful action of Lilian, as he had last beheld her.   Nearest and dearest to his heart, she rendered the memory of his native land still more beloved, for she yet trod its soil and breathed its air, and he knew that daily she could gaze on those blue hills which are the first landmarks of the child in youth, and the last of the man in age, and to the recollection of which the emigrant and the exile cling with the tenacity of life.

The current of his thoughts was interrupted, and his cheek flushed. The great and striking brick façade of the old castle of St. Germain, with its turrets shining in the setting sun, arose before him. There dwelt *he* on whom the hopes of half a nation rested, and Walter drew breath more freely as he progressed; his eye sparkled, and his cheek flushed with animation, for now other and less painful thoughts were occurring to his fancy. With the buoyancy natural to youth, sorrow gave way as hope spread its rainbow before him; and bright visions of the king's triumphant return and restoration by the swords of the cavaliers or Jacobites, mingled with his own dreams of love and honour. Fired with ardour, he often grasped his sword, and springing forward, longed to throw himself at the foot of James VII., and pour forth in transport that singularly deep and burning passion of loyalty which animated every member of his faction.

"And this is the palace of our king!" he exclaimed, with enthusiasm. "Heaven grant I may yet greet him in his old ancestral dome of Holyrood!" But the fever of his naturally excitable spirits subsided when approaching the edifice, for the air of silence and gloom that pervaded it struck a chill on his anxious heart.

"Ah," thought he, "if James should be dead!"

At the distance of twelve miles from Paris, this ancient brick chateau or palace is beautifully situated on the slope of a verdant hill, at the base of which flows the Seine, and opposite lies an immense forest. From the earliest ages, St. Germain-en-laye had been a hunting-seat of the French kings; but in compliment to his mistress, whose name was Diana, Francis I. (a monarch unequalled in gallantry, generosity, and magnificence), built the present palace in form of the letter D, with five towers, the vanes of which were gleaming like gold in the setting sun as Walter approached. A dry fosse crossed by drawbridges surrounded this noble chateau, which had on one side a range of beautiful arcades, built by Henry IV and Louis XIII., and a magnificent terrace. 2,700 yards long and 50 broad, extending by the side of the dark-green forest, and from which, as our exile traversed it, he had a full view of the Seine winding through a beautiful country, bor-

dered on each side by waving meadows, vineyards of the
deepest green, and cornfields of the brightest yellow, villages
of white cottages thatched with light-coloured straw, that
clustered round the turreted chateaux, or the ramparted
châtelets of a noblesse that were then the most aristocratic in
Europe.

But Walter saw only the home of the exiled Stuarts. On
the ruddy brick-walls, the latticed casements, and gothic
towers, the setting sun was pouring a flood of light as it set at
the cloundless horizon. From the summit of the edifice, the
royal standard of Britain hung down listlessly and still, and
the same absence of life seemed to pervade all beneath it. The
ditch was overgrown with luxuriant weeds, and long tufts of
pendant grass waved in the joints of the masonry; great
branches of vine and ivy had clambered up the walls of the
palace, and flourished in masses on its terraced roofs and bal-
conies.   There was no one visible at any of the windows; the
gateway, which was surmounted by a stone salamandre (the cog-
nizance of Francis I.), was shut, and save two sentinels of the
French guards, who stood motionless as statues on each side,
and an old Jacobite gentleman or two, in full-bottomed wigs
and laced coats, promenading slowly and thoughtfully on the
terrace, the old chateau seemed lifeless and uninhabited.

As Walter crossed the bridge, and approached the gate
with a beating heart, one of the sentinels, after giving a
haughty glance at his faded and travel-stained attire, his
weary aspect, and bundle, ported his musket across, and said
politely, but firmly—"Pardonnez, monsieur."

Walter's heart swelled: had he travelled thus far, and
reached the palace of his king, only to be repulsed from its
gates? His colour came and went, as, with a painful mixture
of pride and humility, he replied—

"Mon camarade, I am a poor Scots officer, exiled from his
native country, and who has come here to take service in
France." The face of the Frenchman flushed, and his eye
glistened, as he drew himself up, and presented arms.

"Behold my commission," continued Walter; "I would
speak with my noble lord and colonel the earl of Dunbarton."

"Aha," replied the sentinel, "il est bon soldat, Monsieur
Dunbartong. Passez, monsieur officier; un gentilhomme est
toujours un gentilhomme, et les braves officiers Ecossais
sont l'admiration de la France!"

Walter bowed at this compliment, the gate was opened by
the porters, and, with a heart full of thoughts too deep for

words, he found himself within the gloomy quadrangle of the palace of St. Germain-en-laye.

Left for some minutes to himself, he stood, bundle in hand, irresolutely surveying, with a dejected and crest-fallen air, the great and silent court. A gentleman in very plain attire, with a short wig, a well-worn beaver, and steel-hilted sword, who was slowly promenading under the arcade, suddenly turned, and the wanderer was greeted by his old friend Finland.

"Welcome to the poor cheer of St. Germain-en-laye!" cried this merry soldier (whom no fall of fortune could daunt), grasping Walter's hand. "My bon camarade, welcome to France. By all the devils, I was often grieved for thee, poor lad, and deemed thou wert doing penance in some rascally Tolbooth for our brave camisade in the north."

Walter was so much oppressed in spirit, and so weak in mind and body, that the tears rushed into his eyes, and he could only press his hand in silence.

"What the devil—— my poor lad, thou seemest very faint and exhausted!"

"I have travelled on foot from Boulogne-sur-mer. I spent my last franc at St. Juste, my last sou an hour ago for a glass of vin ordinaire, and for three days no food has passed my lips."

"My God!" exclaimed Finland, striking his flushed forehead, "and my last tester went for dinner to-day! how shall I assist you? Travelling for three days without food! Surely the fortunes of the cavaliers are now at the lowest ebb."

"Then the tide must flow again."

"I now begin to fear it will flow no more for us. What says the player?

'There is a tide in the affairs of men,
Which taken at the flood, leads on to fortune.'

Once at least in life, every man's fortune will be at the flood, and if he misses the tide his bark is stranded on the shore for ever. But thee, poor lad! how shall I get thee food?— we are all as poor as kirk rats here. There are not less than two hundred officers of Dundee's army, and other loyal gentlemen of the life guards and Scottish brigade, subsisting here on the small bounty of our gracious king, (whom Heaven in its mercy bless!) until some turn of fortune again draws forth their swords. We have each but fourpence a-day, and are in great misery from lack of the most common necessaries of life. Yet we never forget that we are Scottish gentlemen,

2 c 2

and daily attend the king's *levée*, with as gallant an air as if we trod the long gallery of Holyrood in our feathers and lace as of old. His grace of Gordon, my lords of Maitland, Dunbarton, Abercorn, and others dine daily at a poor restaurateur's, on plain stew and cabbage broth, while I have to content myself with bread and onions, and a keen appetite for sauce; while it affords me no consolation to reflect that my old ancestral tower of Finland—the gift of the Black Douglas to his favourite son—and all the fertile lands that spread around it, are now possessed by some vile, canting crop-ear. The earl of Dunbarton——"

"Whilom our gallant colonel—how I long for an interview!"

"He is gone to Versailles to visit Le Mareschal Noailles, anent the unfortunate gentlemen who are starving here around us. He will be back to-morrow. Oh, Walter, when I see how might can triumph over *right*, and wickedness over more than Spartan virtue, I am almost tempted to believe there is no governing power in this wretched world; that all this is the effect of chance or fate."

"Chance and fate are the reverse of each other, and this sentiment agrees not with your previous idea of ' the tide in the affairs of men.' "

"Tush! I am in a dozen minds in an hour. Let us leave these topics to such men as Mr. Ichabod Bummel. You remember that apostle of the covenant? ha, ha! A word in your ear. You saw our fair ones ere you left Scotland, I doubt not?"

" Alas, no."

" The deuce! how came that to pass? But you must dine, and where? for I have not a brass bodle, as we say at home in poor old Scotland, (God bless her, with all her errors!) I have it! the officer of the guard will lend me—or give—'tis all one; they are fine fellows, these French, and share their poor pay with us, in a spirit of charity that the apostles could not have surpassed. The gentleman and the soldier seldom seek a boon from each other in vain."

Finland calculated rightly; the French chevalier commanding the guard, on learning the cause of his present necessity, at once divided the contents of his purse, and enabled the happy borrower to lead his wearied friend to a tavern, where dinner was ordered and discussed with wonderful celerity.

"Now, Walter, I shall be glad to hear thy adventures," said Finland, when the waiting girl had cleared the dinner board and laid a decanter of wine, from which he filled their glasses. "Frontiniac dashed with brandy—you remember how often we have drank a bottle of it at Hughie Blair's. and the White Horse hostel. How the times are changed since then! I was not at the Haughs o' Cromdale, being *en route* for Ireland, to crave succour from James——"

"After the dispersion consequent to that ill-managed affair, I wandered from place to place, enduring such miseries as few can conceive, and was a thousand times in danger of being captured by Mackay's dragoons, who were riding down the country in every direction. Assisted by the kind and beautiful countess of Dunbarton (who is yet intriguing in England), I procured some money, and, disguised as a Norlan drover, reached the western borders, for escape by sea from Scotland was impossible, the whole coast being watched by the English and Dutch fleet. In England my money was soon spent, and I despaired of ever reaching the port of Colchester, where I heard there lay a ship that in secret frequently transported our persecuted people to France. My bonnet and grey plaid, though they ensured my safety in the Lowlands, caused me to be viewed with hatred, jealousy, and mistrust, as soon as the Cheviot hills were left behind me, and I had not money wherewith to procure a change of costume. I travelled principally by night, and slept in ditches or thickets by day, for the villagers assailed me with stones and abuse whenever they saw me, using every bitter epithet that national animosity could inspire, while every country boor that had a couple of beagles at hand, uncoupled them to track and hunt me."

"Would to heaven I had been with thee, lad! Well."

"I remember with what bitterness I changed my last penny for a poor roll at Rippon, and eat it by the side of a ditch, near the princely castle of one who had gained a coronet by his political apostacy. I had still many miles before me, but trusting to Providence, continued my journey. Travelling by night and lying *perdu* by day, I found myself in a waste moorland near Cawood, in the West Riding of Yorkshire. The moon was rising; but I found that hunger, fatigue, and humiliation, had done their worst upon me, and that I could achieve no more. Despair entered my heart, and I threw myself down in that bleak spot to die, cursing the rebellion of our countrymen, the inhospita'... of the English, and my own bad fortune. From a stupor that for some time weighed down every sense, I was roused by the trampling of a horse, and a deep bass voice, crying,

"'Hollo Gaffer, art dead, or dead drunk only? Get up with a murrain, for my nag will neither stand or pass; steady —so so—gently, zounds! gently.'

" I started, and instinctively grasped my staff, on perceiving a tall stout fellow muffled in a dark rocquelaure, with his face masked, and a hat flapped over his eyes. He rode a strong, fleet, and active horse, and carried long holsters.

" 'Crush me, if it isn't a Scotch jockey—a pedlar, I warrant!' said he, drawing a pistol from his saddlebow; 'they never travel without the ready; so hand over the bright Jacobuses or William's guilders, or else I may pop this bullet through your brain.'

" I was desperate, and replied, 'Fire! and rid me of an existence that is worthless. I have nothing to give but my life, and it is no longer of value to me.'

" 'A gentleman, by this light!' replied the other, withdrawing his pistol, 'some cavalier in disguise, I warrant.'

" 'You have guessed rightly; so now lead me to the nearest justice of the peace for a reward, if you will.'

" 'For what do you take me?' said he, angrily. 'God bless King James, and may the great devil choke his son-in-law! Ah, had the good Dundee (a Scot though he was) survived that brave day's work, in your infernal pass of what d' ye call it? 'twould have been another case with us both to-day, perhaps. So thou art a Scottish cavalier?'

" 'Once I was so—to-night I am a beggar, perishing by want, and without a roof to shelter me.'

" 'Hast thou no money, lad?'

" 'Not a penny, and have two hundred miles to travel.

" 'Hast thou no friends among the English here?'

" 'Have I not said that I am poor?'

" 'Right! I have learned in my time that the poor have no friends.'

" 'Save God and their own hands.'

" 'Right again, say I; though a highwayman, I love thee, lad, for we have suffered in common from this accursed usurper, who sits in the throne of our king. Here are thirty guineas; 'tis the half of all I have in the world, but to-morrow night may bring me better luck; take them with welcome, and spend them without scruple; but two hours ago they were in the purse of that rascally whig, Marmaduke Langstone, of Langstone-hall. Keep to the right, and an hour's brisk walking will bring you to a hedge alehouse. Whisper my name to the wench at the bar (kiss her for me), and she will put thee on the right road for Colchester; the girl is true as steel to the good old cause.'

" 'Whom shall I thank—whom remember?'

" 'They call me "Highflying Tom" now, eastward of

Temple-bar,' said he in a tone of bitterness ; ' but when King James sat in his own chair, I was Thomas Butler, *Esquire*, of a long pedigree and an empty purse—devil else—but a gentleman every inch, sir ; one that has shot his man, played at cavagnole with King Charles, and ombre with the queen ; drank many a bout with Rochester, ruffled it with Buckingham, and handed the fair Castlemaine and fairer Cleveland through a crowded cotillon. But it's all over now ; and, d—n me! I am plain Bully Butler the highwayman. So, sir, your servant ;' and dashing spurs into his horse, he galloped away over the heath."

"Thomas Butler, of the princely house of Ormond—and twas he!" said Finland ; " a braver spark old Ireland never sent forth to glory or disgrace. His father was a stout old Royalist, and shed his blood for King James on the banks of the Boyne. And so he hath taken to the road, the madcap! That is riding at the gallows full tilt with a vengeance !"

" But for that rencontre, I must have expired. The meeting gave me renewed energy ; and (to be brief) I reached —not Colchester, but the seaport of Saltfleet, where, in the disguise of a poor Scottish mariner, I embarked on board a smuggling craft, which landed me at Boulogne ; and so—I am here.''

CHAPTER LIII.

THE CAVALIERS OF DUNDEE.

In the cause of right engaged,
　Wrongs injurious to redress ;
Honour's war we strongly waged,
　But the heavens denied success.
Ruin's wheel has driven o'er us,
　Not a hope that dare attend ;
The world wide is all before us,
　But a world without a friend.
STRATHALLAN'S LAMENT.

THE magnanimity of those unfortunate officers of the Scottish army who remained loyal to James VII., and had shared his misfortunes and exile, was equally worthy of ancient Caledonia and of the most glorious ages of Athens and of Sparta. They were about one hundred and fifty in number, all men of noble spirit, unblemished honour, and high birth,—for they were the representatives of some of the first families in Scotland. Enthusiastically attached to the king, they gloried in the sufferings their principles had brought upon them.

On their first arrival in France, small pensions were assigned them by Louis XIV.; but these were shortly afterwards withdrawn, on the paltry pretext of public expedience; and the whole of those unfortunate gentlemen, who by their incorruptible loyalty and indomitable patriotism had forfeited their commissions, when they might have purchased new honours in the ranks of the invader, and many of whom had lost titles and estates by their expatriation, were thus thrown destitute in a foreign land.

It is related that, with a noble spirit of generosity, they shared their little funds for the benefit of those who were in greater destitution; and those who had raised money by the sale of their gilt corslets, jewels, laced uniforms, rings, &c., readily shared it with others who were penniless. But these occasional funds soon became exhausted; the king soon found it impossible, from the pittance allowed him, to maintain the numerous exiles and ruined dependants who made his court of St. Germain their rallying point. The poor Scottish officers, finding the horrors of starvation before them, petitioned James for leave to form themselves into a company of private soldiers for the service of the French king, asking no other favour than permission to choose their own leaders; their former general, Dunbarton, to be their captain; their serjeants to be lieutenant-colonels; and so forth. The king reluctantly consented.

Those high-spirited cavaliers were immediately furnished with the clothing and arms of French soldiers; and previously to their incorporation with the army of Mareschal Noailles, repaired to St. Germain, to be reviewed by the king, and to take a long—to many a last—adieu of him.

It was the day after Walter's arrival; and the summer morning rose beautifully on the Gothic towers of St. Germain, the crystal windings of the Seine, and on the dense dark woodlands that, interspersed with blooming vineyards and waving fields, imparted such charms to the landscape.

James VII. had become passionately fond of the chase since the loss of his kingdom; for his brave and restless spirit always sought excitement when not absorbed in the austere duties of religion, in the course of which he often subjected himself to the most severe penances. Kind, affable, and easy to all around him, religion improved the virtues of his heart, subdued the fire of his spirit, and by imparting a monk-like gentleness to his demeanour, endeared him to his

enthusiastic followers. The butcheries of Kirke and Claverhouse, and the tyrannies of Jefferies and Rosehaugh, were
forgotten. Though his uncompromising b.gotry remained,
all his arbitrary spirit had vanished ; and when he laid aside
his visions of worldly grandeur and kingly power, nothing
could be more blameless and amiable than the life he led.

He frequently visited the poor monks of La Trappe, whom
he surprised by the piety and humility of his deportment ;
but there were times when the sparkling eye, the flushed
cheek, the forward stride, and the clanked sword, showed
how regal a spirit and bold a heart misfortune had crushed
and fanaticism clouded. He was an enthusiast in the pleasures of the chase, which he enjoyed after the good old English
fashion ; and on the morning in question, the baying of dogs,
the neighing of horses, and the merry ringing of the clear
bugle-horn, awoke the echoes of the woods, the gloomy
arcades, and quadrangle of St. Germain.

On each side of the archway were drawn up a guard of
honour of *Les Gardes Français*, in their white hoquetons
laced with gold, powdered wigs, little hats looped on three
sides, and surmounted with plumes of feathers, and having
the white banner of Bourbon displayed. The porters unclosed
the heavy folding-doors, and a merry troop of huntsmen in
green galloped forth, with their dogs barking and straining
in the leashes, as the blasts of the shrill horns were poured
to the morning wind, and roused their English blood. The
heavy drawbridge clanked into its place across the grass-
grown moat, the planks resounded to iron hoofs, the French
guard presented arms, the oriflamme of St. Denis was lowered, the drums beat a march, and James VII., raising his
plumed hat, sallied forth at the head of his train, and advanced
along the spacious and magnificent terrace. The earl of
Dunbarton rode by his side ; and as they caracoled along the
level terrace, by the margin of the beautiful Seine, a body of
soldiers in French uniform was seen in front, drawn up in
steady array, with their fixed bayonets shining in the morning
sun. They presented arms as the king approached, upon
which he immediately reined up, and raised his hat.

" My Lord Dunbarton," said he, " what troops are
these ?"

" They are your majesty's most faithful subjects and devoted followers," replied Dunbarton in a faltering voice,
" Yesterday they were Scottish gentlemen of coat-armour and
bearers of your majesty's commission ; to-day they are but
poor privates in the army of Louis of France."

"My God!" said the king; "and, in the levity of the chase, am I so oblivious of the misfortunes of those unhappy gentlemen?"

Instantly leaping from his horse with a heart that swelled by its emotions, he approached them and raised his hat.

Every heart was full in that silent line before him, and every eye glistened. Walter Fenton, who now for the first time beheld that king for whom he had suffered so much, felt his bosom glow with the most intense loyalty and ardour,— a gush of sentiment that would have enabled him to hail with joy the terrors of a scaffold or the dangers of a battle-field.

"Gentlemen," said the king, "bitter though my own misfortunes be, yours lie nearer my heart, which is grieved, beyond what language can express, to behold so many men of valour and worth, from being the officers of my Scottish army, reduced by their loyalty to the station of private soldiers. Nothing but this more than Spartan devotion on the part of the few, but gallant and leal, makes my life worth preserving. Deeply, deeply indeed is my heart impressed with the sense of all you have undergone for my sake; and if it should ever please the blessed God"—(removing his hat) —"to restore me to the throne of my fathers, your sufferings, your services, and your devotion, shall not be forgotten,— never, oh, never! The prince my son, he shares your northern blood. Oh, may he likewise inherit your spirit of bravery and truth!

"At your own desire, gentlemen, you are now going on a long and perilous march, far distant from me, to encounter privation, danger, and death. To the utmost of my small means, I have provided you with money, shoes, and stockings. Heaven knoweth how great are my own necessities. I can no more. . . .

"Fear God—love one another, and you will ever find me your parent, if I cannot be your king."

The eyes of James VII. were full of tears, and a long pause ensued.

"There is a gentleman here who arrived only yesterday," said Lord Dunbarton, who had also dismounted. "He is the bearer of two relics to your majesty: the first is the despatch of the expiring Dundee; the second will bear witness of his own zeal and courage in your cause at the victory of Killy-crankie."

"Let him approach," said the king, covering his face to hide his emotion

"Mr. Fenton," said the earl, "his majesty would speak with you;" and Walter, whose heart trembled from the depth of his emotions, grounded his musket, and, kneeling before James, placed in his hands the long-treasured despatch of Dundee, and the Dutch standard of Mackay's regiment.

"My brave Dundee!" exclaimed James in a low voice, as he kissed and perused the brief letter which had been hurriedly penned amid the agonies of death; "'tis stained with his loyal and noble blood! Oh! never had a king a subject more devoted, more loyal, or more true! Accept my thanks, young gentleman, for the services you have performed, the valour you have displayed, and the fidelity you evince; accept my thanks, for misfortune has left me nothing else wherewith to reward the faithful and the brave, who have followed me to exile and obscurity. This standard I will retain; one day, perhaps, in Holyrood or Windsor, I may replace it in your hands with such rewards as a king alone can give."

Walter strove to speak, but his voice failed him, on which Lord Dunbarton said,—

"Like his brothers in misfortune, my young friend seeks no other reward than the honour of serving your majesty, and the satisfaction of doing that which is right."

The king drew his sword.

"What is your name, sir!" he asked.

"Fenton—Walter Fenton, of Dunbarton's Foot."

"No kinsman, I hope, of Fenton of that ilk, who is so active in his treason against us?"

"Alas, no!" replied Walter, colouring in painful humility; "may it please your majesty I am but a poor *protégé* of the noble Dunbarton. I know not my family, my name, or my origin."

"It matters not; I shall render honour to all who deserve it; arise *Sir* Walter Fenton, knight banneret—of this power, at least, my son William cannot deprive me."

Startled by the suddenness of the action, Walter, whose heart leaped within him at the words of the king, could only kiss his hand and resume his place in the ranks of his cavalier comrades, who with difficulty repressed a shout of applause. Walter felt giddy and confused; the king still seemed to be addressing him.

The temporary excitement which had led James through this painful interview, now passed away, and his features became overclouded with a sad and bitter expression, as he went slowly along the line asking each officer his name, inserting it in his note book, and returning him personal thanks. Meanwhile the troop of huntsmen, equerries, and whippers-in, with their packs of panting hounds, were grouped about the terrace, and quite forgotten in the excitement of this sorrowful review.

" Your name, sir—yesterday you were at my *levée* in a garb more suitable to your rank," said James, to a tall and very handsome man, whose fashionably curled wig consorted ill with the coarse looped hat and plain blue coat of a French musketeer ; " your name, sir, if you please ? "

" John Ogilvie, of the house of Airly—late a captain in your majesty's Life Guard."

" Sir, I thank you ; the day may come when you shall command that Life Guard," replied James, writing down his name ; " and your's, sir ? " he asked of the next.

" Grant of Dunlugais—a captain of Mar's Fusileers."

" Then you have lost an estate in my service ? "

" I have lost nothing that I can regret in such a cause."

" May I live to requite it ! 'Tis an ancient house, and one of unblemished honour. Are you Catholic ? "

" No, I am a Presbyterian."

" Then the greater honour is due to you for disinterested loyalty. And your's, sir ? "

" Douglas of Finland—a lieutenant under the Lord Dunbarton."

" Another forfeiture ! " exclaimed James, striking his breast, " and your's, sir ? "

" Drumquhasel—first major to the same noble earl," replied the tall cavalier, on whose breast sparkled the cross of St. Louis.

" Another, and another ! Oh, gentlemen, your sufferings and your losses, your loyalty and your truth—God may requite them adequately, but I never can ! " exclaimed James, in a troubled voice ; and when he had inserted the names of the whole hundred and fifty in his note book, he moved again to the front, and taking off his hat, bowed profoundly with an air in which thankfulness and respect were exquisitely blended with dignity and majesty. He then retired pensively towards the palace ; but painfully aware of the misery of those who suffered for him, and still unwilling to leave them, with sensations too deep for utterance, the unhappy king returned once more, and bowing to them again and again, covered his face with his handkerchief, and burst into tears. Animated by one sympathetic impulse, the whole line sank at once upon their knees and bowed their heads; the spirit of many a brave man was subdued; several wept, and there was not an un-moistened eye among them. The king, in particular, was deeply affected; his sobs were audible; and again removing his hat, he raised his eyes to heaven, and exclaimed, in the words of the last chapter of Lamentations,—

"Remember, O Lord, what is come upon us! Consider and behold our reproach! *Our inheritance is returned to strangers—our houses to aliens!*"

He repeatedly smote himself upon the breast in an energetic fashion he had acquired among the Jesuits, who had been too much about him for his own fortune; and a long pause suc-ceeded, until Lord Dunbarton gave for the last time the word of command. The Scottish officers resumed their aspect of steadiness and order, and marched past the king, whom nearly all of them were fated to behold no more; for death on the field, disease in the camp, poverty and despair, did their work surely and rapidly, and few of that brave but forlorn band ever returned from the frontiers of Spain.

From Versailles this company of unfortunate cavaliers re-ceived an order to join the army of Mareschal Noailles; and, next day, they set out from St. Germain, on their long and weary march of nine hundred miles, which they performed on foot, heavily accoutred, bearing their own camp-kettles and equipages, and accompanied by miseries and mortifications that baffle all description; but which by the indomitable spirit and ardour that animated them, they seldom failed to surmount.

Louis of France was now plunged in a war, into which his mistaken policy had hurried him. In a long persecution of the unhappy Protestants, he had weakened his kingdom by the expatriation of thousands of his best and most industrious subjects, who wandered as refugees throughout other coun-tries, and justly inflamed all Europe against him. To crush him, there had been formed at Augsburg a powerful league, to which the whole empire of Germany, Spain, Holland, Savoy, Sweden, and Denmark were parties; but, in no way daunted, he anticipated this great confederation by invading the empire and laying siege to Philipsburg. The recent revolution in England had given a new turn to this religious war, and Ireland became the theatre of a contest which ended on the banks of the Boyne, where William triumphed over his unfortunate father-in-law.

It may be that the great expenses of the war in which he

was now involved prevented Louis XIV. from remunerating adequately to their merit the officers of Dundee's army; but when they joined the standard of Noailles on the Spanish frontier, they were in a state of lamentable destitution and misery. The coarse uniform in which they had marched from St. Germain was worn to rags; they were shoeless, shirtless, and emaciated by hardships, privations, and want of the most common necessaries of life; for by the selfishness and duplicity of individuals to whom their little commissariat was entrusted, they were cheated of their poor supplies, the few presents the generous had sent them, and even of a small pittance (a few pence daily) which James, amid all his own necessities, endeavoured to pay them; yet they were never known to utter a complaint, for the misfortunes of their sovereign pressed heavier on their hearts than their own.

Wherever they marched they were beheld with pity and remembered with sorrow. The kind ladies of Perpignan presented them with a purse containing 200 pistoles, and bought all their rings as relics of *Les officiers Ecossais.* "Wherever they passed they were received with tears by the women and admiration by the men. They were the foremost in the battle, and the last in retreat, and of all the troops in the service of France they were most obedient to orders."

There is nothing in the history of ancient or modern times to equal their admirable bearing, heroic ardour, and devoted loyalty. They endured the most severe humiliation and privations without uttering a murmur, and performed actions of heroism outdoing the deeds of romance; for to their inborn daring was united a spirit of desperation, and a longing to be honorably rid of a life that was without a charm and without a ray of hope.

The French were touched by their misfortunes and sufferings; a universal shout rent the camp of Noailles on their marching into it, and with that generosity which is so characteristic of soldiers, the chevaliers and officers immediately subscribed for them, each furnishing shirts, clothing, and money, and none was more liberal with his purse than the noble marcschal himself; but even of these presents the unhappy Scots officers were cheated by the villany of one to whom they were entrusted, and thus the kind efforts to alleviate their miseries failed.

On the route to Catalonia, near Montpelier, when fording a mountain torrent swollen by the recent rains, Walter Fenton and three other cavaliers were swept away. Catching hold of some alders that overhung the bank they kept them-selves above the current, and called on the peasantry to save them. It is related, that though hundreds were there looking on, they never offered the least assistance, but mocked and jibed them in barbarous Catalonian French, while waiting coolly until they were drowned, that they might possess their money, clothes, and arms. But after great toil and danger they were rescued by their comrades.

They were never seen on the field but with their faces to the enemy. On every desperate duty and forlorn hope they led the way, and often too where others dared not *follow*. Death and disease rapidly thinned their ranks, but their ardour never failed; and had the invisible spirit of the fierce Dundee led them as of old, they could not have surpassed the deeds they achieved and the glory they acquired. On Rosas surrendering,

"*Senor Mariscal*," said the Spanish governor, "what sol-diers were those who assailed the breach so valiantly?"

"*Ce sont mes enfans*," replied Noailles, smiling; "they are my children—the king of Britain's Scottish officers, who share his obscurity and exile, and do me the honour to serve under my command."

"By St. James! *they alone* have compelled me to surren-der," replied the noble Spaniard.

They marched from Rosas to Piscador, and, of an army of 26,000 men, 16,000 perished by the wayside of privation. Twice only the Scottish officers were known to disobey orders. The first occasion was at the siege of Rosas, an ancient and well-fortified city, situated upon a gulf about twelve miles from Girona. The air was intensely hot, and the water muddy and unwholesome; the only rations of the Scots officers were horse-beans, garlic, and sardinas; they were utterly penniless, and could procure no better food, conse-quently deadly fevers and fluxes rapidly thinned their ranks, upon which Mareschal Noailles ordered them to leave the camp for the purpose of cantoning in a more healthy locality; but they delayed to obey, and sent Sir Walter Fenton to ac-quaint him that they "considered his order as an affront put upon them as soldiers of fortune and gentlemen of honour."

The second instance was when a strong body of German troops had made a lodgment on an island in the Rhine, from which it was necessary to force them; the marquis de Selle ordered a number of boats to be prepared, under an impres-

sion that the river was too deep and rapid to be fordable, and
the Scottish officers were to lead the way, but were *not to*
move until orders were given to embark. Finding it impossible to restrain their ardour till the arrival of the boats, they
slung their muskets and prepared to cross.

" Come on, Walter !" exclaimed the brave Douglas, as he
.ed the way, " and we will shew these gay chevaliers of France
that we, who have forded the rapid Spey and rocky Forth,
need not shrink on the margin of the Rhine. Join hands,
gentlemen Scots ; forward ! and I will lead you to the dance.
Hurrah !"

Hand in hand, in the Highland fashion, with their muskets
slung, they threw themselves into the rapid and impetuous
stream, where between jagged rocks it urged its foamy way
over a slippery and stony bed ; and thus breaking its force they
stemmed the current, and, though under a fierce cannonade
and storm of musket balls poured on them from the rocks of
the islet, they forced the dangerous passage in the view of
both armies ; the laird of Drumquhasel and Captain Ogilvie*
were shot dead ; but, led on by Finland, the Scottish officers
scaled the rocks, and assailing ten times their number of Ger-
mans, with screwed bayonets and clubbed muskets, drove
them from their intrenchments into the Rhine on the other
side of the island, and reared the French standard on its
summit.

" By St. Denis !" exclaimed the marquis de Selle, " 'tis the
bravest action soldiers ever performed !"

" *Vive les officiers Ecossais !*" cried the French soldiers.
" *Le gentilhomme est toujours gentilhomme ;*" and to this day,
in memory of the Scottish valour. the place is named

L'Isle d'Ecosse.

* Captain Ogilvie was author of a song which is preserved in Hogg's Jacobite reliques,—" *Adieu for evermore.*"

CHAPTER LIV

THE 20TH OF SEPTEMBER, 1692.

But the far mind was absent in pursuit
Of him, her love, in fields where foes contested
The bloody harvest, and a crown the fruit,
Dread fruit, with cares and dangerous joys invested !
Her mind was absent in the distant war.
PEDRO OF CASTILE.

" WHITHER awa', Clermistonlee, ye mad buckie ?" exclaimed
Lord Mersington, as his friend jostled past him under the
great pillars or arcade near the cross, one forenoon, when all
the city were abroad *enjoying* the sunshine ; " whatna way is
that to gliff folk ? is a dun or the deil after ye ?"

" I crave pardon, my lord, but did not observe you ; for
what is all this crowd collected ?"

" The heralds have been proclaiming the ratification of the
new Protestant league against Louis of France."

" A league," added Clermistonlee, scornfully, " which our
pious and glorious William hath tinkered up, that the treasure and blood of his two British kingdoms may be wasted in
defence of the rascally Hollanders and thick-pated Flemings.
By all the devils, my lord, we have brought our political pigs
to a pretty market !" and he began to whistle a cavalier air.

" Wheesht !" said Mersington, glancing furtively around
him ; " this is clean contrary to the act of council ; and mind
ye, my braw billy, if ye aye strut with that long feather and
cocked beaver, your pinkit mantle, and lace o'erlay, like a
ruffling buck o' King Charles' time, instead o' wearing the
sad-coloured garb and sober demeanour of these our present
days, when naething but psalm-singing, swearing in Low
Dutch, and mortifying the spirit, are in vogue, you'll sune hae
the eyes o' the council upon ye, as a Jacobite in disguise, a
hatcher o' plots, conspiracies, and the deil kens what mair—
he, he !"

" Crush me, if I will lessen one curl of my peruke, or one
slash in my doublet, to please any Dutch king or clown that
ever wore breeches !"

" You seem in a braw mood this morning. I warrant you'll
hae pouched a round sum at shovel-board last night in the
Covenant-close."

" A messenger from the court of St. Germain has just been

II.   2 D

arrested by Maclutchy, the macer of council," replied Clermistonlee, watching keenly the sharp visage of the senator ;
"by Jove, you change colour, my gossip !—any correspondence in that quarter, hah ?"

"I trow not," said the other, resuming his immovable
aspect ; " d'ye tak' me for a gomeral ? What is that we see
above the Tolbooth-gable ?"

"The arm of the gibbet."

"Weel," rejoined the judge, drily, "and what news
brought the messenger ?"

"Nought but letters from the exiled lords and gentlemen ;
some of them, I tell thee, Mersington, are deeply touching,
and would harrow up even that impenetrable heart of thine.
They tell of blighted loves and blasted hopes, of sorrow and of
suffering, humiliation and despair ; but of a loyalty and unblemished honour, that shed a glory around the cause for
which they suffer—a glory that makes us intensely despicable
by comparison. There are passages in some of those letters
from the brave cavaliers of Dundee, that have made many of
the council almost weep with compassion. By the heaven
that is above us, I feel that I would be a thousand times more
happy as one of those illustrious exiles, than struggling here
to maintain, by gambling, exactions, and roguery, a hollow
rank, a gilded title, and a career of extravagance on which I
have run too far to return !"

"The only sensible clause in your process," said Mersington, testily. "But you'll hae yoursel laid by the heels yet,
and then you may whistle on your thumb for the braw mains
and revenues of Bruntisfield and the Wrytes, for whilk you've
graned and girned these twa years and mair."

"Right ! 'twas but the feeling of a moment for the misfortunes of our former friends, whose hearts, to their honour
(unlike ours) were better than their heads."

"Puir chields—puir chields—I doubt the act of eighty-
nine presses unco hard on some of them."

"Among other letters, is one from that wild spark, Douglas
of Finland, once a lieutenant in the regiment of Dunbarton,
addressed to his false leman, Mistress Annie Laurie. Poor
credulous fool, to trust in a woman's faith ! He knows not
that she hath become Lady Craigdarroch, and so hath forgot
him in the arms of his friend. I like love-letters, having
written some bushels of them in my time ; but his—by the
devil's beard !—it equals anything in the *Banished Virgin,*
or *Cassandra.* I have taken the liberty to confiscate it to
my own use ; and here it is."

" Hold! a thought strikes me ; the hand is easy of imitation, and for what may ye no add a postscriptum, wnilk may be of service in your love affair, by wedding young Fenton—"

" The devil confound him !"

"To some airy demoiselle ; or knocking him on the head during his French campaign ?"

" 'Tis all one. Excellent ! Juden will deliver it. Annie will fly to her gossip, with every string in her boddice straining with the greatness of her intelligence ; and as we never knew a damsel prefer a dead lover to a living one, we may imagine or hope the issue. 'Tis sublime !"

" I wad rather hae a dead gudewife. I ken—he, he !" said Mersington, as he adjusted his wig, and took his friend's arm, striking his gold-headed cane on the pavement with the air of a man who has said something smart ; "but let us hae nae mair o' your plaguy qualms o' conscience, for they dinna dovetail weel wi' the general tenour o' your way. Weel, anent this postscriptum—he, he !—let us adjourn to——"

" Hugh Blair's, you would say. Poor Hugh ! his *locale* hath changed with the times, and there is nothing now but gloom and obscurity, cobwebs and dust, where all was once courtly merriment and joyous revelry. Who could have imagined that a time would come when this famous coffee-house would be voted 'a den of cavalier iniquity,'—that the buirdly hosteller with whom the noble Perth, the gallant Dunbarton, and the courtly Dundee whiled away the hours at picquet and tric-trac, and pushed the wine from hand to hand, would be accused of those honours as a crime, and thrown into the iron-room of the Tolbooth, there to languish in poverty and misery, while the luscious contents of his well-stored cellars were confiscated to the public use ?"

" It ill beseems ye to condemn the last clause in your interlocutor, my noble gossip, when the maist of the precious contents of Hughie's runlets ran owre your ain craig. My certie ! you had a braw rug at the forfeitures, baith gentle and semple ! "

" Ha, ha ! enough of this—the present business is to procure the use of an inkhorn. I am restricted in wine to drink medicated Hippocras. What art grinning at now ? "

" Your occasional scruples o' conscience—he, he ! Do ye mind the whilly-whaw ye were in anent the spectre of an armed man in the hall of Clermiston ? "

" Why the devil remind me of it ? " exclaimed the other, angrily ; "if it really was a spirit——"

" *If !* we have in profane as weel as sacred writing owre
2 D 2

mony evidences of their reality, and their appearance for various purposes whilk we cannot comprehend; and we have also as many solid proofs that the devil can mak' deid bodies move; but anent this, see Gabrielle Nandæns in his *Apology*, and Delrio in his *Disquisitiones Magicæ*."

"D—n Delrio! Ever pestering me with thy musty learning! but here is a change-house, where it may be that we can get this notable postscriptum concocted."

*   *   *   *   *   *

The summer had passed away, and now brown autumn was once more reddening the heather of the Pentlands, and spreading her dun tints over the woods of Bruntisfield; the sombre eve was closing fast, but the bright fire burned merrily as ever in the chamber-of-dais at the old castellated place, and ruddily its warm light shone through the barred windows into the recesses of the old woodlands, which every passing breeze robbed of some of their crisped foliage, and strewed it over the muirlands to the south. The old manor-house had recovered from the rages of that terrible night in 1688, and was now repaired, and stronger than ever; the windows were more thickly grated, and numerous loopholes and two additional turrets defended the barbican gate.

Lilian and her friend Annie were seated side by side as of old, and opposite sat Lady Grizel—but a change had come over them all. Though the hale old lady recovered from the shock of Lilian's abduction, it had seriously affected her health, and now she was a picture of the helplessness of extreme old age, in her dotage, pale and querulous, but ever gentle and childlike. She occupied the same old fringed chair, with its bobs of parti-coloured silk, in which she had sat every evening for fifty years; her ivory wheel, though now unused, stood on one side of it, and her tall metal-headed cane on the other. Lilian was paler and thinner, and had lost much of her girlish beauty; she had many cares gnawing at her heart, but she was still as adorable and interesting as ever. Annie was, if possible, more so than formerly; the bloom of her beauty had expanded to the utmost; her cheek had a higher colour, and her eye a brighter sparkle; her tall and beautiful figure was more inclined to *embonpoint*. But alas for poor Finland, the fickle Laurie was now the wife of Craigdarroch, who had risen to the rank of colonel of horse in the new Scottish army of William III. Her dress was more matronly and magnificent than formerly, and her rich flower tabby suit, with its brocade stomacher and silver fringes, contrasted with Lilian's plain blue suit of Florence silk with its falls of point d'Espagne.

Ashamed that she had broken her own solemn engagements to her exiled lover, with the natural fickleness of her sex, Annie was labouring to undermine the truth of Lilian, and, Heaven knows why, tormented the poor girl hourly, by urging the suit of Lord Clermistonlee, and left no arguments untried to carry her point, and remove the scruples of her more gentle but less facile friend.

"And poor Walter!" urged Lilian, with a look of great tenderness in her mild and moistened eyes, replying to some observation of Annie.

"Marry come up with your Walter! tush! bethink you, dear Lilian, this gallant never loved you truly, or else, dost think he would have preferred following King James?"

Lilian's eyes sparkled; a terrible retort trembled on her tongue, but her gentleness repressed it, and she could only exclaim with tears—

"Oh, horror! this insinuation is the most unkind of all. The unmerited shame and contumely, the dark and dishonourable suspicions that the malice of Clermistonlee has brought upon me I can bear, for I despise though I mourn them deeply—but a doubt of Walter's faith—oh, Annie, Annie, it sinks like a dagger in my heart. 'Tis the hope of his return, animated by the same spirit of love and truth in which he left me, that makes me rise superior to them all. Oh, yes!" she exclaimed, with girlish ecstasy, "my dear, dear Walter, the hour will yet come, when, with a kiss of affection, I will tell thee that this old manor and all these lands around it are thine, for ever thine!"

"And your heart?" laughed Annie.

"Dearest, that he has already. You see you cannot make me angry."

"And Clermistonlee?"

"Oh, name him not."

"He loves thee truly and fondly," said Annie.

"Dost think he loves me as Walter doth? Dost think he knows what love means? Oh, no; he never conceived it. His passion is a turbulent phantasy, inflamed by rivalry, difficulty, and opposition, sharpened it may be by wounded pride and exasperated revenge. Oh, how can you forget the horrid mystery that involves the fate of his wife—the unhappy Alison Gifford?"

"Pho! she died in France."

"Of a broken heart."

"Gossip, quotha!" laughed Annie, "hearts are never broken except in the pages of De Scuderi. But with his averred evil propensities, I think there is something very noble about Lord Clermistonlee."

" Noble ? "

" Do not his wit, his elegance, and courage excite our admiration ? "

" Yes—but do they make us forget that the villain lurks under that prepossessing exterior ?" rejoined Lilian, scorntully.

" Dear Lilian, I have but one more argument to urge, and 'tis the old one ; remember that your fair fame which his addresses have injured, requires——"

" What ? "

" Marriage," added Annie, quietly. Lilian turned pale ; her spirit of dissent was too strong for words ; she shook her head with a mournful but decided air, and, after a pause, said, " Never, oh, never ! " but Annie only laughed, and a long and unpleasant pause in the conversation ensued. At length Lilian said, shuddering,

" Oh, what a grue came over me just now ! What can it portend ? "

" That an evil spirit is near us," replied Annie, turning pale with the superstition of the time.

" Nay, felt ye a grue, my bairn ? " said Lady Grizel, rousing momentarily from her waking dose ; " then some one is treading on the ground that shall be your grave." Again Lilian shuddered, and throwing her arms around her grandaunt, kissed her, exclaiming,

" 'Tis the first sentence I have heard you utter for a month —and oh, what a terrible one it is ! "

At that moment there was a loud jingle at the great risp on the barbican gate, and Elsie Elshender hobbled in to say that an " auld broken soldier, who had limpit up the gate was speiring for my Lady Craigdarroch, but wadna enter."

" 'Tis a letter from the laird ; his troop are in the north, watching the wild gillies of Braemar. Tush ! what can his message be now ? " said Annie, as she flew to the foot of the staircase, where a man in a tattered red coat, a great scratch wig, with a broad hat flapped over it, one patch on his right eye, and another on his nose, limped forward on a crutch, and presented a letter. " From whence comes it, poor man ? " asked Annie.

" From the frontiers of Alsatia ; blessings on your sweet face, my noble lady," replied the veteran, gruffly. Annie grew pale as death.

" From whom ? " she faltered.

"The brave laird of Finland, Lady Annie; on mony a lang day's march I have trailed my pike by his side, owre the fields o' France and the howmes o' Holland, deil tak' them baith, for there's neither brose nor brochon, nor sowans nor sourocks to be gotten there for love, lear, or money; but I've far to gang this nicht, and maun een march on, so God bless your noble ladyship—mind a puir auld soldier that's faced fire and water baith."

Trembling violently, Annie untied the ribands of her purse and gave him a carolus, which he received with abundance of thanks, and he was limping away when Elsie hobbled forward and presented him with a bicker of ale.

"Drink, puir body," said she, " though the times are sair changit, nane pass this threshold without tasting o' the kindness o' langsyne. We dinna send awa' the naked and the hungry wi' a scrap o' gospel and a screed o' a psalm, like auld Drumdryan or the laird o' Lickspittal owre bye yonder; drink deep, puir body! I once had a son a soldier-lad, (my puir Hab that was killed in the fearfu' times,) and, for his sake, my heart warms to your auld red coat."

"Here's to ye, my bonny lady, and to you, Cummer Elsie, and never may ye be tarbarrelled for a' you're sae runkled and auld; hech, how!" and, drinking the ale to the last drop, this rough and uncourteous old fellow tossed the bicker to Elsie and limped away with great agility.

"Ha, ha!" he laughed, when the barbican gate was angrily banged behind him; "how the gay goshawk pounced at the lure; wha would hae thought I would ever hae hobbit and nobbit wi' lucky Elshender after puir Meg's mischanter among her kale? This carolus comes in gude time, for my pouch is gey empty now. Deil tak' the patches and scratches, the rags and bags," he continued tearing off his disguise; "again I am Juden Stenton,

" And wha daur meddle wi' me ?
Wha daur meddle wi' me ?
My name it's *Juden Stenton,*
And wha daur meddle wi' me ? '

And, light-hearted by the success of his lord's scheme, he sang and laughed as he trudged back to the city.

On rejoining Lilian, Annie was in a flutter of extreme agitation; and, after great reluctance, in which shame and curiosity struggled with some remnant of her former love, and after bursting into tears and then laughing hysterically, she broke the seal and read in a quavering voice as follows :—

" Mine own sweet Annie,

"God knoweth whether the words I am now in. diting will ever be seen by your own dear blue eyes. Never. theless I write (on a drumhead for a desk), and in great haste, for the bearer of this starts for Versailles in an hour. A trench where the dead and dying lie among the blood-stained earth, piled, yea, chin-deep, and where the cannon-balls are re- bounding every instant from the ramparts of Mons, is a very unpleasant place to compose love-speeches; but, believe me that the heart of poor Dick Douglas, in suffering and danger, poverty and exile, is still unchanged, my beloved Annie, and as much thine as ever. Here are we, a company of gallant Scottish gentlemen, in such a plight as you never could con- ceive; and the very appearance of our ragged attire, our emaciated forms, and our exceeding misery, would melt your gentle heart with the softest compassion. My ancient signet ring, the last relic of the house of Finland, I bartered yesterday for a loaf of bread, and now I have nothing left save the lock of thy hair, which shall go with me to the grave. But more glorious by far are our Jacobite rags than the gay bravery we might have worn under that accursed usurper against whom we have sworn to fight to the last gasp.

"The mischances of war are fast reducing the faithful cavaliers of Dundee. Starvation or the bullet daily send some brave heart to its long repose, and the survivors are in such a plight that not even the Westland Whigs could wish them lower. From the frontiers of Spain we have travelled to Alsatia, and from thence to Mons. It was a march of horrors! We were utterly without the necessaries of life, and in the depth of a severe winter, marched nine hundred miles over a country covered with snow. Many of us were barefooted. For many weeks our food was nuts in the woods, roots in the fields, horsebeans and garlic, and thus it is that Louis XIV rewards our loyalty, our patience, our fatigues and achievements.

"Our old friend Walter Fenton is well. Through all the campaigns under Monsieur le Mareschal Noailles and the noble Luxembourg, he hath showed himself worthy of the knighthood King James's sword bestowed. Yesterday he volunteered, with sixty of our unhappy cavaliers, to plant the banner of King Louis on the bastion de Sainte Wandrec, and nobly did he redeem his word. Commend me to all our leal and right honourable friends, and to those who may think kindly of the poor cavaliers for the happy days that have passed away for ever. A time may come—adieu, dearest Annie—the call to arms is sounding along the lines, and we are about to march for Steinkirke, a duty from which few will return. On my mind there weighs a heavy presentiment of what I cannot name to thee. Farewell, my gentle Annie, and may God bless thee! for I fear we shall see the bonnie braes of Maxwelton together no more.

" FINLAND,
" Late Lieut. in the Royall Scotts Ffoot."

There was a tone of sorrowful resignation to a hard and hopeless fate pervading this letter that struck a pang of deep remorse through the heart of Annie—but a pang for one moment only; the volatility of her sex aided her, and smiling through her tears, she said,

"My poor dear lighthearted Dick, would to Heaven I could lessen the miseries you endure!"

"Oh, Annie," said Lilian reproachfully, clasping her hands and weeping, " poor Walter and poor Finland!"

"Tush!" said Annie pettishly, her dark-blue eyes sparkling between shame and sorrow. " Gossip, tease me not."

" Stay, there is something more—oh, read it."

" A postcriptum "—

" It will grieve you much to hear that Walter Fentou hath broken his plighted troth to your fair friend Napier, and married a French woman, a mere camp follower, of evil repute. Right heavy tidings this will be for the heiress of Bruntisfield, but I ever deemed her spark a fool; again I kiss your hand—adieu."

The wicked expression of triumph that flashed in Annie's eyes quickly gave way to one of compassion and regret, on beholding the aspect of Lilian. Pale as death, with her eyes starting from their sockets, her silken curls seeming to twist like knots about her throbbing temples; her nether lip turned from crimson to blue, and quivering convulsively; her bosom heaving with the terrible and sickening sensations that oppressed it. Her little hands were firmly clenched, and her dry hot eyes were full of fire.

" Again, again, read it once more, Annie," she said, in a voice of strange but exquisite cadence.

" Not for worlds!" exclaimed Annie; "Oh, thou wicked letter, thus to mar our peace and hurl us into sorrow. Oh, if Craigdarroch should hear I have had a billet from my former lover, he will kindle up into such a fit of jealousy and rage as the world never saw; to the flames with it!" and she tossed into the fire the letter which poor Finland had so fondly and sorrowfully indited. It was consumed in a moment; and thus all after examination of the postscript was precluded, otherwise the forgery might have been discovered before its effects became too fatal.

"*A camp follower of evil repute!* It is false—impossible; Finland hath lied! Yet—yet—a cup of water, for Heaven's sake—my throat is parched and scorching!" Lilian sank into a chair and covered her face with her hands, but neither wept nor swooned, for her sense of injury was too acute for tears.

How bitter was the palsying sickness of heart—the agony she endured!

Not a tear fell, for the fire that burned in her breast seemed to have absorbed them.

"This is the *third* 20th of September since he first left me. Oh, Walter, Walter, God may forgive thee this great ingratitude and cruelty, but I never can!"

CHAPTER LV

THE EFFECT OF THE POSTSCRIPTUM.

"Women have died and the worms have eaten them, but *not* for love."

LONG, long did poor Lilian grieve and weep, and mourn in the solitude of her gloomy home.

She endured all the complicated agony of endeavouring to rend from her heart its dearest and most wonted thoughts—the hopes and affection she had fostered and cherished for years. No woman ever died for love but the heroine of a romance: so Lilian of course survived it; a month or two beheld her again tranquil and calm, though very sorrowful and subdued in spirit, for *time cures* every grief.

The bitter sentiments of insulted pride and mortified self-esteem which often come so powerfully to the aid of the deserted, and enable them to triumph over the more tender and acute reflections, were kindled and fanned and fostered by the artful sophistry of Annie, who, with her real condolences, threw in such nice little soothing and flattering inuendos, mingled with condemnations of Walter, and pretended rumours of his marriage, the beauty and gallantries of his

French wife, whom some called a countess and others a courtesan, that Lilian first learned to hear her patiently and then with indignation.

With these were mingled occasional praises of Clermistonlee, managed with great tact, for Annie was cunning as a lynx, and never failed to flank all her arguments with the powerful *one*, how necessary it was for the restoration of her own honour, that she should receive the *roué* lord as her husband.

Poor Lilian, though these advices stung her to the soul, learned at last to hear and to think of them with calmness, and (shall we acknowledge it?) to say at last, "that it might be."

With something of that fierce sentiment of desperation and revenge which, like a gage thrown down to fate, makes the ruined gamester place his last stake on the turn of a card, she began deliberately to school herself into thinking of Clermistonlee as her future husband; and though in reality poverty was the real cause of it, Lady Craigdarroch failed not to impress upon Lilian how much he was reformed, how penitent he was, and for three years past had never been engaged in any piece of frolic or wickedness, and wound up by asserting that a reformed rake made the best husband.

What love and perseverance could never accomplish, revenge achieved at last.

> " Alas! the love of women, it is known,
>   To be a lovely and a fearful thing;
> For all of theirs upon the die is thrown,
>   And if 'tis lost, life hath no more to bring "

Long and assiduous were the exertions, the arguments and artifices of Annie, and long and fearful was the struggle that tortured the heart of Lilian, ere she would consent to receive Clermistonlee as her suitor.

At last the fatal words were said.

Annie flew to communicate the joyous tidings, and when next day he rode up the avenue to pay his *devoirs*, the miserable girl nearly swooned. The ring, the little embossed ring of antique gold, the last and only gift of Walter, and which he said contained *the secret* of his life, she had now laid aside, carefully locked up in a cabinet, because it brought too vividly before her the memories she had resolved to banish from her heart for ever.

Gladly will we hurry over this chapter of pain and humiliation.

Clermistonlee had increased his great personal advantages

by all the aid of dress, and in defiance of the sad-coloured fashions of the time, wore a voluminous Monmouth wig, the long curls of which were puffed with aromatic powder, a suit of rose-coloured velvet, laced so thick with gold that the ground of the cloth was scarcely visible, a sword and belt sparkling with jewels. A medal of gold, bearing his coat of arms, was suspended by a chain of the same metal round his neck : it was his last venture in quest of fortune, and his lordship had resolved to spend all he possessed upon the stake.

By the artful Annie he was led forward to the trembling and sinking Lilian, to whom he pleaded his cause, his constancy and perseverance, his raptures and agonies, his hopes and despair, with an ardour that confused, and perhaps flattered, if it did nothing more. These his lordship brought out all at a breath, as he had got the whole by rote, having said the same things to a hundred different women before; but now his natural ardour and spirit of gallantry were greatly increased by the touching character which sorrow, vexation, and disappointment had imparted to the soft beauty of Lilian —and also by the aspect of the comfortable old manor house and the acres of fine arable land that lay around it; while she (shall we confess it?) as bitter thoughts of Walter and his French wife rose up within her, stole glances from time to time at her noble and courtly suitor—glances which he soon perceived, and fired with new animation, threw such an air of devotion into his addresses that he—triumphed.

Annie placed the hand of Lilian within that of Clermiston-lee ; he pressed it to his heart, and she did not withdraw it; but burst into a passion of tears. He then threw his splendid chain, with its medal, around her bending neck, and pressed her to his breast, and so sudden was the revulsion of feeling, that Lilian fainted.

An hour afterwards Clermistonlee, with all his embroidery glittering in the sun, was seen galloping back to the city like a madman ; he dashed through the Portsburgh, and reined up near the Bowfoot, where, at the summit of a ten-storied edifice, dwelt Mr. Ichabod Bummel, minister of the gospel.

" The father of confusion take your long stair ! Why, Mr. Bummel, 'tis like a rascally old steeple," said the lord, breaking breathlessly in upon the lank-haired and long-visaged pastor, who was intent upon *The Hind let loose* of Alexander Sheills.

" Yea, a tower of Babel—but what hath procured me the honour of your lordship's visit?"

"By all the devils, don't think I am come to drub thee for that lecture on the cutty stool—ha, ha! I am about to be married, man, and want you to proclaim the banns and so forth; but my Lord Mersington will see after them for me."

"As my *Bombshell* saith, marriage is an honourable and godly estate——"

"But a deuced poor one, sometimes, Mr. Ichabod. I am about to be married to Lilian, of Bruntisfield, and thou shalt espouse us, because the citizens hold thee to be their first preacher, and it will increase my influence among them."

"But, my lord," began Mr. Ichabod, bowing.

"*But* me nothing—'tis my non-attendance at kirk and my old tricks you aim at—pho! I am a thorough reformado—but, Mr. Ichabod, hast never a drop of wine about thee? 'tis a hot forenoon."

"My dwelling contains nothing but water, and it is a plack the runlet in these dear years; but, my lord," continued the divine, after sundry gasps and contortions of visage, "if I lend all my influence to render popular this intended espousal. whilk I perceive to be the main object of your visit, may I crave your lordship's favour in another particular?"

"Command me in all things save my purse, for 'tis a mere vacuum, if thy philosophy will admit of such a thing. Say forth, my apostle!"

"I love the maiden called Meinic Elshender—yea, I love her powerfully with the carnal love of this world, and the maiden is not altogether indisposed to view me favourably."

"Zounds!" said Clermistonlce, while the minister looked complacently down on his long spindle shanks; "in the name of mischief, who is Meinie Elshender?"

"Handmaiden to the young Madam Lilian, who views me as an abomination."

"By all the devils, thou shalt have her, *bon gré, mal gré,* and after I am fairly wedded, the best kirk in the Lothians to boot— even should I make Juden shoot the present incumbent."

"Heaven reward these generous promises," replied Ichabod, with a smile of incredulity. "Well it is that the maiden hath escaped the snares of her first lover, who was a soldier of antichrist—a musketeer of the bluidy Dunbarton."

"Say rather the most princely earl of the noble house of Douglas! Ha, ha—by my faith! we whigs are winning the false lemans of the cavaliers in glorious style."

"And now, my lord, I have one other boon to crave," said Ichabod, producing a tattered and dog-eared MS. from a bunker. "This is a book of which doubtless your lordship nath heard; my *Bombshell aimet at the taile of the Great Beast*."

" Oh, the devil take thy bombshell—"

" Shame, my lord. It proveth that Jonah——"

" Swallowed the whale ; eh, Master Ichabod?" said the gay lord, pirouetting about and laughing boisterously.

" Oh, my lord, for a centiloquy——"

" Ha, ha ! a what?"

" A hundredfold discourse, to convince thee of the crime of this irreverence and irreligion."

" I crave pardon ; but what do you want, eh?"

" Your lordship's subscription ; 'tis to be published in the imprinting press in the Parliament-close, whenever new irons are brought over from Holland."

" Oh, by all the devils, certainly ; send me a dozen of copies. Faith ! I must be quite pious henceforth. And now, bravo ! see the kirk session about my little affairs, while I ride down the Lawnmarket to old Gideon Grasper, the clerk to the signet, for there will be a mountain of papers to sign and seal, and so forth ; but the banns, the banns, next Sunday, remember ;" and chanting, " With a heylillclu and a how-lo-lan," his lordship danced away out, tripping down the long stair by three steps at a time, and mounting, galloped into the upper part of the city.

CHAPTER LVI.

THE BATTLE OF STEINKIRKE.

As torrents roll increased by numerous rills,
With rage impetuous down their echoing hills ;
Rush to the vales and pour'd along the plain,
Roar through a thousand channels to the main ;
The distant shepherd tremping hears the sound :
So mix both hosts, and so their cries rebound.
                              ILIAD, BOOK IV.

IT was the night before the famous battle of Steinkirke, when the confederates under William III. encountered the gallant and brilliant army of the great François Henri duc de Luxembourg.

In happy ignorance of what was being acted at home by those whose memory lay so near their hearts, Walter Fenton and Douglas of Finland were carousing with their brothers in

war and misfortune around a blazing fire, composed of rafters·
borrowed for the purpose from the roof of a neighbouring
Flemish house.

Intent on crushing the alarming confederation of the protestant powers against him, Louis XIV had taken the field
in person at the head of one hundred and twenty thousand
men. This sensual, selfish, and weak-minded monarch was
accompanied by all the effeminate pomp and tinsel splendour
of an eastern emperor; his women and paramours, numerous
enough for a seraglio; his dancers, players, musicians; his
kitchen, opera, household, and all the ministers of his luxury,
his pleasures, and his tyranny, in themselves a host, crowded
and encumbered the great camp of his splendid army, which,
however, soon captured Namur, a strong city on the Meuse,
though strengthened by all the skill of the great Coehorn, and
defended by the valour of the prince de Brabazon and nine
thousand chosen soldiers.

King William, whose duty it was to have raised the siege
of this important fortress, lay with one hundred thousand men
within gunshot of Louis, but, embued with all the stolid and
phlegmatic stupidity of a Hollander, permitted the place to
be captured, by which his military reputation was as much
injured as that of Louis was increased. The victor of Namur
immediately returned to Versailles, surrounded by triumph·
and adulation, worshipped undeservedly as a hero, and ex-
tolled as a conqueror, while William, whose inertness had at
last given way to necessary activity, excited by shame and
exasperation, having reviewed on the plain of Genappe a fresh
quota of ten battalions of Scottish infantry, pushed forward
against Mareschal Luxembourg, intent on retrieving his
honour.

After basely employing a spy named Millevoix, under pain
of torture and death, to mislead the French commander by
false intelligence of the confederates' movements, William
advanced with his one hundred thousand bayonets to prevent
him from taking up a position between the then obscure
villages of Steinkirke and Enghien, a royal barony of the
house of Bourbon. With his usual bad generalship William
completely failed, for Luxembourg outflanked him, gained
the position, and trusting to the communications of the perfidious (or unfortunate) Millevoix, not anticipating any attack,
confined himself to his tent, as he laboured under severe
indisposition.

Not expecting an *alerte*, the whole of his numerous and
brilliant army lay entrenched among the fertile fields and

pastures of the Flemings, whose thick hedges, solid walls, and comfortable houses, were cut down, torn up, and overthrown without ceremony, to render the position more secure.

The post occupied by the Scottish officers was near the Senne, a slow and sluggish river. The sun had set, and far over the long perspective of the level landscape, that in some parts withdrew to the extreme horizon, shone the red departing flush of the last evening many would behold on earth. In some places the river was reddened by the gleam of the distant fires, whose flickering chain marked out the camp of Luxembourg; the higher eminences were covered by woods and orchards, from which the evening wind came laden with the rich perfume of the summer blossom. Save the hum of the extended camp all was still round Steinkirke, and where the exiled cavaliers were bivouacked there was little more heard than the monotonous ripple of the Senne, as it flowed past its willow-shaded banks on its way to the northern sea.

The Scottish exiles were always more merry than usual on the eve of a battle, for it freed many from a life of humiliation and hardship, to which they deemed an honourable death a thousand times preferable. At times an expression of stern joy, of ghastly merriment, at others of deep abstraction pervaded the little group, as they clustered round the fire that blazed in a little alcove formed by an orchard on the river side. There their arms were piled, and they rolled from hand to hand a keg of Hollands, to which they had helped themselves at the devastation of the Flandrian chateau de Senne. Afar off, above the village spire of Steinkirke, the silver moon rose broadly and resplendently to light the wide and fertile landscape with its glory. The Senne and Tender brightened like two floods of flowing crystal, and the willows that drooped over them seemed the work of magic, as their dewy leaves glittered in the rays of the summer moon.

The stern hearts of that melancholy band were soothed by the beauty of the scenery, the seclusion of their tentless bivouac, the softness of the Flemish moonlight, and a song that Finland sang completed the effect of the place and time. He reclined upon his knapsack, and his fine features, which long privation and toil had sharpened and attenuated, flushed and reddened as he sang of his love that was far away, and felt his brave heart expand with the dear and long-cherished hopes and memories her image stirred within it.

> " Maxwelltoun Braes are bonnie,
> Where early fa's the dew ;
> And blue-eyed Annie Laurie
> Gave me her promise true.

Gave me her promise true,
  That never forgot shall be ;
And for my bonnie Annie Laurie,
  I would lay me down and dee.

" Her locks are like the sunshine,
  Her breast is like the swan ;
Her hand is like the snawdrift,
  And *mine* her waist micht span.
But oh ! that promise true !
  Will ne'er be forgot by me,
And for my blue-eyed Annie Laurie,
  I would lay me down and dee !"

This famous song, which, with its beautiful air, is so chaste and pleasing, and still so much admired in Scotland, poor Finland in his chivalric spirit had composed,. to lighten the toil of many a long and arduous march, and now, inspired by the love and the fond recollections that trembled in his heart, he slowly sang the last verse with great tenderness and pathos.

" Like dew on the gowan lying,
  Is the fa' of her fairy feet ;
And like wind in summer sighing,
  Her voice is low and sweet.
But O that promise true !
  Makes her all the world to me ;
And for my bonnie Annie Laurie,
  I'd lay me down and dee."

Every word seemed to come from his overcharged heart ; and as he sang the beautiful melody silence and sadness stole over the listening group. Softened by the dialect and the music of their fatherland, every heart was melted and every eye grew moist ; the red camp-fires and the shining waters of the Senne, the white tents of Luxembourg, the woodlands and orchards of Steinkirke passed away, and Scotland's hoary hills and pathless valleys rose before them, for their eyes and hearts were in the land from which they were expatriated for ever.

It was the morning of the 24th of July, and in unclouded splendour the sun shone from the far horizon upon the tented camp of Luxembourg, on the standards waving and arms glittering within the rudely and hastily-constructed entrenchments of the great and veteran engineer the Chevalier Antoine de Ville. Like bright snowy clouds the morning vapour curled upwards from the sedges of the Senne, and the dewy foliage of the woods, and rolling lazily along the plain, shrouded everything in a thick and gauze-like veil of white obscurity, which the rays of the sun edged with the hue of gold. Under cover of this, although the French knew it not, the entire force of the allied nations, led by William of England, were coming rapidly on in two dense columns, intent on avenging the disgraces they had endured at Namur. Luxembourg lay within his bannered pavilion on a bed of sickness, and neither he nor his soldiers were aware of the foe's approach until the prince of Wirtemburg, at the head of ten battalions of English, Dutch, and Danes, drove back his outposts on the right, making a furious attack on the camp, which instantly became a scene of greater confusion than king Agramont's.

The patter of the musketry, the roll of the advancing drums, and the bullets whistling through his tent, roused the brave mareschal, who, leaping from his camp-bed, forgot his illness in the ardour and tumult of the moment. Hastily his pages attired and armed him, and throwing his magnificent surcoat above his gilded corslet, he seized his sword and baton, and rushed forth to repair what the artifices of William, the treachery of Millevoix, and the bravery of Wirtemburg had already achieved. To muster, to rally his immense force, and repel the prince of Wirtemburg, were but the work of a few seconds; and the great leader, who five minutes before had lain inert on a couch of illness, was now spurring his caparisoned horse from column to column, with his plumes waving, his accoutrements glittering, and his baton brandished aloft; his features filled with animation, his soul with energy.

The dukes of Bourbon and Vendome, the princes of Turenne and Conté, the duc de Chartres, a youth of fifteen, whose almost girlish beauty made him the sport and the idol of the army, the marquis de Bellefonde, and several thousand chevaliers of noble birth and matchless spirit, by their presence, their ardour, and example, restored perfect order, and in admirable battle array they stood prepared to encounter the host of the Protestant confederation.

As the sun rose higher, the mist which shrouded the whole plain around the village of Steinkirke was gradually exhaled upwards, and as it rolled away the entire army of William III., a hundred thousand strong, were seen in order of battle, advancing as rapidly as the numerous thorn hedges, ditches, and dykes, which intersected the yellow cornfields, would permit.

In defence of a place which it was expected William's brilliant cavalry would assail, the Scottish officers were posted in an abbatis of apple-trees that had been cut down by the pioneers, and made an intricate breastwork all round; and within it, with their arms loaded, they stood in close order, watching with lowering brows and kindling eyes the scarlet ranks of their countrymen, to whom they now—for the first time since their exile—found themselves opposed in battle.

The golden bloom of the ripe and waving cornfields, through which the lines were advancing in triple ranks, with their serried arms and embroidered standards glittering, threw forward the bright scarlet costume in strong relief, and the hearts of the little band of exiles beat with increased excitement as the moment of a general encounter drew nigh.

"Behold yonder fellows in *our* uniform!" exclaimed one, as the Scottish infantry debouched in heavy column on the French left, with their twenty standards displayed, and their drums loading the air with the old march of the Covenanters.

"God knoweth the sorrow, the bitterness, the hatred, and the fierce exultation that swell my heart by turns in this auspicious hour!" said Finland, striking his breast.

"You speak my very thoughts," responded Walter, with a deep sigh; "yonder are the old Royals, but now another than Dunbarton wields his baton over them; yonder are the standards we have carried—but others bear them now. How hard to forget that these are our countrymen! Do not ourselves seem to be marching against us?"

"Enough of this, gentlemen," said the veteran laird of Dunlugals. "In them I behold only the rebels of our king, and the sycophants of an usurper. This day let us remember only that we are fighting under the standard of the first captain of the age, and about to win fresh glories for the most magnificent prince that ever occupied the throne of France!"

The battle was begun by Hugh Mackay of Scoury.

Led by that brave and veteran general, a dense column of British cavalry, accoutred in voluminous red coats, great Dutch hats, looped up, and vast boots of black leather, with slung muskets and brandished swords, rushed at full gallop to the charge on one flank, while the prince of Wirtemburg assailed the other.

The abbatis lay full in front of Mackay, who held aloft his long gilt baton, as he led on this heavy mass of troopers. On they came, horse to horse, and boot to boot, like a moving mountain; but the deadly and deliberate volley poured upon them by the Scottish cavaliers threw them into immediate confusion; the front squadrons, by becoming entangled among their falling horses and riders, recoiled suddenly on the rear, who were still spurring forward; the furious shock produced an immediate and irredeemable confusion, and the whole gave way ere another volley of that leaden rain was poured upon their dense array.

The rear of forty thousand muskets now burst like thunder on the ear, as the prince de Conté and the brave De Chartres, the boy-soldier, at the head of the superb household infantry, assailed the British, and volleying in platoons, continued to press upon them with increasing ardour until within pike's length of each other, when Conté led the whole to the charge. The shock was irresistible. Count Solmes failed to support the English and Scots, who immediately gave way, and a tremendous slaughter was made, especially among the latter.

" *Les Ecossais* retreat !" exclaimed Conté. " 'Tis a miracle. *Tête Dieu !* 'tis surely a bad cause, when the hand of heaven is against them !"

The Scottish regiments of Coutts, Mackay, Angus, Grahame, and Leven, were cut to pieces, and the English Guards nearly shared the same fate. James earl of Angus, a brave youth in his twenty-first year, was shot dead at the head of his Cameronians, William Stuart viscount of Mountjoy, Sir Robert Douglas, Lieutenant-General James Douglas, Sir John Lanier, Colonel Lauder, and many other brave Scottish gentlemen were slain, while the prince de Conté bore all before him.

With the gallant prince of Wirtemburg it fared otherwise. Pressing onward at the head of his English, he carried off some of the French artillery, and after immense slaughter, stormed the entrenchment which covered their position ; but finding himself in danger of being overpowered, he twice sent his aide-de-camp to crave succour from the phlegmatic William and from Count Solmes, a noble of the House of Nassau. Twice over a field that was strewn with thousands of dead and dying, and swept by the fire of so many thousand muskets, cannon, and coehorns, the brave aide spurred his horse to beg succour for the prince his master ; but William neglected, and the Dutch noble derided his request.

" *Vivat* Wirtemburg !" cried Solmes, laughing ; " let us see what sport his English bull-dogs will make."

At length William shook off the inertness that seemed to possess his faculties amid the storm of war that raged around him, and in person ordered Solmes to sustain the advance of the left wing which Wirtemburg had led on so successfully. Thus urged, the unwilling lord of Brunsveldt made an unavailing movement with his cavalry, but left a few English and Danes to sustain the whole brunt of the battle.

Amid the dense smoke that rolled in white clouds and concealed the adverse lines, their carnage and its horrors, again and again the brave old laird of Scoury led his squadrons to the charge, resolved to force the passage, to turn the flank of

Luxembourg, or die ; and again they were repulsed from the abbatis by the courage of the desperate cavaliers. As yet, not one trooper had penetrated among them, though hundreds and their horses lay groaning and rolling in the agonies of death, entangled among the apple-laden branches of the prostrate trees, grasping and rending them with their teeth in the tortures of dissolution. As yet not one of the Scottish exiles had fallen ; but now Mackay ordered a body of his dragoons to dismount, to unsling their short fusees, and from behind the piles of dead and dying men and chargers, to fire upon the abbatis, which could afford no protection against bullets.

A furious fusilade now ensued, and Fenton soon missed Finland from his side ; he turned, and his hot blood cooled for a moment to behold him lying on the bloody turf in the last agonies of death. A ball had pierced his breast; his eyes were glazing, and he was beating the earth with his heels, as he blew from his quivering lips the bells of blood and foam.

Unfortunate Douglas !

Something was clenched in his hand and pressed to his lips ; but as his dying energies relaxed, and his brave spirit fled to heaven, the relic fell on the turf ;—it was Annie Laurie's braid of bright brown hair.

"Farewell, dear Finland," exclaimed Walter, kissing the dead man's hand. "Here end thy love and misfortunes together !" Sorrow, rage, and ardour roused the fury of Fenton to the utmost, and with his clubbed weapon he sprang over the trees of the abbatis, exclaiming, "To the charge, gentlemen Scots !—to the charge ! Never let it be said that the cavaliers of Dundee played at long bowls with those false English churls. Victory and revenge ! "

Fired by his example, and animated by national and political hatred against those who had deserted James VII., and wrought so many miseries to his few adherents, the little band sprang from the abbatis and threw themselves with incredible fury and determination on the dismounted troopers. Onward they pressed over piles of dead and wounded, while every instant the balls that flew thick as drifting rain, thinned their narrow ranks, and added many another item to the vast amount of that day's carnage.

None can be so brave as those for whom life has lost every charm ; and none so reckless as those who have a thousand real or imaginary wrongs to avenge. Thus, heedless alike of the number of their antagonists, who were again pressing up to the attack, the Scottish cavaliers came on pell mell, and a desperate conflict ensued with firelocks and fusils clubbed.

As Walter, forgetful of everything else but to glut a fierce spirit of revenge, pressed onward, he encountered a tall and powerful officer. The nobility of his aspect and the richness of his attire (for his scarlet coat was so richly interlaced with oars of gold as to be almost sword-proof), not less than the vigour with which he kept his soldiers to their duty, made him a marked man; but Walter struck him from his horse and flourished the butt of his musket over him.

"Take these, you tattered villain," said the officer, offering a splendid watch and ring; "take these, and spare my life."

"Insult me not, sir," exclaimed Walter Fenton with undisguised scorn. "I am one of the officers of Viscount Dundee—of Dundee, the brave and loyal."

"The vilest minion of hell and tyranny that ever disgraced his country—then doubly are you traitor!" said the other, starting from the ground and flashing a pistol in Walter's face. Blinded by fury and the smoke of the discharge, he drove his bayonet through the breast of the officer, and fairly pinned him to the turf.

"Curse on the hour that I die by the hand of a base and renegade clown like thee!" exclaimed the dying man, half-choked in his welling blood.

"Traitor!" cried his destroyer furiously; "you die by the hand of Sir Walter Fenton, knight banneret of Scotland!"

"So falls Hugh Mackay, of Scoury!" moaned the other as he sank backward and expired.

"Scoury!" reiterated Walter; "hah! then this hour avenges Dundee—the slaughter of Killycrankie and of Cromdale."

At that moment he was hurled to the earth by a wounded charger as it rushed madly from the conflict. He fell against a tree, and lay stunned and insensible to all that passed around him.

The sun was setting, and still the doubtful battle continued to be waged with undiminished ardour, until Mareschal Boufflers, at the head of a powerful body of cavalry, the French and Scottish *gendarmerie*, and the royal regiment De Rousillon, swept like a torrent over the corpse-strewn plains, with the oriflamme displayed, and decided the fortune of the war just as the sun's broad disc dipped behind the far horizon. William, instead of restoring his tarnished honour, was compelled to retreat in renewed disgrace, leaving many officers of valour and distinction, and three thousand soldiers, slain; while the French, though they had to regret the fall of an equal number, with the prince de Turenne, the marquis de Bellefoude, Tilladete, Fernaçon, and many other chevaliers of noble blood, remained masters of the field, over which they suspended from a lofty gibbet King William's luckless confidant, the spy and intriguer Millevoix.

Paris resounded with joy and acclamation on the tidings of this great victory arriving; the princes and soldiers who had served there were idolized as superior beings by the ladies and women of every rank, whose transports amounted to a species of frenzy; and from that hour, for many a year, every ornament and piece of dress was known by the name of *Steinkirke*.

CHAPTER LVII.

A DISCLOSURE.

'Tis night;—and glittering o'er the trampled heath,
Pale gleams the moonlight on the field of death;
Lights up each well-known spot, where late in blood,
The vanquished yielded, and the victor stood;
When red in clouds the sun of battle rode,
And poured on Britain's front its favouring flood.
                                    LORD GRENVILLE.

AGAIN the summer moon rose brightly over the secluded village of Steinkirke, and poured its cold and steady lustre on cornfields drenched in blood, and trod to gory mire by the charge of the spurred squadrons, the closer movements of the compact squares of infantry, or the artillery's track; on the pale and upturned faces of the dying, the distorted and ghastlier lineaments of the dead,—on a wide battle-field strewn with all the trophies of war and destruction,—misery and agony.

Save where illumined by the gleams of moonlight, by the red flashes of a few distant fire-arms, and the redder glare from a convent burned by the retreating British, the ruddy conflagration of which mingled with the last faint glow of the departed sun, the field seemed gloomy and dark. A narrow lurid streak at the distant horizon showed where the sun had set. The roar of that great battle had now died away, but it had sent forth an echo over France and Britain, denoting joy to one and sorrow to the other. Where, then, was William of Orange, and where his mighty host?

The contest was now over, and, save the distant popping of a few skirmishers or plunderers, every sound of strife had ceased; but the cool night-wind was laden with a sad and wailing murmur, a sound which it is seldom the lot of man to hear—the mingled moans of many thousands of men enduring all the complicated torture of sabre and gunshot wounds and the most excruciating thirst. Many a solemn prayer and pious ejaculation of deep contrition, uttered in many a varied tongue, were then ascending from that moonlit battle-field to the throne of God, while others in their ravings called only on death to ease them of their torments; and long ere sunrise, the stern king of terrors attended the summons of many.

A great cannon royal, drawn by eight horses, and escorted by the artillerists of the brigade de Dauphine, passed near the corpse-heaped abbatis where Walter Fenton lay, and he implored them to remove him from the field. They were passing him unheeded, when one exclaimed—

"*Il est un officier Eccossais !*" upon which the drivers reined up: the soldiers sprang from the tumbril, and placing him beside them, galloped across the field of battle towards the redoubts on the left of Luxembourg's position. The jolting occasioned Walter exquisite agony, and he could not repress a shudder when the cannon-wheels passed over the crackling body of some dead or wounded soldier who lay prostrate in their path.

After riding a mile or two he fell from his seat with violence, and once more became insensible.

"*Il est mort,*" said the Frenchmen, as they whipped up their horses, and thought no more about him.

After lying long in a dreamy state, tormented by a burning thirst, and feeling prickly and shooting pains over his whole body as the blood flowed back into its old channels, Walter made an attempt to rise, but the motion occasioned him exquisite pain, and the whole landscape swam around him. He thought he was mortally wounded; a cold perspiration burst over his temples; a stupor again stole upon his senses, and, believing he was dying, he piously recommended himself to God, closed his eyes, and lay down resigned to his fate.

But the mind was active though the frame remained inert, and he thought of Lilian, of Finland and Annie, and how the hand of death had thrown a cold blight over all their fondest hopes and prospects; and so weak had he become that audible sobs burst from him.

The heavy dew was falling fast, and its moisture refreshed him; he raised his head, and near him saw the figure of a female in a sombre and peculiar garb; she was completely attired in black; a thick veil of the same colour, with a little hood of white linen, were drawn closely round her face, which seemed pale and colourless as that of death in the uncertain rays of a cruise which she carried; but though aged, she was marked by a serenity and air of repose singularly winning and prepossessing. She bent tenderly over him with a face expressive of the deepest commiseration.

" 'Tis a vision!'' was Walter's first thought; " 'tis an Ursuline nun!" was his second.

"Poor youth—unhappy youth!" said the stranger tenderly, and burst into tears.

"Heaven's blessing on you, gentle lady," said Walter, as he endeavoured to rise; "no tears can be more precious in the sight of Heaven than those shed by compassion. God save great Luxembourg! We have this day gained a glorious victory; but at what a price to me!" he continued, in his own language. "Alake! my brave and noble friends, the best blood of Scotland has mingled yonder with the waters of the Senne."

"Scotland!" replied the venerable Ursuline, and her mild eyes became filled with animation and sadness. "I acknowledge with sorrow and pride that your country is also mine; but, alas! I can only remember it with horror and humiliation. Your voice takes me back to the pleasant days of other and happier years, and stirs an echo in the deepest recesses of my heart. Oh, my God! what is this that I feel within me? Intercede for me, blessed Ursula, and save me from my own thoughts! Oh, let not the contentment in which I have dwelt these many years be disturbed by worldly regrets and old unhappiness!"

There was a deep pathos in her voice, an air of subdued sorrow, mildness, and melancholy in her features, and a soft expression in her eye that was very winning, and Walter kissed her hand with a sentiment of affection and respect, and, strange to say, she did not withdraw it.

"I belonged to the convent of Ursulines at Steinkirke. At vesper-time the Count Solmes sacked it with his troopers; (God forgive him and them the sacrilege!) they expelled us with savage violence, and I found shelter in a cottage close by. Your groans drew me forth. Permit me to lead you, my poor son, for indeed you seem very weak. There is one poor fugitive there already, a countrywoman of our own, to whom I hope you will bring pleasant tidings; let us go."

They entered the humble Flemish cottage, the wide kitchen of which was brilliantly illuminated by a blazing fire of turf, that lit the furthest recesses of the great but rude apartment, that strongly resembled those represented by Rembrandt and Teniers, where every imaginable implement and article, garden and household utensil, hang from the beams of the open roof, load the walls, or encumber every available nook and corner ; a heavy Flemish boor, in voluminous brown breeches, arose and doffed his fur cap, and with his wife made way for the sister of St. Ursula, who led Walter to a seat.

Thankfully he drained to the last drop a pewter flagon of water that the housewife gave him, and was about to speak, when his attention was arrested by the sudden appearance of a young lady. She was very beautiful, and had an exquisitely fair complexion, the natural paleness of which grief and fear had very much increased : her blue eyes sparkled with animation, and her half-dishevelled hair was of the brightest and glossiest but palest flaxen. Running to Walter Fenton she took both his hands in hers, and said, with a touching earnestness of manner,

"Ah, sir! come you from the field of battle ?"

"This moment, madam."

"Oh, you are Scottish by your voice, but alas! you wear the garb of Louis."

"My dear madam, it is the garb of loyalty and exile ; of great suffering, and of much endurance."

"Unhappy sir, you are——"

"One of the cavaliers of Dundee."

"Oh, tell me if you know aught of the fate of General Mackay in this day's carnage ; Mackay, the laird of Scoury ?" she added a little proudly.

"Lady," faltered Walter, quite overcome by the question and the aspect of the speaker, "the brave champion of Presbyterianism is no more. I—I saw him slain."

"My father! oh, my father!" cried Margaret Mackay, in a voice that pierced the conscience-stricken Fenton to the heart ; "I shall never see thee more—never behold thy kind old face and silver hair. Oh, my God! I am quite alone in the world, and what will become of me now? Oh, Lady Clermistonlee!" she exclaimed, and pressing against her heart the hand of the nun, sank into a chair and swooned.

"Clermistonlee!" reiterated Walter, starting ; but the helpless condition of his young countrywoman demanded immediate attention, and he was compelled to smother his curiosity for a time, until she had partially recovered, and then the good Ursuline, after attending her with the most motherly care, left her engaged in prayer in another apartment, and turned all her attention to the wound on Walter's head.

With an adroit neatness of hand, a soft insinuating manner which drew the heart of Walter towards her as to a mother, the compassionate nun, assisted by the silent Flemish housewife, bathed the wound, cut away the long clotted locks, and bound it up, while the round-visaged boor, whose mind was wholly absorbed by the loss of a field of corn, which had been cut down by Boufflers' foraging dragoons, sat with his eyes intently fixed on the smoke that curled from his pipe.

Walter had been so little accustomed to kindness, that all the strong feelings of his warm heart now gushed forth.

"A thousand thanks, dear madam!" he exclaimed. "I know not whether it is your kindness, the mere ardour of my heart, or some mysterious influence that heaven alone can see, which calls forth all my fondest and most reverential sentiments towards you."

The Ursuline smiled sadly, and retired a pace.

"Oh, what is this new feeling that stirs within me?" continued Walter, in a half-musing voice. "It seems as if your face bore the long remembered features of some kind friend or dear relative. Like a gleam of sunshine through a mist, they come back to me from the obscurity of the past like those of one whom—but, ah! whither is my enthusiasm carrying me? Dear madam, once more a thousand thanks, for now I must leave, and shall never see you more, but your kindness will ever be remembered by Walter Fenton with gratitude and love."

"Fenton!" said the Ursuline, putting back his hair, and tenderly surveying his emaciated features, "I once had a dear though humble friend of that name, and my heart yearns to thee for her sake. But wherefore this hurry to depart? Your wound?—"

"I know not where I am, lady, and should any of the Stadtholder's people come this way I should assuredly be shot."

"Then, in the name of all that is blessed, away! The fires of the French camp are still visible, and you may gain it ere daybreak."

This passed in French, but the boor understood it; his eyes twinkled, and knocking the ashes from his pipe, he slowly stuck it in his leathern cap, and stole out unperceived.

"And what will be the fate of this poor daughter of the brave Mackay, for everywhere the French are swarming around us?"

"Through a lady of the house of Nassau, who belongs to our now, alas! ruined convent, I will see her consigned to the care of her father's best friend, William of Orange."

"'Tis fortunate. It reminds me of what I scarcely dare to ask. She called you by the name of my bitterest enemy—Clermistonlee," said Walter, biting his lip; "Clermistonlee, who has been my rival and the bane of my existence. Oh, madam, what terrible mystery is concealed under this Ursuline habit!"

As Walter spoke, the blood came and went in the faded

face of the trembling recluse. One moment, when fired by animation, her features seemed almost beautiful, and the next they were withered, rigid, and aged.

"Mr. Fenton," faltered the nun—"Mr. Fenton, for so I presume you are named?"

"I am Sir Walter Fenton, lady, by the king's grace."

The nun bowed slightly.

"My heart warms, Sir Walter, to that dear native land which I shall never behold again, and in a moment of such weakness I revealed myself to that poor fugitive girl, whom fate so happily threw under my protection, when the confederates were defeated and dispersed ——. You know him then, this wicked man, to whom fate in an evil hour gave me as a wife. Oh, Randal! Randal!——. Let me not recall in bitterness the burning thoughts of years long passed and gone —thoughts which I have long since learned to suppress, or endure with calmness and resignation."

"Enough, dear madam, I am animated by no vulgar curiosity, and time presses. Oh, learn rather to forget your earlier griefs than to remember them. Too well do I know the Lord Clermistonlee, and can easily conceive a long and painful history of domestic woe and suffering. You are the unfortunate Alison Gifford?"

"Of the house of Gifford of that ilk in Lothian," continued the recluse, with tearless composure. "In his earlier days, when young, gallant, and winsome, with an honoured name and spotless scutcheon, Randal Clermont became my lover and my husband. Oh, how happy I was for a time; how loving and beloved! But a change came over the unstable heart of my husband. His political intrigues and private excesses soon ruined our fortune, deprived me of his love and him of my esteem. We were driven into exile, and retired to Paris. There he plunged madly into a vortex of the lowest dissipation, and spent the last of my dowry, my jewels, and everything. He became a drunkard, a bully, and a gamester, if not worse. Long, long I endured without a murmur or reproach his pitiless cruelty and cutting contempt, until he eloped with one who in better days had been my companion and attendant, an artful wretch, named Beatrix Gilruth. He joined the army of Mareschal Crecquy as a volunteer, and I saw him no more. Hearing afterwards that he was in Scotland fighting under the standard of the covenant, and being driven to despair by the miseries into which he had plunged me, by leaving me a prey to destitution in a foreign land, I resolved to quit the world for ever; I have come of an old Catholic family, and a convent was my first thought.

"Our child, for we had one, our child was alternately a
source of torment and delight," continued the poor nun, weeping bitterly—"my torment from the resemblance it bore to
its perfidious father, and my delight as the only tie that bound
me to earth; I resolved to see it no more, and sent the poor
infant to Scotland in charge of a faithful female servitor, to
whom I gave a letter for my husband, purporting to be written
on my deathbed, and a ring he had given me in happier days.
In an agony of grief I saw the woman depart, and gave her
all I possessed, a few louis d'ors I had acquired at Paris,
where I had supported myself as a *fleuriste*, and was patro-
nized by the Scottish archers, who were ever very kind to me.
I considered myself as dead to the world from that hour, and
immediately commenced my noviciate in the licensed convent
of St. Ursula, in French Flanders.

"Here again all the wounds of my heart were torn open
by tidings that the ship in which my loved little boy and
his nurse embarked had perished at sea; whether they perished too God alone knoweth, for I heard of them no more.
And now the fierce stings of remorse increased the sadness of
my sorrow, and I upbraided myself with cruelty, with lack
of fortitude and such resignation as became a Christian. I
accused myself of infanticide, and in my thoughts by day
and my dreams by night I had ever before me the sunny eyes
and golden hair of my little child, and its lisping accents in
my dreaming ear awoke me to tears and unavailing sorrow."

Here the poor nun again paused and wept bitterly.

"Time never fails to soften the memory of the most acute
sorrow, and in the convent to which I had fled for refuge
from my own thoughts, the soothing consolations of the sister-
hood, the calm, the pious and blameless tenor of their way,
charmed me as much as their holy meekness of spirit subdued my bitter regrets. After a time I tasted the sweets of
the most perfect contentment, if not of happiness. In the
duties of religion, of industry and charity, I soon learned to
forget Clermistonlee, or to remember him only in my prayers
—to forget that I had been a wife, to forget that I had been
—oh, no! not a mother—never could I forget that."

"Villain that he is! and with the consciousness of your
ladyship's existence, he has, since he was ennobled, wooed
many another to be his bride; but Heaven's hand or his own
vices have always foiled him."

The eyes of the recluse sparkled beneath her veil; but
folding her white hands meekly on her bosom, she said with
exceeding gentleness—

"What have I to do with it now?—besides, **youth, I am**

sure he believes me dead, for some of the Scottish archers told him so—and dead I am to him and to the world."

"It is a very sad history, madam."

"But God has comforted me." Her tears fell fast nevertheless, and a long pause ensued. Walter felt himself moved to tears, and he often sighed deeply, yet knew not why.

The sound of a trumpet roused him; it seemed close by, and came in varying cadence on the passing wind.

"'Tis the trumpet of a Dutch patrole. I must begone, lady, or remain only to die. Farewell; a thousand blessings on you and a thousand more—for we shall never meet again;" and half kneeling he kissed her hand, and, slipping from the cottage, favoured by the darkened moon, hurried away towards the fires of Luxembourg's camp, just as a party of Dutch Ruyters led by the boor halted at the cottage door.

*   *   *   *   *   *

With fifty thousand men the mareschal duke of Luxembourg was posted at Courtray on the Lys; while William, with twice that number, lay at Grammont, inactive, phlegmatic, and afraid to attack him; an inertness which increased the growing ill-humour of Britain against him. Without a dinner and without a sou, abandoned to solitude and dejection, Walter Fenton one evening paced slowly to and fro on the ramparts of Courtray, watching the bright sunset as it lingered long on the level scenery. A page approached, who acquainted him that Monseigneur le Mareschal required his presence in the citadel, whither he immediately repaired, and found the great Henri of Luxembourg, the youthful dukes of Chartres and Vendome, with other chevaliers of distinction, carousing after a sumptuous repast.

As he entered, De Chartres was singing the merry old ditty of *Jean de Nivelle*, while the rest chorused.

> " Jean de Nivelle has three flails ;
> Three palfreys with long manes and tails
> Three blades of a terrible brand,
> Which he never takes into his hand.
>   *Ah! oui vraiment!*
> *Jean de Nivelle est bon enfant!*"

The magnificence of their attire, the happy nonchalance and graceful ease of their manner, contrasted with his own tattered and humble uniform, fallen fortune, and jaded spirit, made Walter's heart sick as he entered; but, assuming somewhat of the old air of a cavalier officer, he bowed to the noble company, and awaited in silence the commands of the mareschal.

"Approach, monsieur," said the handsome young Duc de

Chartres. "*Tête Dieu!* but you look very pale! You were wounded, I believe?"

"It is nearly healed, monseigneur."

"Ah, it is deuced unpleasant work this fighting and beleaguering."

"De Chartres would rather be at Chantilly," said the Duc de Vendome, laughing.

"Or at Versailles," said a chevalier of St. Louis. He is thinking of little Mariette Gondalaurier."

"Or St. Dennis and adorable Isabeau Lagrange."

"Say Paris at once, messieurs," said the boyish *roué,* smiling. "I have beauties everywhere."

"The Scottish officer will drink with us—here, boy, assist our friend to wine," said Luxembourg to his page. "'Tis only Frontiniac, monsieur; but an hour ago it was Dutch William's, and we drink it out of pure spite."

Walter drank the fragrant wine from a massively-embossed cup, and his head swam as he imbibed it, and waited to hear for what desperate duty these noble peers designed him.

"Chevalier," said Luxembourg with his most bland smile, "it is pleasant to reward the brave. Aware that the repulse of the confederate cavalry on my right flank, and consequently the whole success of that glorious day at Steinkirke, was mainly owing to the valour of the Scottish cavaliers animated by your example, King Louis sends you this." And taking from his own neck the sparkling cross of the recently-created order of St. Louis, the duke placed it around the neck of Walter Fenton, who bowed his thanks in silence.

"Go, chevalier—you are a gallant soldier! The Scots were ever brave, and the friends of France. Wear that cross with honour to the most Christian king, to your native country—"

"And to the most sublime Madame Maintenon," said the young duke, and his gay companions laughed.

"Monseigneur!" said Luxembourg warningly.

"*Tête Dieu,* Mareschal! dost think I fear her? Faith, madame, 'tis known, never gives a favour without a most usurious per-centage. She is quite a Jewess in the intrigues of love and politics, ha! ha!"

"Attached to this cross, chevalier, is a pension of four hundred livres yearly, which I doubt not will be acceptable in your present reduced circumstances."

"Oh, believe me, monseigneur le mareschal, and you most noble dukes, it is indeed most acceptable; for with it I may in some sort alleviate the miseries of those gallant gentlemen, my comrades, who share your fortunes in the field."

" By St. Denis, you are a gallant fellow?" cried Luxembourg with kindling eyes. "Your generosity equals your courage. But this must not be. Messieurs your comrades must take the will for the deed. This night you must depart for the court of St. Germain-en-laye, where King James requires your immediate attendance. My secretary will supply you with money, and my master of the horse with a charger—adieu, sir, and God be with you!"

Walter retired.

That night he bade a sad adieu to his comrades, and mounted on one of the mareschal's horses, departed from Courtray.

His brave companions in glory and exile he saw no more. After all their services and their sufferings, their achievements and their chivalry, the few survivors of the war, sixteen in number, were, by a striking example of French ingratitude, disbanded at the peace of Ryswick, on the upper part of the Rhine, far from their native land—without money or any provision to save them from starvation and death. Of these sixteen only *four* survived to return to Scotland in extreme old age, when all fears of the Jacobites had passed away for ever.

Again the unclouded moon was shining over Steinkirke when Walter passed it, and vividly on his mind came back the fierce memories of that impetuous hour. The great plain was deserted, the full-eared corn was waving heavily, and not a sound disturbed the silence of the moonlit scenery save the deep bay of a household dog or the croak of a passing stork.

Thickly on every hand lay the graves of the faithful dead. In some instances he saw great burial mounds; in others there was but one solitary grave secluded among the long grass and reeds, and his horse started instinctively as he passed them.

Fragments of clothing, accoutrements, and other relics, lay among the rank weeds by the side of the fields, under the green hedge-rows, in the wet ditches; and even fleshless bones, bare scalps, fingers and toes, protruded from the soil, imparting an aspect of horror to the moonlighted plain where the battle had been fought.

The abbatis still lay there, but the foliage of the trees that formed it had long since faded and decayed. A great tumulus, on which the young grass was sprouting, lay within it.

" Poor Finland !" muttered Walter, and with a moistened eye and heavy heart he plunged his horse into the Senne and swam to the opposite bank. The cottage where he had found shelter had now disappeared; its foundations, scorched and blackened by fire, alone marked the place where it stood. He thought of the poor Ursuline and her story, and sighed that he could learn nothing more of her fate; he sighed, too, at the memory of the beautiful Margaret Mackay, and felt the keenest remorse for having slain her father.

Of the recluse he never heard more; but the daughter of Mackay reached the camp of William in safety, and in after years became the wife of her kinsman and chief, George, third Lord Reay of Farre.

CHAPTER LVIII.

WALTER FENTON AND THE KING.

To daunton me, and me sae young,
And guid King James's auldest son !
Oh, that's the thing that never can be,
For the man is unborn that'll daunton me
O set me once upon Scottish land,
With my guid braid-sword into my hand,
My bannet blue aboon my bree,
Then shew me the man that'll daunton me !
JACOBITE RELIQUES.

His confessor had just withdrawn, and King James was sitting in his closet involved in gloomy and distracting reverie —immersed in thoughts which even the mild exhortations of the priest had failed to soothe, and with his eyes intently fixed on the morning sun as it rose red and unclouded in the east, he gave way to the sadness that oppressed him.

Alternately he was a prey to a storm of revengeful and bitter political reflections, or to a gloomy fanaticism, which impaired the courage and lessened the magnanimity for which he had once been distinguished. On discovering that he was constantly conferring with the Jesuits upon abstruse theology, the ribald Louis spoke of him in terms of pity mingled with contempt. The French ridiculed, the Romans lampooned him, and, while the sovereign pontiff supplied him liberally with indulgences, the archbishop of Rheims said ironically— "There is a pious man who hath sacrificed *three* crowns for a mass !"

And this was all the unfortunate and mistaken James had gained, by his steady and devoted adherence to a falling faith.

Bestowing a glance of undisguised hostility, not unmingled with contempt, at the follower of St. Ignatius Loyola as he withdrew, the earl of Dunbarton, clad in his old uniform as a Scottish general, entered the apartment of the king. The green riband of St. Andrew was worn over his left shoulder, the star with its four silver points sparkled on his left breast, and around his neck hung the red riband of the Bath, and the magnificent collar of the Garter.

"Good morning, my Lord Dunbarton; you look as if you had something to communicate. Any news from Flanders? Is my dutiful son-in-law still playing at long bowles with Luxembourg? Has Sir Walter Fenton arrived?"

"He awaits your majesty's pleasure in the ante-chamber."

"Let him be introduced at once! Why all this etiquette?"

"Because, please your majesty, it is all that is left to remind me of other days."

"True," said the king, thoughtfully.

"Welcome, my brave and faithful soldier!" he exclaimed, as Walter was introduced by the gentlemen in waiting, and kneeled to kiss his hand. "Welcome from Flanders, that land of fighting and fertility. My poor Sir Walter, you look very pale and emaciated."

"I was wounded at Steinkirke, please your majesty; and with those unfortunate gentlemen, my comrades, have undergone such hardships and humiliations as no imagination can conceive."

Walter's eyes suffused with tears; his voice and his heart trembled. He felt a gush of loyalty and ardour swelling within his breast, that would have enabled him cheerfully to lay his life at the feet of the king. The remark of a celebrated modern writer is indeed a true one. "Unfortunate and unwise as were the Stuart family, there must have been some charm about them, for they had instances of attachment and fidelity shown them of which *no other line of kings could boast.*"

"You have indeed undergone sufferings which God only can reward," said the king, laying a hand kindly on his shoulder; "and your ill-requited valour is a striking example of the falsehood and flattery of the court of Versailles."

"When I consider our achievements," replied Walter, "my soul fires with pride and ardour; but when I think of the friends that have fallen, my heart dies away within me. To the last of my blood and breath I will serve your majesty; but, notwithstanding this gift of the cross of St. Louis, I will follow the banner of the donor no more."

"Louis is a noble prince," said the earl of Dunbarton, "and one who hath raised his realm to the greatest pitch of human grandeur."

"Oh, say not so, my lord! When I remember the cruel

persecution of his subjects after the treaty of Nimguen, his repealing the edict of Nantes, his tyranny over the *noblesse* and the parliament, his unjust wars and usurpations, in which he pours forth so prodigally the blood and the treasures of his people; his blasphemous titles and lewd life; I can only remember with shame that I have served in his army, and from this hour renounce his service for ever. And were it not that this cross hung once on the breast of the gallant Luxembourg, I would hurl it into the Seine."

"The remembrance of your sufferings doubtless animates this unwise train of thought, Sir Walter," said the king, slightly piqued. "But permit me to remark, that to indulge your opinions thus in France, is to run your head into the lion's mouth. How goes the war in Flanders?"

"Still doubtfully, please your majesty; but the recent arrival of the duke of Leinster at Ostend, with fresh troops for William, may turn the fortune of the war against Henri of Luxembourg, and consequently please the people of England, who are not very favourably disposed towards this expensive and unnecessary war for the Dutch interests of the usurper."

"The best proof of this new sentiment is the discontent of the Cameronians in the western districts of Scotland. What dost think, Sir Walter? They have engaged to muster five thousand horse and twenty thousand infantry for my complete restoration, provided Louis will give them only one month's subsidy, beside other supplies, and these he hath solemnly promised me."

"From my soul I thank Heaven that again it is turning the hearts of your subjects towards you. If such is the spirit of the Cameronians, oh, what will be the energy and the ardour of the cavaliers! But trust not in Louis; he has ruined every prince with whom he has been allied, in war or in politics, and assuredly he will shipwreck the interests of your majesty, as he has done those of others."

"Still judging hardly of his most Christian majesty," said James, smiling. "But I have the pledged words of better men. From the noble Drummonds, the gallant Keiths, the Hays, from the Lord Stormont and the Murrays, the gay Gordons and Grahames, I have received the most solemn promises of adherence and loyalty; and I know that the glorious clans of the northern shires will all rush to my standard the moment it is unfurled upon the Highland hills. Oh, yes!" continued the king, while his dark eyes flashed with joyous enthusiasm; "once again as in my father's days the war-cry of the Gaël will ring from Lochness to Lochaber."

"But where is now Montrose, and where Dundee ? " said Lord Dunbarton in a low voice.

"God will raise up other champions for those who have suffered so much in his service as the princes of the House of Stuart," replied the king with catholic fervour and confidence. "Meantime, Sir Walter, I would have you to set out for Scotland forthwith, to negotiate with those distinguished cavaliers, while the minds of my people are still inflamed by the memory of that fiend-like massacre at Glencoe, the defeat of Steinkirke, the slaughter of their soldiers, and all the disgusts incident to the Flemish campaign abroad and William's administration at home. My Lord Dunbarton avers that he will pledge his honour for the loyalty of his old regiment and the Scottish Guards, both horse and foot, for his countess has questioned every man of them. You will not fail to visit Drummond of Hawthorndon; he comes of a leal and true race, and his house, with its deep caverns and secret outlets, is a noble place of rendezvous and security. You will be liberally supplied with money and letters of credit and compliment. You may promise, in my name, everything that seems requisite—titles, honours, pensions,—I will trust to your discretion, from what the Lord Dunbarton has told me of you. Flatter the vain, conciliate the stubborn, secure the wavering, and fire the loyal. Leave nothing undone, and remember that, perhaps on the success of your mission depend the fortune of the prince, my son, the ancient liberties of Scotland, the honour of her people, and the fate of her regal line."

The king ceased, and Walter was so overwhelmed by the magnitude of the diplomacy entrusted to him, and the joy at returning to Scotland, that he remained silent for some moments.

"Oh, with what a mission does your majesty honour me!" he exclaimed, glowing with ambition, gratitude, and joy. "How can I express my thanks for this great confidence reposed in one so poor, so friendless?"

"These are good qualities, Sir Walter, for a Jacobite agent; you may (being friendless and unknown) make your way through Scotland in safety, when a coroneted baron, or the chief of a powerful sept, would soon be discovered and committed to the Castle of Edinburgh or the Tower of London. Go, Sir Walter; Lord Dunbarton and my secretary will arrange the matters you require, and in addition to my holograph letters to the Lowland lords and Highland chiefs, will give you others to Mr. Brown, my English agent, and Father Innes, president of the Scots' college at Paris, who acts for me in Scotland. Go, Sir Walter, and prosper! If ever we meet again, let us hope it will be under very different circumstances. May God and his thrice-blessed mother keep their hands over you, and inspire you for the sake of my dear little son and the people over whom he is to rule! Farewell— I have in some sort rewarded your courage in the field, but if your talent in diplomacy equals it, I swear by the sceptre that my sires have borne for ages, you shall be earl of Dalrulion in the north, and cock your beaver with the best peer in all broad Scotland. Farewell! may we meet again at the head of a loyal and faithful army, or part to meet no more."

Again Walter Fenton kneeled, and after kissing the hand of James, was hurried away by the earl of Dunbarton.

Furnished with a great number of letters addressed to the principal nobles and chiefs in Scotland, Walter artfully sewed them into the lining of his hat and the stiff buckram skirts of his coat, after which, without an hour's delay, he departed on his arduous and dangerous mission—to overturn the established governments of two kingdoms—to hurl down one dynasty and restore another.

Already he had gained a title which formerly he had possessed only in his day-dreams of success and glory; but now decorated by Louis with his new and famous military order, promised a peerage by his king, fired by loyalty, ardour, and love, he seemed to occupy a giddy eminence, from which he viewed distinctly a long and happy future.

It was a far-stretching and glorious vista of triumph and success; the restoration of the king by his means, and oh, far above all,—the exultation of placing a countess's coronet on the bright tresses of Lilian Napier.

CHAPTER LIX.

THE RETURNED EXILE.

Then, Mary, turn awa'
  That bonnie face o' thine
Oh, dinna show the breast
  That never can be mine.

Wi' love's severest pangs
  My heart is laden sair;
And owre my breast the grass maun grow,
  Ere I am free from care.

IN the gloaming of an evening in the autumn of 1693, a man left the western gate of Edinburgh, and, skirting the

suburb of the Highriggs, struck into the roadway between the
fields.

The sickly rays of a yellow sun shining faintly through the
mist after throwing the shadows of the gigantic castle far to
the eastward, had died away, and a deeper gloom succeeding,
denoted the close of the day as the fall of the fluttering leaves
did that of the dreary year.

The stranger was Walter Fenton; but how changed in
aspect and attire! His form was thin and emaciated, his
cheek pale, his eyes sunken from the pain of his wound and
the toil of campaigning; but his step was as free, and his
bearing erect as ever. His attire was of the plainest grey
freize, with great horn buttons; a brown scratch wig and a
plain beaver hat concealed the dark locks that curled beneath
them; he carried a walking staff in lieu of a sword, and
appeared to lean on it a little at times. He was now in the
character of a Low Country merchant, and, favoured by a
passport from the conservator of Scottish privileges at
Campvere, had an hour before landed from the good ship
Fame of Queensferry, at the ancient wooden pier of Leith.

Often he made brief pauses to view the desolate scene
around him; for in that year a heavy curse seemed to have
fallen upon the desolate kingdom of Scotland.

On an evening in the preceding summer, when everything
was blooming and smiling—when the land was rich with
verdure and the woods were heavy with foliage, a cold wind
came from the eastward, and, accompanied by a dense and
sulphureous mist, swept over the face of the country, blighting
whatsoever was touched by its pestilential breath.

The fields seemed to whiten under its baleful influence;
the ripening corn withered, and the land was struck with a
barrenness. Dense, opaque, and palpable, like a chain of
hills, this strange and horrid vapour lay floating in the
valleys for many successive months, and there its effects were
more disastrous. The heat of the sun seemed to diminish,
the insects disappeared from the air and the birds from the
withered woods, which, long ere the last month of summer,
became divested of their faded foliage. The cattle became
dwarfish and meagre, and the flocks perished by scores on
the decaying heather of the blasted mountains. The people
became sickly, ghastly, and prostrated in spirit; for a curse
seemed to have fallen upon the land and all that was in it.

This terrible visitation continued until the year 1701, and
the *dear years* were long remembered with horror in
Scotland.

In some places, January and February became the months

of harvest, and, amid ice and snow, and the sleet that drizzled through that everlasting and sulphureous mist, the half famished people reaped in grief and misery a small part of their scanty produce, while the other was left to rot in the ground Famine, the lord of all, stalked grimly over the land, and strong men and wailing women, yea, and feeble children. fought like wild beasts for a handful of meal in the desolate market places.

"There was many a blank and pale face in Scotland," says Walker, the famous Presbyterian pedlar, "and as the famine waxed sore, wives thought not of their husbands, nor husbands of their wives," and the gloomy superstition and fanatica intolerance of the time added fresh horrors to this ghastly scourge.

The famine was not yet at its height; but there was a desolation in the aspect of the land that deeply impressed the mind of the returned exile, and he sighed in unison with the dreary wind as it swept over the blasted muir, shaking down the crisped leaves and acorns of stately old oaks of Drumsheugh. Save the solitary heron, wading as of old in the lake, not a bird was to be seen, not an insect buzzing about the leafless hedges. The air was dense and cold, and all was very still.

The country seemed to be wasting like a beautiful woman decaying in consumption. Walter felt that the manners of the people were changed; intense gravity and moroseness, real or affected, were visible in every face, while sad-coloured garments, Geneva cloaks, and Dutch fashions were all the rage. Every trace of the smart moustache had disappeared, and with it the slashed doublets, the waving feathers and dashing airs of the gallant cavaliers.

Even the sentinels at the palace gates and the portes of the city, might have passed for those before the Town House or *Rasp Haus* at Amsterdam. The smart steel cap of the old Scottish infantry had now given place to a vast over-shadowing beaver looped up on three sides, and the scarlet doublet slashed with blue, and the jacket of spotless buff, to square tailed and voluminous coats of brick-red, with yellow breeches and belts worn saltier-wise.

Bitterly the reflection came home to the heart of the poor cavalier, that

"The times were changed, old manners gone,
And a *stranger* filled the Stuart's throne!"

Though confident of succeeding in his diplomacy with the loyal lords and chieftains of the Jacobite faction, he was well aware how arduous and difficult was the task to overthrow

two governments so well arranged, ably constituted and supported, as those of England and Scotland. It had long been
the policy of William III. to conciliate domestic enemies,
and, in pursuance of it, he had bestowed several lucrative
offices on the leaders of the discontented and kirk-party. The
Scottish parliament, which had recently met, received from
him an able and cunning letter, replete with flattering and
cajoling expressions, which put all the Presbyterian lords in
such excellent humour, that they returned a most dutiful and
affectionate address—granted him a supply of six new battalions of infantry, a body of seamen, and one hundred and
fifty thousand pounds, to enable him to carry on his useless
wars with new vigour ; but though the parliament was thus
obsequious, the people were far from being pleased ; and the
Jacobites, numerous, enthusiastic, and determined, everywhere fanned the flames of discord and dissension.

The institution of fines and oaths of assurance upon
absentees from parliament, which had direct reference to
certain cavalier lords and lesser barons, exasperated them as
much as the horrible massacre of Glencoe did the commonalty,
who raised throughout the land a cry for vengeance on
William and his government.

Walter Fenton reflected on these things as he walked
onward, and knew that he had come at a critical time. Other
thoughts soon succeeded, and, grasping his staff as he had
often done his sword, he pushed forward with a sparkling eye
and reddening cheek.

Without impairing his nobler sentiments, suffering and
misfortune had powerfully strengthened his loyalty and
virtue, as much as campaigning had improved his bearing
and lent a firmness and manly determination to his aspect ;
but often his brow saddened and the fire of his eye died
away, when he thought of Finland and those he had been
permitted to survive and to mourn.

Glowing with sensations of rapture, and eagerly anticipating the flush of joy that awaited him, he passed the rhinns
of the beautiful loch, the curious gable-ended old house where
once the Regent Murray dwelt, and approached the gate of
Bruntisfield.

His heart beat painfully ; he was deeply agitated. Five
weary years had elapsed since he had stood on that spot, and
it seemed only as yesterday. Through all the hurry of events
that had swept over him, his memory went back to that
memorable eve of September (of which this was now the
anniversary) and to the glorious ardour that animated his
heart on the day he marched for England, when the

long line of the Scottish host wound over yonder hill before him.

Oh, for one hour more of those fierce longings and brave impulses! But alas! the spirit seemed to have passed away for ever.

He approached the avenue. The old gate with its massive arch, its mossy carvings and loopholed wall, had given place to a handsome new erection of more modern architecture, surmounted by a rich coat of arms; and Walter felt every pulse grow still, and every fibre tremble as he surveyed the sculptured blazon.

It bore the saltire of Napier, engrailed between four roses, but quartered, collared, and coroneted with other bearings.

His heart became sick and palsied. Oh, it was a horrible sensation that came over him; he stood long irresolute and apprehensive.

"Of what am I afraid?" he suddenly exclaimed with the enthusiasm of a true and impassioned lover. "There is some mistake here; the house has been sold or gifted away like many another noble patrimony to the slaves of the Stadtholder. Lilian, dear Lilian, when shall I hold thee in my arms?"

He was about to rush forward, when a horseman, the glittering lace on whose bright-coloured suit of triple velvet, and waving ostrich feathers that fluttered in his diamond hatband, formed a strong contrast to the sombre fashions of the time, dashed down the leaf-strewn avenue on a beautiful charger, with the perfumed ringlets of his white peruke dancing in the wind—for white perukes, from a spirit of opposition, were all the rage then, as *black* had been under the three last princes of the old hereditary line. It was Lord Clermistonlee.

"Hollo, fellow," he cried imperiously, "keep out of my horse's way—dost want thy bones broken?" and giving a keen but casual glance at the dejected wanderer, he spurred onward to the city.

Suddenly he reined up so sharply as almost to pull his pawing steed back upon its strained and bending haunches.

"'Tis he!" exclaimed the proud lord, as he thought aloud. "By the great father of confusion, 'tis he! How could I mistake, though truly, poor devil, these last five years have sadly changed him. But on what fool's errand comes he here? By all the furies, I knew his lachrymose visage in a moment, though the despatches of Dalrymple of Stair, to our lords of council, had in some sort prepared me for his return; and for what?—to organize a plot for James's restoration. Poor fool! infatuated in love as in politics. He believes in the faith of

women and the word of kings ; let us see how they will avail
him to-night.

He smiled scornfully, and twisted the heavy dark moustaches, which he still cherished with more than Mahommedan veneration. Alternately sad and bitter thoughts
swelled within him as he remembered the joyous revelry of
King Charles's days, and the tyranny he could then exercise
over all nonconformists, and the hunting and hosting, dragooning and drinking of the Covenanting wars ; then came
feelings of jealousy and revenge that, as they blazed up in
his proud breast, bore all before them.

"How dares he now to prowl before my own gates
Gadso ! if my Lady Lilian sees him once, there will be a
pretty disturbance. A shipload of devils will be nothing to it.
The girl will die, and my own house will become too hot to hold
me. D——nation! too well have I seen the secret passion that
has preyed upon her gentle and affectionate heart—the grief
—the deep consuming grief, that all my magnificent presents
and gentle blandishments have failed to soothe. A thousand
curses on this upstart beggar, and a thousand more on the
mother of mischief, who has raised him up again to cross my
path. By what power hath he escaped war and woe, and
storm and every danger, again to thwart and come in the way
of Clermistonlee, whose purposes were never yet foiled by
man, or woman either? 'Sdeath! the time has come when
the cord of the doomster, or the axe of the maiden, must rid
me for ever of this old source of dark forebodings and secret
inquietude. Ho, for a guard and a warrant of council, and
then Sir Walter Fenton, knight banneret, the Jacobite spy,
chevalier of St. Louis, ex-private soldier, and *soi-disant*
ensign to the Lord Dunbarton, may look to himself. Ha,
ha ! " and dashing spurs into his horse, he galloped madly into
the city.

CHAPTER LX.

THE BUBBLE BURST.

To linger when the sun of life,
  The beam that gilt its path is gone—
To feel the aching bosom's strife,
  When *Hope* is dead, but *Love* lives on.
                              ANONYMOUS.

MEANWHILE, without recognising Clermistonlee, and not
aware that he had been recognised by him, poor Walter, who
was of that temperament which is easily raised and depressed,

turned away from the gate, crushed beneath the load of a thousand fears at the sight of so gay a cavalier caracoling down the avenue of Bruntisfield.

His heart was overcharged with melancholy reflections. " I have been away for five years—in all that time we have never heard of each other. Oh, what if she should have deemed me dead ! "

Drawing his last shilling from his pocket, the unfortunate cavalier entered a poor change-house by the wayside, where a great signboard creaking on an iron rod, and representing a portrait in a red coat and white wig, and having a tremendously hooked nose, imported that it was the " King William's head," kept by Lucky Elshender, who promised good entertainment for " man and beast."

The small clay-floored apartment, with its well-scrubbed bunkers, and rack of shining plates and tin trenchers, kirn-babies on the mantel-piece, and blazing ingle, where turf and wood blazed cheerfully in a clumsy iron basket, supported by four massive legs, looked very snug and comfortable.

A personage evidently a divine, long visaged and dark featured, with his lanky sable hair falling on his Geneva bands and coat of rusty black, sat warming his spindle legs at the warm hearth, and smoking a long pipe, on the bowl of which he fixed his great black lustre eyes with an expression of the deepest abstraction. It was the Reverend Mr. Ichabod Bummel, who came every evening as regularly as six o'clock struck, to smoke a pipe, and hear the passing news at the change-house kept by his aunt-in-law old Elsie, and to bore every traveller who was disposed to hear the abstruse theology and ponderous arguments advanced in his *Bombshell*, for that immortal work had been printed at last, in thick quarto, and a copy of it now lay under his elbow all ready for action against the first good-natured listener or foolhardy disputant.

In person, this redoubtable champion of toleration was as lean as ever, though the goods and chattels of this world had flowed amply upon him of late, notwithstanding the oppression and famine of the time. He had cautiously purchased various tofts and pendicles on the banks of the Powburn, and to these he gave hard and unusual scriptural names, which they bear unto this day, and which the curious may find by consulting the *City Directory*. One he named the land of Canaan, another the land of Goshen, the land of Egypt, Hebron, and so forth, while the little runnel that traverses them was exalted into the waters of Jordan. Meinie, whom he had espoused, had " proved," as he said, " ane fruitful vine," for she had brought him four sons, all long-visaged, hollow-eyed, and sepulchral counterparts of himself, and he named them Shem, Ham, Japhet, and Ichabod.

On the opposite side of the ingle, and far back in a corner, a miserable-looking woman crouched on the stone bench for warmth. A tartan plaid was muffled about her shoulders, and half concealed her hollow cheeks and ghastly visage. She seemed a personification of the famine and misery that reigned so triumphantly in Scotland. Her eyes were full of unnatural lustre; they flashed like diamonds in the light of the fire, but had a scrutinizing and stern expression in them that startled Walter, and he felt uneasy in her vicinity.

"It's only puir Beatrix Gilruth, my winsome gentleman," said Elsie in a low voice; "she is a gomeral—a natural body that bides about the doors, sir; just a puir, harmless, daft creature. She'll no harm you, sir."

In the tumult of his mind Walter did not at first recognise either Elsie or Ichabod, but assuming an air of as much unconcern as he could muster, he called for a bicker of French wine, and took possession of a cutty stool which the slipshod Elsie placed for him hurriedly and officiously opposite the divine, who regarded him with a keen scrutinizing glance, to ascertain his probable station in life, his errand, and objects in coming hither. He saw that he was a traveller, and being on foot must be a poor one.

"Good e'en to your reverence, for, I presume, I have the honour of addressing a clergyman," said Walter, politely.

"Hum—humph!" answered Ichabod, with a short cough, nodding his head, and never once moving his eyes from Walter's face. Every man was then doubtful and suspicious of strangers (the Scots are so to the present hour), and consequently Ichabod was singularly dry and reserved. But Elsie drew near Walter, and looked at him attentively. The grief that preyed upon his heart had imparted a singularly prepossessing mildness to his features, and a winning cadence to the tone of his voice, but the stark preacher neither saw one nor felt the influence of the other.

"A cold night, your reverence."

"Yea," gasped Ichabod; and there was another pause.

"My service to you, sir: wilt taste my wine? 'tis right Gascony, and I should be a judge."

"Yea, having been in those parts where it was produced, probably," observed Ichabod, becoming more curious and communicative as he imbibed the lion's share of Walter's wine pot, and waited for an answer; but there was none given.

"Verily, sir," began Mr. Bummell, "these are times to

chill the souls and bodies of the afflicted. Thou seest how sore the famine waxeth in the land, especially in these our once fertile Lothians, which whilome were wont to be overflowing with milk and honey."

"Ay," chimed in Elsie, "but I've seen them in mair fearfu' times, when they were overflowing wi' blude and soldiers."

"'Tis for that red harvest, woman, that we are visited by this lamentable scourge; plagued even as Egypt was of old. In these three fertile shires of Lothian I have seen a woful change since the last harvest, and my heart grows heavy when I think upon it; but I am about to arise and go forth from them for ever."

"Indeed, sir," said Walter.

"I have gotten a pleasant call from the Lord to another kirk——"

"Wi' a *better* stipend, sir," added the gleeful Elsie.

"Indubitably," said Mr. Bummel.

"Twa hunder pound Scots, a braw glebe, four bolls o' beir," replied Elsie, counting on her crooked and wrinkled fingers, "aucht chalders——"

"Peace, woman Elsie, for this enumeration of thine savours of a love for the things of this life."

"And a braw pulpit. O, but it's grand you'll be, Iehabod, when in full birr under your sounding board. But alake, sir," she added, turning to Walter, "arena' these fearfu' times?"

"Sad indeed, gudewife."

"I was in the mealmarket this morning, and oh, sirs, it was a sight to rend the heart of a nether millstane to see the hungry bairns and wailing mothers worrying about the half-filled pokes. God help them! the puir folk are deeing fast the west country we hear."

"'Tis a scourge on the land for its former sins," said the preacher in his most sepulchral tone; "but let us hope that the faith of its people will save it!"

"You'll hae come from some far awa' country I'm thinking, sir?" said Elsie, inquisitively, for the extreme sadness of Walter interested her extremely.

"True, I have, good woman."

"France, I fancy? that land o' priests and persecution."

"From Holland last. I am a merchant, and deal in broadcloths and cart saddles. From Holland last," he repeated, for their inquisitiveness made him uneasy.

"A blessed land, good youth," said Mr. Bummel. "I sojourned there long when there was a flaming sword over the children of righteousness."

"Reverend sir, canst tell me what are the news among you

here?" asked Walter, who was in an agony of mind to lead the conversation to what lay nearest his heart.

" Verily, sir, nought but the famine—the famine. The west winds hath detained the Flanders mail these two months, and we have heard nothing from London these many weeks, save anent plots of the Jacobites and Papists, of whilk we have ever enough and to spare."

" What have you heard of them of late?"

" 'Tis said that one Walter Fenton, formerly an officer in the regiment of Dunbarton (that bloody oppressor of Israel) is now tarrying among us, plotting in James's cause, or on some such errand of hell."

" The rascal," said Walter, drinking to conceal the confusion that overspread his face.

" Yea," continued Ichabod, puffing vigorously, and luckily involving himself in a cloud of smoke. " This morning the heralds, in their vainglorious trumpery, were proclaiming at the Cross the reward of a thousand merks to any that will bring his head to the privy council; and the Lord Clermistonlee, from the good will and affection he bears his majesty, offers five hundred more!"

" Do you think he will be found?"

" Indubitably. The ports are closed, the guards on the alert; the messengers-at-arms, macers, and halberdiers are all in full chase. He must perish, and so may all who would restore the abominations of idolatry! Here in my *Bombshell* (a work whilk I have lately imprinted with mickle care and toil), if I do not prove, from the epistles to the Thessalonians, that the great master of popery, the bishop of Rome, is the grand antichrist therein referred to, I will be well content to kiss the bloody maiden that stands under the shadow of the Tolbooth gable."

" Hear till him!" cried the delighted Elsie. " Hear till him! O wow, but my Meinie's man is a grand minister—he rides on the rigging of the kirk!"

" I am a stranger here," said Walter, no longer able to repress the torture of his mind; " I know nothing of the vile plot you speak of, having been long in the industrious Low Countries—and—and—canst tell me, your reverence, whose mansion is approached by yonder stately avenue of oaks and sycamores?"

" The house of Bruntisfield—called of old the Wrytes."

" Aich ay," added Elsie, shaking her head mournfully; " but a house o' *wrongs* now."

" Wherefore, gudewife?"

" It is a lang story, honoured sir," replied Elsie, drawing

her stool nearer Walter, and knitting very fast to hide her emotion. "The auld line o' the Napiers ended in a lassic, as bonnie a doo as the Lowdens three could boast o', and mony came frae baith far and near to the wooing and winning o' her; but nane cam speed save a neer-do-weel loon o' a cavalier officer, to whom she plighted heart and troth—and the plight-ing pledge was a dcid woman's ring. As might be expected, the hellicate cavalier gaed awa' to the wars and plundering in the Lowlands of Holland, and sair my young lady sorrowed for him; I ken that weel, for I was her nurse, and mony a lang hour she grat in my arms for her love that was far awa'. At last word came frac Low Germanie that the fause villain had married some unco' papistical woman, and, in a mad fit o' black despair, my lady accepted the most determined, if no the best o' her suitors——"

"Who?" asked Walter, in an unearthly voice, and feeling for the sword he wore no longer. "Who?"

"Randal Lord Clermistonlee, and chow! but sair hath been the change in our gude auld barony since then. Her braw lands and farmsteadings, her auld patrimony, baith haugh and holme, loch and lea, brae and burn, are a' melting and fleeing awa' by the wasterfu' extravagance o' the wildest loon in a' braid Scotland. Hawks and hounds, revellers and roisterers, and ill women, thrang the great ha' house frae ecn to morn, and morn till eenin'; and sae, between the freaks and follies, the pride and caprice o' her lord, my puir doo Lilian leads the life o' a blessed martyr. When mad wi' winc and ill luck at the dice tables, he rampages ower her like a bull o' Bashan; while, at other times, he just doats on her as a faither would on a favourite bairn. But, alake! doating can never remove the misery that has closed over her for the short time she'll likely be amang us—for her heart is breaking fast—it is—it is!"

Here Elsie wept bitterly, and then resumed.

"Her marriage-day was ane o' the darkest dool to a' the barony, for on that miserable day our auld lady died; and a' the leal servitors were soon after expelled to mak' room for the broken horse-coupers, ill women, and vagabonds, that were ever and aye in the train o' the new lord."

While Elsie ran on thus, Walter heard her not. His mind was a perfect chaos of distraction.

Oh, what a shock were these tidings to one whose head was so full of romance and enthusiasm, and whose heart was brimming with scnsibility and love!

He felt an utter prostration of every faculty, and a deadly coldness seemed to pass over the pulses of his heart. He arose, and laying on the table the last coin he possessed in the world, hurried forth without waiting for change, and, bent on some desperate deed, blind and reckless, with anger, agony, and despair in his soul, he entered the dark shadowy avenue, and approached the old castellated mansion—the place of so many tender memories.

CHAPTER LXI.

LOVE AND MARRIAGE ARE TWO.

Oh, these were only marks of joy, forsooth,
For his return in safety! Were they so?
And so ye may believe, and so my words
May fall unheeded! Be it so; what comes
Will nevertheless come.
        AGAMEMNON OF ÆSCHYLUS.

THE shadows of the gloomy evening had deepened as he approached the ancient place of Bruntisfield, and its dark façade, its heavy projecting turrets and barred casements, impressed him with additional sadness.

The wind sighed down the lonely avenue, and whirled the fallen leaves as it passed. Many a raven flapped its wings and screamed discordantly above his head, and all such sounds had a powerful effect on him at the time.

Confused, despairing, and feeling a sentiment of profound contempt and anger, struggling for mastery with his old and passionate love, his heart seemed about to rend with its conflicting emotions.

One sensation was ever present—it was one of desolation and loneliness—that he had nothing more to live for; that the world was all a blank. The light that had long led him on through so many miseries and dangers had vanished from his view: his idol was shattered for ever.

He felt that it was impossible to think with calmness; to tear from his breast the dear image and the cherished hopes he had fostered there so long—to exchange admiration for contempt—love for indifference. Oh, no! it could never be. Ages seemed to have elapsed since the sun had set that evening; while his parting with Lilian, the triumph of Killy-crankie, the carnage of Steinkirke, and his mission from the king, seemed all the events of yesterday.

He felt sick and palsied at heart.

Irresistibly impelled to see her, heedless alike of the dangerous charm of her presence and the risk he ran if discovered, his whole soul was bent upon an interview, that he might upbraid her with her perfidy—hurl upon her a mountain of reprobation and bitterness, of obloquy and scorn, and then leave her presence for ever.

"I am alone in the world," thought he. "This is my native land—the land where I had garnered up my heart, my hopes, and my wishes, though not one foot of it is mine save the sod that must cover me. Of all the tens of thousands that tread its soil, there is not one now with whom I can claim kindred, who would welcome me in coming, or bless me in departing— not one to shed a tear on the grave where I shall lie. Oh! it is very sad to feel one's self so desolate. Where now are all those brave companions with whom I was once so daring, so joyous, and so gay? Alas! on a hundred fields their bones lie scattered, and I alone survive to mourn the glory of the days that are gone for ever! Oh, never more shall the drum beat or trumpet sound for me! Oh, never more shall love or glory fire my heart again! Oh, never more, for the hour is passed and never can return"—and he almost wept, so intensely bitter were his thoughts of sorrow and regret.

The barbican gate stood ajar, and the old and well-remembered doorway at the foot of the tower was also open; they seemed to invite his entrance, and, careless of the consequences, he went mechanically forward.

The old portrait on horseback, the trophy of arms, and the wooden Flemish clock, with its monotonous *tick-tack*, still occupied the vaulted lobby. Everything seemed as he had seen them last. He turned to the left and entered the chamber-of-dais, breathless and trembling, for he seemed instinctively to know that *she* was there.

He entered softly, and overpowered by the violence of his conflicting emotions, stood rooted to the spot. The old chamber, with its massive panelling and rich decorations of the Scoto-French school, was partially lighted by the ruddy glow from the great fireplace, and by the last deep red flush of the departed sun that streamed through its grated windows.

The dark furniture, the grotesque cabinets with their twisted columns, the stark chairs, with their knobby backs and worsted bobs, the grim full-length of Sir Archibald Napier, *cap-a-pie à la cuirassier*, the dormant beam, with its load of lances, swords, and daggers, were all as Walter had last seen them; but the old lady's well-cushioned chair, her long walking cane and ivory virreled spinning-wheel had long since disappeared; and hawk's-hoods, hunting horns, spurs, whips, and stray tobacco-pipes lay in various places, while in lieu of Lady Grizel's sleek and pampered tom cat, a great wiry, red-eyed, sleuth hound slept on the warm hearth-rug.

On all this Walter bestowed not a glance, for his eyes and his soul became immediately rivetted on the figure of Lilian.

With her head leaning on her hand, she sat within the deep recess of a western window, and the faint light of the setting sun lit up her features and edged her ringlets with gold. She was absorbed in deep thought.

Lilian, who for days, and months, and years, in health and in sickness, in danger and in safety, in sorrow and in joy, had never for a moment been absent from his thoughts, was now before him, and yet he had not one word of greeting to bestow. He seemed to be in a trance—to be oppressed by some horrible dream.

He observed her anxiously and narrowly. Nothing could be more tender than the love that was expressed in his eyes, and nothing more acute than the agony expressed by his contracted features.

Lapse of years, change of circumstances and of thought, had considerably altered the appearance of Lilian. The lighthearted, slender, and joyous girl had expanded into a stately, grave, and melancholy matron. Oh, what a change those five sad years had wrought! Her dress was magnificent, as became the wife of a Scottish noble; her figure, though still slight, was fuller and rounder than of old; her face, though still dignified and beautiful, was paler — even sickly. Her blue eyes seemed to have lost much of their former brilliancy, and to have gained only in softness of expression. Her dark lashes were cast down, and her aspect was sad and touching. The bloom of her lip and her cheek had faded away together, for heavily on her affectionate heart had the hand of suffering weighed.

She wept, and the heart of Walter was melted within him. Had all the universe been his he would have given it to have embraced her. He sighed bitterly, but dared not to approach.

"He is gone," said Lilian,—"gone to spend another night in riot and debauchery, while I am left ever alone. Perhaps 'tis well, for often his presence is intolerable. Woe is me! Oh, how different was the future I once pictured to my imagination!"

The sound of that dear voice, which had so often come to him through his dreams in many a far and foreign camp and city, made Walter tremble. He was deeply moved. The fire in the arched chimney, which had been smouldering, now suddenly shot up into a broad and ruddy blaze that lighted the whole chamber. Lilian turned her head, and instantly grew pale as death, for full on the image of him who occupied her thoughts—of Walter Fenton, hollow eyed, emaciated, and supported on a walking-staff—fell the bright stream of that fitful light. He looked so unearthly, so motionless and spectral, that Lilian's blood ran cold.

She would have screamed, but the cry died away upon her lips. After a moment or two her spirit rallied; her respiration, though hurried, became more free; her face blushed scarlet up to the very temples, and then became ashy pale, as before, and her glazed eyes resumed their wild and inquiring expression. She arose, but neither advanced nor spoke. All power seemed to have left her.

"Oh, Lilian! Lilian!" said the poor wanderer, in a voice of great pathos; "after the lapse of five long years of exile and suffering, what a meeting is this for us! Under what a course of perils have the hope of my return and your truth not sustained me? My God! that I should find you thus. Is this the welcome I expected?"

Summoning all her courage and that self-possession which women have in so great a degree, Lilian (though her eyes were full of tears), averted her face, and recalled the fatal letter of Finland, on which had turned the whole of her future fate.

"Look at me, adorable Lilian!" said Walter, kneeling, and stretching his arms towards her.

Lilian dared not to look; but she trembled violently, and sobbed heavily.

"Look at me, beloved one" said Walter, wildly and passionately. "Changed though I am, and though another holds your heart, you cannot have forgotten me, or learned to view me with aversion and contempt. If this lord has won your affection—"

"Oh, say not that, Walter," sobbed Lilian, "do not say my affection."

"Oh, horror! what misery can equal such an avowal? My fatal absence has undone us both."

"Say, rather, your fatal inconstancy."

"Mine?" reiterated Walter.

"Oh, yes, yes; upbraid me not," said Lilian, in a piercing voice. "I was faithful and true until you forsook me for another. To God I appeal," she cried, raising her clasped hands and weeping eyes to heaven, "kneeling I appeal if ever in word, or thought, or hope, I swerved in truth from thee, dear Walter, until tidings of your marriage reached me; when, stung by jealousy, by pride, by disappointment and despair, and urged by the unmerited contumely that had fallen upon me, I yielded to the exhortations of my friends, and in an evil hour ——." She covered her face with her hands, and could say no more.

"Heaven preserve my senses!" ejaculated Walter Fenton, "for here the wiles of hell have been at work. We have been deceived, cruelly deceived, dear Lilian, by some deep-laid plot of villany which this right hand shall yet unravel and revenge. And you are the wife of Clermistonlee? Hear me, unfortunate! You are less than—ah, how shall I say it? You are not and cannot be his wife!"

"You rave, poor Walter. Our doom is irrevocably sealed. Our paths in life must be for ever separate. Oh, for the love of gentle mercy begone, and let us meet no more, for at this moment I feel my brain whirling, and I am trembling on the very verge of madness."

"Lilian, this is the 20th of September," said Walter.

"Cruel, cruel; do not speak of it," said she, wringing her hands. "For heaven's sake leave me, and take back the pledge—the ring, for to retain it longer were a sin, and too long have I sinned in treasuring it as I have done."

Unlocking a cabinet, she drew from a secret drawer a ring to which a riband was attached, and offered it to Walter, but he never approached.

"We have been cruelly duped, dear Lilian; but oh, how could you doubt me, for never did I mistrust you? But hear me, though my words should crush your heart as mine just now is crushed. Alison Gifford, the first wife of Lord Clermistonlee yet lives, though (as she told me) dead to him and to the world for ever!"

"What new horror is this?" said Lilian, pressing her hands upon her temples.

In a few words her unhappy lover explained how he had become acquainted with the existence of Lady Clermistonlee.

"Oh, this is indeed to bruise the bruised—to heap brands upon a burning heart," said Lilian, as she sank into a chair and covered her face with her hands. A long pause ensued, till Walter said in a low and trembling voice,

"Lilian, do you really love this man—this Clermistonlee?"

"He is my husband."

"It is impossible you can love him!"

"Love him!—oh, no! custom has in part overcome the aversion with which I once regarded him, and by his able flattery he has succeeded in soothing me into a temper of kind indifference and quiet resignation—but oh, this interview—"

Walter, who had never dared to diminish the distance between them, gazed wistfully and tenderly upon her; but at that moment an infant that was sleeping in its cradle awoke, and cried aloud. Its voice seemed to sting him to the heart, and he turned abruptly to withdraw.

"Farewell, Lilian," said he ; "I will go, and my presence shall disturb your serenity no more. May you be happy, and may God bless and forgive you for the agony I now endure ! Clermistonlee, like the matchless villain he has been through life, has wronged us both ; but let him tremble in the midst of his success and his treason, for the hour is coming when our king shall enjoy his own again, and remember that in that hour the same hand which rends the baron's coronet from the brow of your betrayer, bestows on me the earldom of Dalrulion ! Farewell," said he through his clenched teeth ; "to me the paths of ambition and revenge are open still, though those of happiness and love are closed, alas, for ever !" He gave her one long glance of agony, and turned to depart ; but at that moment strong hands were laid upon him violently—the room was filled with soldiers and the beagles of justice ; he was dragged down and bound with cords, ere he could make the slightest effort in his own defence.

"An out-and-out Jacobite, Papist, and a' the rest o' it—I ken by the look o' him !" cried Maclutchy, the macer, flourishing his badge of office. "Here will be some grand plots brought to light, that will bring half the country under doom o' forfeiture and fine. Kittle times, lads ! kittle times ! "

"Away with him !" cried Clermistonlee, spurning the manacled unfortunate with his foot ; "away with him. The lords of the privy council meet in an hour. Lose no time— for by all the devils ! the corbies of the Burghmuir shall pick his bones ere the morrow's sun be set."

As Walter was roughly dragged away, Lilian threw her hands above her head, uttered one wild shriek, and fell forward on her face, motionless as if dead.

CHAPTER LXII.

THE RING AND THE SECRET

See the cypress wreath of saddest hue,
The twining destiny threading through ;
And the serpent coil is twisting there—
While regardless of the victim's prayer,
The fiend laughs out o'er the mischief done,
And the canker-worm makes the heart his throne.
THE PROPHECY.

TWELVE o'clock tolled heavily and sadly from the steeple of St. Giles.

It was a bleak and cold night. The lords of the privy

council, muffled up in their well-furred rocquelaures, with
their hats flapped over their periwigs, ascended from the subterranean vaults under the Parliament House, where they
held their dreaded conclaves, and hurried away to their residences in the various deep and steep wynds of the ancient
city. Mersington, who, overcome by sleep and wine, had remained at the table until roused by macer Maclutchy, was
the last to come forth, and he stood rubbing his eyes in the
Parliament-square, and watching the black gigantic statue of
King Charles with steady gravity, for he could have sworn at
that moment that it seemed to be trotting hard towards him.
His rallying faculties were scattered again by a stranger
violently jostling him.

"Haud, ye dyvour loon!" exclaimed the incensed senator;
"I am the Lord Mersington."

"And what art doing here, pumpkinhead?" asked Clermistonlee, who was quite breathless by having rushed up the
Back Stairs, as those flights of steps which ascended from
the Cowgate to the Parliament-square were named. "Are
the proceedings over? Hath the villain confessed? Is he
to die?"

"They are over, and he shall die conform to the act."

"And how went the proceedings?"

"Deil kens; I sleepit the haill time."

"Driveller!" cried Clermistonlee in a towering passion;
"'tis like thee; your head is as empty as my purse——"

"Hee, hee, ye seem a bonnie temper to-night. But what
detained *you* frae the board, when ye knew you were principal
witness?"

"The sudden indisposition of Lady Clermistonlee made it
impossible for me to leave Bruntisfield,—but I have this
moment galloped in from the Place."

"You are a kind and considerate gudeman," said Mersington drily.

"And what did this fellow confess?"

"His abhorrence of you——"

"Ha! ha!"

"His hatred of the present government, and his weariness
o' this life. He spoke unco dreich and sadly, puir callant,—
and sae I fell fast asleep and dozed like a top."

"And did not that goosecap, the king's advocate, give him
a twinge or two of the torture?"

"We brought some braw things to light without the help
o' rack or screw. The tails o' his coat were as fu' o' treason
as an egg's fu' o' meat. There were five-and-twenty auto-
graph letters frae the bluidy and papistical Duke James——'

"Stuff! But lately he was styled His most Sacred Majesty, by the grace of God, and so forth."

"I speak as we wrote it in the council minutes. Five-and-twenty letters to the cut-throat Hicland chiefs, to the Murrays of Stormont, the Drummonds, and others, some slee tod lowries we have long had our een on. But maist of a' was a notable plot of that d——ned jaud Madame Maintenon to assassinate King William."

"Hah!"

"From a paper found, it appears that a certain Monsieur Dumont is now disguised as a soldier in our confederate army in Flanders, watching an opportunity to shoot the king and escape."

"By St. George, I hope the aforesaid Monsieur Dumont is a good shot—a regular candle-snuffer!"

"Our culprit, Fenton, knew not of Maintenon's plot, or of her papers being among those on his person. He looked black dumbfoundered when Maclutchy drew them frae a neuk in his coat-tail."

"And to whom were they directed?"

"To one *Widow Douglas*, whilk the king's advocate avers to be no other than the Lady Dunbarton. Fenton grew red with anger on their being read, and smote his forehead, saying, '*Dupe that I have been! the noble Duc de Chartres warned me to beware of De Maintenon; but let it pass:*' and here, as I said, I fell fast asleep, until a minute ago. But come, let us have a pint of sack; I am clean brainbraised wi' drouth, and I warrant Lucky Dreep, in the Kirk-o'-field-wynd, keeps open-door yet."

"And he dies?" said Clermistonlee, who could think of nothing but glutting his revenge.

"Early to-morrow morning, by the bullet."

"I would rather it had been by the cord. How came our considerate councillors to shoot instead of hang him?"

"Soldiers, ye ken, are often soft-hearted when other men are in stern mood; so auld General Livingstone, after pleading hard for Fenton's life, and failing, procured what he called an honourable commutation of the sentence, for which the puir gomeral cavalier thanked him as if it had been a reprieve."

"Cord or bullet, it matters not. So perish all who would cross the purposes of Randal of Clermistonlee."

His lordship for once resisted the importunities of his friend, and instead of adjourning to a tavern, rode slowly and reluctantly back to his own house. He felt a strange and unaccountable presentiment of impending evil, for which he could not account, but endeavoured to throw it from him. The effort was vain.

He felt himself a villain. A load of long-accumulated wickedness oppressed his proud heart; it was not without its better traits, and writhed as he reflected on some events in his past life.

"Alison! Alison!" he exclaimed, turning his dark eyes upwards to the star-studded firmament, "*now* thy curse is coming heavily upon me."

His principal dread was the death of Lilian, for he had learned to love her with tolerable sincerity, but he knew not the secret which Walter had revealed to her, and the consequent intensity of her horror, aversion, shame, and anger. He knew not the tempest it had raised in her sensitive breast against him.

When he entered the chamber-of-dais, she was seated near a tall silver lamp. The glare of the untrimmed light fell full upon her face, and its ghastly and altered expression struck a mortal chillness on the heart of her husband. He said not a word, but walking straight to a buffet, filled a large silver cup several times with wine, and always drained it to the bottom. The liquor mounted rapidly to his brain; he threw himself into a chair opposite Lilian, and heedless of the perfect scorn that quivered in her beautiful nostrils, and sparkled in her brilliant eyes, began leisurely to unbutton his riding gambadoes of red stamped maroquin, whistling a merry hunting-tune while he did so.

It was easier for him to requite scorn with scorn than give tenderness for love.

"Confusion on the buttons!" he exclaimed. "Juden! Juden! Tush! I forgot: poor Juden hath been with the devil these three years. There is none now of all my rascally household who will share with me the morrow's glut of vengeance as thou wouldst have done, my faithful Juden."

Lilian wrung her attenuated hands; Clermistonlee regarded her sternly, and then bursting into a loud laugh, as he threw away his boots and spurs, chanted a verse from the old black-letter ballad of Gilderoy :—

"Beneath the left ear so fit for a cord
A rope so charming a zone is;
Thy youth in his cart hath air of a lord,
And we cry—there dies an Adonis!"

"Ha! ha! I shall see his head on the Bow-port to-morrow, madam."

"Infamous and wicked!" exclaimed Lilian, feeling all her old love revived with double ardour, and no longer able to restrain her sentiments of grief and indignation. "Walter dear and beloved Walter, how cruelly have I been deceived!" and drawing from her bosom the ring,—his mother's ring, the pledge of his betrothal, she pressed it to her lips with fervour.

The brow of the proud Clermistonlee grew black as thunder, and he grasped her slender arm with the tenacity of a falcon.

"Surrender this bauble, that I may commit it to the flames. Surrender it, madam, lest I dash thee to the earth; for at this moment I feel, by all the devils! my brain spinning like a jenny."

"Give him the ring, Lady Lilian; give it, for the sight of it will arrest his vision, even as the letters of fire arrested the eyes of Belshazzar and smote him with dismay. Sweet lady, let him look upon it," said the voice of a woman.

They turned, and beheld the pale, emaciated, and haggard visage of Beatrix Gilruth, half shaded by a tattered tartan plaid. Taking advantage of Lilian's momentary surprise, her husband snatched the ring from her, and was about to hurl it into the fire, when, incited by the woman's words, and impelled by some mysterious and irresistible curiosity, he looked upon it, and the effect of his single glance acted like magic upon him. He quitted his clutch of Lilian's arm, trembled, grew pale, and turning the ring again and again, surveyed it with intense curiosity.

"How came he to have this ring?" he muttered; "what strange mystery is here? If it should be so—— O, impossible!"

He pressed a spring that must have been known only to himself, for Lilian had never discovered it in all the myriad times she had surveyed it, and Walter himself was ignorant of the secret when he bestowed the trinket upon her. The lapse of years had stiffened the spring; but after a moment's pressure from the finger of Clermistonlee, a little shield of gold unclosed, revealing a minute and beautiful little miniature of himself, which in earlier days had been one of the happiest efforts of the young Medina's pencil.

"'Twas my bridal gift to Alison," he exclaimed in a voice of confusion and remorse. "Oh, Alison, Alison! many have I loved, but never one like thee. Never again did my heart feel the same ardour that fired it when I placed this ring on your adorable hand. Unfortunate Alison!"

"This ring was tied by a riband around the neck of Walter Fenton, when a little child he was found by the side of his dead mother in the Greyfriars churchyard," said Lilian in a breathless voice.

"Confusion and misery! 'tis impossible this can be true; there is some diabolical mistake here. Woman, say forth."

Beatrix gave Clermistonlee a bitter and malicious smile, and addressed Lilian.

"Walter's mother, sweet lady, gave that ring to Elspat Fenton, who, next to myself, was the most trusted of her attendants, and bade her travel from Paris to Scotland, and deliver the child and the bridal gift together to her husband—to Randal of Clermistonlee."

Lilian covered her face, and the fiery lord, whose first emotions were generally those of anger, surveyed Beatrix as if she had been a coiled-up snake. She spoke slowly, and made long pauses, for aware that her words were as daggers she dealt them sparingly.

"After long suffering and great peril by sea and land, this poor woman reached Edinburgh, but failed to meet the father of the infant committed to her care; for then he was in arms with the men of the Covenant, hoping by any civil broil or commotion to repair the splendid patrimony his excesses had dissipated. Elspat being unable to give a very coherent account of herself, was declared a nonconformist by the authorities, and thrown with thousands of others into the Greyfriars kirkyard, where, in that inclement season, she perished; but the child was found and protected by the soldiers of Dunbarton. That child is Walter Fenton; he is your son, Lord Clermistonlee! the child of your once-loved Alison Gifford. I call upon Heaven to witness the truth of my assertion! His own name was Walter (ah! can you have forgotten that?) his nurse's Fenton. *I saw her die*, and I alone knew the secret, and have treasured it till this hour—this hour of vengeance upon thee, thou false and wicked lord! In my wicked spirit of revenge too long have I kept the secret; but now this blameless and noble youth is doomed to death, and fain would I save him, for he is innocent, and good and generous; in all things, oh, how much the reverse of thee!"

"Maniac, thou liest!" exclaimed Clermistonlee, whose heart beat wildly. "I cannot believe this tale of a tub, which is told to affright me. And yet, how dare I reject it?—the ring—Walter—my God!"

"Ha! has Beatrix the wronged, the scorned, the despised, the neglected Beatrix, wrung your heart at last? Fool! fool! Did'st thou never suspect the volcano that slumbered here?" she exclaimed, laying her hand upon her heart. "Did'st thou never perceive the flame that smouldered in my breast—the yearnings, the throbbings, the fierce longing to be adequately revenged on thee who had brought me to ruin and madness, and had abandoned me to penury and privation? Wretch! 'tis twenty-five years since ye betrayed me. Time has rolled on—time, that soothes all sorrows and softens every affliction, and teaches us to forget the wrongs of the living—yea, and the virtues of the dead ; and perhaps to wonder why we hated one and loved the other,—time, I say, has rolled on to many miserable years, until I have become the hideous thing I am, but it never lessened one tithe of my longing for vengeance for the thousand taunts and contumelies that succeeded my first sacrifice for thee. You say I am mad—perhaps I am— but mark me—*a woman's sorrow passes like a summer cloud, but her vengeance endureth for ever !* ''

Clermistonlee smote his forehead, and Beatrix laughed like a hyæna.

"My God—unhappy Walter !" said Lilian in a voice that pierced the heart of him she abhorred to deem her husband. "Then she who saved and nursed thee on the field of Stein-kirke was thy mother—*thy mother*, and she knew it not? Oh, this was the secret sentiment, the heaven-born thought that spoke within her and made her heart so mysteriously yearn towards thee. Unfortunate Walter ! how deeply have we been wronged—how bitterly must we suffer !"

"And till now, thou accursed fiend, this terrible secret has been concealed from me !" said Clermistonlee furiously, as he half drew his sword.

Beatrix laughed and tossed her arms wildly.

"Oh, horror upon horror ! woe upon woe !" said Lilian in a voice of the deepest anguish as she wrung her hands, and, taking up her little infant from the cradle, kissed it tenderly on the forehead, and retired slowly from the room.

"Lilian—Lilian," cried her husband, "whither go ye, lady ?"

"To solitude—to solitude," she murmured. "Anywhere to save me from my own terrible thoughts—anywhere to hide me from the deep disgrace you have brought upon me ; to any place where never again the light of day shall find me."

Clermistonlee heard her light steps on the staircase, and they fell like a knell on his heart : impelled by some secret and mysterious impulse, he followed her to her own apartment, the door of which he had heard close behind her. There was no sound within it.

He entered softly ; but she was not there ; and from that moment she was never beheld again ! Every ultimate search proved fruitless and unavailing. A veil of impenetrable mystery hung over her fate. •   •   •

A sudden thought flashed on the mind of Clermistonlee. The day dawn was breaking as he descended the staircase, after fruitlessly calling on Lilian through various apartments.

"I may, I must save him yet—unfortunate youth, a father's arms shall yet embrace him. Oh, my hapless and deeply-wronged Alison; fortune may yet enable me in some sort to repair the atrocities of which I have been guilty. My horse! my horse!" and, rushing to the stable, he saddled and bridled a fleet steed, and in five minutes was galloping furiously back to the city, the walls and towers of which arose before him, red and sombre in the rays of the morning sun.

CHAPTER LXIII.

THE IRON ROOM—THE DEATH SHOT.

Ay, I had planned full many a sanguine scheme
Of earthly happiness—romantic schemes,
And fraught with loveliness :—and it is hard
To feel the hand of death arrest one's steps,
Throw a chill blight o'er all one's budding prospects,
And hurl one's soul untimely to the shades,
Lost in the gaping gulf of blank oblivion.
HENRY KIRKE WHITE.

THE iron room of the ancient Tolbooth of Edinburgh was a dreary vault of massive stonework, and was named so in consequence of its strength and security. A low heavy arch roofed it, and the walls from which it sprung were composed of great blocks of roughly hewn stone elaborately built. Here and there a chain hung from them. The floor was paved, and the door was a complicated mass of iron bars, locks, bolts, and hinges. A single aperture, high up in the wall, admitted the cold midnight wind through its deep recess.

An iron cruise burned on a clumsy wooden table, near which sat Walter Fenton. the condemned, with his face covered by his hands, and his mind buried in sad and melancholy thoughts.

One bright and solitary star shone down upon him through the grated window, flashing, dilating, and shrinking; often he gazed upon it wistfully—for it was his only companion—the partner or the witness of his solitude and his sorrow. Once he turned to look upon it—but it had passed away.

He reflected that never again would he behold a star shining in the firmament.

Sad, bitter, and solitary reflection—for a few hours was all that was left him now; and, though the sands of life were ebbing fast, one absorbing thought occupied his mind—that

Lilian was false and his rival triumphant; that all his long-cherished schemes and dreams of love and happiness, glory and ambition, were frustrated and blasted irredeemably and for ever.

He was to die!

The infliction of punishment immediately after trial was anciently practised in all criminal cases, and the victim was usually led from the presence of the judge to the scaffold.

Walter had been doomed to death as a traitor, a raiser of sedition, and a deserter from the Scottish forces; the last accusation, in support of which his signed *oath of fealty* to the Estates of Scotland, had been produced in council by general Sir Thomas Livingstone, commander-in-chief of the army, saved him the dishonour of dying on the gibbet.

The door of the iron room was opened stealthily, and the heavy bolts and swinging chains were again rattling into their places, when Walter slowly raised his head. His eye had become haggard, and his face was overspread with a deathly pallor. The tall spare form of the Reverend Mr. Ichabod Bummel stood before him, clad in his ample black coat, with its enormous cuffs and pocket-flaps, his deep waistcoat, and voluminous grey breeches. He removed his broad hat, and smoothed down the long lank hair which was parted in a seam over the top of his cranium, and fell straight upon each shoulder. He did not advance, but continued to press his hat upon his breast with both hands, to turn up his eyes and groan mournfully.

"Poor youth!" he began, after two or three hems; "poor youth! now truly thou lookest like an owl in the desert, yea, verily, even as one overtaken in the Slough of Despond. Now thou seest how atrocious is the crime of rebellion, and how bitter its meed. Now thou seest how wicked is the attempt to overturn our pure and blessed kirk as by law established, and to substitute anarchy and confusion for peace and brotherly love, and to involve the innocent with the guilty in one common destruction. Ewhow! O guilty madness—O miserable infatuation, that for the phantom of kingly and hereditary right, would ruthlessly hurl back the land into the dark abyss of popery, restore the abomination of the mass, and substitute the vile and tyrannical James for that beloved prince of our own persuasion, now seated on Britain's triple throne, if not by that imaginary hereditary right, at least by the laws of the land, and the voice of those that are above it—yea, mark me, youth, *above it*—the ministers of the gospel. The pious and glorious William hath been our saviour from the devilish practices of popery, and the machinations of all those spurious children of Luther and of Calvin, the Seekers, the Libertines and Independents, Brownists, Separatists and Familists, Antitrinitarians, Arians, Socinians, Anti-Scripturists, Anabaptists, Antinomians, Arminians, and a myriad other teachers of heresy, and preachers of schism—whilk, my brethren—my brother, I mean—may Beelzebub confound! Oh, youth, how wicked and ungracious it is in thee to reject the stately fig-tree with its sweetness and good fruit, and raise up the ancient thorn and prickly bramble to reign over us!"

"My good sir," replied Walter, "it is but a poor specimen of Presbyterian charity this, to come hither to a dismal vault, to heap contumely on the head of the fallen, to humble one who is already humbled—to bruise the bruised. Good sir, is it kind or charitable to rail at and exult over me in this my great distress?"

At this unexpected accusation, tears stated into the eyes of Ichabod Bummel, who was really a good man at heart, though his virtues were sadly obscured by the fanaticism of the times.

"Do not misunderstand me, good youth," he replied hurriedly; "and do me not this great injustice. I come in the most humble and Christian spirit, to cheer thy last hour in this gloomy hypogeum, and for that godly purpose have brought with me a copy of my *Bombshell*, a most sweet and savoury comforter to the afflicted mind."

He drew that celebrated quarto from his voluminous pocket, laid it on the table, and opening it at certain places, turned down the corners of the leaves. He then produced a thick little black-letter psalm-book, the board of which bore the very decided impression of a Bothwell-brig bullet; he adjusted a great pair of round horn spectacles on his long hooked nose, and in a shrill voice began his favourite chant :

" I like an owle in desert am," &c.

So much did he resemble the feathered type of wisdom, that Walter could scarcely repress a smile.

"Young man, wherefore dost thou not join with me?" asked the divine, raising his black eyebrows and looking at Walter alternately under, over, and through his barnacles.

"Reverend sir, I never sung a psalm in my life, and really cannot do so now."

"I warrant thou canst sing 'Claver'se and his Cavaliers,' 'King James's March,' 'Rub-a-Dub,' and other profane ditties and camp-songs of thy wicked faction and ungodly profession," said Ichabod reproachfully.

At that moment the deep-mouthed bell of St. Giles, which seemed to swing immediately above their heads, gave one long and sonorous toll.

"It is the first hour of the last morning I shall ever spend on earth!" exclaimed Walter, starting up and striking his letters together in the bitterness of his soul. "Oh, Lilian, Lilian, how little could we have foreseen of all this!"

He wept.

"'Tis well—no tears can be more precious than these," said Mr. Bummel, who thought his exhortations had begun to prove effectual. "Soon, good youth, shalt thou reach the end of this vale of tears! Lo! thy bride already waiteth thee, and these tears ——"

"You deem those of contrition and remorse. They are *not*. I have done nothing to repent of, or for which I ought to feel contrite. I never wronged man nor woman, though many have wronged me in more than a lifetime can repay. These tears spring only from bitterness and unavailing regret. Have I no hope of pardon? I care not for life, but my king and the son of my king require my services, and could my blood restore them I would die happy. Where is old Sir Thomas Dalyel?"

"Gone to a warmer climate than Scotland," said Ichabod spitefully.

"Sir George of Rosehaugh?"

"He is gone where he cannot assist thee."

"Where is old Colin of Balcarris?"

"Fled no one knows whither."

"Where, then, is old Sir Robert of Glenae?"

"Gone to his last account with other persecutors."

"All then are dead or in exile, and none is left to be a friend to the poor cavalier."

"Save one," said Ichabod, pointing upward.

"True, true," replied Walter, and covering his face with his hands he stooped over the table and prayed intently.

Two o'clock struck, three and four followed, but still he remained, as Ichabod thought, absorbed in earnest prayer, and kneeling by his side, the worthy minister joined with true and pious fervour, till his patience became quite exhausted. He stirred him, and Walter, who had fallen asleep, started up.

"Is it time?" he asked.

"Thou hast slept well," said the divine, pettishly; "out of seven hours that were allotted, three have already fled."

"My dear and worthy sir, you see how calm my conscience is. Perhaps it is hard to die so young; but for me life has now lost every charm. Death never has terrors to the brave. He opens the gates to a fame and a life that are eternal, and when the coffin-lid is closed, sorrow and jealousy, envy and woe are excluded for ever. *In four hours more mine will have closed over me.* —— Kingdoms and cities, the trees of the forest, the lakes, the rocks, and the hills themselves, have all their allotted periods of existence, and man has his; for every thing must perish—all must die and all must pass away. Oh, why then this foolish and unavailing regret about a few years more or less?—— Front to front and foot to foot I have often met death on the field of battle, and if without flinching I have faced the volley of a whole brigade, that hurled a thousand brave spirits into eternity at once, shall I shrink from the levelled muskets of twelve base hirelings of the Stadtholder?—— Will Lilian ever look on the grave where this heart moulders that loved her so long and so well? Oh, no, for now she is the wife of another—oh, my God, *another!* In all wide Scotland there is not one to regret me, to shed one tear for me. I disappear from the earth like a bubble on a tide of events, leaving not one being behind me to recall my memory in fondness or regret."

* * * * * * *

The great clock of St. Giles struck the hour of seven.

Muskets rattled on the pavement of the echoing street; the door of the iron room opened, and the gudeman of the Tolbooth presented his stern and sinister visage.

"It is time," he announced briefly.

"I am ready," replied Walter, cheerfully, and, with a soldier on each side of him, and followed by the clergyman, he descended the narrow circular staircase of the prison, and, issuing from an arched doorway at the foot, found himself at the end of the edifice. Here he paused and gazed calmly around him.

An early hour was chosen for his execution, that few might witness it, for there existed in Scotland a strong feeling against William's policy; the massacre of Glencoe, the successive defeats and heavy expenses of the Dutch wars, rankled bitterly in the minds of the people.

The lofty streets were silent and shadowy; scarcely a foot-fall was heard in them, and the dun sunlight of the September morning had not sufficient heat to exhale the haze of the autumnal night.

A company of Argyle's regiment—the perpetrators of the Glencoe atrocity—clad in coarse brick-coloured uniform of the Dutch fashion, were drawn up in double ranks facing inwards on each side of the doorway. They stood with their

arms reversed, and each stooped his head on his hands,
which rested on the butt of his musket. At the head of
this lane were four drummers with their drums muffled and
craped, and a plain deal coffin carried upon the shoulders of
soldiers. Walter, as he gazed steadily along these hostile
ranks, saw only the sourest fanaticism visible in every face,
and in none more so than that of their commander, a hard-
featured and square-shouldered personage, with a black
corslet under his ample red coat, and wearing a red feather
in his broad hat. He introduced himself as—

"Major Duncannon, of the godly regiment of my noble
lord Argyle." Walter bowed.

"Duncannon!" he replied; "your name is familiar to me
as being the man who issued the orders for the massacre of
Glencoe."

Duncannon gave Walter a steady frown in reply to his
glance of undisguised hostility and contempt, and said,—

"I obeyed the royal orders of King William III., to whom
I say be long life—and, like thee, may all his enemies perish
from Dan to Beersheba!"

"I do not acknowledge him; he hath never been crowned
among us, nor sworn the oath a Scottish king should swear.
Shame on you, sir, to rank this false-hearted Dutchman with
our brave King William the Lion. Shame be on you, sir,
and all your faction!" cried Walter, holding up his fettered
hands, while his cheek flushed and his eyes kindled with
energy. "Let our people recollect that the last man whose
limbs were crushed to a jelly by the accursed steel-boots and
grinding thumbscrews, was subjected to their agonizing torture by the 'merciful' William of Orange—by the same wise
prince by whose express orders the bravest of the northern
tribes was massacred in their sleep and in cold blood! Let
our brave soldiers, when the lash that drips with their blood
is flaying them alive, remember that, like scourging round the
fleet and keelhauling the hapless mariner, it is an introduction
of the same pious and magnanimous monarch who planned,
signed, and countersigned the mandate for the ruthless atrocity of Glencoe! Oh, Scotland, Scotland! disloyal and un-
true to the line of your ancient kings, how long will you waste
your treasure and pour forth your gallant sons to the Dutch
and German wars of a brutal tyrant, who at once fears, and
hates, and dreads, though he dare not despise you? But the
hour is coming," and he shook his clenched hand and clanked
his fetters like a fierce prophet—"when war, oppression, ex-
action, and devastation, will be the meed of the actions of
to-day!"

"Silence, traitor!" exclaimed Duncannon, striking him with the hilt of his sword so severely that blood flowed from his mouth.

"Major Duncannon, thou art a coward!" said Walter, turning his eyes of fire upon him. "The brave are ever compassionate and gentle; but thou! away, man—for on thy brow is written the dark curse which the unavenged blood of Glencoe called down from the blessed God!"

Duncannon turned pale.

"Away with him!" he cried. "Drummers, flam off— musketeers, march!" and the procession began.

The dull rolling of the muffled drums, the regulated tap of the burial-march, and the wailing of the fifes, now shrill and high, and anon sweet and low, found a deep echo in Walter's melancholy breast. Sorrowful and solemn was the measure of the psalm, and he felt his beating heart soothed and saddened; but he could only mentally accompany the clergyman who walked bareheaded by his side, and chanted aloud while the soldiers marched.

Walter's cheek reddened, for his fearless heart beat high, and he stepped firmly behind his coffin, the most stately in all that sad procession, though marching to that dread strain which a soldier seldom hears, *his own* death-march. The vast recesses of the great cathedral, and the distant echoes of the central street of the city, with all its diverging wynds, replied mournfully to the roll of the funeral drums.

He whose knell they rung seemed the proudest there among two hundred soldiers. Life now had nearly lost every charm, while religion, courage, and resignation had fully robbed death of all its terrors. Roused by the unusual sound, many a nightcapped citizen peered fearfully forth from his lofty dwelling; but their looks of wonder or of pity were unheeded or unseen by Walter Fenton. He saw only his own coffin borne before him, and the weapons and the hands by which he was to die; but his bold spirit never quailed, and he resolved, with true Jacobite enthusiasm, to fall with honour to the cause for which he suffered.

"Halt!" cried Duncannon, and the coffin rang hollowly as it was placed beside the square stone pedestal of King Charles's statue, and Walter immediately kneeled down within it, confronting the stern Presbyterians of Argyle's regiment with an aspect of coolness and bravery that did not fail to excite their admiration and pity.

A sergeant approached to bind up his eyes.

"Nay, nay, my good fellow," said Walter, waving him away; "I have faced death too often to flinch now. Major

Duncannon, draw up your musketeers, and I will show you how fearlessly a cavalier of honour can die."

While twelve soldiers were drawn up before him and loaded their muskets, Walter turned his eyes for the last time to the glorious autumnal sun, whose red morning rays were shot aslant between two lofty piles of building into the shadowy and gloomy quadrangle formed by the ancient Parliament House, the Goldsmith's Hall, the grotesque piazzas, and the grand cathedral. He gave one rapid glance of adieu around him, and then turned towards his destroyers.

"Farewell, good youth," said Mr. Bummell, as the tears of true and heartfelt sorrow trickled over his long hooked nose. "Farewell! When He from whose hand light went forth over the land, even as the rays of yonder sun—when He, I say, returns in His glory, we will meet again. Till *then*, farewell." Covering his face with his handkerchief, he withdrew a few paces and prayed with kind and sincere devotion.

At that moment the hoofs of a galloping horse, spurred madly down the adjacent street, rang through the vaults and aisles of the great church. Walter's colour changed.

A reprieve!

Alas! it was only Lord Clermistonlee, who, pale, panting, and breathless, dashed into the square to stay the execution; but the cry he would have uttered died away on his parched lips.

"He comes to exult over me," said Walter bitterly. "Behold, ignoble lord," he exclaimed, "how a true cavalier can die! Musketeers," he added, in his old voice of authority, "ready—blow your matches—present—God save King James the Seventh—give fire!"

The death volley rang like thunder in the still quadrangle. Four bullets flattened against the statue, eight were mortal; and with the last convulsive energy of death Walter Fenton threw his hat into the air, and fell forward prostrate into his coffin a bleeding corpse.

———

Here ends our tale.

From that hour Clermistonlee was a changed man. Though given up to dark, corroding care and moody thoughts, he lived to a great old age, and was one of those who sold his country at the union. Soon after that event he died, unregretted and unrespected, and a defaced monument in the east wall of the Greyfriars churchyard still marks the place where he lies.

His gossip, Mersington, would no doubt have obtained a comfortable share of "the compensations" in 1707, had he not (as appears from a passage in Carstairs' *State Papers*) unluckily been found dead one night in the severe winter of 1700, with a half-dr ──d mug of burnt sack clutched in his tenacious grasp.

A few words more of Lilian, and then we part.

From the moment in which, with her child in her arms, she ascended the great staircase of Bruntisfield, she was never again seen.

Every place within the mansion and without, the woods, the lake, the fields, the muir, were searched, but the lady and her child were seen no more.

An impenetrable mystery cast a veil of horror over their fate: but Mr. Ichabod Bummel, and the most learned divines of a kirk that was then in the zenith of its wisdom and power, gave it as their decided opinion that they had been spirited away by the fairies,—an idea that was unanimously adopted by the people; nevertheless, a pale spectre, wailing and pressing a ghastly babe to its attenuated breast, was often visible on moonlight nights, among the old oak-trees, the rocky heronshaws of the Burghmuir, or the reedy rhinns of its beautiful loch; and this terrible fact was solemnly averred and duly sworn to by various decent and sponsible men, such as elders and deacons of the kirk, who chanced to journey that way after nightfall.

In latter years it was to the long gloomy avenue or immediate precincts of the ancient house, that this terrible tenant confined her midnight promenades.

Many sceptical persons, notwithstanding the assertions of the aforesaid elders and deacons, declared the story of the apparition to be downright nonsense. Many more may be disposed to do so at the present day; but we would beg them to withold their decision until they have consulted as carefully as we have done, the *MSS. Session Records* of Mr. Bummel's kirk, entered in his own hand, and attested by the said elders and deacons at full length.

In the year 1800, when the stately and venerable mansion of Bruntisfield was demolished, to make way for the hospital of Gillespie, within a deep alcove, or labyrinth of stone, in the heart of its massive walls, the skeletons of a female and child were discovered; some fragments of velvet, brocade, and a gold ring were found with them.

On touching them, they crumbled into undistinguishable dust.

WYMAN AND SONS, PRINTERS, GREAT QUEEN STREET, LONDON.

Paper Covers.	Limp Cl. Gilt.		Picture Boards.	Cloth or Hf. Roan.
		CROWQUILL, Alfred—		
1/	—	A Bundle of Crowquills ...	—	—
		CUMMINS, M. S.—		Cloth.
1/	1/6	The Lamplighter...	2/	2/6
—	—	Mabel Vaughan ...	2/	2/6
		CUPPLES, Captain—		Hf. Roan.
—	—	The Green Hand ...	2/	2/6
—	—	The Two Frigates	2/	2/6
		DE VIGNY, A.—		
1/	1/6	Cinq Mars	—	—
		DUMAS, Alexandre—		
1/	1/6	Ascanio ...	—	—
1/	1/6	Beau Tancrede ...	—	—
1/	1/6	Black Tulip ...	—	—
1/	1/6	Captain Paul ...	—	—
1/	1/6	Catherine Blum ...	—	—
1/	1/6	Chevalier de Maison Rouge ...	—	—
1/	1/6	Chicot the Jester ...	—	—
1/	1/6	Conspirators ...	—	—
1/	1/6	Countess de Charny ...	—	—
1/	1/6	Dr. Basilius ...	—	—
1/	1/6	Forty-five Guardsmen ...	—	—
—	—	Half Brothers ...	2/	2/6
1/	1/6	Ingenue ...	—	—
1/	1/6	Isabel of Bavaria ...	—	—
—	—	Marguerite de Valois ...	2/	2/6
1/	1/6	Memoirs of a Physician, vol. 1 }	—	
1/	1/6	Do. do. vol. 2 }		3/
1/	1/6	Monte Cristo ... vol. 1 }	—	
1/	1/6	Do. ... vol. 2 }		3/
1/	1/6	Nanon ...	—	—
1/	1/6	Page of the Duke of Savoy	—	—
1/	1/6	Pauline ...	—	—
1/	1/6	Queen's Necklace ...	—	—
1/	1/6	Regent's Daughter ...	—	—
1/	1/6	Russian Gipsy ...	—	—
1/	1/6	Taking the Bastile, vol. 1 }	—	
1/	1/6	Do. vol. 2 }		3/
1/	1/6	Three Musketeers ... }	—	
1/	1/6	Twenty Years After ... }		3/

Paper Covers.	Limp Cl. Gilt.					Picture Boards.	Hf. Roan.
		DUMAS, ALEXANDRE—*continued.*					
1/	1 6	Twin Captains				—	—
1/	1 6	Two Dianas				—	—
—	—	Vicomte de Bragelonne, vol. 1 ...				2/6	3/
—	—	Do. do. vol. 2				2/6	3/
1/	1 6	Watchmaker				—	—

Dumas' Novels, 18 vols., half roan, £2 13s.

EDGEWORTH, Maria—

TALES OF FASHIONABLE LIFE:

1/	—	The Absentee				—	—
1/	—	Ennui				—	—
1/	—	Manœuvring				—	—
1/	—	Vivian				—	—

The Set, in cloth gilt, 4 vols., in a box, 8s.

EDWARDS, Amelia B.—

—	—	Half a Million of Money... ...				2/	2/6
—	—	Ladder of Life				2/	2/6
—	—	My Brother's Wife				2/	2/6

The Set, 3 vols., half roan, 7s. 6d.

FERRIER, Miss—

—	—	Destiny				2/	2/6
—	—	Inheritance				2/	2/6
—	—	Marriage				2/	2/6

The Set, 3 vols., half roan, 7s. 6d.; in boards, 6s.

FIELDING, Thomas—

—	—	Amelia				2/	2/6
—	—	Joseph Andrews				2/	2/6
1/	—	Tom Jones				2/	2/6

Fielding's Novels, 3 vols., half roan, 7s. 6d.; boards, 6s.

See also page 21.

F TIS, Robert S.—

—	—	Gilderoy				2/	2/6

Paper Covers.	Limp Cl. Gilt.		Picture Boards.	Hf. Roan.

FONBLANQUE, Albany, Jun.—

Paper Covers.	Limp Cl. Gilt.		Picture Boards.	Hf. Roan.
—	—	The Man of Fortune	2/	2/6

GERSTAECKER, Fred.—

—	—	Each for Himself...	2/	2/6
—	—	The Feathered Arrow	2/	2/6
—	—	Sailor's Adventures		
—	—	The Haunted House	2/	2/6
—	—	Pirates of the Mississippi ...	2/	2/6
—	—	Two Convicts	2/	2/6
—	—	Wife to Order	2/	2/6

The Set, 6 vols., half roan, 15*s*.

GRANT, James—

Hf. Roan.

—	—	Aide de Camp	2/	2/6
—	—	Arthur Blane ; or, The Hundred Cuirassiers	2/	2/6
—	—	Bothwell : the Days of Mary Queen of Scots	2/	2/6
—	—	Captain of the Guard : the Times of James II.	2/	2/6
—	—	Cavaliers of Fortune ; or, British Heroes in Foreign Wars ...	2/	2/6
—	—	Constable of France	2/	2/6
—	—	Dick Rodney : Adventures of an Eton Boy	2/	2/6
—	—	First Love and Last Love : a Tale of the Indian Mutiny	2/	2/6
—	—	Frank Hilton ; or, The Queen's Own	2/	2/6
—	—	The Girl he Married : Scenes in the Life of a Scotch Laird ...	2/	2/6
—	—	Harry Ogilvie ; or, The Black Dragoons	2/	2/6
—	—	Jack Manly	2/	2/6
—	—	Jane Seton ; or, The King's Advocate	2/	2/6
—	—	King's Own Borderers ; or, 25th Regiment	2/	2/6
—	—	Lady Wedderburn's Wish : a Story of the Crimean War	2/	2/6
—	—	Laura Everingham ; or, The Highlanders of Glen Ora	2/	2/6
—	—	Legends of the Black Watch ; or, The 42nd Regiment	2/	2/6

Paper Covers	Limp Cl. Gilt						Picture Boards.	Hf. Roan.
		GORE, Mrs.—						
—	—	Cecil ...	...	•••	...	...	2/	2/6
—	—	Debutante ...	...	•••	...	...	2/	2/6
—	—	The Dowager	...	•••	...	...	2/	2/6
—	—	Heir of Selwood ...		•••	...	...	2/	2/6
—	—	Money Lender	...	•••	...	...	2/	2/6
—	—	Mothers and Daughters	...		...	...	2/	2/6
—	—	Pin Money	...	•••	...	...	2/	2/6
—	—	Self ...	...	•••	...	...	2/	2/6
—	—	The Soldier of Lyons		...	...	...	2/	2/6

The Set, 9 vols., half roan, £1 2s. 6d.

Paper Covers	Limp Cl. Gilt							
		GREY, Mrs.—						
1/	1/6	The Duke ...	•••	...	...		—	—
1/	1/6	The Little Wife ...		...	...		—	—
1/	1/6	Old Country House		...	...		—	—
1/	1/6	Young Prima Donna		...	...		—	—

The Set, in 4 vols., 6s., cloth gilt.

Paper Covers	Limp Cl. Gilt						Picture Boards.	Hf. Roan.
		HALIBURTON, Judge—						
—	—	The Attaché ...	...	...			2/	2/6
—	—	The Letter-Bag of the Great Western ...	...	...	...		2/	2/6
—	—	Sam Slick, the Clockmaker	...				2/6	3/

Haliburton's Novels, 3 vols., half roan, 8s.; paper covers, or boards, 6s. 6d.

Paper Covers	Limp Cl. Gilt							
		HANNAY, James—						
—	—	Singleton Fontenoy	...	...	...		2/	—
		HARLAND, Marion—						
1/	—	Hidden Path ...	...	...			—	—
		HARTE, Bret—						
		See page 23.						
		HAWTHORNE, Nathaniel—						
1/	1/6	The House of the Seven Gables	..				—	—
1/	1/6	Mosses from an Old Manse	...				—	—
1/	1/6	The Scarlet Letter	...	...			—	—
		HEYSE, Paul (Translated by G. H. Kingsley)—						
1/	—	Love Tales	...	...	...		—	—

NOVELS AT ONE SHILLING.

By CAPTAIN MARRYAT.

Peter Simple.	Jacob Faithful.	Percival Keene.
The King's Own.	The Dog-Fiend.	Valerie.
Midshipman Easy.	Japhet in Search of a	Frank Mildmay.
Rattlin the Reefer.	Father.	Olla Podrida.
Pacha of Many Tales.	The Poacher.	Monsieur Violet.
Newton Forster.	The Phantom Ship.	

By W. H. AINSWORTH.

Windsor Castle.	Guy Fawkes.	Mervyn Clitheroe.
Tower of London.	The Spendthrift.	Ovingdean Grange.
The Miser's Daughter.	James the Second.	St. James's.
Rookwood.	Star Chamber.	Auriol.
Old St. Paul's.	Flitch of Bacon.	Jack Sheppard.
Crichton.	Lancashire Witches.	

By J. FENIMORE COOPER.

The Pilot.	The Waterwitch.	Homeward Bound.
Last of the Mohicans.	Two Admirals.	The Borderers.
The Pioneers.	Satanstoe.	The Sea Lions.
The Red Rover.	Afloat and Ashore.	Heidenmauer.
The Spy.	Wyandotté.	Precaution.
Lionel Lincoln.	Eve Effingham.	Oak Openings.
The Deerslayer.	Miles Wallingford.	Mark's Reef.
The Pathfinder.	The Headsman.	Ned Myers.
The Bravo.	The Prairie.	

By ALEXANDRE DUMAS.

Three Musketeers.	Countess de Charny.	The Conspirators.
Twenty Years After.	Monte Cristo. 2 vols.	Ascanio. [Savoy.
Doctor Basilius.	(1s. each).	Page of the Duke of
The Twin Captains.	Nanon.	Isabel of Bavaria.
Captain Paul.	The Two Dianas.	Beau Tancrede.
Memoirs of a Phy-	The Black Tulip.	Regent's Daughter.
sician. 2 vols. (1s.	Forty - Five Guards-	Pauline.
each).	men.	Catherine Blum.
The Chevalier de Mai-	Taking of the Bastile.	Ingénue.
son Rouge.	2 vols. (1s. each).	Russian Gipsy.
Queen's Necklace.	Chicot the Jester.	Watchmaker.

By MRS. GORE.
The Ambassador's Wife.

By JANE AUSTEN.

Northanger Abbey.	Pride and Prejudice.	Mansfield Park.
Emma.	Sense and Sensibility.	

By MARIA EDGEWORTH.

Ennui.	Vivian.	The Absentee.	Manœuvring.

Published by George Routledge and Sons.

ROUTLEDGE'S SIXPENNY NOVELS.

By CAPTAIN MARRYAT.

The King's Own.	Pacha of Many Tales.	Frank Mildmay.
Peter Simple.	Newton Forster.	Midshipman Easy.
Jacob Faithful.	Japhet in Search of a Father.	The Dog Fiend.

By J. F. COOPER.

The Waterwitch.	Homeward Bound.	Precaution.
The Pathfinder.	The Two Admirals.	Oak Openings.
The Deerslayer.	Miles Wallingford.	The Heidenmauer.
Last of the Mohicans.	The Pioneers.	Mark's Reef.
The Pilot.	Wyandotté.	Ned Myers.
The Prairie.	Lionel Lincoln.	Satanstoe.
Eve Effingham.	Afloat and Ashore.	The Borderers.
The Spy.	The Bravo.	Jack Tier.
The Red Rover.	The Sea Lions.	Mercedes.
	The Headsman.	

By Sir WALTER SCOTT.

Guy Mannering.	Peveril of the Peak.	The Abbot.
The Antiquary.	Heart of Midlothian.	Woodstock.
Ivanhoe.	The Bride of Lam-	Redgauntlet.
The Fortunes of Nigel.	mermoor.	Count Robert of Paris.
Rob Roy.	Waverley.	The Talisman.
Kenilworth.	Quentin Durward.	Surgeon's Daughter.
The Pirate.	St. Ronan's Well.	Fair Maid of Perth.
The Monastery.	Legend of Montrose,	Anne of Geierstein.
Old Mortality.	and Black Dwarf.	The Betrothed.

By VARIOUS AUTHORS.

Robinson Crusoe.	Artemus Ward, his Book.
Uncle Tom's Cabin. *Mrs. Stowe.*	A. Ward among the Mormons.
Colleen Bawn. *Gerald Griffin.*	The Nasby Papers.
The Vicar of Wakefield.	Major Jack Downing.
Sketch Book. *Washington Irving.*	The Biglow Papers.
Tristram Shandy. *Sterne.*	Orpheus C. Kerr.
Sentimental Journey. *Sterne.*	The Wide, Wide World.
The English Opium Eater.	Queechy.
De Quincy.	Gulliver's Travels.
Essays of Elia. *Charles Lamb.*	The Wandering Jew. (3 vols.)
Roderick Random. *Smollett.*	The Mysteries of Paris. (3 vols.)
Autocrat of the Breakfast Table.	The Lamplighter.
Tom Jones. 2 vols. *Fielding.*	Professor at the Breakfast Table.

Published by George Routledge and Sons.

www.ingramcontent.com/pod-product-compliance
Lightning Source LLC
Chambersburg PA
CBHW052331110726

47901CB00005B/1201